Angelica, scowling sligh[...]
her frilled and flounced [...]
one of the heavy silv[...]
smooth the shining blac[...]
she had when Angelica was a little girl. A final burnish with
a white silk scarf, and her hair was immaculate. Thankfully she'd applied only the minimum of make-up; with her
skin and eyes she needed little anyway.

'You look perfect, *chérie*. Let's hope he proposes
tonight.'

She rested her hands on the girl's shoulders and studied
their twin reflections in the mirror. The resemblance
between them had never seemed stronger, but on closer
examination Marianne could see the fine lines of bitterness
and disillusion etched upon her own face, fight them
though she might. As yet young and untried, Angelica's
beauty was flawless. Marianne sent up a silent prayer:
Tonight, God, please let my daughter secure a bright
future for herself, without ever needing to learn of men's
treachery, or the cruel bargains they can drive.

A RICH ALLIANCE

Teresa Marshall de Paoli

Futura

A Futura Book

First published in Great Britain in 1990
by Macdonald & Co (Publishers) Ltd
London & Sydney

This Futura edition published in 1992

Typeset by Leaper & Gard Limited, Bristol, England

Printed and bound in Great Britain by
BPCC Hazell Books
Aylesbury, Bucks, England
Member of BPCC Ltd.

ISBN 0 7088 4998 9

Futura Publications
A Division of
Macdonald & Co (Publishers) Ltd
165 Great Dover Street
London SE1 4YA

A member of Maxwell Macmillan Publishing Corporation

To my darling Michael

ACKNOWLEDGEMENTS

Books are seldom written without an army of people giving their time, expertise and help. I would like therefore to thank my dear friends Valerie and John Knight for encouraging me to write in the first place; Luciana Soloman, Anna Palk and Derek Brierley for their enthusiasm and support; Brian Morris who was always there for me when on occasions I felt like giving up the task; Lynn Curtis for all her assistance; my agent Leslie Gardner for her continuing faith and encouragement; my editor Krystyna Zukowska for knowing how the book should be; Teresa Garraway and Sue Mills and all those close to me for their loving support and understanding during a very long period when the pressure began to build up and I seemed to go through a metamorphosis. And of course my cats who are magical and lay patiently by me.

PROLOGUE

Kingsford Smith Airport, Sydney

The cluster of pressmen gathered at the Flight Facilities Terminal yawned and perspired in the heat of the dying day. What they wouldn't give for a cool beer! It looked like the tip-off from London's Heathrow airport had been wrong. So far the only 'celebrity' they'd intercepted was a twenty-year-old soap star who'd gone over big in Pommieland but was a national joke at home. If no one showed in the next half-hour, there'd be a general exodus to the pub.

'Hold on a minute,' said one of the photographers. 'That 747 coming in . . . Can anyone make out the logo?'

They squinted into the setting sun, straining against the lurid technicolour that dazzled the eyes. 'Looks like a roo to me,' said one. 'Just another Qantas flight.'

'That's no kangaroo,' said another. 'It's a bull, a bloody Brahman bull. Hey, fellers, Rando's back in town!'

A buzz of excitement ran through them. Looked like the long, thirsty wait had been worth it after all. The more seasoned photographers were already jockeying for position with men who moments before they would have described as mates. When it came to snatching a possible front page picture of one of Australia's most famous expatriates, mateship went out the window.

Not long now. Customs and Immigration were there to snarl up the journeys of lesser mortals. Multi millionaires like Lord Dexter Randolph could afford to buy a quick passage through the formalities.

'Here he is!' shouted one of the photographers at the front.

A tall, rangy man, impressive despite the silver-topped stick he leant on, scowled at them and pulled the brim of a battered akubra hat lower down over the famous sky-blue eyes. At his heels, hurrying to keep up with him despite his pronounced limp, came his wife.

Lady Camilla Randolph's delicate porcelain beauty was apparent even beneath the heavy dark glasses and the worried frown she wore. She drew level with her husband, who slid an arm protectively around her shoulders.

'Just hold still a moment, sweetie. Give them the picture they want and they'll crawl back underneath their stones.'

'Want to bet?' yelled a wag at the back. 'You're big news, Rando, you and all the family.'

'Lady Camilla,' called another pressman, sensing the weak link, 'any comments to make about your daughter? Still taking her clothes off for the girlie mags, is she? Suppose marriage to the Prince is out of the question now, eh?'

'Camilla, where's your son? Your youngest boy, Courtney. We hear he's had a few health problems.' A grizzled reporter gave a gargantuan sniff, mimicking a coke addict's greedy snuffling after the white powder.

'What about your mother, Countess Angelica? Hired any toy boy chauffeurs lately?'

Camilla had visibly paled. At that moment a dark blue Bentley Mulsanne pulled up at the kerb ten feet away. Dexter took his wife's arm and started to shoulder the press aside, sensing the questions were about to take an even uglier turn.

'What about this inquest tomorrow, Rando? Is it true you killed an abo for his stake in one of your stations?'

'How will it feel to swop an English stately home for a prison cell back home?'

The pack closed in, pressing microphones into the couple's faces, dazzling them with the glare of flashbulbs as lenses were thrust haphazardly over fellow pressmen's head and shoulders, photographers competing wildly for the shot that would make the morning's news.

A liveried chauffeur got out of the car to open the kerbside door and help Lady Camilla inside. Dexter shook off all attempts at assistance for himself. Leaning on his cane, one foot already inside the car, he put up his hand for silence. When the excited babbling had calmed down, he addressed them in his slow Queensland drawl.

'Gentlemen of the press, there's one question you haven't put to me yet — am I going to clear my name in Brisbane tomorrow? Damn right I am! See you all in court.'

He dropped back into his seat and slammed the door swiftly shut. The car's tinted windows reflected only their own disconsolate faces. The journalists started to drift away, wondering whether it was worth the chase to the house in Darling Point.

'I'll say one thing for the old bastard,' said one reporter. 'He always has known how to make a good exit.'

'Let's hope he can do it in style tomorrow,' his cynical photographer replied. 'I have the strangest feeling that this time he's landed on a square marked "Go to jail".'

'Wonder what his fancy Pommie friends would make of that? Lord Dexter Randolph, descended from an Australian felon, right back where his great-great-granddaddy started from ... Jesus, Jonesy, sometimes my own brilliance astounds me. Get your arse in gear! This is going to make a great feature.'

Book One

ANGELICA

Paris, 1939

Marianne de Bailliencourt rapped upon the polished mahogany door leading to her daughter's suite. When there was no reply, she opened it — and gasped at the sight of the room before her.

Decorated by her friend Madame Castaing in a muted palette of old rose and ivory touched with gold, it was now randomly splashed with pools of vivid colour from the dozen or so full-length evening gowns which lay crumpled and discarded over the furniture or upon the floor.

Worth, Lelong, Patou, Grès ... the foremost designers of Paris seemed to have failed Marianne's daughter Angelica on this night of nights.

'Henriette!'

Hearing voices in the dressing-room beyond, and deciding she could not face the chaos there, Marianne summoned her daughter's maid. The girl appeared, flushed and apologetic.

'*Oui, Madame la Comtesse?*'

'Tell Philippe to bring the car round now. Mademoiselle will be down in fifteen minutes.'

'But, Madame, Mam'selle is still deciding ...'

Marianne merely raised her brows to indicate the girl's impertinence. 'Give Philippe the message and return here in fifteen minutes. Every gown must be thoroughly pressed before you go off duty. Is that clear?'

'*Oui, madame.*'

The maid looked miserable at the thought of the hours of back-breaking work ahead. Then her face brightened.

Although Mam'selle had said she need not, she had decided to wait up tonight anyway. Because tonight, for the umpteenth time this Season, the young mistress was the honoured guest of old Edmond de Selincourt and his son Patrice. Mam'selle Angelica and the young Monsieur de Selincourt made such a handsome couple it was rumoured that he would soon propose. Perhaps tonight ...

When Henriette had scuttled away, smiling, a willowy raven-haired girl appeared at the door of the dressing-room. She was struggling to adjust the side fastening of a dress which, with its daring one-shoulder design and motif of a single huge marguerite hand-painted on to the shocking pink fabric, immediately proclaimed it the work of fashion's new *enfant terrible*.

'Schiaparelli,' Angelica announced, pirouetting so that Marianne could appreciate the gown's severe lines from every angle. 'Tonight, I want to cause a sensation!'

'And in that dress you would, *chérie*. But take it from me — if you want to impress the de Selincourts, a sensation is the last thing you need.'

Marianne closed her eyes wearily, shutting out the sight of the glowing young girl before her. Such style, such precocious sophistication — and such a terrifying failure to appreciate the scale of the stakes they were playing for.

At almost nineteen, there was no denying Angelica's allure. The dress's vivid tones cast a flattering rosy glow over the exposed olive skin of her face, shoulders and arms. Her high cheekbones, slanting green eyes and wavy black hair, now pinned into an elaborate chignon, enhanced the glamorous, almost gipsyish effect. But Marianne knew that if they were to capture the eligible young man on whom both mother and daughter had set their sights, what Angelica needed was the prim and proper appearance of a shy *jeune fille bien élevée*.

'Take off that dress, put on the white Chanel, and take down your hair,' she instructed her daughter.

'But, Maman —'

4

Marianne cut short her protest. 'Do you like living like this? Do you want it to continue?' She looked around at the unabashed luxury of the room whose fine panelled walls were obscured by roll after roll of rose pink *toile de Jouy*. The flowing full-length curtains at the shuttered french windows were of ivory silk, lined and flounced with *bois de rose*. The delicate ceiling mouldings were picked out in gold leaf, and on a fine Hepplewhite sofa table beside Angelica's muslin-draped bed stood one of Armand de Bailliencourt's treasured collection of Fabergé clocks, its golden case enamelled in delicate shades of rose, shell pink and green.

A wave of Marianne's arm also encompassed the crumpled couture gowns and the scent of Joy hanging thick and heavy in the air. As her hand moved, the broad diamond bracelet around her delicate wrist flashed blue fire.

'Well?' she challenged.

'You know I do.' And Angelica went to change.

They had not always lived in this way. Denis d'Alary, Marianne's first husband and Angelica's father, had been the younger son of an old but down-at-heels family. Marianne had married for love and repented at leisure until, at the age of thirty-five, she was left widowed and virtually penniless with a twelve-year-old daughter to provide for.

Two years of living on her wits and Denis' pitifully inadequate army pension had left their mark on Marianne. This was not so much physical, for her beauty had been Marianne's stock in trade and was still jealously guarded. Every day she fought the tell-tale lines of age by carefully massaging her neck and the delicate skin around her mouth and dark expressive eyes — with olive oil when there was no money for expensive face creams. The stray silver hairs that appeared in her jet-black hair were mercilessly plucked, or later artfully disguised, even if the expense of a trip to a decent salon — for Marianne would never allow an inferior hairdresser to touch her hair — meant that mother

5

and daughter went short of food. There was not enough money for a laundress, and, besides, Marianne took better care of their increasingly threadbare clothes, so she did the laundry herself, afterwards frantically smoothing on a thick coat of lanolin and a pair of cotton gloves to remove any tell-tale roughness from her hands.

Against all the odds that penury could stack against her, Marianne kept her looks and reaped many offers from men. Some, including Edmond de Selincourt, a former friend of her husband, expected her to become their unofficial mistress in exchange for evenings at the Opéra or in fashionable restaurants. Others were prepared to pay more handsomely, offering the traditional inducements — jewels, furs, a rented apartment. Marianne gambled that she was worth more than that and turned everybody down, even Edmond with whom she had been more than half in love until he made his businesslike proposition.

At the age of thirty-seven, beautiful still but immeasurably hardened by her years in the social wilderness, Marianne amazed *le tout* Paris by becoming the second wife of Comte Armand de Bailliencourt, an ageing but impeccably well-connected retired diplomat. A widower of forty years' standing, de Bailliencourt was commonly thought to be too interested in his collections of art and antiquities, notably ancient coins, even to notice a flesh and blood woman. But he recognised something unique in the beautiful widow with the fine, wary eyes. Like anything else he admired, Armand knew that Marianne was obtainable — at a price. This time he married the latest addition to his collection of rare and beautiful objects.

The life of the new Comtesse de Bailliencourt was not hard. Her new title gave Marianne an instant *entrée* into the highest circles, and unlimited credit at the couturiers, jewellers and antique shops where she spent her days. There was the gracious Paris house on the Avenue Foch which overlooked the Bois; an estate in the Loire valley; unlimited travel for herself and Angelica ... True, Armand

6

never accompanied them or even seemed to notice their occasional absences. Having roused himself enough to marry her, he took little further notice of Marianne. So long as she was there to grace his occasional dinner parties, dazzling his cronies with her wit and well-preserved beauty, and so long as she granted him access to her bed on demand — which was, God knew, increasingly rarely these days — Armand was happy. He didn't even mind when she took a lover — a skilful, charming and penniless actor from the Comédie-Française. Marianne's female friends frankly envied her, but once or twice a month, as Armand's stick-like bones and sagging folds of skin, wrinkled as an old tortoise, moved against her shrinking flesh, Marianne acknowledged that there was a price to pay for her new life.

But there was no question of going back to the shameful days of poverty. Marianne had won herself a place in Parisian society and intended to see that Angelica did the same. The 'beast' security must come first, of course. Her daughter could only marry a man who offered her the right position, home and lifestyle. Only when these were assured, could personal preference be taken into account.

Marianne was not, however, so blind to a young man's attractiveness that she did not rejoice for her daughter when Angelica succeeded in catching the eye of the handsome Patrice. The fact that the good-looking, highly eligible young man was the son of an admirer who had considered Marianne herself mistress rather than marriage material added a certain piquancy to the situation. Angelica was frankly jubilant at winning the Season's prize. Patrice was everything she had been taught to look for in a man — furthermore, she liked him.

Marianne held before the de Selincourts the twin carrots of Angelica's beauty — unmatched that Season by any other débutante — and the sizeable dowry which Armand had promised. Lately, however, he had been disturbingly vague when Marianne attempted to pin him down to an exact figure.

Edmond seemed inclined to swallow her assurances — 'He simply dotes on the girl, don't worry. I'm sure he'll do something stupendous for her ...' But lately the pace of Patrice's courtship had slackened. What was he doing the rest of the time? Whom was he seeing? Worryingly, a promised invitation to the de Selincourts' Deauville house had failed to appear and it was now the end of June.

But the offer of a seat for Angelica in their box throughout the whole of the Grande Semaine at Longchamp, France's premier race meeting, had gone a long way towards reassuring Marianne. And Edmond had been really quite pressing that she should attend tonight's *soirée* after the Grand Prix, the week's big race, even though her mother could not accompany her.

'Trust Armand to arrange a party for his boring old friends this evening.' Angelica echoed her mother's thoughts.

'Haven't you finished dressing yet? I told Philippe fifteen minutes.'

'I can't find my other shoe and my hair's impossible! Oh, Maman, can't I put it up again?'

When the request was greeted with silence, Angelica reappeared, transformation from gipsy to *ingénue* complete. Her hair curled softly around her shoulders, and in place of the up-to-the-minute Schiaparelli she wore a slim-fitting Chanel gown of white satin charmeuse. The bodice was plain-cut and reached to just below her collar-bone, suspended from rouleau shoulder straps. The contrast between the high neckline and the hint of bareness above was finely calculated to render the wearer both virginal and alluring, while the cinched in waist and full, slightly trailing skirts dotted with random white beadwork, reminded Marianne of nothing so much as a bridal gown. She hoped it would put Patrice in mind of weddings too.

'Hair loose and floating is just right with this dress,' she approved. 'Here, sit down and I'll brush it for you.'

Angelica, scowling slightly, sat before the gilded mirror

8

of her frilled and flounced dressing-table. Marianne picked up one of the heavy silver-backed brushes and began to smooth the shining black silk of her daughter's hair, just as she had when Angelica was a little girl. A final burnish with a white silk scarf, and her hair was immaculate. Thankfully she'd applied only the minimum of make-up; with her skin and eyes she needed little anyway.

'If it's sweet simplicity we're aiming for tonight, I take it your diamonds are out of the question?'

'Definitely *de trop*.' Then, seeing the sulky set to her daughter's mouth, and not wanting anything to spoil her looks or her chances tonight, Marianne conceded, 'But maybe the pearl and diamond earrings.'

These were Angelica's favourite among the de Bailliencourt jewels that Marianne had acquired upon marriage. She intended to ask Armand if her daughter might have them as a bridal gift. But first, she must catch her husband . . .

'You look perfect, *chérie*. Let's hope he proposes tonight.'

She rested her hands on the girl's shoulders and studied their twin reflections in the mirror. The resemblance between them had never seemed stronger, but on closer examination Marianne could see the fine lines of bitterness and disillusion etched upon her own face, fight them though she might. No longer with olive oil, though — Armand's money had seen to that.

As yet young and untried, Angelica's beauty was flawless. Marianne sent up a silent prayer: Tonight, God, please let my daughter secure a bright future for herself, without ever needing to learn of men's treachery, or the cruel bargains they can drive.

Brinsley Alexander Hamilton, sixth Earl of Courtney, Baron Hamilton of Castlemere, twelfth Baron Hamilton in the Barony of Scotland, studied his Boucheron slide watch and sighed faintly. The traffic along the broad tree-lined Allée de Longchamp had slowed to a virtual crawl and the drive from the Plaza-Athénée to the course at Longchamp, normally a matter of ten to fifteen minutes, had already taken half an hour.

The green scent of lime blossom, carried on the warm evening air, enveloped him. Edmond de Selincourt's second chauffeur, who had collected him from the hotel, had lowered the laundalette roof of the elderly Hispano-Suiza and Brinsley had an uninterrupted view through the arching canopy of trees to the stars above. There were, he reflected, worse places to be than Paris this Season — London, for one.

At thirty-eight, Brinsley was a veteran of the London social scene. For more years than he cared to remember he had attended the balls, the house parties, the jaunts to Ascot and Epsom and Goodwood. Each new Season's crop of débutantes, so charming and eager to please, were paid graceful compliments by him, or — the very prettiest — the tribute of a carefully chosen bouquet from Edward Goodyear. Brinsley gained the reputation of a ladies' man but never came close to marrying. Resisting the blandishments of the pot-hunting English mamas, and the none-too-delicate bait they laid, had become second nature to him now. He was however decidedly bored by it, and feeling jaded enough to welcome the prospect of a Parisian jaunt.

Headley, his normally imperturbable manservant, expressed polite surprise when instructed to pack for a trip to France. 'Ahem — I wonder, my lord, if that is perhaps altogether wise in view of the current international situation?'

'You've been reading the yellow press, I see. My very good friend Buster Cardew at the F.O. assures me this Hitler chap is vastly overrated. Good God, the man was a painter and decorator! Hardly a natural leader of men. France at least is quite safe from invasion, mark my words,

10

Headley. And get a move on with that razor, man. The damn bath-water's going cold!'

The slight, self-effacing Headley effortlessly supervised the packing of Brinsley's travelling trunk and valises, and made all the arrangements for the smooth journey from Courtney Park, Brinsley's principal residence in Wiltshire, to the Plaza-Athénée, where he always stayed in Paris.

Brinsley wasted no time in picking up French acquaint-anceships. It was while accompanying Daisy Fellowes to the Grand Prix in the afternoon that he had recognised the rotund but immaculately dressed figure of Edmond de Selincourt, a popular steward in the Société pour l'Encouragement, the French Jockey Club.

'Brinsley, my dear fellow,' Edmond greeted him warmly. 'Why did you not tell us you were in town? Come and join the party in my box. Patrice — my son, you remember? — will be delighted to see you again.'

Brinsley excused himself regretfully. 'Daisy's waiting for me, I'm afraid. I've just been to the Pari-Mutuel to collect her winnings. Bad luck in the big race, old man. But fifth behind Pharis II is really very creditable. Semblat said none of mine would even stay the trip.'

Edmond's normally florid face turned a deeper shade of crimson at the compliment. 'You are too modest, Brinsley. I hear your English string has been unstoppable — a 2,000 Guineas contender, the Gold Cup at Ascot ...'

'Boyd-Rochfort's doing, hardly mine. But seriously, Edmond, I'd love to chew the cud with you one evening, catch up on all the French racing gossip.'

'Are you joining Daisy's party for the soirée this evening?'

'No, actually. She's not feeling quite the thing this afternoon and thought she might give the Nuit de Longchamp a miss this year.'

Edmond's shrewd black eyes narrowed fractionally. 'Then you'd be doing me the most enormous favour if you could join me. I'm one lady too many — well, she's a girl really. She'll be no trouble, and later you and I could have that talk. Patrice will be there, of course, and his fiancée-to-be — only don't say anything about that, will you?' His round face suddenly looked rather anxious, as though he had said too much. 'It's not official yet, you see.'

Brinsley smiled at the memory. The French and their endless protocol! But it had been good of Edmond to send a car for him. So young Patrice was ready to tie the knot ... Despite himself, Brinsley felt a twinge of concern. The privileges of property and title imposed their own obligations. It was his duty to provide an heir for Courtney Park and the Scottish estate, Gilmour. If only he, like Patrice, could meet an acceptable girl ...

Later, Brinsley gave his name to the liveried servant, was announced and then admitted to the spacious main Pelouse, torchlit this evening and packed with party-goers — men in white tie, women in the finest couture and jewels Paris could provide. They were like a flock of fabulous birds, he thought, all strutting and preening and pecking the reputations of their fellows to shreds.

He scanned the politely jostling throng for a glimpse of Edmond and his party. There was a surge of movement and a flash of white caught and held Brinsley's eye. He saw a girl who looked almost too young to be there tonight, standing alone, obviously waiting for somebody. Straight-backed and slender as a reed in her plain white dress, she eclipsed the older women in their sophisticated clothes. Against the girl's natural elegance, their elaborate dresses and coiffures seemed tawdry and contrived.

A hand descended on his shoulder, distracting him from the delightful vision.

'Brinsley! Delighted you could come. Permit me to introduce my other guests.'

Edmond first presented Clara Bibescu, a buxom, overblown Romanian beauty. Brinsley was effortlessly

12

charming to her, and to a family threesome, Monsieur and Madame de Roncesvaux de la Beaune and their daughter Julie, whom Edmond introduced with a flourish. Up from the country, Brinsley deduced from the parents' good but slightly *démodé* evening dress. The daughter too had a slightly bucolic air: blonde, blue-eyed, pretty if you liked the sort. He realised with a sinking feeling that this must be the girl he had been invited to partner.

'Patrice and Angelica will be along soon,' Edmond promised, and proceeded to express an unlikely fascination with what de Roncesvaux had to say about crop rotation.

Since the two women seemed to be making relatively easy small talk, Brinsley struggled to engage the girl in conversation. 'Do you live in town?'

This question prompted an attack of giggles and the eventual admission: 'No, in Normandy. Papa farms.'

Successfully, Brinsley thought, noting the quality of the single strand of pearls she wore above her unflatteringly draped silk chiffon dress.

'And how do you come to know Edmond — or is it Patrice?'

She blushed furiously. 'Edmond has an estate adjoining ours. We see him and — and Patrice, when they are in Normandy. This year Edmond suggested we might visit him — them both — in Paris for the — the —'

'For the racing?' Brinsley suggested hopefully.

Julie's round blue eyes rolled in relief. 'Oh, yes, the racing.'

She was either profoundly stupid or else covering something up. Oh well, another tedious half-hour or so and then he could slip politely away, duty done.

Delivery came sooner. Patrice de Selincourt parted a way through the crush. Five years older than the last time Brinsley had seen him, he now had a matinée-idol profile and dark good looks.

'Brinsley, how good that you could come. I see you've met our neighbour, Julie. And this is Angelica — oh, I'm so

sorry. Do excuse me one moment, won't you? Yes, Papa
...'

As Patrice slid away he revealed the girl who had been standing partly obscured behind him. Brinsley struggled to conceal his sense of pleasurable shock as he recognised her. At close quarters the *ingénue* in white was even more beautiful than he had dared to hope.

The newcomer nodded coolly to Julie whom she had obviously met before, and addressed herself solely to Brinsley — in English, to his great relief. 'Patrice is such a scatterbrain that he didn't fully introduce us — the Countess Angelica de Bailliencourt.'

Unnoticed by Brinsley, who had eyes only for Angelica, Julie raised her eyebrows. Countess, indeed! By all accounts the girl was only the stepdaughter of old de Bailliencourt, who had never formally adopted her.

'Delighted to meet you. Brinsley Hamilton.'

Brinsley, unlike European aristocrats, never used his title when introducing himself, but left that to others. He surprised himself by bowing to kiss Angelica's hand in the French manner, and her by managing it adroitly, kissing the air just above the back of her hand instead of the skin itself as a clumsier Englishman might have done.

'Angelica is a beautiful name, but not a French one.'

'No, I'm named after my great-grandmother on my mother's side. She was Italian. Besides, I much prefer it to the French form — Angélique.'

'So do I,' Brinsley said gallantly, marvelling at the mixture of perfect poise and sophistication with such new-minted beauty.

'Where are you staying?' she asked.

'At the Plaza-Athénée, as usual.'

'Then you visit often? Whom do you know here besides Edmond and Patrice?'

At the roll-call of the rich and fashionable which answered her question, Angelica relaxed. Normally she begrudged every minute of an evening not spent in

14

Patrice's company, but tonight he had been annoyingly stiff with her, discouraging her from sliding her arm through his in her normal proprietorial fashion and letting his father prod him into dancing attendance on that tiresome country trio. Fortunately the girl was a disaster — so fat and unsophisticated.

Two adjectives which could never be applied to the Englishman in his impeccable Savile Row white tie, Angelica realised. He was, in fact, a decidedly attractive man. Too old for her, of course — he must be virtually Maman's age — and shorter than she liked her men. Patrice topped him a good three inches. But with his lean, erect build, smoothly brushed auburn hair and grey-blue eyes, Brinsley Hamilton was undeniably handsome in *le style anglais*.

Angelica preferred Patrice's dark hair and eyes but he was being so boring this evening it would serve him right if she flirted a while with this presentable, well-connected Englishman.

Conversation flowed easily, Brinsley enjoying Angelica's ready wit and the slightly malicious turns of phrase which echoed his own. They were getting along so well that Brinsley felt a twinge of annoyance when Patrice reappeared. Instantly Angelica twined her arm through his and smiled radiantly up at him. Brinsley remembered with a pang that Edmond had talked of Patrice's fiancée-to-be. Lucky fellow, to have landed such a prize! He noted with surprise, however, how quickly the younger man disengaged himself.

'Papa has sent me to remind you both that the firework display will begin soon. If you want a good view it's best to find a seat in the stand. Forgive me, Angelica, but I must show Julie and her father where to go.'

Annoyance flashed across her face, but Angelica was smiling when she glanced coquettishly at Brinsley. 'Since Patrice must do his duty by the country visitors, would you care to watch the fireworks with me, Monsieur Hamilton?'

'Brinsley, please, and nothing would give me greater pleasure.'

'Then you must call me Angelica.'

Brinsley was wondering if he should hint at his knowledge of her forthcoming engagement, force himself to say something complimentary about Patrice — though God knew the puppy didn't deserve it, abandoning such a beautiful girl in so cavalier a fashion. He was saved from any indiscretion by the arrival of Madame de Roncesvaux de la Beaune who had returned from speaking to an acquaintance and was now looking for her husband and daughter.

'Did you happen to notice where they went?'

'Patrice mentioned the stand, madame.'

Brinsley hoped that the woman would make her own way over the lawn but she seemed disposed to linger and talk. There was something gloating in her voice.

'Patrice is such an attentive, well-brought-up young man — a credit to dear Edmond. We've known him from a boy, of course. He and Julie were childhood sweethearts — so romantic! And now, even though poor Edmond has had that slight financial mishap ...'

Brinsley stiffened. He did not approve of tittle-tattle about the state of a friend's finances.

'... what could be more suitable than the joining of two neighbouring estates? Even though Edmond must sell some of his, silly man, and retire to Algeria. My husband intends to give Patrice very sound advice on how to avoid his father's mistakes.'

Brinsley realised that his first impression had been mistaken. He glanced rapidly at Angelica. Despite the ruddy torchlight, her face had paled perceptibly and wore a bewildered expression.

'We thought an autumn wedding,' Madame de Roncesvaux de la Beaune continued remorselessly. 'The quicker the better really, with this awful war they say is coming. They will make their home with us, of course, and if Patrice has to go and fight, Julie will be safe. She's a real help to her father, and takes such an interest in his prize herd of dairy cows . . .'

'How very fitting,' Angelica said faintly, and swayed gently. Brinsley, standing close beside her, unobtrusively steadied her with a hand to her elbow.

Madame de Roncesvaux de la Beaune pondered the remark for a moment, and then her eyes narrowed. Oh yes, she'd got the measure of this ambitious little beauty. Dear Patrice had had a very narrow escape. 'You're quite right, my dear. It is a very fitting match. Of course I must ask you to keep the news to yourselves for a day or two, until the official announcement can be made. Edmond was most insistent it should be done in Paris instead of Normandy — I really can't think why.'

Satisfied with her parting thrust, she pushed her way through the crowd towards the stand. Angelica could not speak for shock and Brinsley realised she was leaning heavily against him. He slid one arm protectively around her narrow waist. A waiter brought a chair and the offer of a glass of water.

Angelica looked dangerously close to fainting, but she waved the man away. 'I'm quite all right, thank you. It was just the talk of war, you understand.'

Brinsley understood more than she realised and his admiration for the girl, so graceful and plucky in defeat, grew stronger by the minute. Tactfully he said, 'The stand looks awfully full. If you're feeling up to it, shall we watch the fireworks down here, from the edge of the lawn? It will be less crowded and hot for you.'

Angelica nodded, grateful not to have to face the rest of the de Selincourt party for a little while longer. The first sensation of disbelief was giving way to one of cold anger by now. How could Patrice had done this to her? Over and over she relived the course of their romance. He had always been so flatteringly attentive, so ardent in their rare moments alone. Edmond and Maman had even got as far as discussing the settlement.

17

It was not that she loved him for himself — Angelica had no idea as yet what being in love really felt like — but Patrice had been easily the handsomest of her potential suitors, and she had willingly envisaged spending the rest of her life with him. They could have made such a stylish couple — and now this little nobody had taken her place!

She wanted to marry. She burned for the freedom and independence it would bring. Damn Patrice for spoiling things! The only consolation was that Edmond had lost his money, and Patrice, who loved town life above all things, was doomed to a country existence with his adoring milk-maid and her parents. Serve him right! Blind to the extravagant display of fireworks, she blinked back tears of outrage. To be left on the shelf at this stage in the Season was insupportable. She would die of shame!

Brinsley stood behind her and slightly to one side so that he could covertly study the purity of her profile. She stood as still as stone, the constantly changing play of light from the brilliant fireworks casting weird colours over her set, beautiful face. He too was almost blind to the display in the sky, more dazzled by Angelica's beauty and bravery. When he saw tears appear in her brilliant, thickly lashed eyes, he took her unresisting hand in his and squeezed it comfortingly.

Angelica's bare shoulder brushed his. Even through the layers of cloth which separated them, her warmth burned and penetrated. He stole another sideways glance, itching to sweep her into his arms and comfort her with kisses.

The display was coming to its finale, rivers of bright colour flowing upwards to form one vast firework still life. Angelica trembled slightly, whether from a chill in the air or from a suppressed sob, Brinsley could not tell. To his horror, the slight movement against him roused him unbearably. He took half a step back, hoping to hide his embarrassment.

At that moment, she realised what the fizzing, jewel-bright colours of the set piece represented: an enormous

18

bouquet of flowers. A bridal bouquet, put there on purpose to mock her ... She turned away from the hateful sight, amazed to realise for the first time that the Englishman was holding her hand. She tugged herself free. Maman ... she would know how to put things right! Angelica wanted her mother.

Through the blue pall of smoke and the scent of gunpowder drifting from the display, she ran. Taken by surprise and still dazzled by the dancing coloured lights, Brinsley was left behind. By the light of the dying torches he saw her, wraith-like in her white dress. He called after her, starting to run, but she seemed not to hear. As she reached the edge of the lawn and passed between two torches, they flickered and died. In the sudden obliterating darkness. Brinsley stumbled and fell.

He scrambled to his feet, and hearing footsteps to his right, raced in that direction. A woman's outline materialised out of the darkness. He grabbed her arm.

'Monsieur!'

An outraged dowager swung round to challenge him but her face softened at his handsomeness and obvious distress. Obviously, an *affaire du coeur*.

An engine roared into life on the other side of the car park and Brinsley cursed himself for his mistake. He started to run, chasing the car's receding tail lights, but the dust from the road clouded his eyes and caught in his throat. Finally, breathless, dusty and dishevelled, he gave up the chase. But only for one night.

He glanced down in amazement at his smeared patent pumps and grubby white waistcoat, then threw back his head and laughed with genuine amusement. After all these years of being chased by women, at last the tables were turned.

Marianne's morning routine was invariable. Breakfast was always served to her in bed at ten, consisting of a glass of

19

hot water flavoured with lemon-peel, and some dry toast. Honorine, her personal maid, then drew her a bath and while Madame la Comtesse soaked in gardenia-scented water, she laid out her mistress's clothes for the morning.

Angelica found her reading her post in the Petit Salon at eleven, dressed informally in a charming dove-grey silk dress and jacket from Patou and matching ropes of grey baroque peals. She was always at her happiest in this room, an eclectic mix of French Empire and English Regency, with touches here and there that were pure Marianne. It was she who had made the bold decision to paint the room's fine panelling and had personally supervised the mixing of an audacious shade of canteloupe. All but one wall was painted, the fourth screened with rare Chinese hand-blocked paper which she had fallen in love with at Mercadé. The decorator had added Chinese Chippendale chairs and fine blue and white export china, combined with heirloom pieces such as the two ormolu-mounted sofas covered in glowing turquoise silk damask and the *bergère* chairs, their *point d'Hongrie* covering stiched by Armand's mother.

This morning Marianne's habitually severe expression was replaced by one of happy anticipation. Angelica had finally lacked the courage to break the news last night and had spent a sleepless night in consequence.

Her mother patted the sofa invitingly. 'Any news? Has he proposed yet?'

Angelica stared dumbly at her, the memory of her humiliation raw within her. Tears rose to her eyes.

'He proposed,' she sobbed, 'but to that hideous frump Julie! I can't understand it, Maman. Everyone knew he was mine.'

'Everyone but the de Roncesvaux, it seems,' Marianne said drily, and passed Angelica a delicate scrap of lace-edged handkerchief. 'Don't cry, *chérie*. So unbecoming.'

Angelica's crying stopped instantly. 'You don't seem very surprised, Maman. I thought you'd have been more annoyed. Patrice has let us down very badly!'

'Of course I'm sorry for your disappointment, *chérie*, but you have to learn sometime that men simply aren't to be trusted. The secret of success with them is to find the one who wants you so badly he'll do anything for you. Obviously Patrice was keener on the de Roncesvaux millions than he was on you. *Tant pis*. You're better off without him.'

'But I was going to marry him!'

'I dare say. You'll be telling me you loved him next. But how could you? You hardly knew him. And who knows? Perhaps it really is for the best. I dismissed them at the time but there have been rumours recently about Edmond's finances.'

Angelica's face brightened. 'I think they're true. Madame de Roncesvaux let something slip when she was telling us the good news — and she just loved doing that!'

'Us?'

'Oh, an Englishman, a friend of Edmond's. But what shall I do now, Maman? All the best *partis* are taken. Maybe we could say I'm not well and retiring from the Season early. There's always next year.'

Marianne's face grew grave. 'I'm sorry, but we can't afford to wait.'

Angelica went cold with horror. 'You mean — there's no money left?'

Her mother smiled faintly. 'Not quite as bad as that. We were entertaining some of Armand's friends from the Quai d'Orsay last night, and they said that Germany is hungry for territorial expansion. War is inevitable, it seems, and it's quite on the cards that Herr Hitler will mount an invasion of France in a year or less.'

As her daughter's eyes widened, Marianne continued: 'Naturally Armand intends to take no chances. He's arranging for all his collections to be packed and stored in the château. If the situation worsens, his friends will tip him off in plenty of time for us to retire to the Loire property. But you see what this means for you?'

'No Season! We'll be hundreds of miles away from all the parties and balls ...'

'No men, *chérie*,' her mother corrected her. 'We'll be overrun or at war, remember? That's why it's so important to get you settled into a good marriage this year.'

'But who *can* I marry?'

Before Marianne could reply, there was a knock at the door and Honorine appeared, carrying a stupendous bouquet of wine red Baccarat roses tied up with a white satin bow.

'For mam'selle,' she explained, detaching the accompanying envelope and handing it to Angelica. The roses were carefully placed with their thorny stems overhanging the edge of a walnut occasional table. The thoroughbred scent quickly filled the small room.

'Patrice!' Angelica cried, her face radiant with relief. It must all have been a ghastly mistake. She'd forgive him and marry him tomorrow — anything rather than lead a spinster's life in the country.

But the card inside the florist's envelope belonged to someone else. 'Brinsley Hamilton' the vellum square read, together with the addresses of his two residences in England and Scotland and that of his London club. On the back of the card he had scribbled: 'I hope very much to see you again', and the number of his suite at the Plaza-Athénée.

'I didn't realise he was titled,' Angelica said thoughtfully.

'And I didn't realise you were.' Her mother indicated the envelope, addressed to 'Comtesse Angelica de Bailliencourt'. 'Really, *cherie*, how often must I tell you? With a shop or a restaurant or anyone of the servant class it's perfectly in order to borrow Armand's title, but never with an aristocrat. Who is this man? You obviously made quite an impression on him.'

'Just an old friend of Edmond's, I told you.'

'How old?'

22

'Ancient! Your age, about.'

Marianne ignored the thrust. 'What is he called?'

For answer, the card was thrust into her hands. Marianne's eyes went straight to the coronet discreetly engraved above the name. 'An Earl! And haven't you heard of the Hamiltons, *petite idiote*? They're one of the wealthiest families in England.'

Belatedly, she remembered the presence of the maid. 'Honorine, go along to my husband's study straight away and see if you can find that copy of *Burke's Peerage* — we must check he's not already married. Oh, and take the flowers and arrange them, please.'

'Do you want them in here, madame?'

'Certainly not! Only white flowers in here. Besides, they are mademoiselle's. Take them up for her.'

When the maid was safely out of the room, Marianne cross-examined her daughter. 'So you told him you were a Countess?'

Angelica nodded guiltily. She knew she had no right to the de Bailliencourt name or rank, Armand never having formally adopted her, but it was such a temptation and usually had a pleasing effect. She should have noticed it barely registered on the ultra-grand Brinsley Hamilton.

'For once you may have done the right thing,' her mother conceded. 'An English Earl might well prefer not to marry beneath him. But if the girl is already a Countess ...' She smiled and hugged her daughter. 'There's not a second to be lost. Ring him immediately to thank him for the flowers, and tell him your mother is holding a small luncheon party tomorrow.'

'Is there time to arrange one?'

'Leave that to me. You, my dear, are to concentrate on your appearance. That means no *maquillage*, and only the simplest hair style and clothes — last year's, before you came out, should be perfect. God knows why, but Englishmen of his class marry girls straight out of the schoolroom, so that is how you must look ...'

23

The next day Brinsley was their guest of honour. Marianne greeted him charmingly, giving an impression of well-bred reserve in her severely cut black dress from Chanel, enlivened only with touches of white at the Puritan collar and cuffs. Her hair was tied back into a black grosgrain bow, and she had abandoned her customary lashings of jewellery and make-up in favour of a softer, more natural look. She wore only a thin platinum wedding band and a discreet diamond engagement ring — Papa's, Angelica noted in surprise. Armand's was much bigger.

'My husband sends his apologies,' Marianne explained with a wistful smile, 'but I'm afraid these days he's much too frail to take part in our social life.'

She prayed that the sound of crates being hammered shut and Armand's shrill instructions to the packers would not reach him.

Marianne had commandeered the attendance of two couples of her acquaintance: dull, respectable, and willing to turn up at the drop of a hat for a good meal in gracious surroundings. An aged cousin of Armand's, who received a small pension from him, was her own escort.

Brinsley, she noticed approvingly, had eyes only for Angelica — chaste and fresh-looking in last year's hastily laundered white *broderie anglaise*. A pity really. In his light-weight Prince of Wales check from Mr Tautz, hand-lasted black brogues, voile shirt and Sulka tie in a fashionable Windsor knot, Brinsley was quite the most stylish Englishman Marianne had encountered since their near neighbour, the disgraced Duke of Windsor. And he was only a few years younger than herself ... But this was no time to be selfish.

'It's such a pleasure for us to receive a visitor from England,' she assured him over coffee in the Grand Salon. Its floor-length shutters and windows stood open to the stone terrace at the back of the house that was artfully lined with painted tubs of clipped greenery.

'My husband was in the diplomatic service and has very fond memories of St James's,' she continued, omitting to mention that Armand had last visited England decades before their marriage. 'We lead such a quiet life nowadays.' She sighed and sat back in her chair, a lonely figure in the vast lemon and pearl-grey salon, its colours chosen to reflect the splendid Aubusson carpet which was the room's focal point.

'I worry about my little girl,' she continued, hazel eyes soft and confiding. 'Sadly, most of her friends at the convent were not Parisians. She misses their companionship so much.'

Brinsley glanced across the room to where Angelica sat, patiently dealing cards for the wizened Cousin Frédéric. He cleared his throat and told a white lie. 'I'm virtually a stranger to Paris myself, Madame, and find myself with time on my hands.' Only that morning he had cancelled his arrangements to drive down to a friend's house in Cannes. 'Would you permit your daughter to accompany me on a few outings while I am here?'

'You are too kind to a lonely young girl. I'm sure Angelica would be delighted.'

And so the charade of seeing the sights of Paris was entered into by both sides. Brinsley had of course visited all the usual attractions before, and Angelica was blasé about them, but it was great fun to drive about town in an ivory-coloured Mercedes-Benz 500K with red glove-leather seats. Brinsley had borrowed it from one of his friends.

Headley, Brinsley's manservant, was quietly amazed. At home, Brinsley never drove himself if he could avoid it, and only ever bought Bentleys. Obviously there was something in the air.

On one occasion Brinsley drove them to the Château of Chantilly for a picnic; the following day to Fontainebleau at dawn where he bid against the cutthroat competition of Paris's restaurateurs to lay at Angelica's feet a bunch of the rare *chasselas*, the fruit from the King's Vine auctioned off each year. Angelica fed him the choicest of the grapes as they drove back to town for breakfast at the Ritz.

There were more active pursuits too — swimming at the Racing Club, tennis in the Bois, and racing, racing, racing at Longchamp, Auteuil, Chantilly. Angelica, whose idea of strenuous exercise was a morning's shopping, was often exhausted after a day in Brinsley's company, but far too clever to let him see it. Not that he was devoid of all appreciation of the finer things in life. He was, she discovered, something of a shop-hound himself and would willingly kill a morning selecting ties from Charvet or replacing a favourite tortoise-handled umbrella at Vedrenne, the only place in Paris for gentlemen's umbrellas.

He drew the line at attending a viewing at Mademoiselle Chanel's famous *salon des glaces* in the Rue Cambon, but arranged lunch afterwards in an intimate *salle privée* for himself, Angelica and her mother. Marianne manufactured an excuse to leave Lapérouse early and allow them some time to themselves but Brinsley was tenderly solicitous of his young escort's reputation and immediately called for the bill.

In fact, Angelica was beginning to despair. They'd been seeing one another for almost a month and in a week's time it would be August. Brinsley would have to leave then. Nobody who was anybody in Parisian society would consent to become an Augustin, simmering in the heat and stink of the city when they could be in a chic mountain or seaside resort. If only Brinsley would declare himself by then!

For he was mad about her, she was certain. He was endlessly entertained by her slightest remarks — when she commented that a zebra in the Jardin d'Acclimatation was '*Très chic*', for instance, or when she confounded him by asking for a *réligieuse* to accompany the *citron pressé* he had ordered for her at the Café Flore. Brinsley's French was not his strongest point and his amazement at being asked to provide a nun quickly changed to roars of delighted laughter when an attentive waiter brought the cake Angelica had requested.

He watched as she ate it with childlike enjoyment, then gently wiped traces of cream from her soft pink mouth with his own spotless handkerchief. His hand shook, she noted with satisfaction. But why hadn't he touched her since?

Sometimes, when he brought her home unfashionably early from the Pré Catalan where they had dined and danced, Angelica had to struggle to stop herself from hurrying things along. She did nothing, of course. Brinsley's image of her vulnerability and innocence would have been shattered. Yet he ached to kiss her, she could tell. After a glass or two of wine, his pale eyes grew cloudy with suppressed passion. Unconsciously his hands would tremble above her bare shoulders as he helped her on or off with a wrap. If only he wasn't such a gentleman. If only he would say or do something to commit himself. Angelica thought she would go mad from suspense.

Marianne too was growing tired of waiting. '*Chérie*, has he kissed you, or even touched you in that certain way?'

'No, Maman. He imagines it would shock a gently bred young girl like me.'

Her mother sighed. 'Then we shall just have to help him along. When he takes you out tomorrow, wear the pale green dress — the one with all the buttons. Then this is what you must do . . .'

The next evening, Brinsley took Angelica to dinner at Maxim's. Albert, the *maître d'*, greeted the English aristocrat by name and showed them straight through to the more fashionable back room, to a table with a banquette seat facing the orchestra. In the red plush comfort of the famous *fin de siècle* restaurant, the seductive ambience heightened by the soft lighting from bronze table-lamps shaped like flowers, Brinsley relaxed and allowed himself to drink slightly more than normal. Angelica barely touched her food and drank less than her customary two glasses of wine. She had to keep her wits about her tonight.

When he drove her back to the house by the Bois, it was still only half-past ten. Angelica made no move to get out of the car but turned appealingly to him.

'Won't you come in for a drink?'

'I'm not sure I should, my dear. Isn't it rather late?'

She pulled a face and ran her hand lightly over his sleeve. 'Oh, Brinsley, do come in. Maman was saying only this morning that she hasn't seen you for a while. Just one drink with her, please.'

Reassured that they were to be chaperoned by the Countess, and hoping he might at last meet Armand de Bailliencourt, who seemed to be confined to his room by a mild indisposition every time Brinsley had called so far, he allowed himself to be cajoled into the house. The butler let them into the marble-flagged entrance hall, where conspicuous upon a Louis XV console table were a man's hat and gloves. A visitor at this hour?

'Madame la Comtesse sends her apologies,' the butler said, 'but Monsieur le Comte is unwell and the doctor has been called. Madame hopes to be able to join you later.'

'Oh,' Angelica breathed, putting her hand to her mouth. 'How is my father? Is he very ill?'

'The doctor says the attack will pass off soon, Mademoiselle. There is no need to concern yourself,' the servant assured her gravely. He'd been tipped handsomely by Madame to locate an old hat and gloves of the master's and place them prominently on the hall table. Then she'd rehearsed him in what he was to say. In reality Armand de Bailliencourt was peacefully asleep in his room.

'I think perhaps I should go,' Brinsley began.

Angelica swayed on her feet. 'I'm afraid I'm feeling a little faint. Perhaps some Cognac . . .'

Brinsley and the butler guided her into the Petit Salon which tonight was softly lit by just two silk-shaded lamps, placed at either end of one of the long sofas.

'Thank you, that will be all,' Angelica said as the butler finished pouring their drinks. There was an awkward silence after he had gone. Brinsley sat stiffly upright in his chair and gulped his Cognac. Angelica ignored hers. She huddled in the middle of one of the long sofas and sank her head into her hands. To his horror, Brinsley saw a slow trail of tears glinting through her fingers. He was on his feet and beside her in a moment.

'Are you concerned for your father, my dear? Bless you for being so tender-hearted, but I'm sure the doctor is right.'

'No,' she faltered, 'it's not just that — although it doesn't help that he is so old and sick. Oh, Brinsley!'

'What is it, my darling?'

Encouraged by the endearment, Angelica inched gradually closer to him. 'You'll think me such a coward,' she murmured.

Brinsley looked down at her tear-streaked face and wet, tangled lashes and his heart turned over. He couldn't bear to see her cry. 'No, I won't, darling. Just tell me what it is, and I'll do anything I can to put things right.'

'B-But you c-can't,' she hiccuped. 'N-No one can. There's going to be a war, and Paris will be invaded and — oh, Brinsley, I'm so frightened.'

She clung to him, pressing her face to his immaculate shirt front. The scent of her, and the intimate sensation of her tears dampening his shirt, were too much him. Pity and love overwhelmed him. He slid his arm around her shoulders. 'You don't have to worry about that any more, my love.'

She caught her breath, her eyes searching his. Nearly ... but not quite. She had to be certain. Slowly she wound her arms around his neck and brought his face close to hers. 'I feel so safe with you,' she whispered, pressing even closer to him.

She could have no idea what she was doing to him, Brinsley thought. The soft swell of her breasts came

29

tantalisingly close to his hand. Angelica sighed and stirred against him, her breath fanning the skin above his shirt collar. Amazed and unbearably excited by her abandon, Brinsley found himself gently tracing the line of buttons at her neckline. Swiftly her hand came up and started to undo them.

He watched speechless as the fabric to either side of the row of tiny buttons fell away, leaving Angelica naked to the waist but for a chemise the colour of cream. Her honey-coloured skin glowed more lustrously than the silk. Through the thin fabric, shell-pink nipples were disturbingly apparent.

'Angelica, do you love me?'

She raised her mouth to his. 'Why else would I be doing this?'

'Darling!'

He groaned and gathered her to him, pressing kisses to her face, neck and shoulders while lowering her back on to the sofa. This was all wrong, he knew. He adored this girl and shouldn't be taking advantage of her before . . .

But Angelica writhed beneath him and one delicate shoulder strap slid down her arm. Gently he cupped the pointed perfect breast she had exposed, then lowered his mouth to its rosy bud.

At the touch of his tongue, Angelica moaned. Patrice had been so clumsy. She had not known that exquisite sensations like this were possible. Maman had never told her. Maman who would stay in her room for twenty minutes after their return and then . . .

There was the sound of the door opening and Marianne's voice enquired silkily, 'I take it there is an explanation for this?'

Angelica and Brinsley sat up in confusion, half blinded by the sudden influx of light from the hall. The Comtesse de Bailliencourt stood in the doorway, her expression unreadable.

Brinsley chivalrously helped Angelica straighten her

30

clothing then got to his feet, brushing back his own dishevelled hair with one hand 'The best explanation in the world,' he said, once more the urbane English gentleman in command of a tricky situation. 'I should be speaking to your husband, of course, Madame. But since he is ill, I should like your permission to ask Angelica for her hand in marriage.'

Brinsley had expected to deal with Armand de Bailliencourt about the legal side of the marriage, perhaps enter into prolonged negotiations, but the Countess — no, Marianne — explained the situation with her customary restraint and dignity. It seemed the poor old fellow was losing ground fast and was far too frail to be bothered with talk of settlements and dowries. All he wanted was to see his little girl married suitably before he died. Surely in this case, and in view of the deteriorating international situation, the lawyers could clear up all the little details *after* the marriage ceremony, which could be held as soon as Brinsley liked? Marianne was surprisingly accommodating about that, too.

'You know, Brinsley, in France it is customary for us to hold two ceremonies — a civil one at the local Mairie, which is legal and binding, and then a second religious ceremony in church. But, *mon cher*, I understand the difficulties this could pose for you. You are not Catholic, I think?'

'My Scottish ancestors were, of course, but I was brought up in the Anglican faith.'

'There's no need to worry. Neither Angelica nor myself would object to the religious ceremony taking place in England, according to your rites. And it would be a chance for you to display your new bride to all your friends and acquaintances there, *n'est-ce pas*? I understand there is a chapel at Courtney Park, or perhaps one of the fashionable London churches? Naturally Armand and I would do our best to attend, but his health and this talk of war ... I really think the sooner the better, don't you? It would be such a tragedy if Angelica were to marry in black.'

She seemed quite unconscious of any irony in her choice of words.

The wedding in the Mairie of the Seizième, Avenue Henri-Martin, took place on Angelica's nineteenth birthday, which was three days after Brinsley became thirty-nine. It was a very quiet affair.

Marianne explained to Brinsley that of course many of their friends were already spending August out of town and it would be no kindness to recall them just for the civil ceremony. A couple of Angelica's school friends arrived from the provinces, also her godparents, Marianne's best friend Isabelle and Cousin Frédéric. None of the d'Alary relatives was notified.

Armand de Bailliencourt was introduced to Brinsley for the first time on the steps of the Mairie. An elegant dandified figure in a frock coat, high wing collar and spats, he looked older even than Brinsley had expected, but with his alert dark eyes and firm handshake not quite the invalid Marianne had painted.

'I'm sorry we haven't met before,' the old man said in a high cracked voice, 'but it's Marianne's business really, and all this packing, you know.' He gestured wearily. 'My congratulations to you both, of course. I always thought her a pretty little thing, though I haven't seen a lot of her during the past three years. School, you understand, then gadding about ... But charming, oh yes, just like her mother. And how lovely they both look.'

If Brinsley momentarily wondered why a doting father should have seen so little of his daughter, the sight of Angelica in her bridal gown was enough to chase away all rational thought.

Marianne had brought her considerable influence to

bear on Elsa Schiaparelli, persuading her to make Angelica's dress in the mere two weeks available. The result was a ravishing gown of oyster-coloured satin. It was not full-length, as Brinsley had expected, nor was it exactly demure. The sleeves and shoulders of the gown, and its scalloped neckline, were of pale Brussels lace, allowing revealing glimpses of the golden skin beneath. The tailored bodice and full skirt of the dress were of heavy silk satin overlaid with the same lace. Matching shoes and a wide-brimmed picture hat had been made specially to complement it, and Angelica's hair had been dressed into soft shoulder-length waves.

A posy of pink camellias was the only hint of colour, but the de Bailliencourt diamonds and pearls flashed at her ears, and on her engagement finger she wore the magnificent twelve-carat ruby ring she had chosen at Cartier — against Brinsley's better judgment. He disliked coloured stones and thought it rather vulgarly large; he offered to send to London for his own mother's diamond engagement ring which was kept in a bank vault there but Angelica had explained very prettily that in France the bride always chose her own engagement ring, and he gave way.

Marianne was dressed by Madame Grès in elaborately draped lilac crêpe de chine. It was last season's, but as she had seen there were no press photographers present ... She wore an outlandish hat trimmed with grey fox, and in August carried an elegant grey fox muff. She also wore far more jewellery than Brinsley was accustomed to seeing her in — emerald and diamond earrings, bangles and dress clips — but he had to admit she looked rather splendid.

On Brinsley's side only Headley attended, a stooping, purse-mouthed figure who stayed in the background. His hearing was acute, however, and his command of French rather better than his master's. A black-suited clerk ushered them to the top of the Mairie stairs and into a dark cavernous room smelling of linoleum polish. A few rapid sentences of French — Marianne had kindly coached

33

Brinsley in his responses — and then the sixth Earl of Courtney slid a slim platinum band on to his new Countess's finger.

As Angelica raised a face of heart-stopping loveliness to receive the first kiss of her married life, Headley wondered why, during the ceremony, the 'Comtesse de Bailliencourt' had given her name as plain Angelica d'Alary.

His wedding night was a revelation to Brinsley. After an elegant wedding breakfast at the Avenue Foch, he and his bride of four hours caught the boat train at the Gare du Nord. Instead of the usual ferry with its cramped un-romantic cabins, they had made special arrangements with a shipping magnate friend of his to take over a vacant stateroom on a Transatlantic liner. The ship was due to berth in Calais for just a few hours to take on fresh supplies for the last leg of the crossing. Angelica and Brinsley were to honeymoon in London, which she had never visited, and afterwards at Courtney Park.

Ever the gentleman, Brinsley decided not to approach her on their first night. It had been a long and tiring day for them both, he decided. As if to prove his point, once inside their reserved compartment on the train, Angelica curled her legs under her, pillowed her head on his shoulder and fell fast asleep. Brinsley spent the next few hours content just to cradle her in his arms, entranced by the length of her curling lashes against the peachbloom of her skin. Even asleep, she was never less than totally alluring.

While they boarded the White Star liner, Headley left his second-class seat on the train and supervised the transfer of their luggage and overnight bags. Once every-thing was safely installed in the great white and gold stateroom, he enquired whether his lordship would be dining that evening?

It was Angelica who replied. 'We have all we need, thank you, Headley.'

Noting the gleam in her brilliant green eyes, the valet quickly bowed himself out.

Brinsley cleared his throat. 'I'll change in the bathroom, darling. Give you some time to yourself.'

Angelica laughed at this British reserve. 'No need, *chéri*. In France it's considered quite usual for a husband to watch his wife undress.'

She stepped out of her demure powder blue and white going-away dress and stood before him, sublimely un-embarrassed, in a pair of skimpy white duchesse satin camiknickers trimmed with tiny blue bows. Still in pearl-grey silk stockings and high-heeled kid shoes, Angelica's legs seemed endless. Around one slim thigh he saw she wore a blue silk garter.

She noted in which direction his eyes had strayed, and smiled. 'Maman gave it to me for luck.'

She omitted to mention that the ever practical Marianne, not trusting merely to luck, had also passed on an unusually detailed 'Marriage Guide'. With sensuality awakened by Brinsley's practised caresses on the night they became engaged, Angelica had studied the book avidly and on her wedding night intended to put as much as possible to the test. Though still a virgin, she had none of the new bride's traditional timorousness. After all, what did she have to be timid about? Every inch of her was eminently desirable, and she knew it.

She ran her fingers lingeringly over the narrow blue garter and said huskily, 'Would you like it as a souvenir of our wedding night?'

When Brinsley still said nothing she stepped boldly forward and began to take off his tie, allowing him a tantalising glimpse of her high round breasts as she leant forward to loosen the knot.

'I know it's difficult for you, *chéri*, without Headley to help you undress,' she teased him, drawing the tie back and forth between her outstretched hands. 'Won't I do instead?'

For answer he pulled her roughly to him. Her mouth opened like a flower in the heat of his kiss, her tongue twining instinctively with his. Nimbly her fingers dealt with the buttons of his shirt which joined the rest of his clothes on the floor.

Brinsley slid the white satin off Angelica's breasts, pausing to suck and tease each nipple into throbbing awareness of his hands' rougher touch. The glassy fabric slid to her feet, revealing pert buttocks and a boyishly flat stomach with an almond-shaped navel. Below gleamed a perfect triangle of close black curls, soft as lamb's fleece.

Brinsley caught his breath. Dressed, Angelica was stunning. Naked, she exuded elegant sensuality, a Cranach Venus who easily surpassed any woman he had known before.

She stepped away from him and teasingly ran her hands over her thrusting breasts while she kicked off her shoes. When she started to unclip one stocking from the white lace suspender belt she still wore, Brinsley spoke for the first time.

'Leave it on.'

He stepped out of his monogrammed silk drawers and she encompassed him in one small cool hand.

'Ravish me,' she breathed, and stretched out on the starched white linen, already moist and ready for him.

London 1939

The stewardess who brought in their early morning tea smiled knowingly. Headley tut-tutted at the sight of his master's best grey alpaca, a tangled mess on the cabin floor. As they disembarked later that morning, every man on deck noticed Angelica's glow of satisfaction and the faint purple shadows beneath her husband's eyes.

Safely installed later that day in the biggest suite of the London Ritz, Angelica decided that hotel life suited her. No need to live by Maman's rigid timetable here. They could breakfast in bed at four in the afternoon or order supper at midnight if they felt like it.

But when three days of this sybaritic existence had passed without their even leaving the hotel, Brinsley began to feel a little restless. He was naturally an energetic man, and even their constant lovemaking could not fully make up for the loss of his usual outdoor pursuits. He stood at the window of their bedroom overlooking Green Park, and said briskly, 'What a wonderful day! Isn't it time I repaid some of your hospitality and showed you the sights of London?'

Angelica barely glanced up from the magazine she was reading in bed. 'That's all right, *chéri*. I'm happy just being with you.' She settled comfortably back in the nest of pillows she had built for herself.

He glanced longingly out at the August sunshine. 'Then how about a spot of riding, darling? I know of a marvellous stables in a mews just off Berkeley Square. You'd love the Row, I know.'

'No clothes,' she said indistinctly, popping into her mouth a rose fondant chocolate from the huge heart-shaped box on the bed beside her. 'They were in the trunks Headley took on.'

'Soon fix that! I'll call Huntsman and ask them to send over a selection in your size.'

Angelica had absolutely no intention of sacrificing her complexion to constant riding, swimming and walking now that she had captured her English sportsman. But she could see it would be wise to let him off the leash, at least for this morning. She stifled a yawn. 'Forgive me, *chéri*. I'm just so tired after last night ...'

Immediately Brinsley was all contrition. He sat on the edge of the bed and squeezed her hands. 'My angel, I'm a brute! Why not rest this morning? I've a few things to sort out in town, and Goodbody's had the infernal cheek to contact me here, saying he must see me. On my honeymoon, if you please! But if you're really tired, my darling ...'

She smiled bravely. 'Don't worry about me. I'll rest for a while, and maybe do a little shopping if I feel up to it later.'

He leant forward to kiss her forehead. 'Jolly good idea. You'll need some country clothes, don't forget.'

Angelica's thoughts were running more on exploring Bond Street for what it had to offer in the way of furs and cosmetics in the shocking colours Maman had never let her wear. She smiled in pleasurable anticipation, and was so busy visualising the treats in store that she quite forgot to enquire who Goodbody was ...

Thomas Goodbody, senior partner of Goodbody, Frayne and Goodbody, warmed his skinny rump before the blazing coal fire he favoured even on a warm August morning. He claimed it was because his office was on the wrong side of the square, the shady side, but his employees maintained that he found the fire a useful device for bringing people into line. Recalcitrant clerks, junior solicitors, even clients who stubbornly ignored Goodbody's advice, all sooner or later found themselves sitting in the button-backed leather chair which Thomas placed close to the fierce flames. It was to this hot seat that the Earl of Courtney was shown on his arrival.

He had passed a pleasant hour or so with his tailor, reviewing the state of his wardrobe, and afterwards picked out a dozen new silks and voiles which Budd, his shirt-maker in Piccadilly Arcade, would make up for him. With the important part of the morning's business taken care of, he decided he might as well see what his lawyer considered so pressing.

Goodbody stood respectfully while his client took a seat, then resumed his own chair behind the scarred partner's desk. No one would have guessed from the studied impartiality of his expression that, like Headley, Thomas Goodbody also had his doubts about Brinsley's marriage.

'The arrangements proceeded according to plan, your lordship?' he established, though he could tell by the glassy-eyed air of satisfaction about his client that they must have.

'Yes indeed, Goodbody. I am now a married man.' Brinsley waited confidently for the lawyer's congratulations.

They were not forthcoming. The lawyer shuffled some correspondence together on his desk and enquired mildly, 'And had you known the young — er — person for long, my lord?'

Brinsley did not miss the piercing glance from above the old man's half-spectacles. 'Less than a month actually. But, good God, with a war threatening, what else could I do?'

His assurances to his valet were water under the bridge by now.

'Quite so, my lord. And the young person herself was

eager for the marriage to proceed quickly, I take it?'

Brinsley began to find the heat of the fire oppressive. He brought out his handkerchief to wipe away the thin film of perspiration that had broken out over his face. He was not, however, sufficiently distracted to miss the implication. 'I'm not sure I care for your tone, Goodbody,' he said in his most lordly drawl. 'I will not have my wife made to sound like a little totty with an eye to the main chance. After all, she was a Countess before she married me.'

The lawyer studied him closely for a moment. Such a noble head. What a pity there was barely a brain in it. Gravely, he dealt his trump card. 'I'm afraid not, my lord. The mother — hmm, Marianne de Bailliencourt — is indeed a Countess by marriage. But the daughter, Angelica —' he stressed the name's foreignness — 'was never formally adopted by her mother's second husband, the Count.'

He kept his eyes on Brinsley's face and pounced, hawk-like, on the flicker of puzzlement he saw there. 'I take it you were in full possession of the facts of your wife's parentage before the marriage was solemnised, my lord? Because if there was any dissimulation, any attempt to hoodwink you into marriage under false pretences, we should have very good grounds indeed for seeking an annulment.'

Goodbody paused, his cynical old eyes intent upon his client. The slightest hint that his suggestion was being seriously considered, and he'd arrange an afternoon conference with London's leading divorce silk.

Brinsley was by now so hot and confused he could barely think straight. What a ghastly mistake to have made, but there must be a perfectly rational explanation. What if he *had* heard Angelica refer to de Bailliencourt as 'Father'? She was a tender-hearted, loving girl, so why should she not address her mother's husband thus, if it pleased them both? Her mother . . .

Brinsley acknowledged to himself that there had indeed

40

been evasiveness in Marianne's behaviour, a marked eagerness to see the match through without his first meeting
Armand de Bailliencourt and learning the full facts. No
innocent deception on her part, then — but Angelica had
not been involved in any of the more businesslike discussions of what 'her father' would do or expect in the way
of dowries or settlements.

A vision of her that morning, adorably flushed and
tousled above the white swansdown-trimmed wrapper she
wore, returned to haunt him. He remembered the generosity with which she had welcomed him to their bed every
night since their marriage, and his loins tingled. It was easy
then to convince himself that his open, loving wife was free
from any taint of conspiracy. The alternative was too
appalling for a man as proud as Brinsley to contemplate.

He looked Goodbody in the eye. 'I was naturally aware
of my wife's circumstances before I married her. I suppose
it was a little remiss of me not to see to the legal side more
clearly, but now that you've heard from her father — her
*step*father — it should be simple enough, I take it.'

The lawyer bowed his head and ferreted out a letter
from the pile before him. 'Couldn't be simpler,' he said
drily. 'It is, however, my professional duty to express
considerable concern at the terms outlined by the Comte
de Bailliencourt's lawyers. In fact, I find it impossible to
believe that if, as you say, you had full knowledge of your
wife's circumstances ...'

Brinsley was by now burning — from the heat of the
fire, and from rage at hearing his word doubted, however
good the cause. He lurched to his feet. 'I must ask you,
Goodbody, to be very careful of the way in which you refer
to my wife,' he said coldly. 'In fact, it may well be necessary for me to reconsider the association between the family
and this firm.'

For the first time the lawyer's composure was shaken.
He drew himself painfully upright. 'I have served the
Hamilton family man and boy for more than forty years,

41

and my father and grandfather before me. I spoke only out of concern, my lord.'

Brinsley felt better away from the heat of the fire. 'I know, Goodbody, but there's really nothing to worry about.' He paused, his hand on the door. 'By the way, what dowry does Angelica's stepfather propose?'

Tactfully the lawyer lowered his eyes to the letter he still clutched in one dry hand, though he remembered the contents perfectly. 'He claims she already has it, my lord. In view of the fact that Angelica d'Alary is not his legally adopted daughter, the Count considers his wedding gift to her — one pair of diamond and pearl earrings, formerly the property of the first Countess — to be dowry enough.'

For the first time that morning there was no trace of bombast or evasiveness in Brinsley's manner. He said quite truthfully, 'Angelica is the only woman I shall ever love. I would have taken her with nothing at all.'

'Quite so, my lord.' Goodbody edged his way around the desk to show the Earl from the office.

'More's the pity,' he added to himself under his breath.

Despite his calm reaction in the solicitor's office, Brinsley's thoughts were in turmoil by the time he reached the hotel. To be so taken in! Not by Angelica, of course — by now he unquestioningly accepted her innocence — but by Marianne de Bailliencourt and her practised evasions. Seething inwardly, he decided to have a stiff whisky before rejoining his wife. As he sat in the lobby, nursing his drink, he saw Angelica push through the swing doors, her jaunty coral-coloured jersey suit and veiled pillbox hat the last word in Parisian chic. Seeing her at a slight distance for the first time in days, Brinsley felt a sensation of shock run through him. She still eclipsed every other woman around, but marriage had changed her already. Her face seemed older, not in years but in experience. Her expression was amused and knowing, that of a woman easy with her newly

42

awakened sensuality. And she wore make-up, he realised, something she had never done in Paris. Her wide, wickedly smiling mouth was painted an intense shade of coral behind the black mesh of her veil.

It was as if she sensed his eyes upon her. In full view of the onlookers in the crowded lobby, Angelica stood still, raised her veil and provocatively ran the tip of her tongue over her full painted lips.

Brinsley knew that every eye in the room would be upon them by now. He should do no more than press his cheek against hers, but Angelica didn't give a damn for convention.

Her lips parted invitingly. 'Kiss me,' she breathed.

He did so, long and hard, in the way no lady should ever be kissed in public. Afterwards, as she preceded him to the lift, walking with the gentle sway of her hips which she knew he found irresistible, he realised the secret of her hold over him. She *was* no lady. She was his Countess, every last tantalising inch of her, and he was her devoted slave.

The intensity of his lovemaking astonished Angelica. 'After only one morning apart, *chéri*!' Afterwards she lay exhausted in the crook of his arm while he called room service and ordered lunch to be sent up.

'Wear something reasonably warm when we go out this afternoon,' he called through to her as she lay soaking in the bath a few minutes later. 'It can be quite chilly in the vault.'

What strange British custom was this? Angelica's voice trembled slightly as she said, 'We are going to visit your family tomb?'

He put his head in at the bathroom door and smiled reassuringly. 'Bank vault, my sweet. And I think you'll like what you find there.'

Angelica was full of suppressed excitement as she was admitted to a narrow eighteenth-century building in Fleet

Street, the inside of which resembled nothing so undignified as a banking hall. Messrs Samuel Hoare conducted their transactions in what appeared to be an immaculately maintained town house.

The manager took them quickly through the formalities.

'And what's to be the limit on her ladyship's account, my lord?'

Brinsley frowned. 'Why none, of course.'

Afterwards the manager conducted them personally downstairs. The basement room was lined entirely with steel safety deposit boxes which struck quite a chill, as Brinsley had warned. But Angelica was too excited to notice. Which of the shallow steel boxes was Brinsley's, and what had he stored inside for her?

The manager went to one corner of the room where the steel drawers gave way to a set of huge floor to ceiling doors, with two keyholes in their shining surface. Simultaneously, he and Brinsley inserted keys. The hollow sound of the lock's tumblers echoed around the room which was silent but for Angelica's shallow breathing.

The manager indicated a graceful Regency table and chairs, striking an incongruous note in the strong-room, and withdrew. Brinsley waited until the door had closed behind him before beginning to display the family treasure.

At first Angelica was disappointed. The rows of deep baize-lined shelves were filled with nothing more exciting than dusty blue drawstring bags or boxes of wood and Morocco leather. Then, as Brinsley pulled out a selection of the bags and opened them, she realised she was looking at the family silver.

'Though only the pieces we can't use at Courtney,' he explained, indicating the solid silver trays, épergnes, bonbonnières, candelabra, and canteen after canteen of cutlery. 'Aunts and uncles keep dying and bequeathing me more of the stuff. It's impossible to keep it all at the house — it just makes more work for the servants — so I store it

44

here. There's so much that I shall have to take another strong box soon — damned nuisance. Are there any pieces you've taken an especial fancy to, my darling? If so, I'll arrange for them to be brought down.'

Angelica's discerning eye had alighted upon a priceless Paul Revere coffee set. 'This is wonderful.'

Brinsley looked doubtful. 'Think so? The American stuff's a bit plain for my taste, but if you like it ...' He fumbled among the jewellery boxes. 'Ah, now, this is more the ticket. What do you make of these, eh?' He flipped open the lid to reveal a ruby necklace and matching bracelet.

'My great-great-grandmother's,' he said proudly.

Angelica looked doubtful. 'The rubies are magnificent if crudely cut,' she agreed, 'but Georgian diamonds are a little dull by today's standards, don't you think?'

The things she knew never ceased to surprise Brinsley, but he picked out another box without comment and displayed its contents. The brilliance and depth of the large square-cut emeralds in the collar and earrings inside nearly took her breath away, but once again the setting was a disappointment, this time heavy and over-elaborate in the Victorian style.

'Think how these would look in a more modern setting,' she sighed, trailing one finger regretfully over the stones' cold surfaces. 'They're so wonderful it seems a pity not to display them better. All those tiny diamonds — not a decent stone among them.'

Brinsley's eyes flicked to a collection of velvet pouches tucked away on a top shelf. He brought them over to the table. 'May I borrow your scarf?' Casually he emptied the pouch's contents on to the silk cushion her scarf provided. 'Should be black velvet for the full effect, of course.'

Slowly she realised what she was looking at. The dull, vaguely yellow stones were not glass, as she had at first supposed, but uncut canary diamonds, hundreds of carats' worth.

45

'Where did you get them?' she breathed, cupping a few of the precious stones in her hands and admiring their muted fire. Cut and polished, they would be sensational.

Brinsley looked uncomfortable. 'One of my more disreputable ancestors served with the East India Company. These were his share of the loot after the putting down of a rebellion in Uzbekistan. No one liked to enquire how the former owner met his end.'

'There are the same number of blue —' he indicated another pouch — 'and a few red and pink. They're the rarest, as you probably know.'

Angelica did, and in her mind's eye was already marrying the splendid rubies from the old Georgian necklace, re-cut, with the red diamonds in an ultra-modern setting. Cartier would be the best jewellers to commission the work from, of course. Something along the lines of the witty pieces they had designed and produced for Wallis Windsor would be perfect. And for the emeralds something really audacious — like the open-ended shooting star torc Coco had designed for herself.

'Do you know what would make me truly happy, Brinsley? I'd like to commission some new pieces, using the rubies and emeralds from these old things and some of the Indian diamonds. Then I'd feel the jewellery was somehow personal, really mine, instead of some other woman's before me.'

'But that's the whole point of family jewels, don't you see?' Brinsley patiently tried to explain about history and continuity within the family, but the French obviously didn't have the same ideas about these things.

Angelica refused to be deflected. She took hold of the lapels of his jacket and pressed the length of her soft pliant body against his. 'I'd make them so beautiful. You'd be proud to be seen with me when I wore them.'

'You'd make anything beautiful,' he agreed, kissing her hungrily. 'All right then,' he sighed. 'I had hoped you'd wear them as they are, but if the resetting's so important...'

46

'Oh, it is.'

'Do you want to pick out the diamonds now?'

'Better take them all — let the cutter decide.' She had no intention of returning any of them to the vault. 'Oh, won't Maman be jealous when she sees my lovely new jewels!'

Brinsley was busily searching the shelves for something else. At her reference to Marianne, he stood still and kept his face averted. 'I went to see Goodbody, my solicitor, today.'

Angelica went cold with horror but managed to keep her voice under control. 'Oh?'

'Yes. He's had a rather disturbing letter from your *step*father.'

Hearing the way he stressed the first syllable slightly, Angelica quickly took her cue, using his Christian name for the first time as though to distance herself from any claim to a blood tie. 'Armand is no worse, I hope?'

Brinsley turned, frowning. 'Not that I know of. Forgive me, Angelica. This is rather difficult. There's no need to concern yourself about the details, but because of what my lawyer has brought to my attention, I'm afraid your mother will never be welcome in my house.'

Angelica stood perfectly still. For the first time in their acquaintance, Brinsley had succeeded in surprising her. Never see Maman again! It seemed, as Marianne had always warned, that every piece of good fortune was closely followed by bad. But she could not agree to ignore her own mother, who had only wanted the best for her daughter.

She opened her mouth to challenge Brinsley, but her mother's voice seemed to prompt her. 'Careful! Never let a man see that you mean to defy him.'

She swallowed her angry retort. When she spoke, her voice was deliberately calm and soft. 'You are my husband, Brinsley. If that is what you want.'

There was an unexpectedly steely expression in his

47

normally mild blue eyes. 'It is. I'm very glad you can be so sensible about it, my dear.' He forced a lighter note into his voice. 'Now, to show how grateful I am for your great good sense, I'd like you to have something very precious to me. Here is your wedding gift — it used to be my mother's.'

He held out a small square box that contained a ring, by the look of it. Numbly Angelica took it. After this afternoon's treasures she had expected something rare and precious and was unprepared for the modest five-carat diamond solitaire on a band of Welsh gold.

Brinsley's expression softened as he gazed at the ring. 'Darling Mama's engagement ring. She gave it to me on her deathbed to pass on to my bride.' He glanced down at the huge ruby on Angelica's left hand. 'I thought that now you have it, perhaps you could wear the ruby as a dress ring occasionally.'

Angelica struggled to keep a grip on her temper. First he had tried to separate her from Maman. Now he was trying to stop her from wearing the ring she loved!

'But I couldn't possibly change engagement rings now,' she said regretfully. 'In France we believe that brings terribly bad luck, and you wouldn't want that for us, would you, Brinsley?'

'Suppose not. Pity.'

He looked regretfully at his mother's ring and left the box on the table while he replaced the diamonds in their pouch. 'Well, I think we've finished here. If you wouldn't mind putting these bags and boxes in your handbag and keeping a very good eye on them ... Hang on, darling, you've forgotten Mama's ring.'

'You're so good to me,' she said automatically, leaving the vault.

And far too besotted to oppose a reconciliation with Maman indefinitely.

But in that, for once, she had misread him. Though Angelica kept in touch with her mother by letter and in later years visited her in Paris, Marianne was never invited to England and for as long as he lived Brinsley refused so much as to speak the name of the woman who had outwitted him.

Angelica's first sight of Courtney Park was breathtaking. For once, reality exceeded her expectations.

Brinsley had chivvied the hotel into packing for them in double quick time, and after visiting the vault they caught a train from Paddington with minutes to spare. At Salisbury station they were met by Brinsley's chauffeur. The fresh-faced country lad wore a smart midnight-blue uniform to match the coachwork and leather interior of the stately Bentley Continental he drove.

'Evenin', My Lord. An' welcome home,' he said, saluting.

'Good evening, Drew. This is her ladyship, my new wife. I want you to take very good care when you drive her, do you hear?'

'That I will, sir.'

The chauffeur bowed to Angelica, then busied himself with their bags. He couldn't resist another sideways glance as she slid into the back of the car. The new ladyship was a real looker, and no mistake! He hadn't known the master had it in him.

Dusk was falling as the car slid through the sleepy country town. Angelica caught glimpses of a cathedral close, streets of small houses, and then the big car purred between country hedgerows, the gentle hills and fields beyond grey in the gathering dusk.

'It's good to be back,' Brinsley said, relaxing in his seat with a sigh of satisfaction.

Angelica strained to see through the fading light. The trouble with the country was that there was so much of it. After the contrived urban countryside of the Bois, the real thing was so empty. What did people *do* in Wiltshire? she wondered, and made her mind up that Brinsley would just have to get used to long spells in town. She'd make him take a house in Mayfair or Belgravia . . .

A high grey stone wall had been obstructing the view to the left for a long time, she realised. 'Are we nearly at Courtney?' she said crossly. 'I'm so tired of staring at that wall.'

Brinsley laughed. 'That *is* Courtney — or rather, the wall around the park.'

Her eyes widened. 'You mean everything behind it is yours?'

Brinsley cleared his throat. 'Everything since we left Salisbury, actually. The house and park are only part of the family holding in Wiltshire. We have over fifteen thousand acres of farmland here, and another thirty thousand in Scotland, though most of that is moor and plantation. I can't wait for you to see Gilmour, darling. You'll love it.'

'Perhaps I'd better get used to Courtney first.'

Still rapt in her conversion of acres to hectares, Angelica was slow to realise they were turning off the road and towards a pair of massive iron gates. Twenty feet high at their curved apex, and surmounted with gold-painted spikes, they also supported the painted figures of a gryphon and unicorn rampant, and a motto — the same device that appeared on the signet ring Brinsley wore on the little finger of his left hand, she realised.

'*Ne plus ultra quam Courtneia.* None finer than Courtney,' Brinsley translated for her.

A flurried woman ran out of the small red-brick lodge cottage, wiping her hands on her apron before dealing with the huge iron bolt. As she swung back the gate for them to enter, she stared curiously at Angelica.

The car swept down a long twisting avenue of elms which met overhead. As they rounded the final bend in the carriageway, Angelica caught her breath. Wreathed in low cloud, and lit by a golden harvest moon, Courtney Park was revealed in all its majesty.

Angelica's hand flew to her mouth. '*Mais c'est d'un conte de fée!* Brinsley — why did you not tell me that Courtney is a castle?'

'Why? Would you have married me sooner if I had?'

She wasn't listening, absorbed in her study of the square central keep with its turrets and towers and narrow slit windows above the massive double doors. From a flagpole high on the battlements, a white standard bearing the Courtney crest gleamed in the moonlight. There was an answering glint of water from the narrow moat before the keep, spanned by a low stone bridge.

Drew pulled up before a shallow flight of stone steps. As Angelica stared out of the car window, the huge nail-studded doors swung open and a double file of servants trooped out to line the steps. The women wore black with frilled white aprons, the men rough outdoor clothing or grey-striped waistcoats and black coats and trousers. Angelica nodded and smiled and met the servants' curious stares with great composure. Brinsley, she noticed, seemed to grow in stature as he received his staff's respectful bobs and bows.

And what a staff! All the estate workers as well as the indoor servants had turned out to welcome the master and new mistress. Gardeners, grooms, estate craftsmen, a second chauffeur, upstairs and downstairs maids, footmen, a cook, a portly butler named Hawkins, and at the top of the stairs, restraining two wildly excited black labradors, stood Headley with a politely welcoming smile on his thin face. The labradors whined frantically as Brinsley approached and stood on their hind legs to slobber affectionately over his face and hands.

He seemed delighted to see them. 'Down! Seek, Fetch — good dogs,' he said, patting their overfed sides. He spent far more time greeting the dogs than he did the staff, Angelica noted with amusement. They melted away, and still Brinsley fussed and patted his dogs. 'Good fellows. Good old chaps. Missed me, did you?'

51

'I didn't realise you were such a dog-lover,' she said, walking inside.

'They're not simply pets,' Brinsley excused himself. 'Working dogs, you know. Earn their keep.' Then he noticed her expression as the grandeur of the marble hall registered. 'It is rather fine, isn't it? And so unexpected after the exterior.'

In a dream, she nodded. Where she had expected to find flagged floors and bare stone walls, her eye was dazzled by a double-storey expanse of blind-arcaded walls in grey-veined marble. Statues lined the niches of the upper storey, gazing sightlessly down upon the black and white chequer-board pattern of the marble floor. Two black marble-topped console tables surmounted by matched pairs of gilt and jasper urns flanked a towering stone chimneypiece on which the Courtney crest appeared again. A log fire blazed in the deep hearth, its warmth a welcome note in all the chilly splendour.

Hawkins politely made known his continuing presence. 'You did say you'd dine in your rooms tonight, my lord? Only, if her ladyship would prefer the dining-room ...'

He gestured through an imposing doorway with carved stone facings. Angelica glimpsed a triple enfilade of huge dimly lit rooms beyond, each twice the size of the Grand Salon at home. There was a similar arrangement to the other side of the hall, she realised. Just how big was the house?

Brinsley took her hand. 'Don't worry, my darling, you'll soon get the hang of it. It's easy really. We never use the state rooms on the ground floor except for parties and entertaining. Mama converted the upper storey of the East Wing into family quarters. I thought we'd dine in my rooms tonight. I take it dinner is ready to be sent up, Hawkins?'

'Yes, my lord. And I chilled a magnum of the Clicquot '29.'

'That will do for tonight, but make a note that her

ladyship prefers Cristal, will you?'

'Very good, my lord.'

Brinsley looked at his watch. 'You can come and serve in an hour's time. Come along, Angelica. There's just time to show you the family rooms before we change.'

He steered her up the broad stone staircase with its carved marble balustrade and tapestry-hung walls. 'The sitting-room, morning-room, dining-room and so on,' he indicated as they turned left at the top of the stairs. The wallpaper and carpets were faded, Angelica noticed, but the pictures that lined the passage were very fine. 'My rooms are at the back of the house,' Brinsley continued, turning to their right. 'I like to watch the wildfowl on the lake out there. Choose any others you like for yourself.'

'But — do I not share yours, Brinsley?'

He gave an embarrassed smile. 'Or I yours, as often as you like. But it's customary for the mistress of the house to have her own rooms. The servants rather expect it. Of course, if you'd rather not ...'

Angelica was quick to weigh up the possible advantages of such an arrangement. 'Very well, *chéri*. If *you* want it that way.'

When she saw his bachelor rooms — acres of polished floorboards relieved by a small rug or two, depressing crimson velvet hangings over the tester bed and threadbare brocade at the windows — she was glad she would not always have to share them.

'Happy with your new home, my darling?' Brinsley enquired anxiously. 'I know it's all a bit daunting at first, but do you think you'll like it here?'

Angelica reflected on the riches she had seen, merely in passing. There were so many treasures still to find, and nearly two dozen servants to see that her every whim was carried out.

'I'm sure I'll get used to it,' she said bravely.

★

In the morning, while Brinsley visited his estate manager, Ralph Hayward, in the office he had converted from a disused tack-room in the stable yard, Angelica set about exploring the house and grounds.

In her glimpse of the previous night she had, if anything, underestimated Courtney's potential, she realised. Hitherto, she had always considered her step-father, with his gracious house on the Avenue Foch, to be a wealthy man. But in comparison with Brinsley's, she quickly realised, Armand's possessions were a mere drop in the ocean.

Courtney was like a giant repository — a storehouse for all that was finest in furniture, paintings, porcelain, silver, textiles ... At every turn of her head Angelica's eyes encountered beautiful and desirable objects. Here a great boule cabinet, there a graceful Hepplewhite secretaire. A small Stubbs *plein air* of some of the Hamilton family of the day out riding together caught her eye. Yes, that would do very well for her own rooms, the cerulean blue of the sky echoing the colour scheme she had already chosen. Her rooms would come first, of course. Then the rest of the house. By daylight she could see that though the house was sound, and by the looks of things comparatively recently decorated, the décor had been planned by someone both colour blind and with no natural eye for good taste.

The state drawing-room was usually referred to as the Grey Room, Hawkins told Angelica as he accompanied her on her first guided tour. She could see why, and wanted to stamp her foot with rage at the lack of imagination that had all but ruined the nobly proportioned room. The ceiling was almost twenty feet high and edged with an elaborately carved cornice. A decorative plaster frieze three feet deep ran round the top of the walls. Someone had thought it rather fun to pick out the acanthus leaf design with tones of sickly green and mustard which clashed horribly with the grey Regency stripe wallpaper, scrolled in gold leaf.

Throughout the house, irritating little occasional tables were strewn with collections of photographs in massive silver frames. There was the occasional portrait of Brinsley as a child or a pathetically young officer in the Great War, and a couple of a bemused man in coronet and ermine-collared cape — his father, James, the fifth Earl, Angelica presumed. There were various affectionately signed portraits of English and European Royalty, but the vast majority of the photographs featured the same soulful-looking woman with masses of badly pinned hair and the pouter pigeon silhouette of the Edwardian era. Whether posing with her baby son or welcoming a visiting Edward VII, Gwendoline Hamilton, Brinsley's mother, looked always to have had the upper hand.

In common with many men of his age and class, Brinsley had hardly known his parents. Raised by a succession of nannies, maids and governesses, and sent off to school at the age of seven, he had retained an almost child-like awe and respect for his father and an exaggeratedly romantic affection for his mother. Yet 'Darling Mama', Angelica suspected, had been the tougher, more dominant partner in his parents' marriage — with a touch of genius when it came to simulating the appearance of a gentle, loving wife and mother.

Angelica saw at once through the misty-eyed romanticism of the poses in which Gwendoline had had herself portrayed, and recognised a kindred spirit. She wondered, with a slight smile, what her chances of capturing Brinsley would have been were his mother still alive. The woman's influence could not be allowed to linger after her death. It was positively unhealthy to keep so many photographs of her. Angelica made up her mind to replace them with flattering studio portraits of herself just as soon as the re-decorating was complete.

But first she must find a good interior decorator. It was no use asking Brinsley to recommend one, she knew. The house had obviously never seen such an exotic species before. But some of his friends must employ them, or at least have heard the names of the most fashionable, and wasn't it time her husband introduced her into his circle?

Over dinner that night in the family dining-room — a gloomy Edwardian room, its walls covered in mustard flock and pictures of dead animals — Angelica taxed him on the subject.

'I still haven't met any of your friends — and what about the service of blessing on our marriage? Can we have it at the chapel? It's so sweet, Brinsley.'

That afternoon she'd visited the twelfth-century Courtney chapel set in magnificent parkland landscaped by Humphrey Repton for the second Earl. Even Angelica could find no fault with Courtney's grounds. They were famous for the vast collection of azaleas and rhododendrons which bloomed there in early summer, the water gardens incorporating the castle moat, and the beautifully planned herbaceous borders set around lawns of billiard table smoothness.

'It's August, darling,' he reminded her. 'Terribly difficult to plan anything with one's friends scattered all over the place, visiting family or shooting and stalking.'

'Couldn't we have a shooting-party here?'

'Hardly! We're supposed to be on honeymoon, remember?' He noticed her downcast expression. 'But if you're desperate for some company, I'll see who I can rope in locally for dinner.'

On the night itself Angelica wished she had not been so insistent. Over drinks in the Grey Room — Angelica had insisted on using the state rooms, though Brinsley could not see why for a party of eight — she was introduced to the Master of the Courtney Hunt and his ruddy-cheeked wife, who strode about the room as if wearing riding-boots beneath her limp biscuit-coloured crêpe de chine. It seemed, however, that Lavinia Forbes-Jefferies taught the local ladies how to ride side-saddle, so Angelica realised that she might have her uses and was moderately charming to her. How much more elegant it would be to ride in a veiled hat and long apron skirt. She told Lavinia she would definitely be in touch to arrange lessons.

The local JP and his wife seemed overawed by the company and the state dining-room, its dinginess flattered by soft candlelight and the brilliant livery and white gloves of the footmen who waited on them.

Over dinner, Angelica cultivated Caroline Rupert, the blonde wife of one of Brinsley's local chums, Lord Reggie Rupert. He had the affable ruddy face and clomping walk of a farmer but was, Brinsley assured her, 'Well thought of in the county.' Caro would be a useful source of information.

'I'd be so grateful for a word or two of advice,' Angelica told her sweetly. 'Could you tell me who one sees about redecorating the house?'

Caro Rupert looked surprised. 'The estate staff, I suppose. Brinsley must have all sorts of wonderful little men who can paint and carpenter and plumb, and so on, tucked away on the estate.'

'You wouldn't think so to look at the place,' Angelica said with a light laugh. 'But I really meant an interior decorator.'

'Well, I suppose it is a *bit* gloomy,' Caro conceded diplomatically. In fact, she thought the house had years of wear in it yet, but judging from the girl's bandbox appearance, it would not be the thing to say so. Goodness, but she was elaborately dressed for a simple dinner with neighbours, and the size of that ruby! Brinsley must be besotted. Yes, obviously the sort to spend thousands on dreary things like wallpaper and curtains instead of decent new bloodstock — and good luck to her.

'John Fowler is probably the best man to see,' Caro volunteered kindly. 'He and Sybil — Lady Sybil Colefax — do all the grandest houses. But will Brinsley agree?'

'Oh, I think so.'

Angelica gave a cat-like smile as Caro helped herself

generously to the bowl of syllabub a footman was handing round. She refused any for herself with a wave of her hand. When Brinsley caught her eye some minutes later, indicating that it was time for the ladies to withdraw, Angelica rose gracefully to her feet. On her way past Brinsley, sitting at the head of the table nearest the door, she rested one hand prettily on his shoulder.

'Don't leave us too long, will you, *chéri*? Oh, and by the way, Caro's solved all our problems, isn't she kind? She's recommended John Fowler to decorate the house.'

Brinsley looked surprised. 'It's only ten years since Mama overhauled it, and *she* never needed a decorator. Still, if Caro recommends him ...'

'Thank you, Brinsley.'

Angelica bent and kissed him warmly before leading the ladies out, with a special smile for Caro.

'Smashing girl, Angelica,' Reggie Rupert commented on their way home later that night. 'Old Brinsley certainly knows how to pick 'em, what?'

'It seems so,' Caro said lightly, but a faint frown creased her forehead.

Angelica spent the beginning of September happily making notes for her meeting with the decorator. So far as the grounds were concerned, she had contented herself with ordering the introduction of masses of sweet-scented old-fashioned roses to be trained along the walls of the path between the wood and the formal gardens.

When she began to feel distinctly queasy in the mornings, she blessed Marianne for advising her to become pregnant as soon as possible. She knew if she provided him with an heir, Brinsley would refuse none of her plans for the house. But, for the moment, she kept her suspicions to herself. She wanted to wait until the right strategic moment.

She was so happily immersed in her own plans that she

did not notice Brinsley's increasingly gloomy expression as he studied *The Times* each morning. Angelica had something far more engrossing than thoughts of war on her mind. For the first time in her life she was in love, with a passion which would outlast any other in her life. She loved Courtney Park; it was a source of endless pleasure and fascination to her, and some of her joy in her new possession spilled over into her treatment of the man who had made her mistress of the house.

On the evening of September 3rd, they dined early and were in bed by ten. When Brinsley switched off the light, Angelica sighed and rested her head against his chest. 'I'm so lucky. This magical house — and you, of course, *chéri.*'

But when she woke late the next morning, to see a grave-faced Brinsley standing beside the bed, she knew her luck had run out.

'Darling, Germany has invaded Poland, and Mr Chamberlain has had no choice but to declare war.'

She sat up, uneasily aware of a seething, bubbling feeling in her stomach.

'Now don't worry,' he said, seeing her anguished expression, 'but I'm going up to London immediately. I want to see whom I can catch at regimental headquarters — thought my old outfit might come up with a wartime commission.'

Through the waves of threatened nausea, Angelica was having difficulty in understanding him. When finally she realised he meant to join up and leave her, she seized both his hands in alarm. 'But you can't,' she cried, terrified. 'What about me? I couldn't bear it without you!' Widowed before she was twenty — the thought was unbearable.

'Darling, calm yourself. It's extremely unlikely I'd be posted abroad. And there'll be plenty to keep you busy here,' he continued, misunderstanding her panic. 'I'll be giving Courtney to the army as a hospital, of course. Mama did during the Great War — she was wonderful with the wounded officers.'

Angelica felt more nauseous by the minute. Wounded, crippled men in her lovely house!

'Might you try a spot of nursing?' Brinsley prompted her.

'I couldn't,' she blurted out, appalled by the thought. 'I mean — I won't be able to. Oh, Brinsley, say you won't go! You can't leave me now — not when I'm expecting a baby.'

His puzzled expression changed to one of incredulous joy. 'My own love, you're the cleverest as well as the most beautiful wife in the world! But are you all right? You're looking very pale —'

'I should think so, after the shock you've given me!'

'Stay in bed, don't move. I'm ringing the family doctor right away — he can give me the name of the very best Harley Street man and we'll have him down to look at you.'

'And you won't go to London?'

'My darling, of course not.' Certainly not before he had the consultant's assurance that the pregnancy was progressing normally.

The gynaecologist arrived the next day and confirmed that the Countess was indeed expecting a child, which should arrive in the following May. After the examination, which revolted Angelica, Brinsley spoke to the consultant in his study.

'How do you find my wife, Mr Frobisher?'

The consultant, a smiling, fatherly man with white hair, thought for a moment. 'Physically she couldn't be better, but she seems a little — ah — highly strung. Her mind seems to be running on this house, rather. She kept telling me how much there was to be done.'

'Poor darling, she's worrying about making it ready for the army — I'm lending it to them for the duration.'

'A splendid gesture! But perhaps, in the circumstances, her ladyship would be better off elsewhere.'

Angelica could barely conceal her rage when Brinsley confirmed his arrangements to hand the house over to the army, who were to use it this time for training purposes. He himself received a wartime commission with his old regiment, the Coldstream Guards, and a posting to a Staff Major's job in Wellington Barracks. He asked for a special dispensation to live out of barracks, and took the lease of a small house in Eaton Terrace.

Angelica didn't realise until the morning they were to leave Courtney Park that she was not to accompany him to London.

'It's out of the question,' he told her, the steely look she had seen once before coming into his eyes. 'Remember, you're carrying the Hamilton heir. There are likely to be bombing raids over London and I would not dream of allowing you to put yourself or the baby at risk.'

'But where shall I go?'

'You've forgotten our other house — or should I say castle? Actually it's the Hamiltons' original family seat. They were clan chieftains there long before my great-great-grandfather lent money to Prinny and received the English title. Much as I love England and Courtney, I shall always prefer Gilmour.'

But, to Angelica, Gilmour was nothing after the splendours of Courtney Park: a grey stone border castle in the lee of the Lammermuir Hills, with a few miserable-looking rose bushes lining the gravelled approach, and nothing but sheep and heather for miles around.

'Mama began the rose garden here — perhaps you could make completing it into your war work?'

Angelica looked out of the car window at the louring grey skies, the trees stunted by constant cruel winds, and doubted she would even leave her room.

When she saw the cheerless stone walls inside the castle, randomly hung with stags' heads, tattered standards and ancient rusting weapons, she lost all composure. She clung to him, weeping. 'It's dreadful, Brinsley. I hate Scotland. Take me back to London with you, please!'

'Nonsense, darling. The place just needs a woman's

touch. You were going to redecorate Courtney, weren't you? Why not start on Gilmour instead?'

Angelica wept and then sobbed, and when tears failed to move him worked herself up into a state of hysteria, shrieking that he was tired of her already and going off to London to enjoy himself without her.

This was so unjust, and his worry and distress at leaving her so keen, that Brinsley lost his temper too. They quarrelled so violently that the noise reached the servants' hall.

'French, you see,' Headley said gloomily to the Gilmour cook-housekeeper, Mrs McPhail.

'Wi' a temper tae match his lordship's,' the old lady said placidly. 'But skirl all she likes, he'll no be taking her back to London wi' him.'

Eventually they were reconciled. Angelica was too wily to allow Brinsley to spend his last night with her in a separate bed. He was shaken by the bitterness of the argument, their first, and worried that in her condition it might have an adverse effect. He spent the rest of a sleepless night assuring her of his love for her.

The next morning, pale and contrite, he left her still abed in the Balmoral-style principal room. She refused even to open her eyes as he tenderly kissed her goodbye.

'I can't, Brinsley. This terrible plaid everywhere has given me a migraine.'

'Take good care of her, won't you? She's not very strong,' Brinsley told Mrs McPhail as she saw him off.

The motherly housekeeper had known him from a boy. 'Och, awa' wi' ye, ye silly man. Her ladyship will be fine, just fine.'

Watching from the bedroom window as Brinsley was driven away to catch the London train, Angelica wept impotently. She hated Scotland, hated being pregnant and feeling so tired and sick all the time. Most of all she hated the child for causing her exile from the things she loved best — the city lights and Courtney Park.

Angelica spent her pregnancy feeling clumsy, bored, and resentful of the housekeeper who clucked around her like an anxious hen. She never grew to love Gilmour and its wind-blasted scenery as her husband did, but, compelled to take some exercise and forbidden by the doctor to ride, she spent her time walking the hills near the castle. She walked doggedly, even when winter drifts had piled snow three feet high against the castle walls, striking such a chill into the stone walls that she scandalised the servants by ordering fires to burn in every room twenty-four hours a day. She had read that frequent exercise during pregnancy would help her regain her figure more quickly after childbirth, and daily walked herself into a state of exhaustion.

One afternoon in her eighth month, out in a soft spring drizzle, she stood by a little burn that had started from the boggy hillside as a result of the winter rain. She missed her footing and tumbled a few feet down the hill. The fall was nothing serious and she was able to get to her feet and resume her walk, but by the time she reached Gilmour, she was too weak to open the castle door. Gasping with pain and fear, she leaned on the bell-pull.

'Whatever's the matter, your ladyship?' Mrs McPhail said, anxiously drawing her inside.

'My back — terrible pain, low down — I fell on the hillside. Oh God! You'd better send a telegram to the doctor in Edinburgh, and to my husband — I think the baby's coming.'

In her torment, Angelica wept and called for her mother. The anguish in her voice brought tears to Mrs McPhail's eyes. She stayed with her mistress throughout the long and difficult birth and only left the shocked and exhausted girl when, towards dawn, the attending consultant admitted Brinsley to the room.

'Ye've a bonnie daughter,' the housekeeper greeted him, gesturing to the white flounced crib at the foot of the bed. 'Will you see her now?'

'Later,' he said hoarsely, with eyes only for the still figure of his wife in the high, canopied bed. The sight of her so deathly pale, with the sickly scent of chloroform still hanging over her, brought tears to his eyes.

'My love, if only I could have been here.'

'I'm sorry it's a girl,' she said, through painfully cracked lips.

'Never mind. All that matters is that you will soon be well.'

Privately Angelica doubted she would ever recover from the horror of the birth. She fell into a deep drugged sleep, relieved that Brinsley did not hold the sex of their child against her. When she opened her eyes twelve hours later, it was to see a pretty, smiling nurse putting a vase of long-stemmed red roses by her bed.

'Where's my husband?' Angelica sat painfully upright, surprised by how much stronger she felt already.

'He's away back to London,' the girl said. 'He's left you something, though.'

She produced a slim leather box. Inside was a thick rope of pearls, blush pink and each the size of a grape, secured with a diamond clasp. It was a gift fit for a queen.

As the nurse brought her whimpering daughter for her first feed, she wondered what the price of a son would be.

They decided to name the baby Camilla Catherine Elizabeth. When she was three months old, Brinsley secured a forty-eight-hour pass to attend her christening in the family chapel at Gilmour. Only one godparent, Caro Rupert, was present, the others being forced to act by proxy since they were away in the forces or in war work and could not make the long journey north.

After the local minister had conducted the ceremony before a congregation of servants and estate workers, whisky was served in the great hall and the family piper, in his dark blue and red Gilmour tartan, played for them.

The kindly Caro Rupert noted, as Angelica did not, the fine lines of exhaustion around Brinsley's eyes and mouth. 'They must be working you hard at the barracks.'

Before he could reply, Angelica cut in with a teasing smile. 'Oh no, it's all the parties and night clubs after his duties there, isn't it?'

'I've told you,' Brinsley protested, 'I'm far too busy to go out on the town enjoying myself. And when I'm not working I'm catching up on my sleep — if the bombing raids permit.'

But Angelica refused to be convinced. From references in the society columns of newspapers and magazines, thin though they were these days, she was convinced that everyone but she was having a whale of a time, war or no. Another three months, and then Camilla would be weaned. Angelica's plans were already laid.

She arrived unexpectedly at the Eaton Terrace house one evening in October. She'd taken the morning train from Melrose, and stoically endured the tedious journey in a compartment crammed with servicemen and women returning from leave. For the last hours of the journey, as darkness fell, stringent blackout procedures were followed on the train. Angelica, unaware, peeled back one corner of the thick black blind at the window.

'The light from this train might help to guide an enemy bomber,' a beefy Wren bawled at her. 'What do you think you're doing?'

Angelica raised one eyebrow. 'If it's any business of yours, I was trying to see where we were — from a signpost or station sign, for instance.'

'Blimey, Princess, they all went months ago,' a cheerful Cockney sergeant told her. 'Where you been — Timbuctoo?'

'Scotland; and it's Countess, actually.' Angelica uncrossed her elegant legs, to the mute admiration of all the men in the carriage. The women noticed the contrast between their own sensible lisle stockings and the quality of her pre-war silk.

Carrying her overnight bag, Angelica pushed her way down the corridor to a squalid lavatory where, ignoring the hammered protests on the door, she spent twenty minutes changing into a spotless white silk blouse and a dashing black and white houndstooth suit. She made up her face carefully and liberally applied Amour-Amour, the scent Brinsley liked best.

She took a taxi from King's Cross and was amazed at the length of time it took to reach Eaton Terrace. Every other street, it seemed, was sealed off by ARP wardens searching for unexploded bombs or shoring up shattered buildings.

'You should see it down the East End,' the cabbie said gloomily. 'More than two hundred poor sods copped it down Shoreditch way last night.'

She barely heard him, too busy with thoughts of her husband and how she would persuade him to let her stay.

It was one of Headley's fire-watching nights. Brinsley had made his own scratch supper and afterwards sat down in the first-floor drawing room. He intended to spend an hour or two reviewing Battalion Orders, but it was a quiet night after the raids of the last few days and exhaustion overcame him. He was fast asleep on the drawing-room sofa when the imperious ringing of the doorbell woke him. When he opened the door, still fuddled with sleep, he thought he was dreaming.

Angelica smiled lovingly at him and said, 'Have you missed me?'

For answer he crushed her to him, oblivious of the cabbie waiting patiently to be paid. Then he realised the full significance of her appearance in London. 'Is everything all right? What are you doing here, and where's Camilla?'

'With Nanny at Gilmour, of course.' Her voice was low

and concerned. 'Naturally I wouldn't dream of bringing her into such danger, but when I heard about these dreadful raids and so many poor people dying — Brinsley, I was so worried for you! I had to come and see for myself that you were all right. Say I can stay for just one night?'

How could he resist such touching concern for him? There were no raids that night to spoil their reunion. Fate seemed to be on Angelica's side. Later, by the light of the rose-shaded lamp in Brinsley's bedroom, he gently traced the faint silvery lines which she had been appalled to find threading her smooth young skin. She had determinedly regained her figure, but the stretch marks remained, a legacy of Camilla.

'Don't look at them — ugly things!'

'They show that you have carried our child, my darling. Besides, how could anything about you be ugly?'

He kissed her stomach and thighs, following the line of each silvery thread with his tongue until Angelica moaned and guided him to the hot, quivering core of her.

In the weeks which followed, Brinsley more than once voiced his concern for her safety if she continued in town, but Angelica made light of the danger. She had been right about one thing, she quickly discovered. Despite the blitz — or perhaps because of it — the London social scene was thriving. Many young and not so young men and women were eager to seize any opportunity for enjoyment, knowing it might be the last they were offered. Even with the blackout and bombing, the shortages of food, clothes, servants and petrol, London was the only place to be. Angelica hung on for Christmas, New Year, the coming of spring ...

The young and dazzlingly beautiful Countess of Courtney cut a swath through the officers stationed or on leave in town. Though nothing improper took place — Angelica was far too clever to arouse Brinsley's anger — she was an accomplished flirt who revelled in the male attention she attracted. For how could she fail to? It was an era of 'utility' — ugly, cork-soled peeptoe sandals and cheap skimpy rayon dresses in harsh 'Victory' blue and 'Flag' red. She had cupboards full of pre-war shoes she had hardly worn in delicate suede and kid and antelope. Cunningly, she had ordered bolts of the finest couture cloth to be sent over to her just before the outbreak of war. She mixed the new clothes she had run up from this with her pre-war wardrobe, and pretended that everything was old.

'Oh no, I've had these rags for years, darling. Of course they look new — I couldn't wear them out in the wilds of Scotland while I was having a baby.'

Her jewellery, too, attracted attention wherever she went. The newly set rubies and emeralds were finer and more avant garde than any woman's in London — and few of them would forgive her for it. But what did she care when all the men adored her, and she adored every officer she met? There was something about a uniform — even the dullest dogs became distinctly attractive in their khaki, navy or airforce blue.

Sitting in the bath one evening in March, up to her neck in water and bubbles, despite the patriotic pleas to use less water, Angelica wondered what Brinsley's friend, Beano Campbell, would be like. He was ten years younger than Brinsley, apparently, and home on leave from serving with the Argyll Yeomanry in the Middle East. Angelica imagined a huge sandy-haired Scot wearing one of those absurd skirts — no, kilts — and laughed aloud.

'I'm glad to see you in such good form,' Brinsley said, coming into the bathroom dressed in his best khaki for the evening ahead. 'I think it's time we had a serious talk, don't you?'

'All right, talk. I can't very well escape, can I?'

Angelica flicked her wrist and sent a shower of foam over Brinsley's immaculate tunic. He brushed it away and adjusted the knife-edge creases of his uniform trousers, perfectly pressed by Headley, as he sat down in a wicker chair by the bath.

'I've just read Nanny Banks's letter.'

She took her cue from his grave expression. 'Oh yes, silly old woman. She's a bit of a — how do you say? — a fusspot, that one. I shouldn't take any notice of what she says.'

'But, darling, Camilla's almost a year old, and in the last six months she's seen her mother twice.'

'She hasn't seen her father at all!'

'But it's different for me. I'd love to see more of Camilla, but my duties —'

Angelica supposed she'd better pay a quick visit to Scotland, to keep Brinsley and Nanny happy. She basked in the warmth of the scented water, juggling dates in her mind. Loelia's birthday wasn't until the end of April, darling Noël in cabaret a week earlier. It would mean missing one of Margaret Argyll's Thursdays but that couldn't be helped. The sacrifices of motherhood!

Besides, Mrs McPhail was a genius with the knitting needles and Angelica had been clever enough to buy — on the black market, naturally — some baby-fine yellow cashmere yarn. A classic twinset, primrose-coloured, with mother of pearl buttons ... yes, a trip to Gilmour might fit in very well. And there was that other matter. Brinsley might notice sooner if she stayed ...

'You're quite right, *chéri*,' she said, smiling contritely. 'It is a very, very difficult position for a mother to find herself in, being forced to choose between her husband and her baby. Of course I don't regret for a minute putting you first, but it *is* time I saw darling Camilla again. If I go next week I can be back for Bunny's embarkation thrash at the Embassy.'

'Angelica, I really meant —'

'Do my back for me, will you, *chéri*?'

She was confident of eventually carrying any argument, however bitter, but did not enjoy being forced to confront Brinsley's terrifying stubborn streak. She had other means of getting her own way....

'What time did you say we'd meet them?' After thirty satisfying minutes, Angelica was dressed for the evening in a new gown with a deep plunging neckline. Motherhood had enhanced her breasts, she noted with satisfaction. The dress was of black slipper satin, bias cut, with clever decorative inserts. Not bad for the Commercial Road — though she would pretend it was pre-war Chanel.

'About nine.' Brinsley had discarded his by now rumpled uniform and was taking another from the wardrobe. 'Shall you wear your pearls?'

'No. I thought the emeralds tonight.'

The emerald and diamond collar with its shooting star motif and daring open-ended design never failed to attract admiring glances.

'But Beano's girl's in the Wrens, darling. I expect she'll be in uniform. Don't you think it might look a little ...'

More fool her! Angelica thought, but said lightly, 'Then I expect she's one of those strapping British girls who look so good in men's clothes. In which case, I don't see why *I* shouldn't look my best, too. Besides, it's my first meeting with Beano, and I want him to see what a good choice you made.'

Captain Bruce 'Beano' Campbell, home on leave for the first time in a year since his posting to the Middle East, was in the mood to enjoy himself. Like many of the revellers in the subterranean club, he and his companion tacitly ignored the shrill keening of the air-raid sirens, and talked above the odd muffled thump of an explosion over to the east. Beano wanted to share supper and champagne with his old friend Brinsley Hamilton, and introduce him to his fiancée, Fiona Payne-Hughes. He was also curious to meet this mysterious French miss whom Brinsley had married so precipitately and carried away to Scotland, though not for the first time he wondered why Brinsley had had to choose a foreigner.

After dancing with Fiona, he led her back to their table, one of the best, facing the band to the right of the stairs. While he was seating her, he glanced towards the great horseshoe-shaped divided staircase which was the central feature of the Café de Paris, and caught his breath in surprise.

Brinsley Hamilton, his hair rather greyer, handsome face a little more lined than formerly, was escorting down the stairs the most ravishing creature Beano had ever set eyes on. She was as dark and alluring as any of the Eastern *houris* he had met on his travels, but carried herself like a queen.

He touched his companion's arm discreetly. 'Look over there, Fiona. No wonder old Brinsley tried to hide her away in Scotland — what a stunner!'

The pretty grey-eyed blonde beside him glanced across at the sultry beauty and then down at her own uniform and heavy shoes. She made an irritated moue. 'If you like the exotic, over-dressed type.'

Beano gave a loud gaffaw. 'I do believe you're jealous!'

'Not until you give me cause.'

He laughed again and quickly kissed her cheek before rising to his feet to greet his old friend and his fascinating new wife.

Fiona seemed a pleasant, sensible sort of girl, Brinsley decided, chatting desultorily to her above the music of Ken 'Snakehips' Johnson and his band. Angelica seemed to be keeping Beano enthralled with an account of her visit to a black market food warehouse.

She took his arm confidingly. 'You've no idea how hard it is for us civilians, Beano. These terrible shortages.'

She was on top form tonight, Brinsley saw. Of course she did rather overshadow poor Fiona, though the girl needn't feel too downcast. With her looks, the clothes she seemed to conjure out of thin air and all the Hamilton

71

jewels at her disposal, Angelica was more than a match for any of the London beauties.

But that was no reason for a servicewoman's night out to be ruined. He noticed one of Fiona's feet beating time to the music, and gallantly stood up. 'I'm itching to dance. Come on, Fiona.'

She was really rather pretty when she smiled, and proved to be a skilful and energetic dancer. She laughed aloud, urging him into a dizzying reverse as the band struck up the opening chord of 'Oh, Johnny'. Out of the corner of his eye he saw Beano escort Angelica on to the floor and take her in his arms.

Suddenly all the lights went out. There was a moment's shocked silence and then a rending, tearing noise from the direction of the ceiling. The dance floor tilted crazily beneath Brinsley's feet. Simultaneously, shock-waves from an enormous explosion overhead sent revellers and staff, furniture and shards of glass from the huge Art Deco mirrors into a deadly *danse macabre*. Fiona was sucked from his arms by the vacuum effect of the blast.

Brinsley's head struck a table that had mysteriously appeared in the middle of the dance floor, and he lost consciousness. He came round, groggy and shocked, to find the sight of his left eye obscured by a trail of something warm and wet. Although everything about him was in darkness, overhead, through the gaping hole that the blast had driven through the building above the basement club, a single light still miraculously shone, casting the faintest silvery illumination on a scene from hell.

He peered at the dark stain on his hand. It was blood, but a cautious probing of his own head, still ringing from the blast, revealed no wound. He realised there was something on the floor beneath him, nudging the small of his back. He felt behind him — and recoiled in horror. A woman's arm, still wearing its long white evening glove, lay grotesquely severed on the splintered boards. All his reflexes seemed to be slower than usual. He couldn't think

72

clearly, but he knew there was something he must do urgently, someone he must find ... In the darkness he could discern vague shadowy figures.

'But he can't be dead,' a woman's voice was saying reasonably. 'He wasn't due to join his unit till next week.'

With a sickening jolt, Brinsley remembered. Angelica! Please God, let her be safe! They'd been sitting at a table at the edge of the dance floor, hadn't they? And there it was, glasses still miraculously upright after the explosion. But there was no one near or underneath it.

It came back to him now. She had been with Beano, on the dance floor. He thought of the severed arm, and shuddered convulsively. 'Angelica!' he shouted into the chaos around him, coughing and choking as he inhaled a mouthful of the dust that hung like mist in the air. 'Angelica, talk to me. Where are you?'

He wandered round the shattered club, bumping into similarly searching figures, and once, appallingly, tripping over something that groaned.

'The band-leader's bought it, poor blighter,' a stranger told him.

A woman clutched his hand. 'Are you a doctor? Please, we must have a doctor over here.'

'Brinsley — Brinsley, is that you?'

The voice was so faint he almost missed it. It seemed to be coming from a banquette on the rear wall, twenty feet or so away. A flash of green in the shadows sent his spirits soaring.

'Darling, is it really you? Oh, thank God!'

Her moan of pain as he put his arms round her sent a trickle of dread through him. He ran his hands gently over her face and body.

She cried out when he touched one arm. 'I think it's broken. No, don't touch it please! Oh God, when will they get us out of here?'

'Soon, my darling. Soon. Where's Beano? Is he all right?'

'I think so. He helped me over here and told me not to move while he went off to find his girl. God, it hurts! When will they come?'

'They'll be on their way,' he soothed, draping his tunic carefully round her. She was still shuddering with shock. 'Lean on me, my love. We might have quite a wait.'

Hours later, as she lay half-conscious against his shoulder, Brinsley distinguished a fireman's helmeted head peering down through the shattered ceiling.

'Hold on down there, mate. Ropes and stretchers are on their way. Soon have you out of there.'

Angelica stirred and moaned.

'Keep still, my darling.'

'But, Brinsley — we have to find Beano.'

She was right. Brinsley was appalled to realise he'd spared barely a moment's concern for his friend since Angelica had told him he'd gone in search of Fiona.

'Of course,' he said in a low, ashamed voice. 'If you're sure you'll be all right for a while, I'll try and track them down. I do hope they're safe.'

'Oh, I'd be so relieved if you could find them. You see, while we were dancing my earrings felt so tight I gave them to Beano to put in his pocket, and he hasn't given them back.'

The doctor in the improvised casualty station in a Leicester Square hotel confirmed that Angelica's arm was broken and asked Brinsley to wait while it was set. Apparently there was also the possibility of internal injury, and they wanted to examine her further. By that time the unscathed but badly shaken Beano and Fiona had taken a taxi back to her Chelsea flat, so Brinsley waited alone, blood-stained and in his shirt sleeves. He was sure there was something he should be doing to help amid the noise and confusion, some example he ought to be setting, but every time he tried to get up his legs shook and his vision swam. If anything should happen to Angelica ...

The doctor reappeared an hour later, grey with fatigue but smiling cheerfully. It was such a change having good news for a relative. 'The arm's set and I'm very glad to say it looks as though the baby's safe.'

Brinsley shook his head in disbelief. That hellish wait, and all the time they'd been examining the wrong woman!

'But that's impossible!' he exclaimed. 'My wife is Angelica Hamilton. There must be some mistake.'

The doctor coloured painfully. Bugger this war! It was difficult to be sure of your ground nowadays.

'Do I take it you're newly returned on leave?' he asked with elephantine tact.

'Damn it, no! I've been stationed in London since the war began. Angelica joined me last year.'

'Then what are you worried about? I expect the little lady wanted to keep it as a surprise. Women get the strangest ideas at times like this. But she's at least three months — you'll have a baby by September. Splendid surprise, eh?'

'Yes, splendid.'

While he waited for Angelica, Brinsley sank his head into his hands, overjoyed yet appalled at the same time. Another baby ... but it could so easily have ended in tragedy. She must have known, couldn't possibly have missed the signs that long. And yet she had said nothing, ignoring the constant bomb alerts, happy to dance until dawn in smoke-filled night clubs while she was carrying a child, possibly the Courtney heir.

He pulled himself wearily upright and went out into the street to find a taxi to take them back to Eaton Terrace.

'Badly injured, is she, your missus?' The cabbie looked worried.

Brinsley's frayed nerves snapped. 'I'd hardly be taking her home in a taxi if she were. She has a broken arm.'

'No blood, then?'

Brinsley looked at the man with dislike. 'Not now.'

The foxy face looked relieved. 'That's all right, then. Only I 'ad a fare earlier, bin caught like you in the old Caffy, and the bloke bled all over me back seat. Got no consideration, some people haven't . . .'

Brinsley didn't bother to reply. Angelica appeared on the pavement, escorted by a nurse, and he settled her in the back of the cab, putting his arm round her to cushion her from any jolts. She seemed to fall asleep immediately, the sable crescents of her lashes the only hint of colour in her chalk-white face.

There were times when she was a mystery to him. The sight of her sleeping when there were so many questions to be answered infuriated him. He wanted to shake her awake, ask what the hell she'd been thinking of, putting their child at risk like that.

Then the dark lashes stirred and fluttered, and Angelica's green eyes were upon him, beautiful and fathomless. 'They told you?'

'Yes, of course. But why didn't you?'

She even cried beautifully. 'Because I knew that, when I did, you'd send me away, and I couldn't bear that. I do love you, Brinsley. Say you forgive me.'

There were few men who could have resisted such an appeal, and Brinsley was not among them. He doubted he would ever fully understand Angelica, but at the sight of her tears he could refuse her nothing. 'Of course I forgive you, my darling, and I love you very much. But you're going to have to be sensible from now on.'

It seemed a small price to pay for escaping with her life, and maybe this time she would give Brinsley a son. Angelica submitted without protest to her second term of exile in Scotland and on September 14th 1941, Alexander Brinsley James Hamilton, Viscount Castlemere, was born.

His father arrived within hours and joyfully received the congratulations of a purse-mouthed obstetrician. The countess had cursed like a French trooper throughout her labour. The doctor, a devotee of the Auld Alliance who spoke the language fluently, wondered how a lady even knew such words.

Brinsley filled Angelica's room with white roses sent specially from Covent Garden on the night train, and presented her with the largest uncut diamond from the Indian hoard. The cutter who had dealt with the emeralds and rubies had said it would be a sin to use that particular stone for the setting, it was so fine. Flawless and uncommonly big, it deserved special treatment.

'I've had it appraised,' Brinsley said, 'and they say you could get sixteen carats of cut stones from it. You can have a brooch, a pendant, a pair of earrings — anything you want made out of it.'

The stone had to be despatched to New York, where a refugee Belgian cutter fashioned a single exquisite Marquise-cut stone. Angelica mounted it on a platinum band and announced her intention of wearing it always.

With the blitz in London, Brinsley was adamant that Angelica should stay safely at Gilmour. Although she pouted and protested, the shock of the Café de Paris bombing was with her still. Perhaps there was a case to be made for staying in Scotland and getting to know her children.

At eighteen months, Lady Camilla was a dark, solemn-faced child who stubbornly resisted all attempts to teach her a little nursery French, preferring to prattle to the devoted Scottish servants with the odious lilt she had picked up from them.

'It will soon pass, My Lady,' Nanny Banks reassured Angelica. 'As soon as this nasty old war is over — and it can't be forever, can it, My Lady? — and Camilla's back with her daddy at Courtney Park away from all these foreigners ... Ooops! Begging your pardon, My Lady, I'm sure. And perhaps a governess, because we can't start educating them too soon, can we, My Lady?'

Not soon enough, Angelica decided. The child's tedious games with her rocking-horse and the dolls in drab, hand-knitted clothes bored her to distraction.

Alexander by contrast was an enchanting sprite of a child, with Angelica's olive skin and green eyes surmounted by a mop of blond curls. He was lively and affectionate but prone to childhood ailments. Nursing her beautiful son belatedly summoned up all Angelica's maternal instincts. She favoured the child shockingly, the servants agreed.

He enjoyed nothing more than sitting beside her in the high canopied bed, a fire blazing in the great stone fireplace in her bedroom, the curtains cosily drawn against the bleak landscape outside. Angelica would take to her bed at the slightest excuse — a frosty day, a damp afternoon, nervous exhaustion from her incessant worry over Brinsley. And Alexander would join her, lying back against his mother's lace-trimmed pillows and parroting snatches of half-remembered nursery rhymes in a high tuneless voice.

Her years of enforced exile grated less than Angelica had expected, but when Hawkins brought news of VJ Day, she despatched Hamish, the factor's son, forty miles to the nearest post office to send Brinsley an urgent wire.

WHEN SOONEST POSSIBLE RETURN COURTNEY STOP TIME ALEXANDER SAW HIS HERITAGE STOP MISSING YOU MADLY STOP ANGELICA

Hamish, who had been invalided out of the army after being blinded in one eye, patiently waited the six hours it took for Brinsley's reply to arrive along the crowded wires.

PATIENCE MY DARLING STOP COURTNEY STILL ON LOAN TO MINISTRY STOP TOGETHER AS SOON AS ARMY WILL RELEASE ME STOP KISSES FOR THE BABIES AND MY BEAUTIFUL WIFE STOP.

78

When Angelica received his answer, she took to her bed for three days and no one, not even Alexander, was allowed into the room.

On the fourth day she got up, dressed becomingly in pristine tweeds and the primrose-coloured sweater, and began to plan a new rose garden with Hamish's help.

He looked dashing, almost piratical in his eye patch, she thought, and so young and virorous. Only her age, too ... Lazily she stood watching the muscles ripple beneath his smoothly tanned skin as he took off his shirt. As he effortlessly turned the hard-packed soil Angelica decided that beds were made for men not roses. Later that afternoon Brinsley was repaid in full for what she saw as her years of exile and neglect. His loyal staff would not let him remain in ignorance for long, she had calculated.

A week later, Brinsley wired the good news — they could return to Courtney. He had moved heaven and earth to secure the early return of the house, instinctively hitting on the one sure way of bringing Angelica to heel.

She returned to the house she loved on a day of leaden skies and constant drizzle. It looked somehow faded. Most of the fine furniture had been safely stowed in the cellars for the duration but here and there she saw evidence of the Army's occupation — a dartboard still hanging from one wall of the Grey Room; a photograph of Betty Grable pinned to the side of a priceless boule cabinet which had been too heavy to move. Everywhere she looked there was evidence of neglect — unpolished windows, smeared marble, moth-eaten brocade.

Luckily the old nurseries at the top of the East Wing were clean and tidy. Angelica ordered Nanny and the children to take an early supper there while Janet, the Scottish nursery maid, did their unpacking and made the beds.

At least the children would be looked after. From the vast staff employed by Brinsley before the war, only four remained. Hawkins had accompanied Angelica in her

Scottish exile, while Headley had remained faithfully by Brinsley's side in London. At the house had been only Mrs Teare, the cook, and Hennessy, a wizened old groom who looked after the pensioned-off horses in the yard.

Angelica awaited her husband's return impatiently. There was so much that needed to be done here, but first she must see how she stood with him. Hawkins had lit a fire in the family drawing-room and she waited there.

Brinsley arrived late that evening, strained and tense from the rush to wind up his military affairs and the consequent loss of face. He was forty-five now, but the war had aged him by another decade. His once auburn hair was mostly grey, and the lines which had sat lightly on his patrician face were seared deep by strain and recent sadness. Angelica felt a twinge of compunction when she saw him. She knew who had been responsible for the sadness.

Without saying a word she stood before him, calm and lovely, ready to fire all guns in her own defence. The white dress she had chosen was calculated to remind him of their first meeting, and did not fail. She was still, despite the depth of his anguish at her betrayal, the only woman who could light up the room simply by smiling — as she was smiling now. Warmly, lovingly ...

'Am I forgiven, *chéri*? He meant nothing, of course. It was the intolerable strain of being apart from you, all those years apart.'

She swayed slightly towards him and her familiar heady scent aroused so many memories. It was a crucial moment. If Brinsley had challenged her then, she would have capitulated and the whole balance of power in their marriage would have been different. As it was, the words of reproach died on his lips. Angelica was, and always would be, the only woman for him.

'I should never have left you. From now on we'll be together always, I promise you.'

He held out his arms and she came to him, confident

that she had carried the day.

Headley tapped on the door. 'The hamper, my lord? Where did you wish me to unpack it?'

Brinsley answered without releasing Angelica. 'My rooms — and that will be all for tonight.'

Later they picnicked in bed on smoked salmon sent down from Gilmour, quails' eggs and a jar of pre-war beluga. Brinsley opened a bottle of Angelica's favourite Roederer Cristal, and they toasted the years ahead at Courtney Park.

'And may I have *carte blanche* to restore the house?' she asked, trailing her fingers through his chest hair — quite grey now, she noted.

'It may not be very easy, my love.'

His tone alarmed her. 'Why? We have money, don't we?'

'Darling, there's more money than you or I could spend in a lifetime,' he laughed, 'though you have to remember a great deal of it is tied up in trusts or depends on the yield from the estates.' He smiled indulgently. 'No, money's no problem, though we may have to spend it rather differently these days. Mr Attlee's government intends to punish people like us for winning the war, apparently. There'll be more taxes to pay than ever there was, not that that need concern you, and I think you'll find that many of the things we took for granted before the war will be a long time reappearing.'

He was right. When she consulted John Fowler, she was outraged to learn that there was no fabric or wallpaper available for her restoration of the house.

'But that's impossible! The war's over.'

'I'm sorry, but all the textile factories switched to producing war supplies. It will take years to adapt back or start importing the fine fabrics we need for decorative purposes. It's the same story with wood-pulp. Lady Onslow was so desperate for something to cover her drawing-room windows with that she used blankets dyed red. It seems

81

they'll have to stay all the rage while rationing continues.'

Forced to delay her plans for the house by several years, Angelica concentrated instead on acquiring more paintings, persuading Brinsley to buy major works by her beloved French impressionists — Monet, Dégas, Renoir, Cézanne — even going so far as to acquire a huge circus scene by Rouault which she hung in his study. She had all the Courtney furniture, silver and *bibelots* catalogued by an expert, and sent for auction any that did not meet her exacting requirements.

'They are family heirlooms,' Brinsley protested. 'One day Alexander might —'

'He shares my tastes,' she countered. 'Besides, I'm replacing everything we sell with better pieces. Can't you tell the difference, Brinsley? Don't tell me all my hard work has been for nothing.'

For work she did, travelling regularly up to sales at the London houses, to auction houses around the country, and once foreign travel restrictions were lifted, abroad. None of her purchases was cheap. Angelica bought only the best.

When Paris couture re-established itself in the late forties, she was one of the first members of English society to receive invitations to the spring and autumn collections. Englishwomen were not noted for their flair with clothes. A lot of the women in Brinsley's milieu were capable of wearing gumboots with one of Chanel's little suits if the going was soft at Ascot. The couturiers did not need that sort of exposure for their designs, but Angelica was a Frenchwoman by birth, with a natural sense of style and elegance. Couturiers clamoured to dress her, some even offering free outfits, such as the Duchess of Windsor received, if Angelica would agree to wear only their designs.

She always refused, for what need had she to save money? When Mademoiselle Chanel lost her touch, Angelica flirted with Balmain, Balenciaga, Jacques Fath and Christian Dior. She was the first to popularise his designs in Britain, to the annoyance of other society figures still thriftily wearing their Utility clothes.

'So extravagant — it'll never catch on,' they murmured when Angelica first appeared in the New Look. The following season they too were in seven-eighths skirts with layers of crackling petticoats beneath, tightly belted waists and box jackets.

Angelica's trips to the couture showings in Paris provided good cover for her visits to her mother, now happily widowed and in sole possession of the Avenue Foch house. Marianne took her banning from Courtney philosophically, though was sorry not to see her grandchildren.

'At least he is good to you,' she said, her eyes on Angelica's jewellery.

'Far better than I deserve.'

For Hamish had been only the beginning. As Brinsley grew older, the pace at which he liked to live inevitably slowed down. Angelica cajoled him into taking holidays as frequently as the Exchange Control regulations allowed — but these days what he enjoyed best of all was a quiet country life at Courtney Park.

Angelica had persuaded him to renew the lease of the London *pied à terre* in Eaton Terrace and made frequent trips there — supposedly to visit the theatre or ballet, neither of which Brinsley cared for, or to go shopping with friends. In reality she was entertaining a string of lovers. She chose elegant young men down on their luck — actors, army officers without private means, gamblers. Brinsley's money supported them for so long as they satisfied Angelica.

But she felt she owed it to her husband to be discreet about the affairs. She always met her lovers at the house, was rarely seen more than once in public with them, and yet somehow Brinsley always got to know about them. Angelica thought at first he might have an informant on the staff. She found constant fault with the chauffeurs, who were best placed to know what she was up to, and regularly replaced them. Her own former maid Henriette, rediscovered on a trip to Paris, widowed and penniless, was above suspicion. And yet, after she had been in London or staying with broad-minded friends at home or abroad for less than a week, Brinsley would telephone her.

'Missing you, darling. Come home and see what I've bought you.'

Another wonderful piece of jewellery, new or re-modelled from the Hamilton family possessions; a Rolls-Royce Silver Cloud II drophead convertible, custom sprayed the colour of her eyes; a string of race horses, each more valuable than the last. Angelica had finally come to share Brinsley's love of the turf — not so much for the courage and beauty of the horses, the aspects that appealed to him, but for the thrill of betting on her own string, hugely and often against the trainer's advice. Angelica loved to bet and Brinsley simply handed over the state-ments of her huge monthly account to Hayward, his estate manager, who dealt with all the bills.

By the mid-1950s, bills were flowing through Hayward's hands thick and fast: from couturiers, jewellers, auction houses, galleries, trainers, restaurants and clubs, and most notably from Angelica's decorator. With suitable fabrics and wall coverings at last available, she gave his creative instincts full rein. The bedroom suites he designed for her and Brinsley were a triumph — if separated by the width of the house, his in the East Wing, hers in the West.

For herself she chose three rooms spanning the depth of the house, with fine views towards the park in front and the wild garden at the back. In summer its artfully planted stands of fine English trees were complemented by banks of rhododendrons and azaleas like pink and white snow drifts.

Angelica's rooms were decorated in four shades of blue, and ivory. She used embroidered blue antique silk for the hangings and cover of her tester bed, plain ivory silk flounced with pleated blue for the long billowing curtains at the windows. Walls and carpet were of two further toning shades of blue, and she chose a long-awaited Colefax and Fowler chintz in blue, white and pink to upholster a comfortable bedroom chair and drape over the circular table at her bedside. This held a collection of photographs in heavy silver frames — of Brinsley and the children, but principally of Angelica herself.

She scoured the house for japanned furniture to use in her rooms. Antique delftware vases were converted into lamps, and her greatest triumph was the discovery in an attic of a pair of eighteenth-century wooden blackamoors supporting shell-shaped urns in which she placed exquisite arrangements of hothouse flowers, always pure white, from the Courtney gardens and greenhouses.

In her personal sitting-room she retained the blue and white chintz from the bedroom at the windows, and toning silk damask for the sofa and two *bergère* chairs. The small Stubbs of the Hamilton family riding together hung over the white marble fireplace, and a charming early Monet of a flower-filled field on the opposite wall. Angelica also displayed pretty pastel portraits of her children. More silver-framed photographs dotted a walnut demi-lune table, and the converted butler's tray table was packed with French and English fashion magazines.

The most important room, her combined bathroom and dressing-room, was concealed behind the ivory painted panelling of her bedroom — a narrow room forty feet long. The porcelain bath, set directly beneath an uncurtained eye window, was boxed in mahogany, and Angelica's perfumes and cosmetics lined a six-foot-long white marble counter beneath a brilliantly lit Venetian mirror.

Row after row of built-in cupboards with hanging rails and shelves filled the other two-thirds of the room. Here Henriette religiously tended and stored her mistress's clothes, brushing, cleaning, pressing and shrouding in white linen each outfit after it had been worn. Angelica's hundred or so pairs of shoes were neatly arranged on rails;

every scarf, handbag, hat or pair of gloves stored in its allotted place. She herself had numbered each outfit and its accessories and handed a list of them to her maid on her first day at work.

'When I ask for number fifteen to be laid out, you will consult this list and see I mean the Balenciaga silk georgette. Its proper accessories are listed and all numbered fifteen. It's quite simple really, but of course we must revise it twice a year when my new season's clothes arrive.'

Brinsley's rooms were overhauled at the same time. His splendid Hepplewhite mahogany four-poster was draped with new Wedgwood blue hangings, lined with the same gold silk which was used to cover the walls and at the windows. A favourite Regency mahogany pedestal desk was placed next to the floor-length window in Brinsley's sitting-room so that when Headley set his breakfast tray down there, he could eat while looking out over the lake. Above the fireplace hung one of the Courtney Gainsboroughs, not a family portrait but a sombre, slightly brooding study of an Italianate garden, an unknown man playing the cello in the foreground.

The next rooms Angelica completed were the White Library and the state dining-room. The library's panelling was stripped back to the original wood and restored with countless applications of linseed oil and beeswax. The fine window shutters, long ago painted into place, were also released and restored. Angelica deliberately kept the rest of the room very plain. Two carved and gilded eighteenth-century sofas were covered in white silk damask, and the decorator installed a new treasure, an Aubusson carpet in deep mustard and pale gold, the colours picked out in the coverings of two George I chairs. The books' bindings were lovingly restored and the most handsome displayed off the shelves on a fine carved wood table which stood along one wall. The library furniture was complemented by a huge antique globe and a free-standing easel on which a Turner landscape was displayed.

The walls of the formal dining-room were used to display more of the Impressionist paintings Angelica had collected. Long sage-green velvet curtains hung at the windows, and the Chippendale dining-chairs were upholstered in the same fabric. The two carver chairs had the family coat of arms embroidered down their padded centre panel. Silver-gilt mirrors and masses of silver candelabra and single candlesticks gave a new, much lighter treatment to the traditional room.

Angelica's redecorating was chic, innovative and appallingly expensive. For the first time ever Hayward expressed concern over the state of the Hamilton family's finances. Brinsley angrily told him to keep his opinions to himself and said that *he* would manage their personal finances from then on. Unfortunately he rarely got further than thrusting the lastest crop of bills into a desk drawer. Reminder notes arrived with irritating regularity. To his amazement, Brinsley found himself forced to think seriously about money. Angelica had, he saw, in the fifteen years they had been married, made staggering inroads into his personal fortune. He was still a wealthy man but no longer one who could afford to spend and spend without a second thought. The renovation of Courtney, of which he only half approved in any case, would have to stop, at least for the time being.

He knew by now what sort of an angry scene or concerted campaign of persuasion to expect if he forbade Angelica outright to proceed with her decorating. He, too, had learned to try the subtler approach.

'Darling, I'm worried about you — you've been looking so tired lately. Why not take a rest from this constant work on the house? Perhaps you could spend some more time with Camilla. I have a feeling she's not quite so happy as she might be in her new school.'

'Camilla is shy and slow to make friends because she's so appallingly fat,' Angelica said crisply. 'I have told her things would improve if she lost some weight, and even offered to plan a *régime* for her, but she won't listen. She prefers the company of that smelly underbred pony to mine.'

'Aren't you being a little hard on her? I always find her very eager to please, and so affectionate.'

'Oh, with darling Daddy, I've no doubt.' Angelica's face twisted scornfully. 'I've done my best, but while she looks like this . . .' She dismissed all thought of her daughter with a wave of her hand. 'Xan is no trouble at all, thank God, and so popular.'

'Will he be back from his friend's in time for the shoot? We're one gun short and it really is time Alexander took part.'

'Oh, *chéri*, don't force him. You know he hates shooting.'

'You spoil him,' Brinsley said bluntly. 'Do him good to get out with a gun.'

'But of course I spoil him. Such a handsome young man — and such a little boy underneath.'

'How, may I ask, does a little boy acquire a tailor's bill that size? When I was at college, Brown's was thought quite good enough for everything except waistcoats. It will be worse when he gets into Pop, you'll see.'

'Don't you mean *if*? The poor darling's desperately worried about it already.'

Brinsley looked amazed. 'Of course he'll get in. Hamiltons always do.'

Angelica took the hint. It was annoying the way Brinsley fussed so over Camilla but her own neglect was brought sharply home one afternoon when Caro Rupert called for tea.

Camilla, who adored her godmother, had been sent to change from her riding clothes that smelled of the stables — though Caro would not have minded if she'd passed sandwiches and cakes still in her jodhpurs and riding-hat. She raised her eyebrows, however, when Camilla returned to the family drawing-room in an ancient Aertex blouse and gym-slip that strained over her adolescent breasts.

'She's just trying on her old school clothes to see what we have to replace,' Angelica said quickly, realising that she had seen Camilla in nothing else but these and her riding clothes throughout the summer holidays. Obviously nothing else fitted her. Something must be done.

The following week she delighted Brinsley by taking Camilla to town to see about some new clothes. Camilla was amazed to receive such attention, but utterly crushed and humiliated when she saw the form it would take.

Her Benenden uniform was renewed to fit her plump figure.

'Goodness! What a fatty you've become, darling.' Angelica's smile deceived the assistant in Harrods' school-outfitting department.

'I expect it's just puppy fat, madam. She'll lose it soon.'

'I know she will.' And Camilla was dragged in her elegant mother's wake to the Junior Miss department.

'You'll need some clothes for association, Camilla. A few dresses, some jumpers and skirts . . . What about this?'

Camilla fell instantly in love with the full-skirted dress in Black Watch tartan with neat Peter Pan collar and cuffs in white piqué.

'It's lovely, Maman, but —'

'Good, we'll take it. And this one, I think. Blue's always been your colour.'

Camilla hung her head so that her mane of fine, light brown hair hid her blushing face and her pale blue eyes filled with tears. Skirts, blouses, cashmere sweaters she'd *die* to wear . . .

'But, Madam,' a salesgirl interrupted with a sideways glance at Camilla, 'I think you'll find these are a size too small.'

'*Two* sizes,' Angelica said with a frosty smile. 'If my daughter wants to wear anything but her school uniform next term, she'll have to diet.'

The girl said nothing but pulled a sympathetic face at

Camilla as she started to pack the lovely clothes.

'Deliver them to our Wiltshire address, will you?' Angelica gave her account number. 'You can catch the train back alone, can't you, Camilla? A big girl like you. Tell Daddy I'll be back in time for the shooting party at the weekend.' After a morning with her daughter she felt desperately in need of the more stimulating company of her latest find — a heterosexual and wonderfully agile male ballet dancer.

Camilla had been made so wretched by her mother's behaviour she didn't eat for the rest of the day. Having survived that, she decided she would follow Maman's wretched diet for the rest of the holiday. By the time she got back to school she would fit her smart new clothes, and then perhaps the constant teasing and name-calling would stop, and she would be a leading light instead of the class blimp. But she would never forget the casual brutality with which her mother had dealt with the problem and doubted she would ever forgive it.

Angelica almost failed to return that weekend. Much as she loved playing Courtney's gracious hostess, shooting parties always bored her to distraction. She liked the look of them — the men so dashing in their tweed knickerbockers and belted Norfolk jackets, Angelica herself in fine heather-mixture tweeds, cut and box-pleated by Dior, and a dashing Loden cape if the weather was foul — which it invariably was. But half an hour's standing in the butts watching the polite rivalry between guns was enough for her.

'Mine, I think.'

'Oh, bad luck, old man.'

'Twenty brace — the fellow's too good a shot for a gentleman.'

Brinsley was inordinately vain of his own skills and hated to be bested by any of his guests. He had recently commissioned a pair of guns from the masters, Purdey, which entailed more trips to their South Audley Street premises for his stance and position to be measured and assessed than any tailor would dare to demand.

Angelica found shooting cold, noisy and vastly over-rated, but infinitely preferred standing on a rain-soaked moor to the hen-pecking conversation of the guns' wives or, worse, their boisterous ill-mannered children whom, unusually among hosts, Brinsley always encouraged them to bring along for the weekend. On the second day, if he judged the game reserves were sufficiently depleted, he would take endless pains teaching the younger guests to shoot clays with specially provided 20-bores.

Angelica's role was to see that the shooting party was handsomely fed, usually a picnic at lunchtime but properly served on Courtney china even if the table was an old barn door mounted on trestles. In the evenings, she would give huge dinner parties for friends from the county as well as the guns, usually seven, and their wives. Breakfast was served in bed to those who preferred or else in the state dining-room. Kedgeree, three kinds of eggs, farm-cured bacon and local sausages would be kept warm in a line of silver chafing-dishes arranged on the sideboard. The guests helped themselves while Hawkins and his staff provided fresh toast, tea and coffee. On Sunday the local vicar would drive out to hold a special service in the chapel for anyone who wished to attend.

Angelica was expecting this weekend to follow the usual course, but she was in for a surprise. Alexander had asked if he might stay longer with his friend, Luis, and at the last minute Brinsley found a replacement gun.

'The most marvellous news,' he told Angelica when she arrived back from London in time for lunch on Friday. 'You'll never guess who's bought himself a place locally? After all these years of calling *me* an effete Southerner!'

'Who has?' Angelica enquired, without much interest.

'Beano!'

'I thought he lived in Scotland.'

'The Laird — his father — does, but Beano's been posted all over the place by the army. You know he stayed in after the war? We've met up now and then at the club, and of course he's been to some of the Gilmour shoots.' Angelica rarely attended these, and Brinsley did not press her to. Hamish had now taken his father's place as factor.

'Scotland's not big enough for him and the Laird, it seems. His mother died recently and left him enough to buy a place down here, bless her. They moved in early this week, so of course when I heard I asked Beano along for this weekend. There's a daughter, too — Imogen. Might do very nicely for Alex in a few years' time.'

Angelica bristled defensively. 'Only if she's very pretty and very rich. And Beano, I think, is not?'

'The heir to one of the oldest titles in Scotland,' Brinsley defended his friend. 'But no, he hasn't a bean until the Laird dies.'

Which made it all the more surprising that when Angelica met Beano Campbell for the second time, later that afternoon, it was a *coup de foudre*.

'Beano — Angelica — you remember one another from that awful night,' Brinsley introduced them.

Angelica couldn't honestly say she did. It was as if she was seeing him with new eyes — a tall, raw-boned, red-haired Scot with an upright military bearing and a pair of the hottest blue eyes she had ever seen.

He took and held her hand more tightly than was necessary, smiling rakishly. 'Angelica, it's been too long.'

She barely noticed his wife and daughter, recognising too clearly the feelings he invoked in her. 'Beano,' her voice was a caress, 'it's so good to see you. I can't think why we haven't bumped into one another since the war.'

Beano, seeing Brinsley's keen, observant gaze upon his hand, which was still holding Angelica's, thought that perhaps he could. 'Neither can I. You've met Fiona already, of course, and this is Imogen, my daughter.'

But she had eyes only for him. Here, she knew, was a man in his prime, as fierce and predatory in love as she was herself. The wild, familiar sweetness mounted in her blood and she broke the self-imposed rule of a lifetime. For the first time she allowed herself to be attracted to a man of the same class. It didn't occur to her that Beano was her husband's best friend. Nor, as his eyes constantly sought her out throughout the whole interminable weekend, did the thought trouble Beano. Each recognised in the other something they must have, whatever the consequences.

They met in secret the next week, while Fiona was visiting her parents with Imogen in tow and Brinsley was touring the tenant farms for the day. Usually Angelica was driven wherever she wished to go, and preferred it that way. To get to Beano she drove herself in a battered old Jaguar that was the most inconspicuous of Courtney's cars. Her face glowed with anticipation. Her arms and legs were bare, and beneath the shell-pink A-line dress, she wore only a cloud of Miss Dior prayed over every last clamouring inch of her.

He was waiting inside the disused estate cottage, shirt and shoes already impatiently discarded. Angelica stepped inside and closed the door behind her. She stared at his smooth hairless chest and freckled arms, each muscle clearly and separately defined. He made no move towards her, but stood and waited.

It was Angelica who broke the silence. *'Tu es magnifique.'* Her voice was husky with desire.

'You too. Take off that dress before I tear it off!'

She laughed, and did as he said. It was only when she looked for somewhere to hang it that she realised there was nothing in the small shabby room but a broken chair and an ancient kitchen table.

'I'll fix it up next week,' he murmured, sliding his arms round her and pulling her hard against him. She ground her pelvis against his and moaned to feel how ready he was for her.

'But what do we do for now?' she asked between feverish kisses as she freed his fierce erection.

'What's wrong with the table?' He grinned and lifted her easily on to the splintered wooden boards. She squealed in protest but he ignored her with a knowing smile which widened as his fingers found the welcome between her legs.

'That's what I like — a woman who knows what she wants.'

And with one practised thrust he was inside her, his hands sliding beneath her to cup her buttocks. She locked her legs around his waist and allowed him to lead her on and on, in a fierce rocking rhythm from which there was only one release. When she was at the summit, gasping to be allowed to fall into velvet oblivion, he wrenched himself free and knelt before her, her legs hooked over his shoulders. He caressed her stomach with featherlike touches of his fingertips while his tongue alternately thrust and lapped at her.

She drummed her fists against the table-top. 'What about you?' she gasped. 'Come inside me again — quickly!'

'This one's all for you, Countess. Besides, I don't think there's time . . .'

Seconds later, with a small scream, Angelica bucked and shuddered against his mouth then lay quite still for a minute or two. Slowly she raised herself to a sitting position and looked down at him, still kneeling between her legs.

'I can never go back,' she said simply.

Beano's eyes narrowed in alarm, and he got to his feet. 'You mean to Brinsley?'

Her full-throated laughter took him by surprise. 'Don't be absurd! He's my husband — I have to go back to *him*. No, I mean the others — they're nothing after you.'

He smiled complacently. 'Why should you need them when you have me?'

'It depends how long I've got you for.'

'For as long as you want, Countess.'

She slid to the bare beaten earth floor and took him in her mouth, tantalising him with the motion of her tongue. Abruptly she released him. He moaned and tried to restrain her by two handfuls of her silky black hair. Angelica pulled herself free and ran one sharp fingernail over his delicate scrotal skin.

'For as long as I want. Do you promise?'

'God! Yes, yes, anything you like, you beautiful bitch. Now put me out of my misery, can't you?'

Her mouth closed willingly over him. She knew then, as he did not, that it would be years before she had enough of him.

Viscount Castlemere didn't wait for the Bentley to finish drawing up but leapt from the still moving car by Courtney's main entrance. He took the steps two at a time, unbuttoning his coat as he ran.

Hawkins materialised before him, a faint smile illuminating his usually sombre face.

'A pleasant half, my lord?'

'My last, Hawkins!' said Alexander. 'Nine months of freedom before Oxford and the House. Is my sister home yet?'

'Lady Camilla returned from Florence on Tuesday. His lordship is in the stables and her ladyship is resting. Shall I ask Henriette to let her know you're back?'

Alexander checked his appearance in the mirror. He ran his fingers through his thick corn-blond hair and smiled disarmingly at the butler.

'I think I'm a little too travel-stained to meet Maman at present. I'll go in later, when I've seen Camilla and changed. Oh, and could you ask Headley to dig out my evening dress and make sure it's pressed for dinner? Guests at Christmas! What will Maman think of next?'

A discreet fit of coughing prevented the butler from making any reply. Alexander grinned and sped up the wide

95

marble staircase to seek out his sister.

Camilla knelt in the family drawing-room, a cosy and rather shabby Edwardian retreat which Brinsley had stubbornly refused to let Angelica touch. Today the room felt warm and welcoming, curtains drawn against the frosty dark and a huge blue spruce in its red paper-covered tub installed in one corner. Alexander smiled to see his sister busily decorating it with gaudy tinsel, glass baubles and tiny red candles in brass holders. The room was filled with the scent of Christmas.

'That looks fun. Need a hand?'

She jumped to her feet and rushed to embrace him. 'Xan, you beast! I was livid to get home and find you'd skipped off to Spain with a school chum.'

He winced. 'Less of the school, please. Scholarship term's over and real life begins. I want to travel as widely as I can before Oxford. I'll want to go back to Spain to start with. The country around Luis's estate is magnificent.'

His sister flicked back her long straight golden-brown hair and looked at him gravely. 'You will stay here for a while, though, won't you? Daddy's so keen for you to learn how the estate is run.'

He dropped heavily into an overstuffed sofa. 'Not you as well, Camilla! It won't take nine months for me to fathom the mysteries of Courtney — I've known all about that since I was ten. Father sits in his study, and Hayward manages the estate. *C'est ça!*'

'Xan, play along with him a little, please. For my sake? I know he's a little hard on you at times, but he loves Courtney so much that he can't seem to take anything about it lightly.'

'All right then. For you. But they'll have to set me free by May at the latest, when they go on holiday. Chartering a yacht for a month doesn't come cheap. Remind me to check the plate, Camilla.'

They were uneasily aware that he was only half-joking. She had fully shared his horror and distress when the previous year Brinsley had announced he was selling at auction three vast silver chandeliers and a fourteenth-century silver reliquary from the chapel. None of the objects had any special sentimental value for his children but for the fact that they belonged to the house, had always been there. Alexander in particular disapproved of any part of his heritage being sold off. Brinsley had played fair with him, notifying him of the reason for the sale — 'Cumbersome, archaic, expensive to insure' — but only last holidays Hayward had let slip in conversation that Brinsley was seriously considering selling off three hundred acres on the borders of the park for development into an 'executive' housing estate. It sounded the sort of scheme the old man usually loathed, but he'd already sold a farm or two and some of the more far-flung holdings. Alexander thought he might be strapped for cash.

For now, he turned his attention on his sister. 'You look very well, Camilla. *La dolce vita* and all that pasta doesn't seem to have fattened you up too much.'

'Not you as well! You can imagine what Maman's first words to me were — almost before she said hello.'

'And are you keeping to your *régime*, darling?' Alexander mimicked his mother's husky tones. 'But looking at you now, she was right in a way, wasn't she?'

Camilla shivered delicately and crossed the room to put another log on the blazing fire. At nineteen, and very much enjoying a spell at a finishing school in Florence, she was a tall, slender, very English beauty. But even now that her daughter's figure was above reproach, Angelica could still find fault with her: dressing too conventionally, or scraping her hair back from her face with a blue velvet band instead of adopting the fashionable bouffant hairstyles. Camilla's social life had improved beyond measure since she had lost weight. Her relationship with her mother had not.

'I seem to suit the Italian taste.' She evaded his question. 'And what of the Spanish? Did Luis's family make you welcome?'

'His family?' Alexander's slanting green eyes were hooded. 'Well, of course they don't go in for Maman's sort of entertaining —'

'Did I hear my name taken in vain?'

Angelica stood poised in the doorway, one delicate dark brow raised in mock reproach. Then she threw her arms wide in welcome and crushed Alexander to her.

'*Chéri*, it's wonderful to see you again — and just in time. Christmas is going to be such fun this year! No more of those boring evenings listening to Papa talking about his childhood Christmases. I'm sure they were charming in their day, but this year we have guests to entertain. You know I asked the de Selincourts — my old beau and his wife Julie? So sad they lost everything in Algeria, and I hear the French estate's looking rocky too so I want you both to be specially kind to them. The Rosses are coming, of course, and the Ruperts. Brinsley's appalling Cousin Eithne — oh, and I've asked that amusing young actor, Jimmy Blair. Such a darling, and very handsome, Camilla. Everyone was delighted to be asked. People get so tired of family Christmases.'

'We don't, Maman,' Alexander told her firmly. 'In fact, it was what I came home for: charades in the Painted Room, carol-singers in the hall, Camilla's tree . . .'

Angelica noticed it for the first time. '*Mais c'est affreux!* How often must I tell you, Camilla. Never more than two colours for the decorations, and that dreadful plastic doll —'

'— will have to go!' Camilla and Alexander chorussed. Maman never changed, even if the Courtney Christmas did.

'What day is it today, Headley?' Brinsley enquired, propped against his three goose-down pillows, morning cup of tea to hand.

Headley, greyer and leaner but still the dapper

gentleman's gentleman, answered gravely: 'It's the 24th of December, my lord. Christmas Eve. Her ladyship's house guests will be arriving this afternoon, and I understand there will be further guests for dinner tonight.'

Brinsley sighed, handed him the cup and got out of bed. 'Then I can't sit around gossiping all day, Headley. Courtney has to be run, whatever the season. It will be the Hunt on Boxing Day, I suppose, then up to Gilmour to see in the New Year, and Hayward will be needing my instructions regardless.'

'Yes indeed, my lord. Shall I ask him to step into your study in one hour?'

'Make it two, Headley. You know I can't abide a hurried bath. Is it ready?'

'Yes, my lord.'

'The brown worsted today, I think.'

'Ahem, I took the liberty, my lord — since your guests may arrive before luncheon — of laying out your grey flannels and blazer.'

'I suppose you're right. Breakfast in half an hour, please.'

Afterwards, Headley held open the door and Brinsley walked downstairs to his study, a cosy club-like room with dark leaf-green walls and heavy red curtains trimmed with dark green braid. The Turkish carpet was red, and two battered leather Chesterfield sofas flanked the carved wooden fireplace where a log fire crackled and spat. Bartle, the English Springer spaniel who had replaced Seek and Fetch when they had eventually died, lay before it. Brinsley knelt to fondle the dog.

'Warm enough for you, old fellow? Let's have another log on, shall we?' The dog thumped its tail.

He fed an applewood log to the greedy flames. No need to distract the maids from their preparations for the house guests. Angelica always liked things to be just so.

Angelica ... Brinsley's handsome well-preserved face softened into a smile as he sat behind his desk and studied the cluster of silver-framed photographs upon it. There were some of Camilla and Alexander — a good-looking pair, though he admitted to himself he preferred Camilla. But the majority of the photographs were of Angelica: languid by Lenare in the forties, a lock of hair drooping seductively across her forehead, or sylph-like in a spangled Hartnell ballgown, photographed starkly against the majestic backdrop of the marble hall. Brinsley had thought it a damn silly place for a photograph, but that Beaton fellow they all raved about had insisted. Then there was Angelica victorious in a froth of lavender silk the year Angel's Wing won the Oaks; elegant in her Peeress's robes before the Coronation; timeless in a recent formal portrait by Baron, her hair elegantly upswept to reveal the swanlike line of her neck.

At almost sixty, Brinsley counted himself lucky to have a wife more beautiful than many a younger man's. Like her husband, Angelica wore her years lightly, only a slight tightening of the skin at the corners of her eyes and mouth, and the becoming streak of silver in her hair, hinting that she might be nearer forty than thirty.

Brinsley rang the bell for Miss Buckmaster, a jolly, capable, spinster who cycled in from the village each day to help deal with his correspondence. She bustled in with a few opened and neatly annotated letters — a subscription here, a request for a donation there — and an unopened letter in the bank's crested envelope which he barely glanced at before opening his desk drawer and dropping it inside. Brinsley handed the rest of the letters back to Miss Buckmaster for her to deal with as she had indicated and sat back in his chair, breathing shallowly. It was the third letter from the bank in as many months.

He knew he ought not to have agreed to Angelica's plan to charter a yacht and spend the month of May cruising the Côte d'Azur with friends — but it had always been impossible for him to refuse his wife.

Bank be hanged! If a month's cruising or the elegant

diamond and topaz earrings he had commissioned from Andrew Grima for her Christmas present brought a smile to Angelica's lovely face, they were cheap at the price.

Longingly he pictured the way she would look when he visited her rooms for their private ritual at Christmas or on her birthday. For her there would be the latest addition to her priceless collection of jewellery; for him, something beyond price — Angelica, naked, warm and welcoming, in exchange for the tribute he laid at her feet.

The keen air caught in her throat and tears pricked in her eyes. At eleven o'clock in the morning thick frost still blanketed the frozen earth. Boxing Day had dawned bitterly cold but clear and fine — perfect weather for hunting.

The guests who had brought riding-clothes with them — pink, black or dark blue jackets worn with boots and tight-fitting white breeches — had been mounted from the Courtney stables. Brinsley, as Honorary Joint Master, and Alexander, as a member of the Courtney Hunt, were entitled to sport half lapels of shocking pink, the hunt's colour, against the deep red hunting pink of their tight-fitting jackets.

Angelica herself was immaculately turned out in a dark blue riding-habit, silk skirt, austere white cravat, and a grey silk topper worn with a veil. She had long ago mastered the art of riding side saddle, first perfected in the court of Richard II where his wife, Anne of Bohemia, set the fashion. So much more becoming than straddling a horse, thighs bulging like pale sausages, as so many of the Hunt's female members did.

She loved the spectacle and excitement of the hunting field. The ceremonial offering of the gleaming stirrup-cup at the crossroads where the members assembled, the noise of jangling harness and the hounds' excited baying, the knowledge that she was far and away the most elegant woman in the field.

' She spurred on Jester to ride ahead of her own party. She usually rode with her whippet, Mistinguette — named for her long elegant legs — running at her horse's heels, but not when the hounds were out, of course. Angelica greeted the members with smiles and nods of greeting. The Courtney was a select hunt — no trade and few professional people. Each application was reviewed by the Hunt committee, of which Angelica as patroness was the most vocal member so she could safely say there was not a single member of whom she did not approve — and one in particular of whom she thought very highly indeed. Her colour heightened as she spotted her quarry.

'Good morning, Fiona. Splendid weather, isn't it? And Beano — you're almost a stranger! Brinsley wondered where you'd got to yesterday morning, though of course it was lovely to see Fiona and Imogen at the drinks party.'

'I did mean to join them later — wouldn't willingly have missed the Courtney Christmas drinks — but I'm afraid we had our own nativity in the stables. It was very good of you to run the girls home yourself. What a shame I didn't hear you. Fiona says you were leaning on the horn for a good five minutes.'

Angelica smiled widely at her, wondering at the same time why Fiona didn't do something about her mousy blonde hair and the broken veins in her cheeks. 'Of course I didn't mind giving you a lift. Oh, look, Fiona, isn't that your friend Liza from the Wrens?'

'So it is. Haven't seen her in ages. Do excuse me, both of you. See you in the field later.'

As Fiona edged out of the press of horses around them, Angelica continued in a conversational tone, 'Half an hour, Thurlow's barn, next to the Hundred Acre Field.'

Beano shot out his hand to seize her wrist, squeezing it painfully. 'No,' he said in an agonised voice. 'I meant what I said. This has got to stop.'

His voice was drowned by the huntsman's horn. The hounds were led off at a smart pace, sniffing out a scent on the frosty ground with yelps of excitement. The riders fell in behind them and Angelica adroitly rejoined the Courtney party, smiling encouragingly at her guests as the pace picked up and the horses broke into a canter.

.They were on to something fast, fortunately for her. She took the first two hedges hell for leather instead of traversing, looking for a lower level or a thinner spot as she usually did. Thurlow's barn was to the west, so she needed to be well to the left of the Hundred Acre Field by the time the pack filtered across the open ground above it. She reached the edge of the field, where the ground shelved sharply down to a deep ditch. Surreptitiously she reined in her mount, which had been relishing the pace and was reluctant to slacken.

From nowhere, just as she was about to drop down into the ditch's cover, Alexander appeared at her side. 'Everything all right, Maman? Jester was nicely into his stride, I thought, but now you're the back marker.'

'He's a little off form, I think,' she said breathlessly, fighting to restrain the horse by digging back sharply with her heels beneath the cover of her long apron skirt. Damn Alexander! He was too observant. 'Don't worry about me, chéri. Aren't you whipping in today? You know how strict John is.'

'If you're sure you're all right?'

'Of course. And, Xan . . .'

'Yes, Maman.'

'Keep an eye out for your father, won't you? He will put Hannibal straight at those five bars, and the animal's past his best years.'

Like his rider, she thought.

The rocking motion of the horse beneath her, and the animal scent that rose from the bay's steaming sides, heightened her anticipation. She stayed in the field till the nearest rider was a hundred yards away then slipped from the saddle and led Jester down into the ditch. She followed the field's perimeter until she reached the shelter of a plantation, then led the snorting horse tamely through a gate and down a sharp incline to the grey weather-boarded barn.

Beano's chestnut hunter was hitched to the low branch of a tree nearby. Angelica tethered Jester a safe distance alongside and picked her way across the rutted earth.

He emerged from the barn at the sound of her arrival. 'All right, I'm here. But I've told you a dozen times — this has got to stop. Christ, I've got a conscience, if you haven't! I'm betraying my wife and my best friend.'

His face was flushed with anger. He had thickened slightly in the years since they had become lovers, but he still had the power to arouse her as no other man could. Even his anger was exhilarating.

'It's no betrayal while they're in ignorance,' she said, laying a gloved hand on his sleeve. 'And we're very discreet.'

He laughed hollowly. 'If you call leaving the hunting field in front of fifty pairs of curious eyes discreet!' He shrugged her off and entered the barn. She followed him, smiling.

He turned away, unable to look her in the face. She moulded herself to the powerful contours of his back, sliding her hands beneath his jacket to the animal warmth beneath.

'Why must we stop? We do no harm, and we have so much fun.'

Beano shook her off and turned to face her, his features twisted with misery and lust. He had known since the first evening they'd met that one day he would have her. She'd been too glorious to pass over. But he'd meant it to be a short, sweet affair, the fulfilment of the promise he'd made himself, and then back to being friends and neighbours. But love with Angelica was potent, intoxicating. She was like no woman he had ever known before, leading him further and further from what he knew to be right.

'Angelica.' He meant to sound commanding, but his voice held a note of pleading.

'Just once more, *chéri*. This once and never again, I promise.'

'Damn you, no! I've heard your promises before.'

She raised her hand abruptly and he saw the thin switch she held cutting straight for his face. He caught her wrist and squeezed it viciously, twisting it behind her back and sending her stumbling. She sagged to her knees, and he put out his free hand to steady her. It brushed against her heaving breasts and he let it lie, her heart hammering like a captive bird at his touch. He was aroused despite himself, the close-fitting riding-breeches emphasising his desire.

'Of course,' she murmured, 'if you're cruel to me, Beano, I might just be heart-broken enough to regret the error of my ways and confess everything to Fiona.'

'You bitch!' he spat. 'All right, then. You asked for this.' With a flick of his wrist he sent her to her knees on the bare earth. He scrambled down behind her and wrenched at the side fastening of the close-fitting breeches she wore beneath the apron skirt of her habit. One powerful tug and Angelica knelt half naked before him, her breeches around her knees, hobbling her. He knelt between her highly polished boots and pressed his hand against her shoulder until her face was inches from the dirt. Swiftly freeing himself from his breeches, he plunged between her barely parted thighs, driving into her furiously again and again.

Aroused from the moment she had seen him at the crossroads, Angelica's climax was swifter even than his. While he shuddered against her, she wondered which gave her the greatest satisfaction: Beano's brutal lovemaking or the knowledge that, whenever she pleased, she could shatter his marriage with a few well-chosen words.

Camilla had opted to stay at home to help amuse the non-riding guests. At two o'clock she instructed Hawkins to open the champagne — her mother's favourite Cristal — as the red-cheeked, mud-spattered riders handed their reins to waiting grooms and thronged into the great hall. It was a tradition that the Boxing Day hunt was a half-day one only, the members assembling afterwards at Courtney for a buffet lunch.

Brinsley was one of the first back. He took the opportunity to check his bandbox appearance in the cloakroom off the hall before confusing Hawkins with a series of contradictory instructions.

Camilla made the introductions betweeen house party and hunt members, soothed Hawkins, and circulated assiduously. Half an hour later she sought out Alexander, a worried look on her face.

'Xan, Maman's still not back. It's not like her when there are guests. Shall I mention it to Daddy?'

'I doubt it's escaped his notice.'

'But what if she's lying injured on the ground somewhere?'

'Don't you know by now? Maman always lands on her feet. And for heaven's sake don't make a fuss. It isn't kind to poor Fiona Campbell.'

'Fiona? What on earth has she to do with it? She looks quite happy, chatting to her friend.'

'I imagine she'd rather be chatting to her husband. Any sign of him yet?'

Camilla scanned the hall for the familiar red-haired figure. 'No, and still no sign of Maman ... Oh, Xan! You don't mean ...?'

'Don't I? See for yourself.'

Just at that moment Angelica strode into the great hall, laughing and clinging to Beano's arm. 'I don't know what came over Jester this morning. He quite ran away with me into the plantation. Beano spent hours catching him for me.'

Brinsley was at once by her side, concern for her evident on his face. 'You're all right, darling? Your arm —'

'My arm is perfectly unharmed, thank you. What I could do with is a glass of champagne and the chance to brush away some of this mud. Look at me! I'm covered.'

Rich red earth smeared the skirt and sleeves of her habit. The undersides of her sleeves, Camilla noted. There was mud on her face, too, yet her normally punctilious mother had made no attempt to wipe it away. Her face was flushed and animated, eyes sparkling with triumph.

'Darling Maman, you must take better care of yourself,' Alexander said solicitously. 'You too, Beano. It seems you had a fall yourself.'

'Fall, me?' Beano looked outraged at the suggestion. 'Why do you say that?'

'Your knees. They're covered in mud — just like Maman's.'

January's Hunt Ball at Courtney was the high point of the Wiltshire social calendar. The extravagance of Angelica's entertaining was legendary. Whole battalions of florists would be drafted in from London to garland the pillars of the ballroom and great hall with lily of the valley and white tiger lilies. The Countess would engage Paul Adams and his orchestra instead of the small dance combos that thriftier neighbours favoured. The skill of the Courtney kitchens was famous and the celebrated cold table would be supplemented by French delicacies flown in from Paris on the morning of the Ball.

As she stood before the tarnished cheval mirror in Beano's dressing-room, checking that the local dressmaker had done a good job of letting out the seams of her one Hardy Amies original, Fiona Campbell hummed softly to herself. How she looked forward to the Ball, and the chance to dance again.

She clasped round her neck her one 'good' piece of jewellery, a four-strand pearl choker with a diamond and sapphire clasp which she adjusted to hang in the middle of her throat. It was the only piece remaining from the collection Beano's mother had bequeathed her. Beano had been forced to sell the rest to add to his inheritance and buy the Grange. It had been a wrench to let the pretty things go, but when at last the Laird died and they could take over the Scottish estates, there'd be jewels enough. She was really a very lucky woman. She had this house, Imogen — and Beano, of course.

The door to the dressing-room opened and he stumbled inside. The unmistakable smell of whisky accompanied him. Fiona forced a smile.

'I feel like driving tonight,' she said brightly. 'Can you remember where we put the fox mascot after the last ball?'

He stared at her blankly.

'No? Well, it doesn't matter. I expect it will turn up. Now make haste and change, darling.'

'No need,' he slurred. 'Not going.'

'Not going to the Hunt Ball?' She was amazed. It wasn't like Beano to pass up one of Angelica's famous shindigs. 'But we have to, darling,' she remonstrated gently, hoping tonight was not going to be one of his difficult nights. 'Brinsley and Angelica are expecting us.'

To her surprise, he laughed until his voice broke on what was almost a sob. She watched him, suddenly afraid.

'You're right,' he said, at last beginning to change — quite efficiently considering the amount of whisky he must have put away.

'Do my tie, will you?' he said, a few minutes later. 'Mustn't keep the Countess waiting — or who knows what she'll do.'

The Earl and Countess of Courtney welcomed their guests inside the newly renovated ballroom. The massive bill for the three year overhaul lay securely in Angelica's writing-desk upstairs. Brinsley would make ominous noises when he saw it, but tonight nothing would spoil her triumph.

She looked superb in a honey-coloured silk georgette ballgown from Balmain, the classical sweep of its draped bodice contrasting with a pale froth of skirts. Beano noticed through a protective haze of alcohol that she was wearing the famous emeralds, just as she had that first night ... She clung embarrassingly to his hand when he and Fiona were announced.

'We're so glad you could both come,' Brinsley welcomed them.

'Yes, lovely to see you,' Angelica echoed. 'Fiona, do you think I might borrow your husband for a while later this evening? We've just had a rather disturbing announcement from Alexander. You know he's gone back to Spain to visit his friend the Duque there, and now apparently they intend to start a tour of the Middle East. He assures me it's quite safe, but naturally a mother worries. I'd so like the opinion of someone who's been there. You won't mind, will you?'

'Not at all — it must be worrying. I know Imo will be sorry not to see Alexander when she returns from college.'

'And how is the secretarial course going? So enterprising to want to work.'

'Oh, she's loving the social side of it and meeting all sorts of highly eligible young men, so we hope it won't actually *be* a question of working. And how is Camilla getting on?'

'Adoring every minute! Her letters are so full of Tommasos and Pieros and Rinaldos, we can't keep up with them, can we, Brinsley?'

'No indeed, my love. But perhaps — our other guests ...'

Reluctantly she released Beano. 'Later,' she mouthed.

The Orangery was locked for the ball, the head gardener fearing drunken damage to his treasured vine. Early that afternoon, Angelica had removed the key from the board in Hawkins' pantry.

At midnight, supper was announced. With his guests

distracted by greed, Brinsley was free to confide in the butler that he felt a little unwell.

'Some fresh air is all you need, my lord. A little turn in the courtyard will soon set you up.'

Hawkins' own feet, in their best black pumps, were throbbing. He looked sympathetically at his master. 'Would you like me to accompany you?'

'Good heavens no, man! There are guests to be seen to.'

Brinsley made his way back through the crowd filing out of the ballroom in search of supper. Inevitably he was waylaid. He made his excuses and returned to the ballroom in time to see a swirl of honey-coloured skirts disappearing through the concealed door in the panelling, the route he had planned to take.

'Angelica — wait for me!'

But Courtney's walls were thick. She did not hear him. It took him a minute or two to find the door's mechanism, then he stepped out into the courtyard behind the West Wing.

After the extravagantly lit ballroom, the darkness was almost total, but Brinsley thought he saw a man's figure lurking by the Orangery. Thank goodness it was locked. He opened his mouth to challenge the stranger when, with a swish of skirts, Angelica materialised beside the man. There was no mistaking her elegant silhouette or the muted flash of green fire from the emeralds at her throat and wrists.

He started across the courtyard towards them — then his footsteps froze. The man had taken Angelica in a fierce embrace. The movement was so sudden and savage that Brinsley expected her to cry out in protest, but she clung to him eagerly. The man had his back to Brinsley. By a feeble sliver of moonlight all Brinsley could see were his wife's pale arms enclosing the man's broad back in its hunting jacket.

He stood totally silent, struggling to come to terms with what he was seeing. For years he had known of her infidelities. The London detective he retained kept him informed. But the men were always young, penniless, of no account ... They had not moved in Brinsley's circles and, though racked with jealousy, he had not feared them. In the past few years he had received no reports from London and had come to the conclusion that Angelica's straying days were over. Now he realised the extent of his self-delusion. All this time she'd kept a lover under his nose, a neighbour, a member of the Courtney Hunt. But who? The moon went behind a cloud and Brinsley watched the shadowy figure of his wife unlock the Orangery door and pull the man inside. He could almost feel the hot humid darkness closing round them ... He felt sick with betrayal.

There were two possible courses he could take: confront his wife and her lover and cause a public scandal, or return to the ball, the perfect host, while his wife cuckolded him with an unknown friend. He realised he was too old and too tired for an ugly scene with Angelica, so he turned on his heel and went back to their guests.

Hawkins, limping over to check that his master felt better, was shocked by the change in his appearance. The lines seemed mysteriously to have deepened on his gaunt face. The sixth Earl was no longer the weathered but handsome man he had been at the beginning of the ball. Like his butler, Brinsley was a tired old man.

Twenty minutes later, the Countess appeared at her husband's side. '*Chéri*, where've you been? I've been looking for you everywhere. Listen, I've had an idea. Poor Fiona's been looking so tired and pale lately I thought she deserved a treat, so I've asked her and Beano to join us on the yacht. Won't that be splendid?'

Fiona and Beano stood tactfully ten feet or so away while Angelica spoke to her husband. Brinsley glanced at the broad outline of his friend's back, familiar in its hunting pink, and stood as if turned to stone.

'Splendid,' he murmured.

The contrast between him and his radiant wife, who glowed like a girl, could not have been more cruel.

★

The ninety-foot *Penelope* was sleek, white and beautiful, as Brinsley had known she would be. At the western Mediterranean charter rate he was paying she damn well ought to be, but still Angelica fussed over the shipboard arrangements like a nervous bride. She set one of the stewards scouring the town for a supply of Scottish marmalade.

She and Brinsley took the master stateroom, ornately decorated in her favourite shade of Wedgwood blue. The Ruperts were to share a spacious double berth; the Campbells were allotted two berths aft.

'Apparently they have to sleep apart. Fiona's a martyr to insomnia, she says, and since we have the space, why not indulge her?'

Swallowing his pride and going along with Angelica had been almost worth it, Brinsley decided over a shipboard dinner three days later. When the guests arrived the previous day they had sailed from Antibes, and berthed overnight at Villefranche. Now they were bound for Monaco, where they were sure to bump into other friends and acquaintances.

Angelica looked relaxed and happy for the first time in weeks. Her olive skin was richly tanned after only a few days of the sun, and splendidly offset by her strapless turquoise dress and simple necklace and bracelet of heavy gold links.

'Just a friendly, informal cold supper tonight, I think,' she had told her guests. After all these years Caro and Fiona had taken her at her word, and consequently felt rather foolish in their second-best cocktail frocks.

Caro caught Brinsley's eye and smiled a touch ruefully. A good sort, he decided, and endlessly patient with dear old Reggie who couldn't, nowadays, be trusted to tell when he had had enough to drink.

'Exshellent bubbly, old man. Simply exshellent. What is it?'

112

Reggie peered short-sightedly at the distinctive yellow-apricot tones of the champagne, named for the crystal bottles in which it was first presented at the Russian court.

'Cristal — Angelica's favourite, of course,' Brinsley said. 'More champers, Fiona?'

Angelica had told the truth about one thing. Fiona had been looking pale and wan when she came aboard, but the Hamiltons' lavish hospitality seemed to have reawakened her sense of fun. She smiled, and took up Brinsley's little joke.

'Marvellous! I could drink it till I dropped! This is heavenly, isn't it, Beano?'

Her gesture took in Angelica's artful *mise en scène*. The sky overhead was darkening, but on deck all was light and elegance. They dined from a circular table draped in a floor-length cloth of blue and white Provençal print. The marzipan scent of the fluffy late mimosa centrepiece was echoed by the perfumed Rigaud candles in their glass jars. The guests sat in high-backed Victorian wicker chairs, painted white and padded with cushions in a contrasting blue and white print.

'Very pretty,' her husband confirmed. He looked ruddily handsome above his white dinner jacket. Brinsley doubted he had noted a single one of Angelica's preparations. He had eyes only for the hostess.

'Gettin' awfully dark, isn't it?' Reggie Rupert remarked as the steward served them with lobster mayonnaise and salads, and then withdrew.

'We are at sea, darling,' Caro patiently reminded him.

'Must be it, then. Pass the champagne, someone.'

Under the influence of a couple more bottles, the party grew riotous. There were shrieks of laughter every time a 'dead man' was removed from the huge silver ice-bucket and tossed over the rails to the black sea beneath.

Angelica moved from animation and smiles to long lingering glances at Beano, whom she had placed on her right. Even when a strong breeze blew off the sea, extinguishing most of the candles and leaving the rest burning dangerously low, there was no mistaking the hungry expression on her face and Beano's answering smile.

Unable to bear the spectacle of her husband's naked interest in another woman, Fiona lurched to her feet. 'I think I'll go and fetch my wrap. This wind's rather chilly.'

As she passed Angelica, a swing of her hand upended a glass of champagne into her lap — as if by accident.

'My dear, I'm so sorry! Your beautiful dress — it's ruined.' But she couldn't disguise the satisfaction in her voice.

Angelica jumped to her feet, eyes flashing. The others held their breath, sensing that something inexcusable was about to be said.

'What a stupid, childish thing to do! Just because Beano and I —'

Fiona drew herself up to her full five feet three. 'I can't think what concern my husband is of yours, but if I ever again see you making sheep's eyes at him, I'll scratch them out!'

Brinsley got to his feet. He had been drinking too much to be clear-headed, but was amazed to find himself unsteady on his feet. 'Angelica, please,' he said, grabbing the table to steady himself. Unbelievably, he appeared to have upset it. China, glasses and silverware were dislodged and clattered in a steady stream on to the scrubbed teak deck.

'You clumsy oaf!' his wife screamed, and then realised that the table was still standing squarely on all four legs. It was the deck that was moving, tilting steeply as a ferocious wind whipped the sea into white-capped peaks and plunging troughs.

'Don't feel awfully well,' Reggie said faintly.

Fiona screamed as a wave coiled over the side, crashing on to the deck in front of her and flecking them all with foam. More waves appeared in quick succession, flooding the deck and rendering it slippery and treacherous.

The steward appeared, holding a storm-lantern. Brinsley grappled to work out what was different about him, and then realised — the man was wearing a life-jacket over his uniform whites.

'Mesdames, Messieurs, the Capitaine requests you go straight to the salon and stay there.'

'Bloody cheek!' Beano began to bluster, but his terrified wife took his arm and shouted above the noise of the wind, 'Beano, don't! If the Captain says so, we must go inside. Just look at the sea.'

Under the wind's relentless scourge the sea had swelled into fantastic walls of water, dark and glassy. The boat which had seemed large and luxurious in harbour suddenly felt like a child's toy.

'Quickly, Reggie. Into the saloon.' Caro guided her husband's faltering steps over the steeply raked deck. The others followed, stumbling and banging themselves as the violent motion of the boat made them lose their footing.

It was worse, if anything, below. Though it was warm and dry, and the steward had drawn the curtains to obscure their view of the sea, the sounds of the heavy swell slamming against the yacht's sides and the thunder growling overhead was distinctly threatening. They were each given a stiff drink and told not to leave the saloon.

'The Capitaine needs to know where you are at all times. Mesdames, Messieurs, for your own safety, please obey his orders.'

Fiona moaned as the steward's meaning sank home. 'He means we might have to take to the lifeboats! Oh, Beano, I'm so frightened.'

Though white-faced, Angelica scorned to show her own fear, or to obey instructions. She opened the door leading to the companionway. 'I won't be a minute, Brinsley. There's something I must fetch.'

He started after her. 'No — don't! The Captain said —'

'Ta gueule, le Capitaine.' Angelica slammed the door behind her.

'Brinsley, can you help me?' Caro, a terrified expression on her face, was struggling to unfasten Reggie's collar, and splashing his face with whisky for want of anything else. 'I can't tell if he's passing out from drink or something worse,' she said, fighting to keep her self-control.

Brinsley supported his friend's considerable weight while Caro determinedly slapped his face. Beano tried to calm a by now hysterical Fiona, his eyes riveted on the door by which Angelica had left.

At that moment it burst open and the Captain appeared, his hair plastered to his skull and foul weather gear dripping puddles of water on to the needlepoint carpet.

'This way please, my lord. We're preparing to launch the lifeboats and you should all be on deck.'

'But my wife —'

The Captain's professional calm deserted him. 'Damn her! Where's she got to? Quickly, man. There's not a second to lose.'

'Our cabin. She went to fetch something.'

'On deck, all of you. I'll find her ladyship. Now — move!'

The scene on deck was terrifying. A crew member thrust bundles of protective clothing at the quaking passengers before rejoining the struggle to winch a lifeboat overboard. Afterwards, painfully slowly, a rope-ladder was secured to cleats and the free end thrown over the side. A crew member in yellow oilskins began to clamber down it, his terrified face a white blur in the darkness. A huge wave began to seethe and boil beneath him. They were powerless to help. It rose, gathering strength, and brushed him casually aside in its relentless climb. His cries were lost in the wind's keening and the roar of the gathering water as it climbed higher and higher.

As the yacht skated down the sheer side of one wave, the giant hung twenty feet above them, still climbing, still gathering momentum. Two figures appeared in the companion-hatch: the Captain in his yellow oilskins;

116

Angelica, frail and unprotected in her blue dress. She was carrying something, Brinsley noticed, and let go of the bulwark he had been clutching. The crewman had given him a set of oilskins for her. He must go to her.

'Brinsley!'

Caro's warning was carried away on the wind. He never heard it, nor the Captain's command as he gazed at the white water appearing on the crest of the giant wave behind.

'I'm coming, my darling,' Brinsley cried, and then the solid wall of water crumpled with sickening force on top of him, blinding him and filling his nose and mouth. As he was swept away into the welcoming blackness, his final thought was of his wife.

Penelope's passengers and crew were picked up at dawn. It had been a freak squall, unpredicted by the meteorologists, but the devastation it had wrought was total. The lifeboat had been knocked to matchwood by the force of the waves. When the patrol boat found them, the survivors were clinging to the partly submerged hull. An elderly couple calmly identified themselves as Lord and Lady Rupert. A huge Scotsman, who had free floated in the water for six hours, helping two women to keep their grip on the wreckage, was acclaimed by them as a hero.

'Which is the Countess of Courtney?' the captain of the rescue boat asked Caro Rupert.

'The one still clinging to her jewel-case.'

The body of the sixth Earl was discovered close by, floating face down amid a mass of splintered spars, rigging and champagne bottles.

Mrs Huntingdon Mercede, the American foundress of a prestigious finishing school in Florence, summoned Lady Camilla Hamilton to her drawing-room later that morning.

Camilla saw the glass of brandy, smelling-salts and linen handkerchiefs laid out in readiness, and received a lesson in the etiquette of breaking bad news.

'My dear, you're going to have to be very brave. I'm afraid it's your father —'

'I don't believe you,' the girl said calmly, and fainted on the marble floor.

Luis, Duque de Luz y Aragon, gazed down at his friend's sleeping face. It was shadowed by the pale blond growth of three days, and the sickly scent of *kif* hung in his unwashed hair.

Life had been simple for them in Tangier, slow and easy. Endless days of smoking and watching the brilliant Moroccan light refract from the red-tiled roofs of the Medina and the endless turquoise sea beyond.

And now the sea had claimed Alex's father. Orphaned at fifteen, Luis knew the pain he would feel and delayed the evil moment as long as he could.

Only when their packing was complete and the flight reservations to England and Spain confirmed did he break the news that Alexander was now the seventh Earl of Courtney.

The funeral was a quiet affair held in the chapel in the grounds of Courtney Park. Afterwards Brinsley's remains were interred with those of his ancestors in the mausoleum beyond the wood. Angelica let it be known that a memorial service would be held at Westminster Abbey at a later date. But first there were family matters to be settled.

Mr Goodbody, the solicitor, the middle-aged son of Thomas, tried to make things as simple as possible for the grieving widow. She was looking very frail in black shadow lace and the pearls her husband had given her when Camilla was born. Goodbody began to read the will.

Brinsley's three faithful servants — Hawkins, Headley and the cook, Mrs Teare — were each to receive full pensions and a bequest of two thousand pounds.

'Bless his poor lordship,' the cook exclaimed, and was led in tears from the room by the two male servants.

As the door closed behind them, the solicitor resumed: 'The Lady Camilla is bequeathed the sum of £250,000, to be held in trust for her until she reaches the age of twenty-five or marries with her mother's consent and approval before that date. Do you understand the terms of the bequest, Lady Camilla?'

Her face was pale and stricken but she answered the lawyer firmly, her chin raised. 'Yes, thank you, Mr Goodbody. It's perfectly clear and more than generous of Daddy.'

'The Courtney and Gilmour estates, and all revenue pertaining thereto, shall devolve upon the heir, Alexander, seventh Earl of Courtney, with the proviso that the widow shall retain possession of the London property for the ten-year extent of the lease, and be assured of a home in Courtney and Gilmour for the rest of her life.'

Alexander squeezed his mother's shoulder. He had never admired her strength of character so much as during this last sad week.

'There was no question of your leaving Courtney even if Papa had not made it a stipulation. You know that, don't you, Maman?'

'What? Oh — yes, thank you, Xan.' She squeezed his hand painfully. 'And the rest of my husband's estate?' she asked the lawyer.

Goodbody cleared his throat. 'You must understand, your ladyship, that your husband made his will over twenty years ago. At that time he provided that, after the paying of all other bequests and death duties, the remainder of his estate should go to you.'

She sat back in her chair. 'That sounds perfectly fair to me. How soon may I expect a statement of accounts?'

She'd been doing her homework, the lawyer realised, and wondered what the grieving widow would make of this.

'I can inform your ladyship of the approximate size of your inheritance now. Not correct to the last penny, of course, but —'

'Exactly how much has my husband left me?' she interrupted.

'His lordship's personal affairs had become a little — er — tangled over the last five years or so. After the payment of the bequests to the staff, death duties, his lordship's personal liabilities, including an overdraft of four hundred thousand pounds, Lady Camilla's trust, and of course our fees, I estimate that the sum of five thousand pounds remains.'

'Five thousand!' For the first time that day, Angelica seemed distraught. 'But that's impossible! My husband was a wealthy man. He loved me. He would never leave me destitute!'

'Hardly destitute, your ladyship. Look on the bright side. You have the London property, a home for life here at Courtney, your jewels and other personal assets, and a lump sum of five thousand pounds. I'm sure, if that is not sufficient, your children would not allow you to suffer actual want.'

'Maman, please don't upset yourself.' Their enmity put aside, Camilla felt desperately sorry for her. 'There'll be the income from my trust, don't forget. You can have it all — I shan't need it. And a bank might lend on it in advance, to be repaid when I'm twenty-five. Perhaps Mr Goodbody could advise us?'

'I certainly would not advise such a course, Lady Camilla.'

'It will hardly be necessary,' Alexander intervened. 'I'm sorry, Maman. I half-expected something like this, and of course I'll be happy to pay you a reasonable allowance out of the Courtney revenue, and bear all running costs myself.

Nothing need change for you, darling. Courtney is still your home, and there'll always be money for anything you need . . .'

Angelica closed her eyes giddily, barely listening to her children. They loved her, she knew, and wanted to see her happy. But already Alexander was talking of 'reasonable' allowances and Camilla of a barebones existence, living off interest. She remembered Brinsley telling her there was 'more money than you or I could ever spend in a lifetime'.

Since her marriage, she had never needed to count the cost. Anything she desired — clothes, jewels, fine paintings, the restoration of the house she loved — Angelica had commanded and it had been hers. Now, that precious freedom was coming to an end. Unless she could do something to save herself . . .

She was beautiful if no longer young, and had never lacked energy or audacity. She fingered the lace dress. Mourning was out for a start — black had never been her colour. Angelica was about to embark on the quest of a lifetime — a man hunt. She needed to look her very best.

She wouldn't be too demanding. The man she was looking for needn't be young, good-looking, amusing or even titled. He'd have to be decisive, though. She needed a man who could make up his mind and act upon it, fast, before the news of her failing fortunes leaked out. Still, Brinsley had met and married her within a month, she remembered.

Poor Brinsley! She glanced at the massive diamond on her right hand. Now that the shock was wearing off, she knew where all the money had gone. It had taken a king's ransom to support her in the style to which she was accustomed.

There was a lesson to be learned there, she realised, as Alexander pressed a glass of brandy into her hand.

She would have to make quite sure that her second husband was even richer than her first.

Book Two

DEXTER

Ballachulish Station, Northern Queensland, 1946

'C'mon, Rando — show 'er yer stick!'

'Keep'em steady longa rails, boss. Thatsa way!'

'C'mon, Cirrus. C'mon, you old dag . . . oh, you beauty!'

A flurry of akubra hats flew into the air and a cheer went up from the crowd which packed the ramshackle grandstand as the sleek grey thoroughbred, her neck and flanks lathered with sweat, streaked past the post to win the Ballachulish Bracelet Race by half a length.

It was a popular victory with the mixed crowd of graziers and their families, ringers, rouseabouts and local bushies. Cirrus had started as favourite, and beaming spectators mobbed the sour-faced bookies and a local station owner who had set up a bush tote under the ironbarks.

But the racegoers admired the rider, Dexter Randolph, for more than his skill as an amateur jockey. It took a special breed to manage a sprawling, largely unfenced thousand-square-mile property with no more than a handful of tribal stockmen for help; the young jackeroos and even the seasoned ringers had, like Dexter's elder brother Lucas, long since answered the call to war. Barely out of the schoolroom, Dexter Randolph had risen to the challenge of managing his inheritance. Now Yelonga prospered and, grudgingly, the Northern Queensland graziers accorded him a man's status.

Their wives and daughters would have been glad to. One glance at his whipcord strength, the striking angularity of a face already deeply tanned and lined by wind and unrelenting sun, and the women of the district voted him number one catch ... or maybe number two. Many of them still had fond memories of Lucas Randolph who had yet to return to the district after his service debrief. He was eight years Dexter's senior but somehow less intimidating. Old and young alike, the women remembered him as a wild but charming larrikin with a smile that could melt ice.

With his throat parched from the whirlwind of red dust the horse's hooves had kicked up, Dexter Randolph longed to join the men in a glass or two, but Cirrus must be made comfortable first. He nodded acknowledgment of the raucous cries of congratulation and invitations to a drink, and started to rub down the mare's heaving sides. Wally, his aboriginal head stockman, materialised soundlessly beside them.

'Me lead her over inna minute, boss. They ready for you inna paddock.'

As Dexter started to force his way through the jovial crowd, a sturdy bow-legged individual raised a glass of rum and water in salute.

'Good on yer, Rando — I'd money on you, mate. Join me in a glass of grog?'

The man looked uncomfortable in a heavy pre-war suit he had outgrown. The high starched collar of his shirt chafed his ruddy perspiring neck, but from his genial rum-sodden expression it was clear he was feeling no pain.

'By and by, Mal. I think I'd better get this presentation over with first.'

Mal Gregson's deepset eyes twinkled rogueishly. 'Ah, man, what's a bloke like you want with a sheila's bracelet?'

'To give it to Lucinda. Any objections?'

Despite the crush about them, the two men stood still, concentrating. Traditionally, the winner of the Ballachulish Bracelet handed it to his wife, fiancée or sweetheart — and if he hadn't had one before, success in the race set the unattached women swarming over him like ants at a picnic.

126

By publicly giving the bracelet to his neighbour's daughter, Dexter would be indicating serious interest in her.

Mal Gregson was a Queenslander born and bred. He took his time considering. Young Randolph had a good head on him, and was steady as they came. He had proved his worth twice over in the war years, running Yelonga and making a mint out of army contacts. He had a half-share in the now prosperous station, and the drive and ambition not to leave it at that. Only one thing worried Gregson: like his grandfather Old Tom before him, Dexter Randolph had the makings of a hard man. If there was one thing Mal Gregson loved more than his bank balance it was his lovely, tender-hearted Lucy. Could he trust Dexter always to be good to her?

The young man's watchful expression softened. 'I know what she means to you and Phemie. Trust me, Mal. I don't care how hard I have to work, Lucinda will always live the way she has with you at Douglas Downs. I love her too much to turn her into a station drab.'

Gregson stuck out his hand. 'That's all I wanted to hear, mate.'

They shook on it, and Dexter grinned with relief. For the first time that day he looked his real age: eighteen. Just too young to have fought, but not too young to believe himself deeply and irrevocably in love.

'Gee, thanks, Mal. You won't regret this.'

'My oath I won't — or I'll bloody well tan your hide for you! But aren't you forgetting something?'

'What?'

'You haven't spoken to Lucy yet. Bracelet or not, if she doesn't want you, my permission's as much use as a tit on a bull!'

Bluey MacGregor, the station owners' red-haired son, interrupted them. 'Dad's refusing to serve any more grog till the presentation's made. You'd better come now, Rando, or there'll be a bloody riot!'

The racegoers had gathered in one corner of the

paddock; brightly dressed women chattered like cockatoos while their menfolk gloomily surveyed their empty glasses. Bluey's mother Flora, all gussied up in her best dress but with an apron still tied round her spreading waist, wasted no time in handing over the dainty bracelet in its Townsville jeweller's box. She gave Dexter an unabashed hug and a kiss.

'And which lucky lassie will ye be presenting this to? If I play my cards right, would I stand a chance myself?'

'Put him down, woman!' roared her cattleman husband Hugh. 'Yelonga needs some young blood in the herd. Come on now, Rando. Plenty of pretty little heifers here — which shall it be?'

While MacGregor roared with laughter at his own wit, the girls and young women in the crowd shifted self-consciously. More than one felt her heart skip a beat. Ruthlessly, Dexter's blue eyes scanned and dismissed them.

'Lucinda Gregson,' he said.

She left her mother's side and stepped hesitantly into the ring of spectators. Sun had burned a golden nimbus into her curling light brown hair and touched her bare legs and arms. She wore a leaf-green dress in some flimsy, floating material. Dexter's breath caught in his throat.

'Och, get on with it, man!' It was the shameless Flora who broke the paralysing silence. 'Put the bracelet on her, and give your sweetheart a kiss.'

'To hell with the bracelet — I'll have the kiss first!'

And for the first time in his life, Dexter kissed a girl. The good-natured crowd urged him on with roars of encouragement, and Dexter found he didn't want to stop. The rougher types started to clap and stamp their feet as he held the girl close. He was still in the sweat-soaked shirt and jodhpurs he had worn for the race, but Lucinda didn't seem to mind, moulding her pliant body to his and making no attempt to escape.

'He's got a nerve,' hissed Euphemia Gregson at her fondly smiling husband. 'Are you going to let him get away with this — making a common spectacle of our daughter in front of these roughnecks?'

'They're our neighbours,' he reminded her genially. 'Dexter's a neighbour too. At least Lucy won't be going far away.'

'You mean ... Mal Gregson, does this mean you've given him permission to marry her?'

Mal began to feel nervous. Phemie on the warpath was not a pretty sight. Not that his gaunt broomstick of a wife with her heavily lined face and slightly protruding grey eyes was an oil-painting at the best of times, but she'd brought him a large dowry, and over the years he'd grown adroit at soft-soaping her.

'Not exactly,' he began.

'You have!' she moaned. 'Oh, Malcolm, how could you? Marry an outback cattleman when my sister had promised her a Season in Melbourne! You've ruined our little girl's chances.'

'Now, hold your horses, woman. Nothing's decided and nothing's ruined. I just implied he could *ask* her. If he doesn't please her, she can always say no, can't she?'

Phemie pounced like a fox on a chook. 'Of course she can. And he hasn't asked yet, you say?'

'Hasn't had a chance, the way you watch her! Poor young bloke's waiting for the ball tonight, I s'pose.'

Phemie had never made any secret of her dislike for the younger Randolph boy though she'd kept her silence as to the reason. The fact was she'd once loved a man just like him, a man with farseeing sky-blue eyes and the wild allure of a hawk. But Euphemia Mitchell, heiress, sighed in vain. Young Tom Randolph, Dexter's father, had preferred a dowryless city chit, painfully out of her element on Yelonga, while Phemie, born to the land, had been forced to make do with the oafish Mal Gregson. When Young Tom crashed his Tiger Moth while bringing mail and supplies back to the station, he had broken Phemie's heart a second time. It was small consolation that his pallid wife had died with him, leaving their two young sons to be brought up by their grandfather on Yelonga. Dexter was the spit of his father as a young man, and a bitter reminder of Phemie's lifelong disappointment. She had no intention of letting him into her family.

She bustled over to Lucinda and took her roughly by the arm. 'Come along now. You must rest before the ball.'

'You'll be dancing with Dexter tonight, sweetheart,' her father told her, sensing Lucinda's disappointment.

Not if I can help it, Euphemia silently promised herself.

While Lucinda reluctantly trailed away to the tent she shared with her mother, Dexter had a few beers and watched the final race on the card, the Black Boys Handicap for aboriginal stockmen. Barely five minutes after Lucinda had gone, he was aching to see her again. If only they could manage some time alone, away from that old witch of a mother . . .

Something slapped painfully against his neck, and he spun round to find Bluey, grinning and snapping a towel in the air.

'Sweet dreams, eh, Rando? Boy, wouldn't I like to be in your shoes tonight! Going to pop the question?'

'Fair go, Blue!'

'Then you'll need to give it your best shot,' Bluey continued the good-natured chi-acking. 'Hot bath wouldn't go amiss, I bet? Coming up to Boiling Billy with me?'

An hour later, scrubbed and reeking of carbolic, Bluey and Dexter lazed in the gently steaming water at the very edge of a sandy-bottomed waterhole. It wasn't safe to go anywhere near the middle, as the hot springs that emerged there were as boiling as their name suggested.

The heat had gone out of the sun, which was dropping fast towards the horizon, the ebbing blue of the sky streaked with fuchsia and gold. With the dying of the day, the mosquitoes emerged.

His red hair and fair freckled skin made Bluey a natural target. 'Bloodthirsty bastards!' he exclaimed, slapping at

130

his neck and shoulders. 'Why'd they never bother you, Rando?'

'Hide's too tough,' Dexter said with a grin. 'Nah, seriously, it was another piece of the old man's bushcraft. When we were just kids he told us we must learn to love the mosquito. Love 'em — huh! He took us into swamp country on a three-day camp-out. The bastard things never touched him but they bit the blue blazes out of Luke and me — his face swelled up like a watermelon. Funny thing, though, after that we've been bitten all right but neither of us has ever felt a thing.'

'Just as well, where Luke was.'

They fell silent a moment, each painfully conscious of the fact that he had been just too young to share the hellish jungle fighting in New Guinea with Lucas and so many other local volunteers. The 9th Division of the Australian Imperial Force had finished the war serving under MacArthur, and sixty per cent of them had died of wounds received in close jungle combat or of mosquito-borne disease like the dreaded dengue fever. Lucas Randolph had indeed been lucky.

'Good old Luke,' Bluey said with a grin. 'Wherever he is, you can bet he'll have smoked out the whisky, women and a pack of cards!'

'In debrief? The bloody army would have something to say to that!'

Bluey stared at his friend, an odd expression on his honest freckled face. 'You can't have heard from him lately, then?'

'Ah, you know what Luke's like. Rather have a tooth pulled than pick up a pen.'

'Yelonga's got a radio.'

'Ah, yeah, but —'

'Rando, the last of the Ninth left debrief in May. Lody Anderson — you know, from Tall Trees — was one of them. He says Luke was long gone by then.'

Instantly Dexter went on the defensive. 'Listen, mate,

so what if Luke has gone off on a spree? Reckon he deserves it after the war he's had.' He remembered Lucas's face as he had arrived on Yelonga for his last leave — gaunt and haggard, his normally laughing brown eyes dark with reflected horror. 'Doesn't worry me how long he stays away,' Dexter continued. 'I've run Yelonga on my own for four years. I can hold out a while longer, no worries.'

But he was preoccupied on the four-mile walk back to the homestead. In the starlit darkness, he picked his way round aromatic trees and shrubs, and over the hummocky ground. Normally he loved the sounds of the bush at night — the grasshoppers' insistent chirr, the bubbling call of the cane toads or the panicked flight of a female kangaroo and her joey through the parched shoulder-high grass. Tonight Dexter barely noticed them.

It was September. In a month or two the first storms would be on them, followed by the Wet in January. He'd been counting on Luke's return by then, whatever he'd said to Bluey. He parted from his friend with a brusque 'See you later, mate' at the beginning of the racegoers' canvas encampment and made his way through the camp, the smell of roasting goanna leading him unerringly to Wally's fire. He was cooking the lizard whole on a spit.

'Smells good.'

Wally broke off a charred leg and held it out to him. 'Tastes good. Wantem, boss? Tea mebbe?'

Two billies full of water were just coming to a boil, propped up with sticks among the flames.

'No thanks, Wally. But I'll have one for shaving-water.'

The stockman nodded. 'Gotta make yourself look good for new missus.'

'I don't know if she's going to be that yet, Wally.'

The aborigine stared into the dancing flames. 'Yes, Miss Lucy gonna be new missus at Yelonga, boss.'

Dexter grinned broadly. 'Well, that's a relief!' Wally had an uncanny ability to get these things right. 'Can you remember where I put Grandpa's suit?' he called, while he was rooting around in his pack for his shaving things.

'Inna cart, boss. You wantem?'

'Sit down, your tucker's ready. I'll get it.'

Though Dexter was on easy terms with all the aboriginal stockmen on the station, and had been since his earliest days when he liked nothing better than to sneak round to the black boys' quarters for an illicit feed of snake or wichetty grubs or a chew of plug tobacco, there was a special bond between him and Wally.

Even more than Dexter's grandfather had been, the head stockman was a fount of bush knowledge. He could cure stock and human ailments with leaves from the bush trees and plants, find water in the most barren surroundings, or warn of a storm to come hours before the sky changed colour and the clouds began to mass. In his short life, Dexter had known two unusually able men. One was his grandfather, Old Tom; the other Wally. Without his help, Dexter would not have been able to turn Yelonga into the prosperous station it was today.

While Wally ate and drank the bitter black tea he had prepared for himself by throwing a handful of leaves and a eucalyptus shoot or two into the boiling billy, whirling it to settle the contents, Dexter crouched before the campfire with razor and mirror and shaved in the shifting light. Afterwards he unpacked his grandfather's evening dress from the naphthalene-scented tin trunk in which it had been stored against attack by white ants. The suit was not a perfect fit — a little too wide across the shoulders, a shade long in the leg — but when Dexter hoisted up his braces and puffed out his chest, he felt he'd look the equal of any man there.

'What do you think?'

Wally sucked on a bone, considering. 'You best-looking feller there, boss. Gins all gonna love you.'

'There's only one girl for me, Wally. You know that.'

The stockman busied himself with his tobacco and did not reply.   Ballachulish homestead was similar in appearance to Yelonga, the Gregsons' Douglas Downs, and countless others in the State: a succession of single-storey buildings, one room deep, raised from the ground on stilts. They were all built of white-painted timber slabs and roofed with stout corrugated iron. The family's accommodation had begun with a small three-room house, still in use as a bedroom wing. But as the station grew and the family prospered, two further wings had been added, linked by a wide shady veranda, so that now the house enclosed on three sides a lovingly tended patch of lawn fringed by flowers and exotic shrubs. Even in the Dry, water was allocated for keeping this precious patch a green oasis in the parched land.

The ballroom, or Flora's Folly as her husband called it, had been tacked on to the back of the big family room. In this room, the family dining-room, tonight an appetising cold table had been set out, and the verandas were dazzlingly lit by acetylene lamps. Their hiss and stink, and the insects they attracted in droves, assailed Dexter as he climbed the veranda steps and looked around for Lucinda.

His suit was far from being the only hand-me-down, yet whether their clothes fitted or not, everybody from the richest grazier or gentleman jackeroo to the poorest rouseabout had done their best to dress for the occasion. Some of the ringers were almost unrecognisable in spit-polished boots and neat water-slicked hair. Their pale foreheads, usually shaded from the sun by battered old hats, gleamed unnaturally bright. It was Flora's party, and she had decreed that tonight no gentleman would wear his hat indoors.

But if the men had made an effort, the women had gone to town. Sunburned tomboys blossomed in pastel-coloured gowns; sober station wives suddenly kicked up their heels in elaborate ruched and flounced creations ordered from a big store or run up on their trusty Singer. Treasured pieces of family jewellery received their yearly airing, and for those without, almond-scented frangipani blossoms or delicate lemon-coloured hibiscus filched from the garden served instead.

Lucinda looked radiant in a soft blue bias-cut gown. Her mother was wearing the same prune-coloured silk she had brought out for the last three Ballachulish balls.

'Evening, Phemie.' Dexter had sense enough to address her first. 'Gee, you look pretty in that dress, Lucy. Where'd you get it — Brissie?'

Phemie replied chillingly, 'My sister bought it for Lucinda in an exclusive shop in Melbourne. They employ a French seamstress.'

There was no mistaking the animosity in her tone, the implication that the Gregsons' girl was used to only the finest things in life. Dexter's palms began to prickle with sweat. There was so much he wanted to say to Lucinda, plans and promises to make, but how could they with her mother standing by, beady-eyed as a brolga?

With an encouraging nod to his young neighbour, a beery Mal Gregson appeared behind his wife and clapped his hands round her waist. 'Phemie, sweetheart, isn't it time you danced with me?' Her shrill protests were drowned by the enthusiastic playing of Russ Haughten and his band.

'Dear old Dad — he knew we wanted some time on our own,' Lucinda said, then lowered her eyes modestly.

But Dexter had noted the tell-tale 'we', and felt encouraged. 'Want to dance?' Before she'd even nodded, his arms were round her. God, she was good to hold, the skin of her bare arms water smooth and her bent honey-coloured head lightly touched with some sweet girlish scent.

'I suppose that came from France too,' he said ruefully.

A puzzled frown creased her wide brow. 'What do you mean?' She looked like a bewildered kitten, he thought, and his heart swelled with love.

'Your perfume. I expect your aunt bought it in the same exclusive Melbourne store.'

'Probably,' she agreed carelessly. 'Mum's the outside of

beyond sometimes! She knows I don't really give a damn about clothes and scent and face powder and things.'

'You don't? You mean, if you had to do without them — just for a little while ... A couple of years, maybe, while we —'

Lucinda raised her wide grey eyes to his. Damn! With her in his arms, it was so easy to jump the gun, start talking about how he saw their life together before he'd actually asked her to —

'Did you ever see yourself leaving here, Lucy?' he backtracked clumsily. 'A girl as lovely as you would have lots of chances. Maybe you want to leave Queensland for one of the cities?'

'Whyever should I?' she asked, puzzled. 'I love this country — the space, the smell of it, the way it can never fully be tamed. Don't you feel that way too?'

It was so exactly the way he felt that any lingering doubts he might still have harboured disappeared like dew.

The band came to the end of 'Love Walked In' and the other dancers politely applauded. Dexter didn't notice, still holding his girl close.

'Lucinda —' To his horror he felt a tap on his shoulder and a rough voice broke in, 'Shove over, mate. It's a gentleman's excuse me.'

Dexter didn't move a muscle. 'Try your luck somewhere else. Me and the lady have things to discuss.'

'Ah, come on, mate. She's the best-looking sheila in the room. Give a poor sex-starved digger a chance.'

Dexter swung round with his fists balled.

'Struth — is this the way to treat a home-coming hero?'

The voice changed, becoming almost familiar, as was the thin unshaven face beneath the army slouch hat.

'Lucas!' Dexter cried, and pulled his brother to him in a bear-hug.

'Good to see you, sport, it's been a long time. You look almost fully grown!'

'What d'you mean — almost! I'm full bloody grown

enough to be running the station. Where've you been these last six months, you bludger!' It had been difficult at first for the partygoers to recognise the travel-stained figure in tattered pants and shirt and forbidden hat, but now a legion of friends crowded eagerly round.

'Luke, you old bastard! How're yer goin'?'

'Here's to you, mate. Welcome back.'

'How many Japs d'you kill, Luke? What was it really like out there?'

Lucas raised his hands protestingly. 'Before I give you blokes the time of day there's one gorgeous woman I have to kiss. Get over here, Flora. Jesus, you're a sight for sore eyes!'

He swept their flushed and beaming hostess into his arms and kissed her full on the mouth. Here it comes, thought Dexter, who had witnessed Lucas's softening-up process before. 'Flora, my darling, would it be all right with you if I grabbed a shower then borrowed a room to change in?' He grimaced at his dusty, sweat-stained clothes. 'I don't want to let you down.'

'You've been fighting for your country, laddie. If you'd turned up in rags you'd not be letting us down,' Flora said with a catch in her voice. 'Bluey, you can move out for tonight. This laddie deserves a bed.'

'Ah, no, I couldn't deprive the boy.'

But Bluey had a bad case of hero worship. ''S'all right, Luke, honest. Where'd you leave your things?'

'In my car.'

Dexter, elbowed aside in the warmth of Luke's reception, managed to make himself heard above the din.

'Did you say — car?'

Lucas gave a smile of pure triumph. 'Want to see her, sport? D'you *all* want to see her?'

Dexter caught hold of Lucinda's hand as the mob stampeded after Luke, down the veranda steps and round the corner of the house to the mechanics' shop and horse tailer's yards. A strange car was parked alongside the rails.

Even caked with red dust the classic lines of a Ford V8 Tourer were unmistakable. The car had navy blue coach-work trimmed with chrome, and inside Dexter could see grey leather seats.

'Stone the crows!' one of the Ballachulish ringers approved.

Bluey was equally enthusiastic. 'She's beaut, Luke!'

Dexter looked dubiously at the car. 'Won't last six months on the roads around Yelonga. Hope you didn't pay much for her.'

Lucas threw back his head and roared with laughter. 'You wowser! But if it bothers you that much, I didn't pay a penny for her. I won her fair and square in a poker school on the train.'

As his cronies roared and stamped their approval, Dexter wondered which train that was. Where exactly had Luke been?

But his brother had turned his attention to Lucinda. 'It couldn't be ... No, it's a trick of the light. But surely — you are Lucinda Gregson, aren't you?'

She smiled shyly. 'That's right.'

'Jesus, you've changed. Such a skinny little thing you were, the last time I clapped eyes on you. D'you remember?'

'No, I —'

'I was due in training camp and I came to say goodbye to Mal before we left for the Tableland. I asked you for a kiss and you said, not until I was a captain!'

She blushed. 'What a brat you must have thought me!'

'Nah, I could see you had potential and I'm a patient man. Remember that promise now. I'm just off to get changed.'

Fifteen minutes later he reappeared, still sporting his rakishly-angled digger hat but otherwise immaculate in khaki. He approached Dexter and Lucinda who, ignoring Phemie's furious stares, had had the next two dances together. 'They bumped me up after the final show,' he

138

explained the stripes on his sleeve. ''Scuse us, sport. To the victor the spoils, eh?' He swung Lucinda away over the dance floor.

Dexter felt a hot flood of jealousy. Get a grip, man, he told himself. You know what he's like with women. Can't stop himself from flirting, and Lucy was first to cross his path. That's all there is to it. But the few minutes the couple spent outside felt like an eternity to him.

He forced down a rum he did not want, then danced with his outstation manager's daughter, who was so breathless at the honour she could not speak. When Lucinda reappeared, Dexter dropped the other girl like a hot coal. He stuck to Lucinda's side all evening but maddeningly Phemie insisted she should dance with all her other admirers, and twice more with Lucas.

Later, when her mother had shepherded Lucinda off to bed, Dexter helped Lucas out with Hugh's carefully hoarded McCallum's whisky; when that had gone, with the rum; and when that had gone, with foaming glasses of beer. Some time in the middle of the drinking Lucas wanted to play cards, but his skill was legendary in Northern Queensland and the others opted for the chancier two-up. Lucas good-naturedly gave in, and just as good-naturedly lost everything in his pockets on the fall of the coins. When his money had all gone, he tapped Dexter for a loan. Without a murmur he handed over everything he had, and stood by and watched Luke drop every penny of that too. His opponent, a slow-talking Ballachulish rouseabout, was embarrassed.

'I dunno, Luke, don't seem right somehow. Your first night back, 'n all.'

'Ah, forget it, man. Plenty more where that came from, eh, sport?'

Dexter nodded and smiled. On the night of Luke's homecoming, he begrudged his brother nothing.

★

Wally woke Dexter at six the next morning with a pannikin of tea.

'S'light, boss. We gonna leave soon?'

'By and by.' Dexter struggled to sit up. 'Jesus!' He felt as if he'd been kicked in the head by a wild Queensland steer, and lived — just. 'Give me a minute and I'll help you strike camp.'

'All finish. You wantem tucker?'

He groaned. 'Think I'll give it a miss, thanks.' The thought of the juicy steak and fried eggs with which he normally started the day was repellent.

Wally eyed him reproachfully. 'Gotta eat, boss. Thirty, forty miles today, mebbe.'

'All right, all right — just let me have a dip first, eh?'

It was already warm when Dexter left the tent, with not a breath of breeze to stir the eucalypts or ruffle the surface of the river, running seasonably low between sandy banks. Washed and dressed, Dexter forced down tea, some Ballachulish oranges and freshly made damper baked in the ashes of their fire overnight. He refused butter on it. The oily mass at the bottom of the tin gave him the heaves.

All around, people were striking camp. The journey home would be in several stages, each undertaken as early or earlier than this, before the heat and dust of the bush trails became unbearable to all but the most hardened stockmen.

After he had eaten, Dexter decided to call in on the Gregsons. It would be his last chance for weeks to see Lucy.

Phemie was bending Mal's ear when Dexter reached their tent. She was so exercised about some trouble with their old Vauxhall that she did not even notice Dexter creep round the side of their tent and tug at Lucinda's hand. She gave a low, delighted laugh and they crept away, tracker style, to sit together on the trunk of a fallen ghost gum by the water.

Lucinda was dressed for travelling today in a plain

cotton dress and sandshoes, her curling hair tied back with a white ribbon. She looked even more beautiful than she had the night before, and a great deal more approachable.

This time the words came out right. 'Lucy, you know what I was trying to say last night. We may have to wait until I've reorganised Yelonga, but will you marry me?'

'Oh, Dexter,' she sighed, and began nervously picking at the loose bark on the tree trunk. 'I'd like to, of course I would —'

He felt the blood drain from his heart. 'But, Lucy, don't you love me?'

She edged closer and rested her head on his shoulder. 'Don't look so down! I love you, or I think I do. But, like Mum says, I'm only seventeen. That's very young to be making up my mind about marriage.'

He pulled away from her. 'I'm eighteen, and I made up my mind two years ago.'

'Did you? When?'

'The day you sewed up my hand.'

She flinched at the memory of the deep crooked gash Dexter had received in his palm when a fencing post had splintered. Gently she took the hand and turned it over. The scar was still livid across his calloused palm.

'You were so brave,' she whispered, her eyes filling with tears.

'You cried that day, too,' he said in a warmer voice, and tilted her chin towards him. 'But not until the job was done. You were so pretty, and so soft and gentle. I knew then you were the only one for me.'

Her tears overflowed then. 'Dexter, I do love you! But Mum's been so awful, you've no idea. Every time she gets me on my own she goes on and on at me not to say yes to you till I've met some more people. She wants me to go to Melbourne!'

She loved him, she really did! It was just that old battle-axe of a mother of hers standing between them.

'Hey, c'mon,' he said, smiling at her tragic tear-stained

141

face. 'Melbourne's not that bad! And you're sure you do love me?'

'Oh, yes! Next to you all the other boys are just — well, boys. None of them matches up.'

'Then kiss me.'

This was no tentative boy and girl caress. Lucinda's sweet ardent lips parted under his, drinking him in. Gently Dexter stroked her ripening breasts. The nipples stiffened and budded under his hand. She made no move to pull away, but sighed and slid her hands under his shirt, to the smooth skin at the base of his back.

He felt a stirring in his groin he was powerless to control. Lucinda's eyes shifted downwards. He blushed with mortification, but she just smiled and moved her hand —

'Lucinda! Where has the girl got to? Do I have to do everything myself?'

Phemie crashed around in the undergrowth like a rogue elephant looking for her young.

Dexter groaned. 'You'd better go, my love. We don't want her seeing us like this.'

The delicate flush receded from her face. 'But what are we going to do? How will we ever be together?'

'We'll just have to sit it out,' he said as he smoothed the ruffled hair back from her face. 'Go to Melbourne if it makes her happy, meet as many men as she likes — just so long as you come home to me.'

'And you will come over and see me just as often as you can, won't you? You can always pretend it's Dad you're visiting. He's on our side.'

'I'll visit whenever I can, that's a promise. Maybe even in a week, on our way to Ten Mile.'

She kissed him again, hurriedly, her worried eyes alert for signs of her mother, and then she was gone. She left him aching but exultant, for now at last he knew: Lucinda loved him.

He waited till he had cooled off, then made his way back to his own tent. He decided not to wave the Gregsons off.

Let Phemie think she had scored over him if it kept her happy.

He found Flora MacGregor striding round the camp, saying goodbye to friends and neighbours she might not see for months or until the next Ballachulish meeting in a year's time.

'G'day! Luke still up at the house?'

Flora looked surprised. 'Why no, he's gone. Just this minute — must have missed you. Phemie was so anxious to reach McMahon's Hotel before noon. You know how fussy she is about travelling.'

'Phemie?' Dexter said stupidly. His head had begun to thump uncomfortably again and his back prickled with sweat. 'Why isn't she travelling with Mal and Lucinda?'

'Lucinda's with her, of course. Can you really see Phemie letting her ewe lamb go unchaperoned, though she'll need her wits about her, travelling with your brother! Serves her right for not waiting.'

Flora glanced behind him and waved. 'Here's Mal now. He'll tell you all about it.'

Apparently a valve had gone in the Vauxhall, and though it was a simple job for the Ballachulish mechanic to grind and fit another, Phemie did not wish to disrupt her timetable by waiting.

'She was madder'n a snake with me,' Mal said, 'so when your brother offered to give 'em both a lift ...' He shrugged. 'Better be off yourself soon, eh? It's getting late.'

'Yes. Well, be seeing you, Mal. Next week when we pass near, probably.'

'Look forward to it, and safe journey.'

But today, for the first time ever, Dexter found himself resenting the time it would take to travel cross country. While he sweated it out with the highly strung thoroughbreds on leading reins behind the camp cart, Luke, in his flashy Ford, would be travelling in style with Lucinda beside him.

★

For the first two days, Wally and Dexter rode MacGregor land. Larger and richer than Yelonga, Ballachulish Station covered almost twelve hundred square miles. For the first day they had an easy time of it, travelling a broad dusty road through rolling downs country liberally spotted with white, red and roan Shorthorn cattle. The Mitchell and red Flinders grass might be parched and overlong by this stage of the Dry, but the water-table beneath the rock was still high from previous seasons' flooding in the Wet. In sandy patches, beefwood and bloodwood flourished and cast a fragrant shade beneath their mass of flowers. Creeks lined with coolabahs provided water for the stock, and when the more succulent feed receded, there was a liberal supply of short prickly spinifex.

At night they would camp close to a creek or waterhole for a welcome sluice among the curious fish and eels. They lit a fire and used the old camp oven to cook a wild turkey Dexter had bagged with his grandfather's old Lee Enfield, or Wally cooked aboriginal tucker such as a whole carpet snake baked whole and coiled in the embers and tasting deliciously of fish. A special treat were the fat white witchetty grubs he gathered from tree bark after observing a flock of red-tailed black cockatoos prising it away with their powerful bills. After eating, they smoked, then slept rolled in their canvas swags close to the fire, which should be enough to ward off the unwelcome attention of a taipan or copperhead. By the third afternoon they were able to water their horses in the river country that marked the eastern boundary of Yelonga.

Among the thousands of acres of trees and scrub were numerous creeks. Some had run dry, but Wally's bushcraft led them unerringly to the small waterholes remaining in the dried up beds. Flocks of wild birds surrounded any source of water — vivid rainbow lorikeets, green red-wing parrots, pink and grey galahs, sulphur-crested white cockatoos, brilliant blue-brown and green bee-eaters. As always, Dexter's heart swelled with pride when he recognised the 'R' branded on the cattle, and the distinctive Randolph clip of their ears.

For the last stage, they climbed gradually upward through three thousand feet of thick ironbark and woolly butt forest, steep red-walled gorges falling away to either side of the trail. The Dry might prevail on the plains below but this inaccessible land was still a world of water with foaming waterfalls from the great table top out-thrusts of basalt and a five-mile creek that never dried.

The trail levelled and the forest thinned until it was possible to make out individual trees: ancient gnarled casuarinas with charred-looking bark, spiky gravillea, bauhinia, and dozens of different eucalypts and acacias. There was nothing but basalt plain between here and the homestead, rich, black-soiled land which teemed with wildlife.

Wally turned to Dexter and gave a gap-toothed smile. 'Home, boss.'

'Feels good,' Dexter agreed, and urged the horses on. He cast a critical eye over the house and yards as they drew nearer. The gate to the home paddock was leaning suspiciously on its hinges, he noted. The stock and pack horses kept there were a docile enough mob, but if panicked by a dingo or a wild brumby stallion come courting, there was a real danger they could kick it down. Dexter's expression grew stern. Samson, Wally's second-in-command, was due for a stiff dressing down. He must be out riding fences, Dexter guessed, because otherwise Rebel, the Queensland Blue-heeler work dog Dexter had lent him, would have caught his master's scent by now and raced five miles to meet them. Before the bougainvillaea-hung gate to the garden, he dismounted and let his horse's reins hang. Hungry and docile, it followed Wally in the cart round the side of the house.

The garden was green and welcoming. Since there was water still in the house dam, it was possible to soak the carefully tended lawn and flowering trees and shrubs —

jacaranda, pecan, bottle and mango — which cast a welcome shade over the peaceful scene.

The area enclosed on three sides by the different wings of the house had, in his grandmother's day, been covered over by a high vaulted roof of timber beams, shingles and white-painted corrugated iron. The ground below had been paved over with flagstones and set around with beds of cool green ferns. For much of the year, meals were taken there in the open air, and sweltering evenings passed in comparative comfort. But the area had never been designated for sleeping. Dexter was surprised and irritated to see the comatose figure of his Chinese cook stretched out comfortably, legs propped on the bare wooden struts of Old Tom's favourite squatter's chair. He was snoring heavily.

'Fu Yin!' Dexter shouted, and clapped his hands.

The cook stirred and twitched and pulled his hat further down over his eyes. A blowfly crawled across his face and settled in the corner of his mouth. Dexter shuddered, snatched the man's battered felt hat off his head and vigorously fanned the fly away. As he did, rum fumes rose to greet him.

'Fu Yin,' he repeated harshly. 'Wake up, man, and tell me where my brother is.'

The cook opened his eyes and stared guiltily up at Dexter. 'Mister Dexter, back alleady?' He heaved himself to his feet. 'I solly, Mister Dexter. So solly. Put water on for tea, chop chop.'

He tried to scuttle past, towards the kitchen tacked on to the back of the house, but Dexter shot out an arm to detain him. 'What the devil's going on here? What do you mean by being drunk on duty?'

'Velly solly, Mister Dexter, but Mister Luke say —'

'Where is he, anyway?'

'Gone away. Brought Missy and Missus in for tea two days gone, then he dlive them back to Douglas Downs.'

'And he's been gone two days? He might have had an accident!'

'No wolly, Mister Dexter. No accident. Thing with bells speak to me yesterday. Mister Lucas stay at Douglas Downs two-three days. I ask what time he get back and he tell me I work too hard, and I must take a dlink.'

Dexter noticed the empty bottle lying on its side under the chair. Fu Yin had had considerably more than the shot Lucas must have meant him to have. He told himself it wasn't really his brother's fault. He'd just spent six years in the company of hard-drinking fighting men. He probably didn't even remember that Fu Yin had a problem with drink — once he started, he couldn't stop. To save him and the aboriginal stockmen from frequent bouts of drunkenness, the station grog was kept under lock and key.

'How did you get this?' Dexter asked.

'Mister Lucas tell me where to find key.'

Foreboding prickled down Dexter's spine. 'Did Samson and the others see you?'

'Oh, no, Mister Dexter. Not good for those men to dlink.'

Dexter almost smiled at the hypocrisy. 'You're not wrong. And it's no good for you either.' He shuddered to think what the consequences could have been if the stockmen had all hit the grog too. He must have a word with Luke about keeping a tighter rein on things.

'Now, Fu Yin, I'd like some tucker, chop chop. And while that's cooking, some tea and johnny-cake or scones wouldn't go amiss. In the office, please. I've a call to place to Douglas Downs.'

The building was a small square detached building, over the cleared grass to the rear of the house. It had two windows, one overlooking the billabong and the other the house stockyards, beautifully morticed post and rail-fenced pens with not so much as a single nail in evidence. They had been constructed in Dexter's great-grandfather's day and with regular maintenance were still just as solid.

The office was a great deal less well ordered. The pine slab walls were kept freshly whitewashed inside and out,

147

but the battered desk was awash with a dusty sea of stock sheets, branding counts, cheque stubs, catalogues from Dalgety's and William Cooper and Nephews, wages records and the horse-book that contained the pedigree and whereabouts of the station's hundreds of stock and thoroughbred horses.

Dexter sighed and lit a Craven A. He lifted the dusty phone receiver and placed his call to Douglas Downs. But as it was a party line, and the gabby overseer's wife on arrawonga was placing the station order with the general store. Dexter had a long wait. He'd finished his tea and sorted the desk into some semblance of order by the time the operator connected him with the Gregsons' station.

'Dexter? We guessed it would be you,' his brother's familiar voice greeted him. 'How're you going?'

'Everything's all right this end, Luke, bar a station cook with a king-size hangover. What'd you give him the keys to the store for? You know he can't hold his rum.'

'You can't nursemaid the staff and run a business.'

'Well, speaking of running a business, maybe you could let me know when to expect you back? There's things we need to settle.'

'Look, sport, I know we've got a helluva lot of ground to go over but it's a bit awkward at present. See, Mal and Phemie have asked me to stay on a few days. There's a tennis tournament coming up for the neighbourhood jackeroos who missed the Ballachulish Meeting. They want me to make up the numbers.'

'Jesus, Luke, can't you get out of it? Samson never pulls his weight without Wally and me keeping after him, and there's a mountain of things to catch up on here.'

Too late, he realised his mistake.

'You've just had a holiday at Ballachulish,' his brother said in his most reasonable tone. 'All I've had for the past six years are forty-eight-hour passes and embarkation leave.'

What about the six months since debrief? Dexter wanted to ask, but it was an open line. Any one of half a dozen stations could be listening in; it was accepted that the switchboard operator always did.

'Okay, Luke, you win. I've got to stick around here for a few days anyway, see to things. Next Thursday, though, we'll be mustering on the way to Ten Mile. We could use another man.'

'I'm on for that, sport! See you Wednesday night at the latest.'

'Give 'em hell, eh?'

'What?'

'In the tournament.'

'Oh, yeah. Sure. See you, sport.'

'Luke ...' Dexter had been about to add, 'Give Lucinda my love,' but his brother had already severed the connection.

Lucas made it home late on Wednesday night. He'd put on weight already and the sickly city pallor of his arrival on Ballachulish had disappeared beneath a healthy tan. With his long square face, curling chestnut-tinged hair and full, smiling mouth he took after their mother's side of the family, whereas Dexter was a raven-haired Celt, a Randolph through and through.

'Good to see you, Luke. Drink?'

Dexter was sitting in front of the house, under the roofed breezeway. A bottle and clean glasses were ready on the table in front of him, together with the station bank-book, some paper and pens.

'Looks like an ambush,' Luke said with his customary easy smile.

'I think we should talk. I couldn't do much more than keep things ticking over while there was a war on.'

Luke looked at him sharply. 'Mal said we'd had a record few years.'

Dexter smiled and opened the bank-book. He slid it across the table towards his brother, who read the total and whistled appreciatively. He poured them both a drink to celebrate.

'Good on yer, kid. Looks like we're in clover.'

Dexter ignored the drink and leant forward eagerly, his lean hawk-like face alive with enthusiasm. 'That's only the tip of the iceberg, Luke. I've been asking around in Townsville and Cairns — Brisbane when I got there last year — and there's changes coming, Luke. Big changes. I want Yelonga to be at the forefront.'

'Whoa there!' his brother said with a tolerant smile. 'These sound like the sort of changes that involve spending money.'

'And we've got it. Remember Grandpa's plans for expansion? Now, for the first time in our lives, we've got the money to start thinking big. For openers, I've got my eye on Maroonda.'

'Old McNaghten's place? You've got to be kidding! It's a bloody desert — he's never done more than scrape by there. I'm surprised he didn't let the land revert years ago.'

'He plans to,' Dexter said, and his brother raised his eyebrows. McNaghten and Old Tom had fallen out fifteen years back over a disputed boundary and the families had not been on speaking terms since.

'Told you I'd been to Brisbane. I met some very informative people, including a secretary at the Land Office. McNaghten's surrendering his lease next year. I've got our names down for it.'

A thoughtful expression crossed Lucas's face. 'Take a lot on yourself, don't you? Suppose I don't agree with the plan?'

'Why wouldn't you? Listen, it's another fifteen hundred square miles.'

'And no bloody water ! Christ, Dexter, it's like the Sahara.'

'There's plenty of water — underground.'

'Which means new artesian bores, lots of 'em. We'll charged like wounded bulls for the drilling, then there's

150

maintenance and repairs — blokes paid to sit around on their arse all day seeing the engine's running. Ah, it gives me the shits, that sort of thing.'

'It's where the future lies,' Dexter told him patiently. 'This is a vast country, but face it: the good land — the land that's easy to work like Yelonga — has all been claimed. But there's more out there, so much more, if only we put our backs into it and make something of it. Think of it, Luke. With McNaghten's spread and our own we'd be the biggest station for a thousand miles.'

Lucas's face set obstinately. 'But what's so damn good about being big if you can't scratch a living from half the bloody place? The old man lost his shirt on those Territories partnerships he had in the thirties.'

'That was partly the Depression, partly the fact that the partnerships didn't vet their managers thoroughly enough. We'd be ahead of them there. We could manage the two stations between us, half a year each on Yelonga, the rest Maroonda.'

'Thanks a million,' Lucas said with a bitter laugh. 'Just what I sweated through the jungle for — the chance to fry my brains out in some Godforsaken desert! You know me. I like a drink, a game of cards, a little female companionship. How'm I going to get those on bloody Maroonda?'

'Marry a poker-playing barmaid and take her with you! Seriously, Luke, don't you think it's time you settled down? I'm planning to.'

'You? You're still wet behind the ears. Besides, what decent-looking sheila would marry a skinny young bastard like you?'

Dexter ignored the ritual insults. 'Lucinda Gregson will — at least, we've an understanding she will once we've brought Phemie round. Mal's already on our side, but you know what *his* opinion counts for.'

Lucas narrowed his eyes. 'You've surprised me, sport. Congratulations. Lucinda Gregson, eh? But, man, she's had the best of everything on Douglas Downs. You can't expect a girl like that to live for months at a go on an isolated hellhole like Maroonda.'

'But it won't be isolated, or not for much longer.' Dexter played his trump card. 'The beef road, the new all-weather route, is planned to pass along Maroonda's boundary. Think what a difference that would make. Visitors and deliveries to the house, and as for the stock ... when they're ready for the meatworks we'd only need to drive them to the edge of our own property. Think what we'll save on drovers' contracts.'

'I still don't get it. What are they going to do when they hit the road?'

'Sorry, I keep forgetting how long you've been away. Forget the old cattle-trucks, Luke. They were fine in their day, but we're talking about a bitumen surface here, remember. They've been experimenting with trailers — huge, two-storey things — and linking a string of them together behind a powerful diesel cab. Road trains, they're called. And where the bitumen is, you'll find road trains.

'Now, think how much weight our stock loses at present, covering so much of the journey to the meatworks on the hoof. Think how many head we lose on the way, and the tonnes of beef that are worked off — all money out of our pocket. At present we only truck them fifty miles or so. I'm talking about making the whole journey in a road train. Only a couple of days' travelling, as opposed to weeks. We'll be quids in.'

Lucas poured himself another drink and studied his brother. 'Sounds like you've already put a lot of thought into this. Any other bright ideas strike you while I was in the jungle?'

Dexter winced at that but let it pass. He hadn't expected this to be easy. He told Lucas about the American jeeps with their amazing four-wheel drive.

'I was with MacArthur's army. I know what a jeep looks like.'

'But think about using them here. Imagine the distance

we could cover in a single day — twice as far as you could on a horse. You've got army contacts. Do you think you could get us a couple, and parts?'

'Maybe. Carry on.'

Dexter told him about the bulldozers he'd seen at the GIs' Tableland camps — 'Think of the difference they'd make for building dams' — and the findings of the previous year's Royal Commission into Cattle Farming. 'Then watering facilities should be more closely spaced so that cattle spread out more. And we shouldn't just rely on indigenous grasses; there are plenty of better-yielding ones we could sow. The Commission wants improved transport, which we'll have, and they reckon new breeding patterns could remove a lot of the trouble we have with ticks and buffalo flies.'

'Look, this is all very interesting and I can see you mean well, but think about it. Is any of it really necessary? Christ knows I don't mean to skite, but that's the best bloody set of accounts Yelonga's ever seen. The old man must be dancing in his grave. Why can't you just be happy with what we've got?'

Dexter felt the cold clutch of disappointment. It had never occurred to him that, once the benefits had been explained, Lucas might not share in his enthusiasm. Grandpa had always said that two things ran through a cattleman's veins — blood and the lust for land. He would have seen the sense in everything Dexter had just said but Lucas obviously did not have his vision. Dexter realised that if he was going to get anywhere at all, he'd better not push his brother too far, too fast. He got to his feet and made a show of yawning and stretching. 'I know it's a lot to hit you with all at once.'

'Too right!'

'And there's no immediate hurry to decide. We're off to Ten Mile in the morning. It's a short muster, but we'll be gone a few weeks. Plenty of time for us to talk things through, eh?'

Lucas nodded doubtfully. Then another thought seemed to strike him. 'Hey, since we're quids in and talking about investing — how about smartening this place up a bit? Christ knows it needs it.'

Dexter felt obscurely hurt, as if any slight on Yelonga was a slight on him personally. There wasn't much about the place that bothered him. The zinc bath, maybe, or the string-operated bucket that was their shower. On his rare visits to the big towns of Cairns and Townsville he'd been struck by the difference in the plumbing there. No back-yard long drop for the townees! 'No harm in thinking about some changes,' he said, to keep his brother happy. There was no point in slamming the door in Luke's face. Once he was back on the land, the feel of it flowing through his veins again, Dexter was confident that his brother would come round to his way of thinking. 'Better turn in,' he reminded Lucas now. 'We leave at half-four, remember?'

'Yeah, no worries. I'll just have another glass or two.'

Dexter padded along the veranda to the bedroom wing. As he turned the corner he caught a glimpse of his brother, sitting with a glass of rum in one hand, smoking an Ardath. His dark unblinking eyes were as expressionless as a lizard's.

The shrilling of his alarm woke Dexter five hours later. It was still full dark outside, and the cane toads and tame carpet snake that invaded the veranda by night glided out of his way as he emerged from his bedroom. Lamp in hand, he made his way to the bathroom. The clattering of pans from the kitchen round the back indicated that Fu Yin was getting ready to serve breakfast in the men's dining-room. He filled the bucket and had a brief dam-water shower. It was freezing, since the chip heater had packed up again. Maybe Lucas had a point about the house ... On his way back from the bathroom, seeing no glimmer of light

154

beneath his brother's door, he knocked and entered.

'Luke — time to show a leg.'

Inside the room, the air was close and stale, redolent of rum and cigarette smoke. Lucas had kept not only the fly-screens closed but the windows too. Wrinkling his nose, Dexter fumbled with the screwtop jar on the night table, removed the matches and lit Luke's lamp for him.

His brother seemed to be awake but lay, unmoving, swathed like a mummy in his heavy army-issue blanket. Dexter bent over him and took a closer look. Luke was bathed in sweat and his teeth were chattering.

'What's up?'

''s n-nothing. Feeling a bit crook, that's all.'

'Is it malaria? I thought you had a rhinoceros hide like me.'

'J-Just a t-touch. B-Box over there.'

Dexter opened the army medical kit he saw on a battered chest of drawers. Lucas sat up, and with trembling fingers extracted a couple of pills from a brown medicine-bottle.

'Shall I bring some water?'

'Nah. Us old s-soldiers crunch these for b-breakfast.'

'Does it last long?'

'F-Few days. Week at the most.'

Dexter's heart sank. He'd been considering postponing their mustering trip, but he couldn't afford to wait that long. It looked like yet more weeks without Lucas's help, and no chance of a diversion to Douglas Downs along the way.

'Listen, I've got to get up to Ten Mile. I'll tell Fu Yin to look in later. Let him know if there's anything special you need. Take it easy and we'll talk again when I get back, okay?'

''kay. Tired ... Sleep now.'

Dexter shut the door quietly and made his way to the men's dining-room. He gulped down porridge, orange juice, and steak and eggs with them. Afterwards he

155

checked the pack horses which Samson and Mick had laden. The country they were to cross was too rough to take the cart. He looked at his watch. Time to saddle up whichever horse he'd be riding today. On a mustering trip each man took several mounts and the surplus were brought along by the horse-tailer.

'Mister Luke's sick,' he told Fu Yin on his way to the saddle shed. 'You leave him sleep four-five hours, then take him hot water for wash, lemon water for drink. Okay?'

'Okay, Mister Dexter. You no wolly. Me number one sick nurse.'

'I'll be back in three weeks or so, if anyone asks.'

Dexter mounted his horse Queensland-style, left hand holding the reins and some of the horse's mane, facing the horse's tail, never its head. The musterers formed up and clattered over the baked earth of the yard, heading for the long dusty trail to Ten Mile.

Four hours later, when Fu Yin knocked at Lucas's door and entered, it was to find him up and about, half dressed and shaving in front of the washstand mirror. The cook stared in astonishment.

'Mister Dexter say you velly sick.'

'Just a touch of the old jungle heebie-jeebies, but I seem to have thrown it off. Must be my iron constitution.' Lucas smiled pleasantly. 'Steak and eggs for breakfast, I think.'

'You want me tell Jimmy saddle up for you? Not too late to catch up Mister Dexter, maybe.'

Lucas's smile faded. 'If I want something, I ask for it. Breakfast, Fu Yin, chop chop.'

He finished dressing. Afterwards he combed back his unruly hair and tested the smoothness of his chin. Not bad, not bad at all ... Pity he'd had to pull the old ipecacuanha trick on Dexter, the soldier's standby when he was late for parade and facing a charge, but the poor sap was too trusting. No mosquito had ever laid Lucas Randolph low.

It looked to him, he reflected as he ordered Fu Yin to serve his breakfast in the family dining-room, not the men's, that Dexter had had his own way on Yelonga for too long. It was time to show him who was the real boss around here.

After he had eaten a hearty breakfast, he picked up his kitbag. 'Be away a while, Fu Yin,' he told the surprised cook. 'You can have another bottle of rum, but don't let my brother catch you with it.'

Fu Yin bowed obsequiously. 'Thank you, Mister Lucas.'

Luke slung his bag into the back seat of the Ford and tooted the horn impatiently for one of the picaninnies from the settlement to open the house gate for him. He chucked the grinning boy a penny and gunned the engine as the youngster bent to pick it up. The kid was engulfed in a cloud of choking red dust. Lucas laughed aloud. Fu Yin, watching curiously from the veranda, noted that his master had turned right, in the direction of Douglas Downs.

The paddock Dexter and the mustering party were heading for provided the station's lushest grazing. Ten miles long, hence the name, and eight wide, it was bisected by the lazily flowing Caroline River and was consequently rich and well-watered, even towards the end of the Dry. When pasture in the other paddocks had long since dried out, there would be new growth along the river banks so long as the mickery system worked. These were lines of logs sunk into the river four feet from the bank, the sand being excavated from the trench in between so that it could fill with water. Dexter and his men were to muster a mob of cattle from the timberland and drive them to Ten Mile. The first day's drive was hard but uneventful, a forty-mile stretch of red volcanic soil plain. The dust choked riders and horses, and to its cloying gritty torment was added the stinging bite of the flies which hung in busy black clouds above the sweating men and their mounts. The second day was far worse. The terrain had shifted and they were once more in black soil basalt country liberally scattered with scrub and timber and flat-topped out-thrusts of rock. Dexter ordered the stockmen to spread out, each a 'cooee's' distance from the next, to drive the cattle from the shelter of the trees. They moved automatically into oblong formation, Samson in the lead, two stockmen riding wing, two on point behind them. Wally brought up the rear, while Dexter, with Rebel at his heels, constantly ranged about overseeing the men and on the alert for stragglers in the timber.

The bush was much quieter than usual, with few birds but crows and magpies. From previous visits Dexter remembered pastel clouds of galahs and pale-bodied lorikeets. They must have flown away in search of water, while the presence of so many carrion birds was not a good omen. Sure enough, he began to find the pathetic dried-out carcasses, worried by dingoes and gouged by scavengers' cruel bills. He counted ten in the gidgee scrub he was scouring before wheeling about with a command to Rebel and checking the other side of the formation.

The ground was dustier than he had ever seen it, all but the poorest nutriment shrivelled and dead. His heart sank as he noted the condition of the emerging Shorthorns being driven by the men and dogs. The cattle's heads hung list-lessly towards the parched grey earth, as if too heavy for the skinny bodies beneath. He could see the ribs of starved heifers, and even the four-year-old bullocks, and the steers — two-year-old castrated males — usually the spirited part of any mob, could respond to Rebel's prompting with only a listless, slack-legged shamble.

At a command from Dexter the big dog isolated a mature roan cow and nipped at her heels, forcing her through the mob until she was at its head. There she set an easy walking pace and the rest of the mob settled docilely behind. They were so weak and dispirited that Rebel and the rest of the dogs had no need to nip and harass them into order. The stragglers that man and dog flushed from the timber settled into a slow cattle pad.

Gripping his horse with muscular legs, Dexter put both hands to his mouth and called to right and left, 'Cooee! Smoko!'

'How many dead?' he asked the musterers when they had brought the mob to a dusty milling halt. Figures were compared until a likely total was reached. At sixty it was high for such a small mob, and would not be the final figure as the scrub was dense enough to hide many more carcasses.

While the men drank their tea, he conferred with Wally.

'At least we've only six miles to the waterhole. Wonder why more of them haven't struck out for themselves.'

'Maybe no reason to, boss. We better drivem slow. Them fellers plenty weak.'

Wally was right. The mob proved slow and intractable. The dogs circled and yelped and nipped, but the pace never picked up beyond a splay-footed walk. The men missed their midday break and afternoon smoko so as to reach the waterhole before darkness, but when they finally left the cover of the trees, they were greeted with a terrible sight. Where Dexter had expected to see water, there was only a dried-out expanse of blistered grey earth. An unpleasant smell hung in the air, and despite the gathering darkness there was the persistent buzzing of flies. He peered through the gloom towards the centre of the dried-up hole. He could just make out the low bloated silhouettes, black against the grey earth in the descending darkness.

'Plenty dead-feller cattle bring dingo and wild pig,' Wally reminded him. 'Dogs gonna be on guard tonight.'

The party pitched camp upwind of the decaying cattle but no one passed an easy night. The dogs set up a warning clamour at each crashing in the bush, whether it was a marauding wild pig or a possum innocently in search of fruit.

Dexter decided not to attempt to draft this mob in the waterhole yards but to use the facilities in Ten Mile.

Nevertheless he was forced to delay their start until first light next day as he needed to assess the number of dead. Wally accompanied him in the gruesome task, which sickened them both.

The black alluvial soil held water longer than any other kind, and so as the waterhole shrank inwards the surrounding earth had retained some moisture and become treacherously boggy. Weakened cattle arriving in search of water had scented it still at the centre and started over the exposed ground, only to find themselves trapped in the shifting waterlogged soil. Held fast, they were sitting targets for dingoes and vicious wild pigs.

Dexter counted another four dozen carcasses, the older ones practically tanned by the action of the sun, the newer still noisome with gaping eye-sockets and pitifully mauled flanks.

When the drive resumed, it was at an even slower pace than the day before. At the rate of five or six miles a day, which was all the stock could manage, it was another four days before they saw the wire and rail fence which marked the boundary of Ten Mile. Without being prompted, the cattle dogs split the mobs into smaller groups and put them gradually through the gate into the paddock. The cattle immediately struck out for the south-east corner, the river's nearest point. The grazing was better in Ten Mile, frail green shoots pricking through beneath the old dried grass. But the cattle had scented water, and pasture was of secondary importance. The old coacher at the front put up her head for the first time in days and broke into a shambling trot. They covered the three miles to the river bank faster than Dexter would have believed possible, and lost only three more head on the way. At a nod from Dexter, Wally drew out the Colt Woodsman which, unusually for an aborigine, he used to put a merciful end to the fallen, who were uselessly scraping the ground with legs too weak to carry them further. Some cattlemen wouldn't have wasted the bullets on stock already written off, but from a child Dexter had shared Wally's belief that animals should not be left to suffer unnecessarily where it could be avoided.

He ordered two of the men to stay with the new mob for a couple of days, keeping an eye out for dingoes which would have scented their weakness, and routinely dredging the mickery at this end of the paddock. The rest of the stockmen ranged over Ten Mile, mustering the stock already in occupation. This was the mob he hoped to sell this year. The contrast between them, lean but sturdy, and the timberland mob was painful. But to have placed all the cattle in the same paddock, even one as good as Ten Mile, would have been to invite worse losses than they had already suffered. As it was, if both mobs were to survive, rain from an early storm was badly needed here to bring up new grass. He looked up into the soaring blue vault of sky. Blazing sun and not a trace of cloud.

Wally noticed him. 'Mebbe tonight she come, boss. Two nights now I hear the Rainbird sing.'

'You reckon?'

That night, he surprised the men by ordering their camp to be pitched in the shelter of a rocky overhang, well away from the course of any dried-up channel or stream-bed. The cattle, too, were driven with whips and dogs away from the river banks and on to higher land. There'd been not so much as a wisp of cloud all day.

After four hours, Dexter was woken by a tremendous crack of thunder overhead, closely followed by a green flash of forked lightning which pitilessly lit their scattered camp. The fire had gone out, embers sizzling in the sudden downpour then sinking into black liquid mud as the parched earth dissolved under the torrential rain. All around men were cursing and scrabbling in their packs for the Smith's oilskins they all carried for wet weather.

In between lightning flashes it was pitch dark, therefore impossible to do anything about the terrified cattle. From time to time as they huddled together under the overhang, the men heard the rattle of hooves against rock on the steep trail down from the outcrop. The scrubbers — wild, unbranded cattle which had never been mustered — were leaving the exposed heights above for the safety of the basalt plain.

But that safety was only illusory. Another jagged fork split the darkness ahead, eerily illuminating the paddock. It seemed to hang in the air, flickered, shifted infinitesimally, then one green branch of light touched the venerable head of a giant Moreton Bay ash. There was a tremendous crack as the trunk was riven in two, then the crash of falling timber. The weird green light was replaced by the blue and orange flicker of dancing flames. Though the fire did not last long in the rain, by its light Dexter was able to scan the paddock.

He patted the big spotted dog which crouched at his feet, wet and shivering. Rebel feared neither man nor beast, but lightning terrified him. 'Looks like we'll have our work cut out for us in the morning, old feller.' He pulled the brim of his hat well down, adjusted his oilskins to keep out as much rain as he could, and settled down on the damp earth and rock to spend the rest of the night in dreams of Lucinda.

At first light, the stockmen rode the riverbank, pulling free those cattle which had been panicked by the lightning into attempting to swim to the other side. The storm had cost Dexter a further six head, but already the ground was sprouting a tender new growth of grass.

Delicate plains flowers and ground and tree orchids had appeared. The rain had dwindled to a light drizzle that was soon to cease entirely, but the land felt renewed, rinsed clean of the dust and despair of the dry months. The store cattle would fatten nicely for a few days on the fruits of the storm, and for the new mob it meant the difference between life and death.

'Any more storms on the way?' Dexter asked Wally hopefully.

'She's gone, boss. 'nother coupla storms November, mebbe. But these-feller cattle last till-a Wet okay now.'

'Yeah, they should. We've been lucky for another year. Wonder how long it'll last.'

Wally lowered his eyes to the ground. It didn't do to call down trouble.

'Hey, boss, boss! Come quick. Samson found big feller scrubber.'

An enraged bellowing from the cornered beast and the crack of a greenhide stockwhip indicated the stockman's whereabouts. The big, over-confident aborigine had located an unbranded bull skulking in some dense acacia scrub. Instead of calling for another man, he'd decided to flush out the beast with only Rebel to assist him. Wild as a hawk at the best of times, this bull was rendered doubly dangerous by the pain from a jagged tear in its shoulder. It must have slipped and gashed itself in the flight down from the basalt.

'No!' Dexter cried, and spurred his horse, but Samson set Rebel on again.

With the speed of his dingo ancestor, the dog lunged to nip at one foreleg, aiming to startle the bull from its cover. In his day there'd been none quicker than Rebel, but he was old now, a gift to Dexter from Old Tom on his tenth birthday.

The bull lashed out with one powerful leg and caught the cattle dog a dreadful crunching blow to his barrel chest. The impetus carried Rebel several feet through the air. He landed in a slack heap, whimpered once, and fell silent.

Samson, who had been relying on the dog, rolled his eyes in alarm and wheeled his horse away from the snorting beast that was pawing the ground, preparing to charge.

'Don't do it!' Dexter yelled. He wanted to go to his dog, but a wounded bull on the rampage in an already crowded paddock was the last thing he needed. The surest way to make that animal charge was to run before it. Samson had

163

to be brought to his senses.

'Jesus, boss!' Wally cried in alarm as Dexter's mount, young and inexperienced, panicked at the rank bull smell and stopped dead in its tracks, throwing him over its head. The enraged bull swivelled its sights from the fleeing stockman and fixed on the fallen man as easier to trample. It put down its deadly horns and charged.

Luckily, Wally's horse was older and more experienced than Dexter's. As the stockman kicked it on, it cut across the charging bull's path, inches from the gleaming lowered horns, and forced it to veer away from the fallen man. Wally wound the plaited strands of his stockwhip round his hand and used the lead-weighted handle as a weapon. He wheeled his horse round to run alongside the galloping bull and whacked it as hard as he could on the horns. Evil red eyes squinted up at him and the animal bucked and reared, slashing the air with razor-sharp hooves. Undaunted, Wally thrashed it again, pitting all his strength against the bull's. It had to be kept away from Dexter.

With the blood-curdling battle yell passed down by his ancestors, he spurred on his horse, wheeled and charged the bull, full on. At the last moment he directed his mount away from the vicious horns and leant sideways from his saddle at an impossible angle. With all his strength he lassoed a strong rope around the bull's neck, half throttling it until its eyes bulged. Dexter pulled back with all his strength as the bull shook its head and slowed down to a trot, bellowing with pain and defeat.

Samson, who had halted in his flight, reached Dexter ahead of Wally and the other stockmen. 'You want me killem, boss?' he asked, waving the camp's ancient rifle with relish.

Dexter looked at him with disgust. 'Just strap him.' He looked the shamefaced stockman in the eye. 'Do you know why I don't want him killed? Because this animal's got guts. He was injured and in pain and just doing what came naturally. You ought to know by now that if you turn and run like a dingo, a scrubber'll come after you. It's not just you that's in danger but your mates too. You know what we all think about that.'

The big man said nothing, but looked down at his dusty boots.

'Apology accepted,' Dexter said grimly. 'And when you've strapped him, see if you can catch my horse. I've got a dog to bury.'

He knew by Rebel's unmoving form that it was all up with him. Ignoring the pain in his ribs, he fetched a spade from the packs and began to dig a hole before the white trunk of a paperbark.

Wally watched while Samson and some of the other men immobilised the bull, then he sent them about their business in the drafting yards. He had something to settle with his second-in-command. Ignoring him, Samson shambled off to mount his horse, that was patiently grazing where he had left it. Wally followed him. When they were out of sight of the rest of the men, he tapped Samson on the shoulder. When he turned round, Wally swung a roundhouse to his jaw that sent the stockman crashing to the ground like a felled tree. Wally spoke a few words in their own tongue, then spat full in his face. He stood over Samson for a few minutes, but the big man stayed down. He preferred more underhand methods of evening the score.

Confident there'd be no more trouble from him, for today at least, Wally went in search of Dexter's hat which had spun away in the fall from his horse. The bull had trampled it. The felt was shredded and ground into the dust, totally unwearable. Wally padded over to the stores packs and pulled out a battered old high-crowned drover's hat. It was not the boss's usual style, but in this sun he couldn't afford to be without protection for long. Wally selected a blanket, too, the cleanest he could find, and used it to cover Rebel's broken body.

Silently he joined Dexter by the grave. He kept his eyes

averted from his boss's face while they lined the pit with sweet-smelling leaves and grass. When they had laid Rebel to rest and packed soil and stout logs on top to protect the body, Dexter stood over the grave, holding the replacement hat.

Finally he gave a crooked smile. 'I dunno, Wal — my hat, my dog. It'll be my woman next!'

Without a mob to drive, the return journey was much easier. The flies haunted them still but the rain had settled the dust. The dead yellow grass was pricked with green and jewelled with patches of tiny ground-hugging bush flowers. Orchids flourished on the sodden bark halfway up tree trunks, and a close carpet of blue water-lilies half-covered the crystal waters of a lagoon where the men stopped for smoko and a swim.

As they breasted a rise in the basalt plain, just before making camp that night, the loveliest sight of all met their eyes. The ground before them was a sea of trumpet-shaped mauve flowers, shivering and dancing on frail green stems above the dead yellow grass. They were rainflowers, one of the bush miracles. By the morning, unless it rained again, they would be gone.

The lavishing of such fragile beauty on these stark surroundings brought memories of Lucinda crowding in. Whatever the rigours of the day, she was never far from Dexter's thoughts. He considered sending the men back to Yelonga, with Wally and himself detouring via Douglas Downs, but it wouldn't be fair. There was bad blood between Wally and his deputy, he was aware. He wanted things to simmer down between them, which meant being on hand to give Samson all his orders direct and not allowing him an opportunity to defy Wally. And there was Luke and his progress to check on. Regretfully, he postponed his thoughts of a trip to see Lucinda but promised himself it was only for a day or two.

★

The house looked subtly different as Dexter approached it. Someone — Luke? — had been busy in the garden. It had an especially well watered look and a froth of white spider-lilies had sprung up in the borders — Yelonga's response to the rain. Besides that, some of the shrubs had been carefully pruned, and the crimson bougainvillaea above the gate was neatly trimmed into its former arch.

As he climbed the veranda steps and walked into the family room, he saw that the screened door and windows stood ajar, as if the rooms were receiving an airing. Simultaneously he saw that the draughty wooden slab walls had been boarded over and papered with a cheerful floral sprig wallpaper. The ceiling was freshly whitened, too. Smells of paint and size hung in the air. The battered sofas and chairs were unrecognisable beneath fresh chintz covers in a pale floral pattern.

'Lucas!' he roared. 'Have you gone out of your mind? Christ — it looks like a tart's parlour in here!'

His voice died as the door to the kitchen swung inward and Lucinda appeared, carrying a Chinese bowl filled with lilies.

She smiled ruefully. 'I'm sorry you don't like it. I'd hoped you would.'

'No, no — it was just a surprise, that's all.' His heartbeat performed astonishing feats. Thank God he hadn't detoured by Douglas Downs. He might have missed her.

'But I don't understand,' he continued clumsily. 'Unless this means it's okay? We can get married now.'

He held out his arms, expecting her to run to him and tell him how she had overcome her mother's resistance. She did not move, but held the bowl of lilies before her like a shield.

'Dexter, please let me explain,' she began.

Lucas's voice interrupted. 'You don't need to, Lucy. Just show him your ring.'

Dexter watched in disbelief as Lucas took the bowl from

167

Lucinda, then slid his arm round her waist.

'But ... she can't be marrying *you*! Lucinda, don't do this to me! You said you loved me.'

She shrank from the agony in his voice and clutched at Lucas for support.

'Would you go and get into the car, sweetie? My little brother and I have a few things to discuss.'

He gave her a dismissive pat and took a step towards Dexter.

'I know this has come as a shock —'

'Too bloody right it has — and *you're* going nowhere!' He seized Lucinda's wrist as she tried to pass him.

She gasped, though not with pain. Even in the face of her terrible betrayal, Dexter took care not to hurt her.

The look on his face was punishment enough, and she faltered, 'I'm sorry. I *did* think I loved you, Dexter. Then Luke came along, and I saw I was wrong. Please don't make this any harder than it already is.'

He stared at her, unable to speak or to relinquish his hold.

'You heard the lady,' Lucas said, and moved lazily forward on the balls of his feet. 'Now let her go, if you know what's good for you.'

Dexter did, but for the sake of Lucinda's obvious distress and not because his brother told him to. They heard her running footsteps, then the distant bang of the car door.

Lucas relaxed. 'Look, sport, there's no need for us to fall out over this. We're brothers, and partners in Yelonga. No bit of fluff's worth —'

He reeled backwards under the force of Dexter's blow, cracking his head against the turned foot of an old mahogany chiffonier. Dexter thought he had killed him and, for a moment, did not care. But dutifully he knelt to inspect Lucas's pulse, then fetched a cloth and a bowl of water from the kitchen, where Fu Yin sat listening, wide-eyed. He soaked the cloth in water and held it to the back of Luke's head. He poured the rest of the bowlful into his brother's face.

Luke came round, spluttering. He winced at the pain in his head but still managed his maddening superior smile. 'You see, you're not right for her. You're still so much of a kid, flying off the handle and throwing your weight around like that. Lucy needs someone more mature, someone who's seen a bit of life.'

'Someone like you? Don't make me laugh!' Dexter stood over his brother with clenched fists, ready to knock the taunting smile from his face, but he could not bring himself to hit a man when he was down. Rage and despair welled inside him until he could barely breathe. 'Why'd you do it, Luke? When you knew I loved her!'

'Lucy and me, we're good together.' The smile widened. 'For such an innocent, she shows remarkable promise — if you get my meaning.'

'You foul-mouthed bastard!' The hateful words conjured up memories of Lucinda on the riverbank. The thought that she could be equally warm and welcoming to his brother caused Dexter to sway dizzily.

'Like I said, still wet behind the ears,' Lucas taunted him, struggling to his feet. 'Under all that sweet girlish front she's just like any other bitch you'd meet. You should have tried your luck while you had the chance.'

'You scum!' Dexter hissed. 'Talking about her like that ... You don't even know her.'

'I know she's heiress to Douglas Downs. What more's to know? You wanted to expand the station, sport. Well, there's more than one way of skinning a cat.'

Dexter reeled with shock. 'Get out,' he gasped. 'Get out of here before I kill you.'

'I intend to. Phemie's waiting to discuss the wedding plans. By the way, she wants you to be best man. Be seeing you.'

And with a mocking laugh he was gone, leaving his brother sick and trembling, knowing that if he stayed on at

Yelonga he would be forced to watch his brother enjoy all he had ever longed to possess.

Dexter went bush for a few weeks before the ceremony, camping out in a cave Wally had once shown him. The head stockman tracked him there the night before the wedding.

Wally was shocked by Dexter's glittering eyes and wild, unshaven face, but he knew better than to comment directly. 'Mister Lucas say you sore loser. Lody Stevens gonna be best man.'

It brought Dexter round, as Wally had calculated. 'My oath he's not!'

Dexter was by his brother's side the next morning in the parlour of Douglas Downs when Father Tom, the visiting bush priest, declared Lucinda Mary Gregson and Lucas James Randolph to be man and wife. Dexter looked on stonily as the priest told Lucas, 'You may now kiss the bride.'

After the ceremony, he held out his hand to his brother. 'Congratulations.'

But a triumphant Phemie Gregson noticed how his blue eyes darkened with misery and he turned away when Lucinda tried to offer a sisterly kiss.

Mal Gregson forced glass after glass of his finest imported malt down Dexter, the only gesture of sympathy he dared make with Phemie's watchful eye on him. Later, Dexter watched in dry-eyed misery while the bridal couple drove away in their flashy blue and silver car, bound for Brisbane and a month's honeymoon touring the coast.

Days later, listlessly trying to order the station's business affairs, Dexter discovered that Lucas had emptied the station bank account.

At first, the loss of the money was purely secondary to the

170

more grievous loss of Lucinda. By the date of the newlyweds' anticipated return, he was in an agony of indecision. Should he arrange to be away from the homestead, knowing that the sight of her sharing his brother's room would be agony? Or should he force himself to bite the bullet and get used to her presence in the house, so close but forever beyond him?

He decided to face up to things and stay, but when the couple failed to appear that week or the next, Dexter realised that yet again he'd been outsmarted. Lucas had taken a considerable sum of money with him, enough to stake even a high roller for more than a month. If the cards were kind to him, he'd stay away indefinitely. Dexter would see his brother only when his luck and their money was exhausted.

He spent that Christmas as he had all the previous ones: in 100-degree heat, sharing the men's Christmas tucker of roast wild turkey and all the trimmings, followed by Fu Yin's leaden plum duff. The station embargo on liquor was lifted for a day, which meant the following three were a write-off.

By the time they were all fit enough to resume their riding of the paddocks, the cows were dropping calves like hailstones. Early storms had seen to it that there was a supply of fresh pasture at the tail end of the Dry, and consequently stock numbers were well up on the year before. All they needed now was the Wet.

It arrived on January 3rd after three agonising days of leaden skies and intense humidity. It was an effort for stock and men even to move in such conditions, but Dexter was taking no chances. The Yelonga mobs would be on high ground, as safe as they could be during the rain's onslaught.

When it came, in solid grey sheets that set the house's iron roof booming hollowly, the rain brought a fall in temperature but confined Dexter and the men to the homestead. It was impossible to ride any distance while the

171

Wet was in its monsoon stage. Though this year the house was not cut off, the sunbaked bush trails had become treacherous quagmires of thick red mud, sticky as honey. Bridges were flooded over, dried-up creeks and riverbeds suddenly churning with muddy foaming water. Dexter spent a month at the homestead, brooding and planning.

Now there was time to react to Lucas's theft. Dexter wrote to the Land Office in Brisbane; to a lawyer there; to the station bank in Cairns, and to the meatworks in Townsville, confirming their inspector's appointment to view the Yelonga stock and place their order. Then he sat back to wait.

Despite the large open fireplaces, even inside the house the air felt clammy. Clothes in Dexter's wardrobe grew mould and had to be repeatedly washed and aired. He left Lucas's to rot but forced himself occasionally to inspect Grandpa's old room which Lucas and Lucinda had redecorated and were to share. The pretty sprigged wallpaper was already dotted with mould, and he found a nest of blue frogs in the filmy white muslin netting draped over the bed. Sighing, he ordered one of the girls to wash out the nets and keep the room clean and well-aired for his brother and sister-in-law's return.

'Mister Lucas come home soon?' the Chinese cook enquired one day, his eyes as sharp and bright as a magpie's.

'I hope so. Him and me have a lot to discuss.'

In February, the rain eased to no more than the occasional drizzle, and work around the station began again in earnest. Old grass was carefully burned off to promote the new growth. Yelonga stretched for mile after mile, fresh and green. The cattle gorged themselves, and grew sleeker and fatter by the day. Dexter was confident of a good sale and calculated his likely profit. There had been no trouble about his borrowing money from the bank to cover the station's running costs, and as the suppliers routinely extended long credit periods, Lucas's appropriation had not affected day-to-day life on Yelonga. But for the successful completion of Dexter's long-term plan he needed a lot more money.

Paddock by paddock, the mobs were rounded up by the men and their dogs and driven to one of the many drafting yards on the property. Inside the receiving yard, working on foot and armed only with whippy green gumsuckers, the men drafted, or sorted, the cattle into their different categories and drove them into separate yards accordingly. Hefty bulls were retained for stud or joined the four-year-old bullocks in the meatworks yard. Later they'd be driven to a paddock where the meatworks inspector could assess them and make his offer. They'd then be shod ready for the long trip cross country on the hoof before they reached the bitumen and were trucked the last fifty miles or so to the meatworks.

Two-year-old steers were assessed for size and most retained for store, to be fattened further before sale. Heifers, or maiden cows, were put into one yard, cows in another. Calves were roped and forced to the ground while the Randolph 'R' was branded into their hide and their ears distinctively clipped. it was always possible for determined cattle-duffers to tamper with a brandmark, but a clip pattern was hard to disguise.

Strangers, or cattle belonging to other stations that had wandered into Dexter's mobs, were allocated for household eating. This was accepted practice, and Dexter's neighbours would be doing the same. The cattleman's maxim was: 'Always eat strangers' cattle.' It was simply too much trouble and expense to get them back to their owner.

After drafting, drenching. The lowing, protesting beasts were forced into a race, a deep trough filled with water containing a strong arsenic-based treatment against flies, ticks and other pests. The meatworks would only buy beasts with clean healthy coats, so this process, which the

173

mobs hated and resisted, was vital.

The inspector reached Yelonga before Lucas. He liked what he saw and placed his best order to date. He seemed only mildly surprised when Dexter asked for the settlement to be made in due course to a new bank account in his own name rather than Yelonga's. It would in any case not arrive until June, July or August, after the meatworks mob had successfully completed their overland trek, been weighed and processed. The inspector quoted Dexter a good price per tonne, and he performed his calculations. There was still a shortfall . . .

He'd hoped to avoid one final course, but Lucas had left him no alternative. Besides, he needed to visit Brisbane to sign some papers. He could kill two birds with one stone. In April, when he had seen the meatworks cattle safely to the drovers' pick-up point, Dexter headed south. He wore his one good suit, uncomfortable shoes instead of elastic-sided stockmen's boots, and carried a heavy suitcase which he kept always within view and slept against at night on the two-day journey.

His business in Brisbane took three interminable days. How townees could stand the life beat him, but he left the State capital a moderately happy man. His homecoming put a stop to that.

The nearest station to Yelonga was a primitive weather-board affair which presided over a single track. The Rockhampton train passed through once a week at six in the morning. Though Dexter had notified no one of his arrival, he recognised the old utility pulled up in the station yard. He didn't ask why Wally had come to meet the train, aware there could be no logical answer. Wally had just *known*.

'G'day, boss.'

'How're yer goin'?' Dexter stretched his cramped limbs and took a deep breath of the scented air. He roped the empty suitcase on to the ute's flatbed and climbed in next to Wally, leaving the window open. 'Good to have some fresh air,' he explained, 'even if it has got a bite to it.'

The sun still had not risen high enough to chase the morning frost from the trees and ground. It was a glittering winter's morning in the outback, Dexter's favourite time of year. Wally glanced sideways at Dexter's sheepskin jacket, slung ready for him round the back of his seat.

'Good on yer.' He shrugged it on. 'So, how's it been? Fencers turned up all right?'

'Everything onna station going well,' Wally said evasively. 'Inna house . . .'

Dexter gripped the sides of his seat. 'They're back,' he said, suddenly blind to the beauty of the morning and deaf to the bush yammer.

'Two days.'

'Is she — I hope they're both well?'

'Yes, boss.'

But Wally's tone said otherwise. His heart thundering, Dexter abandoned the subject. For now. 'Is everyone else behaving? Samson, Fu Yin?'

'Mister Lucas send cookie away yesterday. He go witha mail.'

'What? How will Fu Yin manage?'

'Yeller feller sad, but he tell me his people in Sydney. Missus give him money when Mister Lucas not there.'

'Damn him! Yelonga's been Fu Yin's home for more than thirty years. He deserved better than that. And who's doing the cooking, for Christ's sake?'

'Clara, boss.'

When they were within sight of the house, Dexter leapt from the moving truck and strode for the garden gate. 'Lucas! I want a word with you.'

'Quiet, please, or you'll wake him!'

He spun on his heel to face Lucinda, too astonished by her words to register the deeper implications of seeing her here.

175

'I should bloody well think I will! Sorry, Lucinda, but we have to have a talk. He's been making changes round here without consulting me. Why's he asleep, anyway?'

'He had a bad night.'

Probably had a skinful, Dexter decided, detecting embarrassment in the tell-tale blotches of colour creeping into her cheeks. She looked thinner, and pale even by winter standards. Too many nights hanging out in the city fleshpots and days spent indoors recovering, he supposed. But weren't those worry lines etched around her eyes, and since when had Lucinda bitten her nails?

'Is everything all right?'

'Yes, of course,' she said quickly. 'It's good to see you again, Dexter.'

It was not the word he would have chosen. It was a kind of torment to see her, still beautiful enough to quicken his pulses and thicken his tongue until he spoke pure gibberish. 'Yeah, right ... I mean, good to see you, too. I missed you.' He looked down, cursing himself for his clumsiness, and almost missed her whispered reply.

'I missed you too — so much.'

Her eyes held the sheen of imminent tears. Before he could enquire why, all hell broke out within the house.

'Missus, she's on fire again! Come quick, quick!'

'Oh Lord,' Lucinda groaned, and started to run. 'Use the bucket like I showed you,' she yelled, and then to Dexter: 'Clara's cook now, and she still hasn't got the hang of the range. Luke'll be wild if she burns the dinner again.'

The whole house, more like, Dexter reflected after he had taken control in the kitchen. Clara was one of the most handsome of the station lubras, but not renowned for clear-headedness. She huddled in one corner, her apron to her face, as he snatched the flaming saucepan from the windowsill where she had rested it. He rapidly smothered the flames and doused the smoking window frame. Afterwards he stood by until he was confident there was no further risk of fire. Lucinda set to to mop up the water

176

Clara had spilt on the floor in an ineffectual effort to stem the flames.

Dexter sent the girl in search of Wally. 'Ask him to give you three more buckets from the stores,' he instructed her. 'Until you get the hang of things better, we'll need to be on the safe side.'

'Me nevva learna cook on that thing,' she said with a disdainful glance over her shoulder.

Dexter had the uneasy feeling she would prove herself right. 'Why did Luke sack Fu Yin?' he asked, when Clara was out of earshot.

Lucinda's lashes fluttered uneasily. 'Oh, I couldn't really say. Something about running the station more efficiently. We already support the settlement, after all.'

Dexter laughed bitterly. 'Money's gone, eh? Half of it was mine, by the way. And because he's out of funds he sacks a man who's served this family for thirty years.'

She coloured painfully. 'Please don't talk like that. I can't bear it.'

He couldn't bear to see her defend his reprobate brother, or see her face turn drawn and anxious and her water-reddened hands twist together as she spoke. It was happening already — what he'd feared the day Lucas said he was marrying her. His brother was turning this once radiant girl into a careworn drab. He couldn't simply stand around and watch it happen.

'I'm going out to see Wally, catch up on things,' he said, pushing past her.

She caught at his arm. 'Don't go — I mean, don't you want something to eat? You must be hungry.'

'It'd choke me,' he said truthfully, and gently pulled free. 'Tell Lucas I'll see him at tea. Six o'clock, okay?'

She raised her chin. 'I'm afraid he's changed that. Clara serves dinner at seven now.'

'That,' he said, not caring for the moment how he hurt her, 'will be a bloody miracle. But see you then.'

He strode off to catch Wally, not sure which rankled

more, the alteration in Lucinda or all the changes Lucas had been making on Yelonga.

Lucas was sitting out front under the covered breezeway when his brother returned from the yards, dusty and sweat-stained. He was dressed in a smart city suit, but the top button of his shirt was already undone and he'd loosened the knot of his tie. He'd put on more weight. The handsome features were slightly blurred by fat, and the whites of his eyes finely shot with red.

He welcomed Dexter civilly enough, though he did not get up from his semi-recumbent position in Grandpa's squatter's chair.

'Good to see you, sport. Join me in a rum?'

Dexter glanced down at the table. 'Thanks. I'll get a glass.'

'No need.' He clapped his hands. 'Lucinda, 'nother glass for my brother!' She came running out with it, hot and dishevelled, an apron tied over the flowered silk of her dress. 'Shoddy housekeeping, darling,' Lucas reproved her, and patted her backside lasciviously as she bent to put down the glass. 'Got to keep them in their place,' he said loudly as she turned back to the kitchen. 'So, how's it been, Dexter? I hear we had another good year.'

'Damn good,' he agreed.

A smile widened Lucas's puffy features. 'That's what I like to hear. Knew I could rely on you. Sorry I was away a bit longer than I said —'

'A bit! You've been gone six months.'

His brother gestured vaguely. 'You know how it is. Lucy wanted to visit her aunt in Melbourne, I had a yen to see Sydney again. Bumped into a few cobbers from my old outfit there. They put me on to something promising.'

'A card school, I suppose.'

Lucas took another hefty shot of rum. 'Dexter, you misjudge me. Four-wheel drive vehicles, ex US army ... So

178

if you could point me in the direction of the Yelonga cheque book? I gather we've changed our banking arrangements.'

'Didn't take you long to find out, did it? How long've you been back — two days?'

Lucas smiled blandly. 'I don't think I care for your tone.'

'And I don't give a toss! What did you think, Luke? That you could come in here, spin some phoney yarn about needing money to improve the station, and I'd be green enough to let you waltz off with all the profits again? You've just boozed and gambled your way through four years' worth, *sport*! Well, that's it, finished. You had a hard war so we'll call it quits about that money, but from now on it's time to get our heads down and graft for Yelonga.'

Lucas lurched to his feet, picked up the bottle and waved it menacingly. 'I don't think you quite understand me. I'm the elder, I call the shots round here. Now, give me the money.'

Dexter looked at him pityingly. 'It's no use, Luke. The money's not even in yet, but when it is, it's spoken for. I've taken that lease on Maroonda.'

'You've what? You can't have done!' He took a long swig from the bottle. 'I never agreed to it. We're a partnership, we do things together.'

'Like empty the station account? Half of that money was mine, Luke. I sweated my guts out for it. I can't let you do that to me again and maybe ruin this place for good, so I've invested for our joint future. A Brisbane lawyer's holding Maroonda as my nominee, but naturally I'll cut you in for half if —'

Lucas's face twisted into a snarl. He looked less than human suddenly. 'You can take your godforsaken desert and stuff it up your arse! What the bloody hell are you playing at? I need that money, and I will have it. I've got bills to pay, debts ...'

'Notes of hand?'

179

His silence as good as confirmed it. Dexter tried the gentle approach. 'We'll pay them off gradually, out of next year's profits. When you explain, I'm sure they'll —'

His brother slammed the table, eyes bulging. 'Lucas Randolph never grovels! They'll be paid, in full, from *this* year's profits!'

'No. It's for your own good.'

Lucas's next move took him by surprise. Smashing the bottle against the table edge, he leapt from his seat with the speed of a striking snake. Dexter blocked his arm, deflecting the jagged edge of glass from his throat. It caught the taut skin above his cheekbone and bright blood jetted from the wound. There was a piercing scream from the house behind them. Momentarily distracted, Lucas feinted, missed and went down on the flagstones.

'Dexter! My God, he's hurt you!' Lucinda ran to him, ignoring her husband's inert body, and pressed a lace-edged handkerchief to his face.

'It's nothing,' he said, still keeping a wary eye on his brother.

Lucas sat up painfully, the fight knocked out of him. 'What a touching scene,' he slurred. 'Aren't you going to play the devoted nurse, darling? Aren't you going to tell him what you told me — that you made a terrible mistake and married the wrong brother?'

It was pitiful to see the way shame and humiliation washed over her. She blushed, then turned pale. 'How can you do this to me?' she said in a ragged voice, then ran from them both.

'So now you know,' Lucas said with a twisted smile. 'And there's not a damn thing you can do about it — or is there? If you let me have the money now, I'll go down to Brisbane and Sydney, see a few people. I'll be away a while, and no doubt Lucy will need a little — consolation.'

In a vision from a nightmare, Dexter saw the future Lucas had in mind for them all. Dexter would continue to manage the property while his brother spent all the money.

On Yelonga they'd live hand to mouth, from one year's end to the next, never putting money by against the bad times or investing in stock or equipment. And to keep him sweet to this miserable existence, Lucas was prepared to trade the use of his wife. In a moment of madness, Dexter even considered it.

'Shall we shake on it, sport?' Lucas's voice was oily and insinuating.

When Dexter replied, his voice cracked with the pain of renunciation. 'I guess we've come to the parting of the ways, Luke. You're sick, and I'd be worse than that if I stayed. It breaks my heart to leave Yelonga, after all it's meant to our family.'

'Breaks your heart to turn your back on my wife, more like!'

There was truth in that, but Dexter ignored him. He felt bruised with emotion, his eyes gritty with tears he would not shed in front of Luke. 'I'm renouncing my half share in Yelonga. I'll take Maroonda and this year's profits in full settlement. You can send on any lawyer's papers and I'll sign to make it legal.'

'I'll be sending on more than papers,' Lucas spat. 'I'll have the bloody *law* on you! What about the silver? Mealy-mouthed bastard, canting about our family ... You've just sold what the old man always refused to.'

'I had to. I made an arrangement that we could buy it back within one year, but I needed the money for Maroonda's working capital.'

'I'll go to the police, I'll lay charges —'

'You do that, and you'll force my hand. I've already consulted my lawyer about your misappropriation. Don't you think we'd better call it quits?'

'Honour among thieves, eh? Well, don't expect me to shake your hand. I want you off Yelonga at first light, and for as long as it's mine you're not welcome here. Understood?'

Dexter nodded and went silently to his room. Exile from

the person and place he loved most would be a kind of living death, but it would have been madness to stay.

Sound carries easily in a thin-walled timber house. Sleepless, Dexter heard the slamming of a door; a woman's voice — Lucinda's — raised in protest, lowered in pleading. Then the creaking of bedsprings in a frenzied, unmistakable rhythm. Dexter writhed in his bed, pulling pillows and blankets over his head to drown out the sound. It went on and on. Sometimes he could hear Lucas's voice. The words were indistinct but the gloating tone of them was not. Lucas was revelling in the pain he was causing them both, and prolonging it all he could. He gave a final animal cry and the creaking subsided. Dexter thought he heard Lucinda's muffled sobbing.

And then, shocking in its unexpectedness, Lucas's voice on the veranda outside. 'Did you hear that, sport? Did you hear me taking what's mine? Think of me, won't you, when you're out there in that baking bloody desert. Think of me doing this again and again, whenever I like.' His triumphant laughter was obscene.

Dexter waited until he heard the door of Luke's room close behind him. He couldn't have brought himself to speak to his brother then, but he feared that if he did not react at all the whole ghastly procedure would start again. He dressed hurriedly and left his room, banging the door. He would spend the night in the stockmen's spartan quarters and spare Lucinda further pain and humiliation.

He crept back towards dawn, light as a cat. Rapidly he assembled the few books, clothes and personal possessions there'd be room for in his saddlebags. The last thing he took was the family Bible in which the births and deaths of all the Yelonga Randolphs were recorded. By rights it belonged on the station, but Luke would never miss it. He stepped out of his room into the grey dawn, and started with surprise.

Lucinda was waiting for him, barefoot and wearing a long white nightgown. 'I know I shouldn't have come.'

He took her by the hand and urged her gently into his room. 'Not like that, you shouldn't. Christ, Lucinda, you're freezing.'

'I know. After he'd — after he finished, I spent the night on a chair in our room. He didn't notice; he always sleeps like the dead when he's been drinking. But I couldn't bear to share his bed. Not after that! Hold me, please. Just hold me for the last time.'

They clung together, shaking with cold and grief. 'Oh God, I wish you didn't have to leave,' she moaned, clinging like a vine. 'It's too late for us now, but I want you to know — it's you I love. I did all along, but Lucas put a sort of spell on me. I can't explain it but he dazzled and charmed me and carried me along with his plans for me . . . his and Mum's plans.'

He kissed her and cradled her to him. 'You don't have to explain. I've had years of watching him win people over. And you're sure you don't love him any more?'

She shuddered. 'How could anyone love the way he is when he's drinking — the gambling, the violence . . .'

'You're not saying he hits you?'

'Only once. I told him if he did it again I'd go back to Mum and Dad.'

He stared at her, appalled to think of such fragility at a drunkard's mercy. 'I'd like to kill him, only it'd be too quick. Better to let him stew in a hell of his own making. But not you, my love. Yelonga's no place for you any more.'

'Where else is there? I didn't really mean it about going back to my parents. Mum'd never let me.'

'You could come with me, this minute. Just pack a few things and ride away.'

'No, I can't.'

'I know it's not what I'd planned for you, an outback shack with no friends or neighbours. But you'd have me, Lucy. We'd have each other.' When a smile of piercing regret crossed her face, he knew that he had lost.

Gently she stroked the side of his face. 'You are so dear to me, Dexter. I'll regret until the day I die letting you slip through my fingers, but I'm sorry, I can't go with you.'

'But why? There's nothing to tie you to a drunken bastard like that. He doesn't love you. All he ever cared about was your father's land.'

'Do you think I haven't worked that out by now? But I can't do it. I can't leave him.'

There was a chilling note of resignation in her voice, but still he fought against it. 'For God's sake, why?'

'Adultery's a mortal sin, Dexter. If I go with you, I'm damned.'

Too late he remembered the Catholic wedding, the priest uniting his brother and Lucinda with indissoluble vows. Anger and disappointment put him on the offensive. 'First Lucas, now your God. Why do I always come second with you, Lucinda? And what kind of God is he anyway to force you to stay with a drunken bully who'll never love you like I do?'

'But he'll love our child. Our baby will change him for the better, I'm sure of it.'

Dexter felt the room spin. Lucinda was pale but composed, one arm crossed protectively over her stomach.

'I'm stronger than you think,' she said. 'I love you, but I can live with my mistake. I have to, for my child's sake.'

There was a clatter of hooves on the beaten earth at the back of the house, and faintly from the kitchen a reluctant clattering of pans. The secret part of the morning, when it seemed that anything could be possible, was almost over.

He closed his eyes so as not to see the refusal already on her face. 'Lucinda, I'm asking you for the final time — will you come with me now? I'll bring up the baby as my own. It makes no difference.'

184

She leaned forward and gently kissed his cheek, just beneath the cut that Lucas had inflicted. 'It makes all the difference in the world, and you know it. Be happy, Dexter. Find yourself someone else to love, someone who deserves you better than I ever could.'

There was no point in staying, but pride would not permit him to walk away without having the last word. 'I won't give up, Lucinda. You haven't heard the last from me.'

He picked up the saddlebags and left her standing in his room. Wally had the horses saddled and ready. Silently they took the trail to the back of the house. At the homestead graveyard, Dexter dismounted and knelt for a moment by his grandfather's grave, his hat in his hand.

'Bye, old feller. I've had to leave Luke in charge but, I promise you, one day I'll be back.'

Remounting, he looked back towards the house. The window to his old room stood open, framing a pale figure. She watched, motionless, until Dexter and Wally rounded a bend in the trail and were swallowed up by the vast remorseless bush.

The early days on Maroonda would have broken a lesser man, and the last almost broke Dexter, but in the three years he battled to carve a profitable station out of the fierce red land, he grew to love and respect it.

It was a very different terrain from Yelonga's, a land of red-gold sandhills and exposed soil plains on which the infrequent fences were visible for miles. Dusty eucalypts ringed the few thin creeks and waterholes, and a sparse stand of straggling native pines sheltered the homestead and gave it its name. Apart from these, the harsh land was thinly vegetated, mainly with saltbush and spinifex. In the Wet or after a storm, the desert was said to sprout a carpet of wild flowers — cerise parkelya, yellow button daisies, flamboyant scarlet Desert Pea — but Dexter never saw them. In his three years on Maroonda there was not so much as a drop of rain.

When the Wet failed the first year, his confidence held. The drilling programme had gone as planned. If Lucas had not spent the war years' profits there would have been more, but he was able to pay for a first series of artesian bores which pumped up boiling water from deep within the earth's crust.

The strange life-forms of this new land fascinated him. Where scalding water gushed from the bore mouths, for instance, into the 'turkey neck' earth mounds surrounding them, hundreds of tiny translucent fish seethed and thrived. Yet if he picked these up and threw them further down the irrigation channels, where the water had cooled to air temperature, they instantly went belly up and died. The goannas here grew giant size — six feet long, mottled purple and yellow, and capable of running on their hind legs if startled. They regularly robbed the chook yard, but Dexter and Wally let them be. Any form of life which had adapted to this country was deserving of respect.

Besides the bores, he invested in stock. He would not go to Yelonga for breeders, but Mal Gregson broke the conservative habits of a lifetime and gave Dexter indefinite credit on a sizeable number of Shorthorn cows and heifers. The bulk of the bank loan set aside for stock went into the acquisition of a single Brahman bull, a native Indian breed first imported into Australia in the thirties.

The new acquisition had a high domed forehead, intelligent eyes, and managed to look both humped and sway-backed. He had long pendulous ears and his creamy hide seemed to hang loosely about him, though he was obviously in peak condition. His legs looked too spindly for his powerful quarters and chest.

'Him one ugly-feller bull,' Wally said, scratching his head, the day Dexter drove the animal on to Maroonda.

'You're not wrong! Good name, though. Let's call him Ugly.'

186

The Santa Gertrudis stock Dexter planned to breed by crossing the Shorthorn cows with a Brahman bull would be far more resistant to ticks and pests than the European breeds. Brahmans had other characteristics that appealed to him. When threatened by dingoes or other predators they had an amazing turn of speed; if cornered, Brahman cows would fight to protect their calves, lashing out with hooves and holding off their enemies rather than abandoning their young like other breeds.

When the rains failed for the second year, the natural water sources on the station disappeared completely. The stock, and even Dexter and Wally in their tumbledown old shack, were reliant on artesian water, which, murky and sulphur-smelling, had to be filtered and carefully boiled before it was fit for human consumption. The new season's calves failed to thrive as Dexter had hoped. It took all his and Wally's skilled husbandry to keep them alive during the second year, and the breeding programme dropped away.

It was a hard life, and a lonely one. Although an outback-dweller all his life, Dexter had never known the true meaning of isolation till he came to Maroonda. It had none of the comforts and refinements of Yelonga, but he had expected that. The worst part of life there was the almost complete lack of communication with the outside world. Until the bitumen was extended along the station boundary, which could be a matter of years, reaching Maroonda remained a hazardous business. The mail van called once a month or so but left post and newspapers for collection by Wally and Dexter in a ten-gallon drum miles from the homestead. The mail man refused to come any closer, as the rocky Maroonda roads had already claimed so many of his tyres.

Dexter never heard from Lucas except via his lawyer. He learned that he could not legally resign his half share in Yelonga until he was twenty-one, but signed an interim document empowering the transfer when he reached his majority.

He had hoped Lucinda might write, if only to tell him of his niece or nephew's birth, but there was silence from her, too. A chance meeting with Mal Gregson, when Dexter was on one of his infrequent visits to Cairns, explained why.

'Lucy lost the baby,' Mal said, his face creased with sadness.

'I'm sorry. Will you tell her from me, when you see her?'

'I will. She'll be glad of news of you.'

But the news of Lucinda saddened and enraged Dexter. She'd stayed with his brother at least partly because of the child. The thought of her, childless, continuing to waste herself on Lucas drove him to seek release in the arms of cheap Cairns whores, but it could only be temporary. The loneliness and isolation of his usual lifestyle only increased his yearning for her.

From time to time he wondered how Yelonga was faring in the drought. Since she was blessed with far more natural water than Maroonda, she'd be holding out better presumably. She could hardly do worse.

In their year without rain the water-table shifted and half their expensive bores ran dry. They had to turn off the mechanic who lived for months at a time out at the bore-heads, tending the pumps. There was no more money to pay him. The water supply in the house dwindled to a brackish trickle that looked foul and tasted worse, even when boiled. Dexter and Wally were forced to stand help-lessly by while the stock that was to have laid the foundation of Maroonda's fortunes daily dwindled and died.

When they had lost half the calves, they had an unexpected visitor. He arrived early one morning in a battered dust-covered jeep — US army issue, Dexter noted with a wry smile, the sort of vehicle he'd planned to invest in with the money Lucas had embezzled.

The visitor was a beefy, florid-faced man in a natty khaki safari suit. 'G'day,' he greeted them. 'Glad to have caught you in.'

'We're not going anywhere,' Dexter said tersely. The stock were in the home paddock, too weak to be driven to the next bore. It was just a matter of time before they all died.

'Stuart McFee,' he introduced himself, looking from one to the other of them. 'I'm looking for Mr Dexter Randolph.'

'That's me,' he said reluctantly. Stuart McFee had city timewaster written all over him, and Dexter had dying stock to see to.

McFee produced a card from a silver carrying-case. 'McFee, of Buchanan, Gribble, McFee,' he announced proudly. 'I expect you've heard of us?'

'Can't say that I have. Nice of you to drop by, Mr McFee, but this is a bit of a bad time for us.'

McFee made his pitch quickly. 'Are you a gambling man, Mr Randolph?'

It was an unfortunate choice of words, and Dexter drew himself up stiffly. 'I am not, Mr McFee. And if it's insurance you're selling, you're too damn late. Take a look over there. My stock's dying, the bull's on his knees, and I haven't got a pot to piss in. So you can take your insurance and shove it!'

McFee nervously raised his briefcase. 'Mr Randolph, I haven't come to sell you anything. Quite the contrary. I might — just might — be here to buy.'

'You've got to be out of your mind! Maroonda's ruined me. Don't waste your time even looking round, mate.'

'But that's just what I'd like to do — with your permission, of course. BGM is a mining concern, Mr Randolph, not an insurance company. Our survey plane was out over a Gulf property to the north. He got lost, and ended up over the north-east corner of Maroonda.'

Dexter scratched his head. 'Must have been at least a hundred miles out of his way. Guess it wasn't his lucky day.'

Embarrassment darkened McFee's face a shade or two.

189

'Yes, well, in country as wild as this ... But it may well have been *your* lucky day, Mr Randolph. From the aerial photographs our man took, all the signs are that there is a sizeable deposit of iron ore down in the gorge on your property. BGM would like to take a survey to verify this — at our own expense, naturally.'

'Ah, why the hell not? Just don't damage any fences.'

Privately Dexter doubted if he himself would be around for much longer. With the cattle dropping like flies and his debts mounting, it looked as if he and Wally would have to hire themselves out as drovers. If they left Maroonda, it would revert to the Land Office. No point in telling McFee that, though, not if there was a chance of a bob or two, however long the shot.

Four weeks later, he and Wally were inside the house, holding a wake of sorts over their last bottle of rum. At least, Dexter was drinking rum. Wally, Mission-educated, was drowning his sorrows in tea. They were down to their last few dozen head, and Ugly, barely alive, was tethered in an outbuilding. From overhead came the whine of a light aircraft.

'Looks like the slope-headed pilot's lost again,' Dexter said laconically. 'The gorge is a hundred miles north-east of here.'

The engine sound grew louder. The plane sounded like a giant mosquito as it buzzed the house, setting the windows rattling in their frames.

'What the blue blazes is going on?' Dexter snarled, and flung open the door. The plane banked and circled above him, low enough for him to be able to make out the red-faced figure in a safari suit next to the pilot. McFee leaned out of the plane and tossed something down. He waved goodbye, and the plane climbed steeply out of sight, a tiny speck of yellow swallowed up in an ocean of blue.

Dexter and Wally found the package, neatly wrapped in oilskin, hanging by its string from a branch of Old Man spinifex. Dexter reached for it eagerly and gashed himself on one of the giant spikes in his haste. There was a thick envelope inside.

'I don't believe it,' he said, shaking his head. 'I don't bloody believe it.'

'Bad news, boss?'

Dexter stared at him blankly. 'Christ, no. Good news, the best ever. BGM found iron, wolfram and manga-bloody-nese on Maroonda land. We're rich, Wally! Rich as the king!'

In later years, Dexter was ashamed to think he had signed a contract on the terms BGM offered him, but at the time the money from the mining rights was a lifesaver, with the promise of more to come from royalties. Dexter was able to pay for Ugly and the remnants of the mob to be trucked for agistment to a station far south, on the Queensland/New South Wales border. The rains had not failed there and there was lush and plentiful pasture, at a price.

'Though I can't see why you're bothering, mate,' the station owner told him bluntly. He surveyed the slack-skinned refugee cattle with distaste. 'It's not fattening they need, it's a bloody hospital! If you've got money to burn, why not write these off and buy new stock? It'd be cheaper.'

'Because these cattle are battlers,' Dexter said. 'It's the only thing I respect in man or beast. They may not be beauties, but by God they're tough. They've come through hell so far. In another year or two, when the weather's with us, we'll truck them back to Maroonda and there'll be no stopping them.'

His faith was not misplaced, but when the rain finally fell on Maroonda, he was far away.

'Seems to me when you've got money you can do one of two things,' Dexter had told Wally after paying BGM's first cheque into the bank — not his usual one, to whom he owed a large amount, but another. 'You can play safe, pay off all your debts, set money aside to help you through another sticky patch — but that way you'll never see much of a return. You'll be working for your money, instead of letting it work for you. I know which I'd rather do!'

He kept the news of the Maroonda mineral strike close to his chest, paying off just enough on the station loan to stop the bank from foreclosing. Other station owners were not so lucky, and whenever the banks forced a sale, Dexter and his lawyer were on to it like sharks. He hadn't the money yet to buy up whole stations but he did the next best thing, shrewdly offering over the current odds for blocks of drought-stricken land that were known to be particularly high-yielding in the years when the rain fell.

'They may be dust-bowls now,' he told Wally, 'but the Wet'll be back next year, or the year after. And when it is, the blokes who own the land around will be falling over themselves to bid for mine. You just wait and see.'

Dexter never made his ownership of the blocks public, preferring to use his lawyers as nominees, and he did not mention the change in his fortunes to friends and acquaintances. BGM did not advertise their presence on the out-of-the-way station as they were still trying to steal a march on their competitors by signing up mineral rights on several adjoining properties. He also bought into a couple of station partnerships, acquiring shares in rundown properties in the Kimberley and the Barkly Tablelands.

'Those stations may be beyond the black stump,' he told Wally, 'but Grandpa believed in this land, and communications are improving all the time. After all, when my ancestors settled Yelonga, *that* was the back of beyond.'

His thoughts ran on Yelonga more and more these days. While Wally managed Maroonda, in which Dexter had given him a ten per cent stake, Dexter travelled far and wide, ostensibly looking at stock but secretly acquiring new land. But nothing he saw — channel country, downs, table-

192

land — matched up to his memories of home.

Eventually, on his way north from a sale, he called in at Douglas Downs. The drought years had left their mark on Mal Gregson. He looked old and drawn, formerly thick brown hair receding rapidly and touched with grey. Phemie was away in Victoria visiting relatives, so Mal could talk freely — and bitterly.

'I've come to the end of the road with your brother,' he told Dexter. 'For the past three years I've bailed him out for Lucinda's sake, hoping he'd treat her better.'

'And did he?'

'Like hell! The bastard's gone too far this time. If I had the inclination, I no longer have the cash.'

'It's gambling debts, I take it?'

'Every sort of debt. Hotel bills from his jaunts to Brissie, bar tabs, accounts with this, that and the other supplier. I tell you, Dexter, your brother doesn't spend money – he pisses it away.'

Dexter struggled to keep his voice non-committal. 'Can't be much of a life for Lucinda?'

Mal's anguished expression told him everything. 'Time and again I've begged her to leave him. Who gives a stuff what people say!'

'Do you think she will?' Dexter could hear the longing in his own voice.

Mal was too preoccupied. 'Ah, her mother and those damned nuns who taught her have a lot to answer for! After she lost the baby she turned to religion, clung to it. Now she's convinced herself it's her duty to stick by that layabout. Christ, she's even gone with him to Brisbane, seeing his creditors, lowering herself to beg them to hold off a little longer. It looks as if Luke'll be selling land off this time. About a third of Yelonga, I reckon.'

Dexter sat still. After the lurch of disappointment at hearing that Lucinda was standing by her husband, he could not believe that he was being handed this chance on a plate. Yelonga land was coming on the market, and here he was with money burning a hole in his pocket.

'Listen, Mal, I don't want anyone else to know this but I've come into a bit of money recently ...'

It cost him the sum outstanding on his Douglas Downs starter stock and a fifty per cent cut of any profits made from Mal's working of Yelonga land, but eventually Gregson agreed to 'buy' the land, acting as Dexter's nominee.

'And, remember, keep my name out of this,' Dexter stressed. 'There's no need for Phemie, or even Lucinda, to know you've bought the land, let alone for me. Just tell them you're helping Lucas out temporarily, lending him men and so on. And if Luke wants to know where the money came from, tell him Phemie got it from a maiden aunt or you won it on the sweepstake — tell him any damn thing but keep me out of it. Understand?'

Mal had lost none of his shrewdness. 'Only too well, mate. He's only selling a third now, but you won't rest till you've got the lot.'

Dexter smiled grimly, and Mal realised with a shock of surprise that every trace of the tough but trusting boy he had been was gone. Dexter was a man now, his iron will forged in the fires of experience. Mal doubted that his pursuit of wealth and land would stop at Yelonga, and neither did it.

At the beginning of 1951 the luck was all on Dexter's side. Mal successfully completed his purchase of one-third of Yelonga, including the station's best grazing at Ten Mile and the surrounding paddocks. One week later, the rain returned to Northern Queensland.

Dexter missed the blossoming of the parched land. He was in Sydney, negotiating with a venture capital outfit to re-finance the loans he had outstanding with two Queensland banks and give him a substantial surplus with which to buy out his partners in the two Top End properties.

He hit the other shareholders with his offer at just the

right time. True, rain had fallen at last, bringing new life to the land, but the partnerships were old and moribund. They gladly took the modest profit Dexter was offering. After hiring the best managers and men he could tempt with good conditions and bonuses, he was able at last to introduce the improved land and stock management techniques he had outlined to Lucas so many years before.

They paid off, but he was unable to leave it at that. He could have contented himself with three stations and a sleeping partnership in another. Already he owned over eight thousand square miles of cattle country. But the land, though he loved it, was no longer enough, not while other people were making money out of his efforts. The meatworks, for instance, and the droving and haulage contractors, made their profit on the cattle he bred. That didn't seem right to Dexter.

He sank four years' operating profits into buying his own fleet of road trains, and a meatworks in Darwin. Naturally he also bought in beef from local stations, at a considerable profit, and charged them for trucking in their cattle. He negotiated his own sale of the meat, concentrating on the expanding British and American markets. But the cost of shipping the frozen meat irritated him, particularly when an Australian dockers' strike led to one cargo's being spoiled. He felt it was time to expand his sphere of operations once more. From shipping, he moved laterally into steel production, and from there it was a logical step into mining. He took great pride in his acquisition of BGM, the company that had helped launch his entrepreneurial rise.

The land remained his first love. Dexter liked nothing better than shrugging off his business clothes and pulling on his old stockmen's gear while paying inspection visits to his stations and outstations. But as the scope of his business widened, he was forced to rely more and more upon his station managers. He bought unpretentious homes for himself in Darwin, Townsville and Port Kembla, where the steelworks was situated, but stubbornly resisted putting down roots in Sydney. It was too nose in the air for a country boy like him.

The early to mid-fifties were boom years for the cattle industry. Dexter made money hand over fist and his reputation as a cattle king and entrepreneur was by now firmly established. Shares in Randolph Enterprises were the most widely tipped in the Continent. Mal Gregson, too, recouped all his losses of the drought years and the Yelonga land under his management was more productive than ever. Everyone was doing well, it seemed. Everyone but Lucas Randolph.

His gambling debts constantly outstripped the profits from his badly managed property. He was able enough when he chose to be, but he was constantly away, and Samson, now head stockman, simply wasn't up to the job. Block by block, Lucas stealthily approached his father-in-law with offers to sell. Mal's cheque book seemed always to be open, and after all, it wasn't as if the land was going out of the family. When Mal died, he was bound to leave Yelonga, and all of Douglas Downs, to his only child.

On the day Lucas signed over the last block, including the homestead, he pushed back his chair to leave the lawyer's office and stared Mal insolently in the eye.

'Well, she's all yours, Dad. Now what? I don't suppose you're going to kick your little girl off, are you?'

Mal's face turned scarlet from the effort of keeping his temper. 'You can keep on there for now,' he said. 'No need to alarm Lucy with any of this. Just show my head stockman around when he comes over later this week.'

'White of you.' Lucas carefully angled his akubra over one eye. 'Be seeing you, then.'

'Bloody oath you will! Next Tuesday, lunch at Douglas Downs. And bring Lucinda.'

'Thanks for the invite.'

'It's not a bloody invite! Just be there.'

196

★

Dexter's pilot flew him in to Douglas Downs late on Tuesday morning. Sweating and uncomfortable in a light-weight suit, he straightened the knot of his tie and brushed a film of dust from his sleeves and lapels. It was too hot for these clothes; he'd have been far more comfortable in the shorts and shirt he usually wore to business meetings. But this was different. Special. He'd walked off Yelonga with just his swag and a few stockmen's clothes. Today marked the culmination of the six years' hard graft that had turned a lanky kid into a hard-nosed tycoon. He wanted to look the part — for Lucinda.

Inside the house, Lucas barely reacted to the sound of the plane. No doubt the old goat had a lawyer or two arriving to tie things up about his tenancy of Yelonga. What the hell. The worst of losing it was over now, and Lucas was confident that his father-in-law was too much of a gentleman to talk business in front of the women. Uninvited, he poured himself a second stiff shot of rum, then smiled ingratiatingly at Phemie.

'Mum? Another sherry?'

'Thank you, dear. I didn't know we were expecting visitors, Malcolm.'

Lucinda got up and glanced idly out of the window. She first saw the logo on the Cessna — a hump-backed Brahman bull — and then she saw the man taking the veranda steps two at a time.

'Dexter!'

Phemie rounded on her husband furiously. 'Mal Gregson, what are you thinking of? You know how things stand between poor Lucas and his brother. Why did you invite him?'

''Fraid I invited myself, Phemie. Showed myself in, too. I'm glad to see you don't look a day older.' Dexter stood on the threshold, broad shoulders filling the doorway, and smiled mockingly at his reluctant hostess who seemed to have aged a dozen years at least.

'Well, since you're here you'd better come in,' she said grudgingly. 'Though if you really think it's fair to poor Luke, coming here like this ...'

'Mum!' Lucinda said in an agonised voice.

'... after the way you just upped and left him when the going on Yelonga got too tough.' Naturally she'd swallowed verbatim Lucas's account of their parting.

'It's all right, Lucy,' Dexter said, when it seemed she would intervene. She was still beautiful, he saw, even in the washed-out mail-order dress that was probably the best she could afford.

His smile widened wolfishly at the sight of Lucas. His brother, red-faced and run to seed, slumped in an armchair, slopping rum over himself in surprise. Dexter strode over and righted the glass. 'Shouldn't be so careless, sport. God knows where your next shot's coming from.'

Lucas got clumsily to his feet, bloodshot eyes darting guiltily. 'I don't know what you're talking about,' he blustered. 'Why don't you bugger off back to Sydney and all your pooftah pals there? Leave the real men up here to get on with their work.'

'And what work would that be?' Dexter enquired pleasantly. 'Running Yelonga? Making a living for yourself and your wife?'

'Yelonga, yeah.' Lucas's eyes roamed in the direction of his wife and mother-in-law. They obviously knew nothing about the sale. The privilege of breaking the news fell to Dexter.

'You bloody liar!' he said softly. 'You pathetic, cheating, grog-sodden excuse for a man. You sold it all — land, stock, the roof over your wife's head. *That's* how much you think of her!'

Phemie's head swivelled like a turkey's on its long scrawny neck. 'What's he saying, Malcolm? Do you know about this?'

Mal didn't reply. His concern was all for his daughter, who had turned deathly pale. 'It's all right, Dad,' she whispered. She looked from Dexter, flushed with victory, to her ashen-faced husband. 'Is it true?'

Lucas had to force himself to meet her eyes. His face was contorted with shame.

'Yes,' he said reluctantly. 'But, Lucy, I swear to God it's not as bad as he's made it sound! I sold it to your father. He's not about to turn us off — are you, mate?'

'He certainly will not!' Phemie interrupted, but Mal held up his hand for silence.

'You don't know it all,' he said. 'You see, I wasn't quite straight with you, Luke. You thought I was buying Yelonga on my own account, but I was acting for someone else.'

Lucas stood for a moment, working this out, then seemed to sag with despair. He took one disbelieving look at his brother. 'That's it, then,' he said hoarsely. 'Yelonga's gone. She's really gone.'

His hands came up to cover his face as he sank back into his seat. Apart from his harsh racking sobs, silence filled the room.

It was Lucinda who broke it. She put one hand on Lucas's heaving shoulders and looked at Dexter as if he were dirt.

'You bastard!'

'Now wait a minute, Lucy —'

'Don't Lucy me, you — you bludger!' she cried furiously. 'Just who the hell do you think you are, Dexter Randolph? You bugger off into the blue —'

'Lucinda!' her mother interrupted, scandalised, but the girl ignored her.

'Not a word from you in six years!'

He wasn't sure on whose behalf she was angry: Luke's or her own.

'And then you come creeping back and *use* my father to get what you want behind our backs. I call that despicable. You've changed, Dexter. You're a hard, devious man, not the one I remember.'

Dexter was dumbstruck. This carefully orchestrated

reunion was rapidly spinning out of control. First Lucas's tears, rum-sodden and probably put on, but effective nevertheless. And now Lucinda, spitting at him like a native cat and calling him names, when surely to God she ought to see that he'd done everything for her?

Lucas appeared to pull himself together. He stood up again, and put on a brave smile. 'We'll be off as soon as we can put our things together. Wouldn't want to stay on where we're not wanted, would we, Lucy?'

She smiled at him and rested her head against his shoulder. Dexter's last hope dwindled and died. He saw with sick dismay that it really was too late. Lucas had long since killed her first love for him, the innocent girlish hero worship. But in the years of loneliness and isolation as his wife, it had been replaced by something even more powerful: pity. Lucinda had come to terms with all her husband's failings, every last miserable one, and loved him almost because of them. This love would last because it was based not on infatuation but on experience. Even in his weakness, Lucas triumphed.

There was no question of putting him off Yelonga, not while Lucinda remained with him. 'Stay on and be my manager,' Dexter forced himself to say. 'I won't bother you more than once or twice a year, and I pay decent salary rates and bonuses if you make a go of things. My office will be in touch.'

It looked as though Luke had enough confidence to go through the motions of arguing, but Mal put a stop to that.

'It's a good offer. Think of Lucy.'

'Then it looks as if we stay,' Lucas said with a relieved smile, and kissed Lucinda's cheek.

Her eyes were on Dexter. She seemed to realise some of his inner torment under the stony expression.

'Thanks, Dexter. And — I'm sorry.'

'I'm sorry, too.'

No one else would ever know how many years' dreams he'd just written off.

★

It was time to shake the red dust of Queensland off his feet and make the move to Sydney. He took a suite of offices in the penthouse of a new building at the harbour end of Pitt Street. From his rooftop eyrie he could see the bow-shaped bridge spanning the diamond bright water on which floated ferries, yachts and pleasure cruisers, scaled down to the size of toys.

For a few years he lived in a hotel, but the impersonal politeness and the sheer song and dance every time he ordered so much as a beer got to him. In the summer of 1956, acting on impulse, he drove out to the select eastern suburbs and cruised the streets, looking for a house high-profile enough to match his public image.

He found it in a waterfront property on Darling Point; a sprawling, thirties, white-rendered house with five bedrooms, study, billiards-room, three good-sized rooms for entertaining and a wrapround terrace which on the water side overlooked his own netted-off harbour swimming-pool and private mooring.

He hired a Greek couple to keep house for him, and the three of them rattled round like peas on a drum on the days when Dexter was not entertaining. These were surprisingly few, however, for unexpectedly the rough and ready Queensland grazier turned entrepreneur had become a Sydney social success.

Gradually the male side of the city's coterie had responded to Dexter's blend of laconic humour and cut-and-thrust business sense. Women flocked round him from the outset. Even in elegant imported suits from Richard Hunt and polished city brogues there was still an air of the outback about him, an irresistible combination of confidence and control. Despite the premature wrinkles around his far-seeing pale blue eyes, a legacy of his tough outdoor days, at twenty-eight Dexter was in his prime. He was tireless and demanding in his frequent liaisons, and women adored him for it. More than one indicated she would not be averse to moving into the Yarrabee Road house and playing hostess for him. So far he'd resisted all such offers.

Eliza Haydon, the latest in his long string of conquests, was even more pressing than her predecessors. She wanted marriage into the bargain. Though she did not match up to his idealised memories of Lucinda, Dexter was beginning to see possible advantages to the match. Eliza came from a prominent Melbourne family and was well connected everywhere in New South Wales and Victoria. She had already made her presence felt in his home, advising him on redecoration, caterers, and replacements for the Greeks whom she had discovered were cooking the household accounts as well as his meals. Eliza was a handsome, capable young woman; she was also insatiable in bed. He could, he reflected, do a lot worse.

On one particularly glorious day, Dexter was restless. Outside, the light bounced brilliantly off the turquoise water in the harbour. He was just back from a trip to inspect his Top End stations and had arrived in the office from Mascot, still wearing his country clothes. After only an hour inside, he longed for some fresh air — or as fresh as it came in the city. Unable to settle to work, he told his secretary he'd be out for the rest of the morning and strolled towards Hyde Park.

The patch of green at the city centre was welcome but somehow paltry after the vast open spaces he had just left. He considered pressing on through the Domain and into the Botanical Gardens, but the fine day had brought out shoals of mothers and babies, old-timers and gooey-eyed young couples. Dexter liked his open spaces uninhabited.

The sight of the young lovers brought other matters to mind. He felt a stirring of excitement at the thought of his date with Eliza tonight. Across the park, the landmark bulk of David Jones, Sydney's foremost department store, caught his eye. Eliza loved presents, was always especially loving after receiving one. That ought to be the right place to find a gift for her. He shouldered his way through the heavy swing doors and into the perfumed hush of the cosmetics hall. He wrinkled his nose at the thick miasma that greeted him. Jeez, what a whiff! And row after row of sheilas all dressed up in nurses' white, ready to dispense their different powders and potions. How was a bloke to choose?

'You look lost, sir. Can I be of any assistance?'

It was the accent he noticed first, the slow familiar Queensland drawl a welcome contrast to the rapid Sydney 'Cockney'. Then he took in the eyes — Morning Glory blue — the leonine mass of sun-burnished tawny hair, kissable mouth and voluptuous hourglass figure. She wore a provocative black sheath dress, its draped bodice emphasising the abundance of her breasts. He was puzzled by the outfit, which even he could see was for evening wear, and by the number she wore on a card attached by elastic to one wrist: 54.

'Stone the crows,' he said, after a long up and down look, 'are there fifty-three more like you at home?'

She flung back her head and laughed. He liked the things it did for her barely restrained figure, but even more he liked the sound itself. It was free and uninhibited. Fancy get-up or not, this little ripper was a country girl and he just bet she knew how to enjoy herself around a man.

'It's the dress number,' she explained. 'I'm a mannequin, paid to wander round the store promoting model dresses from the top floor. This is style number 54. Do you like it?'

'I like what's in it better,' he said frankly, and was rewarded with another ripple of full-throated laughter. 'Tell you what — since you look so good in it, I'll buy it for you.'

She obviously didn't take him seriously. 'What's a Queensland boy doing in a place like this?' she asked, wiping tears of merriment from her amazing blue eyes.

'Feeling like a spare part at this minute! But really I'm looking for some fancy smellies to take back home.' He glanced down at his dusty elastic-sided boots and beaten-up moleskins, deliberately playing up the country boy impression. 'I don't suppose you could help me choose, miss?'

'I think that could be arranged,' she said. And, with a demure 'Follow me, sir', she led him forward to the first counter.

'The lady you're buying for, sir — is she young or old?' There was real interest in the mannequin's lovely face.

''Bout your age.'

There was a flash of naked jealousy in her eyes. 'And does she favour light floral scents like this ...?' She squirted a jet of perfume on the underside of one wrist and held it up for him to sniff, provocatively close to her breasts. He bent his head, feeling the wave of scented warmth flowing off her blue-veined skin.

'Jeez, no! Smells like mothballs,' he said to prolong the game. 'Tell me, what would you favour yourself, Miss — ?'

'Linita Tyrone,' she said, in her slow husky voice, 'and I'd favour something a little more exotic. Like this, perhaps?'

She sprayed perfume on the other wrist, but chose to take her time about raising it for his inspection. The assistant behind the counter, effectively cut out by Linita's control of the situation, watched goggle-eyed as the horny-handed bushie actually caught hold of the mannequin's wrist. As he bent his head over it in that disgusting old hat, the assistant could have sworn she saw him press his mouth to Miss Tyrone's pulse point.

Linita's eyelids fluttered for a moment as the man's lips pressed the sensitive skin at her wrist, setting her nerve endings on fire.

'H-How was that?' she enquired, a little less sure of her ground now. He really was remarkably self-assured for a country boy.

'Very nice. But I don't care for the scent,' he told her, poker-faced. 'What else have you got to offer?'

To hell with it, Linita decided. He was by far the most

exciting man she'd met since coming to the city, and she was damned if she was going to let him slip through her fingers. 'I really shouldn't be saying this ...' She paused, letting the tip of her tongue just show behind the cushioned softness of her lower lip.

'C'mon. I'm broad-minded.'

'Your best bet's the French Perfumery Shop in King Street. They have so many exclusive lines. I don't suppose you know where that is, though?'

'Well, I s'pose I could find it,' he began doubtfully. It was about three minutes' walk away, he knew, but the minx had given him the perfect opening. 'You wouldn't happen to have a dinner break coming up, Miss Tyrone? Maybe you could show me the way?'

The interested onlookers rolled their eyes at the country solecism. Dinner, indeed! But it didn't seem to have fazed Miss Tyrone who, they remembered, came from somewhere outlandish herself.

'As a matter of fact I usually take my dinner break around now,' she said breathlessly. 'If you could wait — say, ten minutes? Just while I take this dress back up to Models — I'll meet you at the staff entrance in Market Street. How's that?'

'Bonzer! See you there.'

He watched her take the lift up, calculating he'd have at least twenty minutes by the time she'd changed and fixed her hair and make-up. He gave her five minutes to return the dress, then Dexter, too, took the lift to the top floor.

He was outside by the Market Street entrance when she arrived, but surprised Linita by having a cab waiting alongside.

'King Street's no distance,' she protested.

'Ah, skip that! I thought we'd have a meal together, somewhere special.'

'And where's that?' she asked, getting into the cab.

'My place. You on for that?'

She raised her eyebrows, but didn't say no. 'What about

your friend's perfume?' she remembered, as the taxi turned east.

'Forget her. I already have.'

He gave her a long lingering smile that made her blush and cross her legs until she felt his eyes openly assessing them as well. She felt much less confident now that she was actually in the back of a cab with him. He hadn't, she realised, told her so much as his name.

'Where's your hotel?' she asked nervously as they swept through King's Cross.

'You'll see. Turn off on the left here — saves time,' he told the driver. Sydney cabbies were a notoriously bull-headed bunch but this one, a huge Yugoslav, meekly nodded. Linita's eyes widened as they cruised through wide streets of gracious detached houses, Federation or more recent, each set back in its own sizeable garden.

'But — what are we doing here? This is just for rich people,' she blurted out.

He smiled and patted her hand as the car pulled to a halt. 'Sweetheart, I may not look it, but I *am* rich. This is my home. D'you like it?'

She climbed out of the cab in a dream. A waterfront home on Darling Point? The mysterious man who looked like a down-at-heel ringer wasn't just rich, he must be a millionaire. What had she got herself into?

The cabbie handed over a flat box wrapped in David Jones paper, and Dexter paid him off. As they walked up the gravel path to the front door, it opened before them.

'Lunch for two on the terrace, Maria,' Dexter told the housemaid. 'And — no hurry, eh?'

They waited at the foot of a long curving flight of stairs while the maid clicked down the tiled entry hall and out of sight in the kitchen beyond. Linita felt trapped in the pale blue beam of the man's eyes, drawn like a moth to a candle-flame.

'Are you coming upstairs with me?' he asked, raising one thick black brow.

She stamped her foot, outraged by his presumption. 'I am not! How can I when you haven't even introduced yourself?'

Linita's face flamed as she realised what she had unwittingly revealed. Not that she didn't want to, just that she didn't like to until she knew his name! She was no stranger to men, and she wanted this one so much her legs were shaking. But the situation, and his infuriating assumption that she would dance to his tune, were so strange that she felt scared and out of her depth.

He slid his arms round her. 'I'm sorry,' he said contritely, and pressed the side of his lean, stubbled face against her cheek. 'It's just, from the moment I saw you I knew you were my kind of woman. You've got guts, you've got style and the most kissable mouth — but you're right. A gentleman should always introduce himself first. I'm Dexter Randolph. Now, are you coming upstairs with me? There's something I want you to model again ... afterwards.'

Linita's glorious smile lit up her face like the sun. 'Hello, Dexter Randolph,' she said. 'Hell, yes, I'll go upstairs with you,'

They were every bit as good together as he'd known they would be. Linita had an open, unashamed sensuality that perfectly complemented his skill and vigour. Like fire mixed with air, they flared to new heights with each fresh assault on each other's senses. It was four o'clock before she thought to look at her watch.

'Oh God, they'll sack me!' she moaned, and sprang up in the bed.

He pulled her back to him. 'Call them and tell them you're through. I'll look after you from now on. Besides, you can't go now. What would the servants think?'

For the first time that afternoon, she felt abashed.

'They've made lunch for you,' he finished solemnly.

She pounced on him, straddling his lean hard strength with her golden thighs and pummelling his black-haired chest with her fists. 'Seducer! Kidnapper! Insatiable brute!' she yelled.

His hands came up to cup and caress the pale globes of her breasts.

'And you love me for it, don't you?'

'Of course not, bighead!'

'I don't know about my head, but ... ah, Linita, you certainly know how to do things to a man.'

She moved above him expertly, drawing him deep into her warm silken depths for the fourth time that afternoon. As she stared down at the fierce smile on his face, she shivered with excitement and superstition. Dexter was everything she wanted in a man but all this had happened too easily. Somewhere along the line she knew she would pay for the happiness he brought her.

At Dexter's prompting Linita gave up her mannequin's job. She'd never seen it as more than a stopgap, anyway. Ideally she wanted to work as a photographic model for newspapers and women's magazines and advertisements, but it was so hard to get started in that world. Once it became known that she was the living-in mistress of the formidable Dexter Randolph, though, all sorts of doors opened to her and she acquired an agent, a portfolio of studio shots, and her first job, smiling and holding a new brand of toothpaste in a poster campaign. When that was a success, more offers came flooding in.

'But don't take on too much, sweetie,' Dexter told her. 'You must always look ravishing for our guests, don't forget. I want them to remember the house, the tucker and the hostess as the very best in town.'

It disturbed her sometimes, the way he seemed to think of her as part of the ambience, a beautiful ornament who walked and talked but obviously wasn't expected to feel.

Or not nearly so strongly as she did.

Linita had been under no illusions when she accepted Dexter's invitation to give up her job and live with him in the Darling Point house. He hadn't offered marriage, and in many ways their relationship was businesslike. Her side of the deal was to run his house, charm his friends, warm his bed and be in every way the perfect uncomplaining companion. In return, she could expect to order exclusive clothes from Madame Rocher, and hats from Henrietta LaMotte. In the week she lived at Yarrabbee Road, and they weekended at Dexter's cottage on Church Point or in the homes of friends with similar retreats on the other side of the Barrenjoey Peninsula. She loved the lifestyle, joining Dexter in the early morning surf which pounded up on to the crystalline orange sand of Palm Beach. Afterwards they'd join friends for drinks and lunch from a hamper in the unpretentious weatherboard building that housed the beach's prestigious Cabbage Tree Club.

It was a mark of considerable social acclaim to belong to the club, a feather in Linita's cap even to visit it, but as the first euphoria of being Dexter's constant companion faded, she realised that her acceptance by the smart rich set could only ever be conditional. For as long as Dexter was interested, his friends would pretend to be. But if he ever tired of her ...

Some of the female side of his acquaintanceship didn't even pretend for long. Eliza Haydon, furious at his defection, went out of her way to find out Linita's background, or lack of one. Ingenuously responding to Eliza's show of interest, Linita told her how she'd been born and brought up on a sugar-cane farm just outside Townsville where her father had been killed in an accident when she was only six. He'd been Irish and a regular charmer. Her mother missed him sadly and there'd been a string of 'uncles' before, during the war, her mother became notoriously popular with the American fly-boys stationed there. After her mother's death, to escape nasty small-minded gossip, Linita had come to Sydney and worked in the cosmetics hall of David Jones until a manager had spotted her potential and promoted her to mannequin.

'The banana-bending nobody actually seemed proud of working in a shop!' Eliza broadcast among her bitchy friends. For months afterwards the crueller ones would loudly consult Linita as to whether David Jones stocked their particular favourite brand of stockings or powder or nail polish, as 'After all, dear, you should know.'

When Linita realised they were poking fun at her origins, she tearfully confided in Dexter, but he didn't seem to understand her misery.

'Ah, pay no attention to them — bunch of jealous cats! Their husbands think you're great, Linita. A real looker. They're always asking me where I found you.'

And she would smile and try to mask the hurt she felt at his insensitivity, the way he saw everything about her as in some way reflecting the greater glory that was Dexter Randolph. For all that she loved him, she had few illusions about him.

She had a natural gift for having fun and enjoying life, whatever the surroundings. She enjoyed leading the Sydney high life with Dexter, dressed to the nines and exchanging small-talk with his powerful cronies, but on the rare days when they were neither working nor socialising, she liked nothing better than to sweep him off on impromptu excursions around the city.

They'd leave behind his flashy imported white Mercedes sports to catch a tram to Bondi where they'd watch the daredevil antics of the bronzed musclebound surfers chasing waves. Linita could hold her own in the fancy clubs and restaurants Dexter patronised — they were greeted by name in Prince's and Romano's — but on their days out she was just as pleased to be entertained to traditional beach tucker: shakes and Cola floats in the milk bars, gigantic helpings of fish and chips or a floater — a meat pie swimming in a green lake of mushy peas — served up in a beachside café.

Dexter had started to dabble in horse racing, and had invested in a string of half a dozen or so. In November they'd fly to Melbourne for the Gold Cup, where the female racegoers dressed to kill. Linita was just as happy to put on a cotton dress and mingle with the crowds on ordinary race days at Randwick, or else accompany Dexter through the moleskin- and akubra-clad farmers who came to Sydney each year for the agricultural highlight, the Royal Easter Show.

Once they took a ferry from Circular Quay to Balmain, a narrow promontory jutting into the harbour, surrounded by dockyards and full of narrow streets. The iron roofs and wood or sandstone housefronts were painted in a hotch-potch of old colonial colours — cream, brown, green, ochre — and the mark of a house that was a cut above the rest was an intricate cast iron lacework veranda screen, crafted from leftover ship's ballast.

It was here that Linita had lived on her arrival in Sydney, boarding with a fiercely respectable wharfie's widow in a tiny Federation house in Louisa Street. Mrs O'Leary, her former landlady, was delighted to receive Linita and her 'young man', and entertained them to tea and pumpkin scones in her front parlour. It overlooked a pocket-handkerchief-sized lawn, lined with bottlebrush trees and camellias, on which Mrs O'Leary continued the tradition her boarder had begun of laying out bread for the neighbourhood's raucous flocks of mynahs and kooka-burras.

With Linita, any outing was fun. Dexter frequently congratulated himself for giving way to impulse and inviting her to live with him the day they had met. That, for him, was as far as it went. Marriage was definitely not on the agenda.

'What is it anyway — a ring and a piece of paper?' he'd reply when Linita hinted at what was increasingly on her mind. 'Would it change the way we live? You're having fun, aren't you? Don't rock the boat, Linita.'

And if she sulked or pressed or tried to wheedle him some more, he'd retreat into a stony silence so profound she felt she might as well not be there.

Try as she might, there was something inside him she feared she'd never reach. It was something in his Queensland background, to do with his family there, which had obviously hurt him badly. The family station was called Yelonga, she knew, and he'd speak with open affection of an aboriginal stockman called Wally, and of his neighbour, Mal Gregson. But of his brother, Lucas, and sister-in-law, he never spoke if he could help it. The exceptions were when he announced his twice-yearly inspection of the station.

The first time he mentioned this, she asked if she could go too. She was quite unprepared for the fury of his reaction.

'What the hell use would you be out there? They don't make their living shopping and giving dinner parties on Yelonga, you know.'

'I was raised on a farm,' she reminded him gently. She wasn't always so forbearing; positively enjoyed some of their quarrels which had the habit of ending up in bed. But on the subject of Yelonga, she sensed it would be unwise to push Dexter too hard.

He recognised the effort she was making, and forced a smile. 'I'm sorry, sweetheart. That was uncalled for. But you wouldn't like it, cross my heart. There's nothing there, nothing at all.'

He'd go alone, and return brimful of anecdotes about Wally, whom he'd transferred there from Maroonda, but on the subject of the station manager and his wife, silence.

The first time he talked voluntarily about them was when he returned from a summer trip in 1958. Linita came home from a photographic session for *Australian Woman's Weekly*, dog tired from a day posing under the lights in a

212

succession of heavy woollen cardies. She switched on the light in Dexter's study, his favourite room in the house and the one she naturally gravitated to in his absence. She had not expected him home for another day, and jumped when the lamplight revealed him stretched out on the sofa with a glass in his hand.

'I'm an uncle,' he told her thickly. 'Got to Yelonga this time and found I'm an uncle. After all these years.'

'You don't seem very pleased about it.' She wrinkled her nose at the smell of whisky on his breath. 'Is it a boy or a girl?'

'Boy — Chip. Lucas calls him that because he's a chip off the old block. Christ, poor Lucinda, two of them! He drinks, you know. Lucas drinks. Have I told you that before?'

She sensed her opportunity and sat down on the sofa, cradling his head in her lap. 'No, you haven't. That must be difficult for you all, especially Lucinda.'

'He's made her life hell.' Dexter's voice was raw with emotion. 'This time, while she was lying in bed with a week-old baby, I caught Lucas with Clara — one of the aboriginal girls. My brother the gin jockey! Still, makes a change from rum.'

'Dexter, don't be crude.'

'I think Lucinda knows, though she didn't say anything. She should have divorced him years ago, but she won't — Catholic, you see.'

'Like me,' Linita murmured.

Hurt lanced through her, hearing him speak like this of another woman, but at the same time there was a kind of reassurance in knowing that the someone else in Dexter's life was his brother's wife. She was virtuous and faithful and positively no threat to Linita, only to Dexter's peace of mind. Lovingly she smoothed back the crisp black curls from the widow's peak on his forehead and took the glass from his unresisting fingers.

'Thanks, sweetie. You're good for me, you know.'

213

She knew, and the fact that he admitted it was a good sign. The next time he was due to visit Yelonga, she braced herself for his opposition and told him this time she was definitely going too.

'Ah, sweetheart, be reasonable, it's a rough and ready place. They don't go a bundle on visitors,' he said uneasily.

She put her hands on her hips and faced him down. 'Lucinda's there, isn't she? An outback woman not welcome visitors? You'll be telling me next they've flying pigs on Yelonga!'

Before she could anger him outright by challenging him, she switched to cajolery. He was sitting in his favourite deep leather armchair in the study. Linita sat at his feet and rested her head against his knees.

'Oh, come on, Dexter. I haven't been out of town since you took me ski-ing in the Snowies. It's my State, too, you know. Let me go to Queensland with you — please?' She looked up at him and read the indecision on his face. 'I could make myself very useful.' Languorously her hand crept along the powerful corded muscle of his thigh. She knelt before him and unclasped his heavy buckled belt, deftly freeing him. 'Say I can come,' she murmured, running one finger up and down his shaft.

He groaned. 'All right, you witch. I'm going to regret this, but you can come. Just so long as I can — now.'

If only, Linita thought, as she arched her neck gracefully forward, she was making as much progress on the subject of marriage.

Outwardly Yelonga was as Linita had expected, a low white bush-built structure dwarfed by the limitless Queensland skies. It was the Wet season when they arrived, though with a lighter rainfall than in previous years the ground had not flooded or bogged. As the plane landed on the station strip, the sun was out and the bush was wearing its freshest, greenest face.

Linita breathed in deeply. 'It smells wonderful,' she said. 'You don't get that in Sydney.'

But Dexter didn't answer; he was in one of his distant preoccupied moods.

Inside the homestead she swiftly became aware of the undercurrents. Lucinda, pretty but faded to Linita's way of thinking, welcomed her coolly and made it plain she expected Dexter and his unmarried girlfriend to sleep in separate rooms, though she obviously knew they lived together in the city. Linita was exasperated to see Dexter go along with this without a murmur.

'It's her home, sweetie. We have to respect her way of doing things.'

Lucas welcomed Linita rather more warmly. Dexter had described him as a drinker but she saw no evidence of this; merely a fleshy, once handsome, man with greying hair and unfathomable dark eyes.

The restraint between the brothers was echoed by the coolness between husband and wife. Lucinda made a show of deferring to Lucas but saved her warmth for the child, a sturdy six months, and for Dexter.

Although she knew she was being foolish and that the dutiful Lucinda was no real threat to her, Linita lay awake deep into the night, straining to hear the lightest footfall on the bare wooden boards outside. She heard nothing but the night sounds — toads, grasshoppers, the cry of a hunting frogmouth — and finally fell into a deep sleep from which she did not wake until gone nine.

'Dexter said to leave you,' Lucinda said as she served breakfast for the second time, with a faintly weary air. 'He seemed to think you'd be tired after the journey.'

'Oh, not really,' Linita protested. 'In fact, I was looking forward to getting out today, maybe doing a bit of bush walking.'

'I'm sorry, that's out of the question,' Lucinda said stiffly. 'We can't spare a man to go with you, and visitors mustn't expect to head off unsupervised — it's wild country out there, you know.'

Linita resented the inference that she was a know-nothing townee; resented too the way Lucinda made no attempt to join her even in a companionable cup of tea, simply sat by with folded hands while Linita finished her breakfast of fresh mango from the garden, toast and rosella jam.

'Guess I'll just have to amuse myself,' she said finally. 'Any idea when Dexter will be back?'

'Late, I should think. He and Wally are flying over the western paddocks today, doing a head count. I have to see to Chip. Why don't you ask Lucas to show you round? He's in the office.'

Lucas seemed delighted at the diversion, although his desk was almost bare of papers. He conducted her on a tour of the homestead, differentiating the pioneer parts from later additions. He steered clear of the aboriginal settlement on the other side of the billabong, Linita noticed. She was particularly interested in the station horses, especially the thoroughbreds.

'Do you think I could take one out?' she asked hopefully. 'I am experienced.'

'I can see that.' His eyes lingered appreciatively on the heavy swell of her breasts beneath her check blouse. 'Quite a juicy little piece, in fact. Don't know what my brother's doing, leaving you alone.' He didn't lay a finger on her, but something vicious in his face disturbed her as much as if he had.

'Dexter's here to work,' she said tightly, and turned back to the house.

'And don't we all know it,' he snapped, catching her up. '*I'm* supposed to be the manager here, but between him and that jumped-up coon stockman I don't get a look in. It's not right, setting an abo over me. Have you met Wally yet?'

'No.'

'You will. If you want to borrow a horse, you'll have to

216

speak to him about it. Fusses over them like a bloody mother hen, the sanctimonious black bastard! Why did Dexter have to cut him in to Maroonda? The bastard's richer than Croesus. Is it right, eh? That Dexter should favour him over his own family?'

Lucas's face had flushed to a high colour and was twitching with rage. 'Like I said, I haven't met Wally yet,' she said diplomatically. 'Maybe I'll go and find Lucinda. See if she needs any help with Chip.'

'She won't,' he said sourly. 'Nothing and nobody comes between her and that kid.' And he stumped off back to the office and his highly polished empty desk.

Dexter came back in time for dinner, dusty and sweat-soaked but in high good humour after a day on the land. He knocked on Linita's door.

'Well, I can see *you* had a busy day,' he said, grinning at the pile of discarded magazines by the bedside.

'Oh, I missed you!' She ran to him and pressed her face against the open neck of his shirt, drinking in the warm animal scent of him.

He laughed and held her at arm's length. 'We're staying a week, and this is what one day's done for you? I'll be lucky to get out alive.'

She twisted in his grasp and reached out to unbutton his shirt.

'Oh no you don't,' he said, smartly opening the door. 'Dinner's in twenty minutes. Mustn't keep Lucinda waiting.'

She could barely restrain herself from saying, 'Damn *her*, you're mine now!' but she knew better than to badmouth their hostess. She waited until Dexter had closed the door behind him before pumelling the pillow with her fists.

Things looked less grim in the morning. Linita got up at first pearly light to see the men off in the plane. Dexter took the opportunity to introduce her to Wally, a slight, smiling aborigine in late middle age who treated her with old-world courtesy.

'Boss say you like horses, missus?'

'Oh, yes. Lucas said you might have a mount for me?'

Wally glanced at the rapidly rising sun, then at Dexter. 'Ah, she's apples. Plenty of time to find Linita a safe old nag, stop her getting so bored.'

To her chagrin, Wally ignored the thoroughbreds and picked her out an elderly black workhorse, a giant of eighteen hands. He explained that she should ride only in the two paddocks that abutted on to the house, and should keep a fence within sight at all times. The horse was steady and good-tempered; she should have no problem with him.

'He's a bit old, isn't he? And so big.'

'Old horse is wise horse,' Wally told her, 'and still plenty strong. You tell Samson saddle him after breakfast, orright?'

When she still looked less than enthralled, he explained patiently, 'You need safe horse, missus. Dusty knows this country. Anything happen to you, he come find help.'

'What if something happens to him?'

'You sit tight, missus, and we find you. No account you wander away.'

'But how would you find me?'

'No worries, sweetie. Wally's the best tracker for a thousand miles,' Dexter said, clapping him on the back. 'Got to go, Linita. See you this evening.' He kissed her goodbye. Minutes later she stood watching as the plane climbed into the pink-flushed morning sky and dwindled from sight.

Though she was nervous at first to be riding the bush alone, over the next few days Linita explored the home paddocks thoroughly. Essentially untamed, and teeming with wildlife besides peacefully grazing cattle, every acre brought something new and strange: a flock of emus, startled by her horse, racing away over a plain dotted with white lilies, or a gang of tiny chirping rock wallabies, bright-eyed and inquisitive, who emerged from the cliffs beside a waterfall and tamely took pieces of sandwich from her hand.

In the evenings, after a formally served but badly cooked dinner with Lucinda and Lucas, Dexter would take Linita over the grass to Wally's quarters in the old governess's wing. Out of deference to her, the two men did not talk station business but instead yarned about the old days on Yelonga, and their pioneering of Maroonda. There was electric light in the main house now, but Wally preferred to do without. His small veranda was lit only by the stars and a single kerosene lamp, and there they sat laughing and talking well into the night.

Wally's hands were never idle, Linita saw. He was constantly busy carving strange half-animal, half-human figures out of pieces of wood, or plaiting green kangaroo hide into one of the beautifully crafted stockwhips for which he was famous. When she admired one, he gave it to her, and she knew without Dexter's telling her that this was a mark of approval. Late at night, after they had talked themselves hoarse despite the mugs of strong black tea Wally brewed, Dexter would walk her back across the grass to the house, where they would stand kissing for long breathless minutes until reluctantly they went to their separate beds.

If only Lucinda were not so dog in the manger on the subject of their sharing a room! Newly bronzed by the outback sun, and casually dressed in stockmen's gear, Linita found Dexter intensely desirable and longed to be alone with him. It looked as though her chance had come when a message from the Randolph Enterprises Townsville office was relayed to Yelonga by radio. Dexter was needed there urgently to sign a contract. He offered to take Linita along for the ride. Townsville was her birthplace, after all.

'Will we stay overnight?' she asked eagerly as they took off early in the Cessna.

He laughed and patted her leg. 'Could be — depends

how long the meeting lasts. You'd better pray it's a tough one, sweetie.'

Linita spent the morning walking the familiar streets in an odd, dislocated mood. For twenty years this had been her town and she'd expected to feel a sense of homecoming as the barren red bulk of Castle Hill loomed into view. Once upon a time she'd thought Flinders Street, with its regimental row of tropical palms and colonial architecture, the height of grandeur. As a farm kid, her idea of the high life had been a day trip by ferry to Magnetic Island in the Coral Sea. Townsville had been the limit of her horizon then. Five years later, so much had changed for her. There was a city gloss upon her now. It showed in her made-to-measure clothes and imported shoes, in the carefully manicured nails and expensively styled hair. She'd docked her Queensland accent as well as she could; knew how to behave in the best circles. But, despite all these changes, her essential ambition remained the same: to find a strong, special man and live happily ever after as his wife. In Dexter she had found the man, but the marriage part was a long time coming.

She checked her watch, not wanting to be late for him. He'd told her to come to the office at midday and check his progress. If she hurried, there should just be time for what she had in mind. Linita pulled a headscarf from her bag and tied it over her glorious mane of hair. Then she slipped inside the Sacred Heart Cathedral and knelt to pray with tightly screwed up eyes, as she had done since a child: Oh God, let him come to his senses soon. Let him marry me, please.

When she arrived, on time, at Dexter's tin and timber office in Victoria Street, he was waiting impatiently outside with a car and driver.

'At last! C'mon, hurry it up. If we get back to Yelonga at once I can finish the stock reports with Wally.'

'But I thought the meeting was an all-day one. I thought we'd be staying the night.'

He held open the car door for her. 'No point sticking around here while there's still work to do on Yelonga. Cheer up, it's only for another day or two.'

Linita had to dig her nails into the palms of her hands to stop herself from bursting into tears. Sometimes it seemed that Dexter put everything and everyone else before her: business, Yelonga, Wally, Lucinda . . .

'Why can't Lucas go through the old stock reports?' she grumbled. 'After all, he's manager.'

'In name only. I've trusted Wally's judgment a hundred times. Lucas has never given me a single reason to trust his.'

'Perhaps because you don't let him? I can see he's not the easiest of blokes, but do you think it's wise to put Wally over him as your watchdog? Luke's eaten up with jealousy, reckons he could easily do as good a job.'

'He's up himself! And listen to me, Linita. I don't tell you how to dress yourself up like a Christmas tree and make sheep's-eyes at a camera, so don't you tell me how to run my business — all right?'

The driver was eagerly drinking in every word, relishing the boss's put-down of his fancy sheila. Linita shrank back in her seat, utterly humiliated. She hadn't meant to interfere in Dexter's affairs but, woman-like, she could sense real trouble brewing between Lucas and Wally. Dexter, in his arrogance, was refusing to avert it.

She did not speak on the flight back, longing only to take a bath and change out of the constricting city clothes she had foolishly chosen to wear for her return to Townsville. They arrived back at the homestead in the still of the early afternoon. It was unusually quiet around the yards, she noticed. Wally must have started the mustering camp-out he'd mentioned. Inside the house, all was silence. Dexter and Linita stood in the shade of the roofed court-yard, and he called for Lucinda. They were greeted by Clara instead.

'Missus don' feel good. She gonna bed s'afternoon.'

'Is my brother in the office?'

'Yess, boss. Me fetchem?'

'No, that's all right, Clara. Just bring us a jug of lemon water, will you?

Linita slumped in the hammock, fanning herself listlessly, while Dexter lounged in the squatter's chair. She broke the silence first.

'It's so quiet today.'

'Hmm. Could be our chance.'

She met his eyes and blushed. 'Do you mean it? What about Lucinda?'

'You heard Clara — what the eye doesn't see, eh? Sweetheart, I'm sorry. Let's make up.'

Her heart began to pound and her nipples stiffened visibly beneath the fine silk of her dress. Damn him! He could always have that effect on her with just a look or a few of the right words. 'Your room or mine?' she said huskily.

'Mine, I think. It's further from Lucinda's.'

'Bring me a glass of lemon water when you come.' She bent to kiss him, allowing the fullness of her breasts to brush against him. 'I'll be waiting.'

It was hot and close in Dexter's room with the flyscreens closed and the curtains drawn against the heat. The paddle-shaped blades of the old-fashioned ceiling fan set up a sluggish breeze, and Linita gratefully stripped off her travel-stained clothes and stood beneath it, cooling off. She washed as best as she could, using the basin and jug in the washstand, then lay on Dexter's bed in a fever of impatience.

She heard footsteps and a voice that was deeper than Clara's. Restless with frustration she switched off the fan and listened, hoping that Dexter would get away and come to her soon. It was Lucas who was speaking, she realised. He sounded pleased, as though something had put him in a good mood.

'Worthwhile trip?' he asked Dexter.

'You could say that.' Dexter never divulged business details.

'How was Townsville?'

'How d'you think — hot. I'm beat, Luke. Think I'll catch a few hours sleep.'

'Where's Linita? Does she need anything?'

'In her room, sleeping. Best leave her. See you at dinner.' Linita heard his chair scrape against the flagstones as he got up to leave.

'Dexter, before you go, there's something I have to tell you.' The apologetic note in Lucas's voice masked something else, she was sure. 'It's Wally. I'm afraid you're not going to like this, but I told him to go.'

'You did what?' Dexter's voice was disbelieving. 'Who the bloody hell gave you the right?'

'I am supposed to be manager here.'

Dexter laughed derisively. 'Man or manager, Wally's worth ten of you! I only let you stay for Lucy's sake.'

Linita knew that already, but the words stung her almost as much as they did Lucas. The gloves were off now. His voice was jagged with resentment.

'Do you think I don't know that? Do you think every time you've come up here — listening to *his* opinion, asking *him* what's going on on our family's land — you haven't rubbed my nose deeper in it? All this is your fault, Dexter! You encouraged that black bastard, gave him ideas above his station —'

'You speak about my friend like that once more, and so help me I won't be responsible for my actions! Now, tell me what Wally's supposed to have done and I'll go and sort this whole bloody mess out.'

Lucas's voice was smooth and silky, but Linita could hear the throb of excitement beneath. 'You won't want him back, Dexter. Not when you hear what he called my wife.'

Dexter sounded incredulous. 'Wally, insult a woman? You must be off your head.'

'He insulted Lucinda's good name in front of witnesses — Samson, Peter and Mick.'

'I don't believe you.' Dexter's voice was sharp enough to cut stone. 'So come on, convince me. What did he say that was so bad you took it upon yourself to sack him?'

'Look, he'd been drinking. Maybe he went further than he meant to but he said the only reason I was still on the station was because my wife had been the boss's whore. The others were looking on. I couldn't have Wally speak like that in front of the men, so I told him to roll his swag.'

'When is this supposed to have happened?'

'Mid-morning. Didn't take him long to get his things together. The men will know where he was headed.'

'Where are they?'

'On the way to Ten Mile, mustering. Wally's late there this —'

His brother's voice was like a whiplash. 'Don't badmouth him! Don't dare say another thing against him. I'm going after him. Getting his side of the story.'

Dexter's voice grew fainter. He was obviously going around the side of the house to the stable yard.

'Are you mad? He's gone bush. You'll never find him.'

The only reply was the jingling of harness and Dexter's low whistle to attract his favourite stockhorse.

Lucas laughed softly to himself. 'It's no good. Wally's gone. He's gone for good.'

Linita, listening unseen, recoiled from the note of satisfaction in his voice.

When it was too dark to continue the search, Dexter returned to the station. He refused to eat with Lucas and a puzzled Lucinda. Linita brought food to his room, but he barely touched it.

'You heard Luke's story? It doesn't add up. Wally's Mission-educated. He signed the pledge as a picanninny. I have never heard him use bad language. I can't believe he'd say a thing like that about Lucinda and me.'

'There's no truth in it, then?'

'Of course not! All right, so I was in love with her once, but surely to God anyone could see Lucinda's not that type of woman.'

Linita wondered what type of woman that made *her*, but now was not the time to have things out, not with Dexter puzzled and hurting.

'I've known Wally since I was a kid. None of this makes sense,' he repeated.

'I expect you'll find him in the morning,' she soothed. 'Or couldn't you go after the musterers? Maybe they'll know which way he was heading.'

'I don't need the men to tell me that. If Wally's gone walkabout he'll head for Maroonda. Damn it, he owns ten per cent of it. That's where I'll look tomorrow.'

Despite Dexter's continued sweeps with the plane and radioed instructions to Maroonda to contact him if Wally showed up, there was no trace.

They left Yelonga four days later, Dexter silent and sick at heart. He had hired another pilot and instructed him to keep up the search. Dexter himself was needed back in the city.

Linita was not sorry to depart. Yelonga was beautiful but had her sinister side too. She kept her secrets well.

On their first night back in Sydney, Dexter woke from a dream in the middle of the night.

'Linita, are you awake?'

She was. He'd been shifting so violently in his sleep, sometimes calling out, that he had disturbed her. 'What is it?'

'It's Wally. We can call off the search.'

'Have you remembered something, some place he might be?'

His face was shrouded in darkness but she could hear the catch in his voice. 'Yes, I've remembered something. I was just a kid when Wally told me that one day he would join his ancestors. I didn't know what he was talking about, thought he meant in another settlement or something.

225

Then Grandpa explained it was Wally's way of saying one day he'd die. I cried and said he mustn't go, and he promised me that before he did he'd come to me, wherever I was, and tell me goodbye. I dreamed I saw him tonight. At first I didn't recognise him under the tribal paint, but it was Wally all right, come to say goodbye. He's with his ancestors now, Linita. I may never learn what happened, but I do know I won't see him again.'

Even in the darkness, he hid his face from her, turning away from her in his grief. She did not try to shake him from his belief. The peasant blood of her forebears was too strong for that. Besides, it was not an argument Dexter wanted from her, but the comfort of another body warm against his. She slipped her arms around his waist. When his shaking subsided, she said. 'You're not alone, Dexter. You've got me. You'll always have me.'

There was no answer. Only the regular rise and fall of his chest to tell her he had slipped away from her into sleep.

After the shock of Wally's disappearance, Dexter withdrew from the social whirl and buried himself in work. Linita did not regret the loss of their active social life, much of which had bored her, but she missed the companionship they used to share. Dexter worked longer and longer hours, often refusing to stop for the weekend. When she protested, he would placate her by arranging for her and a girlfriend to go away together, staying for instance at the Hydro Majestic in Medlow Bath. The Edwardian hotel and spa was magnificently situated in the Blue Mountains, on the very brink of the Grand Canyon. It had health treatments, a casino and resident dance-band. If Dexter had been there with her, Linita would have had a good time.

Sometimes he'd hand her a large cheque for food and drink and tell her to entertain a group of her modelling friends at the Church Point house for the weekend. On her own, naturally. Dexter did not care for the photographers, stylists, models and journalists of the fashion and advertising worlds. He regarded the men with deep suspicion, referring to them as a bunch of shirtlifters, and thought the women grabby and hard. But Linita was a good scout, the perfect companion, and he imagined that by making these gestures he was keeping her happy. He was not, of course, but she knew better than to tax him with a long face and demands for attention.

At the start of the new decade, she realised with a shock that they'd been together now for three years. She was twenty-five, and, with her sunny outdoor good looks, at the peak of the Australian modelling profession.

'Not that it compares with working in France or England or America,' she told him wistfully one evening, after studying some of her imported fashion magazines. 'I mean, number one knitting pattern model for Australia doesn't have quite the same ring to it as house model for Christian Dior!'

'I don't know what you're worrying about,' he said, frowning at the snooty-looking models in French *Vogue*. 'Those aren't sheilas, they're stick insects! But tell me, sweetie, would you like a dress like that?'

'Would I!'

'Buy you one, then.'

'They're couture, Dexter — what do you mean? You're not going to Europe! Can I come?'

'I'm going to England, sweetie, on business. I may or may not need to go to France and Germany — depends how I get on with UCS.' She looked puzzled. 'United Consolidated Stores,' he explained patiently. 'They own the biggest chain of retail food stores in Britain. At the moment, Randolph Enterprises ships meat across to Britain, then has to arrange a sale. We pay for frozen storage while we're waiting, and negotiate a new price on

227

each consignment. Sometimes we do well out of it, sometimes not. Now, if I could arrange a link-up with a big chain like UCS, to supply all their fresh meat, Randolph Enterprises would be working with a fixed-price contract, and the buyers would arrange their own shipping and storage.'

She knew she was meant to comment admiringly on his business scheme but couldn't help herself. The mention of Europe was like a red rag to a bull.

'Take me with you, Dexter,' she begged. 'God, I'd give anything to see London — and Paris! You did say you were going to Paris?'

'Only if the UCS thing falls through. And they're in Manchester, for Christ's sake. Look, Linita, this isn't a glamorous world trip. This is business. You'd be bored stiff.'

'How can you say that? I could keep myself busy while you were in meetings —'

'— and bend my ear for me every night about how hard I'm working, and couldn't I take some time off and come shopping? No, thanks!'

She recoiled as if he had struck her, and he realised he had been unfair. Linita wasn't a whinger; she was the least demanding woman he knew, but for some reason he did not fully understand he did not want her along on this trip. He felt they'd been living too much in one another's pockets lately, most of it his fault since he'd put a stop to the socialising. But Linita was beginning to cling like lantana, her influence slowly creeping over every compartment of his life. She was hemming him in, and he didn't like the feeling.

He felt some time and space to himself was called for. He knew it would hurt her, since marriage was very much on her mind these days. Maybe, he rationalised, the separation would actually work to her advantage. If he missed her badly enough, among the new sights and experiences, that would prove once and for all that she was the one he ought to marry.

228

There was another reason for getting away: his deep lingering sadness over Wally. Dexter had not been back to Yelonga since the disappearance. Lucas and Lucinda were running things unaided now, and making a good job of it, according to the Randolph Enterprises station inspector. Lucinda had written to say that they were expecting another child in the summer of 1960 and would Dexter please confirm that Lucas was to continue as manager? The results were good enough to justify it, better than he had expected. There was no real reason to say no. Dexter had confirmed that he wanted them to stay on, but at the back of his mind there was still a nagging distrust of his brother. He shook his head. No use dwelling on unproductive thoughts.

'Linita, don't look like that,' he said, noticing her tears for the first time. Gently he stroked them away. 'You know I hate to see you cry, sweetheart. Another time you and me will go together, just for fun.'

'How long will you be gone?' she asked stiffly.

'Three months or so. A lot of that's travelling time.'

There was a feeling of dread in the pit of her stomach. A lot could happen in three months.

Linita waved him off bravely from the dockside. Dexter was travelling first class on the *Himalaya*. For comfort she took along her new dog, Mignonne, the little Sydney Silky that had been his parting gift.

'To remind you of me,' he'd said, handing over the tiny long-haired dog in a ribbon-tied box.

'As if I'll need reminding,' she sniffed, cuddling the dog close. 'Oh, Dexter, hurry home!'

In his first week in England he wanted to do just that. It was June, high summer over there, though he wouldn't have known it from the leaden skies, sharp breezes and cold continuous rain.

The Poms had a way of making him feel out of place,

229

too. They continually raised their eyebrows at his accent, though God knew it sounded as though they were talking round a mouthful of plums, and maddened him by always referring to him as 'our colonial friend'. It sounded so bloody patronising! What did they have to be so stuck up about, anyway? Their famous English countryside, for instance, what he had seen of it from the train on the way north, had been a big letdown. Everything here was small-scale. Little handkerchief-sized fields, and toytown farms at such regular intervals he wondered how people could stand having their neighbours so close. Even the sky looked lower.

The grim grey streets of Manchester in a rain-sodden summer were worse. Dexter, in his lightweight business suits and suede shoes, had never felt so cold and uncomfortable. It was with a feeling more of relief than triumph that he boarded the London train, his two weeks of negotiations with UCS successfully completed. The contract he had just signed promoted him to the first league of Australian cattle kings, up there with Kidman and the Vesteys. He knew he ought to be celebrating, but without Linita to whoop for joy and share the champagne, there didn't seem a lot of point. God, he really was missing her. There was no point sticking around, he decided. The next morning he would see about his passage home.

He'd booked a riverside suite at the Savoy. That afternoon, after he'd checked in, he decided to take a walk along the Embankment to stretch his legs. He climbed up to Hungerford Bridge for a better view along the river. The rain had stopped, and pale watery sunshine picked out the dome of St Paul's in one direction and the grimy but majestic façade of the Houses of Parliament in the other. There was a sense of weightiness and age about London that was necessarily missing from Australian cities — even Melbourne, whatever it might think. Dexter decided he liked it.

But there was exhilaration and excitement, too. A pretty

girl passed by, long hair swinging, arms and legs bared to the evening sun. Now the weather was smiling, every passer-by looked suddenly less shabby and careworn. What the hell, he thought. He was in London, the capital of the old country. The least he could do was give it a proper go.

Dexter believed the spirit of a place belonged in its people. Not for him the mindless slog of sightseeing. He leafed through his diary. Before he'd left Australia, friends and acquaintances had pressed upon him the names and addresses of virtually everyone they knew in England. Liverpool, Taunton, Newcastle ... most of them were no good to him here, but one name and address stood out.

'Taxi!' he shouted, and gave the cab-driver the Wilton Crescent address of Lord Reggie Rupert.

'Damn!' Caro Rupert exclaimed when the maid brought Dexter's card up to the drawing-room. Reggie was at his club for the first time since their disastrous French holiday, and she'd been looking forward to a peaceful evening alone. The last thing she felt up to was labouring over small-talk with some outlandishly-named colonial.

She looked at the card again. This was too much. It was a business one and inexpressibly vulgar, bearing as it did the company logo of a humpbacked cow. How extraordinary these Australians were! She frowned at her reflection in the mirror over the Adam fireplace and decided she could not be bothered to change. One quick duty drink, and her unwelcome visitor would be sent tactfully on his way.

To her surprise, she found she heartily regretted her decision not to look her best. No one could ever have mistaken Dexter for an English gentleman, but with his rugged, suntanned good looks and innate courtliness towards women, he was undeniably attractive. A pity about the frightful clothes and an accent you could have cut with a knife.

'Those cufflinks are pretty startling,' she commented, as the evening light glinted off what she took to be lumps of solid gold at his wrists.

'These? A bit of a souvenir, really. I picked them up off my first goldfield. Mining company missed it the first time round on Maroonda.'

'And that's your — station, d'you call them?'

'One of them, yeah. Not my biggest. That's in the Barkly Tablelands.'

'How many stations do you have?'

'Five outright. Two in Queensland, two in the Territories and one in Western Australia. And I've shares in quite a few more.'

'That must add up to an awful lot of acres.'

'Well, I don't really figure in acres, Lady Rupert. I tend to think in miles.'

'Goodness! And how many square miles do you own, Mr Randolph?'

''Bout fifteen thousand, at the last count.'

'But that's unbelievable! The size of whole countries.'

'That's why they call us cattle kings, though it's a bit of a stupid expression, if you ask me. We're just regular blokes at heart, Lady Rupert.'

'Caro, please. I can see we're going to be great friends, Dexter. What a pity Reggie isn't here, or I could have asked you to stay to dinner. It was a blessing really. He *was* handsome, but his conversation! Money, land, prize cows . . . now who did that remind her of?

'I'd like to meet his lordship. Maybe another time?' Dexter suggested.

This meeting had gone better than he'd hoped. He didn't fool himself that Caro's apparent friendliness was more than social, but he did admire the way she had so adroitly assumed an air of interest in him, and kept the conversational flow running smoothly.

He was impressed too by the negligent grandeur of their surroundings. The furnishings were slightly faded and

232

thinly scattered with white hairs from the two rat-like Siamese which lay entwined on a sofa. But the only place he'd seen furniture of this quality before was in a museum. Now here he was in a family drawing-room packed with the acquisitions of generation upon generation of wealth and privilege. Dexter, for all his riches, felt raw and unpolished by comparison. He was not used to feeling at a disadvantage and caught himself wondering if you could acquire Caro Rupert's particular skill, or if you were only born with it.

'Will you be in England long?' she was asking.

He hesitated. Only this morning he'd been thinking of booking his passage back.

'A week or two,' he said, refusing to dwell on thoughts of Linita and her loneliness.

'Splendid. Then you simply must join us one day next week for Royal Ascot. Reggie has a box, and all our friends drop in for lunch on one day or another. Now, let me see ...'

She flicked through the pages of a Morocco-bound diary and studied the list of names beside each date. Her eyes rested on one in particular and a slow smile crossed her face. Dexter Randolph really could not have arrived at a better time. Any hostess would welcome a wealthy and attractive single man, but Caro had something rather more important in mind than simply evening up her guest-list. She wanted to save a marriage.

The question currently uppermost in her mind was how to help her good friend Fiona Campbell. Even before Brinsley Hamilton's death, his wife Angelica had openly flaunted her affair with Fiona's randy husband. Now, with no husband to restrain her, she'd got her hooks properly into Beano Campbell, when everyone knew she couldn't possibly want him in the long-term.

It was common knowledge that poor old Brinsley had virtually bankrupted himself to satisfy her craving for luxury. Even when he came into his Scottish baronetcy,

Beano could never afford to support her in that style. The pity of it was that in the meantime he might very well wreck his marriage to Fiona for a woman who frankly wasn't worth it. Unless Angelica could be channelled towards a more worthwhile prospect, even as a purely temporary diversion ...

'It would be most awfully kind if you could come on Thursday,' Caro had told Dexter. 'We'd be thirteen at lunch otherwise, and Reggie would never forgive me.'

She omitted to point out that they were uneven in number because one of their dearest friends, Brinsley Hamilton, had recently drowned in a yachting accident.

When Dexter had finally gone, Caro called Angelica at Courtney Park. 'Just to confirm we'll be seeing you on Thursday ... Yes, wise of you, darling, to put a brave face on and be seen about so soon ... Yes, I know. Of *course* it's what he'd have wanted ... What? Oh, just the usual crowd, you know. And you'll have to forgive us, but we've asked a colonial friend ... No, surprisingly not too bad, and of course he owns half of Australia and lots of goldmines and things ... Well, that's very noble of you, Angelica. In that case, yes, I will put you next to him at lunch.'

Dexter couldn't understand it. He was dressed the same as all the other blokes in the box, and he spoke the same language, or nearly, but his fellow guests were making him feel like a fish out of water. Caro Rupert was as charming as before, and her portly husband gruffly welcoming, but the others ...

'Africa hand?' a man in dove-grey morning dress enquired, on catching sight of Dexter's suntan.

'Pardon?'

The man looked slightly appalled. 'The tan, you know. I wondered if you were just back from Africa.'

'No, Australia.'

The man's gaze slid to the flower in Dexter's buttonhole

and the corners of his mouth twitched uncontrollably. 'Ah, that explains it. Do excuse me, old chap. I've just seen someone.' A few moments later he was clearly directing the attention of some companions in Dexter's direction. He couldn't for the life of him understand why. Bloody Poms!

'Ah, these English,' a strongly accented voice interrupted his thoughts. He looked down to see a female face angled charmingly towards his. The woman was wearing a cartwheel hat of fine black straw, veiled to halfway down her face. Behind the wide black mesh, catlike green eyes openly appraised him. 'You see, they care about the most trivial things. I think if we remove this —' she gestured to his buttonhole with one elegant gloved hand — 'you will find that they stop laughing. May I?'

'Please do.' He was amused at the time she contrived to take — 'But you are so tall!' — before the flower was removed.

'An English flower, a rose or maybe a cornflower, is acceptable. But an orchid — never! Now do you understand?'

'You obviously know what you're talking about.'

'But I don't know what to do with this.' She twisted the orchid in her fingers.

He looked from the waxen white flower to her violet linen three-quarter-length coat over a matching dress.

'Allow me.'

He pinned the orchid to her coat, inwardly fuming. Bloody half-wits! All that fuss over a flower. Thank Christ for a fellow foreigner, even if she wasn't Australian.

'Ah, I see you've met already,' said Caro Rupert.

'Not quite,' said Angelica, though she was certain this had to be the Australian her hostess had mentioned. Who else could possibly have dressed like that? 'I'm wearing this gentleman's flower, but I still don't know his name.'

Like hell, thought Caro. 'Angelica, I'd like you to meet a colonial friend of ours — Dexter Randolph. Dexter, may I introduce Angelica, Lady Courtney.' She smiled at her best friend's widow. 'I'm glad you've met, because I've put you together at lunch,' she continued. 'Do come through when you're ready.'

Dexter stared at his vichysoisse with deep suspicion. Angelica discreetly sent it to be warmed for him, and then set out to fascinate. 'I've never met an Australian before. Aren't you all wild men — convicts and bushrangers and cowboys?'

'We are not! There's no such thing as a cowboy in Australia. And I'll have you know my family came over with the First Fleet.'

'In the navy?'

'No, in irons.'

'Then you *do* have convict blood! I can see I'll have to watch you very closely.'

'I promise you I'm quite safe with the silver.'

She put her hand on his arm. 'I'm sure you are, but there's the blood of scoundrels in your veins. I find that rather exciting.'

As if on cue, the remnants of the cold salmon they had been eating were removed and Angelica duly turned to her other neighbour. All round the table, Dexter saw after a moment's confusion, people were politely breaking off their conversation with one neighbour and turning to the other. He followed suit, but his heart wasn't in it. A crazy idea had occurred to him and would not leave him alone.

Angelica Hamilton, Countess of Courtney, did not, like Caro Rupert, lightly dispense her charm on man and woman alike. She was a man's woman, pure and simple. But he sensed an interest other than sexual in her behaviour towards him. The lady obviously had an ulterior motive for flirting, which was fair enough. So had he.

Like him, she was a foreigner. Unlike him, she was on the inside track. The way his fellow guests had openly laughed at Dexter still rankled with him. Sure, it was only a trivial incident. If it had happened at home he'd have rearranged their faces for them and forgotten it by now.

But that was the point: he wasn't at home but in England, where these things really mattered. Angelica Hamilton was French but occupied a prominent place in English society, playing by the English rules. Dexter didn't even know what they were, but after today's humiliation he was sure of one thing — he was going to learn. He didn't care what it cost or how long it took. For his own satisfaction he was going to put one over on all those toffee-nosed Pommy bastards. Dexter Randolph was going to belong.

He pushed aside the memory of Linita tearfully waving him goodbye and followed Angelica out on to the viewing terrace.

'Will you be in England long, Mr Randolph?'

'That rather depends on you.'

He waited for the put-down, the cutting phrase that would tell him it was a waste of time continuing. Angelica coolly removed a cigarette from a crested silver case and waited for him to light it for her.

'Was that your husband's?' he asked, glancing at the man's case.

She dropped it into her bag. 'Yes. Poor Brinsley, I like to keep a few of his personal things with me as a reminder.'

Funny, he wouldn't have taken her for the sentimental sort. 'When did he die?'

Angelica widened her eyes and glanced down at her subdued clothes. 'Three weeks ago.'

'Struth, *not* the sentimental type, then! The poor bastard was barely cold in his grave and already the merry widow was ready for the next go round. This woman was going to take some careful handling, but she was the one for him: stylish, well-connected, cleverer than a waggon-load of monkeys. And far too tough to be affronted by his proposition.

Dexter took the bull by the horns. 'Listen, this probably isn't the best time, but I'm looking for someone like you.'

She'd heard that Australians were impulsive, but this was fast even by her standards! Tempting, though. Below, the crowd in formal dress broke into loud cheers as the Queen, Prince Philip and other members of the Royal Family were driven down the centre of the course in open carriages.

Inwardly she cursed the interruption, but the correct form must be obeyed. 'Touch your hat,' she hissed.

'That's it! That's just what I want from you,' he yelled, over the crowd's applause. 'When I do something wrong, let me know. When I'm going to be doing something tricky, coach me in advance. I'd pay you for your trouble.'

Angelica's nostrils gently flared, the only evidence of her disappointment. No *coup de foudre* in Dexter Randolph's case, but perhaps his interest in her could be turned to her advantage. 'So this is a business proposal you are making?'

'Sure. What do you say?'

Angelica thought fast. If she fell in with his plan, agreed to launch this muscular six-foot débutante into British Society, she would have every opportunity to cajole and flatter him round to her way of thinking. It would take every ounce of charm, good looks and persuasion she possessed to bring this tough nut to heel, but by the end of the Season, she was sure, Dexter Randolph would be brought to make a very different proposal.

'I will,' she said with a radiant smile.

'Knew you would. Shall we have a drink on it?'

'We shall drink 'to' it, Mr Randolph. And please don't wave to the waiter. A gentleman merely catches his eye.'

They raised glasses of champagne in a toast, each confident they would get the best of this particular deal.

Book Three

CAMILLA

Florence, 1960

The gold and terracotta buildings of the Piazza Torre di Belloguardo basked peacefully, doors and windows shuttered against the brilliant afternoon sun. At four o'clock precisely, with the chimes from a nearby campanile still hanging in the air, the square came alive.

While shop and office workers trailed reluctantly back to their places of business, the girls of the Mercede Finishing School erupted from their stuffy classrooms to congregate outside. In a matter of minutes they were outnumbered three to one by an appreciative audience of boys and young men. The predatory *papagalli*, or pick-up artists, of Florence, smartly dressed and lynx-eyed, were moving in on their blushing, giggling foreign prey.

All but one of them was willing to listen to some extravagantly insincere flattery. Lady Camilla Hamilton flicked back her long sun-streaked brown hair, slid a pair of sunglasses over her clear blue-grey eyes and started to thread her way through the crowd, ignoring the appreciative murmurs of '*Bellissima*' and the occasional straying hand.

She was greeted by a slim golden-skinned young man with a riot of dark curls and the knowing eyes of a Raphael pageboy.

'*Ciao*, Camilla. You are coming to Harry's Bar with us, yes?'

She shook her head. 'Sorry, Luca. Maybe another time.'

She tried to pass, but he quickly sidestepped and barred her way. 'Just one drink,' he pleaded, large liquid eyes

241

fixed beseechingly on hers. 'And afterwards we take a little walk together.'

How odd, she thought. A few weeks ago she'd have been speechless with joy to have Luca even notice her. Now his invitation meant nothing. But how was she to convince him that she wasn't interested without offending his touchy Italian pride?

Julie, her good-natured American room-mate, came to the rescue. Winking at Camilla, she slid her arm through Luca's and tugged gently. 'C'mon, you gorgeous hunk. You promised to sit next to me, remember?'

Happy that one at least of the Mercede's pupils found him irresistible, he allowed himself to be persuaded. A diplomatic distance away, plump red-haired Julie stood on tiptoe to whisper in his ear. Immediately the slightly stagey admiring glance which he was still directing at Camilla faded from his handsome face. A death in the family was always hard, but for a young girl to lose her papa so tragically ... For once Luca's expression of sympathy and concern was entirely genuine, but by then Camilla had made her escape.

She made for the Boboli Gardens, picking her way over the sprawling sunbathers on the grass to a shady out-of-the-way corner where she hoped to find some privacy. She'd been in such a rush to get to Miss Taylor's Etiquette Class this morning — 'Knife *and* fork, girls. You won't see Jackie cutting up her meat, then using her fork like the rest of the vulgar Kennedy clan' — that maybe she'd misunderstood. But no, there it was in her mother's impeccably schooled handwriting:

Goodbody has advanced me the loan you suggested from your trust, *chérie*. So thoughtful of you. I've decided to invest some of it in a stunning new wardrobe for autumn, and to hold a house party after Ascot as we always have done.

This isn't as heartless as it sounds, Camilla. I know how soon it is after Papa's death, but we do have a

position in society to maintain, and I feel we owe it to your poor father not to let word of his mismanagement leak out. Besides, you know how unhappy it would have made him to think that my standard of living would decline . . .

The sheer selfishness of it took away Camilla's breath and blurred her vision. Only weeks since Daddy's death, and already Angelica was back in the social whirl. The worst of it was that her mother was absolutely right. Despite her coldness, extravagance and infidelity, Brinsley had wholeheartedly adored his wife and always agreed with her decisions. Camilla could almost hear his gruff familiar voice: 'Your mother's quite right, darling. *Noblesse oblige*, d'you see?'

She smiled at the memory, and immediately wished she hadn't. A skinny boy of about her own age, with swarthy pitted skin and sharp black eyes, was edging rapidly towards her, openly appraising her rounded figure and long slim legs.

'*Americana?*' he queried hopefully. It was every *papagallo's* dream to acquire an American girlfriend, since they were popularly rumoured to have the deepest pockets and the most flexible morals.

Camilla got to her feet, the picture of outraged dignity. '*Ma no,*' she said in an accent her conversation teacher would have been proud of, '*sono italiana, e ecco la mia nonna.*'

She pointed towards a particularly vicious-looking old crone who happened to be crossing the grass in their direction. Stammering his apologies, her admirer made off without a backward glance.

Camilla watched him out of sight. Cheered to have got the best of the encounter, she decided she deserved tea at Doney's, popular with British expats in the city. She followed the narrow cobbled roads, her sweet pale face eye-catching above the plain sleeveless black dress she wore.

As she crossed the street, there was a sudden squeal of

243

brakes behind her. Camilla jumped in surprise. Horns blared in concert, angry voices were raised, but there was no sickening crunch of metal and she did not turn her head. Florence was a city of mad motorists.

There was no one she knew in Doney's, so she took a table by herself and studied the history of art book she always carried for camouflage in these situations.

There was a flurry of movement at a table next to hers. The waiter practically fell over himself to be of service to the newcomer. '*Buongiorno, Conte. Cosa desidere?*'

'*Te con latte, per piacere.*'

Camilla took a sidelong glance and found herself staring straight into a pair of warm tobacco-brown eyes. He smiled charmingly, got to his feet and approached her table.

'Excuse me, *signorina*. You are English?'

'Yes, how did you know?'

'Oh, only an English girl could have such a beautiful peaches and cream complexion.'

And only an English or American girl would have been reading Berenson in the English-language edition, she knew. But, surprisingly, Camilla found that from this man she did not resent a direct approach. He seemed older than the twenty-year-olds with whom she and her friends at the Mercede usually associated, about twenty-five or -six, she guessed, and he had the confidence to smile disarmingly as he paid her the clichéd compliment. Blushing, she stared down at the tablecloth. But when the waiter returned with the stranger's tea, hovering uneasily between the two tables, she looked up and indicated that he should place it at her table.

When his tea had been poured for him and the waiter dismissed, the young man reached into the inside pocket of his impeccable grey suit and took out a monogrammed silver card-case. 'Allow me to introduce myself — Luciano di Nardi.' He slid a small pasteboard square across the table towards her.

Camilla studied the elegant flowing script with its

addresses in Florence and Rome, beneath the small coronet surmounted by circles, denoting his rank. She smiled faintly, remembering one of the girls at school, an earnest Swiss miss with a quite undemocratic passion for titles: 'Und remember, Camilla, you can see vot titles they hev by their balls.' Luciano was a Count, she saw, and something about him was familiar.

'Camilla Hamilton,' she introduced herself. 'It's Lady, actually, but like you I don't use my title more than is necessary. I'm at the Mercede Finishing School here. Do you live in Florence?'

'I work in Rome, where I manage my father's business. But my mother came from here originally and I often visit. My grandmother is the Principessa Lambardi. Perhaps you know her?'

Who in the small village-like community of Florence did not? The Principessa was one of Tuscany's principal landowners and lent her name to the wines produced commercially in her extensive vineyards.

'That explains it,' Camilla told him. 'Your grandmother's very famous hereabouts. I remember someone introducing us at a party one night. We were just beginning a conversation when she was summoned away. A young man had arrived in a red Ferrari to take her to supper. I was so jealous!'

'To think I refused to come inside that night because I thought the party would be full of crumbling old contessas!' Luciano pulled a tragic face. 'If only I had, we'd have met — when? — about a month ago.'

Camilla's smile faded as, with a stab of guilt, she remembered the intervening events. 'I haven't been around much, these last few weeks. There was bad news from home. My father —'

The treacherous easy tears still lurked, ready to fall at a moment's notice, and she feared she might lose control of herself entirely. To her surprise, Luciano used none of the stock exclamations of surprise and horror to which she had

245

grown accustomed since her return to Florence. Instead, he folded her hand in both of his, imprisoning it in lean brown fingers.

The water watched, goggle-eyed. They'd only just met, and already the Conte was holding the beautiful *signorina*'s hand. *Bravissimo*!

They sat together for an hour, talking in low voices, her hand still trustingly in his. Luciano told her that he too had lost a father, several years before. He had inherited a thriving textiles business and also acted as business adviser to his grandmother. Camilla told him about Courtney Park, her beloved Wiltshire home, and revealed more than she meant to of her relationship with her mother.

'At least you have a brother to look after you.'

'Oh, Xan's a darling; we're very close, and fortunately he and Maman have always been tremendous friends. Surprisingly, he doesn't feel the way we do about Courtney Park — to him, it's just a house. But when he marries I suppose we'll have to leave.'

She looked so woebegone at the thought that Luciano laughed. 'Aren't you forgetting something? When *you* marry, it will be because you want to be with a man all the time, sharing his life, his future — and his bed. Lovely Camilla, don't look away from me like that. I say this not to shock or embarrass you but to remind you of the good things ahead. In time you will put this sadness behind you, and then you will see that life can still be very sweet.'

She forced herself to meet his eyes, and said hesitantly, 'Thank you, Luciano. You're very *simpatico*. It's been enormously kind of you, spending all this time speaking to a stranger.'

'I never thought of you that way, Camilla. From the moment I saw you, crossing the road —'

'You mean — that squeal of brakes?'

He nodded sheepishly. 'What else could I do? I saw a beautiful girl — *the* most beautiful girl! I couldn't risk losing sight of you so I stopped to watch you come in here.

I'd have left the car where it was, but a *carabiniere* came along.'

'Oh, Luciano — you didn't get into trouble because of me?'

The nostrils of his patrician nose flared in surprise. 'A di Nardi in trouble with the law — of course not! I simply gave him 10,000 lire and he agreed to park the car for me in a judge's parking-place. Would you like a lift back to school?'

Weak with laughter at his story, all tears and sadness forgotten in the warmth of his presence, Camilla allowed herself to be led from Doney's on Luciano's arm. Smiling benevolently, their waiter watched them leave — the tall aristocratic Italian and the gentle English *signorina*. As plain a case of *amore al prima vista* as he had ever seen.

Back at the Mercede, Camilla sped upstairs to the pretty green- and yellow-painted room she shared with Julie. Her room-mate had spent a self-indulgent half-hour in Gucci after the drink in Harry's Bar.

'I don't know, 'milla,' she said doubtfully, studying her new leather loafers with their distinctive green and red braid. 'When the Italian girls wear them with no stockings, their legs look so slim and tapering. Mine look more like salamis!'

Camilla was leaning over the balcony rail, staring down into the gravelled courtyard garden. 'Hmmm? Yes,' she said absently.

Julie put her hands on her hips. 'Camilla Hamilton, will you look at me? You didn't hear a word I said, did you? What happened to you this afternoon — sunstroke?'

'In Doney's?'

'Then it's gotta be love. Good Golly, Miss Molly, you met someone, didn't you? I can tell — it's written all over that sweet innocent little English face of yours.'

'Why, thank you,' a third voice drawled from the

doorway. It was the Honourable Marcia Fainlight who shared the adjoining room with a German girl who had an overpowering personal freshness problem. As a result, Marcia spent most of the time she was not busily capitulating to the handsome youth of Florence in Camilla's and Julie's room. As usual she was on the scrounge. Her ancient aristocratic family, having scraped together barely enough to keep her fees paid, could not afford to keep her in the clothes and cosmetics she craved.

'Anyone got any pearl-coloured nail varnish?' she asked, forget-me-not blue eyes rapidly scanning the neatly arranged bottles and tubes on top of the two chests of drawers. The school's Matron, a plump good-natured Irishwoman who would willingly turn a blind eye to the occasional late return became a termagant if the girls' rooms were left untidy. They even had to make their own beds.

'Oh, thanks, Julie,' said Marcia, when the Texan sighed and handed over a small bottle. 'And did I hear you say Camilla's met a man? Do I know him?'

'It wouldn't surprise me, Marcia. You seem to be on *intimate* terms with half the boys in Florence,' Julie snapped.

'He comes from Rome,' Camilla interrupted diplomatically, 'but visits his grandmother here most weekends. His name's Luciano di Nardi — his grandmother's the Principessa Lambardi.'

'Ve—ry nice.' Marcia's pale blue eyes kindled with interest. 'And handsome? Damn you, Camilla, I can see he is! And related to the Principessa, eh? He must be loaded ... Age?'

'Twenty-six.'

'*Perfetto*! Just experienced enough without being jaded. What does he drive?'

The ultimate test. 'A Ferrari, actually.' The ultimate car.

Julie laughed delightedly and clapped her hands. 'Looks

like you scooped the pool! A Ferrari! When's he picking you up?'

'Tomorrow night, about eight. He's taking me to dinner in Borgo Jacopo.'

'How romantic,' breathed Julie. 'Honey, I am so pleased for you. You need some cheering up, after your daddy and all.'

Appalled at her own tactlessness, she broke off and stared at her feet. Despite the glint of tears in her own eyes, Camilla instantly put her friend at her ease. 'You're right, Julie, and thanks. He's going to be good for me, I can tell.'

'Well, there's one infallible test of that!' the irrepressible Marcia butted in. She'd been made distinctly uncomfortable by the sloppy, sentimental talk between the room-mates. Really, between the Italians and her American friend, Camilla was in danger of becoming embarrassingly over-emotional. So un-English. 'How big's his nose?' she enquired.

Camilla looked surprised. 'I didn't really notice, to tell you the truth. But it's the most marvellous shape — strong and patrician. A real Roman nose.'

'Isn't that just wonderful?' breathed Julie loyally. 'And anyway, Marcia, what the hell business is it of yours?'

'Just trying to save Camilla from disappointment, darling. Take it from me, you can infallibly predict the size of a chap's noodle from the size of his nose.'

Camilla blushed painfully, but Julie's curiosity was piqued. 'You mean, small nose, small . . .?'

'Precisely! Remember Tommaso from my first term?'

'There were so many . . . Vaguely.'

'Vaguely is right! A terrific body but the smallest, thinnest nose. And, girls, imagine the disappointment . . . We had a bit of a dip, and even when he was *al dente* I could barely feel more than a tickle! I do hope you're not in for a disappointment like that, Camilla darling!'

★

249

The following night, when Luciano drew up outside the Mercede in his shiny red car, Marcia and Julie were among the appreciative audience of girls hanging over their balconies and making swooning noises as he smiled and waved up at them.

'Oh God,' said Marcia crossly, 'I think I'm going to be jealous. Of Camilla Hamilton, of all people.'

'Hot damn!' said Julie softly as the powerful car roared off down the narrow street. 'Did you see that?'

'Couldn't miss it, darling. The best and biggest nose I've seen all term. It'll be wasted on her.'

Julie shook her head and smiled. 'Bet you my Pucci pyjamas it won't be.'

'You're on!'

Luciano drove them to Borgo Jacopo, a short distance from the famous Ponte Vecchio. At Camillo's, a cheery waiter bid him a cheery '*Buonasera, Signor Conte,*' and led them into the cosy right-hand room, full of a cheerful clutter of bric-à-brac, big bowls of flowers and pictures by local artists, hoping for a sale.

Luciano had ordered their meal in advance: the finest Parma ham with fresh juicy figs was followed by a bowl of plump mushroom-stuffed cushions of fresh ravioli and then a delicious freshwater fish stuffed with fennel and baked with herbs. Without consulting Luciano, the waiter brought a bottle of fragrant golden wine from his grandmother's special reserve.

Camilla had been expecting to feel shy and ill at ease with him; after leaving him, she had been embarrassed to remember how much she had told him about herself. The only other man she'd talked to as freely was her brother — but Camilla didn't kid herself that there was anything fraternal in her feelings for Luciano.

To her relief, she found that they could chat together as easily as yesterday and all the time she found herself studying him with the minutest attention to detail. He had the longest, softest pale brown eyelashes, she saw, and a deep cleft in his strong chin where the razor could not quite reach. His hair was not brown, as she'd remembered, but the richest rarest chestnut, while the wiry hairs on the backs of his strong hands glowed red in the soft light. As for his nose ... Remembering Marcia's tip, Camilla studied it openly, and blushed to the roots of her hair.

Luciano watched her with amusement. 'I don't suppose you want to tell me what you're thinking?'

She shook her head, horrified.

'Then to make it up to me, you must come for a walk before I drive you back.'

'Curfew's at eleven, Luciano. I don't want to get into trouble with Miss Taylor.'

'It is all taken care of.' He left a wad of notes on the table and helped her to her feet. 'My grandmother is a personal friend of Mrs Huntingdon's. She called her this afternoon and the Principal agreed you'd be quite safe out after hours with the grandson of the Principessa Lambardi.'

Then why, Camilla wondered as they strolled arm in arm down the packed streets towards the bridge, were her legs trembling beneath her, her heart pounding like a trapped bird's? Despite her shyness, she was aware of a slow build-up of tension inside her, an unmistakable yearning to do more than politely talk with this handsome, virile man. She shuddered when he momentarily touched her arm to draw her attention to a particularly fine piece of craftsmanship in a jeweller's they were passing.

The flow of conversation had died between them. Speechless, Camilla stared into his proud dark face and prayed he wouldn't be too much of a gentleman, or simply too damned bored, to try for one kiss at least. She couldn't bear it if he didn't. Marcia Fainlight said if an Italian boy didn't kiss you on your first date, it meant he was *cavaletto* — only interested in other boys.

251

On the narrow hump-backed Ponte Vecchio, Luciano stopped walking and drew Camilla aside so that they stood facing one another. 'I suppose you know it was here, on this precise spot, that Dante met his Beatrice for the first time? It's a special place for lovers, Camilla. That's why I wanted to bring you here on our first evening together. I know what you're thinking — just another romantic line in this so romantic city of ours! But believe me, *cara*, it is not. From the moment I saw you I knew you were going to be special for me. I cannot pretend there haven't been others before, but never one like you. Never one I wanted so much. I don't mean now, tonight, but I want you to know that one day soon I intend to make you mine. Do you understand what I'm saying?'

She was a naïve, inexperienced young girl. He'd expected her lovely face to reflect doubt and confusion, though he sensed how attracted to him she was. Instead she lifted her face to his and smiled.

'I'm glad,' was all she said, before his lips came down on hers, making further conversation unnecessary.

Passers-by smiled approvingly. The spirit of Florence's great poet was being celebrated here in a way of which he would heartily have approved.

On the way back from church in the morning her friends relentlessly cross-examined her, but Camilla remained infuriatingly vague on all but the most trivial of details. Yes, his car was fabulous. Yes, he was good-looking, a real man of the world. They'd had a very good dinner and a stroll along the Ponte Vecchio — that was all there was to say. But when they reached the school again a grinning maid was waiting at the front door, barely able to hold a sheaf of wild flowers in delicate pinks and blues and mauves.

'*Da Palazzo Lambardi*,' she said excitedly.

'*Al fiore il più bello*, Camilla Hamilton,' Luciano had

252

written across the back of one of his cards. "To the fairest flower."

'How typically Italian,' said Marcia crossly.

'Don't you try and spoil things for 'milla.' Julie sprang to her friend's defence. 'It's a lovely romantic gesture and Luciano's a catch and a half. You hang on to him, sugar, you hear?'

'Thanks. I intend to.'

Nevertheless, when the same excited maid reappeared to say that Camilla was wanted on the phone, she decided to play it cool despite the excited thumping of her heart.

'*Pronto. Chi parla*?' she said into the phone — for all the world as if she didn't know!

'*Sono Luciano che parla.* Camilla, may I see you for lunch? Grandmother has old friends visiting her today and does not mind if I am not present.'

Joy overcame her pose of cool English reserve. 'I'd love to, Luciano. And thank you for the flowers — they're absolutely lovely.'

'I'm only sorry we had no roses for my perfect English rose. I'll see you in an hour. *Ciao*.'

She spent a frantic hour washing her hair and ransacking her wardrobe but was downstairs, outwardly cool and serene in a blush-pink shirred cotton sundress, when Luciano called for her.

He took the steep hills and treacherous switchbacks up to Fiesole at breathtaking speed. Camilla was so engrossed in the beauty of the day, her surroundings and the man beside her that she forgot to be afraid. As they approached the imposing Villa San Michele, he slowed the car and raised her hand to his lips.

'It won't be today, *cara*, but soon — you understand?' For hours afterwards, the sensitive skin on the back of her hand seemed to burn with his kiss.

They ate outside on a cool, shady terrace, beneath them Italy's most breathtaking view. Florence nestled like a fabulous jewel in the ancient enfolding bosom of the

Etruscan hills. To its citizens, it could feel cramped and enclosed. Today it seemed to float weightless on a heat haze, ethereally lovely in every tone of ancient mellow stone, baked terracotta tiles and green-shadowed copper. Camilla barely noticed what they ate and drank, content just to bask in the splendour of the sight and Luciano's presence.

'I shall have to take you home soon,' he said regretfully. 'I'll be back next weekend — Friday afternoon if I can get away. In the meantime, I'll ring you every night.'

'I'll be waiting,' she promised.

For the next three weekends they were rarely apart. In his haste to get back to her, Luciano set new records for the drive between Rome and Florence, and when they could not be together jammed the students' incoming line with passionate phone calls. The other girls took the inconvenience in good part. Camilla was a general favourite and everyone knew she'd had a bad time recently.

Only Marcia seemed to begrudge her newfound happiness. 'I don't suppose he's introduced you to his grandmother yet?'

'No, but she does seem to be terribly busy, entertaining friends and business guests.'

'But never her beloved grandson's girlfriend. How odd,' commented Marcia waspishly. 'You do realise that none of these old trouts consider an English girl good enough to marry into the family?'

'Since I haven't met her, I couldn't possibly speculate as to that,' Camilla said frostily, but she had entered an unwelcome train of thought. Though Luciano had made it plain he desired her — only the fact that he was too well known in Florence to take a room for them there had so far prevented them from sleeping together — he had never once indicated to her that he had long-term plans for them. Reluctantly she began to wonder whether she had been living in a fool's paradise. Surely, if his intentions were honourable, she'd have been introduced to his family by now?

The following weekend, all her doubts and worries were laid to rest.

'*Cara*, it may be a bit of an ordeal for you — my grandmother doesn't speak much English — but she's been badgering me to bring you to meet her. I was going to wait till Mama could be there as well but my grandmother is most insistent. She would like you to come to tea on Sunday, if that's okay with you.'

'Okay? It's marvellous!' Camilla was transparent in her relief. 'I'll be so glad to meet her properly, Luciano — your mother, too, when she can get up here. And later on, when term's finished, you must come to Courtney and meet Maman and Xan.'

'I look forward to that very much,' he said gravely. 'Camilla, I see I've been insensitive. I've let you worry that because I desired you from the moment we met, perhaps that was all there was between us. *Cara*, of course it is not so! I love you, I want us to be together in every sense, for our families to reach an agreement together. But these things take time to work out, you understand, and in the meantime ... If we could only get you away from that damned school!'

But wily Mrs Huntingdon Mercede was not so dazzled by Luciano di Nardi's manners and breeding as to grant Camilla's repeated requests for permission to spend a weekend away, try though she might to pretend that she intended to pass it in Lerici with Julie. Pupils were allowed to leave the school at weekends, ski-ing at Cortina in the winter or visiting the coast in the summer months — but only in strictly chaperoned parties.

'I'm afraid, my dear,' the Principal told her, 'I would be failing in my duty to your mother if I granted you permission to spend a night away from the school at this time. Although of course if my old friend the Principessa cares to take the responsibility of inviting you under her own roof for a weekend, say ...'

Camilla fervently prayed that they would get on together and an invitation be forthcoming. They were dogged by disappointment. Luciano called her on the morning of the day she was to have visited, saying that his grandmother was ill with bronchial trouble and the tea party would have to be cancelled.

'It's quite serious, I'm afraid. I must stay with her this afternoon, see the nurse has settled in, then drive back to Rome tonight. My grandmother was most disappointed. Said I was to tell you how much she hopes to meet you some other time.'

'I do hope we shall,' Camilla said fervently, 'and that she's better soon. Drive carefully, my darling. *Ti amo.*'

'*Anch'io. Ciao*, Camilla. Till next weekend.'

They had reckoned without Angelica's meeting an Australian millionaire. From the moment she set her sights on Dexter Randolph's millions, Angelica realised she was going to have to play this one very cleverly. She calculated, rightly, that despite his brash exterior and sharp business brain, Dexter was a traditionalist at heart. English history, its ancient customs and fine old houses appealed to some atavistic instinct within him for continuity, heritage, a proud and strong family line. She knew just how to impress him. On the day they met, she invited him to her post-Ascot house party, and that night placed a long-distance call to her daughter's finishing school.

'... What do you mean, you can't miss the last few weeks of term? For goodness' sake, Camilla, why ever not? I am recently widowed, you know. I need you here with me.'

'But, Maman, you sent me back here after Daddy's funeral.'

'It's been much harder than I thought, coping alone. A woman needs her children around her at a time like this. Besides, I told you, I'm having my usual house party after Ascot. It's what Daddy would have wanted, I'm sure, but without him ... Camilla, I need your support.'

The reference to her father weakened Camilla's resolve, as her mother had known it would. 'It's not so much school I hate to leave ...'

Angelica was all ears. 'Is it a man? Have you a serious admirer, Camilla? I hope he's suitable.'

'Eminently, Maman. He's Count Luciano di Nardi. The family owns a textiles company, and his grandmother is the Principessa Lambardi who owns all the vineyards round here. I don't know if he'd be able to get away at short notice, but if so, may I invite him too?'

Angelica thought rapidly. It was one thing to promote an image of family unity, showing off a pretty young daughter; quite another to present one on the verge of matrimony. So ageing.

'I'm sorry, it's quite out of the question. The numbers are too many as it is. I felt so sorry for an Australian I met by chance today that I invited him on the spur of the moment, and you know how over-stretched we are without a full staff. Besides, if you're really keen on this boy, I'd like to meet him some other time, when I can pay him more attention.'

'Hardly a boy Maman. He's twenty-six.'

'My God, what do I pay that school for? They're supposed to keep the wolves at bay —'

'I'm quite safe with Luciano, Maman. Don't fuss.'

But now Angelica had just the lever she needed. 'That's settled it, Camilla. I cannot have a daughter of mine running round with a man to whom I have not been introduced. You are to come home immediately, help me entertain the party, and then afterwards — if I think he sounds suitable — you can invite your friend to stay. Remember, *chérie*, distance lends enchantment ... Now, I want you to catch the train tomorrow. You'll reach Paris on Friday morning, and should be at Courtney for dinner. Mrs Huntingdon will take care of all the arrangements. *Au 'voir*, and don't let me down.'

Camilla was dumb with horror. To leave Florence before the weekend, before she could see Luciano! There was one slim chance ... oh God, please let him be in, she prayed, dialling the number in Rome with trembling hands.

When she broke the news that her mother expected her to take the Paris train in the morning, he surprised her by saying calmly, 'She is your mama, Camilla, of course you must go to her if she needs you. Don't cry, *cara*. I promise we'll see each other before you go, if I have to drive all night.'

'Luciano — be careful.'

But he had already hung up.

Her last night at school was taken up with packing, swopping hugs and addresses with the friends she had made there. She was pretty sure of seeing Marcia again, since they moved in the same circles in England, but it would be Julie she would really miss.

'I'll come with you to the station,' her American friend offered. 'Don't worry — I'll melt right into the woodwork the minute the divinely handsome Conte appears. He is going straight there, I suppose? Not coming to the school?'

'Oh, no! I'm so stupid — I forgot to ask. Julie, what if we miss each other?'

'Quit worrying. We'll leave messages with the maids here, and he knows what train you're getting. God, driving through the night just to say goodbye — he must really love you.'

'And I love him. Oh, Julie, I *love* him! I couldn't bear it if I lost him now.'

In the morning, she couldn't bring herself to take breakfast with the other girls. There had been no word from Luciano. She and Julie hung on at the Mercede later than they had intended, waiting for a message.

Eventually Julie bundled her friend into a taxi. 'C'mon, your old lady'll kill you if you don't get home on time. Besides, I'm willing to bet lover boy's waiting at the station. It'll be just like the movies!'

It was a good thing she hadn't had money on it, Camilla reflected, standing forlornly on the platform beside her reserved sleeper compartment.

Julie's air of calm reassurance had turned to recrimination. 'The jerk! How could he do this to you?'

'Maybe he thought it was for the best this way. Or — I can't bear it! What if something's happened to him on the way?'

Camilla clutched her friend's arm and started back down the platform. There was a last-minute surge of passengers towards the train, a slamming of doors down its length.

'Better get on board,' Julie said gently.

Just then, from the far end of the crowded platform, they heard a faint cry: ''Amilton? *Signorina* 'Amilton, *per favore?*'

A small pageboy in the Excelsior's livery was trotting down the platform towards them, dwarfed by the giant bouquet in his arms.

'*Eccomi!*' Camilla screamed, waving her arms frantically and beginning to thread her way towards him.

Julie restrained her. 'No time,' she insisted. 'Get on board, 'milla. I'll bring them to you.'

Camilla pulled down the window and strained to follow her friend's progress through the frantically jostling crowd. Julie thrust a thousand-lire note at the boy, seized the flowers and started to run back. The train sighed and jolted forward.

'Quick, quick!' Camilla called, stretching out to take the flowers from her panting friend.

'Here — there's a note!' Julie half threw them into her arms. 'Goodbye, Camilla. Take care of yourself.'

'Goodbye — and thanks!'

They waved until they could no longer see each other, and then Camilla sank back on to her narrow berth and hunted feverishly for the message. It was written on a card — not one of Luciano's, but standard hotel florist's issue.

259

The handwriting was not his, either. He had obviously thought better of driving all night and dictated the message over the phone.

'I will think of you fondly,' she read aloud, her heart giving a great lurch of disappointment. It was the sort of message he might have sent to a maiden aunt. After all they'd had together, the promises and hopes for the future, why had he chosen to say goodbye in such a cold, impersonal way? She sat staring at the bright florist's blooms, oversized and garish, utterly different from his pale careful choice for her in the days when he had loved her. Had loved her, she realised. Obviously those days were gone and she had been a fool to put her trust in empty promises.

She spent the whole of the journey locked in her compartment, refusing every offer from the concerned steward of food, some coffee, a doctor perhaps? So that he would not panic and call one anyway, Camilla forced herself to stop crying and accepted the offer of a bottle of mineral water. She drank thirstily, peeled off her creased and travel-stained clothes and washed at the tiny basin.

The sight of the face in the mirror, haggard and red-eyed, shocked her into pulling herself together. She splashed cold water repeatedly over her puffy eyes and disguised them further with a pair of dark glasses. She only hoped her looks would be restored by the time she reached Courtney, or Maman would have something to say.

The kindly steward helped her with her baggage — she had left the flowers on the train — and was directing her towards a waiting room when a deep familiar voice told them: 'That will not be necessary.'

'Luciano?' She took off her glasses, unable to believe her eyes. 'Is it really you? I thought I'd never see you again.'

Laughing and sobbing, for joy this time, she flung herself into his arms. He kissed away her tears, face creased with concern when he saw her swollen eyes and pale face.

'*Cara*, forgive me. I tried my best to get a message to you. Did you not receive my flowers?'

'Yes! And a message: "I will think of you fondly." I thought it was a polite way of saying things were over between us.'

'*Dio mio!*' He clenched his fists in an agony of frustration. 'The message I told them to give you was "I will think of you fondly *until we meet in Paris.*" The idiots left off the most important bit.'

'But I don't understand. I wasn't expecting you to drive here.'

'I didn't. I drove to Florence — or almost. I made good time, and intended to call in on my grandmother, to wash and change there before coming to say goodbye. The car broke down about fifty kilometres from the city. Fortunately I was on my grandmother's land by then, but by the time I'd walked to the nearest telephone and called the house to ask them to send a mechanic, I could see time was wearing on. I had to decide whether to wait for Maurizio to make the repair or take the local taxi into Florence. God help me, I took the taxi. *Cara*, you should have seen it! A beaten-up old Fiat with tyres like glass. By the time I'd realised we weren't going to make the train, you'd left the school. I thought of the Excelsior Flower Shop and promised them a small fortune to get you the flowers and my message before the train departed. Then the taxi-driver took me to my grandmother's, and one of the estate workers drove me to Pisa where I took the plane for Paris. Can you forgive me? I never meant to cause you a moment's pain.'

She closed her eyes and leant against him. 'It wasn't your fault. Besides, I can forgive you anything — as long as you love me.'

'You know I do.'

'Why are things so unfair? Why can't we be together, really together, when I want you so much?'

Gently he took hold of her arms and held her away from

him. 'Do you really? Because, while I was waiting for your train, I did a little detective work. There might be a way.'

An hour later, as the Golden Arrow pulled out of the Gare du Nord, Luciano impatiently tugged down the blind and bolted the door of the cramped sleeping compartment he had booked in the name of the Conte and Contessa di Nardi.

Camilla watched him, leaning against the white-covered bottom berth. The extremity of emotion she'd felt in the last hour — from the depths of despair to overwhelming joy — had left her almost powerless to act.

Gently, Luciano cupped her face in his hands. 'Don't be afraid. I know it's not what we'd hoped for. If you'd rather not —'

'No! I want you more than I've ever wanted anything before. But I'm so ignorant. You'll have to show me the way.'

Slowly and patiently, with infinite skill and tenderness, he conquered her fear and inexperience. Marcia had warned her not to expect too much the first time — 'Hurts like hell and you wonder what all the fuss is about' — but, then, Marcia had never had a lover like Luciano. Afterwards, lying naked and sated in the narrow bed beside him, Camilla was sure that no woman in the world had a lover like hers. With him, even the first time was magical, and the second and third sent her swooping and fluttering over the threshold of unimagined ecstasy. There would never be another man for her, she decided, for there never could be one as unforgettable as this.

When they boarded the train in Paris, Camilla was a green inexperienced girl. At Boulogne, her body still sore and tingling from his caresses, she kissed him goodbye with all the passion and assurance of a woman who loves and knows she is loved.

'*Ti amo*, Luciano,' she said, as they clung together for the final few seconds.

'And I love you. Hold on to that. Until we meet again, I

travel always with you in my heart.'

She stood at the stern of the ferry, staring back to land, until the loved familiar figure blurred and receded and was blotted out by the dazzling glare of sun on sea.

Camilla knew there would be no butler to greet her on her return. As part of the new economy drive, Hawkins had never been replaced. Her mother had instructed her that the housekeeper's husband would be fully occupied meeting guests from the London train, so she was to make her own way to the house. She was surprised, therefore, when a tall rangy man with startlingly blue eyes in a weatherbeaten face emerged from the house to help deal with her luggage.

'Let me,' he said, paying off the taxi and scooping up her cases.

'That's terribly kind of you. I'm afraid we're short staffed at present. I'm Camilla Hamilton, by the way.'

'Dexter Randolph, visiting from Australia. Your mother's asked me down for the weekend.' He managed to shake hands and introduce himself without putting down her suitcases or once breaking stride.

It seemed that this surprising man expected her to go immediately to Angelica's private sitting-room. He was making straight for it, still carrying her cases. 'Er — Mr Randolph?'

'Dexter, please.'

'Dexter, I've just arrived after a long journey. I really think I should wash and change before I go in to Maman. And I don't suppose she'd be very pleased if we took all my luggage into her sitting-room.'

He stopped and considered, looking down at the dust-smeared cases and travelling bag.

'S'pose you're right,' he said cheerfully. 'Will I take them to your room instead?'

'No, honestly. You're a guest. If you just leave them

263

there, the maids will deal with them presently.'

Shrewd blue eyes studied her. 'Are you telling me — ever so politely — that it's not the done thing to lend a hand with the fetching and carrying — not if you're staying in the house?'

The question put her properly on the spot. He *was* a guest, and Brinsley had always taught her that the first duty of the host and his family was to make every guest feel comfortable and at home — however bizarre their behaviour!

'It was terribly helpful of you —'

'But I put my size nines in it again, eh? You can give it to me straight, you know. Your mother's been giving me a crash course in etiquette, and she doesn't pull her punches.'

His thin face was suddenly transformed by a grin so infectious that Camilla found herself smiling in return, even while she wondered what her cold, ultra-correct mother could possibly have in common with this unassuming guest from abroad, who spent his time on the land, if his appearance was anything to go by.

He had an amazing effect on her mother, Camilla noticed, joining them later for tea. Angelica welcomed her with a pretty display of maternal warmth, asking numerous questions about Florence and lightly teasing her about her latest conquest.

'My little girl's becoming so popular,' she said, smiling radiantly for their visitor's benefit.

'I can see why,' he said drily. From the way Angelica talked of her children, he'd expected to find them both of school age. He'd been surprised by the delicately beautiful young woman who had introduced herself as Camilla Hamilton, and could see he'd have to revise his mental estimate of his hostess's age.

'You must tell me all about this latest boy,' Angelica was saying.

'He's called Luciano, and he's —'

'But later. Before my other guests arrive, Dexter and I have a little homework to go over.'

'Shall I leave you to it?' Camilla was beginning to feel distinctly *de trop*. There was an excitement in Angelica's manner which she was newly qualified to recognise.

'No, don't go. I want you and Dexter to become good friends. He's going to need our undivided attention, I can see.' She gave him a nakedly flirtatious smile before, to Camilla's amazement, proceeding to put him through a relentless social catechism.

Titles and other forms of address ... the correct clothes for each occasion ... formalities to be observed when entering or leaving a room, greeting one's fellow guests, dealing with the servants ...

'When a door is opened for you or you are served at dinner, how do you respond, Dexter?'

He frowned, affronted. 'I say "Thanks, mate" of course! D'you think I've got no manners?'

Angelica shook her head vehemently. 'No, that's quite wrong, I'm afraid. In those circumstances, a simple nod of acknowledgment is enough.'

Her tone was the oddest mixture of command and conciliation, thought Camilla, as though she wanted to put Dexter straight while simultaneously charming him. He was after all a very attractive man — if not a patch on Luciano.

'Please don't engage the staff in conversation,' Angelica said with a sweet smile. 'It's unsettling for them and subtly undermines your own authority. The only exception to this rule would be your relationship with your personal manservant, which is bound to be somewhat closer. By the way, I've arranged for you to interview a most suitable candidate tomorrow afternoon. His name's Webster —'

'What time in the arvo's this Mr Webster expected, then?'

'Webster — a servant is never Mr — will be here at three o'clock. He's just what you're looking for, Dexter. Trust me.'

He seemed unconvinced, screwing up his face as if making a difficult decision. 'Ah, I dunno, Angel. I'm not sure I like the idea of having another bloke chasing after me, fussing like a bloody chook. What's he going to do with himself all day?'

'For a start, supervise your new wardrobe.' She looked at the clothes he was wearing and quickly looked away again. 'There wasn't time to do much about them this weekend, but you must realise they won't do?'

He glanced down at himself. 'Well, you did say informal ...'

Camilla felt embarrassed on his behalf. She'd noticed how differently he dressed from the other men she knew, but felt that his open-necked shirt, bleached-looking trousers and soft lace-up suede shoes suited his rangy outdoor looks.

'I meant flannels and a blazer,' Angelica sighed, 'a shirt from a reputable maker — Jeremy Street for preference — and a silk tie or cravat.'

'A cra-what?'

'It would be best if you were to go into this more fully with Webster. He can advise what is required, and even shop for some of your clothes. Of course you'll need fittings for suits, and to be measured for shoes and shirts. Lobb's for shoes, I think. They take months to make a last and deliver, but as you'll be placing such a large order ... Oh, and a pair of those amusing velvet slippers from Tricker's to wear with your evening dress. Without the coronet, in your case.'

'I'm still not convinced I need a nursemaid trailing after me. I mean, what's he going to do when I'm in Australia? If the stockmen catch him fussing about over shirts and shoes, they'll think we're a pair of bloody shirtlifters!'

Angelica lowered her eyes. 'Webster has indicated his willingness to accompany you on your travels, but I rather thought, since you're thinking of setting up a London household, together with the new office, that you might

266

like to leave him in charge of that. Or you could leave him in Sydney while you visited your stations — he could look after your house there.'

'Yeah, maybe.' He still looked very doubtful. 'Let me meet the bloke first, eh? See how we rub along together.'

'And, Dexter, you simply must watch your language,' she reminded him.

'But I never swear in front of ladies!'

'In England, "bloody" is a swear-word. And it's not just a question of profanities. You say "bloke" instead of man; "arvo" for afternoon; "shirtlifter" for ... the sort of man who is not mentioned in polite company.'

'Oh, pardon.'

'I beg your pardon, or sorry, or what — *never* pardon!'

'Sorry, Angel.' Completely unabashed, he grinned at her and Camilla saw her cool and collected mother blush.

'I've already told you, Dexter. It's perfectly all right to call me "Angel" in private, but if they heard you, my friends might get the wrong idea.'

Camilla shifted in her seat. Her mother's open flirtatiousness with another man so soon after Daddy's death was difficult to swallow. She had besides spent an almost sleepless night and a very active few hours on the train to Boulogne. She longed to be alone with her thoughts of Luciano, even perhaps ring him before dinner.

'I think Maman's being hard enough on you,' she told Dexter lightly. 'You don't need me joining in as well. If you'll excuse me?'

With natural good manners, he got up to open the door for her, laying a hand on her arm to detain her while he explained: 'No one's being harder on me than I would be on myself. Meeting you people, I feel like everyone's talking in code. I understand the words but not the real meaning behind them. And I want to understand. I want to make this damn' full-of-itself country work for me! To do that, I need to present myself in the best possible light, and if that means dressing myself up like a tailor's dummy or talking with a plum in my mouth, that's all right by me. Your mum's being a big help, honest.'

'It's "mother" and "honestly",' she corrected him crisply. 'And I'm glad to hear it. It's good to see she's getting over her sadness at my father's very recent death.'

The weekend went far better than any of them had dared to hope. Although Camilla caught a few politely suppressed smiles when Dexter used one of his saltier expressions, he was an apt pupil and rarely made the same mistake twice. He seemed genuine enough, Camilla decided, and it wasn't his fault that Maman had decided to throw her cap over the windmill after him, so indecently quickly. For his own sake, if not Angelica's, Camilla began gently to smooth his passage. Lord Anthony Carstairs, one of Angelica's circle, helped things along when, embarrassingly, Dexter kept referring to him as Lord Carstairs.

'Tony, dear fellow. Tony to m'friends.'

And since the two men shared a common interest in the bloodstock business, they were soon happily swapping yarns about the British and Australian racing scenes. Carstairs' acceptance was the signal to the other male guests in the ten-strong party, all of whom behaved affably.

The women were distinctly impressed.

'Trust Angelica to have an attractive man like that tucked up her sleeve,' Camilla overheard one dowager say.

'You underestimate her, my dear. I'm sure she has him tucked up in a far more interesting place than that!'

Despite his mother's embarrassing flirtatiousness with their guest, Alexander rather took to Dexter, finding him a refreshing change from all the debs' delights and callow Oxbridge contemporaries he usually mixed with. After dinner on Saturday night he told Camilla, 'This is rather unexpected in Maman, bear-leading a rude colonial, but he seems a good enough chap — and, I take it, incredibly wealthy?'

The same thought had occurred to her. 'Bound to be,' she said gloomily. 'He certainly doesn't seem to mind her advising him how to spend his money. He was talking about a London *pied à terre* and she was advising a house in Berkeley Square! I really think she has her sights set on marrying him, once he's house trained. It's awful, so soon after Daddy's death.'

Her brother looked uncomfortable. 'Look, Camilla, Maman's simply not the sort of woman who could be happy without a man in her life. She needs the attention, the excitement ... I know it's difficult for you to understand.'

'Oh, but I do. Better than you think.'

Camilla blushed under her brother's enquiring glance. 'Okay, who is he? Who's been leading my little sister astray? And which is it to be — wedding rings or pistols at dawn?'

'Wedding rings, as soon as it can decently be arranged. His name's Luciano di Nardi, an Italian Count with his own successful textiles company. He's twenty-six with a wonderful strong face and a voice that makes you tingle just to hear it! He's also the sweetest, kindest, most impulsive man.'

She told him the story of the mix-up in Florence and Luciano's miraculous appearance on the station platform in Paris.

'We travelled to Boulogne together, in a sleeping compartment ...'

'Spare me the rest!' Alexander looked thoughtful. 'Does Maman know? That you're serious about him, I mean. She ought to ask him over to stay, start forging the old family alliance, you know the sort of thing.'

'I've tried to mention it a couple of times, but she's so wrapped up in Dexter.'

'Perhaps on Monday, when the guests have gone and she has less on her mind. If things have got that far, Camilla, you ought to be planning ahead.'

'I know — but just for the moment I can't bring myself to waste time on all the boring formalities — the families, the settlement, where we'll live.' She wrapped her arms round her, hugging herself for joy as she turned shining eyes on her brother. 'You'll love him, Xan. He's very special.' A touch of concern tinged her voice. 'But I wonder why he hasn't phoned me tonight. He said he would.'

Alexander laughed. 'From dewy-eyed romanticism to instant reproach! The poor devil's got his work cut out for him. Seriously, though, Camilla, I'm very happy for you both and look forward to meeting Luciano. Don't worry if he doesn't ring tonight. The international lines are always busy — and a letter's so much more romantic.'

She brightened. 'That's a good idea. Do you think Maman will need me any more tonight?'

They glanced across the White Library, where the male diners had rejoined the feminine half of the party. A couple of Regency card tables had been set up, and Angelica was happily engaged in teaching Dexter the rules of bridge. The husband and wife they were playing, both keen practitioners, looked less than enthralled by the time it was taking her to dictate her partner's every move, leaning seductively close to study his hand and pressing her wide smiling mouth to his ear to whisper frequent instructions. Dexter himself was looking oddly imposing this evening, Camilla noted, his tanned face and pale eyes in startling contrast to the severe black and starched white of his evening dress.

'I think I'll go up too,' said Alexander. 'It doesn't look as though I'll be missed.'

It was only six o'clock when Camilla woke the next morning, her half-written letter to Luciano still on the night table beside her bed. Glancing out of the lancet window set in the curve of her charming circular room in a tower bedroom, she decided the morning was much too beautiful for her to lie in bed. She'd finish the letter after breakfast. For now, she intended to take out Sally, her sweet-tempered chestnut mare.

She was prepared to do the saddling up herself, now that Angelica had let all but one ageing 'lad' go, but she did not need to. Crossing the cobbled yard, she heard the jingle of harness and the ring of steel-shod hooves on stone.

At the far side of the yard, by the rows of empty loose-boxes that once had housed the carriage horses, hacks and hunters of Courtney Park's heydey, a solitary rider schooled his horse. Sitting ramrod straight in the saddle, occasionally patting his mount's quivering neck, Dexter brought the big nervy bay hunter totally under his control with expert touches of his hands, heels and muscular thighs.

Camilla stood quite still, not wanting anything to alarm the jittery horse. Hannibal had been her father's favourite hunter and very much a one-man horse. She doubted he'd been ridden since Brinsley's death and was surprised that her mother had not sent him for auction by now. Perhaps his evil reputation had preceded him, yet here was a stranger effortlessly subjugating the big bay's half-ton of muscle, bone and malice.

Dexter noted her arrival and was glad she had the good sense to keep still and quiet. When he was finally satisfied he had Hannibal's measure, he slid out of the saddle and hitched his mount to a post. 'Shall we ride out together? You could show me everything there is to see.'

'I thought Maman had done that pretty exhaustively already.'

'I'm always open to new experiences,' Dexter said blandly, then turned to survey the few occupied boxes. 'Now let me see . . . Ah, yes. I know which one . . .'

Ignoring her mother's showy Arab mare, Alexander's two eventers and a couple of gentle old cobs, Dexter quickly picked out Sally. He seemed to have been as quick to familiarise himself with the location of everything in the yard as in the house, she thought resentfully. The man had a positive flair for making himself fully at home. There was no denying his expertise with horses, however. Sally allowed herself to be saddled and bridled with no more than a token snicker or two, though Camilla knew she must be fresh as paint with little regular exercise.

In a few minutes they were striking out across a field of clover. In unison they jumped a low hawthorn hedge at the far side and found themselves neck and neck over the first of the Humphrey Repton parkland. Dexter's leggy hunter could easily have outpaced hers, Camilla knew, but by his iron control of the reins and a few muttered words, he was ensuring that they rode side by side. She was aware of his strength, of body and of mind, and found herself reaching a reluctant understanding of the attraction he held for her mother.

Dexter's thoughts also were of Angelica. In the few days since they'd met in Caro Rupert's Ascot box, she had dictated what he should say and do, how he should dress, eat, treat everyone around him. Everyone but her. She was not so crass as to tell him how she wished him to treat her. It was more a matter of constant hints, and subtle innuendo. He was not about to let any smart-talking sheila take him over completely, however, even one as glossily well-bred as the dowager Countess of Courtney.

He had missed none of her veiled references to the current state of Courtney Park's finances and her son's determination to live abroad once his studies were over. 'Darling Xan intends to restore the family fortunes as a banker — in America, of all places. He says he's not coming back till he's made his first million. Till then, I shall carry on here in my own sweet way.'

Her behaviour over the cards last night and afterwards, when she had chosen to follow him from the library and closely up the long curving staircase, had left Dexter in no doubt that if he should choose to go corridor-creeping in the middle of the night, he would find her bedroom door already discreetly ajar.

In his own room, restless and keyed up, he had contemplated doing just that. It was seven weeks since he'd left Sydney, and Linita ... He tossed and turned in his darkened room, grappling with the demons of unfocused desire: Linita's lush tawny promise contrasting with Angelica's cool dark perfection.

There were depths of emotion in Linita which, he now realised guiltily, he could never match. Their time apart had been a good thing, for him. It had become apparent to him that their living together was more a matter of habit than of anything else. Linita was a lovely generous woman who would always have the power to stir the earthy sensual side of his nature, but since being in England he realised that he wanted more than that from the woman in his life.

His visit to the old country, and particularly these last few days at Courtney Park, had opened his eyes to so much more. Here was a world of culture and sophistication and civilised excess that he, Dexter Randolph, thirsted to experience to the full. He sensed that Angelica was offering him one means of entrée — but was it the only one? Was it the best? Dexter Randolph never settled for anything less.

'Race you to the Folly,' Camilla shouted, taking him by surprise. He caught a glimpse of her laughing face under its black velvet riding-hat as she issued the challenge over her shoulder. Then she was off, her light-boned mare skimming the emerald turf that rolled before them. For a moment he did not urge his own mount on, caught by a strange sense of *déjà vu*. With her flushed cheeks and air of childish happiness, Camilla had reminded him of somebody ... In a flash he realised it was his first love, Lucinda, before the long years of disillusionment with Lucas had sapped her good looks and gaiety.

'Well, what do you know?' he murmured to himself, and caught Hannibal a smart tap in the ribs which sent him surging after the fleeing mare and her rider. He was in the nick of time. Nearing the Folly, a few hundred yards ahead, Sally's hooves startled a pheasant in a stand of bracken. With a whirring of wings, it flew up straight under her feet. Normally good-mannered, the shock temporarily unhinged the mare, who reared up on her hind legs. Camilla grabbed for her mane to take her weight, losing the reins in the process. She was still hanging on precariously to the plaited hair when Sally's hooves hit the ground, and she was off.

They seemed to cover the ground to the Folly in an instant. It loomed before them, closer, closer — and Camilla remembered with a surge of horror that it was surrounded by a ha-ha or concealed ditch. To her intense relief, Sally suddenly started to veer right, away from the danger. Approaching from her left, Dexter was neatly heading her off, matching Hannibal's longer stride to hers while all the time edging closer.

A lean brown arm shot out to grab the dangling reins, and Sally was hauled to a stop, ten yards from the treacherous ditch.

'Are you all right, Camilla?'

Dexter's face swam into view. In a dream-like state of shock, she studied it. The eyes seemed a deeper colour than she remembered and suddenly less bleak. Warm and welcoming as the bluest sea ...

She started to slew sideways and, in the instant, Dexter was off his horse and holding out his arms to her. 'It's okay, let yourself go, I'll catch you,' he told her. And: 'No more than a featherweight,' he murmured, smiling down at her as he held her.

For a few treacherous moments Camilla allowed herself to enjoy the sensation. The power she had sensed in him was something raw and primitive, not refined by the centuries of breeding and tradition which lent Luciano his charm. Luciano! How could she be allowing this, half enjoying another man's embrace, while at this very moment Luciano was longing only for her? Besides, Dexter

274

was Maman's. Anyone with half an eye could see that.

'Upset over,' she said, coolly detaching herself from his embrace. 'I'm perfectly all right now, thank you.'

'Well, that's a pity,' he said with a deadpan expression on his long narrow face. 'For a moment there I was in danger of enjoying myself.'

Despite her confusion, she had to smile. Dexter's sheer cheek was dangerously attractive at times. 'Come on,' she said, lightening the tension. 'I won't race you this time, but we should be getting back. Maman always comes down for Sunday breakfast.'

For hours Angelica had lain in her wide canopied bed, aching for Dexter's stealthy approach through the sleeping house, his knock at the door and the first thrilling coming together which would follow. In her extensive experience, first times were always the best, and Dexter would be a tough and ruthless lover, she told herself as she shivered with anticipation.

In the merciless grey light of dawn, she reviewed her crumbling hopes. Dexter Randolph was nobody's fool. She'd made it abundantly clear that he would be welcome in her bed. He'd understood the message, but for reasons of his own had chosen not to take up her invitation. Perhaps, whispered a sneering little voice inside her, you no longer have what it takes to attract any man you choose.

Oh God, she needed this man, and not just for his money. Dexter's singular appearance, his outspokenness and aura of self-reliance had brought back excitement to Angelica's life. Not since the early days of her affair with Beano — now sadly run to seed — had she felt so agonisingly drawn to a man. True, Dexter would be Courtney's salvation, but she wanted him for more than that. She wanted him for herself. The sight of him accompanying Camilla into the breakfast-room, both of them laughing and relating the story of her narrow escape, caught her on a raw nerve.

'Camilla,' she hissed, 'I'd be glad if you thought less of your own selfish pleasure and more of our guests. There seems to be some hold-up with the newspapers. Really, it's too bad! See if you can get some sense out of the village shop, can you?'

Properly, in the absence of a butler, the task belonged to the housekeeper, but Camilla knew how overburdened their few remaining staff were by the incursion of weekend guests. Perhaps if her mother had set aside more of the money Camilla had transferred to her for hiring replacement staff, and less on couture clothes, life would have been easier for all of them. But it was only a telephone call, after all.

Just as she picked up the phone in her father's old study, the newspaper van pulled up on the gravel at the side of the house. She went outside to receive the small sack of newspapers for guests and staff, and arranged for those for the guests to be left in the morning-room. She decided not to go back into breakfast, finding herself curiously reluctant to meet Dexter Randolph's searching gaze.

Camilla decided to take a *Sunday Times* up to her room, read it there and finish her letter to Luciano. She crossed the chequered marble floor of the hall, her eyes already lazily scanning the headlines. One in particular caught her eye: *Italian Heir in Car Smash* . . .

26-year-old Count Luciano di Nardi, heir to the Lambardi wine fortune, was killed in an automobile accident yesterday. His Ferrari was struck by a petrol tanker out of control on the Via Bolognese, outside Florence. Both drivers died in the blaze.

Her screams brought people running from every direction. Alexander was the first to reach her. He found her rigid with shock, a discarded newspaper crumpled at her feet.

'What's happened? For goodness' sake, Camilla, tell

me.' She stared at him blankly, her screams fading to low distraught moans. He shook her roughly. 'Camilla? Can you hear me?'

Angelica, who had followed close on his footsteps, was pale with fury. That guests of hers should witness such a scene! 'Of course she can hear you! That's enough, Camilla, do you understand?'

She brought back her hand and struck her daughter across the face. The sharp crack echoed around the hall. In the appalled silence which instantly fell, a sharp intake of breath by one of the shocked female guests was clearly audible.

Too late, Angelica realised the harsh, unsympathetic role in which she had cast herself. 'It's for her own good. Since her father's death, these hysterical outbursts ...' Swiftly she took charge of the situation. Her own maid Henriette was instructed to take Camilla upstairs and put her to bed. The housekeeper was sent to summon the doctor.

'Please go through to the morning-room,' the guests were told. 'Camilla's always been so highly strung. I'm sorry for this little disturbance.'

The English guests withdrew tactfully, taking the platitudes at face value. Dexter was not so easily moved. He had picked up the newspaper and was studying it closely.

'Camilla was at school in Florence, wasn't she?'

'Yes,' said Alexander.

Dexter pointed to the brief Reuter's report. 'Is there a connection with this, do you think?'

Alexander scanned the paragraph and turned pale. 'I don't believe it! Poor, poor Camilla. So soon after Daddy ...'

'Alexander, we have guests. What is this all about?' his mother broke in.

'Camilla's friend, Luciano. He's been killed in a car accident.'

'Luciano? Oh, the Italian boy. It's sad, of course. The

277

family must be desolate. But she can't have been in love with him. They'd only just met.'

It was Dexter who replied. 'Sometimes,' he said thoughtfully, 'that's all it takes.'

The shock of her double bereavement hit Camilla like a runaway express train. She felt crushed and immobilised by grief, unable to do anything but lie in bed, reading and re-reading her own unfinished love letter to Luciano.

On the doctor's advice, Angelica left her largely alone. 'Lady Camilla has suffered a severe shock,' she was told. 'Given peace and understanding, she'll heal in her own time, but I cannot stress enough that no undue stress must be placed on her.'

Angelica took the hint. Camilla's meals were taken up to her; Alexander sat with her for hours at a time; but her mother visited her for no more than a few minutes each day.

After the premature break-up of the house party, Dexter had surprised and delighted his hostess by asking if he might make Courtney Park his base in the short term — until he could buy a suitable London *pied à terre* and office premises.

'Naturally I don't expect you to put me up for free,' he told Angelica. 'I thought in return I might offer to take a closer look at the house and estate for you. You have your own advisers, I know, but a fresh eye ... Do you think Alexander would take offence?'

'He'd be delighted, Dexter. Xan intends to succeed in business himself, and I know he respects your experience.'

Dexter paid frequent visits to London, engaging staff and setting up his London operation with very un-English speed. On his return to Courtney Park, he painstakingly familiarised himself with the precise state of the house, the estate and its accounts. Angelica had indicated that nothing was to be kept back from him.

She was full of plans to complete the refurbishment of the house — once the family fortunes were restored. 'Brinsley was such a traditionalist. He really did prefer things the way his mama ordered them.'

Dexter, who had gained a very clear picture of the Hamilton fortunes from his study of the estate accounts and discussions with Ralph Hayward, the manager, asked her what changes she would like to make, should money be no object.

Instantly, she was all fire and enthusiasm. Dexter thought he had never seen her look so strikingly animated as when she outlined for him the way she would like things to be. She had planned to modernise the family rooms on the first floor, separate from the much colder, grander state rooms below — though naturally those were to be re-vamped too! She also wanted to expand the Hamilton collection of Impressionists, make over the stable wing, and install a heated outdoor swimming-pool.

'What about replacing the lead on the roof, installing a new central heating system, tackling the dry rot?'

'But of course. That goes without saying.'

'But not without paying.'

She smiled wistfully. 'We must all pray that Xan does well. That, or else the House of Hamilton must forge a rich alliance. The French and the British aristocracy have always taken a pragmatic approach to these matters. We are cash poor, but we still have much of value to offer, you understand?'

'Yes indeed, Angelica. I think I understand you very well.'

He was flatteringly attentive to her over the next few days, but departed for London early on the third without saying when he might be expected back. He still had not visited her bedroom.

With unexpected sensitivity, Dexter had made no attempt to force his sympathy on Camilla. Instead, he frequently sought out Alexander and asked after her.

When a week had passed and he thought she would be over her initial shock, he sent her a letter.

My dear Camilla

I'm a plain-speaking sort of bloke, not much good with words, but I want you to know how sorry I am for what's happened.

I lost a woman once. She didn't die, though pretty well as good as. She was lost to me completely and I thought I'd never get over the pain. Believe me, though, the worst of it does fade.

That's probably not what you want to hear right now. I expect you find even the thought of forgetting some sort of betrayal of Luciano. It's not. I believe and pray you'll see that, in time.

Until then you are in the thoughts of
Your friend
Dexter Randolph

It was a thoughtful and deeply-felt letter, and she was constantly surprised by fresh evidence of his solicitude. Not a day passed without some small carefully chosen present arriving at her room: books and records which spoke to her in her grief; a delicate porcelain dove to soothe the eye; a small rosemary bush in an exquisite enamelled cachepot. Rosemary for remembrance.

She would never have believed Dexter capable of such unobtrusive sympathy and kindness and saw now how sadly she'd misjudged him. If Maman were to remarry, Camilla felt she could do a lot worse than Dexter Randolph.

After hiding herself away for a week, Camilla realised she was being selfish, keeping Alexander away from the events of the Season. She ordered him to go up to town. At first he was reluctant to go, realising that his presence acted as a buffer between the rawness of Camilla's grief and Angelica's insensitivity.

'Are you sure you'll be all right?' he asked doubtfully.

'Life must go on,' she said blankly. 'Besides, Dexter keeps Maman pretty occupied, draws her fire. How can he stand her continually ordering him around?'

'Very easily, I should think. Don't worry about our Mr Randolph, Camilla. He's even tougher than he looks, and my guess is he usually gets what he wants.'

Camilla was to remember his words a few days later. Despite her protestations that really she didn't feel up to it, she was steamrollered into guiding Dexter round a few of the local landmarks. Angelica had taken herself off to London to have her hair done when he made his request.

'It's no use trying to fob me off, Camilla. Besides, I thought you Poms believed in looking after your guests. And a day in the open air will do you good.'

'But we'll be driving around in a car for most of it,' she protested.

'My *new* car,' he corrected her. 'They'll be bringing her over any time now.'

It was a sight to behold — a powder blue Rolls-Royce laundalette with navy leather seating. Dexter was like a boy with a new toy, sitting in the driver's seat and playing with every switch on the dashboard. He plainly intended to do the driving.

'Does my mother know about your new car?' Camilla asked innocently.

'Nah — reckoned I'd surprise her.'

'Oh, you'll do that all right,' she said, the corners of her mouth twitching.

He narrowed his eyes suspiciously. 'Come on. What have I done wrong now? A Rolls is a classy English car, isn't it?'

'Generally speaking, yes,' Camilla chose her words with care. 'But the coachwork should be in a rather more — conservative colour, it's usual to employ a chauffeur, and these open roofs are fine if you're Royalty, waving to the crowds and so on, but for us lesser mortals a little ...'

'In other words, it's a total bloody disaster,' he said, and sighed heavily. 'Nothing else for it, then — she goes straight back.'

Suddenly it felt very important to her that his feelings should not be hurt; their day together not be spoiled by something so trivial in any but the narrow circles in which her mother moved. 'Dexter, I just told you what the conventional, rather stuffy, line on the car would be. I didn't say I shared it. Besides, you can't send it back now. Not before I've had a ride!'

Social error or not, he reckoned it had been worth buying the car just to see the colour returning to her wan face and a mischievous sparkle replace the bleak expression in her eyes.

Whether it was the gleaming blue car or the misshapen felt hat Dexter insisted on wearing while driving, they attracted attention wherever they went. Camilla guided him around Stonehenge, Avebury, Savernake Forest and, finally, Salisbury with its picture postcard cathedral close.

'Reckon I'll look around out here for a while,' he said finally, as she stood uncertainly by the cathedral doors.

'Would you, Dexter? I'd like to be on my own in here, just for a moment.'

When she emerged twenty minutes later, after saying prayers for her father and Luciano, he was standing on the spot where she had left him, felt hat pulled down over his eyes, harsh features shadowed in the softening early evening light. She sensed that he was studying her and was glad that she had taken the time to wipe away all traces of the tears she had shed inside. He was not a man before whom to display weakness, she realised.

'You okay?' he asked, taking her arm.

'Fine, thank you.'

'Home, then?'

'I suppose so. Maman will be back by seven.'

'Catch, then!'

'What —?' Camilla looked down at the key-ring with its

distinctive double R motif. 'No, I couldn't!' she said in alarm.

'You could, and you're going to. No more shutting yourself off from things. Get in the car, Camilla.'

In the car park, she begged him to reconsider. Dexter was adamant. He slumped down in the passenger seat, pulled his hat over his eyes and gave every indication of having fallen asleep.

He really was an infuriating man, she decided, tentatively turning the key in the ignition, and gripping the heavy walnut wheel with shaking hands. A gentleman would never have forced her to drive an unfamiliar car so soon after her fiancé's death in a road accident, she thought indignantly, steering the majestic car through streets congested with homegoing traffic. Gaining confidence despite herself, Camilla signalled to turn left, glancing down at the man lounging beside her. She realised he had been sitting very still, studying her every move intently from beneath the brim of his terrible hat.

'Saddle up and remount — is there any other way?' he said laconically. 'You're doing fine, sweetheart — for a woman driver.'

'Right — you deserve this!' She gunned the engine noisily, and took the narrow country roads leading back to Courtney at a speed that whipped tangles into her hair and brilliant colour to her cheeks. Faintly, over the noise of the engine and the rushing of the wind, she heard him murmur, 'That's my girl.'

Over dinner that night Dexter was particularly complimentary to Angelica, commenting favourably on the casual new hairstyle she had adopted. Her thick black hair had been blunt cut to shoulder length and swept off her high forehead, to be secured at the back of her head with a broad diamanté clip and brushed until it flipped softly upward at the ends. The new style enhanced her mother's evergreen appeal, Camilla realised. Basking in the glow of Dexter's attention, she looked younger and softer than Camilla could remember seeing her for years.

After dinner, Angelica proposed that they should take coffee in her private sitting-room, since they were only three.

'Suits me,' Dexter agreed.

Camilla wasn't so sure of her own welcome. There was something in the way her mother looked at their guest — something hot and hungry — which warned her that three might be a crowd. Once in her mother's inner sanctum, Dexter's mood changed. He seemed to turn in on himself, displaying none of the easy good nature of his earlier behaviour. An awkward silence fell between them, and Camilla hastily made her excuses and left.

Angelica was relieved. 'Darling, it was sweet of you to make such an effort with Camilla today,' she purred, setting down her glass of brandy on a Regency sofa table. 'But you know there's no need for you to dance attendance on her. She'll come through this sticky patch so much more quickly if we just leave her to her own devices.'

Dexter leant back in his seat and studied her long and hard. 'I don't agree,' he said finally.

She gave a light, brittle laugh. 'Well, of course, a mother's opinion counts for so little, but in my experience some healthy neglect never hurt a child.'

'I dare say neglect is something you're well qualified to talk about. But motherhood? Don't make me laugh!'

Her eyes were two amazed dark circles in a face frozen with shock. 'I don't have to listen to this from you,' she began, 'an Australian nobody — a cowboy from the back of beyond! How dare you insult me like this in my own home?'

'I don't want to insult you, Angel. Believe me, I've got a lot of respect for you — the way you run this house and your social commitments, the way your clothes are never less than perfect. The way you battle to hold back the years.'

Her pallor suffused by a glint of fury, she raised a hand to strike him for his presumption. 'You bastard!' she cried.

He caught her wrist, squeezing its fragile bones in fingers like steel. She gasped, and at the sound he immediately relaxed his grip, placing her arm carefully by her side and patting it reassuringly. 'Believe me, Angelica, I'm not your enemy, but it's time we got a few things straightened out between us. Number one, you'd better know that I intend to marry your daughter.'

'But you can't! For God's sake, you're twice her age.'

'So, I believe, was your husband.'

'But — but I thought you and I . . .'

'If it's any consolation, for a while so did I. Hell, I'll be straight with you. You're a damned attractive woman. When I saw you here in this place, how well you run it, I did seriously consider asking you to marry me.'

'Big of you,' she jeered, through teeth that were all but chattering with shock. For weeks, she'd stalked Dexter Randolph like a cat. Whatever outcome she'd anticipated, it had not been this dispassionate appraisal and rejection before she'd even had him in her bed. Her skin crawled with horror as she imagined all the tell-tale signs of age that had obviously spoiled her chances with him. To think she'd felt so young and desirable early this evening! Dexter Randolph's words made her feel like a dried-up old hag, and for that she would never forgive him.

She was so busy focusing on her own rage and agony that it took her a while to concentrate on what he was saying.

'. . . Then I saw the way you treated Camilla on the day she heard about the smash. The kid was broken up, destroyed, and you — her own mother — were more concerned to save your guests the embarrassment of any display of emotion. Christ! But yes, you're beautiful still, Angel. Don't worry about that.'

Hearing only the compliment, Angelica rallied. 'You're a newcomer, Dexter, with so much still to learn about the proper way to behave — and frankly I'm not sure that you'll ever fit in. This habit of sermonising, for instance — so terribly middle-class!'

Unmoved, he settled himself more comfortably in his seat. 'Oh, I'll fit in all right. And you, Angel, will be helping me. Every step of the way.'

'Help the man who passes me over in favour of my pale shadow of a daughter? I think not!' A touch of desperation entered her voice. 'For God's sake, Dexter, why? She's not right for you. I ought to know, she's my own flesh and blood, but timid, weak, not nearly woman enough for a man with your appetites.'

'What can you possibly know about those?' he taunted. 'Since the day I met Camilla I've had this in mind. I wasn't going to muddy the waters by sleeping with my future mother-in-law — however desirable.'

As usual, Angelica heard only what concerned her. 'So you admit you find me desirable?'

'You have style, wit, beauty, enormous charm — but you lack one essential qualification in a woman. You have no warmth.'

'What on earth would I need with that? I have Courtney Park!' Her voice sank dramatically. 'And so help me, Dexter, if you and my shrinking violet daughter go through with this travesty of a marriage, I shall see to it that you are never received here again.'

'I doubt it,' he said calmly. 'Not when you hear what else I have to say.'

She sat very still, buffeted by rage and hope.

'Courtney Park needs money, lots of it. The fabric of the house itself is at risk, and the revenue from the estate is frankly a joke. You could be making five or six times what you draw from it at present, but to do so you need capital investment. That's where I come in. If I were to marry into the family, in return for being allowed to make Courtney Park one of my principal homes I would be prepared to sign an agreement assuming sole responsibility for all

286

renovation, re-financing and upkeep of the house and estate for a period of ten years, the arrangement to be renegotiable at the end of that period subject to the agreement of both parties.'

'You've been consulting lawyers, haven't you? You've got a nerve, you colonial upstart!'

'Careful, Angel, you might say something you'll regret. In fact, since the estate is entailed, I've approached Alexander's lawyers. You have the right to live here for the rest of your life, if you choose. No one can take that away from you. But think of it for a moment. What fun will it be, seeing the house fade and decay a little more each year? Never having enough money to entertain decently. Patching and making do when you'd so much rather be starting from scratch, making everything new and beautiful. With my money behind you, you could do everything you've always wanted with this place. Alexander's not interested in it, and I'd not interfere. Christ, why should I? You've more of a feel for that sort of thing than I can ever hope to have.'

'Or Camilla,' she said silkily, the anguished expression replaced by something calmer, more calculating. 'And I should have an absolutely free hand with the renovations?'

'Do as you please. And, besides, an annual budget for entertaining on the understanding that at least part of the time you'll be working to further my entrance into British society. Introducing me to the right people, getting me noticed — you know the sort of thing. I'm not asking them to make me an Earl —'

'Just as well!'

'A peerage, or even a baronetcy, will do me as well. These things can be arranged, I hear, if the price is right.'

Grudgingly, she inclined her head. 'I can't promise, of course. It'll take years of hard work, keeping clear of scandal and donating a great deal of money to all the right charities.'

'You write the cheques, Angel. I'll sign them. Now, do we shake on it?'

She studied his lean muscular body and quirky, strong-featured face. He'd be wasted as a son-in-law. 'Before we do,' she reluctantly agreed, 'there's one point we haven't discussed. Suppose Camilla says no? What do you expect me to do — lock her up and starve her into submission?'

'I wouldn't put it past you! But leave her to me, and there won't be any need for that.'

He got to his feet, more intensely desirable with the light of triumph in his eyes than she had ever known him.

'Night, Angel.' He bent to kiss her chastely on the cheek. She twisted like an eel, twining her arms round his neck and meeting his mouth with hers. For a moment they were evenly matched in the passion of their embrace before he disengaged himself.

'That's very matey of you, Mother-in-law.'

'Bastard!'

'Make that *rich* bastard, the one who's going to pay all the bills — so long as you keep your part of the bargain. Oh, and one other thing — I'm an old-fashioned sort, so don't bother leaving your bedroom door ajar. G'night.'

Breathing raggedly, she snatched up a Rockingham figurine and hurled it after him. It caught the edge of the door as Dexter pulled it to behind him, smashing into a hundred razor-edged fragments, like the pieces of her heart.

When Dexter proposed to Camilla the following morning in the rose garden, at first she thought he was joking.

'But, it's Maman who's looking for a husband. I mean, I never thought of you in that way.'

'Haven't you?' His voice seemed to caress her, though he had made no move towards her.

She remembered their ride together on the morning she had heard about Luciano. 'No,' she said firmly, 'how could I, after everything that's been happening? What sort of woman do you think I am?'

'Delicate, gentle, someone who's been bruised by life and needs the strength and stability I can offer. Marry me, Camilla. I promise you, you'll never regret it.'

It was as though he had hypnotised her. Deny it as she might to him, she knew she had felt vague stirrings of attraction towards him but she had never dreamt that they might come to this. She'd thought it far too soon after Luciano, and Dexter to be her mother's sole province. Now he was telling her it was not so. That he was willing to assuage her loneliness, be a rock for her to lean on. Any moment now he would say he loved her ...

Like a bird into its nest, she went blindly into his arms. Forever afterwards she associated the scent of roses with the sweetness of Dexter's first kiss. He knew better than to alarm her with any display of passion, though when his arms claimed her as his it was all he could do not to shout in exultation. She was everything soft and yielding and innocent, everything he had thought lost from his life with Lucinda. At that moment she meant more to him than he could put into words. The pity of it was that he failed to try.

When, later in the day, a set-faced Angelica explained to her daughter how Dexter had come to her to propose an alliance which could be advantageous to both sides, Camilla's fragile bubble of happiness burst. There was no need to call off the marriage, though. After all, it was a fair trade. Dexter would receive the benefit of an alliance with the Hamiltons: an entrée into society and a home at Courtney Park — in return, she could expect a luxurious, cosseted existence. It had been naïve and greedy of her to expect that the benefits of such a rich alliance could also include love.

Camilla would gladly have opted for a long engagement. Since her marriage to Dexter was not based on romance, more on old-style dynastic principles, she saw no necessity to hurry things. For different reasons, Dexter and her mother disagreed.

'I thought a spring wedding, Maman,' said Camilla a few days after accepting Dexter's proposal. 'Will that give you enough time?'

'Hmm?' Angelica was lost in contemplation of some moire=18- silk swatches, choosing a colour for the walls of the new family sitting-room. 'What do you think — the raspberry or the grenadine?'

'Is there a difference?'

'But of course! Really, Camilla, you have no eye. It's a good thing Dexter has enough money to pay other people to do this sort of thing for you.'

Like you, the girl thought, but obligingly peered at the two near-identical samples.

'And don't screw up your eyes like that. Do you want to be a wrinkled old hag by the time you're thirty?'

'Dexter won't complain.'

'Don't be ridiculous! Dexter Randolph is like every other rich man — only interested in the very best. Take a hint from me, Camilla. Always make an effort to look attractive and soignée, and keep a very keen eye out for rivals. Dexter's rich, well-known, and damned attractive. Having netted him, you'd be a fool to let him slip through your fingers. Which is why I've agreed that you'll marry as soon as possible — Dexter's fixing up a special licence.' She threw down the book of samples. Angrily, thought Camilla.

'It won't be a big society affair, then?'

'I thought the estate chapel. It's big enough for family and close friends. And Dexter and I weren't quite sure he could carry off St Margaret's, Westminster. Not yet, anyway.'

They had, thought Camilla, sorted everything out between them so thoroughly that it was pointless raising any objections.

Thankfully, she remained unaware of the loose ends Dexter was endeavouring to tie up. He was determined to marry Camilla and take her back to Australia as soon as possible. The long sea voyage would be the perfect honeymoon opportunity, a month of constant proximity in which to get to know one another.

Writing to Linita was one of the hardest tasks he had ever undertaken. As he wrote, he could picture her in all her tawny splendour, imagine the shock and horror on her expressive face as she read what he had done to her. His hand slowed and faltered as he wrote. He began to question the wisdom of his decision — and then he glanced around at the tired but lovely morning-room in which he wrote, picturing it newly restored and beautified with his money. He thought of Camilla, his type of woman: beautiful and well-bred, soft and yielding. Quickly he finished the letter and posted it in the box in the hall. He had made his decision and he would stick by it.

He was content to leave all the arrangements for the wedding in Angelica's capable hands. Camilla's dress, eight attendants, the ceremony officiated over by the Bishop of Salisbury and reception afterwards at the house were planned with barely a reference to bride or groom. With the same efficiency and attention to detail with which she had tackled everything else, Angelica drafted the wedding announcement for *The Times*. Remembering the groom's Australian friends, she decided they should be informed too, and cabled a copy of the announcement to the *Sydney Morning Herald*.

Linita woke early that morning, alerted by the pattern of sunlight on water which cast darts of light on the peach-coloured walls. In the twilight state between sleep and waking, she reached towards Dexter's side of the bed and found it cold. Mignonne, sleeping in her basket at the end of the bed, was alerted by the movement. Though this was strictly forbidden when the master of the house was in residence, she knew she was safe today and came creeping

291

up the silk coverlet, silky tail wagging affectionately, eyes pleading for affection.

Linita kissed the smooth fur on the little dog's head. 'I know just how you feel,' she said sadly. Where the hell *was* Dexter? He'd promised to return just as soon as his business was concluded, and in the last letter from Manchester had indicated that he expected that to be by the beginning of July. It was the end of August now and there'd been no further letters, not even a cable giving his date of arrival in Sydney.

In an effort to dispel her gathering anxiety, Linita drew back the ruffled peach taffeta curtains and allowed the cheerful winter sunshine to flood the room. Outside, the smooth waters of the harbour were painted a ravishing blue. It was the first cheerful day for an age.

'Too good to waste on sleeping,' Linita said aloud. 'Come on, Mignonne. You and me's going to the beach.'

She pulled on a pair of hot pink Capri pants and a loose hip-length sweater in searing orange and cerise. They were not the sort of classy imported clothes Dexter liked to see her in, but so what? He wasn't here to see her, damn him.

As she ran a comb impatiently through her heavy mass of hair, the bedside phone started to ring.

'Drat!' she said aloud, and answered it with a brisk: 'Yes?'

'Linita darling, it's me. I don't want to intrude at a time like this but I felt I simply must check how you were.'

It took a while for her to work out that the schooled Melbourne accent belonged to Eliza, Dexter's former girlfriend. 'Sweet of you,' she said, struggling to hide her mystification. 'But I'm fine. Why wouldn't I be?'

'My dear, I'm so sorry! If I'd dreamt he hadn't been in touch himself ... I was worried on your behalf. I know what news like this can do to a woman.'

'News like what, for Pete's sake?' Despite her pretence at briskness, a feeling of cold dread was creeping over her.

'I really don't know how to break this to you ...'

'Just spit it out, Eliza. It's what you called for, isn't it?'

There was a gloating pause before Linita's worst enemy told her: 'It's in the *Morning Herald* today — Dexter's married an English girl, the daughter of an Earl! Well, he always did have his sights set higher than either of us.'

There was a roaring in Linita's ears, a gush of foul-tasting liquid in the back of her throat. She dropped the phone, Eliza's insistent voice still faking concern, and dashed to the bathroom where she retched for minutes on end. Between each painful spasm she told herself: It's a mistake. It can't be true. It must be another Dexter Randolph. But the voice of reason warned her that Eliza would never have called unless she'd been quite sure of her facts.

'Miss Tyrone, shall I leave your tray? Hey — you all right, dear?' It was Joan, the maid, arriving with Linita's breakfast. One glance at her mistress's drawn face told her that something was very wrong.

'Take it away,' Linita said, gesturing violently, 'and bring me the morning paer.'

'You don't look well. Shall I call —'

'*Now!*' Linita was normally the sunniest and least demanding of employers. Joan had no idea why she wanted the newspaper, but brought it at the double.

Linita fumbled through it to the Announcements column. It was there, as she had known it would be, the proof of Dexter's treachery announced in black and white for all the world to see and wonder at Linita Tyrone's public casting-off. A wail of despair burst from her.

Joan, hovering outside the door, came running back in. 'Miss Tyrone, whatever is it? What's upset you like this?'

But Linita was past rational thought or speech. While Joan struggled to locate Dr Ritchie, Linita sobbed, swore and clawed at her face, neck and arms with long manicured nails. By the time the doctor arrived to administer a sedative, she had inflicted more than a dozen shallow wounds on herself. She talked incessantly, as though

Dexter were in the room with her. 'Sweet Jesus, no! Tell me it's not true. You can't do this to me, Dexter, not after all these years. Don't you know how much I love you?'

When he had given her a tranquillising shot, the doctor sat and bathed away the blood which beaded the smooth golden skin of her hands and arms. He decided he dared not leave her until the drug had taken effect, and even then saw that she wept and murmured in her sleep. He gave the rest of the drugs he had prescribed to Joan for safe-keeping. 'She'll need watching closely, maybe even hospitalisation,' he said. 'She's always been so bright and confident. I don't like the look of this. I don't like it at all.'

But on waking twenty-four hours later, though pale and shaking, Linita seemed rational and totally determined. 'Will you help me pack, Joan?' Her own friendly unassuming manner had returned. 'I need to get out of this house.'

It hurt the maid to see her mistress's good looks bleached by her distress. 'Of course I will, sweetheart. But have you anywhere to go?'

'I'll find somewhere, no worries. Dexter may be a ruthless conniving bastard, but he was never mean. I've banked all the fees from my modelling, and now I'll be free to work full-time.'

The desolate sound of her own words brought tears to Linita's eyes. It was hard to believe she'd ever been the Amazonian beauty who'd graced so many advertisements and magazine spreads. She seemed physically to have shrunk since hearing the bad news.

Sympathetic Joan found herself speaking ill of Dexter for the first time since she had worked for him. 'Marrying one woman without so much as a word of goodbye to the last — he's lower than a reptile!'

'Don't you dare say that! Never insult him in front of me.' Tears of hurt still wet on her face, Linita jumped immediately to Dexter's defence.

Joan was amazed. 'I'm sorry, Miss Tyrone, but why waste a second's regret on the bludger?'

Linita gave a wan smile. 'It doesn't seem to make any difference what he does to me. I should have more pride, I know, but if Dexter walked through that door right now I couldn't stop myself from running to him. Where he's concerned, I'm totally without pride.'

'Sounds like it! But there's no sense in your carrying a torch for him, now he's married another girl.'

'Isn't there?' Linita's face, usually so open and sunny, bore a closed, guarded expression. 'I may be out of his house, but if Dexter Randolph thinks I'm out of his life, he's in for a big surprise!'

On the morning of Camilla's wedding, Angelica gave her the pearl and diamond earrings which had been her own mother's bridal gift to her. She helped the shivering girl to dress in the Dior wedding gown of heavy ivory satin oversewn with seed-pearls, and placed the Hamilton tiara over her daughter's veil of heavy Brussels lace.

The recently widowed mother of the bride was calm and composed throughout the ceremony, her guests noted. Only Alexander saw the single swiftly despatched tear that escaped her when the Bishop declared Camilla Alexandra Hamilton and Dexter John Randolph to be man and wife.

For their first night, since they would be leaving from Southampton early the next morning, Angelica had arranged for the newly wedded couple to borrow a small country house in Hampshire. Dexter had insisted on leaving the reception early, overriding his mother-in-law's objections. He had also turned a deaf ear to her strictures on the blue Rolls-Royce convertible. Camilla liked the car and that, as far as he was concerned, was that. He intended to drive them away from Courtney and off on honeymoon himself.

'I'm taking pity on the chauffeur,' he told Camilla solemnly. 'I don't care what your mother says, the poor bloke would feel a regular gooseberry driving a pair of honeymooners. Anyway, bloody good thing I am driving, if you ask me.'

'Why?'

'Because otherwise I wouldn't be able to keep my hands off you.' The glint in his eye left her in no doubt as to his meaning. Her experience of men was limited to those few brief hours with Luciano when his gentleness and patience had been inexhaustible. Dexter was a very different kind of man; patience not one of his virtues. A thrill of unease ran through her. It was not quieted when they drew up outside the rose-red brick façade of a small gem of a William and Mary house.

Dexter turned to her with a wolfish smile. 'Why don't we carry you over the threshold — and straight upstairs? 'Struth, I hadn't bargained on a welcome party!'

A man in butler's grey and black and a woman in a white bibbed apron had opened the front door of the house.

Camilla laughed nervously. 'It's just the couple who "do". I expect they want to know if there's anything we'd like.'

'Too right there is — a bit of bloody privacy! Stay right where you are.'

Obediently she sat still while Dexter approached the smiling couple. They speedily vanished, and Dexter returned to the car.

'Whatever did you say to them?'

'Here's twenty quid. Now bugger off and leave us alone together,' he said, grinning.

'Dexter, you didn't!'

'Music to their ears, believe me. Now out you come. I've waited long enough.' Without stopping to open the door, he leant over the car's open roof and lifted her out.

'I never know what you'll do next,' she said, smiling up at him.

'Give you three guesses!' He carried her straight to the principal bedroom, following the discreet instructions the butler had passed on. Before Camilla could comment on their surroundings, he had kicked open the door and deposited her on the fourposter.

'Christ, you're beautiful. I've waited long enough.' Expertly he dealt with the side-fastening of her silk tussore going-away dress and began to tug it free of her shoulders. Impatiently his hands cupped and appraised her breasts, before sliding behind to unfasten her brassière.

It was all going too fast for Camilla. 'What are you doing?' she said stupidly.

'What do you think I'm doing?' he snapped, eyes misty with passion. 'It's a honeymoon, not a flaming tea-party!'

She shrank from the impatience in his voice. Overcoming his haste for a moment, he kissed the side of her neck. 'It's all right, I'll be gentle,' he whispered. and then his hot mouth covered hers, mastering it with lips and tongue before moving fiercely down over her bare shoulders and breasts.

His hands worked impatiently at her skirts and petticoats. But for her panties and stockings she found herself naked to the man who loomed above her, face distorted by passion. He was a stranger to her, she thought in a panic, and tried to cover herself.

He prevented her, grasping her wrists. 'I'm your husband, Camilla. You hide nothing from me, remember that.'

He had thrown his own clothes on to the floor. She noticed the dark tracing of hair on his muscular chest but could not bring herself to glance lower. He knelt astride her, grasping the top of her silk panties. With a sigh, the thin fabric ripped and parted. Groaning, he lowered himself on top of her, his resolution to take things slowly and gently forgotten in the ungovernable heat of his longing. Camilla was taken aback by this sudden transformation from protector to demanding lover. She stiffened and clenched herself against him, but Dexter would not be denied.

He paused just long enough for his skilful fingers to ease

297

a passage, then drove himself into her, time and time again, until she thought that he would never stop. Where now was all the tender solicitude Camilla had grown used to in him? Dexter knew none of Luciano's teasing seductive arts, just this relentless, hard-driving sexuality which in her innocence she had never encountered before.

'If you're not going to come,' he said through gritted teeth, 'I wish you'd say so, then I could stop being such a bloody gentleman!'

'Is that what you call it?' she gasped.

At the accusing expression in her great grey eyes, he sank his face into the pillow. With a final groan and a tremor which shook his whole body, he subsided on top of her, crushing her with his weight. 'Sorry. Got a bit carried away there,' he mumbled. 'But, bloody hell, Camilla — it's not as though you were a virgin!'

'I never told you I was,' she said proudly, though inwardly shrinking at the trace of accusation in his voice.

For all the admission, her experience of lovemaking had been so brief, and her knowledge of Dexter was so incomplete, that she had gone to him feeling like one. And this was how he had treated her!

'No more you did,' he said, good humour apparently restored. He raised himself to free her of his weight. Lying on his back beside her, he slid one arm beneath her stiff unresponsive shoulders and pulled her to lie against him. She allowed him to position her as he pleased, but had nothing of tenderness or love to say to him while, his passion sated, he was full of both for her. Damn it! If only he was better with words.

He looked ruefully down at the top of her golden-brown head. Her face was averted, pressed close to his chest. He could feel her breathing, soft and regular, stirring the fine hairs on his skin. It would not be long before he was ready to take her again. And this time would be different, he silently promised.

From her manner and upbringing, Dexter had made the

mistake of assuming that Camilla would be a virgin — which made the speed and ferocity of his lovemaking all the more inexcusable, he reflected. He had been surprised to find it not so, and for a crucial moment was affronted to find that she must already have taken at least one lover. Though it was true she had never lied about it to him, he realised. Like so much else between them, it had simply never been discussed.

Mounting pity and tenderness for her mingled sweetly with his rising desire. 'Don't worry,' he said, hugging her close. 'So we didn't get it right that time — so what? We're a long time at sea.'

'Yes,' she dutifully agreed. 'Dexter, would you mind awfully if I went to sleep now? It's been a long day.'

'No, I don't mind,' he said manfully. They had a whole uninterrupted month ahead to work things out between them.

Things turned out not to be so easy. From their first day afloat, Camilla was wretchedly, shiveringly ill.

'One of the worst cases I've ever seen, mate,' the cheerfully irreverent Australian stewardess told him. 'Seasick like you wouldn't believe — unless it's something else, eh?'

'We've only been married a few days,' he told her frostily. The stewardess opened her mouth to reply — and thought better of it.

He was patience and forbearance itself with his suffering wife, seeking out what the ship's doctor and a few old-hand travellers could offer to alleviate her sickness. Finally their advice amounted to leaving her to rest undisturbed. He took another cabin for himself, visiting her from time to time in their stateroom.

'Poor Dexter,' she said weakly, when he had looked in on her one morning. 'Some honeymoon this has turned out to be! Never mind, darling. Once we're on dry land I'll make it up to you, I promise.'

Reassured by his patience when she was ill, Camilla's misgivings on their wedding day faded and vanished. She was far more comfortable with Dexter in his role of protector than as a passionate lover. If she had suspected his secret train of thought, she might have been a little less complacent.

She couldn't help her aversion to sea travel, he told himself. Even weak and debilitated, she still had the power to inspire love and devotion. Their rough and ready stewardess had been effortlessly won over. Of course he did not regret his marriage ... but as the ship sailed on into the heat and light of the southern hemisphere he could not help thinking occasionally of Linita, whose looks and strength and passion had so perfectly complemented his.

Once ashore, Camilla's sickness disappeared, but Sydney was a sad disappointment. Aboard ship, Dexter had painted such a glowing picture of the delights awaiting them there — the people to be met, the parties thrown, the sailing and swimming and trips to the beach house on Barrenjoey. But spring that year was wet and grey, and Dexter's workload, after a four-month absence, heavier than usual. Left alone day after day in the Yarrabbee Road house, Camilla felt lost and disorientated, physically at a low ebb despite the respite from sickness.

She tried first of all to befriend Joan, the maid, who seemed cold and dismissive of all her efforts. A few women — the wives of Dexter's business acquaintances or would-be acquaintances — included Camilla in their ladies' lunches and coffee mornings, but she found the rapid conversation, peppered with words and phrases she did not understand, hard to follow and participate in. Her shyness and lack of understanding was taken for Pommy stand-offishness. Her ladyship thought herself too good for them, obviously.

One woman in particular seemed more determined than the rest to keep in touch, but somehow whenever they met she slyly angled the conversation round to Dexter, revealing in dozens of little ways that she knew him very well. She seemed from the odd waspish comment she let slip to have been supplanted in his affections by a girl with a Spanish-sounding name. Camilla could never quite catch it, and certainly wasn't going to ask. She had never imagined that Dexter had lived the life of a monk previously but did not care to hear the details of his past amours. He was her husband now, and though she doubted he would ever awake in her the romantic passion that had flowered briefly between Luciano and herself, she intended to make the best of their flawed, businesslike marriage.

Things seemed to be looking up a little between them when Dexter suggested she should accompany him on his trip north, travelling via a relay of Randolph Enterprises planes to visit his cattle stations in Queensland and the Top End.

'You'll love it in Queensland,' he enthused. 'The sun up there'll soon have you looking less peaky, depend on it.'

There was sun, it was true. But in addition there were millions of blood-sucking insects which battened greedily on her fair skin until she felt like a human pincushion. Try as she might to smother herself in foul-smelling repellent, their needle bites led to hours of blotched and itching misery.

'Just a few mozzies,' Dexter said.

Fresh horrors seemed to lurk at every turning in the bush or, worse, in the homesteads themselves. Elephant beetles in the bed, blue frogs on the bathroom wall, a carpet snake which, they were warned, lived in the roof above them — 'But he's harmless, really!' The last straw came when, early one morning, crossing the veranda to reach the loathsome outside lavatory, she almost fell over what looked like a small-scale prehistoric monster. It flicked a long pink ribbon of tongue at her before ambling scalily away. Her screams brought Dexter running.

'What a racket over a little lizard.'

'Dexter — it was three feet long!'

'A baby. Where we're going they grow 'em six feet long. I'll see if the boys can catch you one.'

'You will not!' she told him sharply. 'Dexter, I'm sorry,

but this isn't working out. I've got prickly heat, I'm festering with insect bites, and every time I need to go to the — the —'

'Dunny,' he put in helpfully.

'— it's like going on a wildlife safari. I never realised there'd be so many terrifying animals out here.'

'But you loved seeing the kangaroos. And the platypus, and the possums.'

'And I *hated* the dingoes and the crocodiles.'

'Fair go, Camilla! They were freshwater. They wouldn't harm you.'

'I didn't know that!' she shouted, bursting into tears. 'Wherever I go, people are constantly springing these nasty little surprises on me, and laughing when I just about jump out of my skin.'

'Just trying to make you feel at home, sweetheart.'

'That's where I want to be. I want to go home. I'm sorry, but this isn't for me. Take me home, please.'

'There's still so much to see. Don't you even want to see Yelonga, the station where I was born? You'll love it there. It's the best spot on earth. And Lucas and Lucinda'll be offended if we don't go and visit.'

He kept talking to conceal his mounting hurt and disappointment. Camilla's rejection of his country felt almost like a rejection of him. And where did she mean by 'home', he wondered? The house in Sydney, or Courtney Park?

'Is it far to Yelonga?' she asked, blowing her nose.

'A couple of hops on the plane. We were going there next, anyway. You'll find things more comfortable there, sweetheart. It's the Randolph Enterprises showpiece, the last word in comfort. Why don't you stay there and get to know Lucinda while I visit the Top End on my own? I'll get more done that way,' he added tactlessly.

The constant heat and dust and barrage of whining, stinging flies seemed to have exhausted her. She lacked the strength to argue with him and the next day embarked on the journey to Yelonga.

302

It was true that it was a model station — fences strong and carefully monitored, cattle sleek and well-tended, the low iron-roofed homestead freshly painted in honour of their visit. In Dexter's presence, Lucas and Lucinda made a fuss of her. But when her husband flew north, leaving her to get to know them better, she felt ill at ease. Lucas, a blurred and bloated version of his brother, drank steadily through the evenings, paying Camilla heavy-handed, increasingly embarrassing compliments. The prim and ladylike Lucinda affected not to hear them, goading her husband into further indiscretions.

'Pretty little Pom,' he slurred one evening, glugging down another glass of 'grog', or undiluted rum. 'Delicate little English flower. My, but my brother can pick 'em! From dirt-heap princess to the daughter of an Earl ... Not that I didn't have a sneaking fondness for his last piece, the one with all that hair. What was her name, Lucinda? The *real* woman Dexter brought here last time?'

Lucinda looked up from her needlework, frowning. 'I don't think Camilla wants to hear about that, Lucas. What's done is done. Whatever Dexter did in the past, whoever he loved then, he's married to Camilla now.' She broke a thread with a vicious little jerk of her wrist and, not for the first time, Camilla sensed that long ago there had been some romance between this frozen, sad-faced woman and Dexter. Forgotten on his part, she was sure, but not, it seemed, on hers.

Though Camilla managed to befriend her young niece, Rhianne, she could get nowhere with Chip, Lucas and Lucinda's son. He was a wild, headstrong boy who thought nothing of bareback riding the barely broken brumby crosses in the paddock by the house.

'C'mon, Auntie, give it a go!' he encouraged her, but the glint of devilment in the dark brown eyes so like his father's warned her not even to try though she was no mean horsewoman herself. She stuck to riding the more biddable stock horses and touring the bush around the homestead with one of the aboriginal stockmen.

'You belongem boss man like other lubra? One with hair like-a sun?' he asked one day.

Unlike Lucas's mention of the woman, there was no malice in the stockman's reference to her.

'Yes,' said Camilla, after a pause. 'Me belongem boss man.' Though her time outback had been a failure in one way, she felt it had strengthened the ties which bound her to Dexter. Seeing him in his own country, his natural element, she could not fail to be stirred by his power and natural authority. Though she could never feel for the land as he did, she was glad to have seen him on it, and found that she was eagerly awaiting his return. She greeted him with open arms, running to the strip to welcome him back to Yelonga. Delighted and disarmed by such a public display of affection from his normally cool and reserved young wife, he swept her off her feet, showering her face with kisses while Lucas and Lucinda looked on, amused and faintly contemptuous.

Hopeful that at last he might liberate the passionate, giving side to his wife's nature, frozen by the shock of Luciano's death, Dexter longed for the moment they could be alone together. First there was the formal dinner Lucinda had prepared in his honour. It wouldn't be right not to show their appreciation of that.

That night, Camilla couldn't work out what was happening to her. Relief and pleasure at Dexter's homecoming seemed to have stirred other, stronger emotions. As she contrasted Lucas's florid-faced dissipation with her own man's taut good looks, she felt a pang of purely physical need for him, the first she had experienced since their marriage. If only they could get away from this stuffy overfurnished room packed with heavy heirloom furniture and the hideous family silver Dexter had tracked down and restored after his success! Besides the five-branched candelabra, there were clumsy representations of horses, camels, and even a scale model of Yelonga in its earliest days, complete with working mechanical windmill.

She looked down at her watch, then at Dexter. Correctly interpreting the rosy bloom to her skin and bright dilated eyes, he was determined not to disappoint her. The current of attraction which crackled between them was immediately obvious to their hosts.

'Hey, what's this?' said Lucas with fake joviality. 'Wifey tips him the wink and Dexter Randolph goes running?'

'Please don't break up the party so soon,' sighed Lucinda, ignoring Camilla and laying her hand on Dexter's arm. 'We've seen so little of you this time.'

Dexter, smiling at her, seemed to miss her contemptuous intonation on 'you'. Camilla did not.

'C'mon, little brother, have another glass.' Lucas slopped wine over the starched Irish linen cloth. For once his wife ignored the desecration, giving Dexter her sad-eyed smile.

Though his feelings for her had long since died, he never could resist an appeal from Lucinda. 'Why don't you go ahead, sweetie,' he told Camilla. 'There's a few things I need to go over with Luke anyway. Won't take long.'

Seeing Lucinda's tight victorious smile and Lucas's hand hovering close to the bottle, Camilla doubted it, but knew when she was beaten.

With a lumbering display of gallantry, Lucas made much of getting up to open the door and seeing that the way along the veranda was lit for her.

'Tough luck, your ladyship,' he said in a low voice. 'Looks like you'll have to start without him!'

She shrank from the smell of spirits on his breath, the clammy feel of his hand upon her arm. All the warmth and the excitement went out of the evening, leaving her feeling flat and weary. Sleep, however, eluded her. When Dexter stumbled into the room three hours later and saw his wife lying awake in bed, he misread the situation.

'Shorry I'm late. Make it up to you now, shall I?'

She never refused his lovemaking, feeling it was part of

the bargain their marriage had been based on. Tonight, as on all their previous nights together, she failed to enjoy it. And he, despite the haze of alcohol and exhaustion which enveloped him, noticed, and could not but compare memories of Linita Tyrone's warmth and abundant sensuality with his own wife's chilly indifference.

Back in the city, Dexter was soon swallowed up in a round of business meetings. Randolph Enterprises was in the process of acquiring a North American hotel chain, and there were plans to open branch offices in New York and Singapore as well as in London.

To combat the depression and lethargy she felt after the Queensland trip, Camilla decided to follow her mother's example and redecorate their home. Not that it needed it, exactly. It was already attractively, even tastefully, decorated but the taste was not Camilla's. Though she could never hope to equal her mother's flair, she wanted to impress something of herself on her surroundings.

She was supervising a team of decorators one morning, hoping to charm them away from their morning smoko and back into working before she left them to keep an appointment, when the doorbell rang. 'Damn!' she said under her breath, remembering it was the maid's day off. 'Back in a moment,' she said warningly to a foreman who was still exhibiting all the signs of terminal thirst despite three large mugs of tea. 'If you could just make a start on clearing the room, Mr Cates?'

Smoothing her long light brown hair back beneath its customary velvet band, she opened the door to a tall, tanned, outdoor-looking beauty rattling a collection tin.

'Bondi Surf Rescue Team,' the girl said with a smile. 'With a bonzer house like this, I reckon you should be good for a few quid.'

'I expect I would be — if you would explain what a Surf Rescue Team is.'

'You mean, your husband hasn't taken you down to the beach yet?'

Momentarily Camilla wondered why the girl should assume she was married, then caught sight of her own prominent diamond solitaire and wedding rings.

The collector launched into an animated description of the surf rescue teams and their voluntary life-saving work on Sydney's beaches. The competition between rival teams when they met to compare skills was intense, she explained, and the pinnacle for any self-respecting Sydney lifeguard was the coveted red rubber skullcap of the Bondi team.

'You've really never heard about it?' the girl asked incredulously.

'I'm afraid not. I arrived in September from England, and I can see I still have a lot to learn.'

'But surely your husband . . .?'

'He's so taken up with work,' Camilla said wistfully. Then, recollecting herself, 'Please come in. I think you deserve an extra contribution for all your patience with me.'

She stood aside and ushered the collector in. Just as she stepped into the hall, Cates and his white-overalled men staggered past under the weight of an enormous desk. 'We're redecorating,' Camilla called over her shoulder. 'Won't be a minute. I must find my purse.'

She missed the stricken expression which crossed the other woman's face, the sadness in her deep blue eyes as she turned away from the stripped and desolate room visible through the open door.

'That's odd,' said Camilla a few moments later, returning with her purse to find the hall empty and the front door closed. 'Mr Cates, the young lady I just let in . . .?'

'Took one look at us and lit out of here like a cat with a firework up its backside. Pity, she was a good-looker.'

Camilla ignored the other decorators' nods and

murmurs. 'I wonder why she didn't wait?' But there was no time to waste on speculation. Dexter had promised to be home early for once. Camilla intended to keep her own appointment, then return to put the finishing touches to his newly redecorated study.

Throughout the years with Dexter, Linita had made a point of cultivating not only his toffee-nosed friends but also the men and women who worked for him. For her every man was a pushover — there wasn't one worthy of the name who failed to respond to her lush good looks and raw provocative blend of humour. Women, too, responded to her warmth and direct unassuming manner. However much they might have envied her reign as mistress in residence, there was genuine pity and solicitude for her among the female staff at Randolph Enterprises when her dreams of marriage came crashing down. Angie, Dexter's dragon of a secretary, smiled in genuine welcome when, later that day, Linita appeared in the outer office.

'You're looking great!' she exclaimed. 'Your hair really suits you blonde like that. Glad to see the bastard hasn't ground you down.'

'Thanks, Angie. Is he in?'

'Yeah — grappling with some crisis or other. No outside calls, no disturbances of any kind.'

'Be a pal and keep it like that, will you?' Linita gave a broad wink. 'This is definitely do not disturb time.'

'Atta girl. He's got it coming.'

She watched approvingly as Linita threw open the double doors to the inner office and paused before making her entrance.

'Linita — what the hell ...?' Angie heard before the doors crashed to behind her.

'I'm sorry to disturb you, Dexter,' said Linita, looking and sounding anything but. 'Please don't blame Angie. Man eating crocs wouldn't have kept me from you. We

308

have things to discuss, wouldn't you say?'

He'd half expected this confrontation and had his words pat. 'Linita, look, it was a hell of a way to treat you. You deserved so much better ...'

'You're damn right I did!' He still found her remarkably attractive, taking in the flawless golden skin and luscious figure. 'Have you any idea of the pain and humiliation you put me through?' Her breasts heaved beneath the tight cheong-sam she wore. 'Announcing your marriage to that — that tight-arsed little English girl!'

Up till then, Dexter had seemed resigned to his fate. A showdown she was due, and a showdown he was prepared to let her have. But he would not tolerate hearing his wife spoken of in that way. He came round his desk towards her, fury wiping away his wary smile. He seized her arm and shook it. 'Let's get one thing straight between us, shall we? Camilla is my wife. Insult her, and you make a very bad enemy of me. Understand?'

Her face was only inches from his. Weak with longing for him, cursing herself for every kind of fool for losing the upper hand so early in their encounter, she nodded. He let go of her and she sagged limply.

Instantly his hands were on her shoulders, steadying and supporting her. 'Sorry, I shouldn't have lost my temper like that. Damn it, Linita, you always did know how to get to me. Here, have a seat.'

'No thanks. I'd rather stand for what I've come for.'

'Go on, then. I dare say I deserve it.'

Silence fell, broken only by Linita's ragged breathing. Still without speaking she reached out and took his hands in hers. Slowly, very slowly, she drew them down over the smooth uninterrupted lines of her provocative breasts, unsupported beneath the jade Thai silk of her dress. Her hands over his traced the narrow waist and voluptuous curve of her hips. Reluctantly she let his hands go and took a step forward, burying her face in his shoulder.

'I'm sorry I insulted your wife,' she said, her lips almost

309

touching the skin at his throat. He felt himself respond to her, and hoped she would not notice. 'It was wrong of me, I know,' she continued, 'but you can imagine the shock I felt, reading of your engagement in the newspaper?'

'I don't know anything about a newspaper announcement,' he said, frowning. 'I know I wrote to you, explaining.'

'The letter arrived later. The bride's family must have placed the announcement. Eliza rang 'specially to see I hadn't missed it.'

He gave up the fight and cradled her to him, telling himself he was offering no more than consolation for the pain he'd inflicted. 'I'm sorry, Linita. It sounds ridiculous, I know, but I never meant you to be hurt in that way.'

She wanted to cry and scream and stamp her feet, drum into his thick, slope-headed skull just what torture he had put her through, but the physical wounds she had inflicted upon herself in her first desperation were healed now, and she had enough experience of Dexter to know that she must conceal every trace of weakness from him.

'Well, you did hurt me. You hurt me a lot. I don't know how you're ever going to make it up to me,' she sighed, maintaining the pretence that all she was seeking was comfort, while with the slightest movement of her hips she found the evidence of his arousal. 'And the pity of it is,' she said, studying him closely, 'you've hurt yourself as well, haven't you?'

The way he could not meet her eyes proved that she was right. All was not well with his marriage.

'She's no match for you, is she?' He was too busy concentrating on the throbbing ache of desire she had awoken in his loins to prevent her speaking. 'A little school-girl like that,' she continued, more in amusement than in condemnation. 'Can she love you like I did, Dexter? Will she let you love her the way I always would?'

Her hand went to the zip at the neck of her dress. Even with the fastening released it was skintight, the silk slippery and treacherous beneath her fingers. Trembling with a mixture of triumph and desire, Linita sank on to the low couch beside her. The slippery skirt riding up her tanned thighs revealed what he already suspected. She was naked underneath.

'I may not be good enough to be your wife,' she said huskily, 'but I'll be the best damn' mistress you ever had.' Together with her pride, she shed every last inhibition. Moaning softly she slid her hand between her thighs, breathing harshly in an agony of unsatisfied lust. Through half-closed eyes she saw his expression change from one of rejection to near-horrified arousal. 'Tell me you don't want me, and I'll stop,' she gasped.

He could not. With an inarticulate cry he was upon and inside her, driven from height to height of fresh juddering sensation by the twin demons which rode him — lust and guilt.

The light was fading, the outer office long since locked and abandoned, when finally they regained their scattered senses. Sleepy and relaxed as a cat, Linita reached out and picked up her small tote bag. Inside, ornamented with a bow of pink ribbon and a gift tag, was a door-key.

'For you,' she said, pressing it into his hand. He took it reluctantly, opening the tag to read an address in Woollahra.

'My new place,' she explained. 'You're welcome any time.' She stood up and began to shake the creases from her dress. 'Can I call a cab, Dexter? I don't expect you to drive me home. Camilla will be waiting.'

On the ride home, she shed her cool exterior, hugging herself for joy and hope. Dexter had come back to her. Big fish though he was, she had him hooked.

He stood at his penthouse window, watching her cab far below. It had been a fluke, no more than a final settling of accounts, he decided. But if that were so, he asked himself on the short drive home, why had he kept the key? Deprived of its ribbon, it lay safely concealed in the inside pocket of his wallet.

The house was in darkness when he let himself in, a thin bar of light showing beneath the study door. With a stab of guilt he remembered that Linita, too, had always waited up for him there. When he pushed open the door, he saw Camilla, fast asleep, huddled in his high wingbacked chair. The room was filled with the damp and cloying smell of drying wallpaper. She had obviously redecorated his room and sat up waiting to share the surprise with him.

He knelt beside the chair and gently stroked her flushed sleeping face. On a side-table he noticed an unopened bottle of champagne in a bucket awash with molten ice. Two glasses stood beside it. He was touched by an almost unbearable sense of loss. He had wanted this woman to be the only one in his life; already he had betrayed her. He glanced back at the champagne. What a child she was still, eager to make an event of the most trivial of occurrences.

Camilla stirred and opened her eyes. 'At last! I called the office, but Angie said something had cropped up suddenly.'

'Yeah, something like that.' He couldn't meet her innocent eyes.

'Such a pity, tonight of all nights when we're celebrating. Still, you're here now.' She gestured towards the bottle. 'Will you?'

With smooth automatic gestures he poured them each a glass and raised his in a toast. 'To my new study, sweetheart. Thank you very much.'

Eyes brimming with joy, she bumped his glass with hers. 'That too, of course, but we're celebrating much more than that! I went to see Dr. Flanagan today ... Dexter, in March you'll be a father.'

For a long frozen moment he stared at her. When he spoke, there was a tremor in his voice, and a glint in his eyes. 'My darling, I'll love you forever.'

'Even when I'm eating for two and fat as a barrel?'

'Especially then!'

'I'm sorry I've been so feeble lately. I know how disappointed in me you were in Queensland. The truth of it is

I've been feeling vague and fuzzy almost since we arrived in Australia. How idiotic of me not to suspect I might be expecting a baby.'

'You have nothing to apologise for,' he assured her. 'You're giving us our baby and I'm proud of you, Camilla.'

In the light of his wife's announcement, the interlude with Linita seemed tawdry and unreal. She'd have a bloody long wait if she expected him ever to use that key now.

Dexter danced attendance on Camilla — taking time out from the office to shop for maternity clothes with her, months too soon, and interviewing her doctor himself to check that his wife's pregnancy was progressing smoothly. When he began to talk of which Australian schools he intended to put the child down for, the first note of dissension crept in.

'Have you forgotten? You told Maman and Xan you were planning to be in England at least half the year now. Naturally I'd expected that our children would be educated there.'

'And turned into proper little Poms, you mean?'

'They are half-English, and there'll always be a home for them at Courtney Park.'

'Until your brother marries.'

'That won't be for an age yet. Hamilton men always wait till their forties. Look at Daddy.'

'Hmm, you're right ... It would be a shame for them to miss out on that part of their heritage, I suppose. But as soon as they're old enough to appreciate it, the boys're coming out on a long visit to Australia.'

'And to hell with the girls?'

'Now did I say that?'

'No, but I know you're longing for a boy.'

'Girl or boy, my sweetheart, our child will have the very best start in life — parents who love each other.'

Day by day, Dexter and Camilla were growing closer in their shared excitement at the arrival of the child. He was so sweet and attentive, coming home early unbidden and showing her nothing but the most considerate restraint in bed, that Camilla plucked up her courage to seek one more concession.

'Dexter, promise you won't take this the wrong way?'

'I've told you before, princess. Whatever you want you can have.'

'Then I'm afraid I want to go home — to Courtney Park, I mean — to have the baby. Please don't look so upset. It's not that I don't love you and being with you. It's just that it's a sort of tradition with us — whenever possible, the Hamilton family babies are born at Courtney. Maman would see that I had the best man in attendance, of course.'

He scowled at her. 'So you've already discussed this with Angelica?'

'I wrote to her about the baby, naturally, and she wrote back to say she'd decorate the nursery as soon as could be arranged, and our rooms there are ready and waiting. After all, darling, you did say we'd be back in May or June. It's only a few months earlier.'

'Six,' he ground out. 'You'd have to travel in January at the latest if the baby's due in March. I'm sorry, Camilla, it's impossible. I can't leave this end of the business so soon.'

Reluctant to press him further, she turned troubled grey eyes on him.

Dexter looked at her thoughtfully. Family tradition . . . It was partly the allure of Camilla's privileged background which had recommended her so strongly to him. Wouldn't it be hypocritical of him to stop her from sticking to the very sense of tradition he prized in her? But damn it, he would miss her, miss seeing their child grow in her.

'I hadn't realised how much my home and family meant to me — even Maman — until . . .' She patted the gentle swell of her stomach and looked up at him appealingly.

'With this American deal to tie up, I can't travel till February at least,' he told her. 'But if it means that much to you, there's nothing to stop you making the crossing on your own. I could join you later, in time for the birth. Will you be all right, though? You were so ill coming out.'

'I've told Dr Flanagan all about that. Pregnant women are never seasick — isn't it wonderful! I'll hate leaving you behind, but, yes, it means that much to me.'

'All right, then. I'll book your passage today. Straight after New Year's do you?'

She left Sydney on a blazing summer's day in January — leaving the field wide open for Linita Tyrone.

Tipped off by Angie as to both Camilla's pregnancy and departure date, Linita waited until she knew her rival was a week at sea, calculating that for a man like Dexter seven days without female company were six too many.

She rang him at the office, put straight through as she always used to be by her ally Angie. 'You have something that belongs to me,' she attacked, as soon as he picked up the phone.

'I do? What?'

All of you, she wanted to scream at him. Body and soul, you're mine! Hadn't their last encounter proved that to him, as it had to her? She played her cards more cleverly than that, however, trading on a weakness of his which she well remembered. 'My key, lover. If you're not going to use it, there's a construction millionaire just in from Brissie who's itching to get into my — apartment.'

'He's welcome, you conniving bitch! See if I care!'

Later that night she lay expectantly on her bed. It was too hot and sultry for even a single sheet over the carefully arranged folds of the revealing coffee-coloured lace night-dress she had chosen. Not that Linita would have spoiled the open invitation of her pose if it had not been. At half-past twelve, riddled with guilt, Dexter let himself into the apartment, straight into Linita's waiting arms.

His lovemaking was swift and perfunctory — not a

patch on his last performance, she reflected, picking up the lacy garment he had torn in his haste. It didn't matter. The important thing was that this time he had come to her as she intended to keep him coming back — again and again and again.

Though guilty over his betrayal of his wife, Dexter found it all too easy to pick up the threads of his relationship with Linita. Skilfully she smoothed the way — always ready to drop a friend or even a modelling assignment if he told her he was on his way. She was discreet, too, with the sense not to insist on too many public outings when his friends — *their* friends once — and business acquaintances might see them and spread scandal. When they dined out it was at quieter, less fashionable, restaurants where she carefully cultivated the staff so that they were always automatically shown to the most secluded table. She became a dab hand too at assembling impromptu lovers' feasts served to him in bed: blinis, sour cream and Russian caviar, chased with frozen vodka, or a dozen oysters resting on a bed of seaweed, served with the finest imported champagne.

She dressed only to please him, putting away her colourful informal clothes in preference to the slinky, exquisitely tailored French and Italian clothes ordered for her by the most exclusive Sydney boutiques.

She took a close interest in his business, remembering always to ask how a particular meeting or deal had gone. Inevitably her own work suffered. Long hours spent waiting up for Dexter took their toll. Only a couple of sessions missed by her sleeping in gained her a reputation for unreliability. There were, besides, literally dozens of gorgeous, clean-living, wholly biddable girls just burning to step into Linita's size fives. Why should the photographers bother to wait for her?

Linita didn't care. Dexter had opened a bank account in her name and each month paid in a generous allowance. There was no need for her to work at all — though she did

316

miss the company of her modelling friends. She tried to keep in touch with the other girls, meeting them for lunch or drinks and turning every male head in the vicinity. Several times she was asked to accompany them to the sorts of bachelor parties where good-looking model girls were automatically welcome.

'I don't like to see you mentioned in this sort of rag,' Dexter told her one night, angrily indicating a gossip writer's reference to Linita's attendance, together with some friends, at the riotous coming of age celebrations of a big property owner's son. 'Do you have to racket around like that? It looks so cheap.'

'Maybe that's because I *am* cheap,' she flashed back. 'Too damn cheap for you to marry.'

'Linita, don't start all that again.'

'Too right I won't! I bloody well know when I'm well off. What'd I want, marrying a cheating bastard like you? A man who plays around while his wife's expecting their baby?'

She'd made him so angry he almost hit her. She saw it in the rigid set of his jaw, his fists clenching and unclenching. He left her without a word, not returning for several days. She tried to tell herself she was glad she'd spoken out. He had it coming, dictating to her like that! But long before she finally heard his key in the lock, she had acknowledged the bitter truth: there was no woman in the world she envied more than Camilla Randolph.

They were passionately reconciled after their disagreement, but a few days later Linita received a surprise telephone call.

'It's me, Dexter. I'm afraid I won't be able to see you for quite some time.'

'Why? A new deal or something?'

There was an awkward pause. 'No — news from England. Linita, I'm a dad! Angelica wired to say everything went smoothly and I've got a bouncing baby boy to be proud of. Isn't it terrific?'

317

'Terrific. I'm glad for you, Dexter.' She had to force the words out. She gripped the phone, jealousy gnawing at her. At that moment, hearing the man she loved jubilant over the birth of his child to another woman, she felt more of an outsider than she had ever done in her long neglected childhood as the daughter of the Townsville tramp.

'Isn't it a bit sudden?' she asked treacherously. 'I thought you said the baby was due at the end of March. Camilla can barely have arrived in England. How embarrassing for you both — everyone there knowing how you jumped the gun!'

'We certainly did not!'

She couldn't resist it. 'Well, perhaps you were the perfect gentleman, Dexter, but the way I heard it no *lady* gives birth to a bouncing baby seven months after the marriage.'

There was a ghastly silence. Then: 'Damn you, Linita! Damn you to hell. If you ever want to see me again, I'd advise you very strongly to forget you said that.'

'Don't you wish you could?'

The receiver came crashing down at the other end of the line.

In the newly refurnished Rose Room of Courtney Park, all was peace and warmth and silence. Softly diffused light filtered through the silk shade of the bedside lamp. The shifting coals of the high-banked fire cast jewelled reflections on the darkened ceiling. A figure in the high canopied bed barely stirred in the deep sleep of physical exhaustion, until she heard the summons. At the first whimper from the child in the lace-covered cradle at her bedside, Camilla was instantly awake.

She rolled painfully on to her side and stared lovingly down at the wakeful child, silent now that it had attracted her attention. Its tiny fists clenched and unclenched pleadingly.

318

'I know what you want,' she murmured, beginning to undo the neck of her frilled white nightdress.

She was reaching over for the child, one breast bare, when Angelica snapped on the overhead light and came into the room. The child screwed up its eyes and opened its mouth wide, presaging a wail of protest.

'Quick, pass him to me — and switch off that light!'

Surprisingly Angelica obeyed, gently scooping up her grandson and placing him in his mother's arms. His questing mouth found the heavy breast and greed prevailed over anger.

'How extraordinary,' mused Angelica. 'I could never face it myself, but seeing you like that — *chérie*, you're a natural mother. Dexter will be delighted with you and the child.'

'He will, won't he?' Camilla stared adoringly down at her son's fair downy head. 'He has his father's eyes.'

'Babies have blue eyes like dalmatians have spots,' her mother said authoritatively. 'I have to admit it, though, my grandson is remarkably handsome. Well done.'

It was one of the very few times in her life Camilla had actually received praise from her mother. Encouraged, she dared to confide her fears. 'But born so early! I do hope the doctor's right and there'll be no adverse effects. You did set Dexter's mind at rest, didn't you?'

'I simply said he had a bouncing baby boy. No need to bore a man with a lot of unwelcome physical detail. No matter what they say, they're far happier not knowing. Your father would have fainted if I'd told him what I went through with you. You were premature as well. It must run in the family.'

She watched Camilla wince as the baby probed her tender breast with relentless fingers.

'Are you quite sure that's necessary, Camilla? There's a bottle of formula ready in the nursery and Nanny Buggner says —'

'Bugger Nanny Buggner!' Camilla hugged her child

closer. 'He's mine, and I'll decide what's best for him.'

She expected her mother to make a disparaging remark. Instead, she settled herself gracefully on the low button-backed nursing chair at the bedside and looked at her daughter with grudging respect. 'Very well, you seem to be doing a good enough job. But you simply must decide on a name soon. I can't do as Nanny Buggner does and constantly refer to him as "baby". So *déclassé*.'

Camilla sat up straighter. 'I'm sorry, but there's no question of naming him until Dexter's here and can be consulted.'

Angelica looked at her in surprise. The girl who had always been such a disappointment to her — shy and insignificant, sweetly pretty instead of striking — was shaping up into a regular lioness in defence of her family. She doubted whether her daughter had any idea of the picture she presented. Framed by the luscious Colefax chintz of carnations and roses which had been hung as the bed's canopy and curtains, her shoulders bare and cheeks rosy, she was an eye-catching sight. If she had ever doubted Camilla's ability to hold on to Dexter, she did so no longer.

Throughout the long sea voyage, Dexter struggled to force Linita's parting shot from his mind. "No lady gives birth to a bouncing baby boy seven months after her marriage ..." He had always seen Camilla as a lady in every sense of the word, yet when he had married her she had been no virgin. Her reaction to the news of the Italian's death indicated that they must have been lovers. Suppose this baby ...?'

He spent a miserable crossing, tortured by visions of Camilla's sunny guileless face smiling at him as in her arms she cradled a baby — brown-eyed, olive-skinned, the blunt beginnings of a Roman nose plainly visible on its unformed face.

At the first sight of his son, with his fuzz of brown-blond

hair and fierce blue eyes, Dexter laughed at his own folly. 'He's bloody beautiful! Take a look at those eyes.'

Camilla gently rocked the cradle, staring between them in delight. 'Maman says every child is born with blue eyes — but I don't believe it. Look at him — he could only be yours, Dexter.'

A chill of suspicion brushed him again. Was she being just a shade too insistent, drawing his attention to the similarities between them?

Unaware of his thoughts, Camilla picked up the baby. 'You can hold him, you know. It is allowed.'

Dexter took him, fitting the lolling head comfortably into the crook of one arm as Camilla directed. A smile crossed the child's face, and Dexter's doubts disappeared.

'My mother's smile,' he said wonderingly.

'Nanny Buggner would tell you it was wind.'

'Bugger Nanny Buggner!'

'Do you know, that's what I always say? Oh, Dexter, it's so good to see you.'

'For me too, sweetheart. I'm only sorry I couldn't be here for the birth.'

'Probably just as well. Maman says I mustn't bore you with the details.'

'Your mother,' he said, gently replacing the baby in its cot, 'doesn't know everything.'

'Wait till you see what she's done to the house, though.'

'I'd rather see what she's done to our bedroom. I don't suppose you . . .'

'Not yet. But I could always . . .'

'Camilla Randolph, I'm surprised at you!'

Most agreeably surprised, he thought later, watching his wife peacefully asleep beside him in the middle of the afternoon. Though it was too early for them to be able to make love properly, Camilla had been more giving in bed than he had ever known her. It looked as though the time apart might have done them some good. At least he had the next six months with her in England, time enough to wean himself away from the siren call of the voracious mistress who even now, he knew, would be counting the days till his return.

In the end it was nine months before Dexter saw Australia again. After the flurry of his arrival and getting to know his son, there was the pomp of the christening. Princess Marina stood as sponsor, and Alexander was foremost among the godfathers. The baby was named Ashley Thomas Brinsley after his grandfathers, in a touching ceremony in the same chapel where Dexter and Camilla had been married a year before.

Immediately after the service, Angelica approached Dexter purposefully. 'Now that he's been decently named, you'd better hurry up and get his name down for a good school. Traditionally the Hamilton firstborn son goes to Eton, the next to Harrow and so on, turn and turn about. Prevents close comparisons being made, d'you see?'

Dexter felt he was being condescended to. 'Traditionally *all* the Randolph sons are educated at home, but the sorts of teachers we had — fellows who could rope a steer at forty paces or mend a tumbledown fence without using a single nail — are in pretty short supply here. I suppose we'll have to make do with Eton.'

'So Camilla, Ashley and any other children will be making their home permanently at Courtney Park?'

Dexter sighed. 'Looks that way. Camilla doesn't travel well, and she didn't take to Australia. If the kids are to be educated here, I can see it makes sense for her to be at hand. It seems it'll be a long-distance marriage for the Randolphs.'

'Sometimes they can be the best,' said his mother-in-law, a knowing glint in her eyes. 'While we have you here, Dexter, we must make the best use of your time. You're happy with the way the house looks, I take it?'

'Bowled over. I've got to hand it to you, Angel. When

you spend a bloke's money, you spend it with style.'

'Thank you. I have spent a great deal —'

'Plenty more where that came from.'

'— but I have bought only the best. Perhaps you would care to accompany me to the next big Fine Paintings sale at Sotheby's? There's a particularly good private collection of Impressionists coming under the hammer.'

Dexter looked awkward. 'Ah, I dunno. There's a lot to do at the office, and you don't really need me —'

'Of course I don't. It's *you* who need to be seen out and about in public. If we're to build you into a prominent figure here as well as in Australia, you need to become newsworthy. What better way than by splashing out a fortune on some connoisseur-class paintings? Then of course there are all the right parties to attend — don't worry. I've organised invitations — your public support for the pick of the charities, perhaps even founding one yourself ... It's going to be gruelling, Dexter, a long haul to your knighthood. Do you think you're up to it?'

'Just try me!'

He had to hand it to his ma-in-law — she was a trier. Mercilessly she traded on every last family friend and connection, smoothing Dexter's path through the social minefield like a runaway steamroller. Her ambitions for her son-in-law brooked no opposition. Dissenters were simply flattened. It helped that under her stewardship, Alexander being away most of the year studying at Oxford or visiting friends, Courtney Park had become once more one of the nation's showcases for all that was richest and rarest in the field of interior design. Her most expensive caprice was the sumptuous Roman-style swimming pool, modelled on a calidarium, which she had designed herself. It was outdoor, heated all the year round to blood temperature.

'Jesus, what are we burning the boiler on — banknotes?' said Dexter, signing the cheque for the first quarter's bill. But Camilla loved the exercise she could take there and

323

was already taking Ashley, squealing and chortling with delight, into the water with her. The pool was here to stay.

Though Dexter made the occasional protest at his mother-in-law's lavish hand, it was all part of the game between them. He appreciated her efforts on his behalf, especially her masterstroke in arranging the resumption of the Courtney Park shoots in Wiltshire, and shooting and stalking weeks on the Scottish estate. A man could be forgiven a great many gaucheries if he kept a good shoot, she had always heard say, and Dexter poached neighbours' gamekeepers and stocked his land generously. Invitations to shoot with him became highly sought after. Though the consensus was that he was a bit of a rough diamond, guests were happy to accept his hospitality. Female visitors enjoyed the matchless chic created inside the house by Angelica, and the genuine warmth and sweetness of Camilla's welcome. In his first season in the public eye, Dexter caused quite a stir.

'Ten or fifteen more years like this and you'll be home and dry,' Angelica told him.

'If I'm not broke first! As long as that, Angel?'

'It takes some men a lifetime.' She had stopped reproving him for shortening her name, as long as they were in the privacy of the classically simple family apartments she had created on the first floor, with the help of David Hicks.

'And why should Dexter Randolph be on the fast track?'

'Because he has me — and Camilla, of course. It's such a pity you're going back to Australia so soon, just when you were really beginning to catch the public eye. That scheme to allow city boys to get a taste of country living by working on the estate was pure genius.'

'And one I happen to believe in. It's not all for show, you know.'

'I do. And I know how very much Camilla's going to miss you when you go. I'm sure you wouldn't give her any reason to regret your rather unusual marital arrangements?'

324

He poured them both a glass of brandy. 'Don't worry about Camilla. I'd never do anything to hurt her.'

That night, his last with her for six months at least, he possessed Camilla with a ferocity that recalled the early days of their marriage. Warmer and more welcoming though she was these days, she had still not reconciled her need for patience and finesse from a man with the relentless passion of her husband's lovemaking. It left her bruised and breathless rather than satisfied. It also, though she did not realise it at the time, left her pregnant with their second child.

Linita was waiting for him in Sydney, as he had known she would be. He did not consider himself a hypocrite for resuming their relationship. As far as he was concerned, this thing between them was purely physical. She knew he was married to someone else and seemed prepared to take him on those terms. So long as his wife, safely tucked away in Courtney Park, thousands of miles away, never found out, what harm was he doing? He had, of course, totally failed to appreciate the depth of her attachment to him.

She had lost weight in his absence. No more lovers' feasts now. She seemed to have lost interest altogether in eating, and had become more difficult and demanding, too. She was no longer content to stay holed up in her apartment, or to avoid the more fashionable clubs and restaurants.

'C'mon, Dexter. You're not a newly-wed any longer,' she chided him. 'I'm all dressed up and I want to go to this new club opening. Camilla's at home with the baby, everyone knows that. They won't be too surprised to see you turn up with a female escort. They'd be more surprised if you came alone.'

Dexter was amazed at the extent of the blind eye which was turned on them both by his friends and, more particularly, his business acquaintances. None of them really knew Camilla, who had failed to make her mark on Sydney Society. It was no skin off their nose then if Randolph chose to appear publicly with a good-looking party girl in tow.

Outside the apartment they behaved with decorum, never so much as touching before anyone else. She couldn't keep her love and need for him from showing, though. A cameraman snapped their arrival at a Gala Ball in March, a particularly candid shot of Linita walking three paces behind Dexter but looking after him with the pride of possession very clear in her eyes. The picture was picked up by a glossy magazine who published it in their gossip page: "Mr Dexter Randolph and close companion former model Linita Tyrone".

Dexter was furious when he saw it. 'We've got to keep this strictly under wraps in future, do you hear? No more night clubs.'

She laughed throatily. 'Just you and me, lover. Won't we have fun?'

In June he left her for England and his wife, now seven months pregnant with their second child. For Linita, he took the sunshine with him.

Camilla's next child was a full-term baby. Courtney Alexander Charles Randolph, a fine nine-pound boy, was delivered by his father, who confirmed the medical team's impression of him as a barbarian by immediately whisking aside the hospital gown which shrouded Camilla's upper body and placing her newborn child in her arms. The consultant had never seen anything like it.

'Mr Randolph, there are things to do! The cord —'

'It can wait. She's worked hard for this. You can let her have a moment or two's peace for now.'

He spoke with a stockman's instinctive understanding of the bonding process, and would not be swayed. Camilla was so grateful to him for making this birth different from

326

her first forceps delivery that she begged tearfully, 'Please, Dexter, promise you'll be here with me for the next!'

He kissed her forehead. 'Don't you think putting yourself through it twice is enough? We have two strong sons. I'm more than content with that.'

'But a daughter. I'd like one at least, wouldn't you?'

'We'll have to see what we can do. But for now, go to sleep.' He looked down into the cradle set beside the bed. 'We'll both be here when you wake up.'

Privately he'd decided there'd be no more children. Though he had not betrayed his feelings by so much as a flicker, he had been appalled by the torment his gentle wife went through in what was a perfectly normal birth. So far as he was concerned, enough was enough.

Linita Tyrone had other ideas. In Dexter's absence, his Sydney second-in-command, Greg Hightower, took to dropping in on the boss's bit of skirt, to keep her up to date. He'd long been an admirer of hers but reckoned with Dexter around there was no chance. It suited his ulterior motive to bring her the news of Courtney's birth. He found her lying on the couch in her apartment, wearing a sexy pair of black crêpe de chine lounging pyjamas, a glass of wine in her hand.

'Another boy — a whopper!' he announced. 'The boss sounded over the moon in his telegram.' His ingenuous tones contrasted with his sharp-eyed scrutiny of her reaction.

She disappointed him. Her expression was unreadable. 'And his wife?' She took another sip of wine.

'Oh, fine. Talking of number three already, apparently.'

He saw the gleam of her knuckles as her grip tightened on the glass. Without a word or a cry she squeezed the fragile stem until it snapped, driving a sharp splinter deep into the flesh of her palm.

Chilled by the sight, Hightower fetched a cloth and a bowl of water. He removed the splinter and bandaged her hand. It was the closest he had ever been to her, and he

327

found he did not enjoy the experience. There was a crazed, vacant expression in her eyes.

'Now you take care of yourself, you hear?' he said, more relieved to be leaving than he would ever have thought possible.

Despite the fact that sex between them was never more than comfortable and routine, Camilla was still the only woman he could imagine as his wife, Dexter reflected. He liked the way that motherhood had made her more open and assured; loved seeing her with the little boys, patiently cajoling them into the best and most winning infant behaviour. Before he left his family, very reluctantly, she persuaded a talented young assistant of Baron, the Society photographer, to take an informal study of her with her sons. Candid and unposed, Anthony Armstrong-Jones's portrayal of the three of them was a triumph. Dexter carried it in his wallet wherever he went — together with the key to Linita's apartment.

Against his better judgment, he was still seeing her. She was still a knockout, after all. With her blonded hair and sharp tailored clothes, she was a mistress any man could be proud of. It was a pity that, thanks to the need for discretion, their encounters must now be confined to her apartment, where he had arranged to meet her on his first evening back in Sydney.

She looked on top form, he was glad to note. No sign of resentment at his absence. Lovely and obviously delighted to see him, it would have taken a celibate to have withstood her charms. Dexter was anything but. Just the sight of her, ripe and inviting, brought out his animal instincts. First, though, there was some catching-up to do. It didn't seem to upset her to hear him talking about his kids.

'Two sons,' she enthused, 'only eighteen months apart. You're quite a man, Dexter Randolph.'

'I didn't do it on my own,' he pointed out.

Linita permitted herself a small moue of disdain. Though she had no objection to discussing his children, any mention of Camilla was still beyond her. 'Quite a man,' she repeated, unbuttoning his shirt and nuzzling the sensitive skin of his collarbone while her hands continued to undress him.

'You're a witch, do you know that?' he groaned, unbuttoning the cropped silk shantung jacket she wore to reveal her proud pointed breasts beneath, their perfection unmarred by the demands of motherhood ... Instantly he despised himself for such disloyalty to Camilla. 'Every time I see you I tell myself I mustn't come back,' he told her.

'But you do. I wonder why?'

And you always will, she silently promised herself, picturing her diaphragm, still safely stowed away in its pink plastic case. She would see to that.

'You're what? I don't think I heard you right.'

Dexter had let himself into her apartment late one night a few months later, to be met by a bombshell.

'I think you did.' Nervously she pleated the fine chiffon of the formal cocktail dress she had chosen to wear for tonight's announcement. She'd so wanted to look her best, for everything to go just as she had rehearsed it. If only he wouldn't look at her like that. She'd seen his face dark and twisted with anger before, but always at a subordinate or business opponent. Never at her. For the first time she realised the extent of his power to hurt and intimidate.

'Aren't you forgetting something, Linita?' he said in a soft, deadly voice. 'I already have children. I already have a wife.'

'Oh, leave your bloody wife out of this, can't you?' Instantly she could have kicked herself for lapsing into vulgarity. She needed to stay cool and collected to play this hand, but the flinty expression on Dexter's face was frightening. This wasn't how she had planned it to be. She plucked up courage and departed disastrously from her script. 'If she means so much to you, Dexter Randolph, how come you leave her halfway across the world to come sniffing round my skirts? Not that I'm complaining,' she added hastily.

'I should say not,' he said, voice cold and inimical. 'All over me like a bitch in heat the moment I got back, and every chance you've had since . . . Christ, I get it! This isn't an accident, is it?'

'No! It's just a slip-up. Must have been that first night. I was out of practice with my diaphragm . . .'

She had always been a hopeless liar, and Dexter was practised in every nuance of her expressive face. It had been foolish to suppose she could ever pull the wool over his eyes with talk of an accident. Better by far to make a clean breast of it, and not run the risk of forfeiting the rest of his regard for her.

'What the hell for, you silly bitch?' he grated. 'What do you mean, saddling yourself with a bastard? You can't even look after yourself! Unless . . . Surely to God you didn't believe I'd ever leave Camilla for you?'

Although she had never allowed herself to hope as much, his cavalier dismissal of her as quite outside the great Dexter Randolph's scheme of things shattered her tenuous grasp on self-control. All the resentment and bitterness which had festered inside her for so long came spewing out. For the first time he began to gain a dim impression of the extent of the damage he had done her by refusing to let her be more than a beautiful, barren, plaything.

'No,' she said, her voice ringing with sarcasm, 'I never thought the great Dexter Randolph would leave his high-class investment and marry a model who was past her sell-by date. Though God knows, the way I loved you and put you before everything else, you damned well ought to have done. Anyway halfway decent man would never have left me flat, the way you did.'

He retaliated instantly, jabbing his finger aggressively to emphasise his point. 'But when I had, when I came back here a married man, not looking for trouble, *you* threw yourself at me.'

'I didn't exactly twist your arm! You were more than ready for what I had to offer.'

'Look, there've been mistakes on both sides, I won't deny.'

'There's no mistake about this.' Her eyes flashed fire at him. 'I've devoted the last eight years of my life to you. I've given up my career, my friends, any chance of meeting a man who might make me his wife. I'm tired of forever hanging round on the edges of your existence, sweeping up the crumbs you're good enough to leave me. So I'm taking what *I* want, for a change. Yes, I got pregnant on purpose. I want a child, *your* child. Don't you think, after all we've been to each other, you owe me that at least?' To wrong-foot him, she deliberately softened her tone, making it more conciliatory, back on course now to the proposition she'd been meaning to make all along. 'I'm not asking for any more money or any more time. Just visit us whenever you can. I'll make up some story for the kid.'

'Like your mother did for you, I suppose?'

She quailed before the knowledge in his eyes. Throughout all these years she'd assumed he swallowed the story she'd spun about her mother's 'widowhood'. Now it looked as though he had known all along about that shameful entry on her birth certificate: Father Unknown.

'It wouldn't be the same for our child!' she cried desperately. 'It would know its father. You'd still be in our lives, even if we weren't with you always. Don't you understand? I've got to have something in my life. I can't be left alone like this, not any more.' Great shuddering sobs burst from her. 'Don't be hard on me, Dexter, please.'

Too late, he realised how blind he had been. It must have been hell for her, concealing the depths of the despair she felt, continually putting on the act of being his good pal

331

and carefree mistress while all the time her instincts clamoured for her to become a wife and mother. He had to take this gently, curb his anger at her manipulation of him and try and make her see what had to be done.

'Linita, believe me, this isn't the way,' he tried to reason with her. 'You say you could cope with bringing up a child like that — only seeing me occasionally, knowing I could never definitely be there for birthdays and Christmases, spending time with my other family in England half the year. You might be able to swallow that, but think of the child. It would be cruel to expect it to try.'

She recoiled as if he'd struck her, shaking with uncontrollable rage. 'You bloody hypocrite! What about your kids then, and her precious ladyship? They already spend half their lives without you. Why is it different for me and mine?'

He gave it to her straight. 'There's not going to be a child for you, Linita. Not if you want to keep me in your life.'

Her eyes wide with pain and disbelief, she whispered, 'You mean — get rid of it?' She could not believe her beautiful news had turned so sour on her, or the extent of Dexter's blatant selfishness and cruelty. He knew she was a Catholic, that to her abortion counted as a mortal sin. He already had the ultimate power over her body; she would gladly have died for him. Now it seemed he wanted her immortal soul as well. 'I won't do it,' she said, trembling. 'You can't make me.'

'And you can't make me the father of a child I reject. If you want this baby, Linita, go ahead. But leave me out of it. You've betrayed my trust in you. I won't be coming round here again.'

'Go on, then. I shan't beg you to stay. I'll manage by myself.'

He took something from his wallet — the key to her apartment which once she had handed to him in love and hope, tied up with a bow of pink ribbon. Pink for a girl ...

Oh, she did hope so. It would have cut her to the quick to have given birth to a boy with Dexter Randolph's hard unforgiving eyes.

She swallowed, finding her voice with difficulty. 'I suppose this is goodbye, then.'

'Goodbye, Linita. Take care of yourself. And don't worry about money — my lawyers will be in touch.'

'Stuff your money! And stuff you, you double-dealing, sanctimonious, worthless blatherskite!'

She picked up a heavy alabaster lamp-base and hurled it at him with all her strength. He sidestepped easily and it smashed to the floor at his feet. Stepping over the jagged remains, he left without a word.

She heard his slow deliberate footsteps descending the stairs, and as he reached the hall below, dashed on to the landing. 'No, don't go!' She heard the slamming of the outside door. Sobbing desperately, she started to run down the winding staircase. 'I didn't mean it,' she called out. 'I'll do what you say. I'll get rid of it —' As she threw open the front door she heard the familiar deep-throated roar of his powerful car and saw its tail-lights disappear around the bottom of the street.

She could barely drag herself upstairs. She recognised her brave words about managing alone for the smoke-screen they really were. There was no way she could exist without him in her life. No future for her or her child, now he was gone.

In a dream, she sat down at her dressing-table, fixed her hair and face and sprayed herself liberally with her favourite Jolie Madame. She wanted to look her best. Then she lay down on the bed and took the big brown medicine container from her bedside drawer. She emptied its contents into her hand.

The pills would have been easier to swallow if she'd had a glass of water, but she felt too tired to fetch one. She chewed and swallowed, chewed and swallowed. Too tired to register the bitter powdery taste in her mouth, too tired

333

to keep her eyes open a moment longer. Too tired to pick up the phone which rang and rang just inches from her hand.

It was her obstetrician Dr Flanagan who saved her. A pious and upright man, he had at first been disapproving when breaking the news of her pregnancy to his unmarried patient. Linita Tyrone had surprised him, however, by seeming genuinely delighted, tears of gladness sparkling in her eyes. The old bachelor found himself shaken out of his professional reticence. 'What will you do, my dear? The father — is he in a position to marry you?'

'I'm afraid not, Doctor. You see —'

'Married, I suppose.' He sniffed disapprovingly. 'Will he at least provide for you and the child? Because, let us get one thing straight, Miss Tyrone. As a Catholic and a woman it is your duty to have this baby. None of this abortion rubbish here.'

'You don't need to worry about that, Dr Flanagan. I've wanted a child for so long, and Dexter's rich as Croesus, thank God.'

'Dexter? And rich, did you say?' He looked at her sharply, remembering another Dexter who had quizzed him anxiously about a forthcoming birth. 'This wouldn't be Dexter Randolph we're talking about, by any chance?'

Linita flushed guiltily. It was none of the doctor's business who had fathered her child, but she supposed medical ethics would stop him spreading scandal. 'It would, and he'll stick by me, believe me. I can't wait to tell him tonight! But word mustn't get out, Doctor. He's a married man . . .'

'And prefers to sin under a cloak of respectability,' he finished testily. 'This conversation is strictly confidential, I assure you.' With professional detachment he went on to give her advice about her diet, taking extra rest and returning for regular check-ups. His worries he kept to himself. He had met Dexter Randolph and recognised the type at a glance: a hard man, the sort who would not countenance one breath of scandal tainting his public image.

That night, the solitary doctor found his thoughts wandering again and again to his consultation with Miss Tyrone. From what he had seen of her, she was a highly emotional woman, passionate and headstrong. Though it was strictly against his usual practice, he decided to call and reassure himself that everything had gone well for his patient. He rang every ten minutes for an hour or more before, cursing himself for an interfering old fool, he climbed into his car and drove to her Woollahra address to see if the phone was ringing in an unlit, unoccupied apartment.

Outside Linita's block he saw light blazing from her floor. Mercifully, another tenant was just letting himself in at the front door. Explaining that he was a doctor, Flanagan rushed upstairs. The door to her apartment stood open. Inside he could see two untouched drinks standing on a low coffee-table, a door key beside them. On the floor were the smashed remnants of a table lamp. Its shade had rolled on to the landing and lay at his feet. The door to the bedroom was closed. He knew what he would find inside, and prayed to God he was not too late.

Though he had always prided himself on being a man who knew when to cut his losses, stand back from a bad investment, Dexter found himself more shaken by the bitter parting from Linita than he cared to admit. Several times that night and the following morning he caught himself thinking of ringing her, checking that she was all right. But to do so might make her think that he was weakening, changing his mind about the things he had said.

He was not.

Linita, the woman he had thought he'd known inside

335

out, had surprised him by the violence of her emotions last night. In that state, there was no knowing what she might be capable of. Time to limit the damage she might do, and to re-examine his own position.

He saw that he had been foolish to wish this split existence on Camilla and himself. With the boys only babies, it was hard enough to leave them, knowing that in his absence each day would bring fresh developments, changes in their looks and personality. As they grew older and became able to make their feelings apparent, it would be even harder to turn his back on them for months at a time.

Hard on Camilla, too, walled up in the great house with only her witch of a mother for company. Though theirs was not a passionate marriage he knew she loved him, after her own fashion.

Dexter's own childhood had virtually ended with the death of his mother and father. He did not wish to rob his own children of one of the most precious parts of theirs — both parents' loving presence.

After spending the day locked in his office, making plans, Dexter summoned Greg Hightower to him. 'Going to be a few changes round here, Greg,' he said before his deputy had even sat down.

'Yeah?' Hightower said cautiously, not sure whether this was promotion or the bullet.

'Yes.' Dexter surveyed his stocky, square-faced deputy appraisingly. 'From now on you're on your own. I've decided to restructure Randolph Enterprises. The manufacturing operation in Singapore will be headed by "Thin" Harry Lu. My brother Lucas is going to get a chance to show his stuff as MD of the cattle and meat processing division. That leaves shipping and mining, with headquarters in Sydney. What do you say to handling that?'

'I say you picked the right bloody man for the job, of course! But, boss, what are you going to do?'

'Head the Special Projects and Leisure Interests

division, operating from London and New York. I'll be spending a lot more time at Courtney Park, maybe starting a stud there, doing some research into rare breeds. Generally improving my visibility at the UK end and seeing a lot more of my family in the process. Any objections?'

'No. Good on you. It must be hard on the wife, left alone for half the year.'

'It's been hard for us both, Greg.' Dexter gave him a warning look.

'Yeah. But what about Linita — er, Miss Tyrone?' He wished the words unsaid as soon as they left his mouth. Christ, but that was clumsy! The boss could screw sheep on the side for all the business it was of his.

'I'm glad you asked me that,' Dexter surprised him by saying, but from his shark-like smile Greg knew he wasn't going to like the rest. 'There've been a few changes made in that department, too. As of today, I shall not be contacting Miss Tyrone direct again. I'd like you, Greg, to act as my intermediary.' Just his luck. Playing postman between the boss and his screwy sheila! '. . . consulted my lawyer, all watertight,' Dexter was continuing. 'I'm offering a settlement of half a million pounds.'

''Struth! Half a million quid! No woman's worth that much.'

'Her silence is. Make no mistake about this, Greg. I need her out of my life and I want to be sure that there will be no unpleasant comebacks as a result. She and her child, if she decides to have it —'

Greg Hightower's jaw dropped, but he had the sense to stay silent this time.

'— will receive a once and for all payment to provide more than adequately for their needs. With one proviso: the money is to be repaid if any word of my liaison with Miss Tyrone leaks out to the public, press, or my wife and family. It must be made apparent to Miss Tyrone that it is in her own best interests to remain totally discreet. You're just the man for the job.'

337

'Ah, boss, why me?'

'Because I'm buggering off to inspect the stations and break the news of his promotion to my idle bastard of a brother. Hope his wife can keep him up to the mark! When I call you from Darwin, Greg, I want to hear the whole bloody mess is sorted, understand?'

The shadow of a grin appeared on Hightower's face. So the lovely Linita Tyrone had got her marching orders, had she? Who knew how grateful she might be for a little male sympathy and attention . . .

'And, Greg —'

'Hmmm?'

'Lay one bloody finger on her and I'll break you, mate. Okay? Now get out of here, can't you? I must get a letter to England in the next post. Tell them I'm coming home.'

Angelica caused a sensation as she entered the cosy cluttered dining-room of the Randolph Hotel, chosen as their meeting-place because of its name. For an informal visit to her son at university, she had chosen to wear diamond earrings and a full-length cape of sables pieced so cunningly that the surface looked seamless.

'Xan, *chéri*, how lovely to see you!'

Her arrival was as theatrical as ever, but he rose to the occasion, kissing her hand and seating her with old-fashioned courtesy.

'Ravishing as always, Maman. But Oxford in March? I thought you were still in Barbados?'

'February's the chicest month, surely you know that? Besides, there's so much to be done at home, arrangements to be made, decorators briefed . . .'

'Good Lord, I'd have thought Dexter's pocketbook had taken enough of a hammering. He's been quite embarrassingly generous as it is, considering he only uses the place half the year.'

Angelica's eyes glittered. 'But now he intends to use it

338

more, Xan. It's only right that he should pay for the privilege — if you will permit it, of course. He says he wishes to spend more time with Camilla and the boys —'

'Quite right, too.'

'He will concentrate on the English and American sides of the business — "leisure interests", whatever they are.'

'Hotels and holiday camps, I think. Quite the coming thing, apparently. Our Dexter doesn't miss a trick, does he?'

'He'll have to visit America quite often, but he'd like to spend more time at Courtney Park.'

Alexander was genuinely delighted. 'Fantastic. What's the problem?'

'This isn't an estate cottage we're talking about. As the Earl, you own Courtney Park. Dexter and Camilla can only make their home there by your grace and favour. Dexter wanted, quite rightly, to see that you agreed with his plans. He asked me to sound you out.' His mother looked at him severely.

'With your customary charm and diplomacy?'

She smiled faintly. 'It's true. The house and what happens to it is the most important thing in my life — after you and Camilla, of course.'

'Of course,' he agreed gravely. 'Unfortunately, Maman, it is not the same for me. When Dexter first suggested putting money into the place in return for making a home there part of the year, I told him that in all probability I wouldn't be living in Courtney in the foreseeable future. Shearing's Bank in New York has a place for me when I graduate.'

'I do understand. It's wonderful the way you intend to restore the money your father squandered. But I thought, perhaps in several years' time, when you have a family of your own ...'

He looked directly at her. 'Some men never marry.'

She studied her handsome son, possessor of one of the oldest and proudest titles in England. 'It's a little too early to say "never", don't you think? Now, shall we order some tea? You can tell me all about your American plans, and I'll tell you what I intend to do to the ballroom.'

'It was overhauled quite recently. Surely it's not necessary to redecorate again?'

'I cut corners that time. Your father's finances ... If Dexter's going to be around more, we can give balls again. Think of it!'

'Well now, child, do you feel up to a little chat? Sister says I can have just a few minutes.'

Dimly Linita was aware of a bulky black shape at her bedside, a round red face peering down at her. 'Where — Where am I?' she said feebly, feeling a fiery flash of pain as she shifted position, disturbing the IV line attached to her arm.

'At St Cecilia's Hospital. My brother brought you straight here when he found you.'

'Your brother?'

'Yes, Patrick — Dr Flanagan. I'm Father Tom.'

Belatedly, she realised the significance of waking up with a priest at her bedside. 'I'm not going to die, am I?'

'You are not, thanks be to God — though some would say it's more than you deserve. Whatever possessed you, endangering your life and your immortal soul?'

The fuzzy distorted feeling with which she had woken rolled away, leaving Linita's senses sharp and focused. 'Never mind my immortal soul — what about my baby?'

He looked embarrassed. ''Tis a medical matter —'

'Oh God, what have I done? My baby — I've killed my baby!'

There were hurrying footsteps behind her, and a voice said firmly, 'I'm sorry, Father Tom, I'll have to ask you to leave now. The patient is distressed.'

Linita twisted and turned on her pillow, trying to see the nurse who was adjusting the drip stand behind her bed.

340

Mist began to close in at the edge of her vision. Unconsciousness waited to suck her down once more. 'Please, nurse, I must know ... My baby?'

A sweet round face framed by a white coif bent over the bed. 'It's Sister, dear, Sister Margaret Mary. And your child's not been harmed. St Cecilia's is a home for mothers and babies, so you're in good hands, never fear.'

A home for fallen women, Linita thought in grim amusement. How fitting! She fell into a deep restorative sleep.

Later in the day Dr Flanagan came to reassure her that the baby did not seem to have been harmed by her flirtation with death. 'Though you're at an early stage and that's when the damage can be done. Still, we'll not dwell on that now. Can you at least tell me why you did it, Miss Tyrone?'

It hurt the pious doctor who had always unquestioningly accepted the Catholic dogma to see her shrug her shoulders, a hard expression crossing her face. 'Can't you guess? It's a familiar enough story, I'd have thought. He refused to leave his wife, rejected me and the child.'

'So to get back at him, you thought you'd kill yourself?'

'Something like that. It sounds ridiculous now. I'm glad I'm not dead. I want to stay alive to cause the bastard maximum embarrassment!'

He winced to hear profanity cross a woman's lips.

'Sorry, doctor. Not all men are the same, I know. I want to thank you for all the trouble you've taken over a hysterical fool like me. You saved my life and my baby's, and I'll always be grateful.'

He coughed. 'We—ll, that's partly why I came to see you. Do you think, Miss Tyrone, that a woman of your — er, fluctuating — emotions is ideally suited to bring up a child on her own?'

She looked up at him, amazed. 'You're surely not suggesting ...'

'I am not! As I told you before, it is your Catholic duty

341

to give birth to this child, but I do wonder if, after the birth, it might not be as well to surrender the child for adoption. Father Tom and the good sisters here run an agency. The child could be placed at only a few days old. No need for you even to see it if you feel it would be too painful.'

'Too bloody right it would!' He averted his gaze from the agitated heaving of her breasts. 'Look, Doctor, I'm no saint. I've done things in my life I'm not too proud to look back on, but wherever I go from here, whatever I do with the rest of my time, I'm going to make it up to my kid for giving it such a rotten start in life. That's a promise.'

He pursed his lips and got to his feet. 'I won't press you then, Miss Tyrone. It's your own decision entirely.'

She thought she'd carried the day until he wheeled in the heavy guns — Father Tom and Mother Clare, a thickset heavy-browed nun who combined the functions of Matron and Mother Superior.

'I see so many unfortunate young things like you,' said the nun with a forgiving smile. 'Certain they're acting for the best in keeping their babies. But best for whom? In many cases, certainly not the child. The stigma of illegitimacy can be very hard to live with. Are you sure that's what you want for your child?'

'Or wouldn't you rather give it a better start in life?' chimed in the priest. 'With a mammy and a daddy, a secure home life and the acceptance of its little friends. It's painful for you, we know, but you'll get your reward in heaven.'

She was reminded painfully of Dexter's children, safe and secure in the love he had denied their half-sister or -brother. Desolation filled her eyes.

Mother Clare saw her chance. 'No need to commit yourself just yet. Stay here until you're stronger. Speak to the other girls and let them tell you about the good homes we find for all our babies.'

Not your baby, *mine*, she screamed silently. But memories of that last appalling scene with Dexter returned to haunt her.

342

★

Greg Hightower traced her to St Cecilia's a few days before she was to be discharged, Dr Flanagan having persuaded himself she was fit and stable enough to manage on her own. A nun showed him to the patients' sitting-room.

'What the blue blazes are you doing in a dump like this, princess? A rich young woman like you ...'

'Go away, Greg. Whatever you've come to say, I don't want to hear it.'

'Then feast your eyes on that. They say money talks louder than words.'

With the air of a conjuror he pulled a cheque from the breast pocket of his safari-style shirt. It was a warm humid day at the tail-end of summer. The piece of paper felt damp and sticky to her squeamish touch. She did not look at it.

'I don't want a pay-off. I want to speak to Dexter.'

'No dice. He's gone up to Queensland, then the Top End. He sails from Darwin in ten days.'

He got a reaction at last. The hand holding the cheque began to shake.

'For where, Greg?'

'"Home", as he calls it now. England to you and me. He has a wife and kids there, remember?' He could not resist a last twist of the knife.

'But — the business?'

'You're looking at the new Managing Director of Randolph Enterprises, Mining and Shipping. Lucas is boss of the cattle side, God help them, and Dexter will manage the rest from London and New York. Might as well face it, girl, he's not coming back. He's not a tightwad, though. He's left you well provided for.' He gestured towards the cheque which she held in nerveless fingers. 'On certain conditions, of course.'

'Which are?' she asked dully, barely hearing what he was saying. Dexter was leaving Australia. There was no

343

prospect of a reconciliation once the baby was born.

Hightower fumbled in his other pocket and produced two typed documents. For the first time he looked embarrassed. 'Lawyers drew this up ... all the legalese sounds worse than it really is. Can't blame the boss, really. He had to protect himself, see?'

She struggled to absorb the meaning of the cold uncompromising words. For the first time the immensity of the sum of money he was prepared to pay to be free of all responsibility for her and the child filtered through. It was a fortune. Enough to enable her to do anything she pleased. Anything at all ...

'Very well, if that's the way he wants it, I'll sign,' she said.

'You do understand,' Hightower pressed her anxiously, 'this payment of half a million buys your silence, totally and for ever? If you're responsible for any word of this leaking out, to the press, the public, or any member of Mr Randolph's family, the entire sum is repayable. He wants a complete break from you.'

'I understand only too well.'

Dexter thought that by throwing money at a problem and relocating himself far away, he could effectively cut her out of his life as if she had never been part of it. She wouldn't let him. She would take his money and use it wisely. Linita would also travel, and from a distance, across the years, keep a vengeful eye on the man who had robbed her of her youth, her trust, her hopes ... everything. She doubted very much if the terms of this agreement were more than morally binding, but for the moment it suited her to lull Dexter into a false sense of security.

After Hightower had left, she went to Mother Clare's office and arranged that in due course she would deliver her baby at St Cecilia's. Father Tom would arrange suitable adoptive parents for it.

'There's just one thing,' said Linita authoritatively. 'I want to sign the adoption papers now. I don't even want to see the baby when it's born. I want to put all this behind me immediately.'

'I'm afraid it's not quite that simple . . .' The nun's sharp eyes came to rest on the cheque and legal agreement still loosely clasped in Linita's fingers. 'Was it a generous settlement, my dear? Our hospital benevolent fund, you know.'

Linita's eyes narrowed. 'The precise sum is my business, but let's just say I shall be in a position to make a very generous donation — if my request is granted.'

'Then, under the circumstances, Miss Tyrone —' Mother Clare produced the blank forms. The child's birth details would be added later. Linita filled in her own particulars and consent for the child's adoption. In the space allotted to the natural parents' names she wrote: Father Unknown.

While waiting for the baby to be born, she moved to a flat in a quiet unfashionable part of town. She dulled the tawny blonde splendour of her hair with a brown rinse, wore a cheap wedding ring and called herself "Mrs Tooley". The dark unflattering clothes she wore and her general air of sadness bore out her tale of having been recently widowed. The change of name and address was less to honour the terms of her agreement with Dexter than because she could not have borne anyone in her old charmed circle to know the mess he had left her in.

She was alone when her waters broke, alone when she called a cab and told the driver to take her to St Cecilia's. He seemed to know all about the hospital and the circumstances of its female patients, dumping her unceremoniously at the gates with a curt, 'There you go, *Mrs* Tooley.'

She barely registered his lack of civility. The cramping pains in her back were worsening every minute, tormenting her with their iron grip. Inside, she was shown into a brightly lit cubicle to remove her clothes and jewellery. Her shoes seemed welded into place on swollen

345

feet, and when she tried to remove the lying ring, her hands seemed a different shape from usual. It dawned on her that perhaps this was not usual. The pains in her back and heaving belly seemed to be receding, or perhaps they were simply less noticeable beside the excruciating throbbing behind her eyes. She heard a roaring in her ears and sank on the trolley bed, leaning her burning head against its cool metal frame.

'Sister,' she called weakly, 'there's something wrong —'

'Sure, Miss Tyrone, we'll let the doctor be the judge of that, shall we? Come with me now, and we'll have our nice bath.' Sister Margaret Mary put out her arm to help Linita to her feet. She glanced down, saw the hideously swollen ankles and fat sausage-like fingers. 'Holy Mother of God!' she exclaimed, and clapped her hand to her mouth. 'Hold on there, Miss Tyrone. I'm fetching Dr Flanagan — now!'

After that Linita remembered little except for a nightmare ride on a trolley. They seemed to be pushing her far too fast, taking corners at speed and jolting her poor head against the metal handles. She wanted to protest, but the only words to escape her were: 'Dexter! Don't leave me, Dexter.'

The trolley banged open a pair of swinging steel doors. Brilliant lights above her sought out the searing pain in her head and vied with it. She screamed and put up her hands to shield her eyes.

'Pre-eclampsia,' she heard one green-shrouded figure say. 'We'll have to go in quickly. Hold on, Linita.'

It felt as though they were puncturing the skin at the back of her hand with the bluntest needle they could find. She wanted to tell them, but the words dried in her throat. A thin cold trickle of liquid into her vein. For a moment she lay dumb and paralysed, at the mercy of the two conflicting sources of pain, in her head and in her back. Then the blackness rushed over her.

The emergency Caesarian was successful, she was told, but her recovery was retarded by the after-effects of

346

eclampsia. The hospital treated her as they treated all mothers whose babies were being put up for adoption. No one mentioned the child to her, not even to tell her its sex. They concentrated all their reassuring chat on her own plans for once she left hospital. She didn't tell them about the sea passage she had booked, the trunks full of her smart pre-pregnancy clothes packed and stored for her by Joan. "Mrs Tooley's" few possessions she had gladly left behind in the mean suburb. The landlord could throw them out when he repossessed the apartment.

Linita had paid to be given a private room, and was given preferential treatment by the nursing nuns and doctors. They didn't realise, however, that as they swapped notes in the corridor or at the nursing station by the double doors into the main ward, she could hear every word they said.

'No, best not to upset her. It will be the adoptive parents' problem,' she heard Dr Flanagan's distinctive voice saying, before he appeared in her room one day. 'And how are you, my dear? Roses in the cheeks again, I see. Good, good.'

Another time she heard Sister Margaret Mary's voice, tinged with concern: 'The paediatrician called out again in the middle of the night. Let's hope the Melbourne man can do something.'

Without knowing why, Linita became convinced that it was her baby they were discussing. She had tried so hard to avoid every reminder of her motherhood, swallowing the pills they gave her to stop her milk, avoiding the general ward where the mothers who were keeping their babies were taught how to feed and care for them. She wasn't able to avoid the sound of the nuns' marching footsteps and the pathetic crying of the babies as, every three hours, they were taken from the nursery to their mothers for a feed. The thin sounds and, worse, the contented silence which followed, were torture to Linita. She clenched her fists and wept in silence, arms and heart completely empty. She hid

347

her tears from the nursing sisters, who thought her hard and unfeeling.

She knew it was a bad idea, against everything she had arranged with Mother Clare, but she decided she must see her child, just once, and assure herself it was getting the best possible treatment.

Though she was stronger by the day, she could not face making a direct request to Mother Clare, with all the well-intentioned lectures it would give rise to. From her previous stay she knew where the newborns were tended. She chose her time well. In the early hours of the morning, when a crisis was under way in one of the delivery rooms, Linita slipped out of her room.

Thankfully the harassed young sister who had been left in sole charge of the baby unit was new. She did not recognise Linita, even if she had heard her history. She had her hands more than full, juggling two babies, one under each arm, in an effort to calm their crying before the others joined in.

'I heard all the fuss, thought you might like a hand,' offered Linita.

Seeing her nightdress and dressing-gown, the nun said, 'It's against regulations for patients to be up at this hour. But since it's an emergency ... If you could maybe pick up the child in cot three — he's a screamer. Number seventeen's due his feed soon, though how I'll manage with him in an incubator and all these to be seen to as well, I don't know!'

With beating heart, Linita picked up the child from cot three and scrutinised it carefully. Red-faced, red-haired, this couldn't be hers and Dexter's, could it? Around one pudgy wrist it wore a label, she noticed. 'Baby Roberts', thank heaven. But what about the child who was sick, the one in the incubator?

'I heard there was a kiddy not very well,' she said, rocking Baby Roberts against her. 'Poor little blighter. Do they know what it is?'

348

'Hole in the heart from the look of him,' sighed the nun, putting down the babies and picking up two more. 'You can always tell by the blue colour around the mouth. There's only one surgeon in Australia up to the operation, they say, and he'll need to be flown in specially from Melbourne. It's going to cost a fortune.'

A bell jangled on the wall above her head.

'Oh no, time for their feeds already! No wonder they've been so restless,' she said. 'Look, you wouldn't mind keeping an eye on things here, would you?'

'Not at all.'

As soon as the nun had bustled off, carrying her two charges, Linita replaced Baby Roberts in his cot. With dragging footsteps, she approached the incubator. For the past few days, since sensing there was something wrong with her child, she'd been dreading this moment. She'd tried to tell herself she'd given up the baby. It was the hospital's charge, not hers. But she found she could not harden herself against her own flesh, small and sick and helpless.

The incubator looked like a glass coffin, she thought, placing her hands on its heated surface and leaning as close as she could. She studied the dark-haired scrap of a child inside. He showed none of the plump promise of the other children in the nursery. As the nun had said, the skin around his mouth was tinged an alarming shade of blue. His tiny body was swaddled in thick white clothes, a knitted cap on top of the heavy head which hung flowerlike from the delicate stalk of his neck. He looked to be asleep. After a moment one hand stirred, emerging from the folds of his thick jacket. "Baby Tyrone" read the label on her son's wrist.

Tears sprang to her eyes. 'I'm sorry,' she whispered, pressing her mouth to the glass, the nearest she could come to him. 'This is my punishment. If only I hadn't taken the pills ... Don't die, darling. Please don't die.'

She heard the nun's footsteps smartly rapping the

corridor floor. Quickly she wiped away the evidence of her distress and moved away from the incubator, picking up a crying child at random. They were all protesting with hunger. It might as well be this as another. It was a beauty, though, she thought, uninterested.

'You'd never think she was the sister of the other poor little soul, would you?' called the nun.

'His sister?' she said incredulously.

'Twins. One full of health and strength. One sickly. God moves in mysterious ways.' She picked up two more babies, and turned away.

Hardly able to believe what she had heard, Linita turned the label on the little girl's wrist. There it was again: 'Baby Tyrone'. God had not been angry at her, after all. He had sent a second child, a beautiful healthy baby girl. All at once she knew exactly what she had to do. She must not waste time. At any minute now another sister might come on duty, one who would recognise Linita and challenged her business in the baby unit. Or perhaps there was a way around that . . .

The nursing sisters kept clean aprons and starched white coifs in a cupboard beside her room. She had heard them in there one day, chattering excitedly as they rummaged to the back of the shelves to unearth a spare black habit to lend to a sister who had soaked her own. Perhaps it was still there?

Afterwards, she could not work out how she had managed the transformation into a nun in the space of a minute. She seemed to move on automatic pilot, her every movement precise and finely calculated. From her room she removed only her shoes and handbag. From the store-cupboard, a fleecy white blanket.

When the young nun returned to the baby unit a transformed Linita was standing, in nun's habit, with her back half turned from the doorway, apparently writing notes on the clipboard at the end of Baby Tyrone's incubator.

'Ten minutes past, Sister!' she scolded. 'No wonder

they're howling like souls in torment. Well, get a move on, girl.'

'Yes, Sister. Sorry, Sister.' Flustered, the nun picked up two more of her charges and fled. Linita placed the clipboard on top of the incubator where the nurses would easily find it. She had found a spare Moses basket lying abandoned under an empty cot. She wrapped her daughter in the blanket and placed her in the carrying basket. She spared her last few seconds for her son.

'Goodbye, little one. I can't take you with me, you're too sick. We'll meet again one day, I promise.'

When the nun returned, it was to find an unattended nursery.

'Would you believe it? Going off like that and leaving them?' she muttered, ringing for assistance. It was the relief nurse who found Linita's note, clipped to the board on top of the incubator.

Put half of this into the Hospital Benevolent Fund to help other children in need. The rest is to go into a trust fund to be used towards his medical expenses, education and upbringing. His name is David. God bless him.

Beneath the scrawled note, clipped to the board, was a cheque for £100,000.

Dexter's surprise decision to make his home in England from then on did not entirely deceive Camilla. With a pragmatism that would have amazed her husband and mother, she had long since resigned herself to the idea that while he was in Australia he would not deprive himself of any comfort. He was too lusty and virile a man to go for half the year without a lover. So long as his Australian companion did not impinge on his relationship with his family, Camilla decided she could live with the situation. In Ashr and Court she held the trump cards. Dexter's premature return to England, talking of business reorganisation but behaving more lovingly than ever towards her and the children, confirmed the wisdom of her previous decision. He had obviously received some sort of shock. Got into romantic hot water, perhaps? Camilla was not above trading on his sense of guilt — from the purest possible motives.

While they were spending an intimate evening together in their private rooms at Courtney Park, she tackled him. 'Darling, now that you're to be with us most of the time, do you think we could enlarge the family? Wouldn't you love a little girl to twist you round her finger?'

'Just like her mother?' He looked serious for a moment. 'You're quite sure about this? You didn't have an easy time with the boys.'

'I want it more than anything on earth. Oh, Dexter, please say we can!'

'There's no saying we'll succeed ... might be another son. Still, what the hell? We could have a lot of fun trying.'

It was third time lucky for Camilla, as she had always secretly believed it would be. To both parents' delight, Georgianna Elizabeth Louisa Randolph was born on Christmas Eve, 1964, to complete the happiest and most privileged of families.

After completing Immigration and Customs, Linita found herself stranded in New York, a two-month-old child in her arms and absolutely no idea what she should do next. She hadn't thought beyond getting to America. In the cold grey morning Chantel whimpered and wriggled in her arms. Linita had never felt so isolated. Almost she ordered her luggage to be put back on board. Then she remembered that Dexter had left Australia. There was nothing to link her with the country apart from her son who, God willing, would now be cured and with his new parents.

She got a porter to wheel her mountain of luggage and baby equipment to a cab-rank and followed Dexter's usual practice when arriving in a strange town. After all, she had the money. 'Take me to the best hotel you know,' she told the driver.

Apparently it wasn't that simple in New York. 'Lady, I know dozens a good hotels. Depends what sorta joint you want and how much dough you don't mind spending.'

Linita thought for a moment. 'I want somewhere very comfortable and old-established where there'll be no trouble arranging help with my baby. Oh, and I'd like to be close to a garden or a park. Somewhere I can take her for some air. Money's no object.'

He shrugged and thought for a moment. 'Old-established . . . Ya mean old-fashioned? Lady, I got just the place for you.'

He drove Linita straight to the Plaza, the perfect choice. She took a suite overlooking Central Park, delighting in her view out over the greenery and the rows of horse-drawn cabs waiting to take tourists on old-style rides. She relished the hotel's air of ordered calm, the way that nothing was too much trouble for the staff. After the traumas of the past year there was something infinitely seductive in the sensation of sitting back and letting the rhythm of hotel life take her over. She and Chantel, a quiet and placid child, spent long mornings together, lazing around the comfortable suite while Linita ordered brunch from room service. In the afternoons they took walks in the park where spring blossoms and a scattering of green were just appearing on the naked trees. From late afternoon, Chantel slept. It was then that Linita felt her manless state.

It was not that she wanted a lover. The scars inflicted by the break-up with Dexter were still too raw. But at night, staring wistfully out over the darkened park to the towering light-etched skyscrapers beyond, she was painfully aware that there was a whole exciting new life out there. Her money insulated her from worry but not from loneliness. She had come all this way to make a fresh start, only to fall at the last fence. To a woman alone, the town was closed. Linita must have an escort. She never expected to find one as a result of an elevator breakdown ...

One afternoon when Chantel was being untypically unsettled and demanding, Linita cut short their walk, scolding herself for being an anxious mother hen. She wheeled her stately British perambulator into the Plaza's crowded lobby, more congested than usual since all but one of the elevators was temporarily out of service.

She pressed the button to ascend, and stood and waited. There seemed to be some delay on the floor above. Chantel began to whimper and toss herself about in her carriage. Was it Linita's imagination, or was she starting to look flushed?

A man joined her by the elaborate gates. 'You have pressed the button?'

'Yes, but there's some hold-up. I would take the stairs, but —' She gestured ruefully to the pram and its screaming occupant. 'I'm afraid she's a little impatient,' Linita apologised above the din.

'No matter,' he said, and continued to wait with them.

His pleasant smile lightened what might have seemed an attractive but austere appearance. He had a thin, tanned face, regular features and grey-blond hair, neatly parted and swept back off a high intelligent forehead. Linita put his age at a few years less than Dexter's. Damn ... why did everything always come back to him? She concentrated on the stranger for lack of anything else to do. Something about his heavy tortoiseshell-framed glasses and the cut of his suit told her that he was not English or American, though his accent was flawless.

'I do wish they'd hurry up,' she fretted. In her agitated movement inside the carriage Chantel had set it rocking from side to side. Her mother had never seen her do that before.

Her companion sensed her concern. 'You will permit

me?' He placed his hand gently on the baby's forehead. 'She has a slight fever.'

'I knew it! Oh God, I know no one. What am I going to do?'

'Madame, please. I'm sure there is no cause for alarm.'

Linita whirled on him angrily. 'How do you know? You a doctor?'

'As it happens, I did study medicine. It comes in very useful in my present line of work. I'm sure there's nothing wrong with your baby that the mildest infant medication and a good night's sleep can't cure.'

She looked at him imploringly. 'What medication? Please, tell me its name and where to get it and I'll be forever grateful. I haven't found my way around the city yet.'

'The cordial is called Infasol. It's new on the market and at present all the samples in America are in my room. Shall we?'

At last the elevator had appeared and he was ushering her inside. It had to be the most cunning come-on line she had ever heard. Linita was about to refuse indignantly, when a fresh wail of despair issued from a by now seriously uncomfortable Chantel. Tears spilled down her plump cheeks.

'All right,' said Linita, trapped. 'It's very kind of you. Thanks.'

He and the elevator attendant manoeuvred the bulky carriage inside the cramped compartment. Linita, trapped against one wall by its high handlebars, could not reach her daughter to comfort her. She was amazed when the dignified, beautifully dressed stranger reached inside and picked up the screaming child, seeming not to care when tears and worse spilled on to his lapels. Plucking the tortoiseshell glasses from his face, he dangled them in front of the baby, who immediately fell into a silent study of them.

'Say, how d'ya learn that trick?' asked the relieved attendant.

'Years of practice,' laughed the stranger.

Relieved by his easy professional manner with her baby, Linita didn't feel so bad about accompanying him to his suite, which was on the same floor as her own. Inside, he gestured for her to be seated and went into the next room to fetch a soft leather attaché case. He took out a brown medicine-bottle and a clear plastic spoon.

'You're sure this is safe?' asked Linita, nervously eyeing the blank-sided bottle.

'Of course. Here.' He handed over a glossy printed leaflet extolling the virtues of a new infant panacea which could cure colic, colds, sleeplessness and mild stomach ailments. 'And — my card, in case you were wondering what I was doing with all this.'

He was Baron Wolfgang von Stolsenburg, she saw, of Stolsenburg Pharmaceuticals, with headquarters in Munich. He was obviously just being a Good Samaritan, and she felt ashamed of her earlier suspicions.

'Linita Tyrone,' she introduced herself, steadying Chantel on her lap with one hand and extending the other to him.

He bowed and clicked his heels. 'It is a very great pleasure to be introduced to you at last. I have seen you in the lobby downstairs.'

His smile left her in no doubt that 'seen' meant 'admired'. She looked away, embarrassed.

With Chantel he was all professionalism, coaxing her to open her mouth and accept a spoonful of the clear red liquid.

'Tastes good, *liebchen*, doesn't it?'

Chantel fluttered her eyelashes and gave him a goofy grin.

'That should do the trick,' he said. 'But just in case, why don't you take the rest? Another spoonful in six hours wouldn't hurt her.'

'Thank you so much. You've been very kind. Are you sure you won't need it yourself?'

'It only works for infants from one month to five years,' he assured her gravely.

Her full-throated laughter was a delight. Though she obviously had not noticed him coming and going on the same floor, she had caught his eye days before — both for her beauty and her air of sadness. It was the first time he had seen her smile.

'I think that you are staying here on your own?' he said tentatively.

Instantly the smile faded. 'Yes.'

'The Infasol should put Chantel to sleep shortly. I wondered — since we are both strangers in this exciting city, Mrs Tyrone, whether you would do me the great favour of dining with me tonight? I'm sure the hotel could arrange a sitter, and it would be a very great kindness if you would. You've no idea how wearing it gets, spending every night of these trips alone or with a business acquaintance.'

Suave, attractive, Salem-educated Wolfgang von Stolsenburg could have flicked through his little black book and come up with the names and telephone numbers of upwards of a dozen escorts, any one of whom would have been delighted to hear from him. Far from being strange to him, New York was his second city. Usually the knowledge gave him confidence. Tonight he found himself crossing his fingers that the untruth would convince the reclusive Linita Tyrone into accepting his invitation. He found himself quite absurdly committed to bringing that lovely smile back to her troubled face.

She looked down at Chantel, nestling against her. 'Thank you very much. I'd like that. But first there's something you should know. It's not Mrs Tyrone, it's Miss.'

His heart gave a gigantic jump for joy. His face remained impassive. 'The invitation still stands. I should be honoured if you would accept.'

She did not smile again, but there was a lightening of her tense expression. 'In that case, how can I refuse?'

For the rest of his stay in New York, when he was not presenting Stolsenburg Pharmaceuticals to wholesale chemists' chains, von Stolsenburg put away his little black book and devoted himself to Chantel and Linita. He seemed as genuinely delighted to share a messy lunch with the baby in Linita's suite as he was to whisk her mother off to an impromptu dinner at 21 or dancing at El Morocco. She quickly realised the deception he had practised upon her. Wolfie, as she had learned to call him, was a familiar figure to the *maître d*'s around town. With his European elegance and obvious breeding, he acquired friends and acquaintances wherever he went. Generously he introduced Linita widely among his New York circle, and on his recommendation the wealthy 'widow' from Australia was made welcome.

She had in fact confided some of the details of her story to him. He knew all about the long running affair, though not the man's name, his surprise marriage, Linita's pregnancy and suicide bid. The only thing she kept completely from him was David, left behind in Australia but very much a presence still in her grieving heart.

Wolfie extended his stay by several days, but finally felt he must return to Munich. Though they had not exchanged so much as a single kiss, he felt he had grown closer to Linita than to any woman previously. The fact that she was an unmarried mother, far from detracting from her charms, only intensified them for him.

They dined in his suite on his last night. 'My dear,' he said unexpectedly, 'this is going to sound crazy — but come with me tomorrow. There's nothing to keep you here, is there? I could show you Schloss Stolsenburg —' the fifteenth-century Bavarian castle owned by his family — 'and introduce you to my mother and friends. They would welcome you.'

'With my history?'

'Well — we might have to amend one or two small details . . .'

'No, Wolfie, there'll be no more sweeping things under the carpet for me. We've always been honest with each other and that's why I can tell you this now — I'm going to miss you very much when you go. Your companionship has meant a lot to me. With you I've started to see and do all the things I came to America for. It's a great place, and I want to put down roots here. This afternoon I had a realtor show me around some apartments on the Upper East Side. I've found a beauty on Fifth Avenue with a great view over the Park — guess I've got used to it, living here.'

His face remained expressionless. 'That's great, Linita. I'm glad for you. Hotel living's fine in its way, but a child needs a proper home.'

The sort he would gladly have given her.

'I agree. I'll be interviewing for a suitable nanny for her, someone I can trust to live with us in the apartment, and when I've got a routine going there I intend to branch out on my own account, perhaps start up a business.

'It's all due to you. Without your kindness and support I'd never have decided to get this all started. I'm sorry I can't come with you to Europe, but you can see it's not the right time for me, can't you?'

If ever a man's good deed had rebounded on him! There was so much he wanted to explain to her, but he sensed that if he pushed her now he could undo all the progress he had made in gaining her trust. Better to put some space and time between them, though she would still fill his thoughts, he knew.

'I'll be back in the Fall,' he said casually. 'Let me have your new address. You have mine?'

'Of course. And, Wolfie — thanks. For everything.'

He kissed her hand at the door to her suite and left, reluctantly. He caught the early morning flight without seeing her again.

It was torture, but he stayed away for six months. In October he received a bright and bubbling letter which told him that her new apartment was redecorated — at last! —

and she had been so impressed with the interior designer's skills that she had decided to go into partnership with him. His name was Georges Monceau.

"He'll be doing the buying and designing, naturally. I'm too much of a dumb bunny to be trusted with that! But he keeps me busy chasing stock and tradesmen, introducing potential clients and writing cheques. Jewel takes good care of Chantel, who's growing every day. Write me when you'll next be in New York and we'll roll out the red carpet."

Wolfie re-read the letter. Georges Monceau . . . why did that ring a bell? He dialled the number of the private investigator Stolsenburg Pharmaceuticals retained. 'Herr Gross, this is von Stolsenburg speaking. Something a little different for you — an interior decorator living in New York. The name's Georges Monceau. A friend of mine has recently gone into business with him. I want to check he's on the level.'

When Wolfie received Gross's report forty-eight hours later, he booked himself on to the first available flight for New York. From the airport he had himself driven straight to Linita's apartment. It was fabulous, a showcase for the fine English antiques and French provincial pieces that Monceau Associates also dealt in, she told him.

She seemed very glad to see him again, kissing his cheek and clinging to him for a moment before taking his arm and leading him on a conducted tour. He was more interested in Chantel and the progress she had made into All-American baby. Linita and her nanny had dressed her in striped blue and white dungarees, a sweatshirt and tiny baseball boots. She smiled to see Wolfie, and offered him a sticky piece of peanut butter and jelly sandwich from her feeding-tray.

Linita intercepted it. 'That's very kind of you, honey-bunch, but Wolfie's not hungry . . . Oh, I forgot to ask. *Are* you hungry, by any chance? I never was after getting off a plane, but Jewel could fix you something. Sure?'

She seemed to talk just a shade more than he remembered, and there were dark circles under her eyes. Burning the candles at both ends? he wondered. But she seemed to have no social engagements that night or on any of the subsequent ones.

On the fifth evening, hating himself for his deception, he called to break their date. 'I'm sorry, but a client just got into town. Tonight's the only chance we'll have. I've sent you flowers to make up.'

'Sweet of you, but don't worry. There's always tomorrow.'

Later that afternoon an enormous bunch of white freesias arrived at the apartment. 'Sign here,' said the liveried messenger. He seemed pretty grand for a florist's boy, thought Linita — and discovered she was signing a delivery note from Tiffany. There was a baby-blue satin ribbon tied round the bouquet. Beneath it, neatly clipped to the stems, the most fabulous pair of ruby and diamond earrings. It was too much, far more than was necessary to make up for a single missed appointment. She rang the Plaza to tell him so, but the switchboard told her the Baron was unavailable.

The following afternoon the same deliveryman arrived with another bouquet — scented white orchids this time, and nestling among their waxen blooms a thick ruby and pavé diamond bracelet to match the earrings. There was a note this time:

'*Mein Schatz*, duty calls again. A thousand apologies. I will call tomorrow, without fail. W.'

The irony of her situation was almost more than she could bear, Linita reflected the next day as she took delivery of Wolfie's greatest extravagance to date — a ruby and diamond pendant suspended from the branches of a bunch of white lilac.

The months without him had shown her how foolish she had been to let him slip through her fingers so easily before, but this display of his wealth and trust had come at the worst possible time for her.

361

There was another card. "Wear this for me tonight. I'll call for you at 9. W."

When Jewel showed him in later that evening, Linita had not changed out of her brown wool afternoon dress. His presents to her lay on a table before her. Wolfie ignored them. He made no move to offer her his usual affectionate kiss of greeting but seemed strained and ill at ease.

'There's something I must know,' he began. 'Have you missed me these past three days?'

'Yes,' she said in a thin voice, 'I've missed you like hell. But, Wolfie, it's no good —'

'Thank God for that!' he exclaimed, dropping to one knee beside her and taking her hands in his. 'I've missed you, and Chantel, ever since I left here in the spring. Listen, I have a confession to make.'

She snatched her hands away, guilty tears welling in her eyes. 'No, I'm the one who should confess. Let me talk, Wolfie, then you'll see why it's impossible for us to go on seeing each other.'

She was broke, she explained. The partner, Georges Monceau, who was supposed to introduce her to the business world, had systematically conned and defrauded her, getting her to lend larger and larger sums of money to the business on the promise of repayment with interest when the clients to whom she had introduced him settled their bills for the work he had done. Ten days ago he had skipped the country, taking with him his creepy boyfriend — Wolfie smiled with relief to hear it — and all the proceeds of the work done so far on her friends' unfinished apartments. The stock he had left in her apartment as surety turned out to have been borrowed from various European antique dealers for sale to clients on a commission basis. The rightful owners would be removing it as soon as shipment could be arranged.

'I've lost everything,' she explained tearfully. 'I shall have to sell this place to repay the clients Georges has

362

defrauded and let me down. I introduced them to him. It's only right I should pay. I'm ruined, Wolfie. Not at all the sort of woman you want to get mixed up with.'

'That's nonsense!' He sat down beside her and put an arm round her waist. 'You're the woman I've longed for all my life,' he murmured. 'And I did say *I* had something to confess. When you wrote to me, naming Monceau, I did a bit of checking up. Monsieur Monceau, it turns out, is known to Interpol. He has pulled off similar deceptions of rich single women in five other cities. I got here as soon as I could, hoping to save you from his clutches, but the bird had flown. It's no good. You'll just have to marry me now.'

'You mean — you really don't mind that I'm a penniless, simple-minded hick with a child, who's probably only marrying you for your money — you do have money, I take it?'

'Only you would have failed to check me out by now — *that's* why I love you.' He did not tell her that he had checked the details of her own past and now knew the identity of Chantel's father. Let her confide that in her own time. 'Of course I have money, you goose!' He gestured towards the jewellery. 'These didn't come out of a five and dime, you know! But there are things far more important than money.'

'Spoken like a true aristocrat,' she teased, leaning her head against his shoulder.

He twisted in his seat so that she could see his face. Suddenly it looked sad.

'Wolfie, what is it? You're not ill or anything?'

'Not now, but a childhood illness ... I'm afraid there could never be children for us, Linita. At least we'll have Chantel. I love her almost as much as I love her mother. Marry me?'

She did not reply, but made it apparent that she was waiting for him to kiss her, which he did at satisfying length. 'Have I convinced you yet?'

'I'm still thinking ...'

About David, for one thing. A letter from St Cecilia's, whom she had contacted, told her that he had received his operation, which had been a success. He was now happily established with a childless couple who loved him dearly. Although she would always blame herself for surrendering him, she did not believe there was anything to be gained from uprooting him now. Her son was loved. So were she and Chantel.

'What will we say — that you're Chantel's father?'

'I think it would be easiest all round. My family, you know ... Later, perhaps, when she's grown up, we could tell her the truth. I hope it would not come as too much of a jolt then. I mean to be the best father a little girl ever had.'

Linita kissed him again. 'You are the kindest, dearest man ... Of course I'll marry you — on one condition.'

'Name it.'

'You do a lot of business here, don't you? I wondered — could we make our home here, in the States? I've grown to love it, and so does Chantel. I don't want to uproot her again.'

He thought for a moment. 'So long as we visit Mutti once or twice a year, it would be a positive advantage. The firm is building a new manufacturing plant in northern New Jersey. I hear there are some splendid estates there. Will that suit you?'

'Perfectly, Wolfie. And I do love you, you know.'

'I knew all along — I just had to make you see how much.'

It was almost true, thought Linita. She'd never find another man as magnanimous and devoted. She would make him a good wife and never, ever, betray him. But her main reason for remaining in America was that Dexter Randolph had business interests here. He had none in Europe. From this vantage-point she could keep a watchful eye on his progress. And when the time was ripe and he was least expecting her attack, Linita would take her revenge.

Georgianna and her brothers were having an idyllic child-hood. Safe, enclosed and matchlessly beautiful, Courtney Park was one gigantic playground to them, Dexter and Camilla the most generous and indulgent parents. In their earliest days, the children's nannies dressed them in the best that the White House, Harrods and Liberty had to offer. Exquisite clothes, many of them hand sewn, in old-fashioned lawns and cambrics, softest wool and velvets. When they grew older and more active, Dexter delighted them by sending over to his New York office for a selection of tough and practical denim jeans, sweatshirts, caps and baseball jackets. Camilla wanted to keep Georgie in the prettiest hand-smocked Liberty prints with lace-trimmed collars, but when she appealed to her father with tears in her eyes, he intervened, as the child had known he would. Though he could be strict with his sons, one pleading glance from his daughter's wide-set hazel eyes, and Dexter was putty in her hands.

Despite his frequent absences on business, Dexter took care when he was at home to spend hours with his children, teaching them all to ride, drive, shoot and swim, and to excel at any game, irrespective of their sex. Georgie grew up a regular tomboy. She also grew up more lively and self-reliant than many other girls on her age and background.

Dexter spent with a lavish hand on them all — children's parties at Courtney Park were famous for their ingenuity. For Court's tenth birthday, Dexter hired an entire fair for the night, complete with Ferris wheel, carousels, and a hot-dog stand dispensing free hot dogs and candyfloss. Mothers cursed, but for a month Courtney Randolph was the most popular child in the county. Ash's birthday treat on turning twelve was a day at the races in one of Dexter's private boxes, entertaining his friends to a specially ordered lunch of hamburgers, chocolate mousse and Coca-Cola. When Georgie indicated that she would like a proper tutu in which to practise her ballet steps,

Dexter had a whole wardrobe of dresses created for her, and persuaded two Royal Ballet soloists to dance before an audience of enraptured little girls at her birthday tea.

He even got over his disappointment when, at the age of twelve, she flatly refused to hunt with him a second time after the ordeal of her 'blooding'. Dexter was now Honorary Master of the Courtney Hunt, Georgie a gifted and plucky rider. Her defection hurt his feelings.

'I'm sorry, Daddy, but my headmistress says it's principles that count,' she told him gravely. She had just transferred to Heathfield, and took her new 'big' school very seriously.

'And it's against your principles to have fun riding Puffin?'

'No, I shall continue to ride him in gymkhanas. And, Daddy, when I'm a bit bigger, maybe I could ride in point-to-points like you and the boys ...'

'Maybe,' he growled reluctantly. He hated to think of his little nut-brown girl risking her neck like that. 'Anyway, hunting's the best preparation there is for point-to-point. Why won't you come out with us?'

'Because joining in blood sports, the killing of innocent animals for human entertainment, is against my principles. You do understand, don't you?'

'Then I take it you won't be joining the shoots any more?'

Georgie swallowed. She had loved her days out with the guns and their dogs, the camaraderie of rough shooting and the ceremony of the drives. There was no denying, however, that animals were killed for entertainment as much as for the pot. 'No, I'll stand by what I said. I'm afraid I won't be coming out any more.'

She had thought he might be angry with her, or at least a little cool. Dexter was by now a legendary shot, and his three gifted children, with their specially commissioned 20-bores, were shaping up to follow in his footsteps. He surprised her by saying, 'Good on you, Georgie. If you speak up for what you believe in, other people will respect you — even if they don't agree.' He and Ash and Court continued to shoot, but never teased or argued with her over her decision.

Though Camilla played the most active part in her children's upbringing, their grandmother's elegant acerbic presence was a constant in their lives. Angelica was indulgent enough towards her grandchildren to be an entertaining if occasionally alarming companion. She did not believe in pulling her punches. If a child asked a question of her, it got a straightforward answer. Georgie's enquiring mind and firm stand against what she saw as cruel and wrong was responsible, when she was twelve, for causing a major upheaval in Randolph Enterprises and raising her father's public profile.

'Grandmama, I don't think I'll be eating any more meat,' she told Angelica one day.

'Don't be ridiculous, Georgie! The daughter of a cattle baron not eat meat! What's put that idea into your head?'

Georgianna produced a newspaper clipping. In it, a reporter gave a factual account of slaughterhouse procedures. It made far from easy reading. 'Do you think it's the same in Daddy's works?' she asked.

For once, Angelica found herself at a loss for words. What would the child come up with next? 'My dear, I've never even thought about it.'

'Then I think you should, Grandmama. I shan't be eating meat again until you or Daddy can assure me these things have been stopped. I haven't bothered Mummy with it. It would only upset her.'

Angelica rang Dexter, who was away on a tour of his American hotels. She faxed across a copy of the article, which recommended the introduction of a new type of humane killer. Dexter conveyed instructions to Lucas, ordering him to institute the measures immediately. To his surprise, the move received a great deal of free, unmanipulated publicity. Georgie had tapped into a vein of genuine public concern and her stand had caused her father to come up smelling of roses. Seeing the attention that he was receiving, other major meat companies swiftly announced they would be following Randolph Enterprises' initiative. Dexter found himself credited with the introduction of a new humanitarian era in meat production. It was just the boost he needed for his campaign towards a peerage.

Angelica heard from her Honours List contact that his name was being given serious consideration for inclusion among the candidates put before the Sovereign.

'And all because of my clever little girl!' he crowed. 'Come here, sweetheart, and give Lord Randolph a kiss.'

'Don't get your hopes up too high,' his mother-in-law warned.

'No, it's all right. We've cracked it this time. I can feel it in my water.'

It seemed he was right. Angelica was bidden to invite him to an off-the-record interview with her friend Lord St Aubrey, chairman of the Honours Committee. Over a glass of Pimm's on the Terrace of the House, Dexter was un-officially informed that his name would be put forward for inclusion on the next New Year's list.

'Of course,' his lordship indicated, 'it would be no bad thing if your name had recently hit the headlines again in some, shall we say charitable, connection?'

Dexter could take a hint. The funding of a new ward for the Royal Marsden did the trick. In January 1980, Dexter Randolph, a cattle baron from the Australian outback, achieved the virtually impossible. He was granted a life peerage for services to charity and the meat industry, styling himself Lord Randolph of Stoneham, the nearest village. The appellation Courtney — like the house — belonged to Alexander.

The seventh Earl of Courtney arrived in New York at about the same time as Linita. His introduction to

American society was very different. Everyone wanted to know him. In the Wall Street offices of Shearing's he was treated like any other young trainee investment banker — almost. They gave him an office of his own, not because his lowly status merited it but because it gave the bank's chairman such a buzz to walk past and see the name "Alex Hamilton", with a coronet painted above it.

Outside office hours, he began to feel a certain sympathy for the polar bear and other endangered species. He was hunted remorselessly; persecuted by phone calls from society matrons he had never met; his mailbox jammed with invitations to openings, private viewings, charity and cotillion balls, dinner parties, lunch parties and brunches — whatever they were. On any weekend he could choose between an embarrassment of invitations: whether to play polo in Florida or ski in Aspen, sail off Rhode Island or hunt in Virginia?

He was pursued by countless clear-eyed, square-jawed beauties with perfect teeth and poisonous mothers, none of whom seemed to believe him when he explained he could not take time off from the bank on a whim to join them in Acapulco or the Bahamas. His first priority was to learn the business of banking, he told them. Unfortunately, this sometimes meant he'd be unavailable at evenings or weekends. It was a very convenient smokescreen.

He was in fact genuinely fascinated by the complicated world of finance. To a young man like Alexander, born with every advantage, an automatic insider, it was stimulating to find himself thrust out on a limb, struggling every day to crack the code and truly belong to this brash new world of poison pills, White Knights and companies in play. The deal was the thing, he learned. Everything else took second place — including the banker's love life. It suited Alexander very well. To him, love had always been a vague and shadowy concept.

He rose swiftly within Shearing's. He was bright, presentable, biddable, and the Chairman liked nothing better than introducing him to the bank's clients. 'You've met Alex, of course? No? Well, Art —' or Ted or Bert or Frank or Bill — 'I'd like for you to meet Lord Courtney. Alex here is very big on leverage buyouts, aren't you, my boy?'

Because it would have given rise to talk and speculation if he had not, Xan reluctantly accepted a tenth of the invitations he received, and took out a succession of starry-eyed Muffys and Barbras, Missys and Nancys. Three outings with the same girl seemed to be his limit. "Three times Courtney" he came to be nicknamed on the débutante circuit, and to the girls themselves, if not their mothers, Xan began to be looked upon as a non-starter. Sure he was good-looking in a clean-cut British way, beautifully dressed and mannered. But, increasingly, there seemed to be something quaint and old-fashioned about him at a time when beads, bangles and colourful hippy clothes were becoming the order of the day for both sexes.

Hard rock, soft drugs and freewheelin' love were *de rigueur*, even for the children of the Five Hundred. Xan might politely bop to the Beatles — yawn, yawn! — but you'd never catch a stiff like him flying down to catch a Stones concert. Impossible to imagine him in faded jeans and tie-dyes, cowboy boots and a Zapata moustache. He wouldn't even grow his hair, for Chrissakes! Xan didn't queue to eat hash browns, mingle with the divinely decadent in Andy Warhol's Factory, shout slogans to end the most unjust war of all.

As the sixties became the seventies, most of the girls from his earliest days in New York were well into their first marriage — or divorce. Their younger sisters and relatives had grown used to seeing the Earl of Courtney on the scene, a useful walker or window-dressing if their mothers got too heavy, but no player. He was too damned straight! Xan knew what they thought, and it amused him.

In the mid-seventies he was surprised to receive a tele-phone call at work one day from Luis de Luz y Aragon. His

370

friend from Eton and Oxford was in New York and suggested they meet later that day.

'I'm staying at the Kensington,' said Luis. 'We could have a drink there, maybe go out clubbing?'

'Sounds good, but I should warn you that I'm not really into late nights and heavy scenes, Luis. I'm a banker now, remember.'

'Still the same old Xan! Lighten up a little! After all, we haven't seen each other for — what is it? — six or seven years.'

It was more than ten, the friendship foundering naturally when Luis was sent down from Christ Church without graduating after a scandal he could hardly have forgotten, hushed up though it had been. Since then, Xan had heard he'd led a lotus-eating existence on his own Spanish estates and in the villa in Tangiers.

'Okay, I'll call for you at the Kensington at eight. Why stay there, though? It's a bit tacky, isn't it?'

Luis laughed. 'Deliciously "decadent" would be the word I'd choose. Don't be late, Xan. There's someone I can't wait for you to meet.'

Xan was thoughtful and withdrawn for the rest of the day. Normally when meeting someone after work he would have gone along dressed as he had been for the office. For Luis and Greenwich Village he went home after work and changed into his weekend clothes, not the smart flannels, loafers and navy blazer of his society outings but the *other* weekend clothes, the ones he kept for very special occasions.

The hotel was as dimly lit and dingy as he remembered from previous visits. In the lobby, a visiting British punk band, all torn clothes, backcombed hair and safetypins worn rather amusingly in their earlobes, were trying to cause a scene.

'If you don't fuckin' get us a fuckin' limo, mate, fuckin' pronto, we'll smash the whole fuckin' place apart.' They could have saved their breath.

371

'Be my guest,' sighed the desk clerk, busy varnishing his nails. 'Like, I only work here, guys.'

The Kensington never changed, but the alteration in Luis took Xan's breath away. He looked so much older. The once rangy body beneath a showy suit of white vicuna, brocade vest and open-necked shirt had run alarmingly to seed. The olive skin of his puffy face looked simultaneously tight and scored with lines, notably around the eyes and mouth, which had been expertly and heavily made up.

Luis stood back from the door, casting an appraising eye over his visitor. 'Darling boy, you haven't changed. How terribly unfair!'

Xan wondered if he was meant to reciprocate, but couldn't bring himself to.

'Sweet of you to dress down for us —' Luis indicated the tight faded jeans and US army issue parachute jacket Xan had changed into — 'but I can see you're every inch the banker underneath. Not like that little beast Kevin ... Ah, there you are, sweetness.' He was addressing a surly-looking boy of maybe seventeen or eighteen, dressed head to toe in biker's black leathers. Skintight trousers, jacket, boots, gloves ... everything but the helmet.

The boy scowled and threw himself on to a couch next to Luis. 'Don't suppose you've got any H on you?' were his first words to Xan.

'Sorry. I don't use it.'

'Jesus Christ!' The boy turned savagely on Luis. 'You useless old queen. You said he'd be bound to help me out.'

Though he was easily ten years older and much bigger than Kevin, Luis looked terrified of him. 'My dear, calm yourself.' He turned imploring eyes on Xan. 'I thought you'd know a club, perhaps, where he could go to score. You *do* know the gay clubs here?'

'Of course.'

'Then where are we most likely to solve Kevin's little problem?'

'Any of them, but at The Pit it's practically mandatory.

Safest, too. They pay the cops a fortune to stay away.'

Kevin's nervous fingers fiddled with the zips at his wrist. Xan saw the trackmarks in his veins standing out against the hairless, boy's, skin. 'Useless old cunts,' he was murmuring to himself, shivering violently inside the tight shiny jacket.

'Let's skip the drink, shall we?' said Xan.

Luis rose gratefully to his feet. 'Good idea. Is it far?'

'No — we can walk it.'

Luis took the boy's arm. 'Come on, poppet. Won't be long now.'

Xan was appalled by the violence with which Kevin shoved him away. 'Take your filthy hands off me! I've told you, I don't want you touching me. I'm going to get me works.'

He stumbled into the bedroom. Luis laughed, rubbing his arm. 'Don't think too badly of him,' he said. 'Change of scene and supplier — he's not his usual sunny self.'

Xan doubted the boy was ever anything more than a bullying little tough, but obviously that was the way Luis preferred it. He took them straight to The Pit, one of the Village's toughest leather bars. He didn't plan to stay long himself.

Kevin caught a dealer's eye almost immediately, and disappeared. Xan had a drink with his friend, for old time's sake, then looked at his watch. A huge musclebound biker, draped in chains and bursting out of his sleeveless jerkin and leather pants, was giving him the eye.

'Sorry, got to go,' said Xan. 'A call to take from Tokyo.'

Luis looked wistful. 'So soon? I've heard all about the back room here. Thought you and I might sample its delights together.'

Xan looked at his old friend's painted, lascivious face. 'I'm afraid it's not my scene any more,' he said, realising that he meant it. At the door, he looked back. Luis was already deep in conversation with the Incredible Hulk. Xan shivered, and left.

It was not a question of ceasing to be gay. Alexander doubted if the attraction he felt towards certain kinds of boys — young, dark and delicate — would ever fade. But the gay club and bar scene — that was definitely losing its allure. Once irresistible as forbidden fruit, now encounters there seemed merely brutal and dangerous. There had to be an alternative, he decided, but to live openly with another man would finish him at the bank. Trapped again.

Part of his motive in coming to New York had been to spare his family the opprobrium they would suffer if his inclinations became common knowledge in British society. Although these days there was a little more tolerance towards men of his sort, he knew it was always particularly distressing for a great family when it seemed the name would not be carried on. It was true he had come to New York hoping to restore the family fortunes. He had also hoped that by staying there unmarried for long enough the truth would gradually become apparent to his family without the need for any distressing revelations.

A few days later he was to be more glad than ever that he had not chosen to come clean to Camilla and their mother. He was surprised to receive a telephone call in the middle of the night. His sister's soft familiar voice apologised for waking him.

'I know it's three in the morning or something there, but I had to call you at once. I'm afraid something awful's happened — it's in all the papers this morning. It's Luis de Luz y Aragon — have you seen him lately?'

'Yes, a couple of days ago. Why?'

'Did he have a — a friend with him?'

'He mentioned he was travelling with someone. We never met,' Alexander lied glibly. 'Are you going to tell me what this is all about?' He had a sick certainty he knew.

She chose her words with care, knowing that they had once been good friends. 'I hate to be the one to tell you this, but he's dead. Murdered. They found him battered to

374

death in his hotel room. It seemed his — companion — had a drug habit and a history of violence towards the men who supported him. We mustn't judge, I know, but it's all so sordid — a dreadful way to die. I didn't want you to pick up the newspaper and read it without any warning.'

Tears began to roll down Alexander's face. He had seen what sort of trouble Luis was in, and failed to give him any warning. 'Thanks. It was thoughtful of you,' he said unsteadily. 'You won't mind if I don't talk any more?'

'I understand. And, Xan, I'm very sorry.'

Not half as sorry as he was. He could have helped Luis. Instead, he had turned his back.

He spent a sleepless night. In the morning he called in sick and spent a nauseating day claiming Luis's body, braving the sneers and taunts about queer-bashing being too good for his kind. He arranged for Luis to be flown home and buried on his family estates. These would now pass to a distant cousin. The last of the de Luz y Aragon line was dead, and with him the once proud family name.

Though their lifestyles had been poles apart, Luis's death brought home to Alexander the reality of his own position. He doubted he could ever enjoy more than companionship with a woman, but it seemed to him now that for the sake of the Hamilton family line he should at least try. For him there would always be men, but perhaps if he chose the right sort of woman — someone understanding and discreet — there might also be a wife? The only other essential qualification was that she must be able to bear him an heir.

In the late seventies and early eighties Alexander took a string of slim dark 'houseboys', who also served as occasional lovers. In public he amazed the matrons of New York, Boston and San Francisco by once again playing the singles scene. Rumour had it that at long last the dishy Earl of Courtney was seriously looking for a wife. He made it plain that, unlike the Prince of Wales, he was not interested in cradle-snatching. He was on the lookout for someone attractive, presentable, worldly. In Sloane de Havilland, he seemed to have met his ideal.

He was weekending on Long Island in the home of stores heiress Lissy van Long when she suggested he might be interested to visit a neighbour's estate for cocktails.

'Sloane's just back from a shopping trip in Europe. Spends a lot of time there, and she's crazy about England, too. You've got something else in common, also.'

'Oh?'

'Yeah, banking. You work for Shearing's; Sloane's old man owns de Havilland. And the house is just fabulous. You have to see it!'

Sloane de Havilland was a few years younger than him, a slender chic strawberry blonde with a European gloss over her American directness. 'Glad to meet you, Lord Courtney,' she greeted him. 'I've been crazy for Lissy to introduce us.' She was one of the few people he'd met who automatically used his proper style.

'The pleasure's mine. You have a marvellous place here.'

A low sprawling contemporary construction in bleached wood and plate glass, fronting the ocean, it was decorated throughout in the softest greys and aquamarines, the colour of her eyes. Against the watery translucence of the walls shone a dazzling selection of American Abstract Expressionists: Rothko, Pollock, Gorky.

'Why, thank you! When I divorcd Gianni, he tried to go for a cash settlement. I insisted I keep the American house and apartment and all the paintings in them. It more than paid off, believe me!' She laughed, revealing the usual perfect teeth. Her pale blonde looks contrasted appealingly with her air of toughness, of being nobody's fool.

She seemed gratifyingly reluctant to waste time on any of the other visitors. Cocktails turned into an impromptu supper of the choicest Italian food: creamy pale green *zuppa freddo* aromatic with garlic and basil; beautifully arranged salads of beef tomatoes, mozzarella and olives, or

376

frisé, fennel and radiccio, served with thinly sliced *carpaccio* and shavings of Parmesan or piquant *vitello al tonnato*. She ate very little herself, but saw to it that her own glass and Alexander's were kept constantly topped up with a potent, full-bodied Amarone. He liked her style, he decided, actually enjoying the company of a woman for once. He found himself asking if he could see her again, and was pleased when she said yes.

They fell into an easy friendship. Sloane made most of the running. Alexander never had to waste a moment's thought on where they should meet, what they should do. She seemed to enjoy making all the arrangements for them to meet at fun places like Un Deux Trois, Orso, Elaine's or the Canal Bar.

'Can't stand the stuffy old Four Seasons and those places — full of my father's friends,' she told him. She was an inveterate night-clubber, too. When he confessed that the last club he had visited had been Studio 54, she introduced him to Nell's, MK, and several up-and-coming places.

The de Havilland name alone would have secured them admission to the jealously guarded private rooms, but coupled with that of a British Earl ... Sloane's stock in café society had never been so high. Which was fine, but it wasn't the British aristocracy.

Alexander couldn't remember having so much uncomplicated fun in a long time. His regular telephone calls home to Angelica and Camilla began to reflect this, and his mother decided to do a little discreet checking up. 'A divorcée, fantastically wealthy, thanks to her banker father, but decidedly *louche*,' was the verdict.

Camilla laughed. 'Things are a little different now, Maman. No stigma attaches to divorce these days.'

'I know that,' snapped Angelica. 'It's not so much the fact that Sloane de Havilland's been divorced as what she was doing marrying in the first place. Gianni Montebello was a notorious homosexual.'

Sloane was canny enough to realise that rumours of her colourful past would eventually reach Xan. A pre-emptive strike was called for, she decided. After a long evening table-hopping at Mortimer's and dancing till the small hours at a new club in SoHo, she told him that there was something she needed to explain. Would it be possible for her to come back to the apartment?

It was four in the morning and Xan had a heavy meeting the next day, but she seemed upset and he felt he couldn't refuse.

'I want to tell you about my past,' she began when he had poured them both a nightcap. 'Would you do something for me, please? Would you hold my hand while I talk?'

There seemed nothing sexual in the request, just a simple plea for shared warmth and comfort. He held Sloane's hand while in a halting voice she described her upbringing and how it had led to the disastrous marriage in Italy.

Her father had been a remote authoritarian figure who expected her to shore up the family millions by marrying safely into another banking fortune. When Sloane fell deeply in love with her mathematics professor, she was summarily removed from Smith and sent to Europe, out of harm's way. Her teacher wrote her a brief note, saying maybe it was best for both of them. A few weeks later a friend wrote to tell her that her former lover had bought a new apartment — for cash.

She was sick of her father's narrow-minded conservatism, sickened by her lover's easy betrayal of her. In Europe she began to find an alternative lifestyle. Everything seemed slower and easier there, attitudes more tolerant and refined by the passage of the centuries.

'I didn't want to go back. I knew, if I did, my father would only start on me again. When Gianni offered me a way out, I jumped at it. Under the terms of a family trust he stood to inherit a fortune on his thirtieth birthday — so

378

long as he was married. So, fine, find a wife. The problem was, Gianni was gay. It started off between us as a simple business arrangement. I was looking for an escape route from my family, he needed a *mariage blanc*. We were getting along fine, Gianni, me and our boyfriends, until he turned nasty on me.'

'My dear . . .' Xan interrupted, horrified.

'He came into his fortune okay, I had the income from my trust fund. For years we spent half our time together in Italy or America, half our time apart with our different friends. I'd taken a lover by that time — quite openly, with my husband's blessing. Unexpectedly I became pregnant, and was crazy enough to tell Gianni. I really wanted a child, but he freaked out about it. He said he wouldn't allow a baby to mess up our streamlined existence. It didn't fit his image at all. He expected me to get rid of it or else he would sue me for my flagrant infidelity. *My* infidelity! Naturally I fought back. My father helped me find a very high-powered lawyer, Bradford Carter, when Gianni decided to get greedy over the settlement. Our "civilised" arrangement was blown right out of the water in court. I was totally stressed out, not thinking straight, when I accepted an invitation to spend the weekend with my folks in Connecticut. I went out riding, though I was six months' pregnant at the time. You can guess the rest. I don't think I've ever gotten over losing that child. I wanted it so much! That bastard Gianni spoiled everything for me, but he paid! Bradford really took him to the cleaners. It wasn't much of a consolation in the end. My lover left me, my father's started introducing me to banking nerds again . . . I feel so useless and so old. My last chance for a child, and I blew it.'

Xan squeezed her hand. 'You're hardly old. There's still time for you. Women can have children into their forties nowadays.'

Sloane laughed bitterly. 'Not on their own, they can't! What man worth having is going to take me on — a fag hag with a past?' There, she'd made her pitch. Mentally she crossed her fingers, praying she'd read him right.

Xan could hear the stirring of the logs in the fire. Kim, the latest houseboy, had lit it for them before Xan had told him to go back to bed, he wouldn't be needed that night — code for his own bed.

'As it happens,' he said at last, 'I'm looking for a wife like you. I'd very much like an heir for Courtney Park. But there's something you should know about me, first.'

She breathed easier. 'You mean you're gay?' she said with an encouraging smile.

'How did you know?' She'd succeeded in rattling him. Perhaps if *she* could tell, the bank . . .?

'Oh, Xan, after what I just told you? Don't worry. My qualifications for being able to tell are pretty unique, after all. So you'd like an heir, would you? Does this mean the prospect of sleeping with a woman doesn't turn you off completely?'

He coloured painfully. 'I don't know. I've never really thought about it before.'

'Care to think about it now? Maybe even give it a try? It'd be a logical first step.'

She made no move to pressure him with any overt physical display. Sloane was practised in the art of seduction. She knew when to come on strong and when to give every appearance of cool unthreatening pragmatism.

'Shall we go to your room? Don't worry. I'm not expecting the earth to move. We don't even need to do anything, if you'd rather not. We could just share the same bed, get used to each other before we make the next move.'

In fact she had no intention of letting him off the hook so easily. Between the sheets, Sloane subtly led and Xan followed. She was unthreateningly small and slight, he was glad to see. No wobbling breasts or thighs to emphasise her alien femininity. Her skin was a delight, softer and smoother than any boy's. Her strong pervasive perfume masked the faintly jarring scent of a woman's arousal.

'Lie back,' she told him. 'I'll take care of things.'

He floated on a soft cloud of unfamiliar sensations. A woman's pointed breasts lightly grazing his chest. Rounded thighs instead of muscular straddling his own. He felt her light-fingered touch at his groin, and then the warm teasing pressure of her lips and tongue. He felt himself slowly swelling, responding. Expertly she brought him to the brink before, in the final few seconds, sheathing herself on his hard glistening erection. He kept his eyes closed, his thoughts on graceful plaint boys, his consciousness of her as something new and strange receding in the long drawn-out ecstasy of coming.

'Don't worry. We wouldn't have to do that very often,' she teased him, staring down at his stunned face. She hoped it wouldn't always be totally without a thrill for her, but kept the thought to herself. 'I'm not very highly sexed,' she lied. 'I wouldn't be any more of a bother to you than you wanted me to be. Frankly, I'd rather eat candy if it didn't make me fat! Did I make you happy, Xan? Do you honestly think we could make a happy life together? I wouldn't be difficult or demanding. You could go pretty well your own way. All I want is to be a wife and mother.'

And Countess of Courtney.

He pulled her down to lie beside him. She was so small and light, he marvelled. She made everything between them seem natural and easy. Perhaps there'd be more pleasure in this marriage business than he'd thought.

The wedding was arranged quickly and quietly. In the interim, Alexander moved in with Sloane at her Gracie Square house, which was larger and better equipped for entertaining than his Sutton Place apartment. He'd wondered about bringing Kim with him. Sloane told him it wouldn't be necessary. She had her own Caribbean couple.

A few days before the ceremony, Alexander presented Sloane with a document. 'Something my lawyer suggested.'

381

'What's this?' she laughed. 'A pre-nuptial agreement?'

'Yes, actually. Don't worry, darling, it's nothing draconian — quite the reverse, in fact. It simply says that should the marriage fail for any reason, neither party is to have any claim on the other's income or estate. You have far more money than I, so this is very much to your advantage. Get Bradford to take a look. He'll confirm that, I'm sure.'

'It also says I shall "use my best endeavours to produce an heir." Really, Xan, what do you think I am? Some sort of brood mare?'

He was amazed to see her look so upset. 'Darling, I'm sorry, but I thought we were both agreed on that.'

'Well, yes, but seeing it all set out in a contract . . .' He made no attempt to back down, and after a moment, she sighed. 'It's okay, I guess, just a little unromantic. I'll have Bradford look it through, but I don't think there'll be any problems.'

Angelica and Camilla came over for the wedding, accompanied by Ashley, Courtney and Georgianna. Business kept Dexter in England. Alexander's heart sank when he saw that his nephews and niece were already young people instead of the lovely children he always remembered. Ashley was about to go and work as a jackeroo on his father's cattle properties, get a taste for the land on which Dexter was raised. Courtney's plans were more vague. He mentioned to his uncle that he might be looking for a banking job himself. Georgie, in her last term at a Swiss finishing school, was a delight — a tall, slender girl with waist-length chestnut-brown hair and an enchanting smile. They did Dexter and Camilla credit, Alexander thought, and hoped he and Sloane had not left it too late.

Angelica did not seem to take to her new daughter-in-law, though Camilla doubted she would have felt warmly towards any woman who supplanted her as Countess of

Courtney. Privately, Camilla thought that Sloane looked ravishing in one of her three diamond necklaces, matching earrings and a full-length white gown specially commissioned from Oscar de la Renta.

'Diamonds in the daytime, and white for a second wedding. There's something bogus about her,' snorted Angelica. She didn't approve either of the massive emerald cut diamond Sloane had chosen to mark her engagement. 'Alexander's meant to be making a fortune here, not spending one!'

'I think she has one of her own, Maman.' Camilla was overjoyed that after so long Xan had finally found a woman with whom he could be happy. She found Sloane gracious towards her — if a little too conscious of her newfound status as Countess of Courtney.

During the reception at the Carlyle, Sloane made a point of seeking her out to reassure her: 'I want you to know that there's absolutely no problem about you and your husband continuing to make your home at Courtney Park — for the time being.'

Camilla didn't much care for that 'time being'. Besides, Xan had never breathed a word about their possibly having to relocate.

'I don't suppose I shall want to change very much,' Sloane gushed. 'I hear Angelica's taste is pretty good ... Perhaps just a few innovations. Those personal touches.'

Camilla foresaw a battle royal ahead of them, and tried to change the subject slightly. 'Do you plan to visit Courtney Park often?'

Sloane's face froze. 'We plan to make Xan's *home* our principal residence. That's if the rest of his family have no objections!'

Help! thought Camilla. Why on earth didn't Xan tell me?

He approached them, grinning and holding out two glasses of champagne. 'To my sister and my wife, a very pretty sight,' he said expansively, sliding an arm round each of them.

'Just as well you think so if we're all going to be living together,' said Camilla jokily.

He seemed nonplussed by her words. 'Well, we'll be visiting, of course. Sloane was very keen for us to spend our honeymoon at Courtney as a matter of fact, but I thought somewhere more romantic, didn't I, darling?'

'You did, you meanie. You know I just can't wait to settle down on those ancestral acres of yours.'

It was the very first he'd heard of it. So far, all the plans they'd made together revolved around New York. 'But — we're keeping on Gracie Square, we decided. I thought maybe a few weeks in Courtney Park in the summer — for Ascot and Wimbledon, say — and perhaps another at Christmas. That way, we'd have the best of both worlds.'

'I intend to, darling. But I thought we'd make Courtney Park our principal residence and keep Gracie Square and the Long Island house for our American base.'

'But what about my job? You know I've just been promoted to Senior Vice-President of Mergers and Acquisitions. I couldn't possibly walk out on Shearing's now.'

Sloane's jaw set rigidly. 'Phooey! If you insist on working, I'm sure my father could always use an extra consultant. But why bother? I've got more than enough money for us both. Enough to turn Courtney Park into an international showplace.'

Alexander stared at his animated wife, realising the ghastly truth behind their marriage. The house was obviously a far bigger attraction than he had realised. Greater even than her desire for a child?

Camilla felt embarrassed to witness their disagreement so soon after the ceremony. What on earth had her brother been thinking of, she wondered, not even discussing vital questions like where he and his wife would make their home?

Reluctantly she decided that her mother was right. There *was* something bogus about Sloane — all sweet ingratiating smiles one moment, hard as nails the next. She could only pray that Xan and his new wife would work things out between them speedily.

After the wedding, Angelica, Camilla, Court and Georgie flew back to England. Ash was to go straight on to Australia. The newlyweds were to spend a hideaway few weeks in a privately owned villa on Mustique which Alexander had borrowed.

Not wishing to sour the atmosphere, neither he nor Sloane mentioned their future plans, content to bask in the sun, drink rum-sodden cocktails and occasionally make love. Alexander was lying poolside, watching Sloane meticulously observe her daily exercise régime, when the houseboy brought out the telephone.

'Xan? Camilla here ... Something terrible's happened.'

'Maman?' he queried, catching the edge of panic in her voice.

'No — Dexter. A hunting accident. He broke his back ... He's in a special spinal injuries unit and they're talking about permanent paralysis.'

'My God, this is bloody terrible! Poor darling, I'm so sorry. If there's anything we can do, anything at all. You've found the very best neurologist, of course?'

'Yes — or rather Maman did,' she said in a strange jerky voice. 'The best psychiatrist too.'

'Psychiatrist? For the shock, you mean?'

'No.' There was a desperate silence, and then Camilla explained, 'The accident didn't damage only his back — it seems to have produced a total character change! You wouldn't know him, Xan. He's violent, abusive, and he's got this simply mad idea into his head. He rants at me whenever I go near him, swearing and accusing me of the most dreadful things.'

'Such as?' he probed gently.

'Oh — that I'm a liar, whore, betrayer of his trust.' She sounded close to hysteria.

Alexander was frankly mystified. 'There must be more to it than this.'

'Well, he always knew I had a lover before we married. Luciano, remember?'

'Yes, but what's he got to do with this?'

'The accident seems to have addled Dexter's wits or something. He's got it firmly into his head that Ashley is Luciano's son. That all these years I've been passing off another man's child as his. No matter what I say, how often I swear that Ashley *is* our son, he says he's a bastard and none of his. Thank God poor Ash is safely out of it in Australia! It would break him. Xan, I hate to ask you this on your honeymoon, but please could you come home and help me? Maman agrees. We need you at Courtney Park.'

When he broke the news to Sloane, he expected at least a few words of reret for their curtailed honeymoon. She surprised him. All smooth efficiency, she uncomplainingly arranged their packing and booked their flights to England.

'Thanks, darling, for not making this difficult,' he told her, squeezing her hand as the little local plane hopped off the island and took them on their first leg.

She turned her most dazzling smile on him. 'Why on earth should I? It's what I've wanted all along. A honeymoon at Courtney Park.'

Her insensitivity left him breathless. Never mind that a man lay half paralysed, his sister's life in shreds and his nephew due for a traumatic rejection. Sloane had got what she wanted. That was all that mattered to her.

Book Four

GEORGIANNA

Courtney Park, Wiltshire

One length still go to and every muscle was on fire. One less than yesterday wouldn't kill ... The powerful raking crawl slowed. Head tilted to one side a fraction too long, the swimmer lost momentum.

'Hey, Georgie, forgotten how to count to fifty?'

Ignoring the sharp sting of the chlorinated water against reddened eyes, legs trawling and arms rhythmically cleaning the water, Dexter Randolph's favourite child rose to the challenge. Ignoring Webster's murmured protests, Dexter recklessly punched the controls of his electronic wheelchair and beat her to the touch.

'By a short head,' he laughed, holding out his hand to her.

Still gasping for breath, the Honourable Georgianna Randolph slicked her long chestnut-brown hair back into two wet wings. Avoiding the cuff of his silk shirt, she clasped both her hands round her father's and levered herself out of the pool.

Despite his paralysis below the waist, the powerful lines of Dexter's shoulders and chest and the sinewy strength of his arms remained unaltered. He made few concessions to his crippled condition.

'I didn't know it was a race, Daddy,' his daughter protested when she had caught her breath.

'Like hell you didn't!'

He smiled fondly at her. She was a chip off the old block, all right. Hated to be caught out. She'd been just about to duck the last of her daily fifty lengths, but one word from him and she shot up the pool like a shark was on her tail. Looking more closely at her abbreviated swimsuit, he realised that any self-respecting two-legged variety would be bound to give chase, too.

'Call that decent?' he said gruffly, indicating one of Liza Bruce's minimal creations in jade-green Lycra, cut hipbone high at the sides and provocatively slashed front and back.

Georgianna narrowed her eyes against the fierce light reflected from the pool's azure tiles, and grinned up at him. 'It's a bit late in the day for you to turn prude, isn't it, Daddy?' she enquired with an impudent grin, but nevertheless slid her arms into the towelling wrap that Webster, ever obedient to the slightest nuance in his employer's voice, was holding out. 'If you haven't had breakfast yet, let's eat together out here. It's such a lovely morning, and we hardly ever get the chance to sit down without —'

'Sloane poking her nose in,' Dexter grinned. His daughter would have referred to her American aunt much more tactfully — that fancy school they'd sent her to would have seen to that — but she knew as well as he the difference that Sloane and Alexander had made to the household: the servants in a dither as to who now was master after Dexter's years in command; his wife and mother-in-law standing on their dignity while Sloane jockeyed shamelessly for the mistress's prerogatives. Yes, it would be good to escape the fraught atmosphere inside the house and sit in the sunshine with his daughter.

'Webster, Miss Georgianna will take orange juice, coffee, scrambled eggs, bacon and tomato. I'll take my usual.'

'Any news from Ash?' Georgianna asked. She and Courtney were more similar in looks and temperament, but she found herself missing her elder brother's level-headed, moderating influence more and more since he'd left to supervise the Australian end of Dexter's business.

'Had a call from him last night. Seems to be enjoying himself, tear-arsing around with those no-good cousins of his when he should be out on the stations, or breathing down those damned accountants' necks!'

'But you said last week that the canning operation's figures were up on last year.'

'Don't miss much, do you? Ash is doing okay, I suppose,' he conceded reluctantly. 'At least he's ready to put his back into something — unlike his brother.'

'Daddy, you're too tough on them.' Georgie's fair skin flushed with annoyance under its light honey tan.

'Maybe you're right.'

She knew in her heart that this was the best she could hope for. 'I'm glad to have caught you alone,' she began nervously.

Dexter was too quick for her. He caught the note of pleading even before her request was made. 'Hell's teeth, Georgie, not that damned gallery again!' He clattered his cup into its saucer in his annoyance.

'Look, it's not some hare-brained scheme. We've gone into it all very thoroughly — found premises, got estimates for the conversion, figures for running costs, staff and publicity. With Court's American contacts, and my experience helping Catharine —'

'In a gallery which failed,' he said levelly.

Georgianna shrugged. 'It failed because she was under-capitalised, scrimped on promotion when she should have splashed out. I wouldn't make the same mistakes, Daddy. I know how to spend money wisely.'

'Darling, I know it, but what about Court?'

'You have to trust him, Daddy. If you expect him to fail every time he makes a move ...'

Dexter slammed his fist against the wrought iron table, setting their dishes rattling noisily. 'Because he damn well *does* fail, every time! I pulled more strings than a goddamned harpist to get him into the best broker's on Wall Street and what does he do? Courtney Randolph, big shot, turns his back on it to play at movie producer with his arty-farty actor friends. Christ, they must have seen him

391

coming! And when the movie bombs — as anyone but Courtney could have predicted — who picks up the tab while your brother's sunning himself at Palm Beach?'

Georgianna wasn't going to let that go unchallenged. 'Helping out Nicky, one of his best friends, you mean. The team needed a fourth man urgently when Johnno broke his leg.'

'Okay, okay, so he couldn't let down a mate. But what about his family? He's let us down plenty, wouldn't you say?'

Tears of frustration welled in her eyes. It was true that Court had a reckless streak, but from whom did Daddy suppose he had inherited it? 'Look, I'd be the first to admit that Court's done some idiotic things —'

'Still doing them, Georgie, make no mistake. I just need positive proof.'

She looked at him, startled. It couldn't be true. Courtney had promised her. Only this morning he had begged her to buttonhole their father once more on the gallery scheme, which he seemed to think was his big chance to redeem himself. She wasn't going to let her brother down.

'Half a million, and I know we could pay you back.'

'In two years' time from *your* trust, I presume? Court will blow his the minute he gets his hands on it — that's only months away, Georgie. Haven't you stopped to wonder why he's so desperate to hurry the gallery scheme along now instead of waiting? He's no better now than he's ever been.'

'I want the money just as much as he does.'

'But for very different reasons, darling, believe me.' The harshness had gone from Dexter's voice but not from the implacable lines of his face. He was a handsome man still, despite the frost of silver in his thick dark hair, the lines of pain and disappointment etched around his wide mouth and deepset eyes. He sighed, and patted his daughter's hand. 'I'm sorry, Georgie, but I've made up my mind. There'll be no money for any of Courtney's schemes.'

*

'*De nada,* Sis. You tried your best.'

'I know. And I wish *you'd* try to cut down on the street talk. You said you would.'

'You should know better than to believe anything I promise.' But he smiled brilliantly, belying the warning. The Honourable Courtney Randolph unfolded his lanky six-foot frame from Georgianna's bed, where she had found him lounging on her return from breakfast. Humming tunelessly to himself, he restlessly prowled her room, oblivious to its cool green and white Nina Campbell prettiness. He halted before her frilled dressing-table and raked through the hoard of art deco jewellery which Georgianna kept strewn across it.

'You know, you ought to be more careful with this stuff, Georgie. Some of it's quite valuable.

'And some of it's rubbish — only you and I know which pieces aren't. Besides, you surely aren't suggesting the servants can't be trusted?'

'No, of course not.' Courtney sighed and pushed back the thick lock of tawny hair which had tumbled across his forehead. It could do with a wash, Georgianna noticed, and the Versace suit designed to look casually crumpled surely wasn't meant to be set into concertina creases.

'Heavy night last night?' she queried. He'd arrived in Wiltshire in the early hours, waking her at seven for a dawn raid on the kitchen, where he'd eaten slice after slice of bread and honey while rehearsing again his plans for spending the money he was sure Georgie could talk out of the old man.

'Heavy few days.' He shrugged and lurched back to the bed, sinking on to it like a stone.

Georgianna went into the bathroom to rinse the smell of chlorine from her hair. If he knew she was nearby, bathing and making up her face for the day, he would probably allow himself a short nap. If she insisted he return to his own room, he'd probably get sidetracked on the way,

393

decide to call a friend and see what party was on that night, or visit the stable yard which he'd loved from a boy. Nowadays, Courtney Park Stud and stables employed a fair proportion of girl grooms, and Court had cut a swathe through them. Even in his unwashed, unshaven state with the smoke smell from last night's club or party still clinging to his hair and clothes, he was capable of charming almost any women he chose.

Georgie slipped on a filmy silk wrap, deciding to creep into her bedroom and choose something to wear while Court slept. As she opened the bathroom door, however, she was surprised to see him sitting cross-legged on the antique lace coverlet of her bed, speaking animatedly into the phone.

'Great news!' he announced, slamming down the receiver triumphantly. His tiredness seemed to have evaporated and a wide smile brightened his previously drawn face. 'I just rang Nicky, and he's desperate for a fourth for the Zendans this afternoon at Windsor. Johnno's scooted off to Tuscany, apparently, and Nicky got the last-minute chance of a match against the Guerreros today. You'll come and watch, of course?'

She was impressed, despite herself. Polo had always seemed a rather dull game to her — 'Croquet on horse-back' she'd once dismissed it. But even she knew that the chance to play at Smith's Lawn, home of the Guards Polo Club, against the crack team who were the holders of last year's Cartier Cup and Lord Cowdray's Gold Cup, was an exciting one. She was surprised, though, that Courtney seemed to have forgotten his disappointment over the gallery scheme so quickly.

'I thought you were going to ring Harry at Cazenove's today, sound him out about backing us,' she reminded him.

He waved his hand and bounded off the bed. 'Another day. It's not important.'

It wasn't at all what he'd been saying in the early hours, but she decided to leave it at that. Tomorrow would do as well for ringing round the merchant banks, trying to raise the backing for the gallery. Today they might as well capitalise on the glorious weather and an afternoon at Windsor Great Park.

By the time they reached the polo ground, Sammy and Sharon, Court's two devoted girl grooms, had arrived and parked the trailer, and were intent on putting the finishing touches to his Argentinian ponies.

'Sammy, you're a miracle,' Court greeted the head groom, kissing her casually on one freckled cheek.

The girl blushed furiously and bent down immediately to finish bandaging one of Goblin's forehocks. 'Your kit's in the changing-room,' she told him briskly, 'and you're to join the others as soon as you've changed. Tactics runthrough.'

'Thanks, Sammy. Take the beasts down to the lines when you've finished, will you?'

''Course. And they'll be lined up in playing order, Goblin first as usual,' she said reproachfully. There was no need to tell Sammy anything about horses or polo. Her stocky red-haired figure had been a familiar sight at polo matches or point-to-points as she accompanied Ashley, Courtney or Georgianna, once upon a time Dexter, to the equestrian events at which all Randolphs excelled.

'They look terrific, Sammy. Really do you credit,' Georgianna said with a smile before hurrying to catch up with Court. He strode quickly over the rough ground, scanning the throng of purposeful grooms and wide-eyed female spectators, obviously looking for someone.

'You'd better change, Court,' she urged him, then saw fifty yards or so ahead of them the distinctive head and shoulders of the team captain. 'Oh, look,' she said, pointing. 'Would you like to introduce us now?'

'Of course, you've never met Nicky properly, have you?'

'I've never been able to jump the queue!'

She had caught the odd glimpse of Courtney's charismatic friend at clubs and parties. In even the most glittering crowd he stood out from the admiring throng — most of them women — which always surrounded him. Perhaps it had something to do with his height — he stood head and shoulders above his male friends — perhaps it was the piercing gentian blue of his eyes. Perhaps it was because Nicolas of Malivia was a prince, heir to one of Europe's most ancient and blue-bloodied pocket principalites.

'Could we do it later? He'll want to check over the ponies, and I'd better go and change. You can find your way to the stand?'

'I'll manage. Don't worry about me.' Poor Court! He really did look jittery, pale-faced and with his hands visibly shaking as he stuffed them into his pockets. Once on horseback he'd be fine, though. Dexter had brought them up to be fearless riders.

Georgianna was making her way back along the pony lines towards the members' stand where she knew champagne, courtesy of the series sponsors, would be on offer, when she caught a glimpse of a distinctive crumpled suit and shirt. Court still hadn't changed and seemed to be deep in conversation with a showy redhead in a leopard-print dress. Georgianna smiled to herself. No wonder he'd had no time for Nicky! She started to walk towards them, intent on urging Courtney to change right away, when a knot of giggling girls chose that moment to mob Hector de Laszlo, the darkly handsome Argentinian captain of the Guerreros. It took Georgianna a few seconds to negotiate them. When she looked up again and along the side of the horsebox where her brother had been standing, there was only the girl, fiddling with the clasp of the large satchel-like bag she carried over one shoulder.

Relieved to see that her brother had at last gone to change, Georgianna headed instead for the marquee. After a discreet glance at the members' metal badge pinned to the shoulder of her dress, a steward stood aside for her to enter. Waitresses were circulating with glasses of Pimm's and champagne, but Georgie asked for some mineral water. She was waiting for her drink when she heard a familiar voice — 'Georgie, I don't believe it!' — and a blonde in a slightly too tight polka-dotted dress abandoned her escort and started pushing through the crowd to reach her.

Georgie's heart sank. Lizzie Fellowes was a lively good-hearted girl whose company she had enjoyed since they were at Heathfield, but two weeks ago Courtney had ditched her, his constant companion of the previous five months. Georgianna feared she was in for a soul-baring session.

Not that Lizzie looked wan and dejected as she advanced purposefully, smiling beguilingly at a man whose champagne glass she jolted and taking another glass for herself from a passing waiter. 'Phew, what a crush,' she announced, reaching Georgie at last. 'Still, it *is* the Guerreros — and I heart Court's playing for Nicky again. He must be thrilled.'

'Yes, but terribly jumpy — he didn't touch his lunch and was shaking like a leaf when I left him.'

Lizzie's candid grey eyes clouded slightly. She was doing a grand job of disguising her feelings, Georgie decided, but she obviously wasn't over Court yet.

'Did he tell you about us?' the girl asked, lowering her voice from its usual social screech.

'I heard that you'd broken up,' Georgianna said tact-fully. 'You mustn't mind too much. Court's my brother and I love him dearly, but I know how totally heartless he can be when it suits him.'

Lizzie blinked. 'What exactly did he say?' she asked.

Georgianna was beginning to feel distinctly uncomfort-able. Damn Court for getting her to do his dirty work for him! 'Well, just that he'd decided to move on, play the field a little more. Don't be upset, Lizzie. He lasted longer with you than with anyone before, you know.'

Lizzie took a gulp of champagne and studied Georgianna thoughtfully over the rim of her glass. Then she appeared to decide to change the subject. 'Did you see who I was with?'

'Yes. Isn't it Giles Stopforth? He's looking very well indeed. The last I heard he'd been in Farm Place for months. Oh, sorry, Lizzie. You did know about that, I hope?'

'That Giles has been treated for heroin addiction? Yes, I did. Look, this obviously isn't the right time or place, Georgie, but before you go, you and I must talk. Oh, look, Giles is waving. I'll have to get back. The poor love's off alcohol, too, now and it takes my eagle eye on him from time to time to keep him on the straight and narrow. We'll talk after the match, right? There's something you really ought to know.'

'Well, yes, of course.'

'Super, Talk to you later. 'Bye.'

Georgianna made for the exit, absent-mindedly still clutching her glass. As she reached the canvas flap, a tall dark-haired man ducked swiftly through it, cannoning into her and splashing mineral water all over his gleaming knee-length boots. Georgianna stumbled and would have fallen, but two sinewy arms shot out to grasp her narrow waist, steadying her until she had regained her balance. She recognised the canary yellow and white Zendan colours before realising that this inauspicious beginning was her introduction to Prince Nicolas himself.

'I'm so sorry. I wasn't thinking,' she began, stepping sideways to disengage herself. He took his time over relinquishing her, then plucked the empty glass from her hand. A waitress appeared as if by magic to remove it.

'There's no need to apologise.' His deep blue, almost violet, gaze frankly appraised her, from her startled hazel eyes, green-spotted Belville Sassoon dress to her slim bare legs. 'Throwing cold water has a distinct rarity value —

most women prefer to throw themselves. I congratulate you on a novel approach.'

He had arrogantly mistaken her for one of the polo predators. When Georgie was angry, her porcelain skin always coloured. Mortified, she realised it must look as though she were blushing guiltily.

'You don't understand,' she said hastily. 'Please allow me to introduce myself.'

'Ah, now you *are* being predictable,' he said, a note of regret in his deep, rich voice. His eyes flickered away from her to scan the wafer-thin Audemars Piaget on his wrist. 'I look forward very much to our formal introduction, but please excuse me for now. I'm busy tracking down one of my team. Unless I find him in the next couple of minutes, the match will have to be scratched.'

She opened her mouth to assure him that Courtney was on his way, must have been delayed by having to squeeze into his fiendishly tight boots, when Nicolas took her breath away.

'But it's worked. Yours is definitely the best offer I've had all afternoon! Join me after the match. There'll be a small gathering for drinks in my trailer, and afterwards we'll drive into town for dinner.'

'But I'm with someone. It's —'

'Then you'll just have to get rid of him. You'll find a way, I'm sure, a resourceful girl like you. Throw some cold water over him or something.' With a faintly mocking inclination of his head, Nicolas ducked out of the tent again, leaving her furious at his arrogance but distinctly looking forward to their next meeting.

A few minutes later there was a general exodus towards the stand. Georgianna narrowly avoided sitting next to a flock of polo predators, as brightly dressed as parakeets, and slipped into the same row as a family party, mother, father and two children, who must all have been sweltering inside their identical green quilted waistcoats. The girls in the row behind were the first to spot the players mounting up.

'There they are. Over there, look!'

'Oh, isn't Hector de Laszlo the dreamiest thing on two legs, even under that silly helmet.'

'If you go for the swarthy type, Vanessa. I suppose so. Where's ... Ah, there he is. Look, shaking Prince Charles's hand. Of course, Nicky of Malivia leaves the others standing.'

Not Court, Georgianna thought loyally, but as the two four-man teams lined up for the first chukka she found herself reluctantly agreeing that Nicolas on horseback was an impressive sight indeed. He was impressive in action, too, easily matching the flair and vigour of the three top high goal players, the de Laszlo brothers, on the opposing team. With a handicap of seven he rated high enough as a player to have turned 'hired assassin' or professional like the Argentinians, but as heir to a proud European throne there was, of course, no question of that. Nicolas would not play for a fee, nor accept the sponsorship and funding of super-rich enthusiasts like Galen Weston and Mrs Helen Boehm, wealthier though they were by far. So he fielded his own team of gentlemen amateurs, each of whom met his own expenses, and remained the Zendans' undisputed star.

Courtney put in a few useful strokes in the first chukka, his finest pass to Nicky being instrumental in winning the first point of the match for the Zendans. Georgianna sat tight while some of the spectators and their dogs dutifully trod back the divots while the riders remounted on fresh ponies for the second assault.

Emmanual de Laszlo took the next point easily and so quickly that the players did not bother to dismount but played on, their second ponies still fresh after barely a minute's exercise. The fourth Guerrero, American Jake Silvester, took the next point, and the girls behind Georgianna, with typical British empathy with the underdog, became vociferous in their support of the Zendans.

'Come on, Nicky. Show them how it's done.'

'Well *done* the Zendans!'

Prince Nicolas, intercepting a wide pass from Silver to Carlos de Laszlo, drew level with their section of the stand. He was close enough for Georgianna to see the beads of sweat glistening on his tanned forehead. By now his yellow and white shirt was soaked with perspiration and clung to his muscular chest and arms like a second skin. Georgianna watched, mesmerised, as he lined up for the shot which would equal the score.

And then Courtney appeared out of nowhere. Georgianna thought she recognised the pony under him as Goblin, but surely it couldn't be? He was Court's first string and must already have been ridden. The animal's bay sides were dark with sweat and its bit flecked with foam as Courtney kicked it on. He, too, had his stick raised to strike, bearing down on the ball which was, by all the rules of etiquette and the game, Nicky's to play.

There was a murmur of consternation from the crowd and Nicolas, momentarily disconcerted, swung wide of the ball. At that moment Goblin cannoned into his pony's quarters. The impact sent Nicky's stick flying from his hand though he skilfully kept his seat. Courtney craned sideways, obviously intent on scoring, but his mount, thoroughly unnerved by this time, suddenly missed his footing and sent his rider clean over his head.

'Serves him right,' one of the girls behind muttered angrily. 'Butting in that. It wasn't his ball, it was Nicky's.'

It was neither man's by now. Carlos de Laszlo neatly retrieved the wooden ball and sent it skimming up the pitch for Hector to slam home at the Guerreros' end. There was a rather stilted round of applause as the players trickled off the field to remount, and then cries of outrage as the spectators' attention was diverted to the two players still on the field by the Zendan goal-mouth. Courtney had picked himself up and, in his ungovernable rage and disappointment, was beating his distressed pony, flailing at its

401

heaving flanks and sides with his stick. Finally, to the crowd's voluble disgust, he struck it hard over the eyes.

'Shame!' the horsy mother in Georgianna's row exclaimed. 'Don't look, darlings. The man ought to be shot.'

At that moment Nicky, who had dismounted to pick up his stick, realised what Courtney was doing. Dropping his own pony's reins, he ran the ten yards or so which separated them in time to catch the stick as it descended in another brutal downward arc. His gesture as he pointed off the field was unmistakable. The two men remounted and rode off at a gallop, to a buzz of gleeful speculation from the onlookers.

Georgianna saw it all indistinctly. Only she knew how uncharacteristic Courtney's behaviour had been. He loved horses and especially Goblin, his favourite of his first pair of ponies. Still numb with shock, she got to her feet and forced her way past the indignant family who were lumbering to their feet in readiness to do their duty tramping in the pitch. The players were just visible at the far side of the pitch and seemed to be straggling back towards the changing-rooms. At that moment an imperturbable voice over the loudspeaker announced that the match had been abandoned and the next would begin in twenty minutes.

She ran as fast as she could towards the pony lines. She found Sammy first, white-faced and almost in tears as she held Goblin's head and murmured to him soothingly. The pony's eyes were still wild and rolling, and Georgianna noticed with sick disgust the thin bloody weal above his eyes.

'Shh, Goblin. Shh, Boy. 'S all right now. Sammy's here,' the groom said, working to calm the pony through her own tears.

'Sammy, I —'

The girl would not meet Georgianna's eyes. 'Tell Mr Courtney something from me, would you? Tell him I'll take the ponies back to the House, but after that I'm finished.' The grim tone of her voice contrasted sharply with the tender, gentling touch of her hands against the pony's neck and head.

'I'll tell him, of course, but won't you reconsider, Sammy? He's not himself today.'

'Hasn't been for some time, if you ask me, and that's why I'll be on my way. You'll find him in his car, I expect. He won't have dared show his face in the clubhouse.'

She found him slumped in the front of his vintage E-type, still in breeches and boots, obviously too dazed to have changed.

'Courtney.'

For a moment he wouldn't look at her, obviously ashamed. She put her hand gently on his shoulder and his brown eyes met hers, puzzled and desolate as a child's. 'I shouldn't have done it, I know, Sis. I wouldn't have, but —'

'I know, Court. I understand.' Being a child of Dexter Randolph's was a burden all three of them must carry. On Ash and Georgianna it weighed lightly, but the burden of his father's misplaced expectations was slowly crippling Court. Georgianna had never felt so sorry for him as she did at this moment. She bent to kiss his cheek consolingly and at that moment a familiar voice hailed them.

'There you are, Randolph. And where else would you be skulking, after all? You won't be welcome in the clubhouse for a very long time.'

Prince Nicolas strode between the rows of parked cars towards them. He was close enough for her to notice his eyes widen as he recognised her. He surveyed them both, coldly and contemptuously, the expression on his face almost more than she could bear. She quailed before his anger, though what *she* had done to deserve it she did not know. 'So this is your little playmate, is it, Randolph?' Prince Nicolas addressed Courtney. 'How touching that she sticks by you in your hour of need — not at all the sort of behaviour I'd have expected from someone of her kind. Neither is her appearance, come to that, but then, the most dangerous things can be the most attractive, as you know. Here, this should keep you both happy for some time, and out of decent people's sight.'

He tossed a folded piece of paper into the car. Georgianna watched wordlessly as it fluttered to rest on the seat beside Courtney.

'Fifty thousand — a fair price for your ponies. I'll take on Sammy, too. She'll be more than happy to work for me. You're not fit to have charge of animals. You're little better than one yourself.'

Georgianna waited for Courtney to defend himself, but he sat silent.

'Nothing to say for yourself, I see,' Nicolas said after a pause. 'Well, I hope it's a very long time before we meet again. And the same goes for you,' he said, swinging round to stare at Georgianna. 'Your sort makes me sick to the stomach.'

As he walked away, she shook Courtney's shoulder. 'You're not going to let him get away with that, Court. Why don't you explain?'

'What could I possibly say?'

'Well, he's not going to get away with insulting *me* like that.'

She ran after Nicolas, threading her way between parked cars and a handful of interested onlookers until she was directly behind him. 'Prince Nicolas, wait!'

No one before had ever treated her with such contempt. Courtney's behaviour on the field had been inexcusable, but there had been something else behind Nicolas's attack on her and she needed to know what it was, just what he believed her guilty of. He ignored her cries for him to stop, lengthening his stride instead, broad back still set irrevocably against her. She couldn't bear to prolong the humiliation, and stood still, brushing away tears with one hand as Nicolas was swallowed up in the crowd.

The car was a few hundred yards away by now. As she trailed back to it she saw a woman approach it from much closer. She was red-haired and wore a leopard-print dress. Leaning over the side, she picked something up from the passenger seat. As Georgianna watched incredulously, the women gestured to Courtney to move over and herself took the driver's seat. Georgianna waved frantically and started to run towards the car. It looked horribly as though she was about to be left behind, but Courtney would never permit that, surely. Her foot caught against a bumpy patch of grass and she fell headlong on the grass. She picked herself up in time to see the E-type powering its way through the Park gates.

Giles and Lizzie couldn't have been more solicitous. They insisted on driving her all the way to Courtney Park where, amazingly, nothing seemed to have changed. Webster greeted her gravely in the marble hall, hurrying about Dexter's business as usual. Georgianna passed Camilla on the stairs up to the family floor and managed to dismiss her mother's protest of 'I though you were staying in town, darling' with a murmured, 'Oh, Court was asked on a stag night, and I got a lift back.'

In her room she stepped out of the once favourite dress and wadded it into a tight ball which she pushed to the back of her wardrobe. She would never be able to wear it again. She remembered the conversation in Giles's car, Lizzie's earnest face and his nods of agreement. Their voices played round and round in her head: so kind, so well-meaning, so utterly devastating. And in less than an hour she must go into dinner with her divided family and act as though nothing had happened.

She showered, and dressed to match her mood in a stark black Balenciaga gown that had once been Angelica's. Afterwards she sat down in front of her dressing-table mirror, studying her face for signs of the day's traumas while fingering the piles of jewellery before her, seeking the stylish lines of a bold arrow-shaped diamond and black onyx brooch, a Cartier original from the twenties and the pride of her collection.

It wasn't there. Sitting quite still, gazing at the pile of jewellery, she could hear Lizzie's gently inquisitorial voice again. 'Has he been short of money lately?' She remembered, too, the mysterious redhead adjusting the flap of her bag. Putting something away, perhaps? Something that only Georgianna and Courtney had known the value of.

Alexander poured himself a stiff gin. He needed it after two hours of Sloane's non-stop extolling the virtues of her lawyer friend, Bradford Carter. The sooner she realised there was no question of his enforcing his legal right to sole possession of Courtney Park, the better it would be for all of them. The pile-driving force of her monotonous voice had eventually driven him from their suite and into the family sitting-room, where he was sitting, outwardly composed, over a copy of *Country Life* when Georgianna entered the room.

'Uncle Xan, can I talk to you about something?' Nervously she pleated the full skirt of her dress as she spoke — Maman would have had a fit if she'd seen her.

'Of course, Georgie. Why don't you stop destroying your gown and come and sit down? It sounds rather serious. Boyfriend trouble?' Something he was well qualified to advise on, did she but know it.

Georgianna shook her head. The sudden movement sent a tear trickling down one cheek. 'It's Courtney. This afternoon he — Oh, Xan, it's awful!'

Shameful though it was, Courtney's behaviour at Smith's Lawn was the easy part of the story. By the time she'd finished that, however, her uncle's face already looked pinched with disapproval. But there was worse to come, much worse.

'And when I got back my favourite brooch was gone —
my diamond arrow. He knows how much it means to me.'

'I'm so sorry, my dear,' he floundered, appalled by her
description of Courtney's brutality. 'I can see how
upsetting it must have been, and now on top of it all you've
lost your brooch. But don't worry. I'll buy you another the
next time I'm up in London.'

'You're very kind, Uncle Xan, but I don't think you
could. It was an antique ... But it's not the brooch, don't
you see? It's Courtney. He —' Misery overwhelmed her.
Alexander slid a comforting arm around her. She wept like
a child, making no attempt to stem the flow of her tears,
narrow shoulders shuddering.

'Well now, if this isn't the most *touching* scene. The oh
so Honourable Georgianna caught in the middle of her
act.'

Sloane's usual drawl was slower and more slurred
tonight. She'd obviously been at the whisky already, or
maybe it was her slimming pills. Maybe it was both.
Alexander no longer cared how his wife abused herself, but
he wasn't going to sit idly by while she abused his niece.

'As usual, you're jumping to quite the wrong con-
clusions, Sloane. Georgianna has had a very distressing
day and I was simply trying to comfort her.'

Sloane lurched into the room. She was overdressed as
usual in a glittering silver sequinned sheath from Calvin
Klein. The designer had meant its wearer to walk in tiny
floating steps and to stay upright at all times. It was hardly
the thing for a mid-week family dinner, and particularly
not when the wearer was unsteady on her feet. 'I just *bet*
she needed comforting,' she hissed. 'Pity I didn't come in
five minutes later. That *would* have been one for the
family album!'

'Sloane, please.' Alexander sprang to his feet and took
his wife's arm, hoping to steer her from the room before
she could do any more damage.

'Can't you see, you fool? *They* put her up to it. That

simpering wimp of a sister and the old witch herself —'

'That will do, Sloane.' Angelica stood in the open doorway, regal in a floor-length magenta silk tunic. Her long hair, defiantly black still, was piled high on top of her head, emphasising her slender height. She leaned lightly on an ebony stick she had affected since arthritis struck in one hip, but there was nothing in the least frail or faded about her. She summed up the scene before her in an instant. 'Xan, take your wife to her bedroom. She seems a trifle overwrought and will no doubt wish to take dinner in her room tonight. Good night, Sloane. I trust your headache won't be too debilitating in the morning.'

She stood aside as Alexander helped away an unprotesting Sloane, stung into silence by being caught in so unladylike a scene. When they were safely out of the room, Angelica closed the door behind them, then joined Georgianna on the sofa.

'Now, why don't you tell Grandmama all about it?'

Over the years there had been three face-lifts that Georgianna knew of, resulting in an inability to smile more than slightly thanks to the tightness of her skin after various nips and tucks; a certain expressionlessness to the still beautiful face. Only her eyes, the deep smoky green of tourmalines, revealed the blend of intuition and low cunning which, against all the odds, had kept her châtelaine of Courtney Park for more than forty years.

Georgianna thought rapidly. Nothing she could say would shock or disconcert her grandmother, she was sure, but the truth would certainly sadden and upset her. Worse, she might feel it her duty to share it with her daughter. That mustn't happen. Mummy had enough on her plate at the moment with Sloane's scheming and Daddy's constant inexplicable coldness to her. She herself would tackle Courtney just as soon as he came home.

'It was nothing really, Grandmama,' she said, forcing a lightness and confidence she was far from feeling into her voice. 'I had a silly quarrel with Court this afternoon. He drove off and I had to beg a ride back with friends. Not very dignified. And then, to cap it all, I found that one of my favourite diamond brooches is missing. The pin always was unreliable. I kept meaning to have it fixed.'

Angelica sat back in her seat, eyes still fixed on Georgianna's face. 'Well, if you're sure that's all, Georgie.' She was not convinced, but she had the good sense not to press further. You're obviously tired, darling. You haven't been away from here for more than a night or two since February. Why not take a holiday? Follow the sun somewhere hot and chic and terribly expensive? A change of scene, away from this house and all of us, would do you so much good. Say you'll think about it, at least.'

'I'll see if any of my friends are free,' Georgianna promised dutifully. She had no intention even of checking with them until her business with Courtney was over, but there was no harm in setting her grandmother's mind at rest in the short term.

The telephone rang, and Angelica glanced crossly at the ormolu clock on the carved stone overmantel. 'Eight o'clock! What civilised person would call just as we're about to go into dinner?'

'I'll take it, Grandmama,' Georgianna volunteered, glad to put an end to the awkward conversation. 'You go down and I'll join you in a minute.'

Angelica walked more slowly than was necessary towards the door, leaning heavily on her stick for effect. She heard Georgianna's exclamation of delight as she recognised the caller's voice, saw the smile that curved her wide mouth as she began to speak into the receiver.

When Georgianna came in late for dinner, bubbling with excitement, her obvious elation lifted everyone's spirits. Camilla thankfully broke off the long polite conversation she and Maman had been struggling to make to mask the almost total silence between Xan and Dexter, to ask: 'Well, darling? You've had some good news, I can see it in your face.'

'An invitation from Guy de Rennes. Isn't it wonderful?'

Camilla frowned doubtfully. 'Which one is he, darling?'

'You met him once. He came to Chester Square to take me on to Mark's Club one evening. I met him in St Moritz, Mummy, you remember.'

Camilla's face cleared. 'Of course. Charming, soigné, a real Parisian. You'd have approved, Maman. I didn't know you'd been seeing a lot of him, though, Georgie?'

She sighed. 'That's the problem! I've seen him three or four times so far, usually when he's over here on business for Trident Oil and once when I was in Paris for Didier Voisin's party. He has a fantastic flat in the Rue de la Pompe — all steel and glass and white linen. Andrée Putman's a friend of his mother's.'

'Sounds ghastly,' said her grandmother. Then she got to the heart of the matter. 'So you've visited it, then?'

They'd left the party early at Guy's suggestion. Travelling up to his flat in the lift, her knees had been weak from too much champagne and the warmth of his kisses. She'd barely noticed the spectacular penthouse or the view from its wall of glass, too intent on Guy and the delicious messages his hands and mouth were sending. At his suggestion she'd sipped a rare old armagnac, sitting with his arm about her on a wickedly wide white sofa — and then, to her lasting shame and regret, she'd lapsed into sleep.

At first incredulous and then amused, he'd watched Georgianna sleep for an hour before waking her with kisses and delivering her, dazed and heavy-eyed, to their host's apartment. To her great relief he had contacted her the next day, sending a great sheaf of flowers to '*La Belle au Bois Endormie*', but that night she had to be back in London and he was caught up in time-consuming Middle Eastern oil negotiations. He'd been travelling constantly since April, calling her frequently but, until now had been frustratingly unable to predict when they might next meet.

'He's been given a week's holiday before his wretched

company send him back on the pipeline negotiations, and he wants me to join him in Cannes. La Colombe d'Or tomorrow night — *two* rooms, Daddy,' she added, seeing Dexter open his mouth to ask. 'After that, we'll just drift. Guy has a friend we could stay with, or else we'll drive from place to place. He knows some lovely old *auberges*, apparently.'

'We can do better than that for you,' Dexter said vehemently. 'Leave those flea-bitten old dives to the tourists and take *Randolph 1* out. She's moored at Cannes right now, fitting out — I spoke to Captain Rogers today. Take her to Sardinia. You've been saying how much you'd like to go back there.'

'Daddy, you're a darling. Thanks so much.' Georgianna bent down to kiss his cheek. She knew what a concession this was. Dexter normally guarded *Randolph 1*, his graceful custom-designed 120-foot yacht, as jealously as a miser. She was his special toy, and use of her even by the family was by invitation only.

'No need to swamp me, girl,' he said gruffly, but smiled for the first time that evening, glad to have made his daughter happy.

The phone on her night-stand rang at two o'clock. Camilla noted the hour as she reluctantly surfaced from sleep, and reached out to fumble for the receiver in the darkened room.

'Courtney here, Mums. Did I wake you?'

'Well, yes, darling. But it's lovely to hear from you.'

'I'm sorry I didn't get a chance to see you today, but Georgie explained, I expect.'

'Of course, darling. And how did the match go? With all Georgie's news, I quite forgot to ask her.'

There was silence for a moment and then Courtney said, sounding relieved, 'Oh, brilliantly. I'm surprised she didn't say.'

Camilla laughed indulgently. 'She's had good news of her own. Guy de Rennes rang. He wants her to join him in Cannes tomorrow for a week. Daddy's told her she can have *Randolph 1*. Guy's going to meet her from the plane and they're having a night at the Colombe d'Or first. Sounds heavenly.'

There was silence for a moment and then, 'Yes, Georgie's a lucky girl, all right.'

Camilla could have kicked herself for her clumsiness. She knew how strained relations were between Courtney and his father; how more than unlikely it was that Dexter would ever offer his younger son exclusive use of his prized yacht. 'And what about you, darling? Any holiday plans of your own, or shall we seeing you here soon? Or in town, perhaps? Grandmama and I are coming up on Thursday.'

'Sorry, no can do. That's why I called you. I'm going away with friends for a while. It's the Monaco Grand Prix, and we'll be hanging out there for a few days, then going on to someone's villa.'

'Sounds lovely.' Camilla forced enthusiasm into her voice at this news of Courtney's continued absence. 'What a pity Georgie's taking the yacht to Sardinia, or you might have met up with her and Guy.'

He laughed sardonically. 'Oh, wouldn't want to interrupt the idyll. Look, I've got to go now. Be seeing you all in a few weeks, okay? And, Mums, don't worry about me.'

'No, of course not, Courtney.'

He hung up abruptly. Camilla sat shivering, listening to the echoing of the empty line for several minutes before she told herself not to be stupid and to get some sleep.

Georgianna spent almost the entire flight from Heathrow to Cannes studying her face and clothes minutely. She hadn't a trace of vanity. The close-up inspection was to still the nervousness that overwhelmed her the minute she had boarded. Was she doing the right thing? Would Guy be as

412

wonderful as she'd remembered from their brief times together? Most important of all, was she doing the right thing in putting aside the question of Courtney for a week?

Her hand shook slightly so that she smudged the coat of brilliant pink lip-gloss she was applying to the tender curve of her mouth. Mindful of the brilliant Riveria light and the constant assault on the senses from nature's clashing colours, Georgie had dressed to compete in crisp white linen pedalpushers and a cutaway white T-shirt topped with a loose, unstructured St Laurent silk jacket in glowing green, turquoise and hot pink. She applied waterproof mascara — there might be time for a swim later — and a faint line of navy-blue kohl to the inside of her eyelids, enhancing the luminosity of her hazel eyes.

Frightened eyes, she thought crossly, checking her appearance for the umpteenth time. Oh God, this meeting was going to be a disaster, she knew it. And she'd waited so long . . .

'Coming in to land in two minutes, Miss Georgianna,' the steward called through the door of the private jet.

'Thanks, Be out in a moment.' George took several deep breaths to slow her racing heart, then resumed her seat for touchdown. While the steward fussed with the steps down from the plane she checked her reflection one last time and stepped down to the tarmac of the runway with a carefree smile.

'Georgianna! Georgie!'

The greeting was coming from the direction of the customs shed. First she noticed the uniformed customs official striding across the runway to check the jet's manifest. Then she saw that the stocky *douanier* was accompanied by a taller, slighter man, his slightly long brown hair brushed neatly away from a high forehead. A pair of impenetrable Raybans masked grey eyes she would have recognised anywhere. Guy glanced enquiringly at the customs officer, who shrugged good-naturedly, allowing him to break into a run towards Georgianna.

It's all right, she thought. He's just as gorgeous as I remember him.

Then his arms were round her, pulling her almost off her feet as he gave her two quick kisses on either cheek, and then a third, long and lingering, on her softly parted mouth. He kept one arm round her shoulders as they strolled slowly across the tarmac, through a half-hearted customs check and out to Guy's silver open-topped Mercedes.

'What shall we do first?' she asked, sinking back into the luxurious leather seat and waiting for the steward to wheel out her luggage.

'Lunch here,' he said practically. 'Afterwards, maybe you'd like to confirm with your father's captain the arrangements for tomorrow?'

'It shouldn't take long, and afterwards maybe there'll be time for a swim?'

'And a drink at Eden Roc,' Guy said at once. 'And after that, a leisurely drive through the hills to the hotel for dinner. How does that sound? It's a lot for one day, perhaps, but after that we shall be at sea.'

'It sounds perfect.'

Over a delicious seafood lunch in the Carlton, the last of Georgianna's nervousness disappeared. Guy had solicitously seated her facing into the room, but it could have been a brick wall for all she cared. She had eyes only for him, and in the few moments she was not concentrating on his lean, dark-tanned face she noticed the frankly appraising glances cast in his direction by several soignée fellow diners.

He could only be French, she thought dreamily, after three glasses of the delicious lemon-scented wine he had ordered. It wasn't his clothes — the stylish broad blue and white stripes of his open-necked shirt and the baggy, creased natural linen suit were in fact Ralph Lauren's interpretation of *le style anglais* — but the clean lines of his jaw, straight brows and immaculately cut hair stirred her as the blond boyish good looks of the Englishmen she had dated never had. He made her feel with every glance and gesture deliciously cherished and desired.

After their long lunch they walked lazily down the Croisette towards the Old Marina, glancing into the windows of the single-storey shops closed while their owners took a long South of France siesta. Georgianna stopped short before a striking window display of a single stark white *maillot*, artfully displayed against a backdrop of silver-painted shells. Strapless, and with high-cut legs, what little that remained of the swimsuit was embellished with hundreds of tiny translucent crystal beads which caught the light like droplets of water even before the suit got wet.

'Perfect,' Guy agreed, 'or it would be with you inside it. If the shop's open when we return from the boat, I'll buy it for you.'

'If the shop's open, I'll buy it myself,' she said firmly. And then, with a shy upward glance, 'Because I want to be beautiful for you.'

He lifted her hand to his mouth and pressed his warm lips into her palm. She shuddered with delight, all trepidation gone.

Guy drove them over to the new waterfront development. Ten minutes later, on the sun-bleached planks of the marina boardwalk, she came down to earth with a bang. The berth where she had expected to find *Randolph 1*, shipshape, ready and waiting, was empty.

'*Mais non, mademoiselle,*' the harbourmaster said regretfully. If he could have been of positive assistance to the slender brown-eyed girl before him he would have jumped at the chance, but he had only bad news for her. 'It is not possible for me to reach *Randolph 1* while she is at sea. Usually of course, yes, but she has radio trouble, I know. The captain says so when he presents his papers two hours

415

ago. It is most irregular to put out without a radio and I tell him so, but he promised he would have the repairs done at Monte Carlo.'

'*Randolph 1* has gone there, but why? She's supposed to wait for us here till tomorrow.' Georgianna was on the verge of tears, amazed and disappointed that there had been this hitch.

'Don't worry, Georgie. I'm sure there is a perfectly simple explanation,' Guy soothed her. 'Nothing is spoilt. Perhaps the captain knows he can get a replacement part for the radio more easily in Monte Carlo —' the harbour-master pulled a dubious face at this, but Guy ignored him — 'and we can just as easily join the ship there as here.' He turned to the official. 'I take it we can contact the harbour office in Monte Carlo from here?'

'*Bien sûr, m'sieur.*'

'If you would help us to do that, we could leave a message for *Randolph 1*'s captain to contact us at our hotel tonight. There should be no difficulty over that, should there?'

The call was swiftly made and Georgianna left the harbourmaster's office feeling almost reassured. Guy worked hard to re-create the mood of lunchtime, driving her back up the palm-tree-lined Croisette to the boutique where she had admired the swimsuit.

Two hours later they sat luxuriously at their ease in the shade of one of the Eden Roc's giant white umbrellas. While she sipped an early glass of Kir Royal, Georgianna gazed down at the sea and the open-air pool on the promontory. They had swum there, and sunbathed, and swum again before laboriously climbing the steep stone steps cut into the rockface.

'How long will it take us to reach Monte Carlo tomorrow?' she asked idly.

'No time,' Guy assured her. 'Don't worry! The captain won't dare to leave without us again. We can take our time, have another swim, have lunch somewhere on the way. Now stop worrying and tell me, what do you see out here?'

'Just the sea,' she said, puzzled.

'So unromantic,' he said, rolling his eyes comically. 'Whereas I, Georgie, see Sardinia at the other side of it. Emerald green sea and deserted coves of white sand. You won't need your new suit there!'

She smiled, but asked him seriously, 'Guy, I've been meaning to ask. The hotel reservation —'

'Is for two rooms, naturally. Although of course I hope we shall only need one of them.'

'We will.'

'But I knew your father's fearsome reputation for protectiveness and took two. It was an extraordinary stroke of luck getting any at this time of year, of course, but they'd had a sudden cancellation.'

'I'm very glad you asked me,' she said frankly.

'I'm glad, too. Shall we go and decide which of our two rooms we shall be using?'

The air cooled rapidly as they drove up through the hills towards Saint-Paul de Vence. Georgie was glad of her light jacket and no longer needed the protection of her dark glasses as the sun quite suddenly sank from view, leaving a last blaze of red along the horizon. The soft violet twilight obscured her view of gnarled olive trees, stunted thorn bushes and low staked vines clinging to the precipitous hillsides. Guy slowed several times to drive through little villages of roughly plastered, red-roofed houses. She heard the faint click of colliding *boules*, the players competing by street-light; smelt the distinctive odours of Provençal cookery, rich in tomatoes and garlic and herbs, wafting on the breeze from the village kitchens.

The hotel was as beautiful as she'd remembered from a previous visit with her parents before Dexter's accident, its air of timelessness the same. Its mellow walls and stone traceried windows gave it a monastic air.

Inside, and in the hotel grounds, it was a different story.

Although the furnishings were simple native Provençal, there was nothing austere about the colourful upholstery in glowing local prints, the fine old pieces of furniture, or the magnificent collection of art by modern masters. Georgianna strolled on to the veranda to renew her acquaintance with the mural by Léger, while Guy spoke to the desk clerk. Returning, she saw him glance worriedly at her over his shoulder, and felt her heart sink as he walked rapidly over out of earshot of the studiedly incurious clerk.

'It seems it's not our day today,' he began.

'Don't tell me they haven't had our reservation?'

'It's not as bad as that. I just want to assure you, Georgie, that I didn't plan it like a cheap seducer, but there's been a mix-up. I know I told them two rooms, but they swear I said two people, and so they saved us one double room. It's the classic excuse, isn't it, but I didn't engineer this. You do believe me, don't you?'

He looked so anxious, and she was so relieved that they did not, after all, have to leave the welcoming warmth of the hotel that she threw her arms round his neck.

'Of course I don't think you planned it like this, any more than I planned *Randolph 1*'s not being there. Besides, it was terribly selfish of us to plan to take two rooms when we knew we'd only use one. Tell that nosy clerk over there we'll just have to make do.'

The clerk handed them the key without batting an eyelid and an aproned porter made heavy weather of carrying their suitcases to their room, charming with low beams and a private terrace. When the solid wooden door finally swung to behind him, Guy closed Georgianna in his arms and looked intently at her.

'Darling, can I tell you something else?'

'What?' she whispered fearfully.

'I am suddenly and shamefully overwhelmingly hungry, far too hungry to make love to you as slowly and carefully as I want to. So why don't we change for dinner? The sooner we eat, the sooner we'll be back here.'

418

Georgianna used the bathroom first and while Guy was showering slipped on a pale cobweb of a dress in shimmering blue-grey silk chiffon. It was slashed cunningly to reveal tantalising asymmetrical glimpses of her back and shoulders, and her legs as she walked. While she was smoothing her dress, Guy emerged from the bathroom wearing nothing but a pair of white boxer shorts. After one glance at his smooth lean chest and long athlete's legs, she looked away and busied herself searching through her jewellery roll with unsteady fingers, looking for the moonstone and pearl pendant she usually wore with this dress.

He hadn't guessed, she realised, covertly studying him in the mirror as he padded unselfconsciously about, unpacking a lightweight grey suit from one of his cases. She'd played the part of the experienced woman of the world so convincingly that he had no idea how momentous a night this was for her. Despite being admired and pursued by men since her fourteenth birthday, the Honourable Georgianna Randolph was still a virgin.

They dined in the softly-lit rustic dining-room, its walls hung with exquisite oil-paintings depicting scenes in Provance. Warmed by a glass of the champagne Guy had ordered, Georgianna looked about her in unstudied delight.

The light meal of *langoustes au gingembre* and spit-roasted lamb was deftly served. Guy drank most of the champagne, its only effect on him a slight smokiness in his eyes, an even more apealing huskiness to his voice. She shivered as he reached across the table to take her hand. It seemed to be the invitation he had been waiting for.

'Madame is cold,' he told their grave-faced waiter. 'Will you bring coffee and your best armagnac to our room straight away?'

'*Mais bien sûr, m'sieur. Bonne nuit, mam'selle.*'

'A last stroll?' Guy suggested, tucking Georgianna's arm under his and leading her outside. There was a golden disc of a moon above, and the scent of jasmine. They stood arm

419

in arm, surveying the mountains and the almost sheer drop below, obscured in velvet darkness except for the hundreds of tiny pinpricks of light from hidden houses.

Georgianna shivered in earnest this time. She told herself it was because they had left the warmth of the hotel but she knew that there was another reason. Guy's warm hands had found one of the gaps in the back of her dress and were gently caressing her bare skin. He felt her involuntary shudder.

'Come inside and I'll warm you,' he murmured.

As they passed through the lobby on their way to their room, the desk clerk, busily talking on the phone, waved in their direction.

'Phone for the Honourable Mademoiselle Randolph,' he said unctuously, and gestured towards an extension set discreetly beside a low chair.

'It must be the boat.' Guy said. 'I'll go on ahead while you speak to the captain. You'll find the room on your own?'

'Yes, of course. Won't be a minute.'

Counting her blessings that the call had not arrived ten minutes later, she picked up the receiver. There was a click as the desk clerk connected her with the familiar gravelly tones of *Randolph 1*'s full-time captain.

'Masters here, Miss Georgianna. I gather you missed the boat.'

She felt a surge of irritation at the man's offhand manner. 'You mean you left me stranded high and dry, Captain,' she said crisply. 'My father is not going to like this.'

'And I doubt very much if he'd approve of what's going on on his boat either!'

Something had obviously upset Captain Masters. His manner was habitually gruff and forthright, but he was too experienced in dealing with wealthy, capricious employers to sail quite so close to the wind without severe provocation, she realised.

'Is there something wrong, Captain Masters?' she enquired in milder tones. 'We thought that perhaps you'd gone on to Monte Carlo to find a spare radio part.'

'I went to Monte Carlo, despite my express reservations about sailing without a radio, on your brother's orders. He said you'd catch us up there, if you came at all.'

For a moment Georgianna did not understand what the captain was saying. 'My *brother*...? You mean, Courtney's on board?'

'With a very mixed bunch of friends, if you get my drift,' Masters said heavily. 'I am sorry for the mistake, but Mr Courtney said —'

'He must have misunderstood what I told him,' she said smoothly. There was no need for Masters to know that she had not expected Courtney or his party at all. When Daddy found out, though, the fur would really fly ...

'Would you tell my brother hat we shall be joining the boat tomorrow?' she said clearly. 'And, Captain Masters —'

'Yes?'

'You needn't stand any nonsense from my brother's friends.'

'I'd no intention of doing so, Miss Georgianna, and I'll be very pleased to welcome you aboard. Good evening to you, and a safe journey tomorrow.'

Georgianna barely noticed the desk clerk's ingratiating smile as she replaced the receiver and stood up. Courtney installed on *Randolph 1*? Somehow he must have learned of her father's indulgence towards her and seized the opportunity to entertain a group of friends at her expense. 'A mixed bunch' Masters had called them, and she had no doubt they were. What stung far worse, however, was Courtney's utter disregard of her feelings. The week was supposed to be a chance for Guy and her to become better acquainted. She could have done without her brother and his free-loading friends. But there was a brighter side to his virtual hijack of the yacht, she realised. By tomorrow night

421

at the latest she'd see him again, and then she could really go to work on him.

'At last,' Guy said as Georgianna opened the door to their room. 'I was just about to come and find you.'

She noticed that he had lit the log fire laid ready in the grate. Its flickering flames and the soft rose-shaded bedside lamps were the only light in the room. The bedclothes were turned invitingly back. Guy had thrown his jacket and tie carelessly across a chair, and kicked off his shoes. Barefoot, his shirt open at the neck to reveal the firm column of his throat, he bent down to a low table and picked up two glasses.

'Shall we drink our brandy by the fire?'

'None for me, thank you. Is there coffee?'

'Of course. Sit down here. I'll pour.'

Georgianna knelt on the rug before the hearth, warming her hands before the dancing flames. Sensitive as always to her mood, Guy merely handed her a cup of coffee, making no move to touch her. He sat on the floor a few feet away, clasping his hands around his knees and studying her face.

'You've had bad news, I see. Was *Randolph 1* not at Monte Carlo?'

'She's there all right, but we have uninvited guests on board — my brother Courtney and some hangers-on. It was he who ordered the captain to put out to sea this afternoon. It doesn't look as though we'll reach Sardinia after all, Guy. I'm terribly sorry.'

He reached across and took her hand. 'You can hardly evict your brother,' he said calmly. 'But don't worry, we can still have a good time. After all, I'd originally planned to tour by car. Now we'll be doing it by boat, that's all. Admittedly with rather more company than we'd planned, but they won't be with us every minute of the day — or night.'

Georgianna squeezed his hand. She knew that once aboard the boat with Courtney in his present mood things would be far from simple, but she was reluctant to spoil the mood between Guy and herself further. When he pulled her to him she willed herself to forget all about Courtney and this new betrayal.

'Relax,' he whispered, smoothing the rich fall of nut-brown hair away from her tense face and softly kissing the side of her neck. 'You smell delicious,' he murmured against silky, sun-warmed skin. 'How do we unfasten this dress?'

'I — I'll do it.' She had to stand to find the web of concealed hooks that held the dress together.

Guy leant back in his chair and lifted his glass, savouring the perfumed warmth of the spirit against his tongue, through his veins. He could no longer tell if it was the armagnac having this effect on him, or the sight of the girl, shrugging off a silken skein of a dress to stand before him in the briefest pair of flesh-coloured panties.

He drained his brandy and knelt before her, pulling her gently resisting body round to face him fully. His hands circled her waist while he traced a line of kisses downward from her navel, then pulled her down on her knees on the rug before him. He sank back on his heels and gently closed his mouth around each perfect rose-tipped breast in turn.

With a mouth still burning from the spirit, Guy's tongue gently teased each nipple to tingling pleasure. Georgianna sighed, then stiffened, as his hands began to side downward. He eased her gently on to her back before the hearth and she instinctively raised her hips to allow him to slide away the last barrier to her nakedness.

He knelt between her parted knees, smiling down at her, and began to undo his belt.

She stared up at him, eyes wider than ever. It was not desire he saw there, but something that looked more like fear.

'Georgie?' He looked down at her, puzzled. 'You wouldn't by any chance be a virgin?'

Mute with embarrassment, she nodded

'But why on earth didn't you tell me? I thought you knew what you were getting into here.'

The delicious languourous tide on which she had been floating swiftly receded, leaving her shivering with embarrassment and frustration. Tears welled in her eyes. On top of the disappointment over the boat, it seemed her first night of love was not to live up to her romantic imaginings.

He was instantly contrite, helping her to her feet and then to bed. He stroked her cheek, looking down at her tenderly. 'There's no need to hurry things. You should be very sure, *chérie*. The man to whom you lose your virginity should be special to you. I hope it will be me. Maybe later, when we've spent more time together.' He slid into bed beside her, kissing her a chaste goodnight.

Other men had tried to make love to her, believing wrongly that in the heat of the moment she'd forget all her nonsense about hanging on to her virginity. She never had, clinging to the determination to save herself for the right man. How ironic, she decided, drifting finally into a troubled sleep, that when she thought she'd finally found him, he had refused the gift.

Georgianna started awake. She'd been dreaming for what felt like hours. Courtney, adrift in a rowing-boat on a vast empty ocean, was calling desperately for help . . .

When she opened her eyes, it was Guy who smiled down at her. He was freshly shaved and showered, and dressed casually for travelling. He seemed to bear her no ill-will for their less than perfect night.

'Come on, sleepyhead. It's nearly eleven. Breakfast is out on the terrace.'

Heavy-eyed, she nevertheless hurried to shower and change into a simple yellow batiste dress. Yesterday's sun had given a glow to her skin which hardly needed enhancing. She quickly brushed on mascara and lip-gloss, sprayed on some of her favourite Penhaligon Bluebell scent, and was ready.

Guy was seated at a table on the terrace, obviously immersed in a newspaper and oblivious of the breathtaking view behind him. 'I ordered you coffee and brioches,' he said. 'Is there anything else you'd like?'

'Just coffee will be fine.' She waited while the waiter filled a bowl with fresh *café au lait*, then asked Guy, 'Is it all right if we drive straight to the boat?'

Guy looked surprised. 'What's the hurry? I'd thought a leisurely drive through Eze, then lunch at the African Queen. The clerk's booking it now.'

'Would you cancel it, please?' She abandoned all pretence at eating the brioche which lay crumbled on the plate, and stared fixedly at the view ahead.

'Well, of course, if you feel like that about it.'

She smiled gratefully.

'But, if so, I insist you eat breakfast now,' he said firmly. He realised there was something on her mind, the same thing that had troubled her yesterday, perhaps, when she had been so upset about the yacht? He had the feeling that if he sat quietly and waited, Georgianna would unburden herself.

She sat silently for a few minutes, gazing at the beauty of the scene. Beyond the terrace where they sat, majestic hills rolled down to the valley floor hundreds of feet below.

He followed the direction of her gaze. 'It is beautiful,' he agreed, as if she had spoken. 'And like all the truly beautiful things in life, it has an air of timelessness. Some women have that — you, for instance, Georgie. It's in the bones, I think, the lines of your face and the way you carry yourself. You will be old some day, but to me you will never be less than beautiful.'

The sincerity of his voice, the calm and beauty of the scene before her, most of all his reference to the years ahead, undid her. Silently she began to weep, and Guy knew that now he would get the truth from her.

425

'It's your brother, isn't it?'

'Yes,' she said, shuddering with the effort to speak sensibly. 'It's drugs, I'm afraid. Again. This time, I'm terrified he won't be strong enough to stop.'

Guy's face was grave. 'I had no idea it was something so serious. It must be a great sadness to all your family.'

She smiled wryly. 'They don't even know! Oh, the last time, they did. Mummy was wonderful, and Daddy paid all the bills for the best clinics. But now ... Guy, I'm so afraid!'

'Tell me how it started,' he prompted her gently. 'It will help you to talk about it.'

She sighed. 'Courtney decided years ago that the only way he'd match Daddy's reputation was for hell-raising. When he was just fifteen, a master at his school found him and two of his friends smoking pot. The only reason he wasn't expelled then and there was because one of the other boys involved was the son of a cabinet minister and the gutter press would have crucified him over that. Daddy made a huge donation to the bursar's fund, then beat Courtney black and blue. Mummy cried for two days, but Court refused to.'

'Your father's reputation is well deserved, I see,' Guy said drily. 'A couple of joints is hardly becoming addicted!'

'Wait. There's a lot worse to come. In his first term at Oxford, Courtney was sent down from Christ Church. He and some friends smashed up a restaurant after drinking steadily since eleven in the morning. It's always been one of Daddy's fondest boasts, you see, that a Randolph can hold his liquor, only Courtney can't. He just doesn't have Daddy's head for it. When the manager of the restaurant protested, one of my brother's friends hit the man hard enough to put him in hospital. It wasn't Court — even Daddy believed that — but when the police arrived they found him unconscious at one end of the restaurant, and the manager at the other. There was such an outcry in the town that the college authorities were forced to make an example of him and send him down. This time Mummy was furious too. Ash had chosen to study in America, which Daddy approved of, but her side of the family, the Hamiltons, have gone to Christ Church for hundreds of years.'

'So what happened then?' Guy interposed gently

'Daddy didn't beat him this time. It was worse than that. He told Court that the only chance he had of redeeming himself in the family's eyes was to go off to London, find a job — anything would do — and stick at it for one year minimum. We hardly saw him for six months, though he'd been in touch to say he was working for an insurance company, then we had a phone call from an old family friend, Fiona Campbell. Did we know that Courtney was living in a squat with a very undesirable crowd? Her grand-daughter had visited it for a party, and had been shocked by the change in him. Mummy and Grandmama went tearing up to town to see him, and were horrified. He was holding down a job, just, living rent-free in the squat and hardly ever eating. He didn't want to. His entire salary went on drugs — amphetamines mainly, but he admitted to chasing the dragon when he had the money. They got him into the Regent's Park Clinic straight away. It took months, but at the end of it he was pretty well the same old Court. Mummy and Grandmama could see that Daddy's taking a tough line hadn't worked, so they begged him to use his influence to get Court a proper job with real prospects, a chance to build up some confidence in himself. He agreed on one condition: if he ever heard of Courtney taking drugs again, he'd not only cut off his allowance but disinherit him immediately. We don't come into our trusts till rather late, so he's had that hold over Court for a while. Next year it will be gone.' Her voice broke.

'Court dropped out in New York, too, despite the good job Daddy got him with a broker. It wasn't drugs this time, just the traditional square peg in a round hole. Court couldn't be a yuppie if he tried; it's just not his style. Next, he tried his hand at film producing. It bombed, but it didn't deserve to. Daddy pretty well gave up on him then, but because he hadn't been doing drugs couldn't stop his allowance. Instead, he withdrew something else: his attention. It isn't that he dislikes Court exactly, it's just that he doesn't interest Daddy. If he's in the room, Daddy will talk to anyone else, even Sloane, rather than to him. Every time Courtney tries something new, Daddy listens politely to his plans then changes the subject with absolutely no comment. It's painful to see. Court's tried so many things over the past few years but none has lasted more than a few months. Now he spends his time clubbing and partying in London, living at Chester Square or at friends' houses. Since his accident, Daddy's been so cold to both the boys. It seems he can't stand to see Court particularly healthy, and able to walk and ride and drive fast cars, all the things Daddy loved to do, while he fails at everything else . . .'

'But this is dreadful, Georgie,' Guy interrupted, amazed. 'Can't your father see what he's doing to your family — not just to Courtney but to you and your mother?'

'Mummy and I are a lot tougher than we look,' Georgianna told him with a bleak smile, 'and of course we have Grandmama to buck us up. Ash is the lucky one. He got away at the time of the accident because the Australian end needed an extra man. Courtney's the real casualty, and we've all been so blind to it — except, perhaps, Daddy himself.'

She remembered the conversation with Dexter by the pool, was it only two mornings ago? 'I want the money just as much as he does,' she'd told him. 'But for very different reasons,' he'd replied. He must have his suspicions already. If he found out for sure . . . 'It seems that for some time now he's been taking cocaine,' she told Guy painfully. 'I had no idea, never dreamed he'd risk everything by taking drugs again. But on Tuesday there was an appalling scene while he was playing polo. It seemed he'd met a dealer before the match and his behaviour that afternoon was just brutal. So unlike the real Court.' She outlined the events of the match and afterwards, including her own humiliation at Prince Nicolas's hands and Lizzie's revelations on the car ride home.

Guy's face hardened. 'So, this brother of yours is brutal as well as an addict?'

She did not reply, but continued, 'Giles and Lizzie found me after Court had driven off, stranding me. They were so kind and concerned, I felt guilty ever to have supposed that Lizzie was just another jilted girlfriend. He hadn't broken with her, of course. She'd left him, driven to it by his paranoid behaviour — manic highs when he had to take massive doses of tranquillisers to bring him down enough to sleep. There was a doctor in South Kensington, apparently, who'd prescribe them in quantity for a fee. Court used to ask Lizzie to go to the doctor's for him every three days for a repeat prescription, and then to a different chemist every time so they wouldn't get suspicious. On a high, he'd talk to friends on the phone for hours — no wonder Daddy's been hitting the roof about the Chester Square phone-bills. Lizzie stuck with him as long as she could, but it got too much for her. She'd known Giles before, and heard he'd come out of Farm Place after a cure. So she went to him to talk about Court. I'm sorry. It seems dreadful to be telling you this, on a perfect day in a perfect place, but can you see why I'm feeling so damned guilty? I was furious with Court for leaving me, and stealing from me, and then you phoned, and I did want to see you. But I should have stayed with him, shouldn't I?'

He took her hand. 'I think it was a very good thing you came to me, because now there are two of us who know the truth and can help your brother.'

'Thanks. It's such a relief to talk frankly to someone. I did try to tell Uncle Alex, but his loathsome wife interrupted us and got quite the wrong idea. Running away and taking *Randolph 1* is another example of Courtney's not thinking properly. He must know the trouble he'll be in when Daddy finds out — or ordinarily he would. Things are obviously getting out of hand fast if he can't work that out for himself. I must go to him. I've left it too long already.'

Guy was sad, more for Georgianna and the ordeal she faced than for her addict brother. But she was brave and determined enough to see this out, and he cared enough about her to want to help. It looked very much as though their holiday was blown, but what the hell? There'd be others, hopefully still with Georgie.

'Go and get your things packed while I pay the bill,' he said, pulling her to her feet. 'And thank God the crash barriers are in place in Monte Carlo. We're driving to beat the record today.'

Courtney woke to a familiar sound. His dealer, Suzy, wearing only a flame red monokini, was sitting at the leather-topped writing desk, busily cutting a day's supply with a razorblade.

He shivered, though the curtains were drawn back from the open portholes to allow sunshine the colour of liquid gold to flood into *Randolph 1*'s stateroom. He eyed the rumpled clothes, Suzy's and his, which were strewn all over the floor and cascading from half a dozen partially unpacked suitcases. On the night-table by the huge six-foot bed, two empty bottles floated upended in silver buckets, jostling for place with a cluster of pill bottles. On Suzy's side of the bed, a half-eaten croissant lay abandoned on the crumpled sheets. He closed his eyes wearily. Why did it always get like this wherever he lived? And why the hell didn't Suzy hurry up with their morning lines? 'What time is it?' he asked, closing his eyes.

'Nearly one. You really crashed out last night, didn't you? I told you to go easy on those 'ludes.'

'Nice of you to care,' he murmured.

'Hey, what *is* this?' Instantly on the alert, Suzy put down the razorblade. She'd been told to give this sucker the VIP treatment, spend all the time she wanted with him, even sleep with him if he was able to. Jade Kennedy's instructions had been quite specific: 'Fast lane for this one, Suze. His old man's got almost as many eyes and ears reporting to him as I have. If he gets wind of this, Dexter Randolph will kill the goose that lays the golden eggs, so bring sonny boy along fast.'

When Suzy had told her that Courtney never seemed to have much cash, just a batch of credit cards and a monthly allowance he ran through in a week, Jade snorted contemptuously. 'His sort of spoiled brat *never* has cash, sweetie. Give their daddies credit for some sense, the tough old bastards! But the kids can lay their hands on more money than you've ever dreamed of simply by hocking granny's pearls or disposing of the Stubbs their godfather left them. Everything's convertible, love — at my usual rates of commission, of course.'

Jade Kennedy got all of the money, eventually. The fencing side of her business was wonderfully diverse and international. Her clients knew that there was no danger that something Jade had paid out on would turn up at the next Sotheby's or Christie's sale, identifiable and traceable back to them. No, their paintings and jewellery and family silver were discreetly placed with private clients, and the vendors paid a steep commission for the service as well as for the others she pedalled — call-girls such as Suzy had been, beautiful boys, and drugs of every sort. Her drugs, like her whores, were always the best. Suzy was smart and had graduated from basic call-girl to one of Jade's most trusted pushers. The commission she made was so good that she planned to open her own club before she was thirty, but Courtney, her latest assignment, wasn't turning out to be quite the pushover she'd anticipated.

'Don't throw a moody on me, Court,' she pleaded in a little-girl voice, stroking his face with long red-tipped fingers. If her red hair was a little over-highlighted and her suntan spoke of hours on a sunbed rather than in the more expensive West Indies or Côte d'Azur sunshine, she had a great figure. She loved to wear monokinis, since her breasts, large and round and eyecatching, needed no support at all. 'You know how much I care for you,' she said, twitching back the sheet that covered him. 'Lie back. Momma's got something for you, something you'll like.' She lifted his cold hands towards her breasts and started to unclip her side-fastening bikini bottom.

Courtney sighed irritably. 'There's only one thing I like about you, Suzy,' he said, need overcoming discretion.

She followed the direction of his hungry gaze, towards the mound of piled snow she had left covered with a protective glass dome on the writing-desk. The jerk had insulted her again. Suzy took a deep breath and kept her cool. He was already into them for ten thousand and still refusing to endorse Prince Nicolas's cheque over. Jade had said to bring him on fast, and Suzy was greedy for her commission.

'You don't want that any more, lover,' she said with a good humour she was far from feeling. Her brown leather bag lay conveniently beside the bed and she bent down to pick it up, breasts bobbing. 'I've got something else with me, something I've been saving just for you,' she crooned. 'Close your eyes and you won't feel a thing — just a little prick ...' Like you, she thought contemptuously, gazing down at his tense expectant face.

Guy reached Monte Carlo even earlier than predicted. They took the main road down into town almost at racing speed, winning a chorus of claps and cheers from a gang of bare-chested road workers busily erecting crash barriers for the Grand Prix. Descending the town's steep streets, Georgianna had a brief impression of its hodge-podge architecture: gracious nineteenth-century stucco, pastel-painted or embellished with graceful wrought iron, stood wall to wall with rearing monstrosities in plate-glass and steel. The gardens and window-boxes teeming with tropical abundance. Everywhere she looked there were palms, solid thickets of hibiscus or bougainvillaea, climbing fuchsias and swarming geraniums.

Guy traced the steep crowded road down to the marina, where they parked with a fine disregard for regulations. 'The stewards will come and take the car on board,' she assured him, searching the clustered yachts and motor launches for the familiar graceful lines of *Randolph 1*. 'That's her,' she said, pointing to the second biggest yacht berthed in the harbour. 'Leave the cases. They can hoist them aboard with the car.'

'Which staterooms are Monsieur de Rennes and I in?' she asked Herbert, her favourite steward.

'Number four and the two cabins, Miss Georgie. They're the only ones left.'

She drew a deep breath. It was pointless becoming angry with Courtney before she even saw him. They had more serious matters to discuss than his selfishness in taking over *Randolph 1* and giving the staterooms and only decent cabins to his friends, leaving the inferior accommodation for herself and Guy.

'We'd like lunch on deck, please,' she said, and led Guy away to choose between the two worst cabins on the boat.

After lunch they changed into swimwear and lay basking on the sundeck. Drowsy from wine and lulled by the strong sunshine, Guy drifted into sleep, lying on his stomach. Georgianna propped herself on one arm and studied his thick black lashes, the lean athletic lines of his shoulders and back above snug-fitting black trunks. She leant across and kissed his cheek. He murmured in his sleep and reached for her hand, but did not wake.

Too restless to lie still any longer, she went below and decided to take a long bath. She washed and dried her hair, painted her nails, flicked through a magazine or two. When

433

a glance at her bedside clock told her that it was just after six, she decided to dress informally for the evening, choosing to wear an old favourite St Laurent catsuit in violet silk. Deceptively baggy on the hanger, it was transformed when Georgie stepped into it. Its neckline was modest, and her arms and legs swathed in folds of fabric to wrist and ankle, but the silk was so sheer she could wear neither bra nor panties beneath it, and subtly but unmistakably it showed.

Guy was awake when she went back on deck. He whistled when he saw her, but could see from the set of her face that she was in no mood for gallantry. 'I'll go and change, and we'll wait here together,' he said instead.

But she was alone on deck, trying to appear absorbed in the latest paperback shocker she'd found abandoned there, when Courtney and his party returned.

'Sis, you made it,' she heard him call from the companionway as he caught sight of her, for all the world as though he had been given use of the yacht and she had simply tagged along. He grinned and waved and shepherded his companions straight up to meet her, the picture of the jovial host.

'Rupe and Dick I think you know ...' Georgianna nodded and acknowledged Rupert Knight and Dick Fairburn, pleasant enough but, like Courtney, unable to occupy themselves except with clubs and parties and frequent changes of scene.

'Shelley and Dee are with Rupert and Dick,' Courtney continued.

'Pleased to meet you,' chirped two near-identical blondes in this season's resort uniform of fringed suede boots, short shorts and shorter T-shirts. The girls looked, and presumably were, interchangeable, as Courtney had not indicated which of them was accompanying which man.

'And this is my very good friend Suzy,' he said last of all. Georgianna immediately recognised the flaming red hair of the girl who had driven Courtney away from

434

Smith's Lawn. She was older than Court, wary and watchful, but she took care to smile warmly at Georgianna.

'It's great you could join us,' she said, in a carefully flat drawl that could have been anything from Chelsea to Croydon. 'Will you eat aboard with us tonight? I told Chief to make enough for eight.'

Georgianna had already had enough of this pretence that there'd been nothing wrong in hijacking *Randolph 1*. She was damned if she was going to sit quietly and watch his girlfriend, or whatever she was, playing hostess on their father's boat. 'That's kind of you,' she said stiffly, 'but Guy and I have already decided to eat ashore.'

'Perhaps we could all meet up in the Sporting Club later,' Dick Fairburn suggested to smooth over a rather awkward silence. He'd suspected there was something not *quite* about dear old Court's mad scramble to get them all aboard and out of Cannes at twelve hours' notice, and Georgianna's behaviour confirmed it.

'You've got to come gambling,' Shelley or Dee said breathlessly. 'Rupe got terribly lucky last night.'

'In more ways than one,' he said with an unpleasant leer.

'Who's for a drink before we change?' Suzy enquired quickly.

'Oh, rather.'

'Good idea.'

'Can we have scrummy Bellinis again?'

'Perhaps you and I could have a word?' Georgianna suggested to Courtney, hoping to persuade him into the privacy of her cabin.

He wasn't going to be budged, however. 'Sure, Sis. What's the problem? Cabins OK?' he asked, sinking into a canvas chair which he had tilted to catch the last rays of evening sun. With the rest of the party, apart from Suzy who had gone to find a steward, all interested onlookers, Georgianna could hardly begin to question Courtney about his habit.

'How are you?' she asked weakly, studying him closely.

435

He *looked* well enough, tanned and fit, and seemingly quite calm and collected.

'I'm fine, Georgie. You saw me just the other day, remember?'

His eyes met hers boldly and she read the challenge. He was daring her to tackle him in front of his friends. If she did, however justifiably, remind him of his behaviour, he would engineer a scene and vanish quickly and completely. She couldn't risk it. It was better just to sit this out and get him alone later. 'Well, a lot has happened since then,' she said blandly. 'You know I'm with Guy, of course?'

'And here he is now.'

Guy climbed easily up to join them and Georgianna introduced him to her brother and his guests. She saw that he shook Court's hand for a fraction longer than was necessary, studying him intently for a split second before breaking into his charming, lop-sided smile. 'Georgie's told me so much about you.'

'I'll just bet she has,' Courtney said coolly.

Antagonism flared between them, but the awkwardness was broken by Herbert's arrival, taking the steep companionway with a tray of glasses and bottles. Suzy followed with a jug — of Bellinis, presumably, from the way Shelley and Dee swooped on it. After one drink, Guy and Georgianna left *Randolph 1*. She wanted to get as far away as possible from the atmosphere on board: the vacuous jokes of Courtney's friends, inanely giggling girls and Suzy's hard-eyed stare.

There were worse places to kill time than the dining-room of the Hôtel de Paris, with its spectacular views across the botanical gardens and the illuminated horseshoe of the harbour, the lights on every boat berthed or moored there adding to the galaxy, or later Jimmez's, where they danced cheek to cheek, forgetting for a few hours the confrontation to come.

But back aboard *Randolph 1*, it seemed Court had managed to evade them after all. Loud music blared from the saloon where Rupe and Dick and partners were busy making up for the evening's disappointment at the tables with several bottles of vintage Krug and a party that looked as though it would become quite uninhibited.

'Where's my brother?' Georgianna yelled above the din.

Dickie looked at her blearily. 'Crashed out. Suzy's putting him to bed now. Strictly do not disturb time, I'd say.'

He winked meaningfully and Georgianna turned away, disgusted. She was sure Courtney was not sleeping, not even with Suzy, but she could hardly go breaking into his cabin to find out. At that moment, Suzy herself appeared. A battered brown leather bag slung over one shoulder struck a rather incongruous note against the strapless white floor-length evening dress she was wearing. It was slit almost to the crotch, but what caught Georgianna's attention was her single piece of jewellery: a diamond brooch in the shape of an arrow, Cartier original, circa 1920.

Shit, Suzie thought, immediately interpreting the direction of Georgianna's gaze. Court had sworn it was an old piece of his grandmother's he'd found at the back of a drawer, but she should have known better than to trust the word of a junkie. There just might be a way out of it, though. 'Court's out for the count,' she announced, 'but he wants you all to enjoy yourselves.'

Deftly she unpacked a flat round mirror and emptied on to it the contents of a vial full of white powder. 'Seven of us,' she announced, and began busily separating the powder into smaller heaps, then, using the blunt side of a razorblade, straightening each mound into a line until there were fourteen, precisely spaced in a spoke pattern over the surface of the mirror. The others began to cluster eagerly round. Dick had already produced a clean new 100-franc note which he was rolling into a tube.

'Will you join us?' Suzy said invitingly. 'It's pure Thai. Nothing but the best for Court and his friends.'

'Of course,' Georgianna said to Guy's surprise. 'But, first, would you excuse me for a moment?'

'No need to powder your nose,' Shelley called after her, spluttering with laughter.

'Hey, wait a minute!' With a backward glance at her stock, Suzy tried to push through the crowd around her to intercept Georgie. Guy was too quick for her. While the others crowded round the mirror, bending down to inhale greedily, he took her roughly by the arm.

'No fuss, Suzy, there's a good girl. You can fly out tomorrow, no questions asked, but any trouble tonight, and I will ask the police to investigate a most regrettable scene which Miss Randolph and I discovered on our return from a night club. Even Monégasque prisons are far from picturesque, so why don't we just sit down over here, tête à tête, and wait for Georgie to get back?'

Georgianna ran to the stateroom, knocked and waited. There was no answer or even a sound from inside. She tried the handle, but found it locked. She knelt and saw from the lock that there was no key on the inside so Suzy must have locked Court in. Clever, but not clever enough. She knew where a duplicate set of keys was kept in the stewards' galley. Don't be so dramatic, she tried to tell herself. This isn't life or death. A good shaking, and he'll wake up.

Inside, the cabin was in darkness apart from the feeble light of one bedside lamp. Courtney lay on his back, obviously out for the count. Georgianna wrinkled her nose at the sharp, vaguely medicinal, smell in the room. She picked her way over mounds of clothes and shoes and magazines and shook his shoulder,. He lay limp and unresponsive, even when she said loudly in his ear, 'Wake up, Court, it's me, Georgie.' After two sharp slaps the palm of her hand stung agonisingly, but there was no response from him. Maybe it was the dim light, but it was hard to

438

tell if he was breathing. Cold with fear, she felt for a pulse in his wrist. Damn! She could never find her own, let alone an unconscious person's. She sprang from the bed and stumbled to the open door, groping for the light. She found a triple switch and pressed them all. As she turned back to the bed, the boat rolled slightly with the sea swell and the floor of the cabin tilted fractionally. Georgianna stumbled and almost fell. Catching her balance, she saw something small and cylindrical roll from beneath the bed ...

Her screams were heard throughout the boat. Guy jostled for entry to the cabin with the captain and two goggle-eyed stewards while the other guests, bright-eyed but strangely subdued, stood outside in the corridor.

Georgianna was kneeling on the floor, cradling her barely breathing brother in her arms. On the bed beside him, where her nerveless fingers had dropped it, lay an empty syringe.

At the hospital, Georgianna ran beside the trolley which two green-suited attendants wheeled rapidly towards a treatment room. A nurse kindly but firmly barred her way and led her instead to a small, bare waiting-room where Guy joined her several minutes later.

'I've told them that he's Charles Hamilton, and that he lives at my Paris address,' he told her in an undertone. 'If anyone asks, you are his girlfriend, but don't give them your real name — give them Suzy's. If he comes through the next few hours ...'

Georgianna gasped, and he took her hand. 'I think he has a good chance. You caught him just in time, and he's not a regular heroin-user — I checked for track-marks on his arms. Suzy must have introduced him to the needle days ago at the most.'

'She's no better than a murderer! When I see her again, I'll —'

'She'll be long gone by now, and better for everyone

that way. By the time the hospital notifies the police here, I hope to have "Charles" safely on his way to Paris.'

By mid-morning, Courtney's condition had stabilised sufficiently for the doctors to agree reluctantly to Guy's plans for transferring the patient to the Clinique Malmaison, an addiction therapy centre a short distance away from Napoleon's favourite palace outside Paris. He pulled strings to secure a private ambulance jet for the journey to Paris, and borrowed a hospital office so that Georgianna could make a call in private. At the sound of her mother's warm, welcoming voice, she felt such an upsurge of guilt and relief that she could hardly speak.

'Darling, what a lovely surprise,' Camilla said as the operator connected them person to person. 'But what are you doing in Monaco? I thought you were Sardinia bound.'

'It's Courtney, Mummy. He —'

'Courtney?' Camilla was instantly alert. 'Tell me quickly, Georgie.'

'He's in hospital here, Mummy, but Guy's arranging a transfer to Paris this afternoon. It's bad news, I'm afraid. The worst.'

Georgianna could hardly speak for a moment, wondering how to go on, but Camilla forestalled her. Speaking very clearly and rapidly she said, 'That *is* bad news, Georgie. Poor Court. That wretched appendix! Give me the name and address of the clinic and I'll join you there as soon as I'm able — by tonight at the latest.'

Georgianna gave it to her, and the fact that she should ask for 'Charles Hamilton'. Camilla read back every fact but the last and continued, with only the slightest tremor in her voice. 'Thank goodness they're finally going to operate. He'll be much better off without it.'

'Mummy, it's not —'

'Don't worry, darling. Any surgery it alarming, but he's young and fit and he'll easily pull through. I'll be with you soon. 'Bye till then.'

She had rung off before Georgianna worked out what

440

must have happened. Daddy had obviously been around when the call came through, and Camilla had instantly acted to protect her son.

There could be no cover-up at the Malmaison, but confidentiality was the keynote of the establishment. The clinic had a surgical wing as well as its addiction centre, so the cover story of an appendix operation that Camilla had given Dexter was perfectly credible, in the short term at least.

'How long will he have to stay here, Doctor?' she asked Courtney's consultant that evening. She was pale and red-eyed after the shock of seeing her unconscious son, but otherwise perfectly composed and in control of herself.

'It's difficult to say, Lady Camilla. For the first few weeks he will be receiving heavy doses of medication to calm the pains of withdrawal. Fortunately, his addiction is to cocaine. The heroin overdose was only his second fix. In order for us to cure him fully, however, he will need many weeks of counselling, group therapy, and a structured, sheltered environment. Part of our cure includes giving Courtney the chance to "earn" hospital privileges such as the chance to wear his own clothes, read new books and newspapers, eventually pass days and weekends on parole out of the hospital. But that won't be for a long time. I can't promise an instant miracle cure, however much I'd like to.'

'I can only stay a few days, Doctor,' Camilla said painfully. 'Any longer, and my husband would begin to wonder why Court was taking so long to recover from a routine operation. But Georgie's going to stay on in Paris and will visit her brother as often as is practical. We shall tell her father that she and Court have gone to join friends in Villefranche while he recuperates, and after several weeks of that excuse we shall just have to think of another.'

The doctor was moved to say sympathetically, 'You may

call me whenever you like to discuss your son's progress. I am usually in my office every day between three and five, so it's probably easiest to call me then.' Camilla thanked him, and he called an orderly to escort them to Courtney's room for a last look at him.

The stark white-painted single ward, with its high hospital bed, polished floor and single high-backed chair was a shock after the director's opulent consulting-room, but for the moment Courtney was equally oblivious of surroundings or visitors.

Camilla stroked the long sun-bleached hair gently away from his forehead and smoothed the unwrinkled sheet over him. 'You're quite sure you can cope alone, Georgie?' she asked finally, raising anxious eyes to her daughter's face.

'I'll help him through, Mummy. I owe him that much. I realised what was wrong and did nothing about it for those crucial few days. If he'd died —'

Camilla was round the bed in an instant to comfort and reassure the child who had never caused her a moment's worry. 'You mustn't blame yourself. Court's been very weak and foolish, but thank God you caught him in time. He will get better, I know it, and I'm so grateful that you'll be here to help. Guy's been marvellous too, arranging all this and putting us up. Are you sure you won't reconsider and stay on at his flat after he's back in Qatar?'

'I'd better not, Mummy. Sooner or later in that part of town I'd meet someone I knew and they'd be all agog to hear that I was living in Guy's flat, and doubly curious when they heard he wasn't even in town. I think it would be best for the Honourable Georgianna Randolph to drop right out of sight for a while.'

'What do you mean?'

'It's very simple, I shall be Arabella Hamilton, aspiring model, living on the Left Bank and making absolutely no attempt to find work.'

*

'Is there a letter for me? Arabella Hamilton.'

'Is there any mail today — Chantel von Stolsenburg.'

The two girls so eagerly enquiring after news from home broke off in confusion. L'Hôtel's desk clerk eyed them sympathetically. Mademoiselle Hamilton had problems — anyone could see that from her shadowed eyes and pale face. She'd been with them two months now, and spent too much time alone in her room. Her passport said she was really the Honourable Georgianna Randolph, but that was her business. Mademoiselle von Stolsenburg, too, was lonely. She went out more than the other girl, received more visits and telephone calls, but no one as eager as she was for letters from home could truly be enjoying herself in Paris.

'I'm so sorry, mam'selle, mam'selle,' he said with a nod to each of them, 'but today there is nothing for either of you.'

'Darn,' said the pretty strawberry blonde in an accent that Georgie found hard to decipher. 'Just another boring day of brilliant sunshine, I suppose.'

'Sorry?' Georgianna said absently. 'Oh, yes, I suppose so.'

Another day of avoiding the popular shops and restaurants that old friends might visit on a stopover in Paris, walking by the side of the Seine or reading on a park bench.

'Are you staying here on your own?' the other girl asked. Georgianna nodded. 'Because if you're not doing anything special today, I could sure use some company. Would you like a ride out of town, perhaps? We could go to Fontainebleau, take a picnic. There are miles and miles of woods there. Think about it — grass under your feet instead of those goddamned cobblestones.'

Georgianna laughed. 'You sound thoroughly disenchanted. Okay, thanks, I'd love a day out of town.'

The blonde held out her hand. 'Chantel von Stolsenburg, delighted to meet you.'

Georgianna hesitated a moment, then shook hands under the clerk's knowing eye. 'Arabella Hamilton from London,' she said firmly.

In twenty minutes, they were on their way. Chantel proved to have absorbed more of the French style of driving than she had the language, clearing the centre of Paris in fifteen heart-stopping minutes. 'Sorry about that,' she said airily, as they hit a comparatively quiet stretch of road. 'I have to wear these for driving —' she pointed to the large blue-framed glasses she had put on as soon as they got into the car — 'and it always puts me in a lousy mood. But you'll be used to traffic, living in London. What do you do there, anyway?'

'I model a little,' Georgianna said, hating herself for the lie.

'Should have guessed,' Chantel said, taking her eyes alarmingly off the road to study her appraisingly. 'You've got the look all right, but have you been ill or something recently? Sorry — I didn't mean you looked less than beautiful, just a little tired or something.'

'Yes, things have been a bit rough lately,' Georgie hedged. Courtney, too weak to do more than hold her hand before drifting into a drugged sleep again on the first two visits she was allowed; grey-faced and trembling violently, in between begging her to get him out of there on her last visit.

'For me, too.' Chantel's open face was shadowed for a moment. 'But why spoil today? Tell me about London. Do you get much work there?'

Georgianna improvised wildly, vaguely remembering the knowledgeable chatter of two would-be professional models she had shared a dressing-room with for a Berkeley Dress Show some years before. 'Oh, fashion shows and magazine work mostly,' she said. 'Middle-of-the-road stuff really — you know, the women's drearies and the occasional dress show for a charity ball or reception. My agent thought a spell in Paris might be good for me, give me a little more of an edge.'

'Did she send your card round in advance, or are you doing the cattle calls?' Chantel asked.

'Sorry?'

'Cattle calls — isn't that what they arrange when they need a girl for an ad or a cover and they want to see as many new faces as possible?'

'Oh, right, yes — sorry. I must have misheard. Look, isn't that the road we want, over there?' Georgie felt happier to endure Chantel's traffic-defying manoeuvrings than she did another minute of the conversation about modelling. She determinedly changed the subject once they were en route for Fontainebleau and kept up a stream of relentless chatter, pretending a light-heartedness she was far from feeling.

They parked near the village square and made the obligatory guided tour of the palace. After the lived-in luxury of Courtney Park, Georgianna found it all rather over-elaborate and soulless, while Chantel seemed far more interested in the views over lake and trees from the palace's massive windows than she was in Napoleon's throne-room.

'I could do with a drink,' she muttered, when their guide finally released them. 'Let's hope they remembered to pack us some wine.'

The insulated bag which they opened in a sunny clearing ten kilometres outside the village proved to contain a bottle of chilled white burgundy and a light meal of chicken wings, smoked ham in crusty baguettes, salad and white peaches. Chantel's mood seemed to have changed from the sunny, outgoing one of the morning. She drank two glasses of wine, but didn't touch the food.

'Did you say you were American?' Georgie asked to break a suddenly awkward silence.

Chantel absently fingered a lock of hair. 'Sort of. Mom and Dad live there now because his company — Stolsenburg Pharmaceuticals — has its biggest plants there, but Dad's German by birth. He has a castle in Bavaria — all dark oak and stag's heads and these creepy medieval weapons on the wall. Mom and I think it's kind of gross, so we don't go there very often.'

'Then your mother's German, too?'

'Hell, no, she's Australian.'

'That's odd,' Georgie said without thinking. 'We're both half-Australian. My father's Australian, but he rarely goes back there these days.'

'Mom refuses ever to go back at all.' Chantel said. 'I'd really like to see it all: Townsville, where she was born — on a farm, I think — and Sydney, where she lived in the sixties. She was quite a famous model then, Linita Tyrone. That's how I know about modelling.'

The sky-blue eyes had lost their bleak expression and Chantel seemed ready to talk again. Fearing a return to the subject of modelling, Georgie asked, 'Whereabouts in American are you from?'

'Northern New Jersey, where I'd rather be right now if I wasn't too darned scared people would laugh at me.'

To Georgianna's consternation, Chantel's voice wobbled distinctly and she stared fixedly away across the clearing, obviously furious with herself for having nearly broken down in front of a complete stranger.

'Would it help to talk about it?'

'It might, if you're sure you want to hear?' Chantel smiled shakily and began: 'It's an old, old story, I'm afraid. Girl meets the man of her dreams at college — I was Radcliffe, he was at Harvard Law. Mark seemed to be everything I wanted: great-looking, popular, a brain *and* a body. At the beginning of my last semester he proposed, and I accepted. He wanted a summer wedding straight after graduation, so we could take a honeymoon right before he started with the law firm in New York who'd already accepted him. The first weekend we could, we went down to Bernardsville — to break the news to my folks — Mark didn't have any of his own. He was adopted as a little boy. Mom was delighted for me, and I though Dad would be too, but something happened between him and Mark — I still don't know what. They'd always got on great before, but that weekend Dad took Mark off fishing on the lake. Mark was really looking forward to it, but when they came back Dad was so angry he could hardly speak. Mark just packed his things and left without me.'

'But why . . .?' Georgianna asked.

'When I asked Dad what had happened, he wouldn't tell me, just said I'd understand one day and would be glad of my escape. That weekend I kept trying to call Mark, but his room-mate said he hadn't got back. I went around there on Monday but no Mark. In the library, studying, I was told — and on Tuesday, and on Wednesday. On Thursday, by accident, I saw him through a coffee-shop window. I went inside, sure there'd been some ghastly mistake — and saw him holding hands with Katherine Porter, a friend of mine, I'd thought. Her Daddy just happens to own a Boston bank. Four weeks later their engagement was announced. I flunked school but couldn't face hanging round at home. All our friends there knew I'd expected to marry Mark and it was just too humiliating. You know what date it is today?'

'August 18th, I think.'

'Mark and Katherine's wedding day.'

Georgie was sorry for Chantel. She seemed a genuine, trusting sort of girl and it was easy to see how she might have been taken in by someone who was obviously a social climber. She had met enough of them herself to recognise the breed at a hundred yards, but Chantel, she sensed, had in some ways led a more sheltered life. Of one thing, though, Georgie was sure: she was a wealthy girl. Her jewellery and clothes were designer, and she, like Arabella, had enough money to live at L'Hôtel which, though Left Bank, was far from cheap. It obviously wasn't lack of money in her background that had driven Mark away, so what had?

Chantel echoed her thoughts. 'How could he do it to me, Arabella? What's wrong with me that he could stop loving me overnight?'

She was crying unashamedly now, scrabbling in her bag

for a handkerchief. Georgie found one in her own and passed it over. Chantel's story could so easily have been hers; their home backgrounds were similar, and each had an Australian parent. And there was something about the girl, an openness and honesty, that had instantly attracted Georgianna. She felt thoroughly unhappy about receiving her confidences when she herself was acting deceitfully, lying about her name and her reason for being in Paris.

'Chantel, I'm sorry, but I'm going to have to disillusion you, too,' she said, deciding to come clean before she got in any deeper. 'You see, I lied. I'm not a model at all, and my name isn't Arabella Hamilton. I'm —'

'You're Georgianna Randolph,' Chantel astonished her by saying. 'I thought so the moment I saw you in the lobby this morning, but then when you gave me that story about being Arabella, for a while I wasn't sure.'

'How did you recognise me?' Georgie asked, dismayed that her cover was so easy to penetrate.

'Don't look so scared. It's not that you're notorious or anything, but Mom has a passion for glossy magazines. She takes all the imported British fashion and society titles — she says it's professional interest in models today, but we think she's a closet royalist. Anyway, she just loves to read all about the private lives of the British aristocracy in the society pages of *Harper's* and *Tatler*, and one day I caught her deep in an article about your family. There was a picture of you with your mother and grandmother, and a story about how they've restored your family home. What's it called . . .?'

'Courtney Park,' Georgianna said, and a wave of homesickness for the house and her parents rolled over her.

'I told you everything,' Chantel reminded her. 'Now it's your turn.'

She was a good listener, neither condemning Dexter for his hard line with Courtney nor condoning it. 'And is your brother getting better now?' she asked finally when Georgie's story was told.

'A little. They've stopped tranquillising him so heavily, but that's worse for him in a way because now he can feel and remember what he's missing. I hate seeing him like that. He used to be such good fun. Chantel, promise me, word of honour, you won't breathe a word of this to anyone — not even your mother. If word got out to Daddy it would be ruin for Court.'

'I promise. Could you maybe use some company on your next visit?' Chantel offered tentatively. 'If the Clinic allows it, I'd be happy to go with you.'

'It's very good of you, but I couldn't possibly ...'

'You know what you sound like, Georgie?'

'Arabella, please, when there's company. No, what do I sound like?'

'A whingeing Pom,' Chantel said, mischievously echoing her Australian mother. Linita Tyrone, a model in Sydney ... Georgie decided that when she returned home, she'd ask her father if the name was familiar.

That afternoon was the first of many outings for the two girls. Chantel had a few friends in Paris, American college acquaintances mainly, but tactfully kept them away from Georgie in case their mothers too might have a weakness for imported English magazines.

'You see, it's very important that absolutely nobody learns I'm in Paris,' Georgie reminded her over lunch at the Brasserie Lipp one day later the following week.

'Don't look now,' Chantel said through a mouthful of the restaurant's famous *choucroute*, 'but there's a real hunk sitting in the corner over there who can't take his eyes off you. Know him?'

Georgianna gazed apprehensively to her left. A man was sitting alone at a table, obviously waiting for somebody to join him. He was undeniably attractive and knew it, she decided. Who but a man vain of his startling good looks would have dressed from head to toe in the latest, starkest black Gaultier in the middle of the sweltering heat of July? He could carry off the extreme design, though, his pale blond hair and piercing silver eyes the only accent notes in a studiedly monochrome appearance. He looked — dangerous, Georgie reflected, then stiffened in surprise as she noticed the cameras ranged over the banquette beside him. *Paparazzo*, a sixth sense inside her screamed.

'Chantel, he's a photographer, and I think he's recognised me,' she hissed. 'Look, I've got to get away. Settle up will you, please, and I'll meet you back at the hotel.'

She thought she'd got away with it, threading her way quickly through the packed tables and speeding waiters towards the front door. She was almost clear. Only the glassed-in pavement tables to go . . .

'*Mademoiselle, mademoiselle, je vous supplie! Je suis photographe —*'

Georgianna looked back over her shoulder and saw the photographer hurrying after her, Nikon slung around his neck. 'No,' she shouted. 'Leave me alone.' Fear lent wings to her feet. She was outside and running down the Boulevard Saint-Germain before her pursuer could speak again.

'Chantel, thank goodness! Heavens, you must have raided a florist's. Where did you get those roses?'

'*I* didn't get so much as a daisy,' her friend said ruefully. 'Here, these are for you, a peace-offering for an interrupted lunch.'

'Who from?' Georgie said suspiciously.

'Christian Neggar, fashion photographer. Here's his card.' And Chantel pointed to the printed card neatly sellotaped to the cellophane covering the dozen perfect white roses in Georgianna's arms.

'Oh God, you didn't talk to him!' she said despairingly. 'This "fashion" photography is just an excuse.'

'Cool it, can't you? First, he is for sure who he says he is. Mom and her magazines, remember? Christian Neggar's fashion photography is getting to be as famous as

Avedon's or Bailey's. Here, he sent this for you to take a look at.'

Chantel produced the latest issue of French *Elle* and flicked through it till she found a sequence of arresting images: a sinuous black girl in a Cleopatra wig modelled swimwear against a white marble floor, while beside her, and once actually against her smooth chocolate brown skin, exotically patterned snakes writhed and undulated. The most terrifying shot of all was of the girl on hands and knees wearing a silver lamé haltertop swimsuit, seemingly eye to eye with a Giant King Cobra poised to strike.

'It's behind glass,' Chantel said knowledgeably. 'Christian explained to me exactly how they did it. Three seconds later, and the screen was covered in venom, apparently.'

Georgianna shuddered. 'They're terrific photographs, but I don't see what any of this has to do with me.'

'Work and money, sweetest, that's what.'

'But I don't need either.'

'Georgianna Randolph may not, but when Christian Neggar asked me who you were, I naturally told him Arabella Hamilton, aspiring fashion model — well, what other story did I have? It's not my fault he's looking for a new face for his next assignment and thinks you'd be just perfect. You'll have to do it, otherwise you've blown your cover.'

'At first I said no,' Georgianna told Courtney on her visit to him the next day. 'I don't know why he thinks I could model.

'You're beautiful, Sis, and Neggar must be able to show you exactly what he wants or he wouldn't risk using you. He's a professional, so he wouldn't have approached a total amateur like you unless he was confident of the result.'

'Thanks for that total amateur! Just what I needed.'

'I also called you beautiful, remember, and there's quite

451

a few other things while we're on the subject: generous, loving, concerned, forgiving ... I've given you a lot to forgive in the last few months, haven't I, and I'm truly sorry.'

'Stop it, Court. You're embarrassing me.' She squeezed his hand gently. 'There's no need to apologise. It's enough just to see you like this again.'

The last week had brought a dramatic improvement. Courtney's initial distress and antagonism at finding himself in a bare hospital room had been hard to witness, but over the last few weeks he had become fit enough to attend the Clinic's group therapy sessions. Regular attendance at these, and progress in his individual counselling, had earned him a series of 'rewards'. He was now wearing his own clothes instead of a white hospital gown and had a new, much better furnished room on the ground floor, overlooking the hospital garden.

'There's one thing about taking this job, though,' Georgie said tentatively. 'It means I'll have to be out of town on Thursday, the next visiting day. I hate to think of you alone on visiting day.'

'I needn't be, if you'd ask your friend Chantel to come in. I liked her a lot when you brought her before.'

Georgianna stared at him. 'You seem to be making giant strides!'

Courtney grinned. 'She's fun, she makes me laugh and I can talk to her almost as easily as I can to you.'

'And your interest in her has nothing whatsoever to do with the fact that she's stunningly pretty, I suppose?'

'Well, I wouldn't say that.'

After they'd exhausted the topic of Chantel, 'Did Mums reach you last night?' he asked.

'No, we were out till late celebrating my first modelling assignment. Any news from home?'

'Scandal more like! Guess who's taken up polo-watching in a big way?'

'Mummy's started going to polo?'

'No. Our beloved Aunt Sloane has just realised what she's been missing. Or rather who.'

'Sorry, but I don't understand.'

'Who but my old friend Nicky recently crossed Sloane's path? Mums says he came to the house just after you'd left for France. Sloane bumped into him, liked what she saw, and before he knew it poor old Uncle Xan was squiring her to the next meeting at Cowdray Park. Now she goes on her own regularly, apparently, and there's always a "party in town" afterwards. Sometimes it lasts for days, apparently. Mums was cock-a-hoop about it.'

'Yes, but poor Xan.'

'You don't suppose it's the first time, do you?'

'No, but —'

It had never been Nicolas before ... Georgianna realised with surprise that she was annoyed to hear of the unholy alliance, less for the pain it might cause her uncle than for the distinct feeling of jealousy it aroused in her.

Christian Neggar had told Georgianna she would be picked up from L'Hôtel at nine the next morning. She was ready for eight-thirty. By ten she was beginning to think she'd misunderstood the arrangements. By just before eleven, she was furious. Then the desk clerk rang to say that a gentleman was waiting for her downstairs and that he'd appreciate her hurrying. Two hours late himself, and he expected *her* to rush after him!

There was no sign of Christian in the lobby, but as Georgianna stood by the lift, case in hand, a slight, red-haired young man swooped down on her.

'Angel! You really did pack the mimimum. *Wicked* old Gilles kept me waiting for *hours* while he got his bag of tricks together.'

'But where's Christian? I thought he'd be taking me?'

The redhead smiled maliciously. 'Oh, the mean old editrice of *Le Style* doesn't run to plane-fares for the likes of us. Gilles — he's make-up and hair, very versatile — the model and Christian's invaluable assistant — yours truly — must motor down in advance while His Nibs and the fashion editor fly later today.'

'Oh, I see,' Georgianna said, receiving her first valuable lesson in the hierarchy of the fashion world. 'You're not French, are you?' she commented.

'And you're frightfully quick on the uptake, love! But unless we fly, *les cops* will get tough with Gilles, and let's not give him the satisfaction.'

The desk clerk looked sadly after them as they left reception. He'd hoped that Georgianna would meet a man, not a *pédéraste*.

Gilles proved to be perfectly pleasant if a slightly one-track conversationalist. He was a little wizened man of fifty or so, sitting in the back of the white Citroën outside surrounded by innumerable suitcases, towels and travelling bags.

'Bonjour, Arabella. You have the lovely 'airs. Roger' — pronounced as in Thesaurus, Georgianna noticed with amusement — 'Arabella sits with you and I study her 'airs on the journey.'

'Roger Heathcoat-Smith, dear,' the driver introduced himself finally as they pulled suicidally out in front of a container truck. 'Christian thought it would be classy to have an English assistant. I've been with him for six years now, and it don't seem a day over ten.'

Georgianna became uncomfortably aware of a soft stroking sensation against the back of her head and instinctively sat up straighter. Gilles tut-tutted in annoyance and yanked her head back again. 'Sit still, silly girl. This is work, not a pleasure, I assure you. I have to assess the 'airs, decide what must be done with them. Tell me, have you used colour lately?'

'Certainly not.'

'Ah, that is the problem. When we arrive, the 'ighlights, then a mud pack, lash dye, manicure ... Better sleep now.

We're going to be very busy.'

She slept, and when they reached the hotel, a charming creeper-clad old inn in the hills above Grasse, later that evening, she was glad she had. She was not permitted time even to unpack her bag. Gilles needed two hours to colour her hair and they would not eat until Christian arrived.

Gilles converted his bathroom into an impromptu salon, and sat Georgie, swathed in a voluminous lilac gown, on a chair by the washbasin while he began mixing strong-smelling chemicals in a succession of plastic pots. Roger was put to tearing a roll of cooking-foil into broad strips. When what felt like hundreds of fine strands of hair had been painstakingly separated, coated in dye then folded into foil parcels, Roger went off for a nice lie-down and Gilles busied himself slapping mud all over her face and neck, giving her a manicure, a pedicure, a half-leg wax ...

He was almost finished when Roger stuck his head around the door and announced dramatically: 'Guess what? Christian and Marie-Jeanne have been unavoidably detained. They're going to be very, very late and we're not to wait up for them.'

Gilles grunted but seemed unperturbed. Roger was obviously delighted. 'Goodie. That means I can order whatever wine I like for dinner without old fishface reminding me with every mouthful that *Le Style* is picking up the tab. What do you say to a nice Grand-Cantenac, Gilles?'

'*Parfait!* We'll be another hour here, and then I'll change. It should be just right by then.'

The subtle hints of gold and copper that Gilles had skilfully woven into her own chestnut brown shade looked amazingly natural, Georgianna conceded when he had finished drying her hair with his fingers and a low-heat hairdryer. Then he made her stand while he painstakingly trimmed two inches off the length before declaring himself satisfied — for the moment.

'In the morning, at five o'clock, you will come back here

and I will put in the curls,' he ordered. 'Now, you wish to eat with Roger and me?'

'Oh, in my room, I think, if it's possible,' she said. After three hours of Gilles's ministrations she was fit for nothing but a bath and then bed.

'Entrez!' Gilles, dapper in black Levis and a Marlon Brando tee-shirt, was irritatingly fresh and energetic when Georgianna crawled into his room at five minutes past five the next morning. Fortunately he did not expect her to speak while he began her make-up.

'Very light and fresh, he said,' he murmured thoughtfully.

If this was a light make-up, Georgianna thought resentfully thirty back-aching minutes later, after she had looked up, looked down, sat immobile, eyes fixed on the ceiling, tossed her head, pursed her lips . . .

'*Et voilà,*' Gilles announced after painting on the fourth shade of lipstick and fixing it with sticky gloss.

Georgianna was just about to return to her room, hopeful of summoning some coffee before they set out, when Christian came in.

His eyes widened appreciatively as he took in every detail of her appearance. '*Chérie*, how beautiful you look,' he told her. 'I was desolate not to have seen you last night, but Toinette — Marie-Jeanne's editor — kept us hanging around for hours before we could get her to okay our ideas.'

'You mean, you don't just take the pictures then show them to her afterwards?'

He laughed aloud, eyes startlingly pale above a well-worn denim work-shirt.'You have so much to learn, Arabella. I can see it's going to be fun teaching you. You'll come in my car,' he told her. 'Gilles, ask Roger to bring Marie-Jeanne. I'll be taking a few Polaroids while we wait for you.'

By the first light of day they passed fields of roses, staked against poles and trellises as far as the eye could see. Their heady fragrance filled the car and Christian breathed in deeply.

'They're not all white, Arabella. You should only have white roses. But whenever I smell that perfume again, I shall think of you.'

From anyone else she would have thought the compliment stagey and insincere but in Christian's charming, lilting accent the words rang like a declaration. Georgianna blushed and looked down at her hands. Christian laughed, delighted. 'There's no need to be shy with me. That's why I brought you out alone, ahead of the others. We're about to do the most intimate thing in the world, you and I,' he told her. When her wide-eyed stare convinced him that he had her full attention, he continued: 'I don't mean make love. You don't need to be talented or beautiful to do that, and you and I, Arabella, are both those things.' He spoke matter-of-factly, eyes straight ahead on the road. 'Because we are talented and beautiful we can make magic with our photographs, we can make them speak. When the others arrive, let them do what they have to do but concentrate on *me*. Do what I tell you, and what you feel, and we'll have the greatest shoot Toinette has seen in years.'

He was pulling in beside an overgrown meadow as he spoke. They had left behind all the farmed flowers and chosen instead an expanse of waist-high grass in which pink willowherb and long-stemmed buttercups ran riot. In the background, like a solid red sea, hundreds of red poppies swayed in the early morning breeze.

'Just a few Polaroids to gauge the light and distance,' he said, fully professional. 'Stand there, looking half away from me. You're expecting someone to come around the corner at any moment ... Yes, that's it. Hold that. Good! Now, you're shy but you want me. Come on, Arabella, let me see how much.'

Georgianna stood still, at a loss. She ran her tongue

457

over dry lips, threw back her head and stared at him.

'No, too defiant, too harsh. You want me, remember? Try a smile.'

She tried, but it felt stiff and unconvincing.

'Loosen up, *chérie*. Here, try this.' Christian snatched up a buttercup and gently tickled her under the chin with it. She laughed and held out her hand for the flower but Christian crumpled it in his fist and dropped it, pulling her to him instead. Still laughing, she fell into his arms. The touch of his lips on her mouth was exquisitely light and soft but incredibly knowing. They kissed for a long time, Christian refusing to let her catch her breath, his own increasingly harsh and ragged. Finally he stood back from her, taking in her windswept hair, dilated eyes and mouth softened by kisses. 'That's perfect,' he said approvingly. 'Hold it right there.' He was still busily snapping when Roger's car drew up and a curvaceous blonde got out and strode purposefully towards them.

'Marie-Jeanne, at last you're here,' he said, ignoring her scowl. 'This is Arabella, our model. Arabella, meet Marie-Jeanne, fashion editor and stylist.'

'*Bonjour,*' Georgie said politely.

'You're English, aren't you?' the French girl said. 'It would be easier if we spoke in the language you understand. Christian, I want a word with you.'

'You can have two minutes, no more. We have to catch the light. Gilles, fix Arabella's make-up, will you? Roger, my films are loaded?'

'So far. Though at the rate you run through them —'

'Good. Then props, please. We'll start in a minute.'

Roger's task was to embellish the cornfield with more flowers, silk ones, Georgianna noticed with amusement. 'Aren't there enough already?' she asked, wincing as Gilles backcombed her hair and sprayed it with evil-smelling lacquer.

'Not enough colours,' he said briskly. 'Nature can always be improved upon, you know. What have you been

458

doing to your mouth? Gilles, her lipstick's crooked. Wonder why?' His archly lifted eyebrow made it quite plain that he knew why.

Georgie tried to change the subject. 'If we're just using a field and some silk flowers as a setting, why did we have to come so far from Paris? Wouldn't a field much nearer have worked just as well?'

'Of *course* not,' Roger protested vigorously. 'A field in Paris would have been nowhere near Christian's darling little home from home. You've seen it, I take it?'

'No.'

'You will, and before the day is out, or my name's not Mother Shipton. Look, Marie-Jeanne's waving to you.'

'I wonder what she wants?'

'Stick her knife in, I shouldn't wonder! It's all right, love, only teasing. Better get over there fast, though. Hates to be kept waiting, our Marie-Jeanne.'

The stylist had opened the boot of Roger's Citroën to reveal the clothes that Georgie was to model. Next spring's rural styles looked a rather flat and disappointing collection of pastels and floral prints with some authentic-looking smocked calico and obviously antique bits and pieces of lace-trimmed linen thrown in.

'Strip,' ordered Marie-Jeanne coldly, busily unbuttoning the back of a fine lawn blouse.

Georgianna involuntarily glanced over her shoulder at the three men not twenty feet away.

'Don't be absurd,' Marie-Jeanne snapped. 'Two of them couldn't care less if you walked around stark naked, and the other's seen better bodies by far, I can vouch for that.'

She glanced slyly down at her own pronounced curves and then disparagingly at Georgianna's slender figure in the boyish jeans and tee-shirt she had worn to travel to the shoot. There was no option but to change where they stood, Georgie realised, so stripped quickly to her bra and panties.

'That goes too,' Marie-Jeanne said, indicating her bra.

459

'Well, come on. We can't have it showing through the fabric, can we?'

'Aren't you ready yet?' Christian called. 'Come on, we've a lot to do before the light changes.'

Walking barefoot through the grass; sitting cross-legged in it, skirts hiked past her knees; weaving daisy chains, leaning indolently back against a gatepost, Georgianna concentrated only on Christian. She ignored Marie-Jeanne's waspish comments, the probably deliberate jab of a safety-pin which she was ostensibly using to secure the surplus fabric in a blouse. Gilles fussed over her 'airs and make-up, darting at her from time to time with a large brush charged with powder or a dangerous-looking tail comb, but it was only Christian she noticed. He was constantly on the move, altering an angle or a lens, adjusting the tripod, thrusting cameras into Roger's hands for reloading once a film was used up.

For the last few shots he asked Georgianna to lie back on the grass and look straight up at him while he took some head and shoulders studies for make-up credits. Accustomed by now to obeying him, she sank unprotestingly into the still damp grass, oblivious of the teeming insect life within it.

'Throw your arms back over your head,' he told her. 'You've been asleep, dreaming. Close your eyes. Now, open them again, slowly, slowly . . .'

She was glad to keep her eyes half-closed against the glare of the sun, higher in the sky by now. The vivid light cast a dazzling nimbus around Christian's silver-gilt hair as he stood over her, rapidly clicking off shot after shot. After their hours of working so closely, Georgianna felt she'd known him for ever.

'That's right, *chérie*,' he said, stepping so that he had one booted foot to each side of her narrow waist, and angling a shot straight down on to her upturned face. 'Come on, smile. And again. Beautiful! You're so beautiful. Now I can see what you'll look like when you've just made love.'

460

He stepped over her and dropped to his knees. Under cover of the long grass he leant down to kiss her. Her lips instinctively parted, and in an instant he was lying beside her in the damp, sweet-smelling grass. His hand came up to caress her breast and one knee slid expertly between hers, edging the full skirts of a white lawn dress higher up her thighs.

'That is a Martine Sitbon original, and if there are grass-stains on it *Le Style* will send you the bill,' a voice said from somewhere high above them.

Christian sat up and smiled disarmingly into Marie-Jeanne's set face. 'Sorry to keep you waiting.' He jumped to his feet and reached down to pull Georgie to hers. 'Arabella, give Marie-Jeanne her dress, then I'll drive you back to the hotel to pick up your things.'

'Will I have time for a shower before we set off for Paris?'

'Who said anything about Paris?' He draped an arm casually round her shoulders as they followed a stiff-backed Marie-Jeanne back to the Citroën. 'I though we might pay a visit to my farmhouse in the hills above St Trop. Have you visited the area before?'

'Never,' she lied.

'You'll love it.'

'What you see of it,' Roger murmured behind them.

Any minute now, thought Georgianna, stealing a glance at Christian's perfect profile as he steered his grey BMW around another hairpin bend in the road. Another minute, and I'm going to start feeling very frightened indeed.

They had been driving in silence for an hour. 'You don't mind if I don't talk while I drive, do you?' Christian had asked, and strangely she found that she didn't. Alone in a car after a bare few hours' acquaintance with any other man, she knew she would have felt uneasy, babbled to cover the awkward silence, but with Christian there was no

461

awkwardness, no need for words. After two meetings and a morning's work with him, Georgianna had accepted an invitation to visit his home, and an unspoken one to share his bed. Her only moment of nervousness came when they reached St Tropez and Christian started looking for a parking space.

'I thought you said your place was up in the hills?' Georgie said.

'It is, but there'll be no food there. After getting up with the birds, aren't you even a little hungry?'

'Not particularly.'

'So you'd rather not stop to have lunch?'

'Much,' she agreed quickly. The last thing she needed was for 'Arabella' to be recognised by one of Georgianna Randolph's chums. It was unlikely that many of them would be in St Tropez towards the beginning of August, the tourist month, but she felt it would be best to play safe and avoid the smarter restaurants.

'Perhaps you're right,' he agreed. 'We'll just pick up a few things to eat, then drive on to the house. Why waste time, after all?'

It was a relief to leave behind the streets of smartly painted houses and bars and the crowded harbour. As Christian's BMW left the town once more to climb into the cool green wooded hills above it, Georgianna breathed a sigh of relief. She was surprised when, after only ten minutes' driving, he drew up suddenly on a grass verge beneath an overhanging oak.

'I promised you flowers,' he explained, and slid out of the car to vanish into the roadside trees. A few minutes later he was back, clutching something in his hand. Georgie leant out of the car window to examine the perfect posy he had picked for her.

'Wood anemones,' he said as she exclaimed over the freshness and pallor of the lightly scented white flowers, delicately veined in green. 'I picked only a few,' he murmured. 'Like all things naturally beautiful, they are very rare.' He leant inside the car to brush their petals lightly against her cheek. Their fragrance seemed to fill the car as, for a long moment, Christian's mouth held hers prisoner. By the time they reached his house, her hand was damp and sticky from the flowers' sap.

He turned down a narrow unmetalled lane and drew up almost at once before a sprawling whitewashed building. Single-storey and built of rough local stone, it had the characteristic small shuttered windows of the district. Inside, however, it was far from typical. Accustomed as she was to beautiful interiors, Georgie could not remember seeing anything more right than the perfect blend of antique and contemporary style before her. Inside as well as out, the walls were whitewashed, their starkness relieved by the occasional exposed beam in bleached oak. A massive stone fireplace as old as the house was surmounted by a single particularly huge beam — 'From a ship,' Christian explained — from which hung bunches of dried flowers in the same colours of apricot and white as the room's loose covers and heavy quilted curtains. He strode rapidly towards the window, his footsteps echoing loudly against the pale honey-coloured tiles of the floor. He pulled a cord, and Georgianna gasped with delight. The curtains slid apart to reveal french doors which Christian immediately unlocked and threw open, allowing the scent of the lemon-trees in the small walled garden beyond to flood the room.

'Would you like to sunbathe?' he asked, gesturing outside.

Tempting though the garden looked, with its bougain-villaea-clad walls, dovecote and rickety trellis overhung with cottage roses, Georgie shook her head. 'Perhaps later. What I'd really love is a bath, if that's all right? It's been a very long morning, and I'm still wearing all that gunk on my face.'

Christian led her past a small open-plan kitchen and down a narrow corridor. The closed door they passed must be his bedroom, she guessed. There was a second door at the end of the corridor. He opened it and gestured for Georgianna to step inside. The bathroom was huge, almost the size of the sitting-room. It had the same honey-coloured local tiles on the floor, the same full-length apricot and white curtains at the window which Christian whisked aside to give another view on to the garden. A corner fireplace with logs invitingly arranged in it was another unusual feature, but the focal point of the room was an enormous circular sunken bath. He turned on the water and indicated the jacuzzi taps.

'Why don't you start without me? I'll bring in our things, and be in to join you in a few minutes.'

When he left the door open behind him, Georgianna wondered whether to shut it, then decided she was being absurd. 'He's seen hundreds of bodies better than yours,' Marie-Jeanne had told her only that morning. Georgianna had no doubt that was true. Christian had probably known and loved many women, and she had never supposed herself to be beautiful, but the memory of Marie-Jeanne's words thrilled rather than hurt her now. Christian had talked her into modelling for him, picked her out of a crowd and whisked her away from under Marie-Jeanne's supercilious nose. He knew the world's most beautiful women and yet he wanted her, and she was in no doubt that she wanted him.

Georgianna slid out of her dusty shirt and tight constricting jeans. Her wisp of a bra and pants soon joined the rest of her clothes on the bathroom's tiled floor. She rummaged in a well-stocked bathroom cabinet and poured a generous measure of gardenia-scented bath oil into the water. Swiftly she creamed off the heavy make-up and secured her hair in a white towelling bandeau. Then she stepped down into the bath and turned on the jacuzzi. She sank back into the warm whirling water, leaning her head against the bath's circular side and closing her eyes blissfully.

Christian came into the room silently on bare feet. For a

464

moment he stared expressionlessly at the smiling girl in the bath, and then began to undo his faded blue workshirt. The sound of it dropping to the floor was the first Georgianna knew of his presence. She opened her eyes and smiled at him. 'Are you coming in? It's fantastic.'

'In a minute. I'm enjoying the view from here.'

She was more lovely than he'd dared to hope, he decided, studying the graceful lines of her long limbs, the proud tilt of her long, slender neck and the small but deliciously rounded breasts.

'Like apples,' he said aloud, kneeling by the bath and reaching down to cup one as he spoke.

Georgianna sat perfectly still, leaning back against the side of the tub, legs splayed slightly apart by the thrust of the bubbling water beneath and around her. She glanced down at Christian's hand on her breast. It was a strong hand, sun-tanned and flecked with fine white-blond hairs. As his square-tipped fingers stroked and kneaded, she glanced sideways and saw the thick blond hair which covered his chest, found herself wondering what it would feel like against her skin — slightly rough and wiry, or fine and smooth as silk? In her imagination she could feel it exquisitely roughening her already sensitive nipples. There was warmth and welcome around and inside her, a liquid surge of pleasure as Christian's hand slid to her other breast.

'Stand up,' he said huskily. 'I want to see all of you.'

Her legs were shaking, though whether from desire or fear it was impossible to tell. Christian leant forward and snatched away the bandeau which bound her hair. The long chestnut mane tumbled down, sticking to her glistening foam-flecked skin. 'You're like a statue,' he murmured, 'so pale and perfect. Let me wash you.'

A bar of yellow soap lay close to hand in one of the bath's recesses. As Christian lathered it, a faint scent of lavender and honey hung in the steaming air, then his hands were upon her, soaping and caressing every contour of her body. He turned her away from him and started at her shoulders, his powerful hands teasing the last knots of tension from her neck and shoulderblades. Her breasts, already stimulated by his touch, ached pleasurably as his slippery, lather-coated hands circled them rhythmically, then moved downward to her ribcage, waist, the small of her back, the curve of her buttocks . . .

'Turn round.'

She could hardly stand, but she managed to turn. Instantly Christian knelt on the side of the bath. The lather stung slightly as he gently parted her slick pubic hair, then slid his fingers against her lips. His hand moved rapidly in a demanding circular movement. The sensation of heat and lather and Christian's fingers against her sensitive bud was almost unbearable. Georgie moaned and stumbled slightly in the hot silken water, but Christian shot out a hand to steady her without steadying the fierce rhythms of his other fingers against her quivering flesh. They were entering her now, gliding in a warm liquid welcome until — '*Chérie, tu es vierge?*' He slid away his hands and sat back on his heels.

Georgianna couldn't believe it. She couldn't be so unlucky a second time! Mutely, she nodded, afraid to speak in case she sobbed with frustration.

'There's no need to be afraid.' He stood up, hands fumbling urgently with his fly-fronted jeans. His unmistakable erection strained to be free of the tight blue denim. In his urgency to free himself, a button was wrenched off and hit the floor with a metallic sound. He peeled off his jeans and minuscule white briefs and plunged into the bath.

She was more than ready for him. As he sank into the foam and guided her astride him, his fingers brought her to such a peak of ecstasy that she barely noticed his sharp downward tug on her waist. There was pressure for a moment and then he was fully inside her, pumping and shivering in an ecstasy as violent as her own.

'Christian,' she breathed, cradling his blond head to her

466

wet breast when their trembling had ceased.

'Little Arabella, how does it feel to be an ex-virgin?'

'Wonderful.'

'And I didn't hurt you?'

'Of course not.'

'Let me see. *Chérie*, you're bleeding.'

She kissed him. 'It's nothing, really.'

'You must go to bed at once. I'll bring some champagne and we can —'

'Lose my virginity all over again?'

Christian kissed her for the first time. 'It's gone. There's no going back.'

'I wouldn't want to,' she said truthfully. 'Now that I have you.'

They spent a long lazy afternoon and evening drinking champagne, picnicking in bed, or just lying quietly beneath Christian's ice-blue sheets, wrapped in one another's arms.

When she awoke the next morning, he was not in bed, or in the bathroom, or the sitting-room.

'Christian,' she called anxiously.

For the first time she noticed a third door, leading from the kitchen into what was obviously a converted outhouse or deep pantry. After a few minutes he appeared through it, triumphantly waving a piece of paper.

'They're even better than I'd dared to hope,' he said.

'What are?'

'Your photographs, of course. I couldn't wait to see them, so I left you sleeping. Forgive me?'

'Of course. Let me see.'

'Don't touch! The contacts are still wet. Let me put them down on the counter, then we can see how beautiful you are.'

Georgianna examined the rows of tiny 2 by 2-inch shots of herself for a full ten seconds before announcing that she was hungry.

'Coffee's there,' Christian said, pointing to a blue earthenware jar. 'Make me some, too, will you? There's some bread and fruit from yesterday. When you've eaten, we'll be on our way.'

'Where are we going?' Georgie asked blankly. It was another flawless day, and she'd envisaged sunbathing in Christian's garden, then a drive out to one of the quieter beaches. Later, drinks and dinner in one of the smaller hillside villages, away from the jet set's beaten track.

'Back to Paris, of course,' he said surprised. 'If I don't deliver these tonight, Toinette will string me up.'

'You have to work on a Saturday night?' Georgie said incredulously.

'Oh, I wouldn't call Toinette work — more my bread and butter. She's the editor of *Le Style* and a very important lady.' He saw her crestfallen expression, 'Come here, *chérie*, and I'll explain.' He wrapped his arms round her and rocked her. 'I'm a freelance photographer, which means I rely for work on the goodwill of a handful of highly influential, temperamental people in the fashion field. Toinette Mercier gives me some of my best and highest-paying jobs. She's a workaholic herself — lives, eats, and breathes fashion. Since she works every day of the week, she sees no reason why her contributors should not also. I want to work for *Le Style*, so I go along with it. You'll have to as well, once we've got you launched.'

'Do you really think other people will want to use me?'

'They'll stop at nothing once they see these shots. In fact, I think it would be a good idea for you to get an agent right away. When we get to Paris, I'll call Kitty and she can get in touch with you at L'Hôtel. Yes, she owes me a favour or two ... Now, come on and move that lovely butt of yours. We've got work to do.'

'So when are you seeing him again?' Chantel demanded, after listening spellbound to an edited account of Georgie's first assignment and its aftermath.

'He said he'd call me.'

'When. Tonight, tomorrow, a week next Tuesday? When's he going to call you?'

'Tonight, I suppose.'

'What time tonight?'

'Oh, I don't know. Does it matter? I'll be in anyway.'

'Hair-washing night, I suppose? Oh, come on, Georgie. The gang's going to the Café Flore tonight and I hoped my famous model friend Arabella might come along too. They're dying to meet you.'

'It's sweet of you, Chantel, but I really do feel like an early night.'

Chantel wasn't fooled. She knew very well that if Christian were to phone, Georgie would be dressed to kill and ready to party all night at a few minutes' notice. But somehow, from her slightly wider experience of men, she doubted he'd be calling that night.

Georgianna stayed in all the next day, and it was only with difficulty that Chantel got her out to the Malmasion Clinic the next afternoon. But she was glad she had made the effort when she saw the progress Courtney had made in only a week. His skin was clear and tanned, and after learning that the clinic had its own small gym, he had begun a fitness programme, the results of which already showed. He was keen to hear every detail of Georgianna's modelling trip that she would reveal, and guessed the rest.

'He'd better be good to my little sister, this Christian Neggar, or I'll take care of him,' he joked, flexing newly-developed biceps. Even Georgie, despite her sadness that Christian had not rung, managed a smile. Chantel grabbed his hand playfully, intent on proving she could still beat him at arm-wrestling any day. When the laughter had died down and the conversation turned to Camilla and the latest news from Courtney Park, Chantel and her brother still held hands, Georgie noticed with a pang. Where, oh where, was Christian, and why had he not contacted her?

★

469

'There were three calls for you, mam'selle,' Albert the desk clerk announced as the girls reached L'Hôtel later that afternoon. 'All from the same person.'

Georgianna almost snatched the messages from his hand and was bitterly disappointed to read only: 'Call Kitty' and a Paris number.

'From Christian?' Chantel asked.

'No, someone called Kitty. I don't even know a Kitty. It's probably a mistake.'

But when she dialled the number and gave her name, there was no mistaking the reaction at the other end of the line.

'At last!' a strident voice exclaimed. 'Arabella, I've seen the Grasse shoot and we have *got* to meet. Can you get round here this afternoon?'

'I'm sorry,' a bewildered Georgianna replied. 'but who are you, and why should we meet?'

'Oh, I thought Christian had explained to you, love. I'm a model's agent, best in Paris though I say it myself, and you need representation. Christian says you're going to be big, and that boy's got a nose like a truffle hound. Got a pencil? Okay, I'm at Avenue Franklin Roosevelt. Hawk's Agency. Where are you?'

'L'Hôtel.'

'Slumming it in style, I see. Okay, see you in half an hour. 'Bye.'

In the anteroom to the agent's offices, two strikingly attractive girls, one black and one white, were gabbling into phones in rapid-fire French while simultaneously flicking through loose-leaf folders of photographs and consulting charts featuring lists of girls' names. When the black girl spotted Georgianna standing nervously in the doorway, she put down the phone with a peremptory '*Attends un moment*', and snapped, '*Oui. Vous avez une entrevue?*'

470

'Yes — I mean, *oui. Je suis Georg- Arabella.*'

'*Madame vous attend. Avancez.*'

The girl gestured curtly towards double doors painted palest green, then resumed her conversation over the phone.

In her latest Maud Frizon stilettos, Kitty Hawk was a striking six foot. With her long glossy ash-blonde hair, jutting cheekbones, the lean Borzoi lines of her worked-out, played-out body, she looked every inch the top Parisian model she had been in the sixties and early seventies. When she opened her mouth, she was pure White-chapel. 'Park your bum, love,' she said, gesturing towards a thirties tub chair. She continued a phone conversation in execrable French, but her round china-blue eyes studied Georgianna minutely while she continued to speak fast and persuasively. '*Oui, oui. Je t'assure . . . Elle est actuellement ici en ce moment . . . J'en suis sûre . . . Jeudi, oui, chez Christian. Oui, merci. A bientôt, Toinette.*'

She slammed down the receiver and got to her feet in one fluid movement, stalking around her curved blond-wood Art Déco desk. Feeling distinctly at a disadvantage in her low chair, Georgie glanced up apprehensively. Without a word, Kitty reached out one long exquisitely manicured hand and tilted up Georgianna's chin.

Half-embarrassed and half-afraid, she looked the Amazon straight in the eye and said, 'If you'd like me to tilt my head, you've only to say so. It's not necessary to touch me, surely?'

Kitty's eyes narrowed incredulously for a moment. Who did the little bitch think she was? Did she want to work or didn't she? Then her sharp eyes took in the unmistakable lines of Georgie's simple stone-coloured gabardine dress — this season's Ferre unless she was very much mistaken — and the flawless black pearls of her earrings, discreetly diamond set. She bit back a very pithy retort and slowly relinquished her hold on the girl's proudly tilted chin. From the quiet confidence with which she spoke, and the

471

grace with which she wore her designer clothes, this girl didn't need to work at all.

Her height, the set of her head and shoulders and the strong, clean lines of her chin and jaw gave her the usual don't-give-a-damn fashion model's air, but the thick-lashed liquid brown eyes told a different story, revealing the almost unique blend of innocence and arrogance which had permitted her to address Paris's foremost modelling agent so brusquely.

'Sorry, love,' Kitty said, and only she knew how rare such an apology was. 'Just had to check for myself that you lived up to all those luscious photographs Christian's been touting around. That boy's got more tricks than a barrel-load of monkeys when it comes to disguising a girl's bad points, bless him. But he really didn't have to try with you, did he? So, you want to be a model ...'

She was about to launch into her usual spiel: about the hard work, uncertain rewards, short lifespan and willingness to hand over 15 per cent of all fees, whether a job had been negotiated by her agency or not, when Georgianna stopped her in her tracks.

'Not really, Miss Hawk. I mean, it was wonderful working with Christian, but ...'

'So all my girls tell me,' Kitty murmured caustically.

'... in the end, it's tiring, rather dull, work and I'm not sure I really like people painting my face and pinning me into clothes as if I'm some life-size doll.'

'Struth! Agent's contract or not, Kitty had just committed her to two further sessions for *Le Style* and already there'd been a couple of breezy phone calls from particularly *branché* fashion and art editors who obviously bribed the right people in *Le Style's* art department and had heard all about the stunning new English model. But gently did it. Sybil Hammerstein, aka Kitty Hawk, hadn't gone from Old Chapel Street to Avenue Franklin Roosevelt without learning to think on her feet. Her face remained inscrutable as she thought rapidly, and then — of course!

472

Christian, with whom it had been wonderful . . .

'This is terrible, love. He's going to be devastated,' she said, managing to sound sympathetic but resigned.

'Who is?'

'Christian, of course. Who else do you think put me on to you? Didn't he tell you he was going to contact me on your behalf?'

'Oh, yes, now I think about it I do remember him saying something about a Kitty.'

Kitty drew in her breath sharply. Christ, the little cow was making her sound like some fleabitten old moggie! '*The* Kitty, though I say it myself,' she said with a touch of asperity. 'This is the best modelling agency in Paris. The two girls outside are my bookers, fixing for our girls to work for newspapers, magazines, advertising, catalogues — some of them even make it into films. Christian's so excited about you. He talked to me on Saturday at —' just in time she stopped herself from saying "Toinette's party" — 'ten at night, just raving about you. He thinks you deserve the best representation, and of course he's mad to work with you again.'

The instantaneous softening of the girl's expression, the sparkle in her eyes, told Kitty that once again she'd played a trump card. Miss Fancy Pants had obviously been on the receiving end of Neggar's famous telescopic lens and was panting for more. Well, there was no accounting for taste.

'In fact,' Kitty weighed in regretfully, 'Christian did tell me that he hoped very much to work with you later this week when he gets back from his Moroccan trip.'

'He's in Morocco? That explains it.'

Didn't call her, I suppose, the agent was shrewdly deciding. Christ, some of the cock-stricken cows wouldn't recognise the brush-off from a broom. Too busy concentrating on the other end . . .

She smiled kindly. 'Yes, the poor boy was called out on an assignment at the last minute.' It was a lie, but the girl would never know it. 'He's back in a day or two — I expect he'll give you a call then.' Or would do if Kitty Hawk had anything to do with it. That first shoot for *Le Style* had been sensational, and it was in no one's interests for Arabella to tire of modelling before it tired of her. 'But, of course, if you think you're not really cut out for the work ...'

Georgianna was stung, as Kitty had intended her to be, and the news about Christian had buoyed her up so high that she said airily, 'Oh, it has its compensations, I suppose. I wouldn't mind the life for a month or two.'

Kitty hoped it would be a bit longer than that but said nothing, swiftly pulling out a drawer of her desk in which she stored the standard contract form between herself and her 'girls'.

'If you wouldn't mind signing that for me, love, just to put things on a proper business footing between us,' she said with a wide smile. 'And fill in your personal details too, would you? Celeste or Rachelle will give you a call later with the details on Thursday, and the editor of *Le Style* did mention to me there might be more work on the way.'

Afterwards Georgianna found herself escorted to the double doors and given a rather lingering kiss on either cheek in front of the bookers in the outer office. She didn't care. Christian was coming back soon and he wanted to see her again.

He called her on Wednesday afternoon. At the sound of his voice, she was so breathless she could hardly speak. 'At last,' was all she managed to say.

'Missed me?' His low laughter brought her out in goose pimples.

'So much. How did the shoot go? Kitty explained you'd been called away at short notice.'

'What? Oh — yes. It went well, but not so well as ours. Toinette was delighted with it. You know she wants you for tomorrow?'

'Yes, Rachelle called with the arrangements, so I'll see you at ten unless —'

'That's just why I'm calling. Will you come out tonight? There's a launch for a new group at Régine's tonight. Everyone will be there and it will be good for you to be seen around.'

'Sounds great.' Actually it sounded dire, but she'd have dressed up and smiled and danced at a village hop if Christian were to be there.

'I'll pick you up at eight,' he said. 'Dinner first, then we'll go on. See you later.'

'I can't wait.'

As soon as she put down the receiver, Georgianna looked at her watch. Her hair and make-up would take an hour and a half, which meant she had two hours to scour the boutiques for the perfect dress.

She seldom wore red. Grandmama had always said it was not a colour for a lady and certainly not for a young girl, but she was a woman now, and tonight she wanted her man to see her at her most desirable. In Karl Lagerfield's shop, an assistant produced a sensational scarlet gown. Its plunging bodice, supported by narrow shoestring straps, just barely covered her nipples and was entirely covered in thousands of tiny bugle beads. The softly draped tulle skirts frothed to calf-length, and the assistant produced red velvet shoes and a clutch bag to match. She was instructed to wear pale flesh-coloured silk stockings, and to keep her hair loose.

Later, descending to the foyer after receiving Albert's summons, Georgie was glad she had followed Chantel's advice not to take a wrap. Christian stood motionless, staring, for several moments too long as the lift doors opened to reveal her, then swept her into his arms. He'd omitted to shave, she realised, but revelled in the roughness of his beard against her skin, the smooth silkiness of his newly-washed hair beneath her fingers.

'That dress is a marvel on you,' he said, at last releasing

her, to the relief of Albert who was beginning to fear for the dignity of the hotel. 'That particular shade of blood red ... So many people try to wear it, and so few succeed. I shall have to watch you closely tonight, or someone will steal you from me.'

But Georgianna had eyes for no one but him. In the downstairs bar of Laserre the beautiful girl in the red dress caused a sensation. Christian noticed and revelled in the buzz of appreciation around them, but Georgianna, floating on a cloud of champagne and happiness, remained oblivious.

Later, in a club filled with spectacular women and their less spectacular escorts, she attracted dozens of speculative glances. Christian was obviously a favoured club member. He secured a table next to the dance floor and his own bottle of whisky was brought to him immediately, together with Georgianna's glass of champagne. The playing of the promoted record was mercifully brief, and the leather-clad group called a halt to the photo session after ten minutes. Seeing a posse of celebrity-hunting photographers beginning to range the tables, Georgianna got hurriedly to her feet and made her excuses. On her return from the powder-room, she found that her seat at their table had been taken by a strikingly attractive girl in an abbreviated silver lamé skirt and jacket. Like the fairy on a Christmas tree, she decided, and at the table stood pointedly beside her former seat.

Christian jumped to his feet immediately. 'Take mine. But first, let me introduce you to Karen. She's one of Kitty's girls, too. Karen, this is Arabella.'

'Glad to know you,' the girl said in a Texan drawl. 'Maybe we can get together sometime. I know *we* will,' she said with a smile for Christian. 'But I got to go now. My A-rab's giving me the evil eye. Be seeing you.'

Without a backward glance for Georgianna, she uncrossed her perfect silver-clad legs and crossed the dance floor to a table occupied by a group of four or five white-dressed and bearded men.

'I wonder how she knows which one is hers,' Georgianna mused. 'Not that it would matter to her, I suppose.'

Christian laughed. 'I love it when you're jealous,' he teased. 'Come and dance with me. It's too long since I held you in my arms.'

He danced as expertly as he made love, drawing Georgianna's hips into tantalising contact with his own. She danced in a dreamy silence, head resting against his shoulder. After a while, she had no idea how long, he led her back to their table, ordered more champagne and tried to interest her in their fellow guests. The Eurasian model in the white Armani dress had just been offered a six-figure TV ad; the bearded man in the white tux was Marc Stein, the second-best photographer in town; the elderly man with the cigar and the gold-framed glasses . . .

But Georgie wasn't really interested. 'It's getting late,' she hinted.

He glanced at his watch. 'So it is, and you're on call at ten. We'd better go home.'

But on their way out of the club, they were separated by a sudden influx of new arrivals. Glancing back over her shoulder, Georgie saw that Christian had been waylaid by a raven-haired girl whose generous curves were barely covered by a too small pink velvet *bustier*. She had her hand on Christian's arm and kept laughing and throwing back her head in between talking fast and eagerly. Noticing Georgie, Christian said something to the woman, kissed her casually and pressed through the throng.

'Another model?' Georgie asked, raising one eyebrow.

'Does she look like one? No, that's Chloe. She lives in one of the flats below mine. She's always inviting me to parties and dinners at her place, but what can you do when it's a neighbour?' He shrugged, and Georgie felt a momentary pang of sympathy for the girl, for all the girls who were attracted to Christian but couldn't have him because he was hers.

'Are we going to the studio?' she asked as they waited for his car to be brought round.

He looked at her in surprise. '*We* are going nowhere. *You* are going back to L'Hôtel.'

'But, Christian!'

He put both hands on her waist and pulled her towards him, speaking slowly and firmly. 'No buts. There is the small matter of a modelling session tomorrow, remember? You shouldn't have been out this late, as it is. It was selfish of me to ask you.'

'But I wanted to see you.' she said, moving gently against him to let him know how much.

'And I to see you. But now you must sleep, or tomorrow there'll be dark shadows under your eyes and *Le Style* will blame me.'

He gently disengaged her arms which she had slid round his waist, frowning to feel how cold they were.

'Tomorrow night,' she persisted, heedless of the cold.

'Perhaps. Here, put this on.' His jacket was warm and smelt deliciously of his cologne. Christian was smiling at the absurd picture she presented, the jacket dangling down to her knees over the exquisite dress, sleeves scraping her knuckles, when the car jockey brought round his BMW. He slid into the driver's seat as the attendant held the door for Georgianna, but the jacket restricted her movements and made her slow getting into the car. A horn tooted impatiently behind them and Georgie glanced over her shoulder to catch sight of the driver in a hurry.

'Isn't that your neighbour?' she asked idly. 'But she's only just arrived.'

'Shouldn't think so,' he said, adjusting the mirror. 'She drives a pink Porsche. Come on, we're holding everybody up.'

Georgianna climbed reluctantly into his car, and even more reluctantly out again, when they reached L'Hôtel. Albert was so delighted to see her safely home again, pressing the lift button and telling her how sensational the dress looked, that she managed to mask her disappointment and went smiling to her room. But for all Christian's good intentions in taking her home to sleep, she tossed and turned for a long time, burning for his touch and making do, finally, with her own.

'Where *have* you been?' Roger declaimed theatrically as he opened the studio door to her next morning.

'I'm sorry. At the last minute I couldn't get a taxi so I had to walk all the way. I'm only a quarter of an hour late, aren't I?'

'*Only* she says. Darling, when His Nibs is in one of his creative furies, fifteen minutes can be a lifetime, as you'll see for yourself,' he said, steering her into the brilliantly lit studio. 'Here she is, Christian,' he announced with desperate jollity. 'What's it to be — thirty lashes or ordeal by eyebrow tweezing?'

Christian materialised silently behind them, dramatic and slightly sinister today in a high-buttoned white shirt and baggy black suit.

'Darling, why so grim?' Georgie said immediately. 'You look like an undertaker.'

Roger groaned to himself. Arabella had so much to learn . . .

Face stiff with fury, Christian strode past her, refusing to kiss or even look at her. 'You're twenty minutes late,' he ground out over his shoulder. 'You're so careless and unprofessional you've kept a very expensive stylist and hairdresser waiting.'

Unfortunately Christian's dark mood seemed to have affected everyone in the studio. The stylist, a jolly plump girl called Michelle, spent fifty minutes supervising Georgie's make-up only for Christian to give it the thumbs down.

'Far too pale,' he said, scowling at her as if she was a stranger. 'She's meant to be a vamp, not a vampire. Start again, and try and get some life into her.'

Then her hair came under criticism. 'Too tame,' Christian decreed when Gilles showed him the neat waves he had painstakingly created. 'I want something wilder, more wanton. Look — like this.' He seized a handful of Georgie's long hair, screwed it up and squeezed it in his fist.

It took two hours for him to be satisfied with Georgianna's appearance, and then one of the lamps illuminating the set blew a bulb. Christian heaped coals of fire on Roger's head when it was discovered that they were out of spares.

While he went off to buy more, Philippe made sandwiches for everybody, but Georgie was not allowed to eat in case her make-up suffered. Christian retired to his office while the others ate in the dressing-room. Gilles lent Georgie his copy of the *Tatler*, and she tried to ignore the eating and drinking going on around her by concentrating on the 'Bystander' pages. Even in the depths of her misery at Christian's abominable mood she smiled to see a photograph of Sloane, overdressed as usual, at a charity ball, then frowned as she recognised her aunt's partner. Even three-quarters turned from the camera there was no mistaking the crisp black curls and regal bearing of Prince Nicolas of Malivia.

'If you can tear yourself away from your magazine, Arabella, we're waiting,' Christian called imperiously from the studio.

She slipped quickly into her first outfit, an oyster-coloured silk teddy over which the stylist slipped a diaphanous negligée in grey shadow lace. Pink marabou-trimmed slippers with Louis heels completed the look. Georgie stared wide-eyed at herself. In her opinion the combination of make-up, dishevelled hair and sensuous materials made her look tawdry and cheap, but when she hesitantly said as much to Christian, he snapped, 'Exactly! That's the effect we want — a divine slut, beauty *and* a beast. Now, sprawl on the bed. No — not like that! Get your legs wider, kick off one slipper. Michelle, Gilles, her nose is shiny. Do something about it, for heaven's sake.'

Georgianna lolled and pouted and sulked and simmered through a succession of abbreviated camisoles, cami-knickers, teddies, bras, and petticoats. The colours and fabrics were wonderful and the designs just this side of decent, but Georgianna hated the feel of this shoot. In his cold and angry mood, Christian seemed intent on photo-graphing a painted trollop, not a warm desirable woman. The others on the set were worried, too, she could tell. Out of the corner of her eye Georgie noted Gilles and Michelle frowning as they studied some Polaroids.

'Tilt your chin up,' Christian was calling to her. 'Wet your lips and look over your shoulder. Damn! It's still not right. You're supposed to be sexy, Arabella, not a fright-ened little rabbit. Slide that strap down.'

Georgianna knew that a certain degree of nudity was usual in fashion photography these days. She was modelling underwear, after all, and there was no real reason for her to feel embarrassed about baring a breast in front of the stylist or Christian's assistants, neither of whom were likely to be in the least interested. But the last time she had worked for Christian had been so different, *he* had been so different. Tears of humiliation and exhaustion swam in her eyes. It was four o'clock in the afternoon and she hadn't eaten all day. Her fingers felt cold and clumsy as she fumbled with the ribbon straps tied over one shoulder.

'Come on, come on, we haven't got all day,' Christian exclaimed.

A tear rolled out of one eye and cut through the heavy powder on her cheek. Georgie glanced at Christian appealingly, but he was crouching behind the camera, face lost to view.

'The bed's wrong,' he said impatiently. 'Michelle, put it right, can't you? What the hell are you being paid for? Get out of the way, Arabella. Are you stupid or something?'

She swung her legs over the side of the bed and tried to get up, but the bright lights all around seemed to intensify suddenly, stunning her with their force. She closed her eyes against the agonising jolt of pain in her head, and fell into darkness.

'Arabella, *chérie*, I'm so sorry. I had bad news today and I took it out on you.'

Georgie opened her eyes. She was lying on a bed, but a different one this time. There was a soft grey cashmere and fur blanket beneath her in place of rumpled silk sheets. In place of the harsh studio glare a couple of original Lalique glass table lamps bathed the room in a soft light. She noticed the stark grey walls, the floor-length red watered silk curtains drawn against the afternoon light and a magnificent red japanned dressing chest, the only notes of colour.

'Where am I?' she asked shakily. 'Did I faint?'

'I'm afraid you did, and it was my fault. We've brought you through to the flat to recover. Say you forgive me.'

Christian stretched out on the bed beside her and tentatively stroked her cheek. Georgie sighed deeply and pulled him towards her. He was so gentle with her; only the lightest of kisses on her lips and jawline and throat, a minimal pressure of his warm fingers against her lace-covered breasts and bare thighs. She moaned in response and tried to clasp him tighter, but Christian caught and held her hands, gently pressing them back over her head and imprisoning them in one of his. With his free hand he deftly untied the silk ribbons that supported the bodice of her filmy, butter-coloured silk camisole. The material slithered away from her shoulders. Christian bent his head to her breast and simultaneously slid his hand under the delicate fabric around her hips.

'That must be why they call them French knickers,' she said with a low laugh, then gasped with pleasure as his fingers slid inside her. Aware only of the circling movement of his tongue against her nipple and the intimate caress of his fingers, Georgie was deaf to the knocking on the bedroom door.

'Christian, is everything all right?' Roger's high-pitched voice enquired. After setting down the unconscious girl on his bed, His Nibs had told him to leave them alone together for ten minutes and not a second longer.

'Everything's fine,' Christian called. 'We'll be back in a few minutes, but tell Michelle and Gilles they can go now. Arabella looks just the way I want her.'

As Christian took the last shots, he felt that familiar tingle of excitement he recognised from his first shoot with Isabella Rossellini, or the session with Paloma Picasso for American *Vogue*. The second set of pictures of Arabella were winners, he was sure. Like all the best fashion photography, they showed more than just a beautiful girl in the latest clothes. The pictures told a story of tears and teasing and newly awakened sensuality. They were his best work of the year so far, and he was in a mood to be generous.

'Why not go through to the flat and relax?' he suggested to Georgie when they had finished. 'I'll have to supervise things in the dark-room for a while, but you could go through, have a drink or a shower. Whatever you like. I won't be long.'

Normally, he didn't allow a woman to stay unattended in his private apartment. Many women had visited it, of course, but always as players in the well-rehearsed ritual of Christian's private pleasures. They arrived, they did as he and they desired, and then they left. Those women were useful for only one reason, and the less he saw of them in between times, the better he liked it. Arabella was different. Gauche and inexperienced a model as she was, in the right circumstances she photographed like a dream. In a week or two she'd be a very hot property indeed, he knew. Eager fashion editors would be falling over themselves to book her, and if the latest modelling sensation asked only to be photographed by Neggar, they'd have to give in.

For a while, Georgie roamed the vast living area of Christian's private apartment. Like the rest of the loft, it was decorated in cool greys and ivory, with the by now familiar splashes of scarlet. At one end of the long narrow room a collection of magnificent eighteenth-century *sang de boeuf* porcelain was ranged on perspex shelving which was lit so cunningly that the great dishes and funerary urns seemed to hang in space. On the opposite wall hung a silky Persian rug, worn in places, but obviously a treasure. The rugs strewn about the polished floorboards were Eileen Grey originals, as was some of the stark simple furniture. She found the bathroom leading off Christian's bedroom. It was the same pristine white as the kitchen, but in a recessed cupboard she located a pile of thick scarlet Turkish towels and decided to take a shower.

He found her forty minutes later, curled up on his bed wearing nothing but a towel and brushing her hair with his silver-backed brush. 'I'm sorry, but when we started to develop the film the shots looked so marvellous I had to stay. Say you forgive me?'

'Show me how sexy you've made me look, and I'll think about it.'

'I'm sorry, my darling, but I can't. There was time only to make transparencies, not prints, and *Le Style* are waiting for them tonight. Roger has taken them round now. They'll be calling up in an hour or so.'

The telephone standing on the low lacquered table by his beside interrupted them. 'That can't be them already — Roger's only just left,' he said with a frown. 'Would you answer it for me, please? Unless it's Toinette or Marie-Jeanne from *Le Style*, get rid of them, will you?'

Georgianna lifted the receiver.

484

'Hello, Christian?' It was a woman's voice, and one she vaguely recognised.

'I'm sorry. He's not here at the moment. May I take a message for him?'

'Well, now, isn't that kind? Will you tell him that Karen called, and says she hasn't seen him for weeks — a month, in fact.'

'But we saw you only last night at Régine's — I'm Arabella Hamilton, remember?'

There was silence for a moment, and then low mocking laughter. 'Guess you're still very new on the scene, honey. Just give him my message, will you? He'll understand.'

'If you say so. 'Bye.'

''Bye, now.' Karen seemed still to be laughing as she put down the phone.

Georgianna said, puzzled, 'As you probably gathered, that was Karen. We saw her just last night, yet she asked me to tell you she hasn't seen you for a month.'

Christian shrugged and turned away. 'She's always so dramatic. Just one of the reasons I tired of her.'

Georgianna shivered slightly. His voice held only contempt when he spoke of the beautiful girl, though they had plainly once been lovers.

'You must be cold.' He slid a hand behind a tapestry which hung on one wall and the concealed entrance to a brightly lit dressing-room beyond slid open. He stepped inside and emerged with a long grey silk kimono that he handed to her. 'Put this on, and come and have a drink while I cook dinner,' he said.

She sipped chilled white burgundy while he prepared spit roast poussin, wild rice and a huge salad. She felt completely happy and at peace, just sitting watching the simple domestic scene. 'I'd never have guessed you were a cook,' she said with a smile.

He smiled widely. 'There's a lot about me you haven't guessed yet.' Later he produced a plate of cheeses and a second bottle of wine. Afterwards, he offered to make coffee.

Georgie shook her head. 'Thank you, Christian, but no. I know it's supposed to keep you awake, but I shan't need any tonight, not with you in my bed.'

He looked at his watch, an expression of surprise on his face. 'But it's still so early. I thought perhaps a club?'

'I've nothing to wear. And, besides, I'd rather be here with you. Come to bed, Christian.'

Georgianna peeled off the silk robe and lay back. He kicked off his shoes and lay beside her, still fully clothed.

Georgie giggled. 'Aren't you going to undress?'

'Do it for me.'

She was startled by the brusqueness of the command, but her hands moved obediently to unknot his tie and unbutton the stiff pearl buttons of his shirt. When she had pulled it off, she knelt beside him and ran her hands lightly over the thick blond hair of his chest. Christian groaned and pulled her down on top of him, crushing her to him for a moment before winding his hand into her hair and toppling her on to her back. He kissed her repeatedly on her neck and breasts while his hands roughly parted her legs.

Georgie was more than ready for him, but sensed that there was something wrong. 'Aren't you going to take these off?' she said, sliding one hand towards the waistband of his trousers.

He pushed it away. 'No need,' he said fiercely.

'No need?'

'It wouldn't do any good, not tonight. It's been a long day. That quarrel with *Vogue*, and I've drunk too much. It doesn't matter.'

'Yes, it does. Please, Christian. It will be all right, I know it.'

He looked at her for a moment, then stood up to take off the rest of his clothes. When he lay beside her, naked and perfect, she thought he was the most beautiful man she had ever seen. He was also completely unaroused.

'It happens,' he said dismissively. 'Another time it will be perfect, I promise.'

486

She was amazed and disappointed, particularly after the afternoon, but decided it would be kindest to say nothing. They lay in each other's arms until her lids began to droop.

'Shall we sleep?' he suggested.

She slid to her feet and he pulled back the heavy coverlet. Georgianna glanced down and gasped with surprise. Against one of the white lace-edged pillowcases lay a single gleaming black hair. Christian bent over the bed and brushed it away. 'It must be Maria's, the maid's. I'll speak to her about it in the morning.'

Reassured, she slid into bed. 'Well, while you are, better tell her not to use your hair-brushes either. The one I borrowed was full of black hairs.'

'Okay, I'll tell her. Good night, *chérie*.'

'Night, Christian.'

The evening had not turned out the way she had expected, but just being with him was happiness enough for one night.

The telephone woke them at half-past eight the next morning. Christian sat up in bed and groggily began a conversation in Italian.

'*Si, si. Quell'altra ragazza, capisco lo Faro'oggi?*'

His expression was stormy as he replaced the receiver and looked down at Georgie. 'That was Italian *Vogue*. It seems I'll be back in favour if I agree to a reshoot, using a different model — the publisher's girlfriend, apparently, and only sixteen years old. I *hate* working with those dumb kid models, but I'll have to do it to keep in with *Vogue*. It'll mean flying this afternoon. I'll have to reschedule two other sessions ... Damn!'

'Oh, Christian,' Georgie wailed at the prospect of another endless weekend without him. 'When will you be back?'

'Oh, Thursday, Friday ... it depends. We're doing

beauty shots, too. I'll give you a call as soon as I get back, I promise.'

'But what shall I do while you're away?'

Rachelle, Kitty Hawks' imperturbable booker, had the answer. Ten minutes later the phone rang again and Georgie picked it up as Christian was in the shower. An animated voice immediately greeted her by name.

'Arabella, hi! This is Rachelle at the agency. *Le Style* loved your latest, and word's really started to get around. *Elle* want to book you too — isn't that great? They've got a provisional for next Tuesday, and a new magazine, *Boom!*, very avant-garde, wants you for next Friday. It's terrific! I'm so pleased for you.'

'But — I don't understand. How did you know to find me here?'

'Oh, darling, *everyone* knows you're Christian Neggar's new *petite amie* — don't worry about it! At least it makes you easy to get hold of. Is he there? I could tip him off that *Le Style* and *Boom!* will be handing out some assignments.'

'He won't be here,' Georgianna realised, dismayed. 'He's got to go back to Morocco on a reshoot.'

'Oh, yes. We heard about that little disaster. Poor Christian. Never mind. I expect you'll get Marc for *Elle* at least. He's a sweetie to work for, so don't worry.'

Christian's eyes narrowed in annoyance when he emerged from the bathroom to hear about the two new sessions he couldn't bid for. Interest in Arabella seemed to be snowballing even quicker than he'd anticipated, and if he wasn't careful he'd lose even more lucrative jobs.

'I don't know how I'll manage without you,' Georgie said sadly. 'If you're not there to help me, I'll freeze up, I know. I wish you could always be my photographer.'

He remembered the pile of unpaid bills in his office, and wished it, too. 'Can't be helped this time,' he began, 'but there is something you could try.'

'What? Tell me.'

'After the session next week, have a word with Kitty.

Tell her you didn't feel happy with way they went — the photographers were rude to you, worked you too hard, anything you like. I could be wrong, Arabella, but I'm almost sure you're going to be very big, and if you really take off you could be in a position to name your own terms for a job — including the choice of photographer.'

'I'd ask for you every time, darling. But do you really think they'd listen?'

'Don't get your hopes up too high yet. See how many new bookings come in next week and what the response is to the new shoots. If it's good, speak to Kitty and see what she thinks. If I'm right about you, you could be on to a fortune.' He cupped her face in his hands and kissed it hungrily.

Georgie clung to him. She didn't need a fortune, she had one already, but she wanted to be a success for Christian, because he believed in her. She dressed and brought him coffee and orange juice while he packed, then followed him through to the studio where he began to sort through cameras and equipment, cursing Roger for being late that morning of all mornings.

'I'd better go,' she said sadly, seeing his preoccupied expression. 'I can tell you've got a lot to see to.'

'I'm sorry, but we'll be together next weekend, I promise. I'll come down with you — I must get some currency from the bank.'

On one of the several flights of stairs between Christian's loft and street level, he nodded good morning to a thin grey-haired woman shabbily dressed in a wraround pinafore.

'Who was that?' Georgie asked idly.

'Maria, my cleaner. She comes every day. I share her with Chloe.'

They had reached the street and Christian held open the door for her. Georgie looked puzzled. 'I thought Maria —'

He flagged down a cruising taxi and pulled her to him. 'One last kiss to remember you by.' It left her breathless and light-headed. She knew there was something she ought to be asking him, but he was busily instructing the cab-driver, paying him in advance. 'Take care of yourself. I'll call on Thursday or as soon as I can. Goodbye.'

Georgie waved to him as he stood staring after her taxi. Christian smiled, waved once and waited till the car was out of sight before hailing a second cab. He'd call Roger later with instructions to pick up their tickets and Moroccan dinars. Before they left, he had some other business to take care of.

Tuesday's assignment was another studio session. Georgianna posed before two stark backdrops, black while she modelled next summer's range of white garments, white to reflect her lean black-clad silhouette in the latest matador pants, short peplumed jackets and sinuous silk jersey dresses.

'It's minimal chic — streamlined and very cool,' the stylist explained. 'If you could look sort of bored, that would be great.'

Georgianna found she could co-operate effortlessly. Marc Stein, a slight, uncharismatic figure, made few demands on her. Christian had described him as the second-best photographer in Paris and, free by three o'clock, she decided he was definitely the quickest. Christian made so many more demands on her — in terms of time, energy, emotion — but working with him felt so much more worthwhile. Even with her limited experience she sensed that today's photographs, though no doubt professionally accomplished, would seem flat and dull in comparison to the two previous shoots with Christian. She would definitely speak to Kitty and see if they were in a position to make the use of Christian as photographer a condition of hiring Arabella to model.

On Wednesday morning, Chantel and Georgie drove out to the Malmaison Clinic to collect Courtney, who had been given a two-day parole. He was waiting impatiently for them in his room, a bulging overnight bag packed and ready by the door.

'Let's go!' he exclaimed the second they reached his room. 'I thought we'd have drinks at the Café de la Jatte, and did you book for lunch, Chantel?'

'Of course.'

'Okay, After that I'd like some new shirts — you can help choose those, Georgie — and I need music. That last collection of tapes you brought has just about worn through. And what are we doing tonight? Trying out Le Palace?'

Georgie sank on to his bed in mock exhaustion. 'Take it easy, Court! I'm a working model, remember? Two days of hectic socialising and I'll be a wreck that no one will want to photograph.'

'You could never be a wreck,' he said loyally. 'And I'm sure Christian agrees. When am I meeting him, by the way?'

'Not until tomorrow night, if then,' she said with a sigh. 'He's away on a job, I'm afraid, but he should ring me then.'

'Too bad, Georgie. You'll have to play gooseberry to Chantel and me. Now come on!' Courtney slung his overnight bag over his shoulder and seized each girl by the hand, pulling them after him down the hospital's long gleaming corridors.

Fortunately for Courtney, treatment at the Malmaison did not stipulate that patients should give up all stimulants, only controlled substances. His first night out was a Bacchanalian affair of drinks at the Ritz Bar, followed by dinner at Taillevent, then more drinks and dancing at Le Palace. Courtney seemed amazingly unaffected by the alcohol or the lateness of the hour, but by two o'clock both Georgie and Chantel were drooping.

'I won't come out with you tomorrow, Chantel,' Georgie said as Courtney was fetching their wraps. 'I mean, much as I love Court, I find more than one day of him totally exhausting when he's like this. And wouldn't you like to spend some time alone together?'

Chantel squeezed her hand. 'That's so thoughtful, Georgie, thanks. But won't you at least join us tomorrow evening? We'll have had a whole day together by then. We might be sick of the sight of one another.'

'I don't think so somehow, and anyway I'm not really a clubber.' Georgie felt guilty that Chantel thought she was being selfless when in fact she wanted to stay by the telephone all day in case Christian called. By eight o'clock the following evening, when Courtney and Chantel were ready to go out to dinner, he still had not been in touch.

'Are you sure you won't come out, Sis?' Courtney prompted. 'It is my last night.'

'You're very welcome,' Chantel assured her.

But Georgie was adamant. 'It's sweet of you both, but please don't worry about me. Christian may call later — perhaps his flight's been delayed or something. He did say it might be Friday instead ... In any case, I'll see you early tomorrow, Court.'

'Not too early,' he protested.

'*Very* early. I'm modelling on the steps of Sacré Coeur, and we have to be well advanced by the time the tourists come streaming by. See you tomorrow, then, and have a super time tonight.'

After a romantic candlelit dinner at Maxim's, Chantel was quite ready to return to L'Hôtel but Courtney pleaded, 'Just a quick look into Castel's, a very quick one? It'll be a while before Fournault gives me another exeat — Christ, listen to me, I sound like a schoolkid.'

'You're not a kid, I can vouch for that,' she said with a wicked smile. 'But okay, if it will make you happy, Castel's for one hour, and afterwards ...'

Thirty minutes later, sitting in an alcove overlooking the

dance floor while waiting for Courtney to rejoin her, Chantel looked around — and froze. A spotlight had picked out an exceptionally attractive couple on the floor. A tall tanned man with silver-blond hair was dancing with a slight Titian-haired beauty, her skin biscuity brown above a strapless cream-coloured dress. The man looked horribly like Christian Neggar.

The morning's session was a circus. From Georgie's arrival at the liaison point, her stylist and hairdresser were at loggerheads. Hardly able to understand their vitriolic flow of words, she gathered that the magazine's stylist, a gaunt and charmless girl in second-hand Piaf black, wanted a white on white approach to her make-up — pale foundation, matte powder, palest of pale eye-shadow and no lipstick. The hairdresser cum make-up artist, on the other hand, intimidatingly tall, dark and much more macho than was the rule, wanted instead to turn her into a clown using bright primary shades and geometric patterns painted on to her face. 'That way the girl's face is an incidental, a mask. The reader will concentrate on the things she's supposed to — the clothes,' he argued.

There was going to be no fear of anyone recognising her from this session, Georgie realised. Both make-up approaches sounded dire, and the clothes were little better.

'Aren't you going to iron them?' Georgie asked, and then mimed her question.

'I-ron! Of course not. It is the textured look, *le style pionnier*. The clothes are meant to look like this! Now you must stand still for *le maquillage*. We have no chair.'

The distressingly young-looking photographer turned up alone, just in time to witness the stylist winning the make-up war.

'*C'est un revenant,*' he announced tactlessly, then busied himself with intrusive camera angles as Georgianna very publicly changed into her first outfit.

With no assistant to load and unload film for him, the young photographer had frequently to stop shooting. By about nine o'clock the mild morning light had disappeared and the stylist was sighing and tut-tutting over Georgianna's pallor in full daylight. The hair and make-up artist smiled smugly as he applied yet more gel to the teased and tangled mess he had made of Georgie's hair.

With a brusque nod, the stylist gave in. 'Okay, we do it your way now.'

Georgianna stood immobile for another half-hour while he transformed her features with a modified clown's make-up. She refused even to look into the hand-mirror he offered her, convinced she looked ghastly, and climbed grimly into the next example of sackcloth and ashes.

By eleven o'clock they managed to finish the session. By then Georgie's legs were wobbly from fatigue and a dull throbbing pain had begun in the small of her back. When the photographer finally announced, '*C'est fini*', she sank on to the nearest step, only to be reminded by the stylist. 'That *is* a Yoshiburo coat, you know. We'll have to buy it if it gets dirty.'

'I shouldn't think for one moment they'd notice,' Georgie reassured her before stepping behind the hateful screen to change for the last time into her own clothes. She begged some cleansing lotion from the make-up artist and hastily scrubbed his artistry from her face. 'Do you know where the nearest phone is?' she asked.

Scrabbling through her handbag for a *jeton*, she reasoned that if Christian had arrived back in Paris last night, too late to call her, he was probably still asleep. She rang the private number Kitty had given her. If he was in, he could answer from bed. He was there, and from the sound of his voice still fuddled with sleep.

'Christian, it's me!' she exclaimed. 'I've just finished a shoot. Can I come round right away?'

'*Quoi?*'

'It's me, Arabella. Did I wake you? I'm so sorry.'

By now he sounded rather more alert. '*Chérie*, how did you get this number? I don't remember giving it to you.'

'You're always in such a rush, darling, but fortunately Kitty let me have it some time ago. Lucky, wasn't it?'

'Very.' There was a moment's silence before he asked rather formally, 'How are you, anyway?'

'Dying to see you. Do you have a job today?'

'No, but —'

'That's okay then. I'll be with you in half an hour. I'll bring some croissants and we can have breakfast together. See you soon, darling.'

After he had crashed down the receiver, Christian cursed Kitty aloud. She knew damn well that his private line was strictly for business, and for certain women who had graduated to it. Normally he would never have given it to a girl like Arabella, the clinging, over-dependent type he usually tried to avoid. But she did have one overwhelming point in her favour, he admitted as he slipped into his grey silk robe, then stripped and remade the bed. In modelling terms, she was hot property and there was money to be made from photographing her. He sighed and made his way to the kitchen. He was drinking a large glass of grapefruit juice when Georgianna rang the bell.

She rushed to kiss him where he sat at the kitchen table. 'I'm such a brute to wake you early after last night,' she said. 'Did you get in very late?'

'Yes, very.'

'I'm sorry. I wanted to see you so much I just couldn't wait. Aren't you pleased to see me, Christian?'

He patted her hand. 'Of course. How did it go this morning?'

'Terrible! The stylist was a thwarted theatrical director and the make-up man seemed to think I was a clown. And as for the photographer ... Marc Stein on Tuesday was better, but not a patch on you. You're quite right. If Kitty thinks she can swing it, I shall ask her to make sure that you are used on all my bookings from now on.'

He pulled down on to his knee and closed his arms round her. 'I'll hold you to that.'

'You can hold me to anything you like. I've missed you so much. Can we go to bed right now?'

'Arabella, I —'

'But first I simply must have a shower. I've had so much make-up trowelled on to me this morning, I must look dreadful. Shan't be long, darling. Wait for me in bed.'

When she was safely out of the room, Christian opened a kitchen cabinet and took out a bottle of cognac. A quick jolt of alcohol could sometimes do the trick ... He was lying in bed, hands behind his head and the sheet pulled up to his waist, when Georgianna came out of the bathroom, wrapped in one of his scarlet towels.

'Christian, I'm sorry, but I don't think I'd better come to bed after all.

He stared at her. 'Why not?'

She couldn't meet his eye but stared at the carpet in embarrassment. 'I've — It seems my period has started. I'm sorry to disappoint you.'

He rolled over on to one elbow and reached out his free hand to stroke her arm. 'Don't be shy, Arabella. It really doesn't matter.'

'That's sweet of you, but I couldn't.'

His fingers clamped over her wrist. 'But I want you, Arabella, and I want you now.'

His expression was fierce and through the fine linen sheet Georgianna could see his jutting erection. It was so unfair, when she wanted him so desperately and he so obviously wanted her. Christian suddenly yanked her wrist, pulling her off balance and on to the bed beside him. When she began to protest, he clamped his mouth over hers and pulled away the towel. When he told her to raise her hips so that he could pull it from under her, she barely recognised his voice which was hoarse with passion. He fastened his mouth greedily over one of her breasts and prised her knees apart. His breathing was harsh and she cradled him in her arms, feeling the tremors which shook him as he covered her body with his. Today, he was displaying none of the sensuous technique with which he had so memorably seduced her. Then he had been very much in command, of her and of himself, but now his arousal was of a deeper, more primitive kind. She had always thrilled to his practised fingers, but found this evidence of his overwhelming need for her even more enthralling. Christian seemed too excited even to guide himself into her and moaned as Georgianna took charge. He began to move jerkily inside her then seemed to recollect himself, fumbling to bring her to the same pitch of excitement.

His unusual clumsiness did not deter her. Under his frantic touch she climaxed almost immediately. Christian shuddered and the rhythmic circling of his hips changed to a desperate driving motion. She found herself sinking again into a whirlpool of sensation and then Christian was lifting her higher and higher ...

As she reached her second shattering climax she opened her eyes. His face hung above her, twisted with passion.

'I love you,' she said.

For an instant their eyes met, his glazed and remote, and then his hips ground frantically against hers and he sank, shuddering, face down in the pillow.

She was exhausted from the morning's work and Christian's passionate onslaught. As he rolled to his side of the bed, she closed her eyes and for several minutes seemed to drift in and out of consciousness. A shrill ringing sounded in her head, but it was too far away for her to worry about. She felt Christian stir beside her and drowsily reached out to him. 'Don't go.'

He patted her hand and slid out of bed. 'Sleep, Arabella. I won't be long.' As she drifted into sleep, he was still talking to her: '*Chérie, c'est toi ...*'

★

They spent the whole weekend together, Georgianna returning only once to L'Hôtel to pick up some clothes. Chantel was out with friends but had left a note to say that Courtney was expecting the two of them on Monday. There were four other messages — three from Kitty, peremptory demands for Georgie to call her at once, and one from Guy. 'Flying back next week. Can't wait to see you. All my love.'

She stuffed the message-slip to the bottom of her bag, wishing it were as simple to shrug off her feelings of guilt over Guy. He had been so good to her on their ill-fated holiday, and only a few months ago she'd been more than ready to fall in love with him. What a mistake that would have been! Her feelings for Christian ran deeper than anything she could have felt for Guy, but she knew that when he returned to Paris she owed him the gentlest of explanations.

Christian's lovemaking overwhelmed her that weekend. They hardly left the flat, where the telephone for once was still. In the middle of the vast city Georgianna felt no desire to see or speak to anyone else. Christian too, seemed happy to stay in, mostly in bed, for the whole two days.

On Monday morning, however, it was back to work with a vengeance. Christian said he had a session due to start in the studio at nine o'clock and Georgianna had to be back at L'Hôtel in time to join Chantel on the visit to Court, though she could not, of course, tell Christian that.

'Don't forget to call Kitty,' he reminded her as he tenderly kissed her goodbye.

'I will. And, Christian — don't forget to call *me*. I'll be in from four o'clock or so. Maybe we can do something tonight?'

'I'll phone you. Don't worry.'

Kitty was caustically delighted that Georgie had finally condescended to call her back. 'Still, it seems you're now a star, love, and I suppose I shouldn't expect anything different. I've seen the *Elle* and *Boom!* shots and the fashion editors are raving over them, though frankly I thought you looked like death warmed up in the location pix. What did you let them do to you?'

'I thought the client was always right?'

'Not in this business, and especially not with a star model.'

'I've been thinking about that, Kitty. Could we make it a condition of hiring me that the client also hires a particular photographer?'

Kitty sounded amused rather than angered by the request. 'It has been done,' she conceded. 'No one but Bailey photographed Marie Helvin for years, and it didn't do her any harm. But Christian's no Bailey, even if he thinks he is. American *Vogue* are in town soon and they're bringing Albert Watson with them. Wouldn't you like me to send them your composites?'

'You can show them my card, Kitty, but until I say differently the deal is that only Christian photographs me. If a client can't go along with that, too bad.'

'Message understood. Oh — I almost forgot. *Le Style* want you again on Thursday afternoon. They'd already booked Christian, so that was lucky. His studio again, so you'll feel right at home.'

Kitty's insinuating tone set Georgie's teeth on edge. 'That's fine,' she said. 'I'll see Christian on Thursday, then. Speak to you soon, Kitty.'

The thought that she would in fact be seeing Christian much sooner put her in such high spirits that the visit to Courtney seemed to flash by. Some time before visiting hours were officially over, Georgie kissed him goodbye and discreetly went to wait in Chantel's car, allowing her brother and friend to be alone together for a while.

'You free tonight?' Chantel asked, rejoining her in the car looking suspiciously tousled and pink-cheeked.

'No, sorry. Christian's phoning me later, and I expect we'll go out somewhere.'

'That's a pity. I was wondering if you'd like to come

along on the gang's last night out? College starts up again early next month, and there are arrangements to be made, parents to pacify, so it's best to go now. I'm really going to miss them all.'

Georgianna twisted in her seat. 'When do *you* have to leave?' she asked. 'Court will miss you terribly, I know, but we can't expect you to stay on once term begins in September. You've got a semester's credits to make up, haven't you?'

Chantel smiled. 'That's right, but I thought it would be kind of embarrassing going back over the same old courses, being the oldest face in class, so I did a bit of research and found I could start some college-approved courses at the Sorbonne in two weeks' time. I can be near Court and still get my credits, isn't that great? Even Mom and Dad are pleased, thinking I'm soaking up some European culture. So if you've had enough of Paris, Georgie, I'm going to be around till at least December, when hopefully Court can leave the Clinic. If you wanted a change of scene, he'll be okay with me around.'

Georgianna was amazed Chantel could imagine she was ready to leave. 'It's wonderful that you're staying, of course, but I've no intention of moving on. There's my modelling, for one thing, and Christian. He's got exclusive photography rights to me now, and I couldn't let him down.'

Chantel opened her mouth to reply, then seemed to think better of it. 'But what about your parents?' she asked after a pause. 'Sooner or later they've got to find about the modelling. The shoots you're doing now are for three or four months ahead, aren't they? Someone will notice them then.'

'I've been thinking about that.' Georgie admitted. 'And I've decided I'm going to come clean. Oh, Daddy will rage and pound the table and say "No daughter of mine ...", but he'll get over it. And Mummy won't mind really, not once she's met Christian. We're going to have to say some-

500

thing else to Daddy soon, anyway. He must be wondering what's going on. I've never been away from Courtney Park for so long before.'

'Do you still miss it?'

'Yes, very much, but I've decided I'm not going back until I can tell Christian the truth and take him back with me.'

When they got back to L'Hôtel, Georgianna checked for messages but found only a slip from Rachelle confirming Thursday's booking. She had a drink with Chantel, then went to her room. She spun out a long leisurely bath, then a mud-pack conditioning treatment on her hair until half-past seven. Christian still hadn't rung by then so, against the grain though it went, she decided to phone him. After ringing both the studio and the private numbers for ten minutes, she gave up in annoyance. She painted her finger- and toe-nails meticulously, tried to read a magazine, failed, and threw it at the wastebin. At nine she called room service and ordered a light meal, which she barely touched. She tried Christian's number once more, then took her own phone off the hook for the night; when he tried to call her later on he'd get no reply. Let *him* do the waiting, for a change.

But her good intentions evaporated the next morning when his call woke her at ten o'clock.

'Christian! Where have you been? I was worried ... When I left you, you said you'd ring.'

'I'm ringing you now, aren't I? Something urgent came up; I was busy.' From the brusque tone of his voice it was obvious he didn't intend to tell her anything more, but Georgianna unwisely pressed him.

'What was the job?'

'Damn it, Arabella, must you know my every movement?'

Stunned by the coldness of his voice, she was silent.

'And don't sulk, you silly girl,' he said, exasperated.

'I — I'm not sulking.' She fought to control the tremor

in her voice; the shock and hurt she was feeling that Christian could treat *her* like a stranger.

Sounding more himself, he continued: 'Anyway, I was ringing to see whether you'd like to come out tonight? There's a new club opening, and there'll be someone there I'd like you to meet.'

Relief flooded over her. 'I'd love to come. What time shall I expect you?'

'You couldn't come round to the studio? I'll be tied up here till late — say ten. Maybe you could call round then?'

'All right,' she said.

'And, Arabella —'

'Yes?'

'Wear something really *codé* for once, can't you? I'm tired of seeing you in all that grand couturier stuff. It'll be too formal for the place we're going.'

She swallowed the hurt she felt at the implied criticism of her dress sense. 'Okay. Christian — I did miss you, you know.'

He laughed indulgently. 'Silly girl. It's been no time. See you tonight then.'

When she rang his bell that evening, his voice over the entryphone told her not to come up, he'd be right down. She waited uneasily on the street, ignoring the appreciative leers of some male passers-by. When Christian appeared several minutes later she saw that he had had his hair cut into a fashionably short crop. She preferred it longer, but refrained from telling him so.

'You look sensational, Arabella,' he greeted her, after appraising her skintight chocolate brown Alaia.

'Glad you approve.'

'Just make sure you don't spill anything down it. I know we're doing rather well, but Alaias aren't cheap.'

More than anything then she wanted to tell him that money didn't matter a damn to Dexter Randolph's daughter, but she stopped herself. His behaviour on the phone earlier had shocked her. It was true he had given her no claim over him but ever since they had met she had felt there was something special between them. And yet she had never trusted him with her identity, confided even in her lover the truth about Georgianna Randolph. No wonder things seemed to be going awry between them. Their whole relationship was built on a falsehood of her creation. It was up to her to set the record straight, then maybe the closeness of the weekend would return.

LouLou's was just the sort of club Georgianna hated. Acres and acres of stark white rubber flooring covered the ground floor of a converted warehouse in the Pigalle district. There was a forty-foot steel bar behind which stood barmen in futuristic silver suits, and rows of glass and steel refrigerators. Tonight, all they held was jug after jug of LouLou's special cocktail, a nauseating white concoction of baccardi, kümmel and coconut liqueur. That and Perrier was all that was available to drink on the opening night. Georgie stuck to Perrier, but Christian drained three glasses of the cloyingly sweet drink while his eyes scanned the vast crowded club.

Georgie recognised many of the beautiful girls standing in the throng around them as fellow models, and there was the usual complement of rock stars, fading or hot, several rather battered-looking French actors, and the latest American brat-pack hero surrounded by a gang of giggling nymphets.

She jumped when Christian suddenly took her arm and began steering her purposefully between crowded tables to the far side of the dance floor. At first she thought he was making for an empty table, then she realised that the girl she had thought belonged to a party on the next table was in fact sitting waiting for them to join her on a narrow black banquette. She waved animatedly to them both and Georgie said, 'Goodness, she's just a child. Is she old enough to be in a club like this?'

The girl was very young indeed, though delightful to look at. Her smooth skin was deep-tanned and the hair piled precariously on top of her head was a gorgeous titian, but she had the prominent collarbones and waif-like body of a child. Her voice, too, when she greeted Christian in fluent Italian, was breathless as a little girl's.

He bent to kiss her. '*In inglese*,' he said strictly. 'I know you speak it, Giovanna, so no games. Arabella, I'd like you to meet Giovanna — we worked together in Morocco last week. Giovanna, this is Arabella Hamilton, the English model I was telling you about.'

Giovanna put her head to one side and looked her up and down frankly before sticking out her hand and grinning disarmingly. 'You're just as Christian described you,' she said. 'Dark hair, dark eyes, not really interested in clubs and parties at all.'

Georgie shook hands politely, but was oddly disturbed to hear that Christian had been discussing her with this precocious child. 'Are you in Paris for long?' she asked as she sat down in a chair opposite the girl.

'It depends,' Giovanna answered evasively. 'I've been here almost a week already and my fiancé's beginning to complain.'

'Giovanna's engaged to a magazine publisher in Rome,' Christian explained.

'So young?' Georgianna enquired.

'I'm old for my years, aren't I, Christian?' The girl looked at him sidelong. 'May I have another drink, please?'

He sprang to his feet. 'There are never any waiters at these places. I'll see what I can do. Arabella?'

Georgianna nodded silently. She almost froze with disbelief. The girl said she'd been in Paris a week, yet Christian had never so much as mentioned her.

'It must have been a nuisance your flight from Morocco being delayed like that?' she hazarded.

Giovanna nodded vehemently. 'I know. I was dead to the world all of Thursday, but by the evening I'd come round enough to go dancing with Christian. He took me to

Castel's and we had a marvellous time. You know, I really envy you,' she said.

'*You* envy *me*?' Georgianna said faintly.

'Yes, working only with Christian like you do. He told me how he'd managed to fix it. I'd give anything to be photographed only by him, but Luca would have a fit.'

'Your fiancé, I suppose?'

'That's right. The wedding's at Christmas. He can't wait.'

'Your drink, *chérie*,' Christian said, appearing silently behind them and leaning past Georgianna to hand Giovanna's drink to her. *Chérie* . . . Georgianna felt sick. Christian had lied to her about the date of his return from Morocco. In conversation he'd twisted the facts about his exclusive photography right to Georgianna, somehow implying that he was granting her unlimited work instead of the other way round. He hadn't even bothered to lie about his whereabouts on Monday. With a hollow feeling, Georgianna remembered the phone call he'd answered. She'd been half asleep at the time, not even sure it was really the phone or just a dream. But while she lay naked in his bed, sated with lovemaking, he had left the room and greeted the caller the way he always greeted *her*: '*Chérie*'. Or, rather the way he always used to greet her. Tonight, she noticed, she had become simply 'Arabella', whereas Giovanna . . .

'Would you excuse me a minute?'

Giovanna started to get to her feet, too, obviously concerned by Georgie's pallor and strained expression. 'Are you all right?' she enquired. 'Shall I come with you?'

'She'll be fine,' Christian said, pulling Giovanna down on to the banquette beside him. 'Don't be long, Arabella, will you? Giovanna hasn't eaten yet, and I thought we'd get out of this place and try Le Square. You'd like it there, *chérie*,' he said with a smile for the girl.

Georgie walked stiffly away, moving like an automaton. She reached the powder-room safely, determined not to make a spectacle of herself in public. The spartan black and white room was deserted when she reached it, and she leaned gratefully against the wall. To her dismay, however, she heard the sharp staccato rap of female footsteps fast approaching. Glancing around, she slipped into one of the empty stalls and bolted the door.

The pain of Christian's betrayal was awful, but there was worse to come. The two women who had followed her into the powder-room had obviously embarked on a lengthy overhaul of their make-up, simultaneously swopping the latest scandal. Georgie was sure she recognised one of the voices.

'There is nothing — but *nothing* — sleazier than a sheikh on the make. In the end I gave him the goddamned bracelet back, and who do you suppose I saw wearing it the next day?'

The other girl's shrieks of laughter drowned the name, but Georgianna, a reluctant eavesdropper, caught the next part of the conversation and immediately wished she hadn't.

'And speaking of sleaze, did you notice who's here tonight, Karen? Your old flame Christian Neggar.'

This time Georgie recognised the Texan model's voice. 'He has his uses still, believe me. I just wish he wasn't such a bastard in between times.'

'He's not just a bastard, he's sick!' the other girl protested. 'Josephine told me he can't get it up unless the girl's a virgin or having a period. They call him the Blood Merchant, apparently.'

'Tell me something I don't know, honey. Like I said, he has his uses.'

'You're no virgin, Karen . . .'

'It may surprise you to know that I was until I met Christian. He was real sweet at first — you know, a romantic weekend at his place at St Trop, bunches of these little white flowers, candlelight, soft music, the works. I was really crazy for him for months, but after that

506

weekend I saw him less and less. Finally, he spelt it out for me. I was glad, by that time. At least it meant there was nothing wrong with me, and he said I could give him a call from time to time, on his private number.'

'You mean . . .?'

''S right. I call him once a month, and so does his neighbour Chloe — that fat little brunette who's always slavering over him. And then there's Lydia, Hélène, Bibi, Josephine . . . why else do you think we've all got his private number?'

'Karen, this is so *tacky*! I can't believe all you girls know about each other.'

'So what would be the point of getting jealous? He'll never change, and we know it. But when the time is right he's the best ever lay, so who's he hurting? I saw him last week, on his way to the airport — good thing he's a fast worker. And guess who obligingly passed on my message? Arabella, his new English girl. I thought she knew all about him, but from the look on her face tonight I guess she's just finding out.'

'Poor thing! Someone should have warned her.'

'She wouldn't have thanked us, even if she'd believed it, but I guess it is sad. He's obviously chasing after that Italian kid now.'

The slamming of a door marked the two girls' departure. Georgianna emerged from her prison and caught a glimpse of her white horrified face above the stark brown dress. She was too stunned even to cry again but of one thing she was quite sure: she was damned if she would walk meekly back and watch Christian practising all his charm on another victim. The cloakroom attendant accepted a lavish tip to deliver a note to him — 'Sorry, migraine coming on. Had to go back. A.'

She was back at L'Hôtel before midnight with no intention of sleeping. Horrifying though the girls' conversation had been, she was glad to have heard it. If she had not, like the younger, more innocent Karen, she would have begun to blame herself for Christian's waning interest, wasted months of her life trailing after him in despair when the truth was the man's veins ran with ice-water. It was inhuman the way he had managed to deceive her, turning on all that tenderness and passion and charm. She shuddered at the memory of their last weekend together. The Blood Merchant ... It was horrible, unbelievable. And to think the time before that she'd felt sorry for him, believed the story that he was tired and worried about work.

Work ... For two hours, she sat rapt in thought. Christian was going to pay for his deception of her, and for the way he'd treated so many girls before. Some, like Karen, and Chloe, obviously managed to adjust to the outrageous way he used women, using him in return. That long black hair in his bed the night after Chloe had stopped him in Régine's ...

But there must have been more, so many more girls who'd been totally taken in by his dazzling looks and heartless lies. For their sake as much as for her own, she'd be revenged on him. Christian liked money, she knew that by now. She shivered at the memory of how close she'd come to telling him her real identity. One way of punishing him would be to sever their business connection. Photographers, she knew by now, earned far more than the model for each session they worked on. Georgie reached for the phone. Kitty would not complain at a call from one of her top models, even after midnight. But then she had second thoughts. If she acted now, she'd be showing her hand, letting Christian know she was on to him. And even if he did lose the work with her, he was a well-known name, meeting countless beautiful women every day. There'd soon be another star he could hitch his wagon to, whereas she wanted him stopped for good. There had to be a subtler approach, one that would really hurt.

★

She was restless the following morning, keyed up before the afternoon's test of will. Dressed plainly in a favourite old Salmon and Greene dress, sailor-style navy and white cotton — Christian would hate it, she realised with a smile of satisfaction — she took the lift down to the foyer. Her heart jumped at the sight of the lean sun-tanned man waiting to catch it.

'Guy!'

She didn't know whether to laugh or cry — there was something so comforting about the feeling of his arms about her.

'I called last night after I'd flown in, but you were out and I told them not to leave a message, I'd rather surprise you. When I turned up just now, the desk clerk agreed I could go up. The only thing was, he seemed to think my name was Neggar.'

There was no reproach in his voice and his smile was warm as ever, but Georgianna could sense his hurt. 'Let's have breakfast together,' she said quietly. 'There's a lot I need to explain to you.'

He heard the news that she had taken a lover calmly. 'It had to happen,' he told her. 'A girl as lovely as you ... I just hope the lucky man appreciates you.'

But when Georgianna recounted Christian's deception of her, leaving out some of the worst details, Guy's face twisted with rage. 'My God, this is too much. Tell me the bastard's name again and I'll take care of him!'

'There's no need; I can do that for myself. Besides, weren't you listening? We're still working together. Or at least we shall be this afternoon.'

'A photographer,' Guy mused, 'and his name was Naggar, I think the clerk said. No, Negger ... Oh, God. Christian Neggar, of course!' He leant back in his chair and groaned. 'If only I'd been here. Then, if you'd just mentioned his name and the fact that he was a photographer, I could have warned you. The man has a foul reputation around town, I remember hearing all about it now. I'm surprised no one else thought of tipping you off.'

'I've had to keep a low profile because of Court,' Georgie reminded him.

'Ah, yes. How is he? Better, I hope.'

'Marvellous — and in love. Chantel, the girl who lives here too, has been such a friend to me, and rather more to Court. He's determined to be fully cured as soon as possible just so he can be with her.'

'And didn't she know about this Neggar fellow?'

'Chantel's not French, despite the name, but a funny mixture of Australian, German and American. She's a newcomer to Paris, too, so she couldn't have known, though I've sensed in the past few days that she somehow disapproved of Christian. I suppose she's just a better judge of character.'

'She sounds a sensible girl,' Guy agreed feelingly.

'I know I've been a fool.'

'Georgie, I didn't mean —'

She shook her head. 'It's all right — I know you didn't. You've been a good friend to me too, and I want to say how sorry I am that it was nothing more.'

'Later, perhaps. I shan't give up hope. In the meantime, Georgie, I'll be here for you. Anything I can do, you have only to ask.'

'Thank you. And actually there is something. Would you be free tonight, around six o'clock?'

Buoyed up by the reunion with Guy, Georgie's afternoon session went better than she had anticipated. A slightly sheepish-looking Roger rather overdid her welcome to the studio.

'Arabella, darlingest, lovely to see you again.'

'It's lovely to see you too, Roger.'

He studied her anxiously. He'd been prepared for tears, hysterics, even suicide threats. They'd had them all before, God knew, when His Nibs began to tire of a conquest. But

510

this delicate-looking English girl seemed to have taken it on the chin. 'I gather you met up last night,' he probed.

'We did, yes, but unfortunately I had to leave the club early with a migraine. Is he here yet? I'd like to say sorry before I change.'

Roger glanced towards the door. 'Actually, he's not. A very important lunch date.'

'I'll change, then. Who's styling and make-up?'

'Gilles is hair and make-up, and Marie-Jeanne's the stylist. You've all worked together before so that's nice, isn't it?'

'Very.' Georgie's memories of the girl were not particularly pleasant, but at least she now understood the reason for the girl's antipathy to her. A fellow sufferer, obviously. Or maybe even a name on Christian's 'sometimes' list. Thinking back, there had been that suspiciously late arrival in Grasse . . .

In fact, apart from briefly indicating the cream wool Jasper Conran dress Georgianna was to wear with each of the six model hats they were photographing that afternoon, Marie-Jeanne seemed more intent on her conversation with Gilles than with trying to make Georgie feel small. Her French had progressed in leaps and bounds during the past few weeks so she was able to make out the sense of their conversation and eventually take part.

'It's always the same when an editor leaves,' Marie-Jeanne was complaining. 'A new broom comes in, starts raising the dust everywhere. Why do we use so-and-so for hair when he costs an extra 500 francs a day? Do we really need a third foreign location trip this year? Are these overtime claims justified? Why do we give so much free-lance work to him or to her? You'd better watch out, Gilles.'

'Me?' he protested, spiking the tip of Georgianna's ear-lobe with a needle-sharp hairpin with which he was securing her hair in a severe French pleat. 'I do hair *and* make-up for one fee. Toinette knew what good value I give.'

'Yes, but she's gone, stupid! She didn't like all these rumours that Lamier are looking for a buyer for *Le Style*, and when *Vanity* headhunted her . . .'

'But a fashion editor only, when she's been used to running her own ship.'

'A failing one,' Marie-Jeanne pointed out. 'Sure, it's well respected in the business, but the feeling in the street and in the marketing polls is that *Boom!* is where it's at.'

Georgianna, shuddering to remember the session for them, interrupted. 'Do they have a new editor for *Le Style* yet?'

'No. Her deputy's been appointed acting editor, but management are hanging fire so long on a new permanent appointment that it's adding fuel to the rumours that they plan to sell. It's bad enough when a new editor comes in, but a new proprietor can really rock the boat. Look at Murdoch and *Elle*. There'll be trouble for the permanent staff as well as the freelance workers, you mark my words.'

'I can see it must be worrying,' Georgie agreed, then leant back in the chair, eyes closed, as Gilles blended a fine line of grey kohl next to her lashes. 'Okay, not hurting you, am I?' he asked after a moment, but she was deep in thought and did not reply.

When she was dressed and her hair finished, the stylist led her through to the studio.

'About time, Christian,' Marie-Jeanne snapped on seeing him. '*Le Style* pays you for the whole afternoon, you know. We could have started half an hour ago.'

It was an exaggeration and Christian knew it, but he automatically began to flatter and charm Marie-Jeanne. Georgianna watched expressionlessly until it was her turn.

'Arabella, as beautiful as always,' he greeted her. 'We were worried about you last night.'

But not enough to ring me, she thought, nevertheless smiling at him as she said, 'I was fine, thanks. I get the wretched things occasionally, and there's nothing for it but to go to bed and sleep them off.'

'If you two are ready,' Marie-Jeanne interrupted. 'I thought of something very *My Fair Lady*. Did you ever see it, Arabella? I want the same feeling as the Ascot scene for this. Can we try a few poses, please?'

Georgianna set her head in an imitation of Grandmama on Ladies' Day, and the stylist clapped her hands. 'Perfect. Don't miss it, Christian.'

The formal poses were boring to hold but at least they necessitated a minimum of encouragement from him. She remembered last week's lingerie session, and an involuntary flicker of distaste crossed her features. Christian called out, 'Hey! You look as if you've stepped in something.'

That just about sums it up, she thought, and smiled charmingly.

'Too happy,' Marie-Jeanne immediately told her. 'Come on, Arabella, concentrate. This is the last hat.'

Georgie resumed her expression of glazed disinterest and the session swiftly wound up. Afterwards, while she was cleansing her face, Christian put his head round the dressing-room door.

'If you're not doing anything tonight, I thought —'

She glanced at him over her shoulder and smiled apologetically. 'Sorry, Christian, but I am. A friend just got back to town and I promised I'd drop *everything* for him.'

'A Monsieur de Rennes for you, Arabella,' Philippe called from the studio.

'Oh, Guy's here already. Must dash, Christian. See you soon, I expect.'

'Arabella! I wanted a quick word with you about —'

She waved at him distractedly. 'Give me a ring, why don't you? I should be in after midday tomorrow. Speak to you then. 'Bye.'

In fact, Georgianna had no intention of staying the night in Guy's flat, but she was eager to reach it as soon as possible after leaving the studio.

'Is it all right if I phone England?' she said as soon as they were inside.

513

'Go ahead. Can I get you a drink?'

'Something long would be a good idea. I've a feeling the call is going to be.'

If Ford the butler was surprised to be asked by Miss Georgianna to connect her to her uncle, but only if her aunt was not in the same room, his imperturbable voice did not betray it.

There was a long and agonising pause during which Georgianna prayed that Alexander would be run to ground alone, and then her uncle was greeting her with delight. 'Georgie, how lovely to hear from you. You're quite a stranger these days. Camilla tells me you're in Ville-franche, you lucky girl.'

'Paris now, actually, doing a spot of modelling — but not a word to Mummy or Daddy, please. I need to break it to them gently.'

'Understood. And what's this call in aid of — I take it it isn't purely social?'

Georgianna drew a deep breath and began in a business-like tone: 'I need your professional help, Uncle Xan. I want you to help me to buy a magazine.'

It was a longer call even than she'd anticipated, but by the time Georgie rang off she had managed to convince Alexander that the acquisition of *Le Style* might well be a shrewd business move. The magazine was high profile enough to have earned the goodwill of all the couturiers and manufacturers, but as the only 'exotic' title in a stable of business and technical titles it had suffered over the past few years from an unimaginative management and devel-opment policy.

When Alexander asked how she intended to combine modelling with running a magazine, about which she knew nothing, she triumphantly referred him to two of her London chums, Jane Wilson and Jamie Spencer, currently sweating it out as assistant editors on *Harper's*. Fizzing with energy and ideas, she was confident they'd jump at the chance of joint editorship of a glossy new style leader in

Paris, the most style-conscious of cities. She was sure that under their editorship *Le Style* could quickly be turned around to become a major publishing force once more, and furthermore could probably be re-sold more than profitably to one of the major magazine chains in a year or two.

Alexander was relieved to hear she was thinking in terms of a short-term loan only and agreed to put a couple of accountants on to investigating the title and the Paris magazine scene in general to see if her idea was feasible.

As Georgianna wearily hung up, Guy replaced her spritzer with a glass of champagne.

'It's still a little early for celebrations,' she said, laughing. 'I haven't got what I want yet.'

'Neither have I,' he reminded her, 'but I'm still hoping.'

She looked away in confusion, and Guy did not press his point that evening or the next day when Georgie took him to the Malmaison and introduced him to Courtney and Chantel.

'We met in Monte Carlo, but I'm ashamed to say I remember very little of it,' Court said frankly. 'But I know I nearly died, and Georgie has told me how much I owe you, for getting me treated so quickly and for covering our tracks. I owe you a gigantic favour, de Rennes. Is there anything I can do for you — short of handing over Chantel?'

'That will not be necessary,' Guy assured him with a smile. 'But if you could persuade your sister to come out with me tomorrow . . .?'

Courtney and Chantel looked uncomfortable, obviously thinking of Christian. Georgie took a deep breath and told them, 'By the way, it's all over between Christian and me. I made a bad mistake there. He wasn't at all what I thought he was.'

Chantel's blue eyes were alight with fellow feeling. 'Damn it, Georgie, he's really hurt you, hasn't he? I should have warned you . . . Remember when we went to Castel's on Court's last night?'

'I expect you saw him out with someone else,' Georgie said painfully. 'Was she a redhead? Yes, that was Giovanna. They worked together in Morocco and got back to town a day earlier than Christian admitted to me.'

'I am sorry,' Chantel said, taking her hand. 'I only saw them for a few seconds, and not very clearly. I thought it looked like Christian, but I wasn't sure and didn't like to spread gossip.'

'Why didn't you let me know?' Court interrupted. 'All you had to do was point the bastard out to me and I'd have given him something to regret.'

'*And* made the gossip columns, *and* blown your cover,' Georgie reminded him. 'It's all right, Court. I've a scheme in mind for getting more than even with Mr Neggar.'

'You're still seeing him, then?'

'For as long as it suits me, and no longer. Then he'll wish he'd never set eyes on me.'

On Monday Rachelle rang with news of two more assignments, both with Christian as photographer. Georgianna thanked her sweetly and jotted down the details. She was surprised when, later that day, reception rang to say that she had a visitor.

'A Mam'selle 'awk,' Albert announced. 'You will see her?'

Georgianna sighed. 'Okay, Albert. Order some tea for us, will you, and I'll come down.' She ran a comb through her hair and quickly applied some make-up, wondering idly what had brought her agent out of her lair, a rare occurrence, apparently. Whatever it was, it was obviously important, Georgie decided five minutes later, enduring a very public display of affection from Kitty.

'Who's a clever girl, then?' Kitty's scarlet lips grazed Georgianna's cheeks and dipped dangerously towards her mouth. Appalled, she sat down suddenly on a low sofa and Kitty immediately concertinaed her long legs and sat cosily next to her.

'We did it, love,' she announced in low, thrilling tones. 'You and me have really cracked it this time. Heard of Sarong?'

'Well, yes, it's a piece of cloth you —'

Kitty threw back her head and guffawed. 'You slay me, Arabella, you really do. The *perfume*, silly, Esmée Kovacs's latest. You should read the trades.' She tapped Georgianna's knee reprovingly, then let her hand linger as she continued, 'Remember I told you American *Vogue* was going to be in town? Well, they didn't want you, silly prats, but Albert Watson's got more strings to his bow than tinpot magazine assignments. He saw your card and loved it. He passed it on to the advertising agency who've retained him on the new Sarong promotion. Now, I know you and Christian are having a thing, but . . .'

'Not any more,' Georgianna said.

'He's given you the elbow already. Oh, sorry. I mean . . .'

'That's all right, we both know what you mean, and actually he hasn't formally given me up. I'm still the goose that lays the golden eggs so far as he's concerned. I think he means to keep me dangling on a string a while longer, but I happen to know he's already turned his attention elsewhere.'

'Where *exactly*?' Kitty asked, avid for the latest scandal.

'A young Italian model — Giovanna. He met her in Morocco on that re-shoot for Italian *Vogue*. She's been on my conscience, actually,' Georgianna admitted. 'I know what he's like, and she's so young and innocent. I ought to warn her.'

'I knew just what he was like but would *you* have believed *me*?' Kitty pointed out practically. 'Anyway, love, if this Giovanna's the scrubber I think she is — carroty hair, no tits, silly little voice — she's well able to take care of herself, don't you worry. You don't go from the slums of Naples to an engagement with one of Italy's wealthiest bachelors without learning to keep your hand on your halfpenny. Her fiancé won't take damaged goods, and she'll know that, never fear. And I happen to know she travels everywhere with Mama in tow. They're camped out in the Plaza-Athénée, apparently, and rumour has it that Mama *sews* her into her knickers every morning.'

She laughed uproariously again but patted Georgianna's knee kindly this time, and even took her hand away. She seemed genuinely sympathetic for the first time since they'd met, Georgianna decided.

'You were saying something about a perfume?' she prompted.

'My God, yes.' Kitty swooped on her handbag and brought out a list of statistics which she proceeded to reel off in an excited gabble. 'Sarong will be launched with a ten-million-dollar promotional budget. Unprecedented advertising coverage has been secured in America, Canada, the UK, Europe and South Africa. The campaign will be the longest running in the history of cosmetics advertising, with a brand new TV commercial and stills each month for six months,. Each will feature a different exotic location — Fiji, Goa, Bali, Sri Lanka, Barbados and the Virgin Islands — think how at home Christian would feel there. Whoops! Me and my mouth.'

'It's okay. But I don't understand about Sarong. What's Christian got to do with all this?'

Kitty fanned herself with the sheet of statistics. Christ! The girl must be the biggest moron in her entire stable, but now she was a major money-spinner and Kitty had better play this straight. 'How much he has to do with Sarong depends entirely on you, sweetest. They've got Juien Temple for the TV commercials and Watson for the stills, but if you'd wanted Christian on board as associate photographer ...'

'If *I* wanted him? You mean ...'

'Why else do you think I'd come schlepping round here in this heat? They want *you* for Sarong Girl. Isn't it great?'

Georgianna couldn't believe her luck. 'It's fantastic,

Kitty, and far more than I'd hoped for.'

Le Style and the Sarong job. Luck seemed to be going her way at last. One thing she was certain of: it definitely wasn't going Christian's.

In his call to her the next day, Christian pressed her to come out with him that night. 'We've got business to discuss, *chérie*,' he reminded her.

So she was '*chérie*' again as soon as the prospect of a major contract loomed, or had Giovanna flown back to her millionaire?

'Sorry, but I can't come out tonight,' she said.

'Your friend of the other night, I suppose; Monsieur de Rennes?' he said knowledgeably.

'No, it's someone else actually. Alexander lives in England, but he's over here on business and I promised to show him the town.'

'Tomorrow, then. We must talk about the new job.'

'But there's plenty of time, Christian. The meeting isn't till next week, and that's only a preliminary. I'll be in touch later this week, and that's a promise.'

If Xan could move as quickly as he'd indicated on the phone the night before, Christian would definitely be hearing from her.

She met her uncle from Charles de Gaulle and they talked business in the back of his hired limousine on the way to the Ritz. The conversation was so satisfactory that Georgianna was able to sign the enabling documentation as soon as they reached his suite.

'It's terribly good of you to lend me the money yourself,' she protested.

Alexander shook his head. 'It's nothing of the sort — you've seen the projection for yourself. This way I'll get 50 per cent of the action on a re-sale as well as interest, don't forget.'

'But you're putting up all the purchase money immediately and charging me very nominal interest on my share. Don't try and tell me a bank would have been so generous.'

He shrugged it off. 'The project interested me, that's all. I've always hankered after some publishing holdings, and your pals in London really impressed me. *Le Style*'s projection checked out, and it seemed such a damn good thing I didn't want to risk putting it through the bank's credit committee and running the risk of word leaking out. My Paris lawyers are in a meeting with Lamier's now. They promised to call as soon as it breaks up. If my offer is accepted, they'll go for the quickest possible handover. Effective control of *Le Style* could be ours by tomorrow.'

Four hours later Georgianna had bitten her nails to the quick and her restless pacing had worn discernible tracks in the thick piled carpet. Alexander sat imperturbably at the desk, shirt-sleeves rolled back neatly and a pair of gold-rimmed half-glasses perched on the end of his aquiline nose as he checked through some documentation.

When the phone on the low table by the window rang, they collided, each trying to be first to answer. Since it was her uncle's lawyers calling, however, Georgianna reluctantly relinquished the receiver to Alexander. He spoke in rapid colloquial French peppered with technical phrases about tax warranties, indemnities and transfers.

Georgie tugged at his sleeve. 'Have we got it?' she hissed.

He waved his hand reprovingly at her and carried on his conversation. She sank on to a chair and gestured to him beseechingly for a shake of the head, a thumbs up or down, anything. With a final crisp '*Au 'voir, et merci pour tous vos efforts,*' Alexander terminated the conversation.

'Well?' she said, holding her breath.

'Our offer is accepted. The legal side will take two weeks to complete —'

'But I don't *have* two weeks!'

'If you'd let me finish, Georgie? However, as we have arranged to hand over the entire purchase price to Lamier's lawyers in escrow, they have agreed to relinquish managerial control from tomorrow. Shall I call Jamie and Jane, or will you?'

'We *did* it! You don't know what this means to me!' Or to Christian, she thought gleefully.

She hugged her uncle excitedly and kissed his cheek. 'Will you call Jamie and Jane, please? They're friends of mine, so business talk would come better from you. And when you've done that, I want you to get ready for a night on the town. We've got some celebrating to do.'

They allowed the magazine to go one day without word of the new management, calculating quite deliberately that by midday the buzz that *Le Style* had new absentee owners would be all over town. Jane and Jamie arrived on the evening flight. They each had a month's notice to work in London and agreed that Georgianna and Alexander had followed the best course by asking the acting editor to remain, at least for the next few weeks.

'If you've no objection to running up some pretty hefty courier service bills, we can ask her to send over future dummies, roughs, even page layouts for the next few issues, and send them back to her with our comments and amendments overnight,' Jamie said. 'I take it we shall be able to meet her tomorrow morning as planned? She hasn't stormed out in a huff at the thought of new English editors? I must admit to feeling a bit sorry for her.'

'Jamie,' Jane said quickly, 'your killer-diller, hot-shot editor image is slipping just a wee bit. Keep this up, and Georgie will suspect you're really a pussycat.'

Georgianna smiled reassuringly at them both: Jamie, with his shock of carroty hair and permanently worried expression; Jane with her sleek short haircut and carefully understated clothes. She knew very well that Jane's hard-headed managerial ability would keep Jamie's natural affability in check, and that his unerring nose for a timely story or an innovative style of layout would put *Le Style* back on the map.

'I have every confidence in you both,' she told them. 'So

much so, that I've no hesitation in asking for your help, in strictest secrecy, please. It may sound as though I'm interfering in editorial decision-making, but I assure you this will be the first and only time. Tomorrow, when you see Elise, our acting editor, would you please ask her for a full list of all *Le Style*'s freelance contributors — writers, layout artists, stylists, hair and make-up people, photographers and so on? I've roughed out a letter I'd like you to send them all. Could you see they go out without fail?'

On Thursday morning, when she calculated that all the letters from *Le Style* would have been received, Georgie rang Kitty to see if there was any news on her meeting with the American advertising agency who would be handling the Sarong campaign.

'They've just this minute called, love. Early next Monday evening okay for you? And I dare say His Nibs will drop anything — or anyone — to be there too.'

'That's why I rang, Kitty. I've been giving my career a lot of thought in the past few days, and I've decided that it really wouldn't do my reputation a lot of good for word to get around that I'm difficult, insisting on working with my own photographer and so on. I really hate doing this, but —'

There was a telling pause, then Kitty laughed throatily. 'Neggar can boil his head. Shall I break the glad tidings, or will you?'

'Would you be an angel, Kitty?'

'Darling, in all my years of dealing with him, *nothing* will have given me greater pleasure. See you on Monday, then, six o'clock in my office. I'll have the champagne on ice.'

Twenty minutes later, the hotel switchboard buzzed Georgie. 'There's a call for you from Monsieur Christian Neggar. He says it's urgent.'

'I'm not in to Monsieur Neggar, on the phone or in person. Would you see that reception know that, please?'

'Certainly, Miss Hamilton. Monsieur Neggar will not bother you again.'

Georgianna sighed. Just the thought of him still had the power to disturb her, whether she spoke to him or not. It was surely a bad omen that the very first man she loved, had given herself to in every sense, should turn out to be someone like him, a man who used women, enjoyed the pursuit of them but not the possession. She could still remember the force of the physical attraction he had held for her, even though the thought of ever being in his bed again left her cold with distaste. Next time she loved, it would be someone very different, someone she knew and could trust, who would prize her for herself and not her novelty value. Meanwhile, she had one last message for Christian.

She dialled *Le Style*'s offices where, as publisher-in-charge and co-owner, the Honourable Georgianna Randolph had been allocated her own penthouse office and a secretary. So far, of course, none of the magazine's staff had actually seen her, as it was vital that none of them should be able to make the connection between the magazine's new owners and the British model Arabella, but she kept in touch with developments every day by telephone.

If her as yet unseen secretary was surprised by the two letters Georgianna now dictated to her, she gave no hint of it but took them down in rapid shorthand and efficiently read them back.

'A copy of the first letter is to go to every freelance contributor *except* one,' Georgianna instructed her. 'The second letter is to go to Monsieur Christian Neggar only — Marie-Jeanne, the fashion editor, will have his address. Check with her that you have it absolutely right, will you? And I want you to make certain that all the letters are despatched tonight. Is that clear?'

'Would you like me to wait for you on Monday evening?' The secretary tried to sound merely cool and efficient, but her eagerness to see her mysterious new employer for herself was almost palpable.

Georgianna smiled. 'Thank you, but that won't be necessary. I wouldn't want to keep you so late. There is one thing more you could do for me, though.'

'Oui, Mademoiselle Randolph.'

'Make sure there's a bottle of Cristal on ice, will you? I should have something to celebrate.'

Kitty was confused. Before the meeting, she had thought the girl would need nursemaiding through every stage. Instead, Arabella had introduced herself to the creative head of Manson and Da Silva, one of America's foremost advertising agencies, an agency executive, and the marketing manager of Esmée Kovacs with an assurance which had left her open-mouthed.

'The contract is a two-part one,' Ivan Czerny, the Account Executive, began to explain. 'The first part covers a development period of three months — we'd want to kick that off pretty quickly, say in three or four weeks at the most. We'll be working initially on product packaging, as every Sarong product will bear an image of the Sarong Girl. At the end of three months, there'll be a campaign assessment. For instance, if you found that you were unhappy in the work —'

Georgianna raised an eyebrow. 'Such concern for a model's welfare is touching, gentlemen, but don't you think it sounds a little bogus? Now let's get down to business, shall we? The contract is in two parts so that, if *you* want, you can cut your losses after three months if it turns out you've made a mistake in hiring me. True, you'd have spent a lot of money in those three months — your creative team's salary and the initial payment to me, which incidentally isn't enough. Fifty thousand pounds would be more like it, wouldn't you say, Kitty?'

The agent thought rapidly. If she'd known in advance the little bitch was going to try it on like this, she'd have shaken her till every perfect tooth rattled, but from the bemused, even admiring, expressions on the negotiating team's faces, Arabella's approach was working, and 15 per cent of an additional thirty thousand pounds . . .

'For exclusive use at this crucial stage in a highly promising career, that sounds about right to me,' Kitty confirmed, crossing her flawless legs which was so much more effective and less obvious than crossing her fingers.

'Now hold on there, little lady,' Ellis Kramer, the cosmetics company marketing man, intervened. 'Let's not get too greedy here. You're a great-looking kid, sure, but —'

'But you're still not prepared to sign me up for two years right now. That's all right, I understand, and I see why you feel you must protect yourself with the three-month try-out period. What I do not understand is how you can reasonably expect me to agree today part two of the contract, a figure for my exclusive two-year services, when you yourselves haven't definitely committed yourself to engage me. Your two-part contract is more than a little one-sided, it seems to me.'

Two of the team reacted with polite smiles of interest to her summary but the third man, the agency's creative head, Burt Johnson, began to panic at the idea of his perfect Sarong Girl slipping away from them.

'I'm sure there's a way round this, Miss Hamilton,' he began. 'In fact, I imagine you've already thought of an alternative approach?'

Georgianna smiled charmingly. 'I have indeed. In fact, I'm prepared to sign the first part of the contract today, offering my exclusive services for a period of three months, for a fee of fifty thousand pounds. I am not, however, prepared to commit myself in advance to continuing as Sarong Girl for the next twenty-one months, but would prefer a more open-ended arrangement. If, at the end of three months, you feel that you wish to retain me further, we can negotiate a continuance figure then.'

Her throwaway tone resulted, of course, from the fact

that it couldn't have mattered to her less if she worked for the next three months or the full two years. Kitty, however, felt the cold clutch of fear. Oh God, the greedy cow was going to blow it for both of them!

Kramer nodded almost imperceptibly in Czerny's direction. No way would the client agree to an open-ended arrangement in the model's favour. All that money on R & D and *then* have to negotiate her fee — it would be handing her a stick to beat them with. As Czerny opened his mouth to refuse categorically, Burt Johnson leant over and whispered in his ear. The Account Executive swallowed nervously and turned two shades paler. The client expected him to stay on top of the situation, but Johnson was a director of the company which employed him, paid him a six-figure salary and could squeeze his balls when it damned well felt like it. Johnson had just told him that unless he secured Arabella Hamilton, he could start looking for another job. Czerny took a big gamble.

'Miss Hamilton, we clearly cannot commit ourselves to an open-ended contract. For budgetary reasons there has to be a ceiling on our allocation to the model.' He shot a cautious sideways glance at Kramer's smugly smiling face. The marketing man wasn't going to like his next move, but it was cards-on-the-table time. At the planning stages, when they had discussed the highest sum of money they might be prepared to offer the model, the figure of two million dollars had been mentioned — 'For the right girl only, and of course we'd expect you to do your best to bring her in for less.' Well, he'd done his best, but this was some tough cookie and he didn't dare lose her now.

'We're prepared to sign an agreement today that we are prepared to negotiate a separate renewal fee at the end of three months, up to a ceiling of two million dollars. I must stress at this point that two million is the most you can expect, but our negotiations in three months' time won't necessarily reach that figure.'

It was a sop to the furious Kramer, of course.

Georgianna's gamble had paid off royally. She certainly hadn't expected them to agree to give her the whip hand in leaving the renewal figure to a later date, but she had hoped to scare out of them the absolute top figure to which they were prepared to agree, and it looked as though she'd succeeded. Kramer could hardly conceal his fury.

She smiled disarmingly. 'That sounds fine to me, gentlemen. What about you, Kitty?' The agent nodded dumbly. 'Okay, would you please amend the first part of the contract accordingly and initial it? Kitty, may we have the girls in to witness our signatures?'

Kitty went to summon them herself. She could have buzzed through, but she had to tell someone the amazing news before she burst. Arabella, the silly little English girl who'd fallen so crazily for Christian Neggar, had just made her three hundred thousand dollars in commission! Kitty was staggering in under a trayful of glasses and two bottles in a silver ice-bucket, when Rachelle noticed something odd.

'Why didn't you sign yourself "Arabella Hamilton"?' she asked.

'Because my real name is Georgianna Randolph. That's right, isn't it, gentlemen, you should always sign a legal document in your full legal name?'

'Right,' Czerny agreed brightly. 'Randolph, hey? That sounds kind of familiar.'

'Georgianna Randolph?' Kitty said faintly, and her best Baccarat champagne flutes skidded crazily on the tray as she plonked it down on her desk top. 'Your father's Dexter Randolph, the tycoon, and your parents own a bloody big mansion somewhere in England, right?' she said.

'We don't actually own Courtney Park,' Georgianna demurred.

'But your Dad was made a Lord not so long ago, and your Ma's a lady in her own right,' Kitty pressed. 'That makes you an Honourable, doesn't it?'

Czerny felt a great weight of anxiety lift from his

shoulders. He seized a brimming glass of champagne and passed it graciously to Kramer. 'There we are, Ellis,' he said. 'It seems I've secured a genuine English aristocrat to promote your product for you. Just think of the mileage we're going to get from that — and absolutely free.'

After two hours of solitary drinking, Christian left the Crillon Bar in the same state of anger and confusion in which he'd entered it. He was also spoiling for a fight. Arabella's dropping of him had been a blow to his self-esteem — it was literally years since a woman had tired of him before he was finished with her, and already rumours were spreading around town that Neggar must be losing his touch. Arabella had been a financial loss, too. The magazines were crazy for her, and he didn't even want to think about the advertising deal he'd missed out on just when he needed to make some real money.

And then, out of the blue, there'd been the final blow. Thursday's post had brought a letter from *Le Style* advising all freelance contributors that commissions were temporarily frozen while the magazine's new management conducted their own study of the publication's running costs. A few discreet telephone calls to other people in the business confirmed to Christian that they were all in the same boat.

'But it can only be temporary,' Marc Stein assured him 'A bit less work for the freelance stylists, maybe, and more doubling up on hair and make-up, but there are very few staff photographers, and none who can do the work we do. *Le Style* can't do without us, and they'll soon realise it.'

Christian knew it was true, but something about that letter had sent a shiver of foreboding through him. On Saturday, a second letter bearing *Le Style*'s distinctive franking on the envelope had arrived. It hadn't taken them long to climb down, he reflected, slitting open the envelope, but the tone of the letter inside was far from conciliatory. Someone — a secretary, probably — was writing to let him know that *Le Style*'s new publisher expected him to attend a meeting at eight o'clock on Monday evening in her office. Expected! No courtesies were extended; there was no suggestion that date and time might be altered to suit his convenience. Still smarting at the letter's peremptory tone, its bland assumption that he would not risk offending the magazine's new proprietors, Christian called Stein again.

'Had the latest from *Le Style*?' he enquired.

'Yes, total climb-down, isn't it? What did I tell you: "Invoices will be closely monitored, but all existing commissions are confirmed." I told you they couldn't do without us. Any juicy titbits about the new setup from your little English girl — Araminta, isn't it?'

'Arabella, you mean. No, we're not seeing so much of each other, remember? Your letter was from the editors, then?'

'Wasn't yours?' Stein's elaborately casual tones immediately alerted Christian.

'Well, obviously a secretary signed it. They're in London aren't they?'

'But keeping in close touch with Elise, apparently. The poor girl has to air courier over the day's correspondence, minutes of meetings, even press pages, and they call her back the next morning at eight o'clock with their instructions. *And* they're monitoring invoices, damn them! I guess there won't be quite so much of a profit to be made out of *Le Style* nowadays. What do you think?'

Christian was beginning to wonder if there would be any profit for him at all. All existing commissions had been confirmed — except his. He alone had heard from the magazine's publisher, a faceless nameless individual who 'expected' him at eight o'clock on Monday evening. It was a strange time for a business meeting.

He stumbled as he left the Crillon and realised he was more drunk than he'd supposed. One of the fountains in the Place de la Concorde caught his eye and he lurched towards it, splashing his flushed face and rinsing the whisky taint from his mouth. On the way to *Le Style*'s offices he dived into a *bar tabac* and ordered two cups of strong black coffee. As he spooned sugar into the second, he noticed that his cuffs were soaked through and that his hands were trembling. Only Christian knew how important it was he should keep the work from *Le Style*, and how well over the odds Toinette had always paid him for it in recognition of other services rendered. If an interfering busybody of a new publisher chose to get sticky about his fees, Christian could find himself in financial hot water pretty damn fast.

The porter had to be summoned to unlock the door to *Le Style*'s offices. The man confirmed that Monsieur Neggar was expected, and insisted on riding up in the lift with him to the fifth floor where the editors and publisher's offices were situated. The corridor was in darkness when the lift doors opened and the porter stepped out and located the light-switch without a word, but not before Christian had noticed a strip of light under one of the closed doors.

'This must be the one I want,' he said, indicating the door he now saw was marked 'Publisher.'

The porter nodded, still without speaking, and sat down on one of the low sofas in the reception area by the lift.

'I'm sure there's no need to wait,' Christian assured him.

'Mam'selle has given me my orders,' the man said gruffly, and took a folded evening paper from his tunic pocket.

Christian shrugged, his spirits lifting at the news that the mysterious publisher was a woman. This was going to be considerably easier than he'd feared. He knocked sharply, and a woman's voice, muffled by the thickness of the door, called out in English: 'Come in.'

It was dark inside the room, the only illumination a pool

of light from a halogen desk-lamp, turned to its lowest level. A high-backed swivel chair behind the desk was turned away from the door and towards the picture window.

Christian cleared his throat to indicate his presence and began to cross the pale wooden floor, his footsteps unnaturally loud in the still quiet room. 'Good evening,' he said in his most lilting accent. 'I'm Christian Neggar —'

'I know who you are, and you know me, so we'll dispense with the introductions, shall we?'

He peered into the gloom surrounding the desk, half-suspecting whom he was hearing, but unable to believe it. Slowly the swivel chair spun round and its occupant leaned forwards to adjust the desk-lamp. Brilliant light flooded around her in a pool, and Christian saw that there had been no mistake. Georgianna had dressed simply for the meeting in a favourite blue crêpe Jean Muir and a dazzling diamond pendant and earrings which she had asked Alexander to bring over specially from the Courtney Park safe when he came.

Christian laughed nervously. 'Arabella, it's lovely to see you again, especially when you've been avoiding my calls. But I don't understand ... I was expecting to meet the new publisher of the magazine.'

'You're looking at her — publisher and co-owner, with my uncle, Lord Courtney.'

Christian was at a loss for words. There'd been no final parting from this woman, none of the tears and threats her predecessors had regaled him with so many times. He floundered, unsure of his ground. 'Arabella, I —'

'My name's not Arabella.' She smiled at the effect of her words and sat back in her chair, light refracting from the magnificent diamonds as she moved, leaving him in no doubt that they were real. 'There's something you ought to know, Christian. Hamilton is a family name — it's Uncle Xan's, for instance — but it's not mine. Neither am I Arabella — I took the name from a portrait of a favourite ancestor. My real name is Georgianna Randolph.'

When he still looked blank, she continued softly, 'Perhaps you've heard of my father, or maybe of his companies? He's Dexter Randolph, of Randolph Enterprises.'

He put out his hands and began to walk towards her. '*Chérie*, Georgianna is such a charming name, why did you keep it from me?'

How could the soft-toned insinuation of his voice ever have blinded me to the calculating light in those icy eyes? Georgianna wondered. She shivered with affront. That he actually dared to try and charm her now, after all he had done to her! The loathing in her voice stopped him in his tracks.

'Do you know,' she said incredulously, 'I did actually feel guilty about keeping it from you? When I think about all the things you kept from me!'

'What things? What did I keep from you? I took some wonderful photographs of you, launched you into a highly profitable career. I didn't notice you thanking me for that when you refused my calls last week.'

For a moment Georgianna was speechless, then the full force of her anger over Christian like a tidal wave. 'You have the effrontery to expect me to thank *you*, after the way you treated me! You stole my virginity, tricked me into believing I was special to you. You do it to all your conquests, apparently — the same flowers, the same compliments, the same weekends at your seedy little love-nest. Like the fool I was, I loved you. I believed you loved me, but it was all a game. Do you even know the meaning of the word?'

From the blank expression on his face, she could read her answer. 'You've had a lot of practice, haven't you?' Georgie continued. 'You enjoy having girls run after you. It feeds your ego to leave a chain of broken hearts. The only difference is, this time I got out before you'd quite finished with me. You'd already chosen my successor, but I was still useful to you, wasn't I? Arabella brought you profitable work, so you were prepared to put up with her hanging around you for as long as the money lasted. How long would it have been, Christian, before you changed the number of your private line and gave me the new only if I'd agree to play your sick little games?'

His face paled perceptibly, but he'd obviously decided to bluff this one out. 'What do you mean? What games? Someone's been telling malicious lies, poisoning you against me.'

'Nobody told me anything about you, but I overheard plenty, and thank God for it! You couldn't contact me last week because I'd already decided I wanted you off the Sarong Girl contract. We finalised it today, by the way, for a record-breaking fee. Your name wasn't mentioned. And now I own *Le Style*, and find from the books that you are one of our most favoured photographers at fees that far outstrip those of the other contributors. What do you suppose I'm going to do about that?'

He was round the desk and pulling her to her feet quicker than she had thought possible. For a terrifying moment she thought he intended to hit her, but his next words sickened her even more than the threat of violence.

'Forget about the work — I don't need it. There's only one thing I care about and that's you, *chérie*. I love you.'

She wrenched herself free. 'Yes, I believe you could care for Georgianna — after all, she's got enough money to keep you for the rest of your life. You wouldn't need to work with her to look after you, would you? God, you're so transparent, Christian! Did you really think I'd swallow that? You had your chance to love me as Arabella, but I meant nothing to you then — I don't believe any woman ever will. And now, we seem to be one photographer too many on *Le Style*, and as you don't need the work . . .'

He sank into the chair she had vacated, his face ghastly. Days of worry over his failing finances had etched lines of strain around his pale eyes. Georgianna realised she'd never asked his age. It must be more than she'd imagined.

'Don't,' he said hollowly. 'Don't take the work away. If you do, I'll be bankrupt in a month or two. Is that what you want, Georgianna? Would it make a rich girl like you happy to know that you've broken me? I'll beg, if that's what turns you on, but don't take that work away.'

There were actually tears in his eyes and a strong smell of whisky hung in the air around him. His usually immaculate appearance was marred by three days' growth of patchy stubble and his Comme des Garçons jacket and shirt were darkened randomly by patches of damp. Georgianna looked steadily down at him and felt absolutely nothing. There was no pity — he'd hurt her too much for that — but the burning need for revenge seemed to have faded. She pressed a concealed button on the underside of her desk.

'You'd better go now, Christian. Georges is waiting to see you out. I won't take the work away from you immediately — you're too good a photographer for that — but we'll pay you the same rate as we pay the others, and from time to time I'll ask Marie-Jeanne for news of you. There are women who'll accept you on your own terms, I know, but if I hear of you taking up with any new young inexperienced girls as innocent as I was, you will never work for *Le Style* again, and I will use all of my family's considerable influence to make sure you never work in London or New York either. I don't like being abused, *chéri*. Now get out!'

Christian nodded, and the door to her office opened. 'Monsieur Neggar is going now, Georges,' she told the doorman. 'Would you show him out, please?'

When she heard the lift beginning its descent, she opened the door into the compact little galley kitchen off her office. The small fridge was empty but for a single bottle of Roederer Cristal, for which Georgianna had inherited her grandmother's taste. Two crystal flutes stood nearby on the worktop. She smiled, and looked at her watch. Any minute now ...

534

The wall-mounted phone beside her rang once. 'Your second visitor is here, mam'selle. Shall I show him up?'

'No thanks, Georges, he can find his own way.'

'Very well, mam'selle.'

'Oh, and Georges, we won't be needing you again this evening.'

Georgianna had lowered the lights and poured the champagne when Guy entered her office. He glanced around him, bemused. 'Are we celebrating something else?' he asked, smiling.

'Catching up, if you still want to,' she told him, and stood up to kiss him hello. Much later they toasted each other in glasses of flat champagne.

'You know what I'd like,' he murmured, winding a strand of her red-brown hair round one finger. 'I'd like you to stay here in Paris, run your magazine and live with me. But you won't, will you?'

'You've forgotten my modelling contract,' she reminded him. 'For the next three months at least I'm committed to being the Sarong Girl.'

'But there's something else, too'

She told him half the truth. 'There's my family, and Courtney Park. I've never been away from them so long before and I hate leaving them all, particularly with Sloane on the prowl.'

Guy laughed and kissed her. 'You English are so funny. The wicked aunt with her too smart clothes and too young lovers. What harm could she possibly do you, *ma belle*?'

'The lovers and the clothes don't matter. My aunt's plans for Courtney Park do,' Georgie insisted, but a sudden vivid mental image gave the lie to her words. She wasn't thinking of Courtney Park at all but of a tall broad-shouldered man striding angrily away from her, black hair ruffled by the breeze. The last time they'd met, Nicky had misjudged her badly, but Court had written to him from the Malmaison to set the record straight and she had a premonition that their next meeting could be very different, if Sloane would permit it.

'Georgie,' Guy said wistfully, 'you will be coming back to Paris?'

She hugged him. 'Of course I'm coming back — try and stop me! There's the magazine, and Court and Chantel — and of course there's you. You'll always be one of my dearest friends.'

'But not *the* dearest?'

Georgianna thought for a moment. Her time with Christian had taught her many things, principally that people lied for one of two reasons: to betray or to be kind.

'Maybe, one day,' she said, and hardly knew if she was being kind or telling the truth.

Book Five

SLOANE

Alexander sat at a Shaker table studiously examining the entries in a Sotheby's catalogue of Indian and Asian Art. In a house whose walls were jewelled with museum-quality French Impressionists, and in the teeth of Sloane's expertise in the field of contemporary art, Alexander had decided to choose one of his own in which to specialise. One of his latest acquisitions — a serene Khmer head — looked incongruous among the colourful contrasting chintzes and Early American furniture which Sloane had insisted on importing on the advice of one of Sister Parish's bright young men.

In the years they had been married, Alexander had come to realise that his wife throve on flouting any opposition she was offered. Far from shrinking from a fight and the resulting bad feeling, she waded in, pennants flying, and proceeded to make the life of everyone around her a living hell until she got exactly what she wanted. He had long ceased to offer any opposition to his wife's plans. He put up none this morning when she strode into their private sitting-room, reed slim in a tailored Versace suit cut sharp as a knife.

'I can't think why you bother with that ethnic sleaze,' she said, looking over his shoulder and shuddering at a particularly explicit Indian minature.

Alexander closed the catalogue and studied her instead. 'You're looking extremely smart today, my dear.'

'Yes, I've got a lunch,' she said evasively. 'Before I go there's something I need to discuss with you.'

Something she wanted, in other words. Alexander stifled an impulse to close his eyes in weariness. It was not that she expected him to pay for any of her wild and extravagant notions, but he was required to pass on the news to

Angelica and overcome the objections she always made — on the grounds of tradition or simple good taste. He was tired of being caught between the twin implacably opposed forces of his wife and mother. Every day he could feel his energy and will wearing a little thinner. 'What is it this time?'

She turned mild blue-grey eyes on him, the colour they always went when she chose to charm a concession out of him instead of demanding it. 'There's no need to sound like that, Xan. It's just a little thing, really. It's my birthday in November and I was thinking wouldn't it be fine to have a grand birthday ball, here at Courtney Park?'

A ball to mark the end of his wife's fourth decade ... It was not an unreasonable request.

'I don't see why not, darling.' He was pleased to find her in a softer, more reasonable, frame of mind than he had seen her for weeks. 'It'd be a big affair, I take it?'

Her lips curved into a smile. 'Naturally. I have friends the world over. But don't worry, Xan, I'm not expecting you to bankroll it.'

It was a cheap shot, since he had given up his post at Shearing's at her insistence. It was true that after Dexter's accident, while he was in hospital and afterwards undergoing extensive physiotherapy, Alexander had had his hands full just getting to grips with the enormous amount of administration involved in running a great house and estate. But with Dexter's return on the scene, able to get about and make his viewpoint known, even if he seemed unlikely to regain the use of his legs, Alexander had begun to feel more and more redundant in his own home. It was his wife, however, who still would not hear of his returning to New York, the city he loved, and working full-time - and now she was taunting him with his relative penury.

She must have seen the flash of anger in her husband's handsome face. 'Darling, that was mean of me. I didn't mean anything by it, okay?'

They both knew it was not true. The fact of Sloane's

superior wealth shadowed a relationship already strained by basic incompatibility.

'So you agree to my birthday ball?' she pressed.

'November 20th ... yes, that should be fine for Courtney and Georgianna. They'll both be back from France by then.' Georgie was more or less finished there already, he knew, but Courtney's secret release from the Malmaison Clinic would not take place till late that month. 'Ash should be able to find some business reason to fly back from Australia, and I'm sure Maman can give you all sorts of useful pointers about the catering and the florists and so on. She's had so much experience of party-throwing here.'

Sloane's patience, thin at the best of times, reached snapping-point. 'For gosh sakes, they're not *our* kids! Who cares if they can make it or not? If they're around, fine. If not, who gives a damn? I'm sick of always pussyfooting around the Randolphs and your mother. Why can't I throw a ball, when and how I like, in my own goddamned house!'

He looked affronted. 'I do wish you'd try and get on with my family, Sloane. It would make life so much easier for us all.'

Her thin face was flushed with anger and her eyes glittered the colour of ice, the way they always did when she encountered opposition.

'What would make *my* life easier would be if *your* family got the hell out of here,' she spat. 'What's the matter with you, anyway? Why don't you ever assert yourself? Don't you want this house to be for *us* and *our* family?'

'My dear, after years of trying, and undergoing those humiliating tests, nothing would give me greater pleasure than to hear that you and I were expecting a child. Until then, given the enormous amount of money and time Dexter has lavished on this place, it would seem a little dog-in-the-mangerish to insist on turning him and my sister out.'

She was breathing rapidly now, her chest rising and falling beneath the rich cerise silk of her Hermès blouse. 'So it's all down to me, is that what you're saying?' She was building up to one of her hysterical rages. 'You're trying to put the responsibility for solving this whole crazy situation on *my* shoulders? Well, all right, if that's what you want. I'll show your entire free-loading family where this particular gravy-train stops!'

She stomped out of the room, crashing the door behind her. Alexander sighed, too dispirited to pick up his pen and carry on marking up his catalogue. The phone rang.

'My lord?' The estate manager's quavering tones were instantly recognisable. Ralph Hayward coughed deferentially. 'Lord Randolph and I were wondering if you had forgotten our usual meeting? His lordship and I are in his office downstairs.'

Alexander looked at his watch, ashamed to realise he had forgotten their usual bi-weekly meeting. 'Thank you, Hayward. I'll be with you in a minute.'

He put down the receiver, already getting to his feet, then stopped and frowned. Why was it always Dexter's office? It was, as Sloane was constantly reminding him, *his* house. Why did they never come to him?

He began to dial Dexter's number to countermand the arrangement, then realised how churlish he would seem, standing on his dignity in front of his crippled brother-in-law. Dexter loathed using the special invalid lift Angelica had had installed, confining his visits upstairs to once a day when he was usually to be found at dinner in the family dining-room. Downstairs his mother-in-law had created for him not only a state-of-the-art office but an entire suite of specially adapted rooms where he could be largely independent, with few painful reminders of the life he had forfeited.

On the way downstairs, Alexander glanced idly out of a window and saw his wife's midnight blue Aston Martin rocketing down the drive. He hoped that she was lunching locally but knew that she had made virtually no friends in the county. Which meant, he supposed, that she was on her way to another assignation with her lover in London, whoever he might be.

There was no lunch date for Sloane, who considered that people who ate before nightfall were self-indulgent and deserved to be fat. At the Chester Square house, which was owned by Dexter but put at the disposal of the whole extended family, she spent half an hour with her personal beautician, Rosa. When she was satisfied that her face was flawless, she went on foot to Knightsbridge. She let herself into the small mews house, which was unfurnished except for one room, and looked at her watch. Good, she had time for her second bath of the day, though she was careful to keep her face free from water. While she was soaking, she examined the results of her latest breast implant, lifting up each small round globe to inspect the hairline scar beneath. Hmm, not bad. Barely noticeable at all, in fact, except in a harsh light or from an unflattering angle — and Sloane was much too canny to permit either.

After her bath she patted into her skin a layer of rich scented cream, then opened the closet where she kept a few clothes. She pulled on a soft Indian robe of billowing white muslin heavily encrusted with gold Rajput embroidery. She enjoyed the snagging of the metallic thread against her sensitised breasts. She would have liked a massage before this assignation — they always left her totally relaxed and ready for sex — but the scene with Xan had slowed her down. At the memory, she could not prevent a frown.

She glanced impatiently at the enamelled carriage-clock at the bedside. In New York, Bradford Carter should just be starting work. With any luck she'd be among the first of the hundreds of callers who besieged his relay of secretaries all day long. If they knew what was good for them, they'd put The Countess of Courtney, straight through.

Her lawyer greeted her with easy familiarity. 'Sloane, baby, how's it going?'

Anyone else would have been frozen for their presumption. Use of her newly-acquired title was very important to Sloane, but Brad was one of the two people on earth with whom she could not stand on ceremony. 'Just fine, thank you,' she replied. 'And you, and Jo-Ann and the children — I hope you're all okay?'

'Just great, thanks.'

A shade too much heartiness to his voice? She really couldn't be bothered thinking about other people's problems but launched straight in to an account of her own concerns.

'— I mean it's just grisly, Brad, you have no idea. Locked into this situation where my brother-in-law calls all the shots. Okay, so he was tragically crippled in an accident — de-da-de-da-de-da — but that was years ago, for goodness' sake. He's continually in a foul temper and his behaviour is so inappropriate. He barely speaks to Xan's sister — not that she has any conversation other than the boring lives of her boring babies, all of whom use the place like a hotel. One's in Australia, thank God, the cokehead's in some fancy clinic, though they don't realise I know that. The spoiled brat of a daughter's flying in next week and already they're rolling out the red carpet — *my* red carpet.'

There was real bitchery in Sloane's voice. She still had not forgotten the scene with Georgie and Xan in which she had so disastrously lost her dignity.

'Hmm, sounds quite a household,' Brad commented, 'I take it you're looking for an out from this family togetherness?'

'Oh, Brad, you know me too well.'

'That's right.'

She had a moment's uncomfortable recall of just how much he did know about her.

'I'll need to consult with our English associates on this,' he continued urbanely. 'British land law's a little out of my usual field, Sloane.'

'Sure, I understand. Consult with them by all means —

544

but, Brad, I expect you to handle this matter personally.' Time to jerk his strings just a little, pay him back for that crack about knowing her past. 'I know how indispensible you are to Daddy —' subtly reminding him that if Daddy's little girl said so, he could just as easily be let go — 'but I'm sure I can talk him into using one of your assistants while you're in England on my business. 'Besides,'' she lightened up a little, 'that would mean you'd be here for my birthday ball, the weekend of November 20th. Don't forget, now.'

Bradford had not become a top New York litigator by failing to recognise a client's veiled command. 'Sure, Sloane. Just let me clear a few things with Jo-Ann and the office, and I'll be with you shortly. *Bye for now.*'

He put down the receiver and buzzed for his personal assistant. Jo-Ann was the least of his difficulties. So long as she and the kids could continue to drive between the cripplingly expensive Connecticut estate and the cripplingly expensive Connecticut country club where they played golf, tennis and in the sand-pit, he doubted he'd even be missed. His packed appointments schedule was another matter.

'Looks like you and me'll have to wing it a little,' he told his assistant, who raised one immaculately plucked eyebrow as he drew a line through the last two weeks in November.

'But ...'

Grimly he pencilled in the name Sloane de Havilland — the way he always thought of her, despite the two marriages.

'Sure,' said his assistant. Anyone else, Bradford would have told to go screw themselves.

Meanwhile, back in London, already moist with anticipation of her lover, Sloane was doing exactly that. Her fiery impetuous stud liked her ready and receptive.

She lay back on the blue-scalloped linen sheets from

Frette and reached into the drawer of the night-table where she kept a few very personal things. The slightly larger than life, exquisitely modelled, jade dildo had been a wedding present from Gianni, together with a card reading: '*Carissima*, use this, and *don't* think of me!'

She smiled reminiscently. Bastard though he had been, at least Gianni was a realist, whereas Xan ... But no, she refused to allow thoughts of her husband to spoil her afternoon. Relaxing her muscles, she guided the smooth cold shaft deep inside her. There was always that moment when it felt just too big and then she thought of Nicky, her royal lover — the powerful thrust of his loins, his bold eyes under their fierce black brows — and the juices began to flow. Her jade lover eased in and out of her pulsating warmth. Time and again it and Sloane's fingertips brought her to the brink. Each time she forced herself to hold off, enjoying the ache of desire which only one man could satisfy.

She heard the slam of the door, his rapid footsteps on the uncarpeted stairs. She thrust the cold comfort of his substitute out of sight and sprawled naked across the linen sheets, legs apart, waiting for her lover to blaze between them.

The door opened and Crown Prince Nicolas of Malivia appeared, raindrops glinting on his jet-black curls. He stood in the doorway without speaking. He looked so heart-stoppingly handsome, so male, so very young ...

'Good afternoon — sir.' It always gave her an extra buzz to obey the stuffy conventions in these circumstances. She raised herself more becomingly on one elbow, angling her chin so that the effects of its cosmetically neatened lines would not be wasted.

'No, don't move,' he said. 'You're exactly how I like a woman — on her back and waiting for me.'

She laughed and lay back, angling her head on the pillow so that she could watch him undress. He knew how much it always turned her on. With maddening slowness and thoroughness he took off his jacket, shirt and tie, his

546

shoes and socks ... When he had taken off the rest he stayed perfectly still, hands by his sides. Even unaroused, his thick sturdy rod was memorable. Feasting her eyes on it, Sloane widened her legs in anticipation, showing him the extent of her arousal.

Nicky's strong-boned face held the fierce concentration of a hunter closing in on its prey. He reared into magnificent erection and knelt by the side of the bed. Eyes dilated, she slithered across the sheets towards him. He hooked her legs over his shoulders, slid his hands beneath her buttocks. Half lifting her, he plunged into the furnace heat, answering fire with fire. Sloane convulsed, drumming his back and shoulders with her heels as he slammed into her — once, twice, three times more, and she felt him come in a fierce scalding rain.

'That's what I like about married women,' he drawled afterwards. 'They don't waste a man's time.'

She knew that before the aftershock of his loving had fully faded, he'd be ready again. Nicky always liked a brief interlude, to start. The second time his lovemaking would be slow and overwhelmingly satisfying. She must speak to him now, while she still had the energy. Quickly she poured them both a glass of champagne — a small fridge was concealed in the panelling beside the bed — and asked him if he planned to be around at the end of November.

'Perhaps. Why do you ask?'

'It's my birthday on the 20th —' she didn't mention which one, naturally — 'and I'm throwing a ball at Courtney. It'll be tremendous fun, a costume affair, I thought. You wouldn't even need to dress up, Nicky. You could come in one of those divine uniforms of yours.'

He glowered at her. 'The robes of high office are not a joke in my country.'

She widened her eyes ingenuously. 'Darling, of course they're not. Forget I even said it — but promise me you'll come, pretty please? My evening wouldn't be the same without you.'

Nicky remained silent. He hated being forced into any commitment, however trivial. The discreet married women — older than himself — with whom he conducted his longer running affairs — the one-nighters he reserved for the eager nymphets of the polo circuit — always started so well, not making any demands on him, thrilled and flattered to have a handsome young man, let alone a prince, in their beds. Until now, Sloane had been everything he appreciated — blandly polite in public; frankly lascivious in private. Now, as they always did, she was going one step too far, trying to include him in her own petty socialising.

Fortunately for her, she did not realise the direction his thoughts were taking. 'I'm sure your attendance wouldn't give rise to any gossip, sir,' she said cleverly. 'It's common knowledge you're a friend of Xan's nephew Courtney — he's flying over from France specially.'

Without realising it, she'd said just the right thing. Nicky was too discreet to mention it, but he knew where Court had spent the last months. It would be good to see his friend now that he had recovered. Even better if he was accompanied by the sister Nicky remembered from their last meeting.

He pulled a slim diary from the inside picket of his alpaca jacket. 'What date did you say?'

In the space for November 20th he noted: 'Ball, CP. Georgianna?'

His Royal Highness Prince Nicolas of Malivia left Sloane in the early evening for a reception at Buckingham Palace. No woman ever got more than a few hours of Nicky's undivided attention — but then a few hours of him was worth a whole week of a lesser lover.

Sated and weak, Sloane made her own way back to Chester Square where she went straight to bed, ordering the housekeeper to bring her up a chilled bottle of her favourite Chablis. After a few minutes, she realised that the international time-zones were on her side. She could reach her friends in Argentina, Brazil, the West Coast. The formal invitations would go out as soon as the party planners had had them engraved but she wanted to make sure of her dozen or so most famous friends, any one of whom would command front-page headlines on their arrival in England. On November 20th she wanted them all to be at Courtney Park, making it the most memorable ball of the year.

She dialled and talked, dialled and talked. It was thirsty work, catching up on the gossip of three continents. She ordered up a second bottle of wine and drank it all, toasting her own brilliant future as châtelaine of Courtney Park and royal mistress.

By the time she returned to Wiltshire three days later, preparations for the ball were well advanced — at least so far as the London end was concerned.

Alexander greeted her coolly. 'You said you had a lunch, Sloane. You didn't mention you'd be gone so long.'

'I didn't know. I ran into some old friends from Italy, went out with them a few times.' Nicky had been able to visit her twice more. The memory made her quiver inside her silk underwear. 'For goodness' sake,' she said, rattled by his air of censure, 'it's not as though there was anything special going on here.'

'No, but aren't you forgetting something? By my calculation Thursday was the day you were due to ovulate. We should have made love then.'

Sloane's face tightened with annoyance. 'If you can call it making love!' She had grown to dread Alexander's earnest but totally uninspired efforts. He did nothing for her in bed, and she knew very well that he only managed the limp account he gave of himself by fantasising about raven haired, tight-buttocked boys. She suspected he had a thing with one of the grooms from the stud, a chirpy lad, Black Irish and graceful. The sexual side of their marriage was a farce, but she could not afford to turn her back on it completely.

Instead she resorted to the usual get out — tears. 'It's terrible being ruled by the calendar like this,' she sniffed. 'So humiliating, dehumanising. And every month that awful reminder that time is running out.'

Alexander was instantly contrite. He pressed his handkerchief into her hand. 'Darling, I'm a brute. It was wrong of me to pressure you like that. Of course you must feel free to go up to town whenever you feel like it — but it has begun to be rather noticeable how long you stay there. Maman was commenting only the other day.'

She chose not to comment on that, zeroing in instead on the topic of chief concern to her. 'Elizabeth Anson's agreed to take charge of everything — isn't that marvellous? We thought we'd model it on a Venetian *ridotto* ... She's arranging for a wonderful structural engineer to see if he can create a miniature canal in the ballroom, complete with gondolas! It's amazing what can be done, she says ...'

She poured herself a whisky, chattering about the costume she would wear, the guests she was expecting. Alexander felt his jaw and shoulders tighten with worry. The ballroom was his mother's pride and joy. The thought of water within a hundred yards of its venerable floor would be anathema to her, he knew. This was going to take very diplomatic handling. 'I'm sure Maman could be terribly helpful to you —'

'Forget it!' she snarled, pouring herself another three fingers of whisky.

It was only four in the afternoon, but he knew that now she had started drinking there would be no stopping her. With any luck she'd have passed out by the time family dinner was served at 8.15.

Sloane stared at him fiercely in an effort to focus her eyes. 'Your mother is not to lay a finger on the arrangements for my party — is that clear?'

'Perfectly. Now, if you'll excuse me, I have some figures to go over with Hayward.'

It was a face-saving excuse, they both knew. The truth of it was he couldn't stand to sit and watch her drink, knowing she was spoiling for a fight with his mother which he was powerless to prevent.

It seemed it would not take place that night, however. When Alexander glanced into their sitting-room in the early evening it was empty, and Sloane's personal maid told him the Countess had taken to her bed with 'one of her 'eads'. He changed in his own room and joined his mother and sister for a drink in the family sitting-room, feeling light-hearted at his reprieve.

Camilla was cockahoop at the prospect of Georgie's imminent arrival. 'She's just called to confirm her flight and says she has some very exciting news.'

Alexander, who had recently visited Paris and invested his own cash in Georgie's purchase of *Le Style*, kept the news to himself. 'I wonder what it is,' he said affably.

'And what about Courtney?' said Angelica sharply. 'He's up to no good, I can tell.'

Camilla crossed her fingers behind her back. Although she knew her mother would not let slip to Dexter any word of Courtney's temporary slide back into addiction, she had a superstitious dread of discussing his problem. This time his cure seemed so deep-rooted and complete, things would go better for him, she was sure. 'He's met a super new girl, apparently.'

Alexander seized the bull by the horns, 'Well, I hope they can both get themselves over here by the 20th November. Sloane's planning a grand birthday ball for about a million of her closest friends. Should be quite a bash.'

Angelica's mouth pursed in annoyance. 'But that's impossible — I have a house party planned for that date. Some Japanese business associates of Dexter's ...'

Alexander looked uneasy. 'It *is* the date of Sloane's birthday, Maman. We can hardly ask her to change that. Surely it's possible to move the house party to another weekend?'

551

'She should have consulted the bible,' said his mother stubbornly. She was referring to the Courtney Park events diary in which family members recorded details of their movements and engagements as far ahead as possible, so as to avoid exactly the sort of clash which had just taken place.

Camilla the peacemaker intervened: 'I'm sure it can be rearranged, Maman. I'm going downstairs to tell Dexter when to expect Georgie. He'll be so thrilled about that I doubt he'll make too much fuss about putting off the weekend.'

For the second time that week, Alexander felt himself growing annoyed at the way Dexter's wishes seemed to be paramount in everyone's mind. Anyone would think *he* was the Earl of Courtney instead of a life peer who had more or less bribed his way into the Honours List, he caught himself thinking bitterly.

'It's not working out, is it — this game of Happy Families?'

As usual, his mother's astuteness caught him on the hop. He poured her another drink, choosing his words with care. 'Let's just say I find Dexter's manner a trifle wearing at times. And Sloane —'

'— would be happy to show all of us the door. Thank God your father got one thing right at least, protecting my position here under the terms of his will.'

'Now, now, Maman,' he soothed her, 'things aren't nearly as black as that. You're both very strong characters and bound to clash from time to time. I'm sure Sloane would never make you less than welcome, though.'

His mother gave him an old-fashioned look, but did not comment further. They went down to dinner soon afterwards, Alexander telling Ford, the butler, to clear away a place as the Countess would not be joining them.

Unfortunately, he was wrong. Sloane drank just enough to make her drowsy. Her maid saw her to bed and switched off the light, believing she was out for the count. In fact, a light sleep restored her, if not to sense, at least to a state of light-headed euphoria. At 8.15 she snapped on the light, got out of bed and dressed herself in an extravagent Carolina Herrera creation of red velvet. Its neckline was far too cutaway and flirty for a quiet family dinner but accurately reflected the way she was feeling. She felt wonderful, on top of the world — until she walked into the family dining-room and saw that her mother-in-law had usurped her place at the bottom of the table.

The others were too polite to comment on the dress or Sloane's weaving walk. Dexter was not. 'Dunno about Sloane — Scarlett's more like it in that rig-out!' To add insult to injury, he actually laughed at her name — Sloane, for a Countess of Courtney!

The alcohol flowing freely through her veins dulled her inhibitions and tinged her words with vitriol. 'Keep your cheap cracks to yourself, you slob.'

Her brother-in-law opened his mouth to let her have it with both barrels, but Camilla jumped from her seat and put her hand imploringly on his arm. Angelica merely picked up the silver bell set before the mistress's setting.

'We weren't expecting you, Sloane. I'll ask Ford to see that another place is set.'

'No, you damn well won't! If there are any orders to be given in my husband's house, *I'll* give them.' She was dimly aware that she had gone too far in snatching the bell from her mother-in-law's hand and ringing it violently, but, damn, it felt good! 'I've had it with you all — cosying up to each other and making me feel like an outsider in my own house. That goes for you too!' she told her husband, who was on his feet and approaching her.

'Dexter didn't mean to hurt your feelings,' Camilla intervened.

'You don't need to speak for me, woman. I'm a cripple, not a mental defective!' he roared, slamming the table and scattering silver.

In answer to Sloane's agitated summons, Ford came

into the room at a discreet trot and stopped short at the scene which met his eyes.

'Ah, Ford,' Angelica greeted him, the only one who seemed in full possession of herself. 'As you can see, Lady Courtney has decided to join us for dinner after all.'

Obligingly he hurried to set a place between Alexander and Camilla while an embarrassed silence filled the room.

'Come and sit by me, darling,' said Alexander in a vain attempt to steer Sloane away from his mother.

She would not be swayed. Her blood was up. Inexcusably, she allowed herself to voice everything that was on her mind. 'Get out of my place,' she hissed at her mother-in-law. 'Yes, you heard me. Your precious son's too weak to say it for himself so I'll do it for him — you're history here. Your days as Countess of Courtney are through. I want you to take your arrogant, interfering face out of my sight — is that clear enough for you?'

She was so buoyed up by the elation of speaking her mind that she barely noticed Angelica's reply.

'You've made yourself more than clear, Sloane — you've made a public spectacle of your dislike for me. Very well. I have no interest in staying somewhere where my presence can give rise to such an appalling display of bad manners. A word of warning though, *ma chère* — you're going to be very sorry indeed for this night's work. 'No — ' she gestured at Camilla who started to follow here out of the room — 'I'm perfectly all right, thank you. Don't worry, I'll see you before I go.'

Bowing, Ford opened the door as she made her slow and stately way out of the room.

Incredibly, Sloane seemed unaffected by the scene which had left the others dumbstruck. Glowing with triumph she seemed to want to make polite small-talk.

'Did I tell you, Xan, I spoke with Bradford Carter a few days ago? He's coming over to England on business, so I invited him to stay with us one weekend — clever of me, no?'

Alexander knew what the lawyer's visit meant and left the rest of his dinner untouched. Sloane was wheeling in the big guns. One unwelcome inhabitant thrust out, only the Randolphs to go.

Dexter's sharp ears and eyes took in all the by-play. Bradford Carter, eh? The name would bear some checking out, he was sure.

Upstairs, Angelica's mind was buzzing with schemes. There was no way she was leaving Courtney Park for good — and no necessity for her to do so. Under the terms of her husband's will she was guaranteed a home for life here. Nevertheless, she felt Sloane's hysterical outburst was best met with a strategic withdrawal, somewhere quiet and peaceful where she could think things through ...

She ordered her clothes to be packed and a car to be called. As a parting shot she arranged for the doors to her rooms to be locked and the keys conveniently 'lost'.

Her luggage was carried down and she gave the chauffeur his orders. Gilmour had been her refuge during one outbreak of hostilities. It would serve excellently as a backdrop to the war of attrition she planned to wage against the upstart Countess of Courtney.

Only Georgianna's return to Courtney Park lightened the atmosphere. For once, Dexter and Camilla were united in happiness. Georgie breezed into her father's ground floor sitting-room, delighted to see her parents awaiting her arrival together.

'Darling, it's been much too long,' her mother welcomed her. Neither mentioned their meeting in Paris at Courtney's clinic.

'Stand back and let me have a look at you, girl,' growled Dexter when his daughter had hugged him hello. He studied her informal clothes — black 501s, hip-length black leather jacket — and disordered mane of hair. 'You look different, somehow ... What have you been up to over there?'

She blushed. 'A great many things — the most exciting is that I've started to model, rather successfully.'

In a long involved explanation she told them all about her accidental modelling début, editing out her subsequent disastrous affair with Christian or the real reason why she had been forced to remain in Paris. 'I never expected it to take off the way it has,' she said truthfully.

'Why ever not?' snorted her father. He didn't really like the thought of her modelling, standing around often skimpily dressed under the eyes of strangers — but any hint that she thought she might have been less than highly successful, and he was immediately her staunchest supporter. As she had anticipated. 'You're a flesh-and-blood beauty, not one of those poor skinny little things I see in those magazines of your mother's. The photographers have come to their senses at last and chosen a real girl, that's all.'

'And not just the photographers,' said Georgie. 'I saved the best till last. One of the top American ad agencies has chosen me to be the figurehead of a major new cosmetics line. I'm to be the Sarong Girl for a fee of two million dollars — how do you like them apples?'

'Oh, that's fantastic! I'm so proud of you.' said her mother.

'You mean there's real money in this taking-your-clothes-off lark?' said her father, then looked at her suspiciously. 'Everything's above board, I take it? Nothing you wouldn't like us to see?'

'It's so above board there's even a morals clause in my contract. And as for not wanting you to see — I've brought my book with me. I've masses of magazine clippings but I got prints of the best.'

She unzipped the large black portfolio she was carrying under one arm and placed the book on her father's knee.

Camilla hung over his shoulder, exclaiming in delight at their daughter's many different faces, all of them beautiful. Dexter frowned at some of the last shots of Georgie — and they were the heavily edited highlights of her underwear session with Christian.

She took back the book. 'No worse than anything you see on the beach at St Trop or Bondi. Don't be such a stick-in-the-mud, Daddy.' Privately she resolved not to show anyone the clippings of the underwear shoot when the magazine finally used them.

'And what do you plan to do with all the money?' her father asked, reverting to his favourite topic. 'Want me to invest it for you?'

'Thank you, Daddy, I've invested it myself,' she said firmly. She'd decided to keep word of her involvement with *Le Style* to herself until she saw how its relaunch was received.

'That's my girl!' Nothing Georgie said or did ever offended Dexter. 'Give that lazy bastard Webster a ring, will you? This calls for champagne.'

'Super. Why don't we ask Grandmama to join us?'

'Because we'd have a bloody long wait. Tell her, Camilla. It's your brother and his precious wife who're responsible.'

'Mother's gone to Gilmour for a rest,' said Camilla tactfully.

'Rest, my arse! Your grandmother and Sloane had a royal falling out, Georgie. Alex did bugger all to intervene and Angel's made a tactical withdrawal. Don't worry, she'll be back.'

Already the peaceful atmosphere of her homecoming was spoiled.

'I refuse to believe Uncle Xan's done anything mean or underhand. What's Sloane been up to?'

Camilla explained, adding painfully, 'It was none of Xan's doing, of course, but I can't help feeling he ought to have stopped Sloane before things got so far out of hand.

Poor Maman, I think I should go up to Gilmour and check that she's all right.'

'I've told you, Camilla, don't be such a worry-guts,' said Dexter. 'The old buzzard'll be happy as Larry, plotting how to get even. You fuss too much. She and Sloane were running true to form, that's all. It's Alex's part in all this that really worries me. He's changed towards me lately. I have a feeling it's not just his dear wife who wants us out of Courtney Park. Why else would they have asked a top litigation lawyer to stay here? I checked their "house-guest" out.'

'I'm sure it's just a coincidence,' said Camilla lamely.

'And pigs might fly! No, I can see their game, and I've arranged a visit from my own lawyers on Monday. If Alex and Sloane want to play rough, they'll find me ready to go to the last round.'

Camilla looked horrified. 'Litigation within the family? It's unthinkable.'

Her husband looked darkly at her. 'It bloody isn't — not with my whole investment in Courtney Park at stake. Your gentleman brother gets us Randolphs out over my dead body!'

Georgianna made her way slowly upstairs, saddened to learn the extent of the rift between the Hamilton and Randolph sides of the family. She still found it hard to believe that her gentle, generous uncle who had been such a help to her in Paris could have played any part in this. It must have been Sloane's doing — subtly poisoning her husband's mind against Dexter while announcing the arrival of her American lawyer friend, a red rag to a bull, so far as Dexter was concerned. Thank God she herself had come home in time to keep an eye on the worsening situation.

Before visiting her uncle, she checked with Sloane's maid that her aunt was out. 'In London again!' said the scandalised local woman. There was no way Georgie would expose herself or him to a repetition of the appalling scene Sloane had made on finding them alone together earlier that year.

Alexander's behaviour towards his niece remained unaltered. He looked and sounded tired but seemed genuinely delighted to have a private chat with her. He asked after the progress of his investment, naturally.

Proudly she produced a pasted-up dummy of the Christmas issue of *Le Style*, with some of the spreads already completed.

'Sensational! It can't fail. You've done marvellously well, Georgie — and, I note, without the aid of a single photograph from the studio of a certain Monsieur Neggar. I don't see him credited anywhere.'

She dimpled mischievously. 'You wouldn't. He's packed up the Paris studio, lock, stock and waterbed, and taken himself off to the Big Apple. He should feel right at home there, with all the other cockroaches!'

Alexander laughed with her. It was good to see her looking happy and confident again, not the shattered lovelorn girl he had visited in Paris only a month before. 'And Guy?'

'Working very hard, but he says he'll make time to meet me whenever I say. The Sarong thing's going to take up a lot of my time once it gets under way, and I'm not looking for a firmer commitment from him — not yet, anyway.'

'I understand. But don't let him slip through your fingers entirely, will you? It can be a mistake just to let things drift.'

'I couldn't agree more. Can't you do something about this appalling business between Sloane and Grandmama? People are bound to notice if she's not back for the ball. A bit shame-making, having the family's dirty linen washed in public.'

Her uncle looked unhappy. 'I've already spoken to them about it, naturally, but you know how stiff-necked they both are. In this case, I really do think it might be best to let things cool off in their own time.'

But Georgie wasn't prepared to let it rest there. She missed her grandmother's acerbic presence. Courtney Park simply wasn't the same without her.

'Can't you put it all behind you, Grandmama?' she pleaded when she rang Gilmour later that evening. 'We really need you here. Uncle Alex is miserable, Daddy's bullying Mummy, and Sloane's going around with the smuggest smile on her face. It's unbearable.'

'Sorry, *chérie*, but I'm far too busy even to see you.'

'In Scotland? In November? What *are* you up to?'

But her grandmother refused to be drawn further. 'You'll know everything when the time is right,' was all she would say on the matter. 'And get Court to phone me, *hein*? I'm beginning to worry about him.' Anxious to head off her grandmother before she asked awkward questions of Dexter, too, Georgie called her brother in his Paris clinic. She gave him all the latest Courtney Park news and told him to ring Scotland immediately.

Courtney sounded his old teasing self when he spoke to his grandmother. 'You've got to climb down off your high horse and come back for the ball, Grandmama. I'm bringing someone very special with me.'

'Oh? What's her name?'

'Chantel.'

'French, eh?'

'Be there and check it out for yourself. I'm only telling you one more thing — it's serious this time.'

'I'm glad for you, Court. Maybe you can both visit Gilmour after the ball. I don't think I'll be attending.'

'C'mon, what's Sloane going to do to you? Have her security men evict you?'

'Security men? How extraordinarily vulgar. The house servants checking invitations was always considered enough in my day.'

'Oh, it's a full production number, apparently — dog

patrols, security gates at every entrance, armed guards in the house, a helipad on the top field. Georgie says the security fees alone would pay for an ordinary ball.'

'It sounds quite dreadful,' said his grandmother. 'Thank heavens I shall not be there.'

Ashley's business commitments in Australia made it unlikely he would be able to reach Courtney Park until the day before the ball. Sloane, frenziedly working out a room plan for the couple of dozen guests she wanted to put up at the house itself, high-handedly tried to requisition his room.

Camilla headed her off firmly, receiving her sister-in-law's most basilisk stare in return. 'I'm sure the Ruperts and the Campbells would offer to hold a house party to tie in with the ball,' she said reassuringly. 'They could accommodate a dozen guests between them.'

Sloane's expression was even more forbidding.

'You *have* asked them, Sloane? The Ruperts and the Campbells always come to Courtney Park balls.'

'Not this one, no way! This is strictly international *glitterati*, not fuddy-duddy old pals of your mother's.'

She went on to rebuff Camilla's every good-natured offer of help. Tired of the frigid atmosphere within the house, and confident that Dexter would not miss her with Georgie to keep him company, Camilla flew up to Scotland to join her mother until the week before the ball.

'Bradford, at last! You would not believe the hassle these people are giving me,' was Sloane's indiscreet greeting to her lawyer when he arrived to stay for the weekend before the ball.

He kissed her cheek, taking in the tweed and leather Ralph Lauren knickerbocker outfit she considered informal country wear. 'Looking good, Sloane. And this is some place you have here. Even better than I imagined it.'

The long vista of the house, visible through the bare

branches of the avenue's trees, had made him catch his breath. The place was fantastic, a jewel. No wonder Sloane was prepared to fight tooth, nail and chequebook to win sole possession for herself and her husband.

'Thanks, Brad, I'm pretty much in love with it myself. How are you feeling? Too tired for me to show you around a little?'

No mention of her husband the Earl displaying his ancestral property, he noticed. 'Nothing I'd like better. Will your husband be joining us? I'm looking forward to meeting him.'

'I thought we'd have a meeting later. Xan's out with his manager, overseeing some improvements they've had made to the estate cottages. I thought it would be a good idea for us to get together first. You'll find Xan a little indecisive when it comes to his family.'

Bradford's heart sank. This was all he needed — Sloane forcing a reluctant spouse into family litigation, the dirtiest, most vicious, sort there is. Outwardly courteous and interested in everything, he exclaimed over each new wonder that she displayed for him, though in fact there was far too much for anyone to take in on one tour around the house. The paintings alone would repay many days' study.

'You have a superb collection of Impressionists.'

'My mother- and brother-in-law's,' she said dismissively. They were looking into the family dining-room, now dragged in subtle stripes of butter yellow against which was displayed a sumptuous Matisse odalisque of almost edible form and colour, and two small Dufy seascapes, full of gaiety and Mediterranean light. 'I wanted to paint this place grey and hang my De Koonings — you'd have thought I was planning a murder. Now, maybe, we can do something to show them who calls the shots in this house.'

Privately Bradford thought that altering a single thing about the lovely light-filled room would be a desecration. He kept quiet. He was paid to win cases, not form opinions on who had right on their side. Nevertheless he found himself most unprofessionally interested to meet the family who bought such ravishing pictures and created an atmosphere both chic and comfortable in even the grandest of rooms. Countless small touches brought the Randolphs' presence to his notice: a girl's sleek black leather jacket abandoned among a row of battered Barbours in the drying-room; an embroidery frame and wool left scattered untidily over a chair in the morning-room. Sloane rang a bell and had the mess tidied away, but Bradford liked the lived-in air the sewing gave to the room. In the deserted family sitting-room a collection of glossy fashion magazines had been left open on a table, all turned to pictures of a particularly striking girl. Sloane tutted in annoyance and flicked them shut, hurrying him past the rows of silver-framed photographs on display.

'I guess I will be meeting your husband's family?' he said casually as they made their way down one branch of the great divided staircase to the marble hall below.

'Can't miss them — all but Angelica.' Her smile told its own story. 'Georgie and Camilla aren't in for lunch. Dexter's around. We'll probably fall over him somewhere. He's always snooping round where you least expect him.'

Sure enough when they reached the chequerboard floor of the hall, Bradford heard the low whine of an electronic wheelchair. He turned round, expecting introductions. Instead, the door leading to a ground-floor wing they had not visited slammed shut.

Sloane shrugged. 'What did I tell you? The guy's a heel. Come on, we've just got time for me to show you what they've been going in the ballroom, ready for next weekend. Then a little drink before lunch.'

The 'little drink' had turned to several before, flushed with and annoyance, Sloane took a call from Alexander. '"Unavoidably delayed"!' she snorted. 'He's too damned laid back to bother to make up a lie. I'm sorry about this, Brad. It looks as though we'll have to postpone our meeting. Now, what shall we do with you this afternoon?'

'If you've no objection,' he got in quickly, looking out on an unseasonably mild and bright November day, 'I could maybe borrow a horse and do a tour of the estate?'

'Okay — since we can't get anything useful done till Xan gets home.' Sloane seemed nervy and distracted. She picked at her food, barely waiting for Bradford to finish his before ringing the bell for Ford to clear away.

'I have some calls to make,' she told her guest. 'A horse will be saddled for you in the yard. Tea's served from four — Ford will show you where. If I don't see you there, I'll catch you at dinner. Have fun — but not too much fun! Remember whose side you're on, Brad.'

He sighed as he went upstairs to change, remembering not whose side he was on but who paid the bills. It looked like being a tough weekend. After only a few hours' exposure to Sloane's hothouse intensity, he needed a break.

Dutifully he inspected the Randolph Stud, the highly successful bloodstock business which Dexter had funded. He visited the rare breeds farm, also a Randolph innovation, and then the Home Farm, equipped with the latest farm machinery. Lord Randolph's money had been freely spent over the years, Bradford could see; Courtney Park was very much the beneficiary. He needed to go through the case law with his firm's English associates in the City, but it seemed to him that a generous *ex gratia* settlement out of court offered Sloane's greatest chance of gaining sole possession. A woman as rich as she could afford to make Randolph a very good offer — but would she want to? Bradford doubted it. Compromise was not a word that featured largely in Sloane's vocabulary.

Turning his horse away from the farm, he struck out across country. 'You could ride for several days in any direction — it's all Courtney Park land,' Sloane had told him. He passed prosperous tenant farms, a small village with its own Hamilton Primary School and Courtney Arms public house. He felt the weather's mildness wane. The air held a chill now and he realised he ought to be thinking about making his way back. In which direction, though? He realised he'd lost track of where he was.

Halfway along a grassy ride he spotted a tethered horse. The rider must be close by, so he could ask directions. He slowed his horse to a walking trot and looked up and down the ride. In the fading light he saw a woman stumbling towards him, using a forked branch for support. He dismounted quickly, hitching his horse to a fallen tree trunk. 'Are you okay?' he asked her. 'Here, let me help.'

'Oh, thank you,' she panted, leaning gratefully on his arm. 'I thought I could just about get myself back to Rosie, but I couldn't think how I was going to mount her.'

She had a British brand of good looks, he saw, a fresh bloom to a face innocent of make-up, long light brown hair tied back at the nape of her neck. A few tendrils had escaped to frame her flushed, slightly tear-stained, face. She was dressed for riding in beige breeches and a canary yellow rollneck sweater, but from the pocket of her Barbour jacket protruded a sketch-pad and a few stocks of charcoal.

'Such a silly thing to have happened. I was sketching — there's a wonderful view of Courtney Park from up here when the trees are bare.' She gestured down the ride. At least he had his bearings now. 'I climbed to the top of the knoll, drew for an hour or so, and then when my fingers started to cramp, I decided to come down. I caught my ankle in a tree-root and must have ricked it. I do hope it isn't broken.'

'Is it hurting you very much?'

'I don't know — I think I'm too cold to tell.'

Bradford saw that her graceful hands with their pale unpainted nails were tinged blue with cold. She must have felt very frightened, cold and alone up on that hill but was bravely trying to make light of the experience. Unthinking, he took her hands and rubbed them between his own, chafing rosy life back into them.

565

'Ouch, that hurts! But it's wonderful to feel my fingers again!' She smiled up at him trustingly, leaving her hands in his.

He was surprised she hadn't protested; he was a stranger, after all. He always underestimated the charm of his square-jawed face, warm brown eyes and voice to match. 'We ought to take a look at that ankle of yours,' he said, seeing the way she balanced one foot gingerly on its toes. 'But it's getting dark, and if you haven't broken anything the boot's support is the best treatment at the moment.'

'Don't tell me you're a doctor?'

'No — just a dad with plenty of experience looking after cuts and scrapes and broken bones. We should get you home quickly. Do you mind?'

Without waiting for her embarrassed refusal, he swept her off her feet and carried her towards her horse. Camilla opened her mouth to protest, then realised she didn't want to. She felt safe and protected in his arms. Something else as well. A haunting memory pricked her. Dexter, whole and strong, had once had the power to make her feel like this — warm and protected. Unbidden, the tears rose to her eyes. Not from pain, but from regret for all that love and trust between them, gone for ever now.

'Have you far to go?' he asked, when he had helped her into the saddle.

'No, there's a short cut down the green lane there — I'll be home in minutes.' She seemed to be pointing away from Courtney Park. Bradford's gentlemanly instincts told him he ought to escort her. 'I'll be fine, honestly,' she insisted. 'Rosie's safe as a lamb. I wouldn't dream of troubling you further.'

That British reserve! Bradford could never tell if he was meant to take it at face value. She was holding out her hand for him to shake, when only a minute before she had been in his arms. Bemused, he took it.

'Thank you very much,' she said. 'I don't know what I'd have done without you.'

If Camilla had been less shaken up after the accident, she would have introduced herself at this point and they could have taken the short cut back to Courtney Park together. As it was, Bradford realised she was shivering with cold and took pity on her. He touched his cap. 'Goodbye, then. I hope we'll meet again.'

'Yes, I hope so, too.' With a shy smile she urged Rosie beneath the green lane's tracery of overhanging branches and left Bradford to take the long way round.

When she was lost to view, he kicked himself for not having asked her name. The remnants of her scent clung to his jacket, haunting him on the long ride back.

Once more at home, Camilla limped painfully to the Rose Room, a haven of comfort and warmth after her ordeal. Pam, her personal maid, took one look at her mistress's wan shivering appearance and went to draw her a hot bath liberally laced with her favourite Chloe. Together they eased Camilla's tight boot over her injured ankle, already shadowed with bruising.

'It does look bad, my lady. Shall I call Dr Brett?'

'I think you'd better. Oh, what a nuisance, just before Sloane's ball! Dexter and I will have to sit out together, a couple of old crocks.'

In the bath, she wept. She'd been in an unsettled state since meeting the handsome stranger on the hill. Now that she thought about it, she'd acted foolishly there, too — allowing him to take her hands; making no protest when he picked her up and carried her. He could have been a burglar, a prowler, anything. But not with those eyes, she decided. She ought to have enquired what he was doing on private land, though. At the very least, asked his name. Now she would never know, she realised with a pang.

The years since Dexter's hunting accident had sapped all the happiness and self-confidence Camilla had gained in the early years of their marriage. Now, in her middle years, she found herself slipping back, living more and more in the vague, sentimentalised fantasy world she had known as a young girl, in love for the first time.

The thought brought back memories of Luciano, her lost love, the man her husband stubbornly persisted in maintaining was Ash's father. That was something that ought to be cleared up once and for all, she decided. Now, while Dr Brett was visiting, would be a good opportunity.

She slipped into a heavy white towelling robe and limped into her bedroom where Pam had drawn the heavy curtains against the dark and chill beyond the glass. It was still known as the Rose Room, but the furnishings had been updated by the introduction of another Colefax chintz, roses and pansies this time, in warm shades of pink, green and violet. The curtains around the bed and at the window were finished with a strikingly pretty petal-cut trim. The walls and two large round tables at either side of the bed were covered in a toning pink, green and ivory chintz. The tables, and the rest of the antique rosewood and yew furniture, bore a selection of family photographs in silver frames and a collection of pretty Battersea enamel boxes.

Camilla sat at her dressing-table, studying her face by the light of the fire Pam had lit while she was in her bath. The mingled scent of roses and orchids from the Courtney Park hothouses filled the room. In the half-light she decided that she looked young for her age, her skin still naturally smooth and firm. When she had lit the two candle-lamps flanking the mirror, however, the illusion was more difficult to sustain. Camilla fingered the fine tracery of wrinkles around her grey eyes and soft mouth. How cruel to have grown old, still with so little knowledge of love.

Pam knocked and came in to say that the doctor had arrived. Quickly Camilla slipped on a pink silk nightgown laid ready for her on the white cotton bedspread, and called for him to come in.

Dr Christopher Brett sat her on a low chair by the fire

and gently probed her ankle and the top of her foot.

'Good news and bad,' he said. 'No broken bones, but you do seem to have torn a ligament. I'll strap it up tonight and give you something for the pain. It'll be a few weeks' mending, I'm afraid. Take a few days' rest, and after that you can hop around on crutches.'

To his surprise, Camilla made no complaint. She seemed far more interested in discussing something else, something which had weighed on her mind for years ...

Bradford arrived back at the house tired and hungry. Following a maid's directions, he made his way to the ground floor drawing room, where a lavish spread of sandwiches, scones, and homemade cakes was laid out for the family to help themselves. The room was deserted. He felt disappointed. That Sloane was not one to indulge herself in the afternoon he could well imagine, but he'd been at Courtney Park for several hours and so far had met none of the family except his hostess.

Ford sailed into the room to enquire: 'Indian or China, sir?'

Bradford ordered Darjeeling and sat down to study *Country Life*. After a few minutes he heard an electronic whirring, and Dexter Randolph appeared in his wheelchair, a lean grey manservant fussing in his wake.

Bradford courteously rose to greet the newcomer.

'I'm Bradford Carter, a friend of Sloane's.' He held out his hand.

'I know your reputation, Carter, and your business in this house is far from friendly.' Dexter made no move to shake hands.

Abashed, Bradford sank back in his seat. Dexter guided himself to a seat by the uncurtained window and half-turned so as to stare out over the floodlit park.

His manservant arranged Lapsang Souchong and a few cucumber sandwiches on a small table by his side.

'Bloody diet,' Dexter muttered, the last words he was to say for some time.

Under cover of reading the magazine, Bradford took the opportunity to study the formidable Lord Randolph. He looked fierce, a naturally forbidding air enhanced by the lines of pain and disappointment etched into his thin face. He would be a tough adversary in any fight over his family's right to inhabit Courtney Park — unless, perhaps, there was some truth in the rumours of trouble within the Randolph Enterprises empire? They were only vague as yet. Bradford understood that Dexter Randolph kept a pretty firm grip on the English and American ends of the business, but Australia could bear some watching, apparently.

Bradford had done some reading up on the business and learned that a few years earlier, shortly after Dexter's accident, Lucas Randolph, his elder brother, had been placed in charge of Randolph Enterprises Australia. The manager of the Mining and Shipping Division, which formerly had been run independently of Lucas's cattle operation, had resigned in protest and gone to join the Packer Organisation. The meat side of the business was much less important these days, the main thrust of the Australian business going into leisure industries, particularly their expansion into the new resorts, mostly in Queensland. Lucas Randolph had advocated the phenomenally expensive purchase from the outgoing Queensland State Premier of an island in the Whitsundays. Chip, his son, had been appointed project manager for Bradbury Island, with a brief to turn it into an exclusive hideaway for Australia's new wave of millionaires. It was to be the last word in luxury, outclassing even Hayman Island. Even if you could trust your lieutenants, Bradford reflected, funding a development like that wasn't chicken-feed. If you couldn't, the project could well become a cross for Randolph Enterprises to bear.

'I know why you're here, Carter,' Dexter's harsh voice broke the silence, 'and I want you to know I think it stinks.'

'Sloane and I have been friends —'

'You don't have to be a cattleman to recognise bullshit! You're here to spy out the land, Carter, so hear this: when my time comes, they'll carry me out of Courtney Park in a box. Till then, it's my home.'

There seemed no point in trying to make polite conversation after that. Bradford got to his feet. 'Delighted to meet you too, Lord Randolph. Perhaps we'll see each other again at dinner?'

He strode out of the room, feeling uncomfortably as though the other man had got the best of their encounter by cutting the crap about Bradford being just another guest. He felt angry with Sloane for dragging him into her tangled family affairs when there was so much else he would rather have been doing. Attending the new production of *Aida* at the Met, for one; he and Jo-Ann had had tickets. Or trying to make some headway with his kids, persuading them that there were more things in life than borrowing his Porsche or owning the largest collection of cashmere sweaters in their class. More than either of those things, though, he'd rather have been rescuing a pretty woman in distress, holding her in his arms again and maybe this time kissing that soft mouth. How stupid not even to know her name.

Reaching the first floor, he took the wrong corridor and had to retrace his steps. A faint familiar scent wafted under one of the doors. He checked in his path, reaching out a hand to knock and see if she was perhaps behind the door. But no, he told himself. He was being stupid. She'd ridden off in another direction, hadn't she? He'd just have to ask around, see if anyone recognised his description of a sweet-faced woman on a bay mare, with a fondness for sketching and an inability to keep both feet on the ground . . . just the way he was feeling now.

Though it was Friday night, not traditionally a dress night

in the country, Bradford felt certain that Sloane as Countess of Courtney, would observe every formality. He dressed accordingly in a dark blue velvet jacket with evening trousers, a blue silk shirt and tie, and slipped on a pair of black velvet evening pumps.

When he reached the White Library, where the butler had informed him that drinks would be served before dinner, he saw he had not been mistaken in dressing formally. The room's only other occupant, a tall slight man with blond hair fading to grey, was wearing exquisitely tailored black tie.

'You must be Carter,' he said, getting to his feet to offer Bradford his hand. 'How do you do? I'm Alexander. Delighted to meet you. My wife's told me all about your past triumphs. May I pour you a drink?'

'Thank you. I'll take a whisky and water, please.'

'I do apologise that I wasn't here to greet you myself. We had something of a crisis on the estate. A long-standing tenant, the elderly widow of an estate worker, had to be persuaded to leave her cottage. She wouldn't agree to move to sheltered housing till the Earl himself convinced her she should. A minor victory, I know, but it's good to feel one's of some use around the place.'

The Earl of Courtney's self-deprecating smile spoke volumes about his character. This was not the go-for-it business brain who would have been a match for Sloane, but a gentle, sensitive man solicitous of others' feelings. If he was reluctant to take a firm line with even his humblest tenant, what would his attitude be towards dispossessing his own family?

'It must be a big responsibility, looking after this house and your sizeable estate.'

'It is; but of course I don't do it on my own. There's Hayward and — oh, good evening, Dexter. Have you met my brother-in-law Lord Randolph?'

'I have had that pleasure.' Bradford raised his glass in greeting.

Dexter nodded a reluctant acknowledgement and turned his chair towards the drinks table.

'Oh no, you don't, you old backslider!' A girl in floating plum-coloured chiffon, draped Renaissance-style around her slim, high-breasted figure, dashed after him and took the whisky decanter from his hand. 'I'll pour. Christopher said no more than three measures a day, didn't he, Daddy? I expect Webster sneaked you a drink while you were dressing, so this is number two.'

'Christ, girl, there's not enough there to drown a gnat!' Amazingly, bad-tempered Dexter Randolph did not seem to resent the girl's interference.

She noticed Bradford studying her. 'Hello, I don't think we've been introduced.'

'Carter, I'd like you to meet my girl Georgie,' said Dexter with obvious pride. 'Ripper, isn't she?'

'Daddy, please! How d'you do, Mr. Carter? You're a friend of Sloane's, I understand?'

'Yes, indeed,' he said, hating the cover story by now. 'I was over here on business and she kindly asked me down to escape the weekend doldrums in town.'

Georgianna Randolph's hazel eyes were clear and expressive. Like her father's, her disbelief was plain to see. His sense of awkwardness was increased when Sloane herself appeared, striking in the Hamilton emeralds above a sinuous Christian Lacroix in green silk jersey so décolleté it only just spared their blushes. Bradford's were not spared for long.

'Bradford, darling!' She kissed him on the lips for rather too long. Her mouth tasted of wine. Afterwards she clung girlishly to his arm. 'You've met my husband, I take it?' Obviously she did not consider the other two occupants of the room worthy of an introduction. 'Xan, don't I get a drink too?'

Silently the Earl poured her a glass of chilled Chablis from the bottle cooled and uncorked in readiness.

Though Sloane was still clinging to his arm, Bradford

was determined not to let her monopolise him. 'I believe you're a model, Miss Randolph?'

'Georgie, please. Yes, quite a recent thing. How did you know?'

'From a collection of fashion magazines, all turned back to a picture of the same girl.'

She laughed in embarrassment. 'How awful! Mummy's doing, I suppose. I'm afraid she won't be joining us tonight, Sloane.'

'That's too bad,' she said mechanically, not asking why.

'She's not ill?' said Alexander.

'A slight accident, Pam said. Nothing to worry about.'

Dexter made no comment, his face remaining expressionless throughout the entire exchange. Bradford would have been willing to bet it was the first he'd heard of his wife's indisposition but, unlike her brother, he expressed no concern. Cold-hearted bastard, he thought, feeling a surge of pity for the unknown woman.

Sloane jerked his arm to demand his attention. 'I hope you're not too tired by your ride, Brad. Since Xan let us down this afternoon, I thought we'd reschedule our meeting for after dinner. Dexter and Georgie will excuse us, I'm sure.'

'With pleasure,' said the girl.

Great, thought Bradford, just what I need to end a perfect day. A midnight meeting with a megalomaniac and a reluctant client.

Sloane had gone to pour herself a refill. Since it looked as though the rest of the evening would be business with a vengeance, Bradford took the opportunity to study his surroundings. The White Library was a study in restraint — except for a full length portrait that hung in an embrasure at the far end of the room. He recognised the camera-clear rendition of Annigoni, which, together with the elaborate off-the-shoulder ballgown the subject wore, dated the picture to the late fifties or early sixties. It was not the hyper-realistic style which drew his attention so much as the subject: he thought it not too fanciful to suppose that the very young girl depicted was wearing her first ballgown. The painter had captured her air of coltish awkwardness inside the draped and flowing dress. The girl's golden-brown hair was piled on top of her head in a bouffant style, but sly tendrils escaped to curl next to her clear pink cheeks. The wide grey-blue eyes were shy but trusting — exactly like those of the woman on the hillside, he realised.

'Lovely, isn't she?' Georgie appeared at his elbow. 'My mother, Camilla.'

'Camilla — that's very beautiful, and very English.'

'Oh, Mummy's that, all right. Never makes a fuss, even though she fell over while she was on the hill today and tore some ligaments. Heaven knows how she made it back to the house.'

Bradford was about to describe his meeting with Camilla when Sloane swept up to them. He did not choose to discuss the details of her sister-in-law's pain and fright. The meeting would remain their secret, he decided, his and Camilla's. Lovely name, lovely lady ... He couldn't wait to see her surprise when they were finally introduced.

He was disappointed, however, descending early to breakfast the next day, to find only Alexander in evidence. Georgie had been and gone, apparently. Dexter and Camilla usually breakfasted in their rooms — separate rooms, Bradford noticed. Perhaps because of Dexter's condition. Perhaps not.

'Sloane sends her apologies, but after last night ... ' Alexander could not meet Bradford's eyes. Sloane had outdrunk them both and was obviously sleeping it off. 'She suggests that you and I go over a few points, but frankly, old chap, I don't see the need. Not yet anyway. I've no objection to your completing a review of the legal implications of our arrangement here, but I'm not convinced, whatever my wife says, that it will ever come to an open rift between Dexter and myself. He's an autocratic, prickly sort, and not always as kind to my sister as I would like, but I'd be the first to acknowledge all the good he has done for the house and estate. We rub along well enough. Of course, if Sloane and I were to start a family . . . '

Bradford's hand jerked, setting the fragile French porcelain of his cup chiming against its saucer.

'I hope I shan't embarrass you too much,' Alexander continued, 'if I tell you, man to man, that things between Sloane and myself are not perhaps all they seem. It's not exactly a *mariage blanc*, but we do both have our little distractions . . . '

Bradford left his Finnan haddock and scrambled egg untouched. 'But you have definitely discussed starting a family?'

'Good lord, yes. We're long past the discussion stage, but despite our best endeavours . . . and neither of us is getting any younger, of course.'

'Forgive my directness, but have you considered seeking a medical opinion?'

'A perfectly sensible question. We each saw separate specialists; each got a clean bill of health.'

'I see,' said Bradford thoughtfully.

'Looks as though we'll just have to soldier on.' Alexander sighed. 'Look, do you mind if I leave you to your own devices this morning? I've some business to attend to in the stables.'

'Not at all.' Bradford got to his feet as his host left the room.

Alexander paused for a moment. 'We've put you in a difficult position, I know, Carter. Just between ourselves, I doubt this action will ever get off the ground. My advice to you is to go through the motions, do the English research Sloane expects, and allow me to work on her from this end. There might always be a perfectly happy outcome, of course. I can't believe my brother-in-law or his family would make real difficulties if it seemed Sloane and I were about to produce a brood of children and decided we needed the place to ourselves. But frankly, old chap, that doesn't seem very likely.'

He left the room, a lean handsome man with a face on which the unmistakable marks of disillusionment were plain. Bradford clenched his fists in frustration. In many ways the relationship between client and lawyer resembles that of patient and doctor. To reveal all that he knew of Sloane, even to her husband, would be a breach of professional confidence. But if anyone had the right to know, it was the decent, deluded Earl of Courtney.

Bradford decided he had no stomach for breakfast. To clear his head, he decided to tour the gardens which Sloane had had no time for yesterday. It was not the best season in which to view them. The famous rose garden had been cut back to ranks of low gnarled stumps. The gardeners had done their best in the wide formal borders, nursing along late roses and petunias and putting on the best show they could with the help of clipped bushes spangled with brilliant red and orange berries. It was a colder, greyer day than yesterday, and Bradford had unthinkingly walked out without a coat.

He was turning back to the house when he noticed the impressive glasshouses in which, Sloane had told him, out of season vegetables, fruit and flowers were grown for use at Courtney Park. Walking around the outside of the giant glass constructions, Bradford soon found the section devoted to flowers. He tried the door and stepped inside, disturbing a little gnome-like man hard at work with a watering-can. He was bending over a huge bank of stargazer lilies, their mottled pink faces turned imploringly towards the light.

'These are fantastic,' said Bradford. 'Are they just for the house?'

'We bought in more for the ball,' the gardener explained, 'but you'll find we have some of most things in usually. Lady Camilla loves her flowers, she does.'

'Is she responsible for the arrangements in the house?'

'That she is — though Lady Courtney has decided to spend a fortune bringing some fancy London chap down for the dance. He's bringing his own blooms, too. Courtney Park flowers is only good enough for the gardens and guest bedrooms, it seems.'

'Did you hear that Lady Camilla had an accident yesterday?' said Bradford craftily.

'Yes, that I did. Shame it was, poor lady.'

'I wonder — do you think it might cheer her up a little if I were to take her some flowers?'

The head gardener looked the American guest up and down. A fine well-set-up chap he looked, and obviously concerned about her ladyship — not like some he could mention.

'It might,' he conceded. 'What was you thinking of, sir?'

Bradford glanced around at the massed lilies, orchids, roses, carnations. They didn't seem right. Too brash, somehow. 'Those,' he said, pointing to some lily-of-the-valley. Shy and discreet, they reminded him of Camilla.

The gardener smiled, and picked a small bunch to make an old-fashioned posy. His soil-stained fingers were precise and delicate about their task. To Bradford's surprise he even produced a length of white satin ribbon from a drawer of his workbench. 'Maybe you should tie this, sir. There — pretty as a picture.'

Bradford thanked him and started to take out his wallet.

'No, sir. That won't be necessary,' said the old man touchily. 'It's always a pleasure picking flowers for Lady Camilla.'

Bradford turned back to the house, where he thoroughly confused Ford by asking for a plain white card to attach to the flowers.

'The gentlemen of the house usually use their own, sir.'

'I know, but it would spoil the surprise.'

Eventually a blank white card and envelope were produced, and Bradford wrote his message. Ford concealed his disapproval when he was asked to send the flowers up to Lady Camilla. He was not aware that the American guest had been introduced to her.

Upstairs, Camilla was sitting listlessly over her embroidery. Pam had lit another cosy fire, the maids had cleaned and tidied her room to perfection while she was in the bath. There was no need for her to feel cross and out of sorts, but she did. Of all the bad luck, injuring herself now! She felt dull and old and neglected. Ford's knock at the door was a welcome distraction. 'Come,' she called.

The butler entered, bearing Bradford's posy on a silver salver. Curious, she took the plain white card from its envelope. Her curiosity deepened as she read: 'We met yesterday afternoon — I hope your ankle is feeling a little better now. May I come up and introduce myself properly?' There was no signature.

Her heart began to beat faster. 'Very well,' she said breathlessly, 'you may show Mr — my visitor up now, Ford.'

'Very good, my lady. Shall I take the flowers and ask Pam to put them in water for you?'

Camilla was nervously twisting the stems between her fingers. 'Sorry? Oh, yes, that would be kind.'

When the butler had gone, she went painfully to her dressing-table and quickly brushed her hair. God, but she was looking pale and uninteresting. She hurried to apply mascara, some pale lipstick and blusher, then a quick puff of her favourite scent. Her heavy peach satin lounging pyjamas and robe were decent enough, she decided. She was back in her chair, feet propped on a low embroidered stool, when Ford knocked again and showed her visitor in.

'We meet again,' he said. 'This time under happier circumstances. I'm glad.'

'I'm glad, too. I'm afraid I was a little distracted yesterday and didn't thank you properly, Mr. —'

'Carter. Bradford Carter.' He was prepared for an antagonistic reaction when she heard his name. Her husband and daughter obviously knew his business in the house.

'Sloane's lawyer friend,' said Camilla, showing that she did, too, but her cordial expression did not alter. He was amazed by the relief he felt.

'Won't you sit down? Can I ring for something for you — some coffee, a drink?'

'No, thanks. I'm fine. I was amazed to learn last night that we were actually under the same roof. I thought you were riding in another direction entirely.'

'A short cut — the path jinks back quite quickly and takes a steep but mercifully short route to the house.'

'And you rode it alone last night?' he reproached her. 'Why didn't you say it was dangerous? I'd never have let you do it.'

'You'd have had to stop me first!' she laughed. 'Mr Carter — '

'Please, Brad.'

'Brad, then — you'd already been very kind to me. Much kinder than I deserved after being so stupid.'

'Don't put yourself down,' he said feelingly. 'You're a very beautiful woman and, I'm willing to bet, not stupid at all.'

'I think I might be about to be.'

Silence fell between them, their eyes speaking for them both. Pam broke the tension, knocking and entering with Brad's flowers prettily arranged in a moss-covered block inside a cream Leedsware basket.

Camilla clapped her hands. 'Oh, lovely!'

He glanced ruefully around the room. He should have realised; the gardener had told him Lady Camilla loved flowers. There were arrangements of pink and white roses, and cymbidiums in wickerwork cachepots, on every flat surface, yet Camilla seemed childishly delighted with his gift. Flushed with pleasure, her small heart-shaped face looked almost girlish. Her smile was radiant and un-affected.

It made Brad angry to realise that in this beleaguered household, caught between's Sloane's bitchery and her husband's neglect, she would have few reasons for smiling. He decided he had nothing to lose. 'Look, I'll come straight to the point. I'm in kind of a difficult position here — '

'You're Sloane's lawyer, and she wants us out,' said Camilla calmly. 'Yes, I know. That's perfectly all right, Brad. I understand you're very talented at your job. You do, of course, realise that if it comes to a court case my husband will retain the finest English QC in the field. In court, we'd be on opposite sides. That doesn't mean we can't be friends in private.'

'That's impossible, I'm afraid,' he said, stern-faced.

Camilla felt her heart sink with disappointment. In a trembling voice, she said, 'Of course, I've no desire to force myself on you.'

He could not bear to see her distress. He took her hand and leaned closer. 'You don't understand. I want, more than anything, to see you again — but I'd be lying if I said I thought we could just be good friends. I want more than that, Camilla. When I held you in my arms yesterday — this is going to sound corny, I know, but —'

'— it felt like coming home. Yes, I felt it, too. I was being dishonest in claiming I wanted you just as a friend. It's more than that between us, isn't it?'

'I think it might be love.'

'I'm a married woman,' she said shakily, 'with a husband who needs me more than he'll ever admit.'

'I'm a married man with a wife who needs me to pay off our home, and her Saks account, and the kids' ortho-dontistry, but otherwise not at all. I'm a hard-nosed, hard-bitten bastard at work — but, in private, I want something else. I want to be loved. Do you think you could love me, Camilla? I know I could love you.'

She touched his cheek. 'Oh, Brad, I don't know. I never dreamed it could happen like this for me again.'

'Will you at least agree to meet me again, somewhere else away from here? I'm about to have myself called away on urgent business. I don't think I could stand another minute of Sloane right now. You'll find me at the St James's Club in town. Call me. I'll meet you any time, any place.'

'I might not be very mobile.'

'You know what they say — love finds a way. I'd better go, before Sloane pours herself breakfast. For now, something to think about.'

Before she could stop him, he had picked her up for the second time in two days. This time he settled her on her bed where he half lay beside her, careful not to jolt her injured ankle while his mouth began to make slow seductive love to hers.

He mastered her with gentleness. She forgot to be embarrassed or afraid. Instead she burned for him to take his caresses further, the breath catching ragged in her throat as very lightly he skimmed the palm of his hand over the thin silk of her robe above her hardening nipples.

'Not like this,' he said huskily. 'We have to give ourselves time — but not too much time, Camilla. I have to be back in the States a few days after the ball. Call me if you want to take this further.'

Even though she knew he was right, it was agony for her to see him go. Brad had stirred something within her she had thought gone forever when Luciano died. She waited a whole day before ringing him at his club. It was a Sunday. She supposed he would not be hard to find.

'Camilla?' His voice came on the line almost immediately. He'd tipped every porter in view to make sure this was one call which would not be misdirected.

'Brad, I'd like us to meet again ... '

'Well, hallelujah! Camilla, that's wonderful. Tell me where and when.

'Only for lunch,' she said quickly. 'Can you get out of London? I know a wonderful place near Oxford. We could meet, just talk ... Would that be enough — for now?'

His voice was low with emotion. 'Just to see your sweet face again would make me the happiest guy I know. You'd better give me directions to this place. I don't want to waste a minute of our time together.'

Sloane had been furious to hear that Bradford Carter had skipped the house on urgent business. She called his club, his London associates, she even called his PA in New York, just to spread the misery around, but Bradford proved elusive.

He finally called her late on Tuesday. 'Sloane, thanks for the hospitality last weekend — '

'Bull, Bradford! What the hell did you mean, walking out on me like that? Why haven't you returned my calls? We have so much still to go over, strategies to discuss.'

'My considered advice to you at the moment is to hang loose. From what I saw of it, the situation at Courtney Park is far from untenable. Alexander's mother has taken herself off; Dexter's a dog, granted, but he seems pretty housetrained. And Georgie and Camilla are delightful.'

'Camilla?' She was on to it like a flash. 'I didn't know you'd met.'

Bradford could have kicked himself. 'I — uh — came across her by chance. A lovely lady. You should make friends of them all, not enemies.'

'Who's speaking here — my lawyer or Dr Ruth? I don't pay you to preach to me. I pay you for results and I want them quick — otherwise I might just have to call up Daddy and let him know how dissatisfied his little girl is with nasty old Bradford.'

He hated it when she used her baby voice on him, and she'd used that threat just once too often lately. He did not want to lose the fee income from Henry de Havilland's business, but the Earl of Courtney had unwittingly given him some very useful ammunition. 'You do that, Sloane, and I might just feel obliged to call your husband with some fascinating facts about you he seems not to know.'

'You wouldn't dare! It would be malpractice.'

'Not if you and your father had fired me. Then I'd owe no professional duty to the de Havilland family.'

'Don't jerk me around, Bradford. You don't want to lose the family's business.'

'And you don't want me to spill the beans. Shall we call it quits? I'm digging up some very interesting precedents here.'

'Okay,' she said grudgingly. 'So long as you promise me you're giving a whole lot of thought to the Randolphs.'

'I think of little else,' he assured her solemnly.

Camilla was up with the birds on the day of her lunch with Brad. She had considered asking Sloane if she might borrow Rosa, but decided there was no need to rouse her sister-in-law's suspicions.

Sloane, she knew, had regular collagen injections to plump out her face and keep the wrinkles at bay, and she and her friends all had their eyes done periodically by Mr Nicol. Camilla had never before considered submitting herself to the knife to hold back the years. Now she was not so sure . . .

She took a long time bathing, then dressed in her white robe, wondering how to fill the empty hours until she could be with Brad. She was too excited to eat, and found her hands shook so much while she was applying pale polish that she had to rub off the first two coats and start again.

This is ridiculous, she told herself, almost weak with excitement. It's just lunch together. A meal and some conversation, that's all. But she knew it was more than that. It felt like a new beginning, after the parched years she had spent deprived of Dexter's love. At ten o'clock she realised she'd been foolish. She had a model in the house. Georgie would know enough of the tricks of the trade to help her mother look her best.

'Hmm, very smart,' said her sharp-eyed daughter, taking in the cinnamon-coloured Maxfield Parish suede trouser outfit — to hide the bandage — and cream cashmere sweater laid out on the bed. Camilla's favourite plain but perfectly beautiful Bulgari gold necklace and earings had been taken from a drawer of her jewel-box and lay in readiness on the dressing-table. 'You're obviously going somewhere very special,' said Georgie. 'Let's see what we can do to make you look even more stunning.'

She used only a minimum of make-up — Camilla's peaches and cream complexion would have been drowned by more — but the blue-grey kohl around the eyes was a revelation. Camilla had never realised her eyes could look so smoky and mysterious.

The transformation took longer than she had bargained for, however. 'My God, look at the time,' she cried, pulling on her clothes anyhow. 'I'm going to be late! Oh, please, don't let me be late.'

She was early. After the chauffeur had carried her down to the car, then carried her up again so she could hunt out a length of brown velvet ribbon to tie to her crutches, she urged him to drive at such a pace that they arrived at the fifteenth-century Oxfordshire house, Le Manoir Aux Quat'Saisons, three-quarters of an hour early.

'Would you like me to drive you back along the scenic route, my lady?' said the chauffeur, not amused by having been ordered to use the motorway.

'Yes ... I mean, no. We might be late — which would be awful after being so early. Oh dear, I don't know what I mean. I think the best thing I can do is go inside and have a drink while I wait.'

She was helped inside, welcomed charmingly and told to her amazement that Mr Carter had already arrived.

'I don't believe it — you're as early as I am!'

'Earlier — and for the same reason, I guess. Camilla, it's very good to see you.'

'Me too, I mean, I'm very glad to see you too.'

'Listen to us. We sound as though we haven't met in years. I thought, in honour of our long parting ... '

A waiter uncorked a bottle of champagne in a clear bottle.

'Cristal — my mother's favourite,' she said. In normal circumstances this reminder of Angelica, sitting out her Scottish exile, would have upset her, but nothing about today was normal. She was about to enjoy a meal in one of the finest most civilised, restaurants in the country with a man who could not help revealing his admiration for her in every fond look.

Though the food was delicious, Camilla barely noticed what they ate. Besides, the hard knot of excited anticipation in her stomach, which she had thought would vanish at seeing Brad again, seemed to be growing, making it hard for her to think of eating.

Would it be today? she could not help wondering. These few hours away from Courtney Park and its clash of personalities had confirmed for them both that the instant affinity they had felt was based on something solid and real. They took delight in one another's company, swopping information and silly jokes. Would they delight in one another's bodies, too?

Brad had considered taking a suite at Le Manoir. He'd heard that they were beautifully appointed and each named after a flower. Camilla's room at Courtney was known as the Rose Room, he remembered, and suddenly realised he could not make her his in the illusory privacy of a rented room, however luxurious. It felt too much like routine expense-account adultery. She deserved better than that.

'I know what you're thinking,' she said, putting her hand on his. 'And you're right. It wouldn't do, not for us. But, oh, I do want you so much! Listen, I think I have the answer. You're coming to Sloane's ball, aren't you?'

'Sure am — as Batman.'

'My hero!'

'I can't wait to see how you get out of this one. What'll it be — Cinderella on crutches? Madame Récamier reclining all night on her sofa?'

'I shan't be there.'

'What! It's the only reason I accepted the darn invitation, thinking I'd get to see you in costume.'

'How would you like to see me out of it?'

'You mean — while everyone's busy at the ball the Caped Crusader hooks his batline to the window of My Lady's chamber ... ?'

'Something like that.'

A doubtful expression crossed his honest face. 'I don't know, it sounds a little tacky to me. With so many people in the house, your husband among them.'

Her tongue loosened by love, she told him: 'If Dexter came across me *in flagrante* with a groom, he'd tell the man off for not paying attention to his work. I'm nothing to him now but a has-been, the mother of his children — even though he stubbornly persists that Ash isn't his! To shut him up, I've finally arranged what I should have done years ago — blood tests and typing for the three of us. I'm going to prove to Dexter once and for all that he and I have three children.'

It was the first Brad had heard of Dexter's strange fixation with the subject of his eldest child's paternity. She'd already told him about her springtime love affair with Luciano in Italy. Briefly she explained the belated legacy of Dexter's jealousy of Luciano for sending him a bride who was no longer a virgin.

'I think the rational part of him knows very well he's barking up the wrong tree,' she said, her eyes brilliant with tears. 'But when he had the accident, it was as if part of Dexter's brain became irrevocably twisted. He must have been secretly hoarding up all that jealousy and resentment — oh, it's horrible to think of it! Maman and I swore to him repeatedly that Ashley was his, born prematurely — it even runs in the family — but he simply refused to listen. He says he's stuck with me now, I'm the mother of his *two* children and so, in his generosity, he won't divorce me. My God, the times I've wished he would! Anything would be better than this cold loveless existence.'

'My dear ...'

'You're right, Brad. Under normal circumstances it would be pretty tacky, coming to me under the roof I share with my husband. But remember, since the accident, that's all I have shared with Dexter. A normal sex life was out of the question, but he denied me even his affection. I don't know if I'll ever forgive him for that.'

'You might,' he told her, more to calm her than to plead Randolph's case for him. From what he'd seen, the man was one hundred per cent stone.

'I don't want to talk about sad things now,' she said, taking his arm and leaning on its comforting strength as they walked out to the car. 'I want to look forward. First of all to Saturday, and from there — who knows? Come to me at midnight, Brad.'

They came within earshot of the chauffeur, who opened the back door for Camilla. Brad handed her inside, mystifying the driver by saying: 'Bats can be a lot of fun, I think you'll find. Cute, cuddlesome, and very, very loving.'

'I can't wait!'

She sat back in her seat. Brad, in the chauffeur's eyeline, waved politely. Camilla wriggled across the back of the car so that she was not and could blow him a single kiss to sweeten his dreams until they were together.

Wednesday was the last time Nicky could use the Knightsbridge house he had borrowed from a friend, the last chance Sloane would have to meet him before her ball. It was an unwritten rule for every mistress of the future King of Malivia that his dignity and privacy must be guarded at all costs. Unthinkable that he might visit her at Chester Square. He might be prepared to share another man's wife, but never under her husband's roof. Nicky was a gentleman.

Sloane was forced to follow the hypocritical protocol, though her craving for him had reached the level of addiction. Normally she let him call all the shots, naming the next time he'd be free. Today, distracted by thoughts of the ball and their coming separation, she made a series of mistakes.

When Nicky entered the bedroom, instead of finding her naked and ready for him as he preferred, he saw she was fully dressed, eyes feverish with concentration, working at the little davenport which stood at the bedside.

'Oh my God, is that time?' she said, looking up from her lists. 'Baby, forgive me. Just a few things to check for the ball. I can't trust any of them to get things right unless I'm constantly breathing down their necks.

'If this is inconvenient for you,' he said stiffly, taken aback by her departure from their normal routine.

Sloane's eyes widened in horror. She was beside him in a second. 'For God's sake, Nicky, stay. I need you to be with me.'

In her haste to show him how much, she offended again, by beginning to undress him. He hated that, reminded of the merciless sexual teasing he had suffered at the hands of a nursemaid in his isolated years in the royal nursery.

He took hold of her wrists and held her firmly away from him. 'Thank you, but I prefer to do this for myself.' Anyone else would have been left in no doubt that he was issuing a command rather than stating a preference.

Careless with craving for him, she did not notice. She scrabbled at the concealed fastening of her svelte Donna Karan body and wraparound skirt, dropping the beautiful clothes where she stood. Nicky was undressing with his usual precision, folding his clothes neatly as he had learnt to do at the Royal Military Academy.

She wrapped her arms around him from behind, rubbing her nakedness against the lean muscled length of his back, his high horseman's buttocks. 'C'mon, it's rude to keep a lady waiting.'

He allowed himself to be pulled to the bed. He was completely unaroused.

Sloane felt she could not bear to follow the usual pattern of their encounters, exciting him by exciting herself. There was no need, in any case. If she so much as brushed herself, she would risk spending the shattering orgasm she could feel building inside her. She decided to take the initiative.

Playfully pushing him back on the bed, she knelt and took him in her mouth. She showed none of the delicacy and finesse he prized in a woman, tackling him with the fervour of a ten-dollar whore desperate to turn another trick. Though the approach appalled him, the warm slick pressure brought him to instant erection. There was also, he realised, folding his hands behind his head, something else to be said for this departure from their usual love-making. At least, this way, she could not talk.

But not for long. She eased him, fully erect, from the haven of her mouth and throat, and slid eel-like across the bed to straddle him with eagerly parted thighs.

'No, let me!' she cried, when he started to slide his hands beneath her buttocks, positioning her for the two or three wild thrusts which he knew would be all it would take. 'I'll do it all,' she breathed, riding the potency of his glistening shaft with long lingering thrusts of her hips. On and on she took them, playing the dominating role long past the point when he could see it as a lover's game. And all the time she talked.

'Oh, that's good! That's so-oo good. Nicky, Nicky, give me all you've got . . . Now!'

She reached behind her, tightening her hand around the taut skin of his scrotum. The added stimulus was all it took to send him hurtling towards a mind-blowing climax. She shuddered and convulsed around him, making weak little mewing sounds of ecstasy. The power of their orgasms left them weak and played out. The difference between them was that Sloane saw this as a cause for celebration, whereas Nicky did not. He liked to remain, if not on top, always in charge. He liked to be silent after lovemaking too, at least for a few minutes it took him to return from the dark and silent place within him which was attained only then.

Sloane draped his arm around her shoulders and lay with her face pressed into his chest, talking, dragging him back to the imperfect real world.

'It's such a nuisance, Nicky! The junkie — sorry, I forgot Court was a friend of yours — but really it's such a pain. He and this French girl of his are coming over for a few days before the ball and taking Chester Square. They want to go shopping, would you believe? Straight over from Paris, and they want to shop here. I can't possibly stay on in London with them in the house, and I'll miss you so much. I won't be able to keep my hands off you at the ball.'

He twisted away from her, angling his head so that she could see his face while he told her: 'I trust you will not be so foolish.'

She pouted and snuggled back against him. 'Oh, Nicky, you know me better than that. But God, it's getting so hard. Every time I leave you and go back to my draggy husband, dangling around after those boys of his, I just want to throw up. He's so damned obvious about it — "business in the stables". Huh!'

Nicky did not want to listen to this. He'd met Alexander on a few occasions and found him dignified and presentable. If he chose to conceal his true preferences behind a dignified façade of heterosexuality, Nicky considered it Sloane's duty as a wife not to spread scandal. After all, if she was so blatantly disrespectful of her husband, how could he himself expect complete unswerving loyalty from her? Marriage was considered the perfect training for a royal mistress. In Sloane's case, it did not seem to have worked. She was becoming too aggressive and demanding for Nicky's taste, and her increasing sexual dependence on him threatened to make her dangerously unstable.

591

Time for their association to draw to its natural close, he decided. But she would need careful handling. Not for her the discreet but costly kiss-off in its Van Cleef and Arpels box. Sloane had more money than the whole of the Malivian Royal Treasury. Besides if she chose to go pouring poison into the ears of the press, she could do him and his image a great deal of harm. This definitely called for a more gradual fade-out. 'It's a pity we won't be able to manage another meeting before the ball,' he said, making his voice regretful. 'Because, after it, I shall be leaving for Malivia.'

She sat up in bed. 'But, Nicky, you can't just leave me like this! How will I manage without you?'

'Like any royal mistress — with dignity and restraint,' he told her, appealing to her sense of pride. He saw with annoyance the tears in her eyes. He hated to see a woman lose her self-possession. 'Calm yourself.' He took her in his arms. That way he did not have to see the damage that her tears were inflicting on her careful maquillage. 'There's no need for this,' he said, feeling faint stirrings of shame since, in fact, there was every need. He had not realised how deep her feelings for him had already gone. His tactical with-drawl had come not a moment too soon. 'I should have gone earlier this week, in fact. I put back my return just so that I could attend your birthday ball.'

She gave him a watery smile. 'Really?'

He nodded, omitting to add that wild horses wouldn't have sent him back to Malivia without the chance to renew his acquaintanceship with her niece.

For Camilla, Thursday and Friday were a joyful round of arrivals. She was mobile enough to leave her room and welcome Courtney, the first of her returning sons. To her surprise, Dexter left a conference call to join her. His parents met Courtney as he and Chantel stepped into the marble hall.

'Darling! You're home at last,' said Camilla, throwing her arms round him.

There was so much she must leave unsaid with Dexter sitting like Solomon in a wheelchair, watching them. Courtney looked marvellous, she saw. Bright-eyed, rested, that old shifty sideways look she had learned to dread quite disappeared.

'Mother, Dad, I'd like you to meet Chantel,' he said, taking a step back to put his arm around the waist of a fresh-faced blonde girl who had been hanging back shyly. 'Chantel, may I introduce my mother and father, Lady Camilla and Lord Randolph.

Camilla was overjoyed to welcome the girl she knew had done so much to help her son's recovery. This was no time to stand on ceremony. She hugged Chantel, too.

Dexter studied the new arrivals closely for a moment, taking in the girl's youthful prettiness, his son's healthy appearance. 'You'll do,' he said to Chantel, wheeling himself forward so that he could take her hand. 'And none of this Lord Randolph and Lady Camilla stuff, eh? We're Dexter and Camilla, and don't you forget it.'

To everyone's surprise, he tugged at Chantel's hand instead of shaking it so that she had to bend down. He gave her a smacking kiss on the cheek. Afterwards he looked up at Courtney and winked. 'Good to see you can still pick 'em, son. Next time don't stay away so long, okay?'

Camilla was keen to capitalise on this unexpected display of warmth. 'We're going to have tea in the sitting-room, Dexter. Shall I take you up in the lift?'

'No, damn it! You know I hate that steel coffin. Once a day's more than enough for me. Besides, we aren't all parasites. Some of us have work to do.'

He wheeled himself off in the direction of his office, leaving them all dumbfounded by the affable welcome and equally crushing put-down.

'Glad to see Pa's running true to form.' said Courtney, putting an arm round the waists of his girlfriend and his mother. 'Chantel would've thought I'd been exaggerating otherwise, wouldn't you?'

'It's okay — he's Australian,' she said. Then, in case Camilla had thought her rude, added hastily, 'I mean they say what they think. At least that way you know where you stand with them. I should know. My mother's Australian, too.'

'How interesting,' said Camilla. 'I'd love to meet her and swop notes one day. Come on, darlings, Georgie's waiting upstairs — she's dying to see you both again.'

If Courtney's homecoming had passed off better than Camilla had expected, Ashley's was far worse. She had never shared with her eldest child Dexter's unreasonable suspicion about his parentage. With natural delicacy she shrank from discussing with her son her own earlier affair. Ashley had of course noticed Dexter's attitude to himself and Courtney, but had not realised that this stemmed from different reasons in each case. He had put it down simply to his father's bitterness at being crippled and deprived of the active lifestyle which he could see his sons enjoying.

Camilla had herself informed immediately of her elder son's arrival in the house. She used Dexter's lift to come down and greet him, only to arrive in the marble hall to see him reluctantly disappearing in the direction of Dexter's office, Webster beckoning him on like an anxious tugboat.

'Ash — wait!' she called. 'We'll go in together. It's so good to see you. Was it an awful flight? You look exhausted.'

'An engine cut out on our approach to Abu Dhabi. We had to sit on the tarmac for three hours while they tinkered with it. I've had a lot worse.'

Dexter did not even glance up as they entered the room. He was studying the British market movements on one screen while another reflected Sydney's closing figures. 'So you finally made it,' was his ungracious greeting. 'We were expecting you earlier.'

'Ashley's flight was delayed,' Camilla began.

'Who told you to poke your nose in?' Dexter asked his wife, erupting into fury even quicker than usual. He turned savagely on Ashley, jabbing a finger in the direction of Randolph Enterprise's red-flagged listing on the screen. 'What the bloody hell are you and your uncle doing out there? Trying to ruin me?'

Camilla had had enough. Her son had arrived, pale and red-eyed, after a long-haul flight made even longer by delay. 'Stop bullying him, Dexter,' she said, trying to keep a light tone to her voice and smooth over the ugliness she could feel bubbling just beneath the surface of the scene.

'Dad, there's a whole lot of things I need to discuss with you,' said Ashley wearily. He took a mass of print out from the attaché case he was holding. 'Look, I'm bushed right now, but before I left Sydney I came across something pretty worrying in the Leisure Division. Uncle Luke wasn't going to give me full access —'

'He'd damn well better! You're my personal representative.'

'— but I dated his secretary Jayne a few times. She's a great girl, gave me the code to his personal files. It looks as if he's been channelling Shipping and Mining profits into Leisure to cover up an enormous deficit on the Bradbury Island project. The figures are mind-boggling, and even with his jiggery-pokery he's only just ahead of the creditors. Some of them have been waiting months, and word's started to leak out — hence the unease you've been noticing in the market. There's just one thing — the files were bugged. The next time Luke accesses, he'll know someone's been in. Won't take him long to work out who.'

'And why the hell shouldn't you? You're a Randolph, for Christ's sake!'

Camilla had a wild impulse to laugh. Oh yes, Ash was a Randolph when it was a question of business. But when it came to any natural family feelings — forget it! 'Surely this can wait, Dexter?' she said fiercely. 'Poor Ash is dead on his feet. He'll be good for nothing if you don't let him rest.'

'We've got the weekend to study these and work out our response — or most of it,' said Ashley. 'I'd be fresher and more able to help if I got some sleep now.'

It was the only sensible course of action, Dexter knew, but the sight of Randolph Enterprises taking a bath because of mismanagement or worse made him clench his fists with fury. 'All right, then. Bugger off and leave me to do all the work,' he said ungraciously.

Ashley looked miserable at his cool reception, but as Camilla bundled him out of the office she could only feel glad that things had not gone a lot worse. With the black dog on him as it was today, Dexter could say the foulest, most humiliating, things. He had not mentioned his suspicions about his eldest son's parentage, but it was only a matter of time, she knew.

Dinner on Friday evening was a sophisticated affair. Sloane's house party comprised one former president of the USA, the deposed head of a South American government, a German baron, a press baron, a man who wore sunglasses even to dinner and was rumoured to be a Colombian drugs baron. There were Hollywood stars of every sex, and a woman who had been married seven times despite her total lack of pretension towards looks, charm or even a personality. She merely paid off each handsome reject more royally than the last.

Sloane had arranged for dinner to be served in the state dining-room, on gold plate brought down specially from the London vault in an armoured car.

'Nice company you keep, Sloane,' Camilla heard her husband say as he wheeled himself away from the Painted Room where drinks had been served before dinner. 'You'll excuse me if I don't come in to dinner? I find the company a little — exalted — for my simple taste.'

Camilla knew that he was itching to get back to Ashley's figures. Sloane took his departure as a calculated insult. As he left, she rounded furiously on Camilla.

'Isn't that just typical! Your husband's completely screwed up my *placement*. I was relying on him to keep DeeDee St John out of mischief. He's the only man here she could play her tiresome under-the-table games with without his even noticing!'

Though she herself had every reason to be angry with Dexter, Camilla rose to his defence. 'I find that remark in very poor taste, Sloane. Dexter's got far more on his mind at present than dangling around after your guests.'

Her sister-in-law spat venom in reply. 'I haven't noticed his drawing the line when it comes to attending the ball tomorrow. In fact, he asked me specifically if Rolf Blanchard of Blanchard et Cie was attending. What's the matter, Camilla? Randolph Enterprises going down the tubes? Too bad, but tell that husband of yours not to embarrass my banker friends by drumming up finance at what is meant to be a social occasion. I'm relying on you to see that he doesn't. Besides, if it's capital he needs, I'd always be happy to strike a private deal. I think you both know what my terms would be.'

Camilla drew herself up proudly. 'Your *placement* has just evened itself up again, Sloane! I'm certainly not going to share a table with you after that insult. And as for tomorrow night, I suggest if you're worried about Dexter, you should keep an eye on him yourself. I shan't be coming to the ball.'

'Not even to see Bradford Carter?'

Sloane's parting taunt stopped Camilla in her tracks. She ducked her head, hoping to conceal a painful blush, but not succeeding.

It was a lucky shot on her sister-in-law's part, but there had been something about Bradford's manner when he'd mentioned his meeting with Camilla. And how had he managed it, anyway, when she was playing invalid up in her room? On Wednesday, when she'd called his office repeatedly, she had finally been told that he was out for the day — at exactly the same time that Camilla disappeared with a chauffeur to a mysterious destination.

Whoever would have thunk it? Sloane asked herself while she hurried with outstretched arms to kiss the air above the carefully powdered cheek of her dozenth closest friend. The virgin martyr herself was having a fling! And with dear old Brad — the man who was supposed to be on Sloane's side. Dexter could make as big a fool of himself as he liked tomorrow, trying to scare up capital from her friends. The man *she* intended to keep a close eye on was Bradford Carter.

After her spat with Sloane the night before, Camilla woke on the morning of the ball feeling jaded and out of sorts. Her mood was not helped when she was told that Ashley and Dexter were in a meeting and did not wish to be disturbed. Only the thought that tonight she would see Brad again kept her going.

The house was in an uproar. Sloane seemed to be in a dozen different places at once: berating the caterers drafted in to help out in the Courtney kitchens — 'Sevruga instead of Beluga. I do not *believe* this!' — insisting on being the first to throw the switch on a complicated series of holograms installed on the West Terrace. These projected an image of a Venetian skyline which would be visible from the windows of the ballroom, to be left unshuttered for the night. She had wanted the room to be candlelit, but the house's insurers had put their foot down at that. Sloane has stamped hers repeatedly, then compromised by having the existing Georgian glass chandeliers taken down and others of Venetian glass installed, just for the evening. They were lent specially after a friend at the Getty Museum had pulled strings. The cost of insuring and transporting them would have paid for a semi in the local village, but Sloane was unrepentant. This was her night. It was going to be special, whatever the cost to her or anyone else.

Ken Turner and his team had surpassed themselves with the flowers. Four enormous facsimiles of the lions of Piazza San Marco had somehow been constructed of dried flowerheads. They were arranged looking out from the centre of the ballroom. It would play havoc with the dancers' freedom of movement, but looked spectacular. Elsewhere the florists had borrowed from Baroque motifs and constructed fantastic swags and still lifes of flowers, wound around the pillars of the ballroom or spilling from giant cornuopiae in the alcoves and embrasures.

Burt Bacharach's orchestra, flown over specially for the occasion, were to play for part of the evening, alternating with cabaret turns from a talented young ex-Footlights duo and an octogenarian torch-singer currently enjoying her third comeback. For the hardier spirits, a disco had been set up in the cellars.

Sloane's own costume was a carefully guarded secret, but Courtney and Chantel reported seeing some strange sights on their way through the house before the ball began.

'We saw Queen Victoria going into Casanova's bedroom,' said Courtney.

'And Harpo Marx let me sound his hooter,' said Chantel.

'I'm not surprised, looking like that,' said Courtney appreciatively.

'Court!'

Camilla was pleased to see the easy way they treated one another. Anyone meeting them for the first time would have supposed them married for years. They had dressed to complement one another as Pierrot and Pierrette. Courtney clowned around in wide white ruffs, black pompoms and a tall white pointed hat. Chantel wore a white and black ballerina-length tutu trimmed with the same pom-poms, and a black velvet ribbon at her throat. She had put up her strawberry blonde hair and pinned a gardenia to the back of it.

There was a knock at the door. 'Come in,' said Camilla. For a moment nothing happened, then the door slowly swung open to frame a living facsimile of their ancestress, Arabella Hamilton, whose portrait by Lely hung on the wall of the great staircase.

'I don't like to move my head too much because of this ridiculous wig!' Georgie said cheerfully. 'And every time I move at more than a snail's pace I leave a storm of baby powder behind me. Otherwise I'm quite pleased with it. What do you think?'

Camilla could have cried. Her daughter looked so fragile, young and ethereally beautiful. Her dress was of ivory slipper satin oversewn with brilliants, simply cut with a low square neck. Below the long fitted waist billowed full skirts with a flash of turquoise and gold at their hem. The white wig, heavily powdered, was ornamented with diamond and enamel clips in the shape of dragonflies and ladybirds, and a cascade of white curls was pulled to one side to droop fetchingly over one shoulder.

'There'll be no one but Chantel to touch you,' said her brother affectionately, going to kiss her.

'Careful! Mind my patch,' she said, pointing to the star-shaped black mark she had painted high on one cheekbone.

'What do you think, Mummy? I know it's a bit *Rebecca* dressing up like a portrait, but while we were in Paris and having to keep quiet about our real names —' Georgie smiled at Courtney and Chantel — 'I used Arabella's. I felt I owed it to her in return to bring her back to life tonight. Do you think that's silly?'

'Of course not, darling. Arabella was very good to Courtney when he needed her. I shan't forget her.'

'Neither shall I,' said Courtney, giving Georgie a careful kiss. 'I do wish you were coming too, Mums, then I'd have all my favourite girls together.'

'Yes, come on, Mummy,' said Georgie. 'Won't you change your mind? If you don't have a costume, I'm sure you could borrow one of Sloane's. Her maid told Webster that her ladyship had had three run up — all c originals, would you believe!'

'I wouldn't ask that woman for the time of day,' Camilla said vehemently. 'Not after the way she talked about your father last night. No sign of him and Ash, I suppose?'

'Not yet. Still closeted in their meeting in Dad's private office. Sloane sent down word that he was to switch off the computer terminals for the duration of the ball — something about them interfering with the disco in the cellar — and he sent a very dusty answer back. But I know he does mean to go. We've seen his costume, haven't we, Chantel?'

'You bet. A Roman emperor, complete with laurel wreath.'

'Wonder which one?' said Camilla.

'Caligula, from the way he's been behaving to Ash. Have you any idea why he's being so rough on the poor guy?'

Camilla looked away. 'Business worries. Something's gone wrong at the Australian end and Dexter's venting his frustration with Uncle Luke on the poor messenger. But don't let's talk about it now, darlings. You don't want to miss any of the fun.'

'Are you sure you'll be all right, Mummy?' Georgie pressed her. 'Is there anything I can have sent up for you?'

'Thank you, I'll be fine. Pam's helping out in the kitchen for tonight, and she's going to bring me up something light later on. I think you should all be going down now. I can hear cars pulling up already.'

'All right, all right, we can take a hint,' said Ashley, knocking on the door of her dressing-room as he passed it. 'It's okay, you can come out now,' he joked. 'You didn't know my mother kept a lover in her dressing-room, did you, Chantel?'

Camilla felt hot with guilt.

When Pam brought up her supper half an hour later, she took the glass of white wine but sent back the smoked

ambled eggs. She put out all the lights
e by the bed and sat at the uncurtained
ching the stately convoy of Rolls Royces,
aimlers and Mercedes winding down the drive.
re handed from their cars by liveried footmen
and a able file of Moorish pages lit the entryway with
flaming torches. From time to time she saw red flashing
lights in the sky and heard the thudding arrival of a
helicopter. Courtney Park's most venerable Rolls Royce,
the emerald green fifties model Brinsley had given Angelica
as a birthday present, ferried helicopter passengers from
the top field to the house.

Were it not for Sloane's part in the proceedings, her
mother would have loved tonight, Camilla reflected, then
all thoughts of Angelica were chased from her mind as she
realised that any one of the cars arriving below might
contain Brad. For a few minutes she craned her neck,
studying the costumes. Micky Mouse, The Sheikh — or
maybe *a* sheikh, Sloane knew several — two rival
Cleopatras, each furiously ignoring the other. She couldn't
see Batman ...

And thank God he couldn't see her! She realised that
with Georgie at the ball, she'd have to manage her own
transformation this evening. She struggled to apply
cosmetics in the way her daughter had shown her. It was
hopeless. In Camilla's shaking hands the kohl pencil turned
itself into an instrument of torture. She stabbed herself
painfully twice in the eye, then gave up, reverting to her
usual artless appearance. Brad had fallen in love with her
like this, after all.

When she was ready, she sat for a long time with folded
hands looking around the room which, before the accident,
she had shared with Dexter. Her eyes skimmed the cluster
of photographs on one of the bedside tables. A wedding
portrait of Dexter and herself; tiny precious studies of each
of her newborn babies; the Anthony Armstrong Jones
portrait of herself and the boys she had given Dexter as a

parting gift when he left her to go to Australia the second time. Then later pictures of the children: Georgie, in riding-kit, grinning toothlessly as she held up a first prize rosette; Court and Ash, two skinny suntanned little boys in shorts on their first visit to Yelonga. And then there was Dexter in his peer's robes on the morning of his investiture. The whole story of her marriage was there — or almost.

From the drawer of her rosewood desk Camilla withdrew another photograph, one she had never displayed out of deference to her husband's feelings. It was a small candid shot she had snatched of him in hospital shortly after the accident, half afraid it might be the last she would take. The old brash confidence of the earlier photographs was missing from this, replaced by an air of uncertainty that tore her heart every time she looked at it. Afterwards, he'd retreated into bitterness and his unreasonable obsession with Ash's parentage, but she had kept the photograph as a reminder to herself of the hidden face behind Dexter's bully's mask. Quickly she dropped the photograph back in the drawer, wondering if she was doing the right thing in hiding her husband's suffering from herself.

Sloane and Alexander received their guests in the marble hall, exchanging kisses and handshakes and amused exclamations over the different costumes. Eventually the flood of arrivals began to die down.

'Don't you think, my dear, we ought to be mingling with our guests by now?' Alexander's fine-drawn good looks and courtly manner perfectly complemented the Cavalier costume he had chosen.

'Please don't tell me how to behave, Xan,' snapped his wife. 'The British aristocracy doesn't have a monopoly on good manners, you know.'

She stood erect, a queenly figure in a Renaissance-style dress of grey velvet, gold lace and sea-green silk. Romeo Gigli had designed it to her commission, working from an old engraving of a costume Catherine de'Medici had worn to a court masquerade. It combined his masterly technique for draping the female form with a witty fantastic 'costume' element. On her head she wore a puffed velvet cap, slightly higher than a tam o'shanter, trimmed with gold-dipped ostrich feathers which drooped becomingly over one eye. To go with the costume she had chosen an austere Elizabethan Gage pendant of Roman intaglio seals, grey and white baroque pearls, opals and brilliants.

She continued to stand in the hall, greeting the stragglers with a strained smile while her eyes returned constantly to the front door. She felt her heart reverberate to hammer-blows of disappointment at each fresh arrival who was not Nicky.

Alexander finally prevailed upon her to join their guests in the ballroom, where Sloane received the second blow of the night. The Randolphs had not, of course, joined the receiving line, even though they as much as Sloane and Alexander were occupants of the house. Courtney, Chantel and Georgianna had already joined the party. Pierrot and Pierrette made a charming couple, wandering hand in hand among the other guests, Chantel finding several European friends of her parents among them. But Georgie — Sloane stood staring at her, eyes at their bleakest and least forgiving.

Sweet simplicity versus contrived effect: Georgie upstaged her hostess without even trying. Wherever she went, her pale fragile prettiness garnered her compliments, admiring glances and invitations to dance. Insult was added to injury when Hank Fosburgh, a Hollywood producer friend of Sloane's, waved animatedly to her through the crowd.

'Hey, Sloane, looking good, baby. Listen, I gotta ask you a favour. Could you please introduce me to that girl in white? Convince her I'm on the level? I made her a serious offer of a screen test, but she must have thought I was coming on to her. Someone said she was your niece.'

Sloane couldn't bear it a second longer. 'Speak to my husband — she's *his* niece.' She left the ballroom, unwilling to share her thunder with Georgie. She stuck to the other rooms, circulating among her guests.

'Sloane, I'm so-oo jealous! The house, the husband — both to die for.'

'Fa-abulous party, darling. Gloria Diehlmann's *green.* She was planning a Renaissance fête, but *après* this . . . '

'Piazza San Marco without the bally pigeons! Brilliant idea, my dear. Simply brilliant. And what a very jolly dress.'

It was one way of describing a £10,000 couture original, she supposed, but her ruffled feelings were soothed.

She couldn't see Bradford Carter, anyway. The trouble with holding a party like this was that half her guests were unrecognisable from their usual selves. Over to her right she saw Fay Wray, a rather shrunken King Kong, and Batman deep in conversation. As Sloane watched, Fay Wray slid her long red manicured nails over Batman's black-cloaked arm. He bent his masked head close to hers while she whispered something to him. Something dirty, if she recognised DeeDee St John behind the thirties glitz! Batman shook his head vigorously and laughed — a warm, vibrant, unmistakable sound. So Bradford Carter had come as the Caped Crusader, had he? Just let him try and fly out of here before she'd had a chance to grill him on the progress of her case.

She started to push her way towards him, but Ford intercepted her. 'I thought you'd like to know, your ladyship, that His Royal Highness Prince Nicolas of Malivia has just arrived.'

Sloane whirled away from Bradford, all thoughts of business forgotten in her haste to reach Nicky and claim him as her very special guest.

He had arrived in a black mood, furious with his father who had insisted on holding a long telephone conversation on wearisome matters of state even though Nicky had plans to be in the country the next day.

'Some things are more important than carousing and chasing after married women's skirts,' said the King in his precise and formal Middle European accent. 'It's time you thought about settling down. The princesses on offer are a sorry collection, it's true, but a European aristocrat — someone with a substantial dowry, of course. You would do well to think about it seriously, my son, if I am seriously to consider abdicating in your favour.'

It was a lure he had thrown countless times before. Nicky lunged after it as he always did, resigning himself to an immensely long and tedious conversation before he would be free to drive down for the ball. He left London far later than he'd intended and in no mood to indulge a jealous mistress's whims.

Dancing seemed to be in full swing when he and his two detectives arrived. Nicky looked around for his hostess, then told himself he'd catch her later, drawn as if on invisible strings to the ballroom. His superior height and striking looks drew attention wherever he went. He'd rejected Sloane's suggestion that he might wear a flashy comic-opera-style uniform and instead chosen to dress as a Regency buck. There was nothing dandyish about him, though. With his broad shoulders, tapering waist and muscular legs, the white shirt and stock, cream chamois waistcoat, fitted tailcoat and white buckskins looked superb. His own slightly too long black curls gave him a dashing Byronic air. His progress through the ballroom gave rise to a few ceremonial bows and curtsies, mainly from the European aristocracy represented at the ball. His younger English friends did not stand on such ceremony.

'Nicky, you old dog,' said Courtney, appearing at his side with Chantel in tow. 'Thank God you're here at last! Now we can really liven things up.' They had met a couple of times in town: for lunch at Drone's, drinks and dancing at Annie's. Chantel was confused, however, at meeting Nicky at this public occasion. She wasn't sure whether to curtsy, shake hands or just say 'Hi'. With a devastating smile, he solved her dilemma. He bent down to kiss her lingeringly, whispering after he had done so. 'I always kiss my friends' girlfriends. A little healthy jealousy works wonders.'

Chantel laughed. Sure enough, Courtney became all proud possessiveness and slid his arm around her waist. 'Come away from that man at once, Chantel. No woman is safe with him.'

'Oh, come, come, Courtney. I'm perfectly safe with any female — so long as she is old and ugly!' Nicky's joking expression altered. 'Do you think we could have a few words somewhere quieter?' He gestured towards an out-of-the-way corner. 'I don't want to cause you any unpleasant memories, Court, but you may recall that the last time I met your sister I got off to a rather sticky start. I was wondering if this time you would introduce us properly? She is here, I take it?'

'Don't you recognise her?' said Courtney. He pointed out onto the crowded floor. Nicky scanned the dancers whirling by in their crazy costumes. His eyes sought a flag of nut-brown hair, a pair of expressive hazel eyes . . .

'Where?' he said impatiently. 'Ah, of course.'

Three times his eyes had lingered over the charming little lady in white. With her patch and powdered wig she looked like an aristocratic shepherdess strayed from a pastoral idyll by Watteau or Fragonard. He had already promised himself the pleasure of making her acquaintance — after he had sought out his prime reason for being here tonight. Now it seemed that he could fulfil both plans in one delightful meeting.

Fortunately the dance was ending. Court was able to walk on to the floor and commandeer his sister from a very disgruntled partner. 'Sorry, but someone very important has to meet you now.'

'Who? Don't be so maddeningly mysterious, Court! Oh—'

She broke off in surprise as she realised whom he

intended to introduce. After the previous easy banter, a strangely formal mood fell over them.

Courtney made an elaborate introduction. 'Sir, I should like to present my sister Georgianna. Georgianna, His Royal Highness Prince Nicolas of Malivia.'

Perhaps it was the effect of the graceful court dress she was wearing; perhaps the piercing glance she intercepted from Nicky's dark blue eyes, but Georgie felt herself sinking into a low curtsy. Chantel caught Courtney's eye, and they slipped away.

Nicolas steadied Georgie as she rose, and kept hold of her hand. 'An introduction between us was not really necessary, was it?'

She shook her head, unable to pretend. She had known who he was the first time they met, and despite his savagery to her then the image of him had remained fresh and intriguing in her mind.

'An apology most definitely is,' he continued. 'When I found out the error I'd made at Windsor I came to Courtney Park immediately, intending to apologise for my mistake. Imagine my chagrin to be told the bird had flown.'

'By my aunt. I gather you've become good friends.' She hoped he would take the hint and not insult her by evading the truth.

His handsome face looked uneasy for a moment. 'It is true that Sloane and I were particular friends — for a time. You must understand it is very difficult for someone in my position. If I am seen out in public with an eligible young girl more than once, the gossip columns scream their speculation: "Nicky and Stephanie — is marriage on the cards?" "Lady Helen and the Playboy Prince — a love match?" To conduct an affair with a young woman in the full glare of the public's interest would be undignified and unfair to her. For this reason I usually do as your own British royalty has done for centuries — confine myself to discreet liaisons with chic older woman blessed with under-standing husbands. It sounds a little cold-blooded, I know.

I assure you, I am anything but.'

She stared at his heavy lidded eyes and full mouth, saying nothing.

'Shall we dance?' he asked. Silently she placed her other hand on his shoulder and they joined the waltz. He was not displeased by her cool manner. It made a welcome change from the excited stream of girlish chatter a prince was usually subject to from women of every age. Under cover of the dance, he pulled her tight against him. The way she caught her breath and refused to meet his bold gaze made it clear that Georgianna Randolph was far from indifferent to him.

They danced in silence, oblivious of the attention they attracted. The two most striking people at the ball had found each other. Fellow dancers faded into the sidelines so that they could watch the beautiful couple.

Sloane's hurrying footsteps were slowed by the crush of spectators. She had to elbow her way through, emerging on the fringes of the crowd slightly breathless. The spectacle that met her eyes was unbelievable — Georgianna throwing herself at poor Nicky, clinging to him with the embarrassing light of calf-love in her eyes. What on earth was the matter with everybody, standing around and letting this embarrassing scene continue? It was her party. She could call the tune. She gestured for the orchestra to stop playing.

'Sir, it's so good to have you here.' She all but elbowed Georgie aside in her urgent desire to claim the Prince. Embarrassed, the girl stepped back as Sloane wound her arms round Nicky's neck and kissed him full on the mouth in full view of the interested onlookers. There was an outbreak of whispers and giggles.

'Dance with me, Nicky.' Sloane's voice was audible throughout the room.

'I shall be delighted to dance with my hostess — after Georgianna and I have finished this waltz.' His voice was perfectly polite, but echoed embarrassingly in the hushed room.

Nicky glanced commandingly at the orchestra leader, watching the scene with raised baton.

'Play on,' said the Prince, and the waltz was reprised.

For an awful moment Sloane was stranded partnerless in the middle of the floor, the two dancers moving gracefully away from her. There was an embarrassed movement among the spectators and, tactfully, more couples appeared on the floor, disguising her partnerless state. The walk off the floor and out of the room for the second time that night felt like the longest she had ever taken.

Alexander had been tipped off by the servants to the Prince's arrival. He had followed his wife into the ballroom and witnessed the humiliating passage, though he had not understood the full implications of it. He caught hold of her arm as she walked past. 'My dear, don't let the young puppy upset you.'

She shook herself free. 'Get out of my way, damn you! I need a drink.'

She snatched a glass of champagne from a silver tray, draining it and substituting another virtually in one movement. She continued to drink and circulate, beginning countless conversations only to drift hazily away when someone more interesting caught her eye. No one half as interesting as Nicky, though, goddamn him. Why was it always the same? she wondered. Why did the men in her life always use and humiliate her?

Through her champagne haze she caught sight of a tall caped figure making his way out into the marble hall.

'Bradford!' she called, but he seemed not to hear her. Glancing quickly around, he began to climb the stairs to the family apartments above. For a moment she could not imagine what he was doing. There were plenty of cloakrooms downstairs. Then something about the guilty speed with which he moved, head down as if to avoid recognition, tipped her off. Bradford Carter was going visiting, and only one person was still occupying her room upstairs ... Her eyes narrowed to ugly slits. Goddamn them all to hell!

Every single man, even the one she paid, let her down. So Bradford thought he could play kissy-kissy with the enemy, did he? She'd see about that!

Camilla heard Brad's discreet knock, and quickly opened the door. He came inside, nervously balling the black mask in his hand.

'I'm sorry I'm late — couldn't get away before. There was some sort of scene in the ballroom. Everyone was talking about it.'

'Anything serious?' she asked, not really wanting to know. All she wanted was to be in the safe haven of his arms, hearing his warm reassuring voice tell her that everything would be all right.

'Something to do with Prince Nicolas and Sloane. Sorry — I didn't get all the details. My mind must have been on other things.' For the first time, he gave her his boyish grin.

Camilla reached up to free the long cape at his throat. 'Love the costume.'

'Love you. Love and want you. God, I've been living for this moment.' His eyes were cloudy with passion but they had not lost their acute perception. 'What is it, Camilla? You haven't changed your mind? You do still want us to be together tonight?'

'Oh, Brad, hold me. This is so difficult when you look at me like that.'

He led her to a couch and sat beside her, holding her hand. 'I thought we agreed days ago that we were going to be lovers. If you don't want me —'

'It's not that! Of course it's not that. You're very dear to me, Brad. I love your crooked smile and all the funny little things you say. I love the way you make me feel when I'm with you.'

He smiled with relief. 'Then what is it?'

'Dexter.' The word fell like a stone, shattering his

hopes. 'When I told you I didn't believe he cared for me, not any more, I wasn't telling you the whole truth,' she said painfully. 'There's always another side to things, isn't there? The truth is, *I* still care for *him*. Oh, not in the romantic shivering-in-my-shoes sort of way I feel for you, my darling. Poor Dexter. He's never had that from me, and now it's too late. But despite all the years of estrangement and neglect, I find I do still care for him very much. Before the accident, when I was very young and badly upset after Luciano's death, you wouldn't believe how gentle and sensitive he was with me. Yes, he's been neglectful since, cruel even, but that's doubly sad because I know that underneath there's a good, caring man. I should have tried harder to reach him, I owed him that much at least. Do you understand what I'm saying, Bradford?'

He laughed bitterly. 'Better than you, it seems. Camilla, sweet Camilla, you're so gentle and good you see the same qualities in everyone else. But it just ain't so! The guy's a classic case of a stony-hearted S-O-B. Believe me, I know.'

She shook her head. 'You've only met him as he is now. You can't really understand him without having known him as he was. I'm sorry, Brad. I didn't intend to run on like this about my husband. I do want us to have this night together — so long as you understand that one night is all it's going to be. One perfect night to look back on and treasure for always when we've gone our separate ways — you back to Jo-Ann, me here with Dexter.'

He opened his mouth to protest, but she silenced him with a finger to his lips.

'Do you agree to my terms, darling? Because, if not, I think it would be better for you to go now.'

It took him an age to reply. The revelation of the attachment she still felt to Randolph surprised and upset him. His emotions fluctuated between regret, jealousy, desire ... principally desire. Brad heard what she said, but the powerful core of self-confidence which made him so effective in court refused to let him believe that a warm, loving woman like Camilla could seriously prefer that stone-faced monument to selfishness to him, her flesh and blood lover. He knew besides that he was a skilful seducer. Wait till I've made her mine, he told himself, then she'll forget she ever told me to go.

'I agree. Conference over. Give me tonight, Camilla, and I won't ask for more.'

Unresisting, she let him take her in his arms. Something was wrong, though. She did not seem to know how to respond to his kisses. With a feeling of disbelief he realised this infinitely desirable woman was practically unawakened. After a week of tantalising awareness, his need for her was acute. That didn't matter now. All that did was that he should make a long, comprehensive seduction of her, raising her to such heights that afterwards she would be unable to force him from her life.

Her maid had turned back the covers of the bed. Brad ignored it, undressing her where she lay on the couch, murmuring an extravagant litany of praise in a voice that was an additional caress. The speedwell-blue velour lounging robe and white lace bra and pants, which were all she wore, were speedily discarded. Camilla reached up to help him undress, but he caught hold of her wrists, gently preventing her. 'Not yet. Lie back, Camilla. This is all for you.'

The feeling of his body, clothed against her nakedness, was exciting in itself. Brad's kisses thrilled her. He seemed to know all the most sensitive places on her face and throat, but was in no hurry to take his caresses further. She found herself initiating the next move, timidly exploring his parted lips with her tongue, gently rocking her hips so that she could feel the hardness at his loins begin to stimulate her.

She loosened her arms around his neck and almost groaned when he slid his body to one side, momentarily breaking the tantalising contact between them. He renewed it in a way that made her gasp and catch at his hair as he lowered his mouth to her breasts, sucking them like the ripe delicious fruit they resembled. He held the rest of his body deliberately out of contact with hers. It was skilful erotic torture, stimulating one part of her to a pitch where she could barely stand the torment of his touch in one place while simultaneously yearning for a more intimate caress.

When she began to roll her head from side to side, in an agony of frustration, Brad abruptly pushed up her knees and opened her for his deepest kiss. He felt an instant's shocked reaction, then the long-suppressed sensuality took over. She forgot everything but the tempo of his flickering tongue, tracing delicate patterns on the furled petals of her sex. She felt herself blossom in a gush of molten heat.

'That wasn't very fair,' she said, when she could speak again. 'The next time will be for you, darling.'

Tenderly she helped him undress and slide between the sheets. The second time was ecstasy. She loved the feeling of him inside her, making them one; enjoyed even more the pleasure of watching his expression turn from one of steady purpose to blissful release. She climaxed a moment later, on and on, enjoying the rollercoaster sensation which he helped to prolong with his fingers and hips and finally his penis, still deep inside, which stirred into life again and thrust her to the threshold between intense pleasure and erotic pain.

'Do you still think you can live without me?' he said at last.

She kissed him, beyond words. She felt as though she had just completed some fantastic journey continents away, beyond the realms of language. Tiredness overwhelmed her. It was bad timing with so much still to say, but for the moment she must sleep . . .

Brad smiled tenderly down at her as she lay in his arms. No matter what she'd said before he made love to her, he felt she was his woman now.

★

It was the DJ who unwittingly led Sloane to her brother-in-law. The languid ex-Etonian from Juliana's approached her warily, recognising all the signs of a hostess who has partied too enthusiastically. 'I'm terribly sorry, but the turntable seems to have packed up again. Frightful bore, but I did warn you that the terminals overhead seemed to be affecting things.'

'What the hell are you talking about?' she said aggressively. 'I gave strict orders that those damned office terminals were to be closed down during the ball. If my brother-in-law's still in there working . . . ' She marched off to Dexter's ground-floor suite, out of bounds to partygoers and usually to members of the family unannounced.

'My lady,' bleated a startled Webster when Sloane crashed into him. 'Was it Lord Randolph you required? I'm afraid his lordship's busy — '

'I know — screwing up my party,' she yelled, and threw open the door to Dexter's private office.

He and Ashley sat opposite each other at a conference table strewn with endless ribbons of print-out. Evidence that they had meant to come to the ball was plain to see. Dexter's toga and laurel wreath hung over the back of a chair while Ashley, tall and tanned, was dressed in Aussie surfing gear, a ripped Hot Tuna T-shirt and fluoro boardshorts. On their consoles, the computer terminals winked like green eyes.

'What the hell is the meaning of this?' thundered Sloane.

'It means we're working,' Dexter retaliated. 'What do you think you're doing, thumping in here like a demented roo? These are my private quarters.'

'Nowhere in Courtney Park is barred to me. This is my house. I call the shots. I gave strict instructions that these terminals were to be switched off. They're interfering with the disco.'

'And your bloody disco's giving me a pain in the arse! Can't you see we're busy?'

'Dad, wait a minute —'

'And you can shut up, you snivelling ineffectual little bastard! About the only consolation in this whole bloody mess you've landed us in is that you're no son of mine.'

Ashley had heard his father rant and curse at him before. This was something different. This was genuine dislike from a man who sounded like a stranger. 'I don't know what you mean!'

'Ask your mother. It's about time she came clean!'

'My, my,' said Sloane, beaming with tipsy malice. 'What a happy family scene. Much as I hate to be the bearer of bad tidings, Dexter, it looks as though your wife might be up to her old tricks.'

The tendons in his throat and neck stood out as he gripped the sides of his chair. 'What d'you mean?'

'Simply that she appears to be entertaining a gentleman caller in her room tonight — Batman, alias Bradford Carter, my lawyer. It's too bad, Dexter. She has absolutely no sense of loyalty.'

'Stuff your pity, and stuff you!' He pressed the button on the arm of his chair, sending himself hurtling out of the room.

With a contemptuous look at Sloane, Ashley followed. He caught up with Dexter at the lift in the hall. The doors opened. 'I'm coming with you, Dad.' Ashley tried to step inside.

With a violent broadside shove, Dexter sent him sprawling. 'Didn't you hear what I said? You're no son of mine. I'm going to see what that worthless whore of a mother of yours is up to. And I'm going on my own'

Ashley scrambled to his feet as the doors clanged to. He started to run, through the house and up the staircase, bumping into guests as he went. The lift reached the first floor only a few doors along from the Rose Room. He pushed aside all thoughts of his father's extraordinary behaviour towards him, praying that his mother would be alone in her room. There had been murder in Dexter's eyes.

'Camilla honey, wake up. I think I should be going.' Brad, fully dressed, shook her out of her sleep.

'What time is it?'

'Almost three. From the sound of it they're still partying, but we have to be careful.'

She sat up in bed, her mind still fuzzy with sleep. There was something she had to say ... 'Brad, I — oh, no!'

The door burst open, slamming into the wall from the force of Dexter's entry. He propelled himself into the room. 'You slut!' he said in a voice that sent a trickle of fear down her spine.

She held the sheet against her nakedness. 'Dexter, I can explain. It's not what it seems —'

Ignoring Bradford, he wheeled himself to the side of the bed. 'My wife naked, a strange man in the room — what the bloody hell else could it be?' He snatched the sheet away.

Any chance she might have had of remaining calm and putting her own case shrivelled and died beneath his pitiless scrutiny.

'You disgust me,' he said, letting the sheet fall back, 'not because of your dishonesty in taking a stud behind my back —'

Bradford approached from behind. 'Now hold on a minute, fella.'

Quicker than a striking snake, Dexter pivoted his chair and landed a punishing blow to Bradford's midriff. Camilla screamed as he sank to his knees, winded.

'Lucky I didn't hit below the belt. *You* certainly know how to, creeping upstairs to another man's wife,' Dexter told him. He turned back to Camilla. 'Like I was saying, what turns my stomach is the thought of all the years you lay in my bed like a block of ice, suffering me to take what you freely gave to others. The Italian, for instance, Ash's father —'

'How can you believe that? You must listen to me!'

He gestured at Bradford, now pale and shaken, levering himself up into a chair. 'That's how I can believe it. Because I turn my back, and this is what happens. Well, I wish you joy of him. You had precious little from me, didn't you, Camilla? Even when I was a real man.' They stared at one another. The anger faded from his eyes to be replaced by a terrible emptiness. 'You can have a divorce,' he said. 'A quick, clean one. I won't waste my time fighting in court. You're not worth it.'

'Please! Oh, please, Dexter.'

He wheeled himself out of the room.

Sobbing, she snatched up her robe and ran after him, stumbling on her weak ankle. When she reached the lift, he had wheeled himself inside. 'You must listen to me!'

He turned his set expressionless face away from her. The lift doors clanged to.

When Ashley appeared, panting for breath, his mother was standing by the lift, shaking with sobs. A man he did not recognise was trying to comfort her.

'Camilla, don't pull away from me now. I'm here for you.'

She seemed not to see him. 'I don't know what I'm doing ... I'm so confused. I can't believe he said that.'

'Don't feel guilty, not about us. He couldn't cope with his disability. That's not your fault.'

'It was! It is! I can't let him go like that. Don't you see, it's Dexter I want? If you love me, Brad, just leave me alone.'

Ashley led her back to her room, stunned by what he had witnessed. His own problems faded into insignificance beside his mother's misery and remorse.

Now! thought Sloane, catching sign of Nicky and Georgianna. The ball was winding down, the older guests retreating to their cars or rooms, but there was still an admiring crowd around Prince Nicolas and his constant companion of the evening, Georgianna Randolph.

'Don't they make a lovely couple?' said one waitress to another, heaping coals of fire on Sloane.

She started to walk towards them, stumbled slightly and changed her mind. Although her brain was dulled by drink, she had not forgotten that earlier humiliation at Nicky's hands. She had wit enough to realise that if she got into a public row with her lover she would lose what few shreds of dignity remained to her. No, better to choose her time more carefully, catch him in private.

It didn't look as if he was going anywhere. He and Georgie and their hangers-on were sitting around a caterer's marble-topped table, every inch of which was covered in spent or current champagne bottles and glasses.

Eventually there was movement at the table. Georgianna was getting to her feet. She bent over Nicky to tell him something. Sloane saw him nod and run one hand possessively down the girl's arm. A shaft of white-hot jealousy transfixed her, followed by a more rational impulse. Why create another scene with Nicky? It would be easier by far to split them up by bringing pressure to bear on Georgie. She snatched at her niece's dress as the girl tried to bypass her. There was a tearing sound.

'For heaven's sake!' said Georgie in annoyance. 'Watch what you're doing, can't you?'

'No, it's you who'd better watch your step. If you know what's good for you.'

Georgie noticed her aunt's unfocused eyes, her seeming lack of control over an expression contorted by rage. She might not care for Sloane's own sake, but for Uncle Xan's Georgie would not allow her to make a fool of herself a second time in public.

'All right, you obviously have something you want to say. Why don't we go into the library and clear the air?'

It was not that she wanted to get into a slanging-match with Sloane, today of all days, but she could see that her aunt would not let this drop until she had had her say. Part of Georgie was actually sorry for her. Despite her wealth and good looks she was a restless, dissatisfied, permanently unhappy woman who made life at least as unpleasant for herself as she did for others. They found the library darkened and deserted, lit only by firelight and a single lamp on a console table at the far end.

Sloane was on the offensive immediately. 'What are you trying to do to me, Georgianna? First it was my husband you were flirting with. It would have been incestuous if it wasn't such a joke!' She laughed harshly. 'There's a whole congregation of other men out there. Why did you have to pick my lover?'

'Maybe I didn't know he was,' said Georgie, choosing her words with care, since in fact she had already heard rumours before Nicky's own admission. But he had said the affair with Sloane was over. Obviously she did not accept that. 'Besides, you're a married woman. Whatever there was between you and Nicky —'

'We've been together for six months, the best months of my life,' said Sloane, seeming not to notice Georgie's use of the past tense. 'I won't let you take him away from me.' While she was speaking, she steadily advanced on Georgie, who backed away. There was something manic about the glitter in Sloane's eyes, the way she held her long manicured nails poised at her sides like daggers ... 'Stay away from him,' she hissed.

The back of Georgie's legs bumped into a chair, and she gave a little cry of fright. Sloane smiled, on top of the situation now that she could see the girl was unnerved. 'Go fool around somewhere else, little girl. Leave the field clear for the major players.'

Her contempt and misplaced pride were too much for Georgie, who finally lost her temper. 'Why don't you open your eyes, Sloane? You're so wrapped up in yourself you're blind to the truth — there was never any future in your relationship with Nicky. A man in his position takes up with a married woman only so long as she remains discreet.

You embarrassed him publicly this evening. He wouldn't be able to ignore that even if he wanted to.'

'What do you know about it? You only just met him tonight. How dare you presume to tell *me* what *my* lover thinks and feels?'

'Because someone has to level with you, Sloane, bring you to your senses before you wreck your marriage with Uncle Xan.'

'I do not believe this!' Sloane threw up her hands in a gesture of rejection. 'I can't stand living like this, not any more, I'm so hacked off with putting on a front so that my husband's precious family don't have to face the facts — he is and always will be a fag! Your uncle's gay. Shows how well you all know him, huh? Only Dexter saw through it.'

'But — he married you.'

'Our marriage is a phoney. Xan gets a respectable cover from it. I get to be Countess of Courtney. Strictly business.'

'Uncle Xan has always said you were hoping to produce an heir for Courtney.'

'Oh, grow up! He wanted to make it look good, so he let it be known we were "hoping" for a child. That didn't mean there was ever any prospect of one arriving.'

'I see.' Georgie sat still for a moment, coming to terms with what she had heard. The fact that her uncle was gay did not shock her so much as the lengths to which he had been driven to keep the fact from his family. Did he have so little faith in their love and trust in him? And could he ever have intended to create this poisonous and powerful Countess, whose main aim in life seemed o be to push them all from Courtney Park? '"Oh, what a tangled web we weave,"' she said slowly.

'Guess you should ask your mother about that.' Sloane gave a drunken laugh.

'Mummy? Do you mean she knew all about this?'

'Who knows? I'm beginning to have second thoughts about my hotpants of a sister-in-law. Another stud before she married your father — yours and Court's that is. Ashley was merely passed off as Dexter's.'

'I don't understand what you're implying with your gutter gossip, but you're wasting your breath! My mother is incapable of doing anything dishonest.'

'Interesting ... That didn't seem to be your father's opinion when I told him I'd seen my good buddy Brad Carter sneaking upstairs to pay her a visit. Come to think of it, Georgie, maybe you should go check that out. Your father looked mad enough to kill.'

'If this is your idea of a joke, Sloane, I'm warning you...'

Her aunt was reckless in her arrogance. 'Let's call this a little foretaste of the hell you and your family can expect if you don't get out of my hair. Leave me my lover, leave me this house, or by God I'll rake up enough dirt to choke you all! A confidential tip-off to one of the gossip columns, perhaps, telling them the Earl of Courtney's guilty secret...'

'You're beneath contempt,' said Georgie to her raddled aunt, who leant back in her seat, eyes closed. 'And I don't believe you will spread gossip about my uncle. Not when you're sober enough to think things through. After all, if you expose your marriage for what it really is, you can hardly go to law in order to reclaim your "family" home. You'd be laughed out of court, like you were laughed off the dance floor tonight. Think about it, Sloane. The Randolphs aren't the only ones with something to lose.'

She swept out, unaware that her last words had been wasted on her aunt. But not, however, on the other occupant of the library.

In the heat of their exchange, neither Sloane nor Georgie had noticed that the high wingback chair close to the fire was occupied. When silence fell after Georgie's exit, the chair was pushed back and its occupant walked to the door. He paused beside Sloane, who lay huddled in her chair, mouth open, breathing deeply in an alcoholic stupor. Her eyes flickered open for a moment, but he did not believe she saw him.

Alexander wondered how he could ever have thought her a charming and gracious companion who would accept him and the civilised arrangement he had proposed. The signs had all been so clear for him to see: the way she always wrung the best for herself out of any deal; the harsh dissatisfied set of her mouth. Their marriage had always been flawed. He had not realised until tonight that he aroused nothing but loathing and contempt in her. He could almost have pitied her, flinging her cap after a young heartbreaker like the Prince, if her outright rejection of his cherished plan to father an heir for Courtney had not stung so much. Hearing that had hardened something within Alexander's gentle soul.

For tonight, and for as long as they had guests in the house, he had his duties as host to perform. They wouldn't stop him making plans, though. He knew who his keenest ally would be in arranging a speedy conclusion to his marriage. When the last visitor left Courtney Park, so would he. Bound for Gilmour and the Dowager Countess of Courtney.

When Georgie reached her mother's room, she found Ashley coming away.

'Thank goodness it's just you,' she blurted out. 'Sloane's just spun me some amazing story about Mummy and Bradford Carter.'

Her brother looked at her, serious-faced. 'I'm afraid it was true, Georgie.'

'I don't believe it,' she said, horror-stricken. 'Not Mummy.'

'I'm afraid so,' he said gently. 'Try not to blame her, Georgie. Life with Dad's been no picnic, and when he found her tonight ...'

Georgie shook her head, confused. This shock, coming on top of Sloane's direct attack on her, was too much. Ashley decided to spare her the details of his conversation with Camilla about their father's painful rejection of him. It didn't look as if she could take in any more tonight.

'I must go to Daddy,' she was saying, distracted. 'He ought not to be left on his own.'

Dexter, it seemed, had other ideas. Though Georgie pleaded with Webster to use his pass key to let her into the sitting-room, he steadfastly refused. 'There's some sights not fit for a lady to see, Miss Georgie. Your father's locked himself away in there with a bottle of Glenfiddich and he does not wish to be disturbed. Don't you worry,' He said kindly, seeing her distress. 'It's happened before when something's upset him. I'll see he comes to no harm. The best thing you can do is get back to the ball. Your uncle's doing the goodbyes on his own. Her ladyship's been taken unwell.'

Georgie knew she ought to go and offer to help her uncle, but could not face him after the evening's revelations. She felt that her beloved Courtney Park had been tainted by so much unhappiness. Her aunt sat like a malevolent spider at the centre of her web, spreading poison along the snares she wove. Though Georgie loved this place at happier times, she needed to get away tonight, somewhere where she could come to terms with everything that had happened.

'Georgianna, at last!'

Prince Nicolas appeared, his detectives at his heels. 'Wait outside,' he told them. 'I'll be with you in a minute.'

Her disappearance had annoyed him, but the words of reproach died on his lips. 'Has something happened?' he asked gently. 'You look as though you've had a shock.'

'I have. Several.' She didn't want to embarrass him or herself by talking about her mother's affairs, but Sloane was one of his. 'My aunt — let's just say she warned me off you in no uncertain terms.'

His expression was thunderous. 'You must accept my most sincere apologies. Usually these things do not get so badly out of hand.'

If there was a certain arrogance and world-weariness about that "usually", in her confused state of mind Georgie did not notice it. She saw only a chance of escape.

'Look, I know this is going to sound dreadful, but I need to get away.' She had in mind a lift back to London, where she could always stay at the Chester Square house.

He bowed. 'Nothing would give me greater pleasure. Shall we go?'

'Thank you. You've saved my life.'

'On the contrary — you have saved me from myself. There will be no more women like your aunt in my life. I'm looking for something more than that.' Blushing, she took his arm. At the great double doors to the house, he left her for a moment to tell his detectives to have the cars sent round.

Georgie approached Ford, who was seeing guests out. 'Get a message to my mother, would you? Tell her I'll ring her tomorrow from London. Prince Nicolas is giving me a lift.'

Solicitously he settled her in the passenger seat of his XJ12. Nicky loved to drive himself — at great speed, thanks to the diplomatic numberplates, always trailed by two detectives on loan from the Met. 'Relax. Go to sleep, if you like. I'll take care of everything.'

She closed her eyes and sank back against the buttersoft leather, comfortable in the warmth of the car. Reassured, she fell asleep.

He glanced across at her, and smiled. His father would never be able to say again that Nicky did not listen to his advice. There she was, a girl who was beautiful and triply eligible. The King's warning and the unpleasantness with Sloane had finally convinced him that it was time to put his bachelor days behind him.

Before they reached London, he took the Heathrow turn-off, driving past the passenger terminals to park on the tarmac only feet away from the single DC10 of the Royal Malivian Flight. Past its best, he thought, glancing up at the plane while his British detectives formally liaised with their Malivian counterparts. Like so much else in his family's tiny pocket principality, the Royal Flight needed an injection of cash. Georgianna Randolph's beauty and aristocratic blood were very strong recommendations in her favour. Her father's wealth was equally compelling.

One of the detectives offered to carry the sleeping girl aboard, but Nicky angrily refused. Despite the calculations his country's well-being forced him to make, he looked upon himself as a romantic. He carried Georgie up the steep metal stairs, picturing her surprise when she woke, not in London as she had expected, but in Malivia, his country, soon to be theirs.

'Where on earth have you brought me?' demanded Georgie, waking from a deep sleep to find herself on the back seat of an unfamiliar car. Instead of driving, Nicky shared it with her. Outside, it was full daylight and their surroundings were snow-covered.

'Home!' he said with a proud smile. 'You did ask me to take you away.'

'I meant to London,' she wailed. 'I can't just take off on a whim. I've got things to take care of — family matters, work. Oh, what a mess!'

The Crown Prince of Malivia was not accustomed to his romantic gestures being met with anything but delight, and certainly not within earshot of his curious driver and bodyguard, sitting in the front of the old Daimler. Belatedly, he slid the glass across. 'I am sorry if my surprise does not please you.'

Georgie glanced out of the car window again. They were riding in a sort of procession, she saw, with motor-cycle outriders and at least two venerable saloons crowded with sturdy men in mackintoshes. The scenery around them was almost too picturesque, like the inside of a child's glass snowscene. They were climbing a steep mountain road, sunlight refracting from the frosted branches of the pines to one side of them. From time to time they would pass a timber chalet, eaves hung with icicles, windows hung with bright curtains and even brighter faces as his people rushed to watch their prince pass by.

'It looks like a Christmas card brought to life. It's lovely, Nicky,' she said.

He smiled proudly. 'I knew you'd like it.'

Nevertheless, he slid aside the glass screen once more and asked the driver in their language to take them not to his parents' home, the Summer Palace, as he had planned, but to his own private hunting-lodge, twenty miles away. She was almost perfect, but it seemed he would have to make a few minor adjustments in Georgie's behaviour before he dare introduce her to the King and Queen.

'Where can she be?' moaned Camilla, who had phoned the Chester Square house for the third time that morning, only to be told that Miss Georgianna still had not arrived. She was close to tears from the strain of trying to trace her daughter, and worry over Dexter. He was still locked in his room, stubbornly refusing to allow anyone but Webster inside.

'I don't think you need to be too concerned,' said Courtney awkwardly. 'We know she left with Nicky. He's probably keeping her — occupied — at his place.'

'But she said she'd phone! She knows the situation here. We really need her to get through to Daddy. God knows she's the only one who can! It's not like her simply to disappear.'

'Do you want me to check Nicky's flat in The Boltons?' said Courtney reluctantly. He couldn't imagine that Prince Nicolas would be overjoyed to receive a call there from a girl's distraught family, but this was an emergency. He made the call but was informed by a housekeeper with a guttural accent that the Prince had returned to his own country after attending a ball last night.

'I suppose she could have gone with him,' suggested Ashley.

'A bit unlikely. The modelling thing starts any day, and with everything that's going on here ... '

'If only she'd call,' fretted Camilla. She could not remember feeling as desperate as this even when Dexter had had his accident and the doctors had at first feared for his life. At least then she had been able to sit by his side and talk to him, even if she had not been sure he could hear. She could not get last night and his final tortured expression out of her mind. If only she could reach him, at least try to explain. But it was useless. Webster guarded his door like Cerberus, and Dexter refused to pick up the phone. They were living in the same house, but she felt he was lost to her.

'I'll give it another go,' said Ashley. 'Dad'll have to let me in some time today. We need to work out our moves for when the Sydney market opens — nine o'clock our time.' With Camilla, he still referred to Dexter as 'Dad'. He wasn't sure he'd dare do so face to face.

'If you don't mind, I thought I'd take Chantel out for the afternoon,' said Courtney apologetically. 'I feel a heel leaving you, but she says she'd love to see Stonehenge. She doesn't have a clue that all this is going on.'

'Thank goodness for that! Of course you must take her out, darling. You don't know how happy it makes me that things are working out for one of us at least.'

When both her sons had left, Camilla's fingers went automatically to the phone. She needed to hear a friendly voice, someone who would be on her side. Brad Carter? She began to dial his London number before realising how cruel of her it would be to call.

Last night had been a dreadful mistake. She should have been content with the knowledge that she could still attract a personable man, and left it at that. It had been self-indulgent and ultimately destructive to sleep with Brad,

628

knowing, as she had all along, that it was Dexter she really loved. If only she could convince *him* of that.

Sloane glanced at her bedside clock, and groaned. The effort of moving her head left her sick and giddy. It took a long time for the room to stop spinning; longer still for the humiliating memories of last night to fade. The only slight consolation was the trouble she had stirred up for Camilla and Brad.

Her maid appeared to say that Sloane's bath was ready. 'Will you be lunching, your ladyship?'

The mere thought of food made her stomach lurch, but she could hardly avoid it. Getting bombed and making a scene was regrettable. Hiding away from houseguests like a whipped puppy was not Sloane's style. 'Yes, of course I'll be lunching with my guests. Bring me a Bullshot in the bath.'

Her only alcohol for the day, she vowed, downing the hangover cure in one. It seemed to work, soothing her queasy stomach. She'd feel even better with a Valium on top, she decided. Of course, you weren't supposed to pop pills and drink, but the minute amount of vodka in her pick-me-up would barely count if she stayed off the wine at lunch.

She descended to meet her guests in a warm tranquillised haze. She checked that everyone had had a good time last night, apologising for her own indisposition. 'A little too much champers,' she explained. 'Darling Xan's a tad displeased with his birthday girl, aren't you, sweetest?'

He blinked and changed the subject, not even enquiring how she felt that morning. He made absolutely no attempt to talk to her other than in general conversation with their guests.

Despite the vodka and the pills, she noticed the withdrawn expression on his face, and it worried her. Without thinking, she sipped from a glass of wine that was poured for her. The chilled white Burgundy tasted good in her parched mouth. It was bull that you couldn't drink and pop Valium, she decided, accepting a second glass, and a third. She chatted animatedly with her guests, feeling herself become more sparkling by the moment. She did not notice the glazed expression on some faces or the way that others glanced surreptitiously at their watches.

All too soon for Sloane, lunch was over. The guests seemed anxious to leave, and quite suddenly she could not have cared less. She was exhausted from the strain of carrying the lunch party while Xan sat silent and disapproving over something or other. She had a vague feeling she could remember what if she got down to it and concentrated, but felt too tired to try. She must go and rest.

On the way to her room she heard a couple of women, roped in from the village to help with the houseguests. They were gossiping about the ball as they turned out a guest bedroom. ' . . . beautiful, really lovely, like something out of a kiddy's story.'

Sloane smiled approvingly.

'And him so handsome, too. Made a smashing couple, they did. No wonder she agreed to go off with him at the drop of a hat. Her mother can't find them nowhere, Pam says . . . '

Sloane pressed her hand to her mouth and hurried away.

Alexander waited until he knew his wife was sleeping it off before going to see his sister. She had sent down her excuses at lunchtime. Dexter, too, had been absent and Alexander wanted to assure himself that there was nothing amiss.

He was shocked to find Camilla looking haggard and distraught. Under his gentle probing, the full story came out. He was sad but not surprised to hear it all. 'Something like this was bound to happen sooner or later, my dear. The real tragedy is that Dexter got to know of it.'

'I still don't understand how he did,' she said, puzzled. 'He hasn't come to me in my room since the accident. I can't imagine who or what prompted him last night.'

'Can't you?' he said grimly. 'Who's responsible for every ounce of bad feeling in this family? Who froze Maman out? Who brought her lawyer in under false pretences? Who's been gunning for Dexter and you since she arrived?'

'You mean — Sloane? Oh, how could she be so cruel!'

'Second nature to her. I won't go into all the painful details, but you weren't the only one to have a surprise visit last night. While I was sitting unobserved in the library I heard a conversation that wasn't meant for my ears. Let's just say it changed my opinion of my wife. I've hidden it from myself for a long time, but last night she did me a gigantic favour — she made me see what a mistake I'd made in marrying her. I'm getting out of this marriage, hopefully with as little damage as possible. I'm going up to Gilmour now to persuade Maman to come back and advise me.'

'I'm glad.' For a moment Camilla's expression brightened.

'I never should have been so weak as to let her go in the first place,' he continued. 'Don't lose heart. We'll soon be back to help you. You know how fond Maman is of Dexter, and he has a lot of time for her beneath all the grumbling. Can't Georgie help out in the meantime?' Camilla's face clouded over again. 'She's vanished. She left with Prince Nicolas last night and hasn't been seen since. Oh, hurry back, Xan, please. Something awful's going to happen. I can feel it in my bones.'

Their arrival at the hunting-lodge had not gone as smoothly as Nicky had hoped. Instead of enthusing over his secluded miniature castle with its pepperpot turrets, blue-painted shutters and high white walls outside, heavy oak furniture and grand but faded tapestries inside, Georgie seemed more interested in getting washed, changed and to a phone.

Nicky summoned a maid to help, a shy blonde who wore her hair in old-fashioned 'earphones'. The girl wore a crudely-embroidered peasant apron over her long black skirt and starched white blouse. She gestured for Georgie to follow her up a wide stone staircase and an echoing stone-flagged corridor lined with stags' heads and other hunting trophies. The chill of centuries seemed to permeate the thick walls. Georgie felt nervous and oppressed, ridiculous in her fancy dress, though the maid did not seem to find it out of place.

'Are there any other clothes I could borrow?' asked Georgie as she was shown into a dark bedroom. By the look of its chase-scene tapestry, fur-coverleted bed and leather-covered furniture in solid masculine colours, she guessed it was Prince Nicolas's.

The girl obligingly opened a door. Georgie glanced inside to discover a spartan white-painted bathroom, steam rising invitingly from an ancient free-standing tub.

'I said — clothes. I'll need something to wear when I get out of here,' said Georgie, pointing to her travel-stained dress.

The maid's face cleared. With a coy smile she flung back the doors of one of the two huge oak clothes-presses. It contained a selection of women's day and evening wear.

The sight made Georgie purse her lips angrily. She'd have something to change into after her bath, but she did not like the thought that Nicky kept them in readiness. Evidently there had been more than one previous recipient of his romantic gestures.

She took off the filthy dress, which was borne away by the maid, and lost no time in climbing into the bath, seeing to her surprise that there were no taps. The girl must have filled it the old-fashioned way. Sure enough she returned a few minutes later bearing a couple of steaming jugs to keep up the temperature — no easy task in a stone-walled room. Crown Prince Nicolas lived among the wealthiest, most sophisticated members of European society, but his mountain retreat was conspicuously spartan.

Georgie decided not to wash her hair. She doubted she could bear the wait for hot water. She hopped out of the bath, wrapping a towel round her, and returned to the bedroom to find Nicolas sprawled by the fire in one of the leather chairs.

'I loved your dress, but that suits you even better,' he said.

Furious to find herself in such a clichéed situation, she pulled the towel tighter and crossed to the clothes-press, flicking quickly through the clothes.

'I'm sure there'll be something to fit you.' He seemed annoyingly sure of himself and of the situation he'd engineered. He didn't expect her to dress at all, she realised, and pulling the door in front of her like a screen began to scramble into the plainest, most practical, outfit she could find: a pair of navy cashmere leggings and a large baggy sweater. See if he could find anything provocative in that particular outfit!

It seemed he could. 'As I thought, a perfect fit.' His eyes seemed to be boring through the clothes to her body beneath.

'Why? Do you specialise in abducting girls just my size?'

'I don't need to abduct them. Usually they're more than eager to come.' Caught for a quick reply, he succeeded in giving the opposite impression to the one he'd intended. He'd decided to leave behind the image of playboy prince, and here he was, rubbing her nose in the evidence of his former mistresses. He had never had for them the plans he nursed for Georgie, but their Malivian interlude seemed to have got off on the wrong foot. 'I don't understand why we're quarrelling,' he said, sounding genuinely puzzled. 'If the clothes upset you, naturally I'll have them taken away. It's very important that everything about my home and my country should please you.'

This uncharacteristically humble approach seemed to soften her. She moved closer, stretching out her hands to the blazing fire. 'I know you meant all this as a splendid romantic gesture, Nicky, and at any other time I'd have been thrilled, honestly. Your home is out of this world —' it certainly felt like it — 'but it's impossible for me to relax and enjoy myself knowing that my mother will be frantic with worry. It's not fair to her.'

He gave her an amused smile. 'This isn't Transylvania. We do have telephones, you know.'

'I'm glad to hear it, but it isn't quite so simple as making one phone-call. You see, something happened between my parents last night . . .'

Her deep sleep on the flight seemed to have cleared her thoughts. She found that last night's revelations no longer shocked her, but she was concerned that the gulf between her parents might even now be widening. Though she hated to discuss family business, she felt she should explain the urgency of her need to return.

'It wasn't really my mother's fault. Daddy's been incredibly difficult to live with since the accident,' she concluded. 'But you do see why I need to get back?'

Nicky's heavy-lidded eyes were almost hooded. He'd never heard the remotest breath of scandal attached to Lady Camilla before. To do so now, while he was considering an alliance with her daughter, was distasteful. Magnanimously, he decided that none of this was Georgie's fault. She was a loyal, generous girl who deserved to be saved from her unsavoury background.

'And then there's Sarong, of course,' she was continuing. 'The preliminary shoot starts in December, and I've promised to start a tan. I don't suppose your girlfriend left a sunbed!'

'Maybe.' He gestured vaguely towards the cupboard's packed interior. 'I'm sorry, I didn't understand that. What's sarong?'

She explained about her contract to become the figurehead in a multi-million-dollar advertising campaign for the Sarong line of cosmetics and perfumes.

'Break it,' he said grandly. 'You can't need the money.'

'You never know. With Sloane revving up to force us out of Courtney Park, Daddy's going to need every penny he can raise to buy somewhere as grand.'

He frowned. 'Your father is in financial difficulties?'

'Joke!' she said, unaware of the latest developments in Australia.

Ashley had tried and failed for a third time to get Dexter to admit him. He was just turning away from the door when Webster emerged from the general office. 'Your cousin Rhianne on the phone, Mr Ashley. She says it's urgent.'

Rhianne was his favourite Australian relative — an open uncomplicated girl who had accompanied him on several memorable evenings' 'raging'.

'Ash? Thank goodness I caught you. All hell's breaking out here. Listen, I don't know exactly what's happening — Dad keeps his mouth shut tighter than his wallet — but the police were round here this morning.' The Lucas Randolphs now lived in Sydney's Double Bay, a prime residential suburb. 'They wanted him to fly up to Yelonga immediately. It seems they've found a body they want him to identify.'

'Bloody hell! That's all Randolph Enterprises needs at the moment. Did you find out what had happened? Was there an accident up there, or something?'

'Not recently, I don't think. As we were leaving, I heard one of the policemen saying there were very few remains. Sounds like something from a long time ago, doesn't it?'

'You could be right.' Ashley's mind went into overdrive. Policemen, bodies, Lucas going back to Queensland ... he had to get in to Dexter.

'Uncle okay?' asked Rhianne, who'd always liked her tough no-nonsense 'English' relative.

'A bit preoccupied. Listen, Rhianne, I can't talk about it now, but keep your eyes and ears open for me, will you?'

'You bet!' She had had a crush on her good-looking super-polite Pommy cousin since he came to work in Australia. 'When are you coming back, Ash? Mum and I are missing you already.'

He glanced out of the window, at trees whipped bare of leaves on an afternoon leaden with the threat of rain. Australia's weather could be just as cruel, but when he thought of his second country it was always as a place of beneficent sunshine and a sky that lifted the spirits just to look at it.

'Can't be soon enough for me,' he said with feeling.

Sloane woke at seven and rang for her maid to bring her a supper of bouillon and chicken salad.

'You can tell my husband I'm dining in my room tonight.'

'His lordship's gone, my lady. He left an hour ago.'

Sloane looked up, startled. 'Left? Did he say where for?'

'No, my lady. I could ask Mr Ford for you.'

'No, I'll speak to him myself. That will be all, thank you.'

Sloane was damned if she would humbly ask the butler where her husband had gone. There were more subtle ways of going about things. She rang Ford on the house phone. 'His lordship seems to have forgotten his wallet. Do you think we should have it sent after him?'

'I hardly think that will be necessary, madam. The Gilmour driver will meet him at Inverness, and even if there were to be a mix-up, I'm sure his lordship's credit in Scotland is beyond doubt.'

'Yes, thank you,' said Sloane thoughtfully.

Gilmour ... So, Mama's boy had gone sneaking off behind her back, had he? She settled comfortably against the pillows. Alexander might think he'd outsmarted her, heading off without a word. In fact, he'd played right into her hands. Without his milktoast presence cramping her style she could take the final steps in her campaign against the Randolphs. She had them demoralised and at each other's throats. Time to move in for the kill.

At five minutes to nine, Dexter rang through to Ash's room. 'You're keeping me waiting. Get down here, we have a company to save.'

There was to be no mention of the previous night's events, Ash saw. He did his best while they were waiting for the Sydney market to open. 'Mama's in a terrible state. Don't you think you're being too hard on her?'

'Let's get one thing straight. You're here to work, not to lecture me on my private life. Understood?'

Dexter looked ghastly, wearing yesterday's clothes and a dark growth of beard. While he keyed in the Randolph Enterprises trace, his hands shook. From whisky or emotion?

'You're the boss.'

'Too bloody right! Well, what are you sitting about on your arse for? Get the line to Lucas open. I want to direct every move he makes this morning.'

'It'll be Chip in charge today. Rhianne phoned. Uncle Luke's been called up to Yelonga.'

Ash was dialling the Sydney headquarters while he spoke. The clock on the screen before them ticked away the last sixty seconds before trading.

'Suffering Christ! Why didn't you tell me before?'

'Because you wouldn't take my bloody calls, you pig-headed old bludger!'

Dexter ignored that. 'Jesus, the one day we need to put on a three-ring circus, and the bloody ringmaster goes off on a jaunt!'

'Hardly,' said Ash, still waiting for the Randolph Enter-prises switchboard to reply. 'It's police business he's on.

Something about identifying some remains ... Hey, are you all right?'

In the green reflected glow of the screens his father's face looked deathly, filmed with sweat.

'I'm — it's all right. Felt a bit crook there for a minute. You see, I think I know who've they've found ... '

'Randolph Enterprises, g'day,' came the switchboard operator's breezy Strine over the speakerphone.

Dexter pulled himself together. He pressed the button to talk to her. 'Put me through to my idle bastard of a nephew, sweetheart. This is Dexter Randolph speaking.'

Ash had always admired his father's toughness in business, but he had never seen such a show as Dexter put on that night. Whatever traumas he had suffered the night before, whatever the signficance of the finding on Yelonga, until the early hours of the following morning Dexter concentrated solely on the fight to save Randolph Enterprises.

The line to Chip Randolph was kept constantly open, Dexter relaying his instructions to his nephew by the minute as he watched the market movement on his screen. 'Tell our brokers to pull their finger out and buy all the paper they can,' he ordered after watching the value of RE stock fall several cents in the first few minutes.

'From the small investors too, Uncle?'

'I don't care if they get it from the nail on the back of the dunny door — I want all the stock we can get! Is that clear enough for you?'

'Yes, but — won't it leave us overextended?'

Dexter momentarily cut the connection to speak privately to Ash. 'Did you hear that? *Now* the clown can add up. Why the hell couldn't he on the Bradbury Island accounts?'

He pressed the button to speak to Chip again. 'No worries. I'm going to cover our arses with some fancy dancing when the New York market opens. Oh, and Chip . . .'

'Yes, Uncle.'

'How's the Island coming along?'

'Couldn't be better.'

'That's what I like to hear. Looking forward to reviewing things with you at the end of the week.'

'Was that wise?' Ash asked in a lull when they could hear Chip busy relaying their instructions on another line. 'With Uncle Luke and Chip, it can be better to catch them unprepared.'

'I'm more interested in saving the company than in recriminations!'

'How serious is it?'

'Put it this way. That offer from Top Hotels for the Miami and Acapulco properties — the one I've been shrugging off for months — today looks like their lucky day. And if the worst comes to the worst, I can always take your auntie up on her offer to buy me out of here.'

'You can't do that! It would break Ma's heart.' He could read his answer in Dexter's hollow eyes. Camilla had broken his heart, hadn't she? Ash could have wept for his parents, separated by no more than this man's stubborn macho pride.

He made up his mind he'd have the blood-test his mother had mentioned just as soon as he could reasonably call out Chris Brett.

When the Australian market closed, Dexter and Ashley had the satisfaction of seeing Randolph Enterprises' share price chased back up. They had made back two-thirds of the previous week's drop — so long as Dexter could find the finance.

Webster brought in a tray of sandwiches and beer. Ash ate and drank hungrily. Dexter barely touched his food, but glanced frequently at his watch. It would be late afternoon in Queensland, a good time to call for news.

'Would you dial Yelonga for me?' he asked.

Ash noticed that his hands, perfectly steady throughout the hours of shoring up Randolph Enterprises, were shaking again. It was not always possible to get straight through to Yelonga, but today the radio phone was co-operative. They expected the station manager to answer. Instead, an unfamiliar voice came over the speakerphone.

'G'day, Yelonga Station.'

'Hello. Who's this speaking?'

'Sergeant Les Mason, Queensland Police. Who's asking?'

'This is Dexter Randolph calling from England. I'd like to know what the hell's going on on my station.'

'Well now, Lord Randolph —' there was a touch of scorn in the policeman's use of his English title — 'good of you to give us a call. We'd have had to get in touch with you ourselves. A little matter of a murder inquiry.'

Dexter did not seem able to reply. Ash cut in instead. 'Hello, this is Ash Randolph speaking. Sergeant Mason, could you explain exactly what's going on there, please? Whose body has been found, and how do you know they were murdered?'

'The remains of an aboriginal male have been found in a gully five miles south of here. We know he was murdered because there's a bloody great bullet-hole in his skull. There was very little left of him, but from an old Colt pistol, his watch and the remains of a stockwhip, Mr Lucas Randolph believes he can positively identify Wallace Wuggalar. I think he worked for you once, Lord Randolph?'

'He did. He was also my friend.'

'But he was fired after a quarrel some time late in '59. Later that day you went out after him. You didn't catch up with him, by any chance?'

Ash wasn't sure he liked the implication behind that. He glanced sideways at Dexter, whose face was contorted by rage and sorrow. 'I did not,' he said. 'But if I had, I'd have brought him back to Yelonga and torn a strip off him till the bugger had more sense than to leave.'

'Even though earlier that day it was you who told him to go after he had insulted Lucinda Randolph, formerly a good friend of yours.'

640

'What's that? You're saying *I* fired him?'

'According to Luke, you did.'

'That's a damned lie! My brother told him to go. Wally was off the property by the time I got back from Townsville. I went after him, but I couldn't trace him.'

'Strange — and you quite the bushman in your time. Lord Randolph, it's more than thirty years, I know, but your memory of events differs from your brother's. We'll need to talk about this some more.'

'I don't think I care to answer any more questions without my lawyer being present.'

'Would that be your English or your Australian lawyer? We can arrange for you to be interviewed in England —'

'Australian, damn you! I'm coming back to find out who killed Wally. Expect me in a few days. I must get my business affairs seen to first.'

'Okay, but don't leave it too long, will you? Else we just might think you had a reason to delay ... G'day, your lordship.' The policeman hung up.

'I didn't like the sound of that at all,' said Ash, concerned. 'Did you notice the way he started out calling Uncle Luke "Mr Randolph" and then it slipped to "Luke"? Seems to me they're pretty friendly. He's going to believe Uncle's version.'

'The Queensland police have always had bottomless pockets,' said Dexter. 'He'll have been on Luke's payroll for years.'

'You'd better tell me what you remember about that last day,' said Ash. 'Wally was the one you used to tell me and Court about, wasn't he? The one who taught you how to track as a kid.'

'And how to ride, how to move a mob of cattle, about the bush plants that heal, the way to find water in a dry place, his people's stories ... Wally and Old Tom brought me up between them. When my grandfather died, Wally was my best friend on Yelonga, and afterwards on Maroonda. He was actually running Yelonga for me when he disappeared. Luke was just a figurehead, then. There's no way I would ever have told Wally to go.'

'How do you remember it happening, Dad?'

Dexter made no reaction to being addressed that way.

'I'd gone up to the station on one of my inspection tours, taking a girlfriend along with me. She was a Townsville girl, and when I had business there we flew over for the day. When I got back, Luke spun me some yarn about Wally insulting Lucinda after he'd had a few too many. There was something odd about that. Wally was Mission-educated, never touched a drop. I went out after him, sent planes up, but we found nothing. That was surprising in itself. Wally left openly. He had no reason to cover his tracks.'

'The girl you took up with you? Can you remember her name?'

Dexter gave a tight smile. 'Can I ever forget! It was Linita, Linita Tyrone. She was my mistress for years before I married your mother.' He did not say that she had been his lover afterwards as well.

'Would she agree with your version of events rather than Uncle Luke's?'

Dexter thought for a moment. 'She did overhear us talking about it. Luke didn't realise she was in my room — waiting for me in bed.' He smiled grimly. 'But don't pin any hopes on Linita. Later on, I gave her every reason to hate my guts. Even if we could trace her, which I doubt, she wouldn't lift a finger to save me.'

'Hello, Mom? Did I catch you at a bad time?'

'I was just on my way out, but it's great to hear from you. How's England?'

'Fantastic! I'm having the best time here. This weekend we went to a costume ball in the country, but we're back in London now.'

'When are you coming home, Chantel? It's been

months, and you know how much we're looking forward to meeting your new boyfriend.'

'We thought next weekend. Charles has a few loose ends to tie up first.'

'Dad might not be here right away. He's in Germany ... Some negotiations or other. But come anyway, darling. I can't wait to see you both. Call me about your flight, and I'll send a car.'

'We'll be in touch. Take care of yourself, Mom.'

Chantel put down the phone, feeling slightly guilty. While preserving Court's alias in Paris, she'd grown used to referring to him as Charles Hamilton. Although there was no longer any need to conceal his true identity, she and Court had decided not to explain the deception to Linita on the phone. They believed it would sound less alarming face to face. Court was determined to come clean with Chantel's parents about his past. He wanted everything above board between them. If only they could do it straight away, she thought uneasily. She hated keeping things from her mother.

'Georgianna, I am truly sorry. Many things in my country are not quite as I would wish. This is most embarrassing.'

Nicky had shown Georgie to his study to make her call while he bathed and changed. She tried to dial direct without success. The local operator had then informed her that since some power lines had been brought down by the heavy snow, international calls were temporarily suspended.

Nicky was mortified. Nothing about this spur-of-the-moment visit was going as he'd intended. The girl he had thought so sweet and impressionable turned out to have an expectedly steely side.

'Then you'll just have to drive me to the frontier. The roads are still passable, I take it?'

'Yes, but it can't be so important, surely? The lines will

643

be mended by morning — it's only a temporary suspension. Your mother won't worry about you for one day — not with so much else on her mind.'

'You don't know Mummy! But I suppose if it really is only a few hours . . . '

'By tomorrow morning, I swear.' In fact Nicky had known the international lines go down for days, but he had no intention of letting Georgie slip through his fingers now. 'Would you like some lunch?'

It was early afternoon, and Georgie had not eaten since the ball. She realised she was starving.

The maid served their meal in his study which, panelled in dark wood, was by far the warmest room in the lodge. The food was plain but good, and Nicky kept Georgie's glass constantly charged with an unusually strong white wine.

After a while, she felt the tension drain away. What did it matter if she was a little late ringing home? A handsome prince had brought her to his secluded castle. She might as well relax and enjoy the fairy tale.

While they were eating, snow began to fall and the light outside quickly faded. The maid began to draw a pair of faded velvet curtains across the high arched window, but Georgie told Nicky: 'Please ask her not to. It looks lovely.'

He spoke sharply to the girl and gestured to the door. She blushed, bobbed a curtsy and left. Georgie finished her wine, watching the fluttering snow dance tinged with rose from the light reflected off the faded grandeur of the Turkish carpet and red velvet-covered chairs and sofa.

'Am I forgiven?' he asked, sensing the softening in her mood.

'For bringing me here? Of course. After all, it was what I longed for last night — some peace and quiet after all the trouble with Sloane and my parents.'

'I'm glad. It's very important to me that you should be happy. Come and sit beside me, Georgianna.'

They sat next to each other on the couch. His knee

644

grazed hers as she came to join him, but apart from that he made no move to touch her. 'Tell me about yourself,' he commanded. 'I want to know everything there is to know.'

His intensity brought a smile to her mouth. 'No, you don't! Why don't we talk about something more interesting? Growing up in a palace, for instance. That must have been fun.'

His expression was sombre. 'I don't believe I knew the meaning of the word until my parents decided I was old enough to leave Malivia and travel on my own. My country means everything to me and I admire and respect my parents, but they were brought up in a very strict code of behaviour. They taught me the same way: duty, dignity and the service of the people. These are good and valuable lessons, but to a young child they can seem harsh and impersonal.'

He was showing her a side of himself she had never dreamt of beneath the confident smile of the Playboy Prince. She found herself moved to pity by this glimpse of a bleak childhood. 'You are an only child, I believe?'

'Yes, my country's only hope.' He smiled and stretched his arms above his head, as though shrugging off a heavy burden. 'You know why I brought you here?' he asked, resting one arm along the back of the couch behind her.

'I think I can guess.'

His face was very close to hers. The reflected glow of the firelight, red over darkest blue, turned his eyes a mysterious amethyst colour.

Why fight it, after all? She had been attracted to him the moment they met. The misunderstanding over Courtney had only postponed the inevitable.

She put up a hand to touch the side of his face. He turned his head, pressing his lips to the inside of her wrist. She shivered and drew back. She had always heard that he was a collector of women on a love-them-and-leave-them basis. The thought did not appall her.

The time with Christian had taught her that a brief

honest encounter with a man could be worth a lot more than the long misery of being used and betrayed. But Nicky was sending signals that confused her. She could almost have sworn that he was asking more from her than a brief romantic fling.

His next words made her smile at her own foolish imaginings. 'Shall we go upstairs? Marte has prepared the room.'

'How did she know we were staying?'

'I told her while we were having lunch. Shall we?'

He took her arm and led her up the stone staircase and down the echoing corridor to his bedroom.

She thrilled to the sight of his powerful male erectness, but found that he made love the way he played polo — hard, fast and by the rules. The touch of his broad calloused hands was infinitely arousing, but he moved them mechanically, as if by rote — here a caress; there a hint of roughness. He evoked a physical response but absolutely no mental connection. She felt he was making love to her in a pattern tried and tested on countless women before. When he had brought her to a swift climax he proceeded to prolong his own pleasure, instructing her exactly what he wanted her to do. She could feel that the routine was unvarying. When he climaxed, with bruising ferocity, she wasn't sure whether to hold him or applaud.

'My love,' he said, 'you pleased me very much. And next time you will please me more because then no explanations will be necessary.'

'No, I'll know just what to expect,' she said, realising with a sinking feeling that she was not going to get away that night.

Making love with Nicky was rather like eating chocolate, she decided: exciting only in anticipation. The reality was cloying. She found herself thinking regretfully of Guy, whom she had abandoned so cavalierly in Paris. When she was back in England and home at Courtney Park, he would be the first she would call, she decided.

Nicky remained unaware of her detachment, sprawling on the bed, arms behind his head, almost as if she were expected to admire him. Maybe that was what the women of her aunt's generation were used to in their men; maybe that was the way he trained them. Georgianna was damned if she would follow the pattern. She kept her mouth shut and found herself thinking more and more fondly of kind unselfish Guy.

Nicky stood up and put on a monogrammed silk dressing-gown. 'We must marry immediately,' he said. 'I see no necessity to wait, do you?'

At first, she did not think she had heard him correctly. 'But — we hardly know one another!'

He smiled, and sat down beside her on the bed, catching her wrists in his strong hands. 'We can soon put that right. I'll have to keep you here till I've explored every last delicious inch of you, my little prisoner.'

'Don't,' she said uneasily, struggling to free herself. 'Nicky, please, I don't find this funny.'

He released her, going to the door, which he unlocked. Outside in the corridor the maid had left a trolley set with chilled wine and cold food. Georgie was not hungry, but he ate with an appetite, outlining his plans for their life together.

'We'll have to spend some time here, naturally, but while my father is king for no more than a few months each year. The rest of the time we can divide between London, Paris, Rome — wherever you like. So long as I'm not playing polo, that is. The wedding will have to be here. The marriage of the heir to the throne is a state occasion. Your parents won't mind, I take it?'

'Never mind my parents! *I* haven't said I want to marry you.'

'But you will,' he said with alarming arrogance. 'Why shouldn't you? Everybody does.'

It took her breath away. Georgie had to remind herself of the more vulnerable side he had revealed to her earlier that evening. He was the typical product of the upbringing he had described to her. Deprived for so long of normal human warmth and affection, he now saw women as wonderful toys, and most of them, flattered by his good looks and the charm of a royal romance, were content to be treated as such. None of it was really Nicky's fault, she reminded herself. He deserved careful and sympathetic handling, not outright rejection.

'Why don't we talk about it in the morning? I'm feeling terribly tired.'

He came back to bed and made love to her again, more tenderly this time, but still moulding her into the little rituals he expected from all his lovers, and would demand from a wife.

Exhausted by her strange day, Georgie slept heavily again. She was half aware of Nicky slipping out of bed hours later and felt him kiss her forehead. She drifted back into sleep, and when she woke Marte was pulling back the curtains and gesturing towards the laden tray she had left on a table by the fire.

'Where's His Highness?' she asked, before realising that of course the girl would not understand. 'Nicolas,' she said slowly, and gestured towards the half of the bed where he had slept.

The girl blushed, and thought for a moment. Then, seeing Georgie's concern, she pointed out of the window. There were crisp tyre-tracks in the fresh new blanket of snow that covered the road from the lodge.

'I hope he won't be long,' Georgie said disconsolately.

The maid gestured towards the bathroom, where hot water was waiting, and towards a clutch of English-language newspapers. They were yesterday's late edition, Georgie saw when she inspected them over a breakfast of hot chocolate, rolls and apricot jam. Still, reading them was less boring than sitting twiddling her thumbs, waiting for Nicky's return. One item on the finance pages caught her eye.

With mounting concern she read of the discovery of a man's body, believed to have died of gunshot wounds, on Yelonga land. The British press had picked up the story from the Australian wire services because of the connection with a British peer. Georgie read that Queensland Police had spoken to her father by phone, and that he was expected to fly to Australia later that week and help them further with their enquiries. She didn't like the sound of that, but even more alarming was the report that Randolph Enterprises share price had been severely affected by the news.

She was appalled by the tone of the story, which subtly indicated that her father was a murder suspect.

She jumped up, determined to try the international lines again. Nicky had said they'd be ready by morning. She could not open the bedroom door, and twisted the unfamiliar handle several times before the truth dawned on her. Nicky had not been joking last night. She *was* his prisoner!

She looked out of the window. Thick snow had fallen during the night, but it was a clear bright day. Ideal escaping weather, if she could nerve herself to try. She considered knotting the sheets and lowering herself to the ground. It looked an awfully long way. There had to be another way.

Nicky's bedroom had two windows, and the maid had uncurtained only one. She tugged aside the thick curtains at the other revealing a floor-length window, the outlook obscured by blue-painted shutters on the outside. She opened the window easily, but the shutters were more difficult. The stiff catch cut into her fingers. Looking around the room, she found what she needed — a poker from the hearth. Using it as a lever, she prised up the rusted catch and pushed the shutters apart. They caught on a wall of snow piled up on the balcony behind, but with a final heave Georgie found herself standing barefoot in the snow. There was a steep drop below, but close by, so close she felt she could lean across with no difficulty, was another balcony. If she could reach it and get into the neighbouring room, there was no reason to suppose that it, too, would be locked ...

She rooted about in the clothes-press, putting on several layers of clothes beneath yesterday's warm leggings and sweater. She found a stout loden topcoat, a ski-hat and mitts, even a pair of dark glasses. She twisted her hair up inside the cap, pulled on two pairs of socks and some moonboots, and as an afterthought put the poker into her deep pocket.

She took a breath to steady herself and swung herself over the side of the balcony, clinging to it with her toes and hands, her back to the drop behind. It was a longer stretch than she had bargained for to reach the neighbouring railings. She was going to have to rely on the halfway house of a crumbling rain-gutter. Don't look down, she told herself, and stepped back into the void.

'She sounds eminently suitable,' said the King, sitting stern-faced and straight-backed in his armless wooden chair. Nicky had been granted an interview in between a deputation of villagers petitioning for a new hospital and a visit from the King's economic adviser. 'Provided her dowry is generous enough, we should be pleased to consider her as a candidate for our daughter by marriage.' He glanced down at the photographs of Georgie that Nicky had found in a glossy magazine he had stopped to buy on the way. The King frowned, and gestured towards the plunging neckline of a dress she was modelling in one picture. 'All this, of course ... '

'Will stop immediately, sire. You have my word on it.'

'I'm glad we understand one another. Where is Miss Randolph now?'

'We stayed at the lodge last night.'

'The Queen must not hear of that. She will expect the

girl to be formally introduced and to stay here in the Summer Palace at all times.'

Nicky glanced round at the comfortless surroundings. Though the public rooms of the Palace were heavy with nineteenth-century grandeur, in their private apartments the ruling monarchs lived austerely. 'Georgianna will need a few things before I bring her here — clothes and so on.'

'She arrived in our country without clothes? I thought you said this girl was well-bred?'

'She is. It was all my fault. I brought her here straight from a ball.'

'I see. And you have known her for how long?'

'At least six months,' said Nicky, dating back to their disastrous encounter at Windsor.

The King looked a little less certain than before. 'I suggest you find Miss Randolph's clothes and bring her here immediately,' he said. 'We shall reserve our judgment till then.'

Nicky hurried home, bursting to share the good news. By his father's exacting standards, the interview had been a success. Now all they needed to do was make Georgie presentable. A quick stop at one of the fashionable boutiques in the ski-ing resort nearby should do it. She could have her other things sent over in due course.

He was totally unprepared for the sight that met his eyes when he reached his bedroom. The door stood open, the window to the balcony ajar. Marte had collapsed into a chair, fat legs askew, and was weeping into her apron.

'What's happened? Has there been an accident?'

'No, worse than that, Your Royal Highness. She's escaped!'

Georgie had noticed the main road from her balcony vantage-point and cut across the fields towards it. She was still congratulating herself on the dexterity with which she had used the poker to shatter the glass behind the shutters

651

on the adjacent balcony and make her way into the room behind, and from there out of the house. She had reached the road, and stood looking down at the hairpin bends beneath and wondering which direction to take, when a terrible thought occurred to her. She was stranded in a strange country with no money and no passport. She almost wept with frustration.

As she stood knee-deep in snow, shivering despite her improvised costume, she heard the grating of gears on the road below. A decrepit lorry was climbing laboriously towards her. As it turned a bend immediately below, she read the sign painted on its side: Fratelli Petucci.

An Italian lorry ... if it was only homeward bound! She snatched off her woolly hat, tossed back her hair and smiled while she held out her thumb in the internationally recognised sign. The lorry driver could not believe his eyes. Hitchhikers were forbidden by law in Malivia. This had to be a trap. He slowed right down to take a closer look. *Dio*, but she was pretty! He shook his head regretfully.

'*Non è possibile*,' he called through the open window. '*È vietato.*'

'*Signore, per piacere* ... ' She ran alongside the cab, eyes fixed imploringly on his.

He sighed, and stopped the engine. '*Dovè? Italia?*'

The girl nodded furiously. '*Si, si.*'

It had been a long and boring drive. The dour village café he had stopped at had had little to offer by way of entertainment. And she did speak Italian ...

'*Va bene, ma presto! La polizia, capisce?*'

The driver looked nervously over his shoulder as she climbed in beside him. Georgie assured her saviour that if they caught sight of a police car she would duck beneath the tarpaulin on the floor of the cab.

It took three hours to reach the Italian frontier. They talked about Paolo's job, his family, his football team. He told Georgie she was by far the most beautiful girl he had ever given a ride to. They talked about heavy goods vehicles, how hard it must be to drive them, the expertise involved. He told her again she was easily the prettiest girl he had seen in a long time, and life on the road was lonely ... She talked about her father, her uncle and her two brothers, and how grateful they were going to be to Paolo for delivering her safely. He smiled, and asked what she was running away from. A man, she explained, a man who treated me badly. He smiled and puffed out his chest and she had no more trouble.

As they approached the border, she offered him her small diamond earrings, the only thing of value she had on her, if he could let her hide on the floor of the cab as she had no passport. He waved them aside, the border guard waved them through. Georgie kissed Paolo and got him to drop her at a hotel near the border, where she charmed the management into letting her make a call to England.

When she had got through to Dexter, the hotel staff fell over themselves to be helpful, volunteering to drive her to the nearest airfield, where the Randolph Enterprises jet was sent to pick her up.

She flew back to England — straight into the lenses of what looked like the world's complement of press photographers. She thought word must have leaked out about her abduction by Nicky, until she saw the copy of the French girlie magazine which one of them was clutching in his hand ...

Having nerved himself up to ask his mother's forgiveness, Alexander found it distinctly annoying to find her absent from Gilmour when he arrived.

The housekeeper said she had driven to Edinburgh for a meeting.

'On a Sunday? Did she seem all right?'

'She seemed awfu' pleased about something,' said the housekeeper. 'She said she'd be back tomorrow evening at the latest. Will you be waiting, your lordship?'

653

'I suppose I shall have to! Really, Maman, what are you up to?'

His mother did not return until late Monday evening. Alexander had expected her to react in one or two ways to news of his arrival: indifference or anger. He bitterly reproached himself for allowing Sloane to drive her out, but did not expect Angelica to be in a forgiving mood. In the event, her reaction surprised him. For a moment, as she hesitated in the doorway, his mother looked guilty.

'You were in Edinburgh, I heard,' he said awkwardly.

'Yes — things to see to. A business matter.'

He was too distracted by thoughts of what he had come to say to think of questioning her then. 'Maman, I came to tell you — Sloane and I, it's all over.'

'Thank God! At last I have my son back again.'

'You may not want him, when you hear what else I have to say.'

'Nothing you could say could possibly shock me, Xan.'

His mother was a genuinely amazing woman, he realised. She showed not a trace of emotion when he confessed the elaborate deception he had practised for years: taking women out while finding satisfaction only with the men he met through gay clubs and bars.

'And you thought I would condemn you for that? But, my son, I knew. I have always known, right from the earliest days with poor Luis.'

'You knew? But why didn't you say anything?'

She shrugged. 'What was there to say? I could not order you how to conduct your sex life. Besides, I will admit, for a time I hoped that perhaps it was something you would grow out of if you experimented. I am ashamed to say that when I realised that that was unlikely, I hoped you might make a marriage with a woman who understood — for the sake of Courtney Park. Then you married Sloane.'

He smiled wryly. 'She was so different when we met, you've no idea. She promised we could make a go of it, allow each other our freedom and at the same time provide an heir. She told me that was what she wanted above everything else. The only thing I regret about the divorce is that now I shall never father a child.'

His mother looked at him sorrowfully. 'My poor boy, it would never have happened, anyway. Don't be annoyed, but after that last scene I started some very thorough checking up on Sloane and her past. An American inquiry agent flew over at the weekend to give me the final proof.'

It was a sad and sordid story. When she had told it, Angelica poured them both a stiff drink and booked their flights back to England in the morning.

On the Edinburgh–London shuttle, the cabin crew ran out of *The Times* and the *Telegraph*. Angelica said that she would manage without. Alexander accepted a tabloid — and froze in horror.

'Good God, it's Georgie! But where on earth did they get this picture? It's pornographic.'

PEER'S DAUGHTER IN STEAMY SEX PIX SHOCKER screamed the *Daily Scoop* over a borderline decent shot of Georgie sprawled on what appeared to be a bed, one breast completely revealed by the sliding strap of her silk camisole.

And this was one of the least suggestive shots! Gorgeous Georgianna Randolph — Georgie to her intimate friends — was supposed to be modelling lingerie for a top French fashion mag. As you can see, seductive Georgie didn't quite pull it off — or should that be on?!!

The photographer, jilted boyfriend Christian Neggar, took his revenge by selling the pix to a soft porn magazine, *La Sexy France*. Was Georgie's face red! Last night the peer's daughter flew into Heathrow from a mystery European jaunt, refusing to comment. Her father, tough Aussie millionaire Lord Dexter Randolph, threatened to horsewhip any newsman found in the grounds of the family's stately home. What was he thinking of — Georgie's reputation or his own?

The article went on to reproduce the substance of

yesterday's scandal-mongering on the discovery of a body on Dexter Randolph's Australian property, Yelonga.

'That bloody Neggar!' said Alexander. 'Poor Georgie fell into his clutches while she was in Paris.'

'Pretty comprehensively from the looks of this,' drawled his mother. 'The other pictures are obviously worse.'

'Only in the context of a girlie magazine,' he said fiercely. 'The high fashion magazines use shots no less explicit than this every month. Put it in *Tatler* or *Vogue*, and no one would think twice.'

'If only Georgie had thought before she agreed to take her clothes off. The family could do without this sort of publicity on top of a murder enquiry.'

'Oh, come on. It's not as bad as that! No one seriously suspects Dexter was mixed up in this killing, do they?'

'After this, *Scoop* readers will,' she pointed out, 'and you can bet this sort of mud-slinging won't do Randolph Enterprises' share prices any good at all. Dexter had better act to clear his name pretty damn quick.'

Sloane woke early on Tuesday and ordered a selection of newspapers to be sent up instead of her usual *Times* and *International Herald Tribune*. The one tabloid she was sent featured a Christian Neggar syndicated shot of Georgie, as the reporters and photographers who had besieged the house yesterday had predicted. She studied the semi-erotic photograph and salacious report, smiling. What with this and the story of her niece's interlude with Prince Nicolas, which Sloane would see was leaked in due course, Georgie's chances of making a respectable marriage looked pretty well over.

She turned her attention to the business pages. All without exception predicted a bumpy ride for Randolph Enterprises in the wake of the revelation that its chairman, Lord Dexter Randolph, had been invited to help Australian police with a murder enquiry. After its temporary rally on

Monday, the company's share-price was plummeting.

A broker friend from New York had called late last night with a very interesting piece of information — the secret sale of Dexter's American hotels. Two locations had definitely been disposed of, with the sale of the flagship New York property under negotiation. Dexter must really be in trouble! It was time to act.

'Ask Lord Randolph, Lady Camilla and their children to come up to my sitting-room at eleven,' she instructed Ford by phone.

'Mr Courtney's in London, and I believe Lord Randolph and Mr Ashley have only just gone to bed, madam. The Sydney market ... '

'Ford, I said tell them all to come up to me at eleven!'

She banged down the receiver, not really angry. It suited her just fine that Dexter would be feeling exhausted after a night of monitoring the slide in Australia. The more beat and demoralised he felt, the smoother her own ride should be. The whole affair would be managed more easily without Xan's scrupulously fairminded presence.

The meeting called for careful stage managing. She had considered summoning Bradford Carter, but decided it would only be inflammatory. Instead, she told her maid to arrange five chairs in a semicircle before her own Early American walnut desk. She seated herself behind it, crisply formal in tailored Bill Blass charcoal-grey wool dress and jacket. With her jewellery restrained to simple diamond ear studs and her great emerald cut diamond ring, she looked every inch the part of a svelte successful lawyer or businesswoman, not the sybaritic Countess of Courtney they thought they knew.

Camilla and Georgie were first to arrive. After hearing of the embarrassing use to which Christian Neggar's pictures of her were to be put, Georgie had refused to look at any of the newspapers that morning. She was annoyed therefore to see a copy of the *Daily Scoop* prominently displayed on her aunt's desk.

Still jaded by her Malivian experience, she was in a confrontational mood. 'I didn't know you read this trash, Sloane. And you'd better have a damn good reason for setting up this little charade! We're all far too busy with our own affairs to waste time on you and your power-tripping.'

Sloane's eyes were guileless as glass. 'Poor Georgie, I do understand. Those darned reporters can be so persistent when they scent a really juicy scandal. Such a pity Nicky tired of you so fast, or you could still be tucked away in his darling little castle.'

It had never occurred to Sloane, hearing of Georgie's precipitate return, that the girl might actually have chosen to leave Nicky. She was about to set her aunt straight when Camilla said, 'Leave it, Georgie. I don't think we need discuss our private affairs any longer.'

Courtney and a yawning Ash were the next to appear. They greeted Sloane politely, but were obviously surprised by her air of formaility.

'You remind me of the lady magistrate who fined me for speeding,' joked Court.

She glanced pointedly at her chunky gold watch.

'Perhaps we could start this without Dad?' suggested Ash. 'He had a pretty rough time last night.'

'I'm sorry,' said Sloane, looking anything but. 'I'm afraid I must insist that your father is present. He is the one most directly affected by what I have to say.'

'Well, spit it out then,' said a gruff voice behind them. Dexter glided soundlessly in. 'Come on, woman. You got me out of bed for this. It had better be good!'

'I think it very well might be, for both of us, Dexter.' Despite her assumed smile, the permafrost never left Sloane's eyes. 'It can come as no surprise to you to hear that my husband and I feel it is time we assumed sole possession of his ancestral home.'

'Hold it right there,' said Dexter. 'It's not that I doubt your word, Your Majesty — ' he could not resist a sly dig after Sloane's use of the Queen's favourite phrase — 'but I'd feel a damn sight happier to hear this straight from the horse's mouth. Where *is* Alex?'

She avoided the question. 'I think you can trust me to speak with my husband's full knowledge and consent. Both Alexander and I recognise your long association with, and contribution to, Courtney Park. This would appear to give you some rights of tenure here, an opinion confirmed by my good friend and attorney Bradford Carter —'

She paused to let her mention of Brad do its work. Dexter glowered at his wife, the first time he had looked at her since entering the room. Georgie squeezed her mother's hand supportively and glared back at him. Camilla stared miserably at the floor. Confident that she had succeeded in her ploy, Sloane continued, 'It is Bradford's opinion that the agreement entered into by you, Dexter, and by my husband's advisers since he was then below the age of majority, was in fact a repairing lease. It ran for an initial period of ten years, I understand?' She glanced down at the notes on a yellow legal pad before her.

'Cut the posturing, Sloane. You know damn well it did, renewable for a similar period subject to the agreement of both parties. We never got around to ratifying a formal renewal. Hell, there was no point. Alex was in New York. He could see all the good work I was doing here, while he had no interest in the place.'

'A situation which has changed, I'm afraid. The Earl of Courtney is entitled to reclaim sole possession of his home.'

'Not without giving me formal notice to quit,' Dexter retaliated.

'Since you've obviously been consulting *your* lawyers you'll know that, while you could perhaps insist, the legal proceedings involved would be long and costly — something I imagine you'd rather avoid right now? If you want to fight, Dexter, go ahead. But I don't think you're in any shape for it, financially or emotionally.' She looked at Camilla as she said that.

'Get to the point,' Dexter rasped, sensing the sub-text to her words, the honeyed inducement after she had wielded the big stick.

'Naturally we don't want to be unreasonable. As I said, we both recognise the valuable contribution you have made here. Bradford has proposed an *ex gratia* sum in settlement. He has still to fine tune his calculations —'

'You'd better keep your tame poodle out of my sight!'

'— but a ballpark figure of around five million pounds sounds right to us. I don't mean to gloat, but with the shape Randolph Enterprises is in, I figure that sum could come in very useful. Think very carefully. The offer stands until midnight tonight. After that, I start revising it downwards.'

The veins in Dexter's face and neck swelled with rage. 'I don't need to think. I can tell you now, you can take your proposal and —'

The house telephone rang. Sloane picked up the receiver and snapped, 'Yes?' She listened, incredulous. 'Yes, that's right. They're all up here with me. But, Xan —'

He had obviously rung off.

'Thank God!' cried Camilla. 'Xan's back. I don't believe he knew you were doing this, Sloane. I know my brother. He'd never kick us out of our home like this.' There were tears of relief on her cheeks. Ash held out his handkerchief, while Georgie patted her back. Dexter made no move to comfort her.

A tense expectant silence fell.

'Heavens, it's like waiting for the Derby,' murmured Court.

They heard footsteps outside in the corridor, the door swung open, and Angelica entered, followed by Alexander.

'Maman!' Camilla embraced her mother fondly. Angelica's grandchildren were equally pleased to see her. Even Dexter managed a crooked smile and a 'Welcome home, Angel.'

Only Sloane failed to react. Irritably, she shuffled the papers on her desk, refusing to meet either newcomer's eyes.

'This all looks very official,' said Alexander. 'Would you mind telling me what the devil's going on, Sloane?'

Dexter interrupted. 'We thought you knew, Alex. Your wife's giving us our marching orders. We're to be paid off, of course, but her ladyship wants us out.'

'How dare you?' Alexander's normally gentle voice cut like a whip.

Sloane paled. 'Xan, please, I think we should discuss this in private. It's for the best —'

'For whom?' His voice was charged with more anger than she had ever heard from him. 'Best for my sister, who was brought up here and loves the house? Best for my brother-in-law, who's devoted a fortune and years of his life to it? Best for my mother, who made it what it is? Or best for you, my cold overbearing cheat of a wife?'

'I don't have to take this from you, you pitiful fag! How could I possibly have cheated you when we agreed right from the start that I'd have my boyfriends and you'd have yours!'

It was the first time Camilla, Dexter and the boys had heard a reference to Alexander's homosexuality. Georgie and Angelica, forewarned, immediately closed ranks.

'Don't you dare insult my uncle like that!'

'There is absolutely nothing to be gained from a display of this kind. My son called you a cheat not because of your extra-marital activities but because of something that took place even before the ceremony.'

'You're talking in riddles, old woman. I don't know what you mean.' Sloane attempted to bluff it out, but her face was wary.

'I'd rather have spared you this embarrassment, but if you insist . . .'

Angelica produced a typewritten sheet of paper from a slim document case. 'Do you recognise this?'

Sloane glanced at it. 'Yes. It's a copy of the pre-nuptial agreement Xan asked me to sign. So what?'

'So you lied, *ma chère*. In this document you agreed under seal to use your best endeavours to provide an heir. You signed it in the full knowledge that there was absolutely no chance of any pregnancy ensuing.'

'Because your gay son couldn't get it up, you mean?'

Angelica's nostrils flared with distaste. 'Because you knew you were barren.'

Sloane pushed back her chair and lurched clumsily to her feet. 'Prove it!' she yelled. 'You can't know that. No one knows . . .'

Angelica turned to a xeroxed sheet of paper. 'My inquiry agent has obtained this copy of the admissions record of Welbury Hospital, Connecticut. In 1985 a certain Suzanne Selby was admitted, suffering from a badly advanced case of syphilis. The child she was carrying was found to be so severely affected that the doctors advised an abortion. Suzanne herself was cured, but her womb had been so badly infected that she was told she would never bear another child. That patient was you, Sloane. Suzanne is your middle name, and your mother's maiden name was Selby.'

Sloane was shaking her head from side to side in frantic denial. 'No, it's circumstantial evidence only. None of this would stand up in court.'

'Except perhaps for a couple more extraordinary coincidences.' There was something very like pity in Angelica's voice as she continued: 'Among the list of the Welbury's benefactors is one highly significant name — Henry de Havilland. Shortly after Suzanne received her treatment, the hospital's accounts show that it received a substantial donation on behalf of an unnamed patient. The transfer was arranged via a New York lawyer — Mr Bradford Carter.'

Alexander took Sloane's arm. 'I don't think we need to prolong this painful discussion, do you?'

Blindly, she shook herself free. 'Please, spare me the pity! You make me sick — fags like you and Gianni and that little creep Franco who did this to me. He was my husband's first, then he got greedy. He soon saw who wrote the cheques, and he was willing to be adaptable. And I — I thought it would be fun to turn the tables on Gianni for once, show him what it was like for me, forever shut out in the cold.'

She began to sob, tearing cries of despair that made the others shift uneasily in their seats. Even Angelica was uncomfortable, staring down at the incriminating file in her hand.

Alexander tried to steer Sloane out and into her room, but she refused to go. 'Take your hands off me! You're like all the rest. Everyone, my whole life through, just wanted to use me — my father for his business; Gianni and Franco for my money; you for the respectability I gave you. But what about me? What do I get out of all this? At last I found something I wanted. I would have given my life, every penny of my money, to this house — and *you won't let me*! All right, I'm out of here. Take back your house — but don't expect your brother-in-law to help you out with the bills. He's going down, and I pray he takes you with him, every last one of you!' Alexander recoiled as she pushed past him and out of the room. The slam of the door echoed for a long time.

It was Dexter who finally broke the silence. 'Alex, mate, I'd say you were well rid of that one.'

In the general slackening of tension, Angelica took control. 'Camilla, Dexter, Xan's told me some of what happened. Would the rest of you leave us, please? We need to get a few things straight.'

'Sure, I have a call to make,' said Ash, who intended to consult Chris Brett on the results of his blood-test straight away.

'Chantel's waiting for me,' said Court. 'Why don't you come and have a drink with us, Georgie? It's early, I know, but after that I could use one.'

'So could I. I'll just check with Ford, to see if the press have slithered back under their stones.'

Leaving him, Georgie glanced over the banisters of the great staircase and caught her breath in horror. In the marble hall below, angrily interrogating the butler, stood Prince Nicolas.

'If Your Royal Highness would consent to wait in the morning-room,' a harried Ford was saying, 'Miss Georgianna and all the family are engaged at present.'

'But I have travelled all night. I must see her!'

Catching sight of her descending the stairs, he side-stepped the butler. 'Georgianna, why did you run out on me? And what is the meaning of these? You made a fool of me!' He strode towards her, brandishing a fistful of news-papers.

She spoke to the butler first. 'That will be all, Ford. Would you tell Mr Courtney I'll join him and his fiancée shortly?'

When he had gone, she addressed Nicolas. 'No one made a fool of you — you did that for yourself, coming on like a heavy seducer in a Victorian melodrama. As far as the newspaper reports are concerned — I'm surprised you even read them! Didn't you tell me yourself that the press exaggerate and distort their coverage of you? Why should you imagine they behave any differently towards me?'

'But — there are pictures.'

'Surely you're not so naive as to believe the camera never lies. These were done for a fashion magazine.'

Nicky felt more at sea than ever before with a woman. She had turned her back and fled from him, wounding his pride, and causing him severe loss of face before his father. These scandalous reports in the newspaper should have been the final death-knell to his infatuation with Georgianna Randolph, but seeing her now, so calm and dignified in the face of his anger, he was won over once more.

'Very well. I shall accept your explanation. But you

must see that your modelling days are over. I cannot run the risk of further embarrassment.'

'*You* can't! What on earth has any of this to do with you?'

He looked amazed. 'You are shortly to be announced as my fiancée, Georgianna. Naturally any scandal attached to your name touches the honour of my country.'

She laughed incredulously. 'You can't be serious? Do you think I'm actually going to marry a man so terminally insecure he has to lock a girl into his bedroom?'

He flinched. 'It was a misunderstanding. The stupid girl thought —'

'I don't care what she thought. It's *you* who need to understand. Nicky, I never at any time gave you any reason to suppose that I was taking your extraordinary proposal seriously.'

'You spent the night with me.'

'So has my aunt, and I don't see you offering to make her Crown Princess of Malivia.'

'You know quite well that's different. She's married.'

'Not for long. She and Alexander are divorcing. Sloane's dowry would be far bigger than mine. Have you thought of that, Nicky?'

'Georgianna, please, it's not a question of money.'

'I don't suppose that was the only consideration,' she said more gently, 'but your country's finances matter to you, don't they? I think I should warn you that my father's business affairs are in a mess. Unless he can pull off a minor miracle, he stands to lose the best part of his fortune.'

She saw his eyes widen with shock, but his pride would not permit him to back down now. 'It makes no difference,' he said stiffly. 'It's you I want.'

'I doubt it,' she said softly. 'You chose a girl with all the attributes you expected of a princess — birth, fortune, good looks. You ticked them off like so many items on a shopping list, but you didn't spare the time to get to know me. I'm not the girl you want, Nicky, believe me. As well as a model, I'm a magazine proprietor, did you know that? I've had one failed love affair with a man who exploited me, and I'm in the middle of another with Guy, a man I respect and care for. It's quite possible that Christian, the creep who used my trust in him to take those silly pictures, will crawl out of the woodwork with something even more damaging. Can you look me in the eye and say you honestly don't care? That you'll love me anyway, whatever happens?'

In the lengthy silence, his eyes could not meet hers.

She sighed and touched his hand. 'I thought not. It was just an illusion, Nicky. A technicolour dream. There's nothing wrong with dreaming, but eventually you need to wake up and get on with real life. I think you should get back to yours — if the press will let you out alive.' A thought dawned on her. 'Do you mean to say you drove right past them on the way in? My God, imagine the head-lines tomorrow!'

'Good heavens, no.' He looked appalled. 'My detectives brought me in over the fields from the home farm.'

'You mean, you weren't so blinded by passion as to run the gauntlet?' she said, and smiled when he blushed faintly.

'Georgianna, you're right. You're far too wise to make a good wife to me. But I hope — I very much hope — that I might consider you a friend?'

'Just good friends with the macho playboy prince? The press will never believe it.'

'To hell with them! And, Georgie —'

'Yes?'

'Tell Guy he's a lucky man.'

'Thank you. One of these days I'll introduce you both.'

'But not too soon, please. Let me nurse my broken heart first.' He was only half joking.

They were interrupted by the sound of the lift descending. Georgianna was delighted to see both her parents inside, talking freely for the first time since the night of the ball. She pulled Nicky's sleeve. 'Come on, they haven't seen us. Let's leave them to make things up. We'll go and find your detectives at the back of the house, shall we?'

Dexter and Camilla came to an awkward halt at the door to his rooms.

'Go to bed now, darling,' she said. 'You look exhausted. We can talk again when you're rested. Ash should have the results of his blood-test by then.'

He caught her hand. 'I don't need them. He's mine, all right. Who else's could he be with a business head like that on his shoulders?' He abandoned his attempt at humour, seeing the pain and confusion on the face that had always remained the dearest in the world to him, however hard and uncaring a front he had put on. 'I'm more sorry than I can say, sweetheart, for all the wasted years. Camilla, I love you very much. I always did, right from the days when you were a big-eyed kid being pushed around by Angel. I was crazy jealous of Luciano, poor bloke, just for being the first. After the accident, I felt broken up inside, totally bloody useless. I knew I could never be a proper husband to you again, and I got to thinking obsessionally about him, the man you loved first. We never quite got it right, did we, Camilla? Even in the good years.' He squeezed her hand, gently demanding the truth.

'It was my fault as much as yours. If I hadn't been so stupidly shy. I should have explained what I needed — shown you.'

'Too late now that I'm less than half a man. That's what drove me to say those things about Ash — to get back at you for the years I'd disappointed you, and the knowledge that now I could only fail you completely. It was cruel and pathetic. Can you forgive me?'

'Of course. I never stopped loving you. Even last Saturday. Brad made me feel young and desirable again. I needed to feel that, Dexter, but it was you I wanted. It's always been you.'

He kissed her hand. 'Thank you, sweetheart. You don't know what it means to hear you say that after everything I've done. We'll talk again, I promise. But first I must get some sleep.'

She made no move to help him, knowing how much he hated to be fussed over or babied in any way. Her heart was bursting with love for him, urging her to stay, but she could see he needed some time alone. She bent to kiss his forehead. 'G'bye for now, darling. Come and see me at any time. I'm just upstairs.'

Dexter had intended to go straight to bed, but once inside the comfortable office-cum-living quarters Angelica had created for him, he found that he was still too keyed up to think of resting.

Despite his cruel treatment of her, Camilla still loved him. The thought brought almost unbearable tenderness, and grief. After he had made his partial recovery, the doctors had told them there was no reason they should not conduct a sex life of a sort. He would not be able to make love to his wife as before, but there were some things he could still do. Camilla had wanted to try then. He had rejected her. He knew that now she would want to try again, but still he shrank from the idea of compromise. He had once been a proud and virile man. Pride lasted, he discovered, where virility did not.

He wheeled himself through to his private office. In the outer room he could hear his secretaries fielding calls: 'I'm sorry, but Randolph Enterprises has no comment to make on that at present.' 'Lord Randolph is unavailable for comment, I'm afraid.' 'There is absolutely no truth in the rumour that Randolph Enterprises will shortly stop trading...'

Dexter wished he were as sure. Wheels had already been put in motion to sell off the last of the American holdings. He ought at this very minute to be sitting down drafting a breezy statement to the effect that Randolph Enterprises was rationalising its holdings, consolidating its foothold into markets where it had always led: Australia, the Far East and England.

He began to dial Ash's number, thinking to ask him to come and help. He changed his mind. He thought back to Saturday, and his callous rejection of the elder son who had always been a pillar of support. Saturday — images of Camilla's rosy satisfied nakedness. He remembered Bradford Carter, too. Caught on the hop, but still able to walk, to ride, to make love to Dexter's wife. However genuinely she loved her husband, Camilla had recent knowledge of a whole man. How long before she tired of a cripple's feeble efforts and found herself another Carter?

Dexter poured himself a measure of his favourite Genfiddich and sat brooding, looking out of the window on to the parkland beyond. He saw Alexander hurrying off to the stables, and smiled sardonically. He might have pretended surprise at Sloane's revelation but he had not felt it, not after years of watching his brother-in-law sneak out to meet a succession of stable lads.

A cripple and a shirtlifter ... not much of a future for Courtney Park.

He stared up at the pair of antique Purdeys on the wall above his desk. They were kept there for show, his own working guns, unused since the accident, oiled and polished and stored on the racks in the gun-room. But Webster was nothing if not a perfectionist. He fussed over every finest detail of his master's clothes and personal possessions. The antique breeches and barrels would have been fastidiously scoured and polished, and it wouldn't surprise Dexter to find them in working order. Funny how he had a notion to feel the heft of a gun in his hands again.

He reached up, clawing at the walls to stretch himself higher, higher. The tips of his fingers grazed the stock of a gun, sending it crashing to the floor.

Instantly he heard his valet's voice outside the door. 'Are you all right, My Lord? Is there anything I can do?'

Dexter had a wild urge to tell him, 'Yes. Fetch me a box of cartridges.' He smiled to think of the fluttering in the dovecote *that* would cause.

'It's okay. I dropped a file, that's all. There is something you can do, though.'

'Yes, My Lord?'

'Go out and see if you can convince that rabble at the gate there's no story for them here. Try the soft approach. Get the girls in the office to help you. Take 'em out some sandwiches and drinks, offer to send for taxis. You know the sort of thing.'

'Very good, My Lord.'

It was a fool's errand, Dexter knew, but it would keep them all busy.

He picked up the gun. It felt awkward and unbalanced in the hands of a seated man. A man doomed to spend the rest of his life a useless cripple. The rest of his life . . .

In a moment of total recall he remembered his old cartridge-belt. Normally scrupulous about returning fire-arms and ammunition to the gun-room, he had been called back to the office unexpectedly from the last shoot he had been able to attend. The belt, almost empty, had got in his way while he took an important call. He had unclipped it and stored it safely out of the way in that little drawer at the bottom of the bureau.

The drawer hadn't been opened in years. It had swollen out of true and stuck when he tried to open it. He cursed under his breath, straining with both hands until he thought the handle would come off — and then the drawer shot open to reveal his old belt, empty but for one live cartridge.

One was all it would take.

Georgie was up in her room. She had just finished talking to Guy, who had rung as soon as he saw the coverage about the photographs. In a long, loving, phone-call he had insisted on flying over at once to be by her side and draw some of the fire.

Smiling, she glanced out of the window — and froze in annoyance. Mark Hayward, the estate manager's son, was sauntering over the park beyond the stables, labrador at his heels, gun cocked over one arm like any gentleman sportsman out for a morning's rough shooting. It was not so much the pretension which annoyed her, though Mark's was an abrasive and difficult personality, so much as the fact that she was forced to witness the slaughter. Despite the bulging game-bag, from which rabbits' feet drooped pathetically, he was even now lining up another shot. She saw the recoil at his shoulder, the puff of cordite upon the still November air. The dog darted off and was back in seconds, its wriggling quarry still alive in its jaws.

Georgie couldn't bear it a second longer. Mark was shooting far too close to the house, and after everything Daddy had told him. It was time Mr Hayward was delivered a stinging reminder. She wanted to have a word with her father anyway, find out where things stood between her parents after their talk. She left her room and ran downstairs.

She could hear the phones ringing unanswered in the outer office. Strange, when they were usually manned or answered by a machine twenty-four hours a day. There was no sign of Webster, either.

The door to her father's bedroom stood slightly ajar. She pushed it and saw the curtains were open, the bed unoccupied. He must be in his office. She tapped at the door once, and received no answer. She knew her father hated to be disturbed at work. Normally she would have tried once, then gone away. Today, something prompted her to knock again. When she still received no answer, she tried the door. He hadn't locked himself in. The handle turned.

She let herself into the room and every sense seemed to function at twice its normal intensity, half its usual speed.

She noticed the strange smell first — fireworks and an odd sweet coppery smell. She saw her father sitting at an unfamiliar angle in his wheelchair, head slumped forward on to his desk.

'Daddy?'

No answer, just a steady drip-drip-drip. On the polished wooden floor, a pool of viscous crimson was widening by the second. Drip-drip-drip. She saw the shotgun poking out from beneath the desk, and at last she understood, and ran screaming into the hall.

'Help me, please! Somebody help! It's Daddy. He's shot himself.'

In the confusion which followed, with servants and family hurrying to call an ambulance, open the gates, deal with Camilla, who fainted from shock, no one noticed the departure of the seventh Countess of Courtney.

Book Six

COURTNEY

'The helicopter will arrive to take Lord Randolph to hospital in ten minutes,' Courtney told the shocked and silent staff whom he had assembled in the marble hall. 'I know it's going to be hard, but the best way you can help the family is by going on with your work as usual. And it goes without saying that no word of this must be allowed to leak out.'

There was a subdued chorus of 'Yes, Mr Courtney' or merely solemn shakes of the head from those too stunned to reply.

'Very well then. Ford, you'll take charge of the landing arrangements?'

'They're in hand, sir. I shall meet the paramedics myself in the Range Rover.'

'Good man. And, Huggins, wait in the hall, please. We shall need you in a moment. The rest of you please carry on. We'll pass on any news of Lord Randolph as soon as we have it.'

He went quickly back to his father's study. Webster and Ashley looked up hopefully.

'Any sign of that helicopter yet? I don't know how much longer he'll last,' said Ashley. His handsome faced was creased with anxiety, and there were splashes of his father's blood on the knees of his trousers where he had knelt beside Dexter's wheelchair.

Webster picked up one of the stack of towels he had brought in. With neat economical movements he wadded one to form a pressure-pad and clapped it to the wound in Dexter's chest. It turned red with shocking suddenness. Unflurried, he dropped the towel to join the rest in a pile at his feet and repeated the process with a fresh pad.

They had not dared to move the wounded man. He still

675

lay as Georgie had found him, with his head and shoulders slumped forward on his desk.

Ashley felt the pulse in his neck. It was still there, but weak and irregular. Why didn't they come? The valet's mechanical movements faltered for an instant.

'Here, let me,' said Ashley, seeing that the elderly man was tiring. He put out a hand to shift aside the gun, which was still protruding from beneath the desk, so that he could kneel at that side of Dexter's chair.

'Don't touch it!' Courtney exclaimed.

Ashley turned, surprised. 'Why not?'

'Hasn't it occurred to you that it's highly unusual for someone to choose to shoot themself in the chest? And even if Dad had chosen to, I really don't see how the barrel of the gun could have fallen quite so far under the desk, can you?'

'You can't mean someone tried to kill him?'

'I don't know. All I'm saying is that it's a possibility. Until the police have ruled it out, we shouldn't touch that gun.'

Ashley nodded, slightly ashamed that for once his brother seemed to have much the clearer grasp of the situation.

Webster had ignored the conversation, folding and pressing. The flow seemed to be getting lighter. He hoped desperately that the wound was clotting, and not the other possibility.

'There's another thing,' Courtney was continuing. 'We're going to have to head off the press.'

Ashley was ashamed to have to think of the business at a time like this, but knew that he must. Their father would expect it. 'You're right. If word gets out that Dad's shot himself — or that someone else did — Randolph Enterprises is finished. But how can we cover it up, with the press camped out at the gates like this?'

'Divert them,' said Courtney immediately. 'They're here to interview one person. It's her they must see. Can you manage here?'

676

Ashley nodded. Courtney went to find their sister. She was in the morning-room with Chantel, a glass of brandy in her hand. She spilled it over herself when he came into the room.

'Daddy! Is he —'

'It's okay, he's hanging in there. It'll take more than one bullet to stop him.'

Courtney forced his grim attempt at humour. It was important that Georgie did not see their father's true condition — grey-faced and barely breathing — or she would not remain strong enough to play her part.

'Look, I hate to ask you, but do you think you could face the lions at the gate? It's important that news about Pa doesn't leak out, and if the press sees a medical team arrive . . . Can you decoy them, d'you think?'

She was on her way instantly. Courtney helped her into a voluminous aubergine-coloured sheepskin jacket, and Chantel thoughtfully fetched a pair of dark glasses. Courtney gave Huggins his instructions. At the gates to Courtney Park the chauffeur was to stop just long enough to let the press see who was inside the car, then take off like a bat out of hell. Once he had eluded the cars which would hopefully pursue them, he was to take Georgie to the Capital Clinic, where her father should be being treated.

Courtney patted his sister's shaking shoulders. 'Do your best, Georgie. We're all counting on you.'

She got into the back of the car, winding one of the tinted windows down halfway so as to leave a good view of her pale, troubled face. Thank God for the dark glasses which concealed her tears of shock and fright! As they slowed for the great double iron gates to be swung open, the press scenting a juicy story clustered round like a pack of hyenas. Questions were called through the half open window; cameras and microphones thrust inside. Some of Georgie's distress communicated itself to the reporters, who thought they were witnessing a daughter in disgrace.

'What's the matter, love? Old man slung you out, has he?'

'Here, darlin', no one's died! Giz a smile, then.'

'You couldn't open your jacket a bit? You *are* meant to be a glamour story!'

She leant across and pressed the switch to lower the window, looking as if she were about to make a statement. Overhead, she heard a helicopter's juddering approach. She rapped on the glass which separated her from the chauffeur.

'Get us out of here — fast!'

Huggins slammed down the accelerator and the dark blue Bentley, one of her father's fleet, shot down the road at a crazy speed. There was a mad scramble for the assortment of press cars parked on the verge, and the pack set off in hot pursuit, missing the biggest scoop of the year — Lord Dexter Randolph's airlift to a London clinic, critically ill from a gunshot wound.

When she heard the helicopter land, nothing her mother or brother could say would dissuade Camilla from accompanying her husband to hospital. Courtney felt it would be quicker to let her go rather than argue, but realised she must be accompanied.

'Can you cope at this end while I go with Mums?' he asked Ashley.

'Sure. I'll join you at the Capital as soon as I can get away.'

From the window of their father's office, Ashley watched the helicopter lift off before dialling the police. When he had made the call, he saw Webster, moving like an automaton, tidying away the bloodied towels.

'No, that's okay. Better leave everything as it is for the moment,' he said, guiding the elderly valet from the room. After his efficient nursing of his wounded master, Webster was trembling with reaction. Ashley sent him to the kitchen to get some tea and brandy, and sat in the outer office with the subdued secretaries until the police arrived.

The Chief Constable of the County, an old friend of his grandmother, expressed concern at hearing of Dexter's injury and pledged his and the force's full co-operation in seeing that a total press embargo was placed on news of Dexter's shooting.

At the Capital Clinic, Courtney and his mother sat in a side sitting-room while Dexter was rushed through for emergency treatment. Courtney saw that his mother was in full control of herself, but he had never seen her look so bereft.

'How could he do it?' she asked after a long time without speaking. 'How could he do this, when at last things were starting to come right between us?'

He hadn't wanted to alarm her with his suspicions, but realised that they might well be easier for her to bear than thinking Dexter had attempted suicide. 'We don't know that he pulled the trigger, Mums.'

'What do you mean?'

He'd expected her to be horror-stricken at the suggestion of attempted murder. Instead, her face lost its desolate expression. 'That must be it,' she said, almost with relief, then stared at him, wide-eyed. 'But, Court, that means someone at Courtney Park . . .'

'I know, Mums, but try not to worry about it now. Pa's safe here, and as soon as the doctor's had a word with us I'm going to see about hiring some security.'

Mr Ferguson, the Consultant, came to see them straight from the treatment-room, removing only his gloves and mask. He took Camilla's hand. 'You're going to have to be very brave, my dear.'

She gave a cry of alarm, and snatched her hand away. 'Please don't say he's dead!'

'He's not,' Ferguson hastened to reassure her. 'In fact, when we'd given him heart massage and a transfusion, he regained consciousness for a few minutes. We can't operate, but he's out of immediate danger.'

'I must go to him. Let me see him,' she demanded.

The consultant looked uneasy. 'I'm afraid we've sedated him for now, but you can of course sit with him. Before you do, there's something you ought to know. The bullet has lodged in a very delicate position next to the spinal cord. There's no question of operating to remove it while he's in this traumatised state. Now it may just be temporary, but the signs are that further damage has been done.'

Courtney was quicker to see the implications than his mother, who was just thankful Dexter was still with them. 'You're telling us he's completely paralysed?'

'For now, I'm afraid so.'

Ashley arrived at the Capital a few hours later to find Courtney and Georgie together in the sitting-room. Camilla was with their father in the intensive care unit.

'She's being marvellous,' Courtney reassured his brother. 'Refuses to believe this paralysis could be anything but temporary. I don't know, though. Given his condition before . . . I don't think it looks too good.'

'When can they operate?'

'He's got to stabilise first. Could be a week, could be a month. It's hard to predict with gunshot wounds, apparently.'

'What did the police say?' Georgie asked.

'You mean they haven't turned up here yet? With me, they took the line that Pa must have shot himself because of business worries.'

'I've been thinking, and I don't believe he would do this to himself,' declared Georgie.

'Which means,' concluded Ashley, 'that he has a dangerous enemy, and we'd better take steps to protect him.'

'Done,' said Courtney. 'I rang Randolph Enterprises Head of Security, and he's recommended a bodyguard service. All ex-SAS. Didn't you notice the musclebound cleaner in the corridor outside?'

'Yes. I thought it was an odd time to be mopping the corridor. Well done, Court!'

Ashley was immensely heartened by the way his brother had acted, heading off publicity and safeguarding their father. If the crisis could be said to have its positive side, it was in the way that Courtney had been revealed in the best possible light after years of being written off as a playboy dilettante. The new mettle his brother had displayed should make Ashley's own suggestion easier to carry out.

'We're all going to have to be very strong about this. You did enormously well, choking off the press,' he squeezed Georgie's hand, 'but Pa's going to be out of action for quite a while.' Ashley refused even to contemplate the possibility that it could be for ever. 'It's vital that the shareholders don't realise how seriously he's injured. When Mr Ferguson thinks he's up to it, I'm going to have a talk with Pa, find out his plans for the company. He doesn't trust Luke any further than he could throw him, which leaves me at the helm. I think I'll be most effective in Australia while the company's in crisis, and there's no time to lose. While I'm holding the fort out there, you'll have to support Mums and see everything goes smoothly here. Do you think you can handle it, keep everything under wraps?'

Courtney flushed angrily. 'Listen, I know my record's nothing to be proud of, but I came through hell this summer and Georgie and I managed to keep that pretty quiet, didn't we? You can trust us with this, too.'

Ashley touched his shoulder. 'If you handle things as brilliantly as you did today, I can see I'll have to be moving over in the business for you.'

Later that evening, Ashley spent a harrowing few minutes alone with his father. Dexter was lying in a glass-walled intensive care cubicle. It was practically at jungle heat inside, and he was naked under a single sheet. He had been given something to control the pain, which seemed to be working, but Ashley saw the size of the dressing on his father's bare chest and inwardly shuddered. Dexter's mind was surprisingly clear while he relayed his business instructions, but when Ashley asked, 'Do you want to talk about it, Pa?' his father's eyes became puzzled.

'There's nothing I'd like better, son, but the devil of it is I can't remember. I know I took the gun off the wall ... After that it's a blank, I'm afraid.'

'Don't push yourself. Just concentrate on building up your strength.'

Dexter gave a tired laugh. 'For what? So I can have the neck and shoulders of a bull while the rest of me withers away? It's no good. Your mother and the quack say I mustn't move and risk dislodging the bullet, but it's all whitewash, isn't it? I couldn't move even if I wanted to. I'm finished, son, but you're not. I want you to do two things: first, save my company, and, when you've done that, find the bastard who did this to me and nail him to the floor. It's what I'm living for, d'you hear?'

Ashley shook his head, unable to speak. There were tears in his eyes as he obeyed the nursing sister's instructions and left his father with a gentle squeeze of his shoulder. In the relatives' seating area he made his good-byes. Camilla was too distracted to do more than kiss him hastily before she left to sit with her husband in intensive care. Ashley, Courtney and Georgie took a little longer together.

'Call me at eight in the evening your time every day — that'll be six in the morning in Sydney. I'll be getting ready to go to the office,' Ashley told them. 'During office hours, my secretary will always know where to find me. Outside, the answering service will be able to let you know.'

'It'll be okay, Ash. Pa's a tough old devil,' Court reassured him. 'He'll pull through.'

Unspoken between them was the thought: Even if he never moves again.

On the drive to Heathrow, Ashley remembered some words of his father's, and was obscurely comforted: 'Find the bastard who did this to me ...' Though Dexter could not remember exactly what had happened, in his subconscious at least he obviously knew that he hadn't pulled the trigger himself. The realisation cheered Ashley while at the same time he prayed that their security cover would be effective. If someone had tried to murder once, they could easily make a second attempt.

He made the quickest possible flight to Sydney, two twelve-hour hops, and arrived, red-eyed and unshaven, at Randolph Enterprises' Sydney headquarters in the early evening. It was after office hours, but the lights were still on on the executive floors. Ashley looked in first on his uncle's office, then Chip's. No sign of either of them, nor in the conference-room. He finally ran them to earth upstairs in Dexter's penthouse suite. His father did not mind it being used in his absence for entertaining, but this looked like something different.

Luke occupied his brother's chair, his back to the fabulous Harbour view, while Chip had his feet up on the other side of the desk. They looked very much at home, thought Ashley.

'Ash!' said Chip, getting to his feet. 'What are you doing here?'

Uncle Lucas was more polished. He slid out from behind Dexter's desk with a fine show of family feeling, clapping his nephew on the back and saying, 'Why didn't you let us know your flight? I'd have sent a car. Want a beer? You look done in.'

Ashley seized his chance, and took his father's seat. 'No, thanks. I didn't tell you the flight, because there wasn't time.' It was a feeble excuse. He hadn't told them because he hadn't wanted them forewarned. 'Glad to find you here, anyway,' he hurried on. 'I think it's time we had that review of Bradbury Island, don't you?'

Chip folded his burly arms and leant back in his seat, openly defying his cousin. 'We don't have to answer to you. The only person who can call us to account is Uncle Dexter. And where's he, eh?'

It was not so much a question, more of a taunt.

Ashley took a deep breath. For a moment he had been pierced by the memory of his father as he had last see him, paralysed and in mental agony. He had to get a grip. For his father's sake, he must stay on top of this situation. Dexter had decreed that no one outside the immediate family must be told what had happened, and that included the Lucas Randolphs. Now Ashley could see why. Any sign that Dexter's grip was slackening, and they'd be in like knives.

'Pa's been unavoidably detained,' he told them, and, looking up, surprised a fleeting change of expression on his uncle's face.

'Well, isn't that a shame?' said Luke, replacing his first unreadable reaction with his customary unctuous smile. 'Nothing serious, I hope? It's just with things going the way they are for Dexter on Yelonga, this is no time to play possum.'

Now Ashley knew what the expression on his uncle's face had reminded him of: a cat sadistically playing with a mouse before biting off its head. He'd long suspected that his uncle had his own network of loyal informants within the Randolph Enterprises offices. Suppose he had one within Courtney Park itself? For somehow Ashley had the strongest feeling that his uncle knew all about Dexter's condition. The only surprise had been his own arrival.

'Pa's been overdoing things,' he said steadily. 'As you know, since the hunting accident he's never been as strong as he'd like to think. Together with all this business over Wally and our bad performance in the market, he's been under considerable stress. The doctors have advised him not to risk a long-haul flight until he's rested. It's nothing serious,' he assured them, though neither had expressed concern, 'and in the meantime I have his mandate to conduct the company affairs as I see fit.'

'And we're to take your word for that, are we?' sneered Chip.

'Well, of course we'll take Ash's word.' His father gave him a warning look, and Chip subsided like a burst balloon. 'After all, if we can't trust one another, what are we doing in business together?'

Ashley bit back the retort he could have made — that the Lucas Randolphs were not in business *with* Dexter but because he had employed them. 'I'd like to review Bradbury,' he repeated.

'I thought you already had done, sport. Someone's been in my files.' Lucas then confused him further by laughingly admitting: 'Okay, okay, you caught us with our pants down on that one. My boy here allowed his enthusiasm to run away with him more than a little. Your dad wanted Bradbury to outclass all the other island resorts, and by God it's going to! But I'm afraid Chip here, in his in-experience, went a little too far with the specifications: expensive imported marble when we could have used local stone. You know the sort of thing. The pool's a miracle — you have to see it to believe it, Ash. Carved out of the rockface, one wall facing out to sea so you feel you could swim out to the horizon. But the contractor took us for a ride on the costing. He said he could do it for a million four. It ended up costing double.'

Ashley tried to stem the tide of this surprising con-fession, but Luke put up his hand to stop him. 'No, you were right first time. It's good we come clean about this. We didn't mean to pull the wool over your eyes — not for ever, that is. My idea was to take some of the sting out of the figures by making certain — ah, adjustments — to the running totals of the other divisions. It was wrong, but what can I say? He's my boy.'

Chip sat in stony silence, making no attempt to speak up for himself, Ashley noticed. 'It may have been criminal, Luke,' he pointed out. 'It completely screws up our tax position, for a start.'

Luke shrugged his shoulders. 'What tax position? With the company the way it is ...'

'Randolph Enterprises is not, I repeat *not*, going under while I'm at the helm. I'd like the precise figures on Bradbury, but since you've come clean with me about it, I think we can do without the inquisition — for the time being, at any rate. Besides, we've got something else on hand. Something even bigger. We're going after Chimera Resorts.'

'You're kidding!'

'What with, exactly?'

For the first time that evening, Ashley sensed he had them on the run.

'I'll level with you. It's all or nothing time. Dad wants me to make a statement about selling out in the States, telling the market here we're going to be concentrating on our Australian, English and Far Eastern interests. If we can back that up with a really major acquisition, there's a chance that market confidence will be restored.'

Lucas frowned. 'But where's the cash coming from? We're in the shit already. This could drag us under.'

'My father and I are pledging our personal fortunes.'

'D'you think that's wise, with the murder and all?'

For a moment, Ashley suffered a nasty jolt. He could have sworn Luke was talking about the attack on Dexter. Then he realised he meant the investigation on Yelonga. 'When my father gets out here, he'll send the police packing.'

Luke shook his head mournfully. 'I wish I could share your confidence about that.' He was trying to give a downbeat impression, but Ashley sensed that he was inwardly fizzing with excitement.

'All your personal fortune, eh? Well, I hope it pays off for you both, I really do.' He got to his feet. 'C'mon, Chip. You know how fussed your mother gets if we're late home to dinner. D'you fancy coming with us, Ash? Rhianne will be glad to see you.'

'No thanks, Uncle. I've a few things to get in motion here, then it's an early night for me. See you both tomorrow morning — with the Bradbury figures, please.'

'No worries. Don't push yourself too hard now.' Lucas's smile didn't quite reach his eyes. He knew, as he had been intended to, that whatever Ashley had said about no inquisitions, the figures would be scrutinised intently. If Ashley could prove only one instance of the widespread collusion he suspected between his Australian relatives and the various contractors they had appointed, then their days with Randolph Enterprises were numbered.

Then again, he reflected, shoulders sagging with exhaustion as the mantle of responsibility pressed down on them, if he didn't pull off this Chimera deal, the company itself might soon cease to exist.

Three days after Dexter's wounding, Courtney travelled to Heathrow with Chantel to see her off on the flight to New York. 'I'm sorry I can't come too, but you do understand why I have to be here, don't you?'

'Of course. I just wish I could stay and see you all through this, but I can't keep putting Mom off. She's getting worried.'

Despite the prohibition on telling people outside the family circle, Courtney had confided everything in Chantel. She had, after all, been in the house on the day of the shooting, and though they had said nothing publicly yet — Courtney insisting that he must win her family's approval first — they regarded themselves as unofficially engaged. He had asked her, though, to share the knowledge with no one else, not even her family. 'It's hard for you, I know.'

She looked lovingly at him, noting the new lines of stress around his tired brown eyes. 'Not half as tough as it has been on you. Oh, Court, I'm so proud of the way you've handled things.'

'Thanks. I'm rather proud of it myself.'

They clung together until the last boarding announcement was made. At the gate she turned and called: 'Remember — I love you.'

'I love you too,' he called after her. Two stewardesses standing at the gate smiled at each other. A party of Japanese late arrivals put down their briefcases and applauded. Courtney blushed. He watched Chantel out of sight, then left the terminal for the car that was waiting to take him back to the clinic.

He arrived in time to relieve Georgie at their father's bedside. The three of them had tacitly agreed that, security guard or no, one of them would always be at Dexter's side. The painkillers and sedatives Ferguson had prescribed left him largely comatose, but Camilla believed that even in sleep he drew comfort from their presence.

'Go and get some rest,' Courtney told his sister now. 'You look whacked.'

'Thanks! Just what a two-million-dollar model wants to hear before an appointment with one of her employers.'

'Shooting starts today?' he asked in concern. Worry and sleeplessness had taken their toll of Georgie's looks.

'No, but the account exec's over here apparently, and he suggested we should touch base. Maybe he just wants someone to be seen with while he's in town. Bit of a nuisance, actually. Guy's flying in tonight.'

'That's great!'

'Yes, it is, and much more than I deserve.'

She smiled, and for the first time in days he could see his sister's old mischievous sparkle. 'Look, don't come in tomorrow,' he said. 'I can do your session as well.'

'Oh no, Court, really. It wouldn't be fair.'

'It's okay, I want to. Father and I have spent so little time together these last few years. When he wakes up and is actually pleased to see me, it means a lot.'

She squeezed his shoulder. 'He never really stopped loving you, not deep down.'

'I think I'm just beginning to realise that.'

She bent and kissed Dexter's sleeping face. 'Take care of yourself, Daddy.'

'He doesn't need to,' said Courtney. 'He's got me now.'

It was quiet in the room, the traffic roar of central London muted by the double glazing. From time to time Courtney heard the rattle of a trolley in the corridor outside or busy footsteps brisk about their business. Inside the room, it was quiet enough to hear his father's gentle breathing. It was a good sign that he had not needed any assistance with that, apparently, but Courtney wondered if it was also significant that there seemed to be longer and longer intervals between his brief periods of wakefulness. Certainly he had shown no sign of regaining consciousness this afternoon.

Courtney looked out into the corridor. Instantly the cleaner checked him out, hands ready to discard the mop and reach for a gun. Courtney smiled at him, and at the nurse on duty at a desk at the far end of the corridor. 'I don't suppose you've got a book or a newspaper I could borrow?'

'Well, I shouldn't have ...' She looked up at him, and dimpled, producing a copy of the *Daily Express* from the bottom drawer of the desk.

'Thanks. I'll let you have it back in a while.'

'Oh, that's all right. Would you like me to get you a cup of tea or something?' she asked eagerly.

All the nurses on that floor thought that the Honourable Courtney Randolph was the dishiest thing on two legs, and so touchingly devoted to his father. Showed how wrong the gossip columns could be, making out they were at daggers drawn.

'That's terribly kind of you,' he said, and produced one of his most effective smiles. 'I don't suppose there's any chance of something to eat? I didn't have time to grab lunch, and it is rather a while till my mother's due to arrive.'

'I'll see what I can find,' she said purposefully. Even if it meant raiding Sister's fridge, it was worth it to make sure he was properly looked after.

When she came into Dexter's room a few minutes later, she was surprised to find Courtney making a phone call. Usually he was careful not to disturb his father in any way.

'Mr Maddigan,' he was saying. 'Yes, a conference delegate. He should be in the ballroom now ... Well, page him, for goodness' sake! This is an emergency.'

He smiled apologetically at the surprised nurse. 'Thanks for the tea — and a sandwich, too. You're an angel.' He made no move to touch either, drumming his fingers in agitation.

'I beg your pardon?' he said into the phone. 'Oh, you mean he's speaking at present. I see. Until when, do you know ...?' He glanced down at his wristwatch. 'Listen, will you do something for me, please? When Mr Maddigan's finished, will you pass him a message asking him to wait for my arrival ... My name? Oh — it's Courtney. Yes, Mr Courtney. I'll be with you in fifteen minutes. Thanks.'

He put down the receiver and glanced regretfully at the tea and sandwich. 'Nurse, you're going to think me terribly rude, but I have to go now. And, Nurse —' he leant over and kissed her quickly on the cheek — 'thank you very much.'

He dashed out of the room with a final glance at his sleeping father. The nurse shook her head, and took the tea and sandwich and the discarded newspaper back to her station. While she leafed through the *Express*, a headline caught her attention:

AUSSIE SUPER SURGEON
AIDS MIRACLE RECOVERY

There was a picture of a handsome dark-haired man crouching down beside a grinning five-year-old in rugger strip. The Australian surgeon had apparently performed a miraculous feat of microsurgery to restore the use of his legs to a little boy crippled in a road smash. The revolutionary techniques which the surgeon, Dane Maddigan, had used were to be the subject of a talk he was giving at a medical conference to be held at the Athenaeum Hotel that day, she saw, and smiled understandingly. Now she knew why Courtney had gone rushing off. She silently wished him luck. The Australian had already pulled off one miracle cure. It was going to take another to restore Dexter Randolph even to semi-mobility, but she didn't blame his family for clutching at straws.

Funny thing, though, she thought, absent-mindedly eating the sandwich, Dane Maddigan looked familiar, somehow . . .

Courtney was lucky to flag down a taxi just outside the Capital; not so lucky in the time it took them to crawl down Harley Street and cut through the congested hell of central London. Thrusting a £10-note at the surprised cabbie, he gave up on the traffic and began to run down Park Lane, cutting through to Piccadilly as soon as he was able. He arrived breathless at the Athenaeum fifteen minutes after the conference had closed.

'Mr Maddigan?' he gasped at the receptionist. 'I left a message for him to wait for me. The name's Courtney.'

The receptionist pointed to a table in the lobby, overlooking the congested double carriageway and Green Park beyond. 'He's over there, having a drink while he waits.'

'That's fantastic! Will you order two more of the same and have them sent over, please?'

691

He smiled when he saw the glass of beer on the table before the surgeon.

'G'day, thanks for waiting, Mr Maddigan.'

The other man got slowly to his feet. He was taller than Courtney, slim but strongly built. Against his deep tan, the glossy dark hair and dark blue eyes were startling. 'That's okay. I felt like a beer and some time to myself. If you want the truth, all this medical shop talk gives me a thirst.'

'I'm afraid this is more of the same,' said Courtney, waving to attract the attention of the waiter with their drinks who made a big deal of pouring the Fosters into two glasses and taking away the cans.

Maddigan looked after him in amusement. 'Probably thinks we'd drink it out of the tin if he left it.'

'I probably would,' laughed Courtney.

'So tell me what a fellow Australian is doing here,' asked Maddigan.

'Half Australian, actually.'

'Oh, "actually", I see that now.' Maddigan grinned good-humouredly. 'C'mon, spit it out. Your message sounded desperate.'

Courtney told him all: about his father's previous accident which had left him half-paralysed; the gunshot wound with the bullet still lodged perilously close to the spinal cord; the total paralysis which might or might not be temporary ... Finally he told Maddigan the family name. Ashley would be furious if he found out, but in Courtney's judgment Maddigan was a man to trust, even without the medical ethics.

There was something about his thin, strong-featured face, angled intently as Courtney told his story, that inspired confidence. He would be far from a soft touch, however. Courtney decided it would be worth the risk of giving the family name to prove to him that they were good for whatever fee he cared to ask for operating.

'It's not the money,' said the Australian, leaning back in his chair.

692

'What then? The challenge? I hope it's not publicity you look for — there couldn't be any in Father's case. It would finish Randolph Enterprises.'

'It's okay, relax. Have another beer, Courtney. I can call you that, can't I?'

'My friends call me Court.'

'And I'm Dane. Okay, I'll level with you. I've got more work on than I can handle right now. A six-month waiting list in Sydney; a year in New York, where I have a visiting professorship. Normally, when a patient or his family approaches me, I tell them to join the queue. It's not high-handedness, just fairness to the hundreds of other cases on my list.'

'But don't you see? We *can't* wait! My father's whole business will collapse unless we can get him fit enough to put in an appearance in Australia soon.'

Maddigan frowned. 'I do realise the problem, and for an exceptional man like Lord Randolph an exception can sometimes be made. I'm glad you told me your real name. As it happens, I know quite a bit about Randolph Enterprises. I come from Sydney, as you can probably tell. My own father worked as a clerk in the shipping division of your dad's business. He died when I was fifteen. I wanted to quit school and help support Mum. The company pension scheme paid out over the odds so that I wouldn't have to — my teachers got on to them, I think. Your father's company helped me through uni and med school. I've never forgotten. That's why, if I think he's strong enough, I'll operate on him.'

Courtney's radiant smile dissolved the worry from his face. He took Maddigan's hand and shook it. 'Thank God! And thank you, Dane Maddigan. I'll never forget this, never.'

'Hey, hold on a minute. I haven't even seen him yet.'

'You'll do it,' said Courtney simply. 'You have to. You're his last chance.'

They left the hotel together and caught a cab back to

the clinic. Despite Courtney's nervous impatience, Maddigan insisted on playing things by the book, refusing even to see Dexter until medical protocol had been observed and he had consulted Mr Ferguson who, fortunately, was expected in for his evening round. Courtney had feared that suggesting another surgeon operate on his father might be tricky. When he introduced Dane Maddigan, however, Ferguson's professional impassiveness gave way to relief.

'I don't know how you pulled this off, young man,' he said, 'but there's only one surgeon to whom I'd willingly relinquish this case. You've found him. Well done.

'Welcome to the Capital, Mr Maddigan. We've been hoping to attract you here for some years. I don't mind confiding,' he said quietly as Courtney hurried ahead of them to break the news to his mother, 'that the patient is giving some grounds for concern. If his condition's no better than it was on my earlier round . . .'

It had deteriorated since Courtney had last seen him. When they entered the small overheated room, Dexter's breathing sounded harsh and laboured, and his cheeks and eyes looked sunken.

Camilla sat beside her husband, talking bravely, though everyone else was sure he'd gone beyond hearing.

Courtney persuaded her to leave with him while the surgeons made their examination. Briefly he explained who Dane Maddigan was and his track record in similar cases requiring microsurgery. 'He's Australian, too. Pa would like that.'

'I don't care if he's a Martian,' snapped his normally mild-mannered mother, 'just so long as he *does* something! Oh, Court, he's slipping away from us. I can feel it.'

Maddigan joined them in the visitors' sitting-room. 'Lady Camilla, I'm pleased to meet you. With your permission, I'll be operating on your husband first thing tomorrow.'

'You have it, of course, but my husband's a very

independent-minded man. It'd come better from him.'

'I'm afraid that won't be possible,' he told her gently. 'Lord Randolph is unlikely to regain consciousness until after we operate.'

If all goes well, was the unspoken caveat.

She swayed dizzily. Before Courtney could reach her, Dane Maddigan steadied her. 'I won't beat about the bush. Lord Randolph's very sick. I can't promise he'll come through, but believe me, I'll have a damned good try at saving him.'

Maybe it was the fighting talk in the familiar Aussie accent, maybe the warmth of his strong, long-fingered hand on hers. Despite her dreadful fear of losing Dexter, Dane Maddigan's presence comforted Camilla. 'Thank you,' she said. 'I know you will.'

Courtney arranged for his mother to spend the night in a visitor's room. Then, glancing at his watch, he realised he was late for his evening call to Ashley. The phone at the other end was picked up on its first ring.

'Court, is that you? I was just about to go to the office. Everything okay that end?'

'Well — yes and no.'

'What's happening?'

'Dad's taken a turn for the worse, but he's in the best possible hands, I promise.'

Briefly Courtney outlined his tracking down of Dane Maddigan and his undertaking to operate the next day.

'I can't think straight right now.' Ash's voice was unsteady. 'But I want you to know, Court, you've done fantastically well persuading Maddigan. He's the best there is, quite a media star here. Did he tell you about himself? How he was so sick as a baby that they thought he'd die, and how he grew up determined to be a doctor and repay that debt.'

'No, he didn't mention it,' said Courtney, realising that his brother was running off at the mouth about Maddigan because he was so concerned their father might not make it.

'Look, I'll call you tomorrow just as soon as we know anything — that's early evening your time. Where will you be?'

'At the office, of course. Oh no, I just remembered. I agreed to go over to Luke's this evening. He's holding a drinks party for some visiting Poms — I think he's trying to shunt one of the Territories stations off on to them. I'm trying to keep up appearances, so I agreed to look in. I'll call you at the clinic at, say, eleven your time. I'd get out of the party, but I don't want to alert Luke and Chip. They've been acting pretty weird since I got back. I have this feeling they know Dad's sick. It's vital they don't find out how sick, or anything could happen.'

'Sure you can handle it?' Courtney was worried. He'd never heard his usually cool and efficient brother sound quite so off the wall.

'It's okay, I'll hack it. It's just — I feel so isolated out here. I can't trust the people I'm supposed to be working with, the Chimera deal's a bastard, and all the time I'm worried sick about Pa and unable to confide in anyone.'

'Hang in there, Ash. I'd put my money on Maddigan every time. By evening, things could look a whole lot brighter for you.'

'Yes, sure. Wish him good luck from me.'

'Will do. And don't worry. It's going to be all right.'

At the office, Ash should have been working on the Chimera contract. Dexter had proposed a generous price, but a complicated scheme of staged payments. The Chimera Group had asked for more time to go through these with their lawyers. Ash could see which terms would prove the sticking-points and was trying to formulate his counter-proposals in advance. He needed this deal, and he needed it fast.

It was no good. With his head full of thoughts of Dexter, he couldn't summon up the concentration. Instead, he took out the Bradbury Island accounts and settled down to a more routine task. When Luke and Chip had presented him with a final print-out a few days before, he had rejected it. He knew his uncle's computer wizardry too well to rely on that. Instead, he had demanded the original documentation: copies of Randolph Enterprises' specifications, tenders, letters of acceptance and all invoices for work in progress or completed.

One sentence from the conversation with Luke and Chip on the evening of his return had stuck in his mind. 'The contractor said he could do it for a million four. It ended up costing us double.' Luke had been so confident of disarming Ashley by apparently coming clean that he'd over-reached himself. Ash had recently read in one of the property magazines about an Olympic size pool constructed by a town in Western Australia. The article had given its finished cost as just over a million. Even allowing for local price differences and the cost of shipping raw materials over to Bradbury, nearly three million for a much smaller pool was an incredible difference. Incompetent though Chip undoubtedly was, Ash doubted that even he would have allowed a contractor to overrun his original estimate by that much — unless he was cut in for a considerable part of the action.

Ash paid special attention to the pool file. One interesting point emerged. On the original letter from the contractors, Funswim, arranging a site inspection, the printed company notepaper listed the directors' names. It was a small family affair from the look of it; every director had the surname Haughton. Strange then that after the initial tender and the letter of confirmation, the rest of the correspondence from Funswim appeared on paper without the name of its directors. The correspondence continued to issue from Funswim's Cairns address, continued to be signed by Tim Haughton, Managing Director. But that change to the paper . . .

Looking thoughtful, Ash slid the original documentation

back into its file. Funswim would definitely bear some more checking out. He opened the bottom drawer of his desk to store the papers near at hand. There was a knock at the door, and Luke strolled in, uninvited.

'What's this?' he said jovially, eyes scanning Ash's desk. 'Can't have you slogging away all night. You haven't forgotten the party, have you?'

'No, I haven't forgotten.' Ash tried surreptitiously to close the desk drawer without drawing Luke's attention to the file within, flagged yellow for Bradbury Island.

'Good man,' said Luke heartily. 'Are you going home first, or do you want a lift? Better not to take your car, maybe. It's going to be quite a shindig.'

'That's okay, Luke. I'll drive myself, thanks. I can't stay long in any case.'

'Oh, why's that, then? Some little bit of fluff warming the sheets for you?'

His uncle's words were genial, but Ashley could see the joshing manner was assumed. 'Pressure of work. This Bradbury project's taking a lot of unravelling.'

He had the satisfaction of seeing his uncle's broken-veined face turn an angrier shade of red, but his voice was as pleasant as ever. 'See you later, then. I can't wait for you to meet Chip's new girl. She's a Pom, and titled too. Anything Dexter can do, eh?'

After his uncle had gone, Ash glanced at his watch. Just after six. In under an hour, his father would be on the operating table. He sorted out a few things to take home with him for the night. He didn't think he'd be able to concentrate on work, but as he sat up they'd give him the illusion of doing something useful. He thought for a moment, then added the Funswim file to the work in his briefcase. There was nothing much he could do with it that evening without access to Companies Records, but he had the feeling it would be safer with him.

Sure enough, when he emerged from his office, his uncle and Chip were still in Luke's room. Waiting for him to leave, thought Ash. Well, if they were intending to remove the Funswim file, they'd find the cupboard bare.

Dane Maddigan glanced up at the Theatre Sister. Though his head moved, his hands were rock steady, poised above their delicate task. She mopped the sweat off his high forehead with a wad of cotton, quickly discarded in the sterile waste bin.

Ferguson glanced at his watch. Two hours ... So far, the operation had gone absolutely by the book. The Australian surgeon had removed the bullet, repairing the damage to three sides of the wound. All textbook stuff. So why the delay before tackling the last stage?

'How much longer can we keep him under?' Maddigan asked the anaesthetist.

'He's had five hours. I can't vouch for him for more than another thirty minutes.'

'I need an hour, damn it. Christ, I thought you Poms were supposed to know your stuff.'

Out of the operating theatre, Maddigan was a commanding but relatively affable figure. Inside, he was formidable.

The anaesthetist gulped. 'I'll see what I can do.'

Mr Ferguson caught Dane Maddigan's eye. 'Is this really necessary? From where I'm standing, the operation looks like a success.'

'Oh, really? Take a look at this.'

Ferguson bent over the screen, which magnified the minute area of damaged tissue on which Maddigan was working. The normally suave consultant had never been heard to swear in theatre. 'Bloody hell!' he said now.

Maddigan nodded. 'That's why I need the extra hour. Better get a message to the relatives. The poor buggers'll be climbing the walls out there. Tell them another hour should do it, one way or the other.'

Ash returned to his house in Paddington to change for the party. He glanced at his watch and phoned his answering service just in case Court had phoned early while he was en route. There was nothing. Might as well make his duty appearance and get it over. He drove to Double Bay, cursing the evening traffic.

It was a fine night, so he knew that drinks and canapés would be served around the pool of the imposing property with its view of the Harbour. Luke's party was very well attended, he saw, and slightly wondered. Though successful businessmen were Australia's aristocracy, there was a strong compulsion to gloat over any fall from grace. The reputations of tall poppies, men who made their mark then overstepped it, were gleefully cut down. Ash had always supposed the same went for their associates, but judging from the crowd of tycoons and politicians from Queensland and New South Wales, no opprobrium had attached itself to Lucas Randolph.

The same could not be said for himself, he saw, noting with amusement the lengths former good friends of his father went to avoid catching his eye. The brashest simply stared through him. Even the Queensland mates, though they nodded affably, seemed disinclined to chew the cud with him. Yet, strangely, they'd all accepted the invitation of Lucas Randolph and his wife.

Aunt Lucinda was, as usual, all in a dither, hurrying between her guests with a harried expression on her face. The transition from outback to town living had not suited her. Raised in the slow and steady rhythm of farm life, she was like a fish out of water among her husband's powerful new friends. And yet she had been one of the guiding forces behind his successful management of Yelonga in earlier days, Ash had heard. He'd never have guessed it to look at her now, a brittle faded woman with anxious grey eyes and the nervous fluttering movements of a bird.

She greeted him with a distracted peck on the cheek.

'Ash, I didn't think you'd come ... I mean, naturally it's lovely to see you.'

Her husband waved to her, frowning. With a hurried, 'Please excuse me,' she left her nephew.

Rhianne's welcome at least was warm. A pretty bouncy girl who had inherited her father's dark eyes and curling chestnut hair, she beamed with pleasure when she saw her good-looking cousin. 'Ash, this is great! Mum and I didn't think you'd come, with uncle being so ill and all.'

Ash's surprise showed, but he managed to cover up its cause. 'My father's not ill, Rhianne, just a little run down. It's really nothing to worry about.' So trivial, in fact, that at that very minute Dexter Randolph was on an operating table, but Ash was not going to acknowledge that, even to his most congenial Australian relative.

She looked puzzled. 'Funny, I got the impression from hearing Dad and Chip talk that Uncle Dexter was pretty crook. When I wanted to ask them about it, Mum stopped me.'

Guesswork on his uncle's part? Luke wondered. Or something else ...

'Anyway, I'm glad Uncle's okay, 'cos that means you'll have lots of free time to spend with me! Hey, do you think we could use the Palm Beach house one weekend? Chip's got this amazing new girlfriend.'

'So I've heard. Where is she?'

Rhianne was a small girl. She peered through the crowd for a moment, then gave up. 'Here, somewhere. Oh, look, that's her father talking to Dad.'

She pointed towards a tall distinguished-looking man with wings of grey hair brushed neatly away from his forehead. The soldierly bearing and aristocratic profile were unmistakable.

'Catch up with you later, Rhianne. I've just seen an old friend,' said Ash happily. He made his way towards his uncle Luke and the English guest — though prey might have been a better word.

701

Lucas was smiling like a shark. 'I promise you, James, it's prime land. The very best. Ah, Ash, allow me to introduce you.'

'We're old acquaintances, in fact. James, how are you?' Ashley shook hands with James Melville, Marquis of Cunningham.

'My dear boy, how very good to see you. I knew of the family connection, of course, but hadn't realised you were out here. Kara and I are looking for an Australian property. Your uncle's been praising one of yours to the skies — can't think why he wants to sell it if it's so good, what?'

'And which one would that be?' Ashley directed the question at Luke, who did not reply.

'Ma — something or other. You must forgive me. I haven't got the hang of these outlandish names yet.'

Ash nearly choked on his drink. Luke was offering Maroonda? How dared he! For sentimental reasons, Dexter would never allow it to be sold off. For one thing, it had been his first independent purchase; for another, at least until the news of Wally's death, he had always considered that ten per cent of it was held in trust for the old aborigine and his descendants. Ash did not intend to cause a scene at Lucas's own party, but this was another bone he had to pick with his uncle.

'. . . been to Hawaii to inspect the farms there,' James Melville was continuing, blithely unaware. 'Kara's done so well with them, and with the ranch in Texas, we're thinking of branching out.'

'As I said, James,' Luke was at his most ingratiating, 'anything Chip or I can do to help.'

'That's terribly kind of you, old man. Look, you mustn't allow me to keep you from your other guests. I've been meaning to have a word with Ashley here about my nominations . . .'

Luke took the hint and left them. They passed a pleasant few minutes discussing Northern Territory, the ten-year-old bay who 'stood' at the Courtney stud, which Ash had persuaded his father to buy. He was now the most sought-after stallion in Europe and James Melville, a keen racehorse owner and Jockey Club steward, had bred a few likely foals from him, and one was about to make his debut as a two-year-old.

Until his father's hunting accident, horses and racing had been Ash's primary love. Though he still retained a very active interest, his long absences in Australia meant that, regretfully, he was forced to take a back seat in the affairs of the stud these days.

'It's very fortunate running into you like this. I don't think you've ever met my daughter, have you?'

'No, she was living in the States the last time we talked. Oh, good evening, Chip.'

His dark saturnine cousin appeared beside them, dogging the heels of a ravishing blonde who smiled and held out her hand in greeting. Her startling turquoise eyes exactly matched the heavy Navaho silver and turquoise belt she was wearing with her tailored white shorts and white silk shirt.

'Ashley, allow me to introduce Kara. Your cousin's been taking very good care of her since we arrived.'

Ash wasn't surprised. She was a genuine Grade A stunner. Maybe he'd misjudged Luke. Maybe the sales talk on Maroonda was just a blind, a talking-point to bring Kara and Chip together. Though his uncle liked to scoff at Dexter for marrying into the British nobility, Ash knew how very much he'd like his son to do the same. Girls and their pursuit were the last things on Ash's mind at the moment, but part of him would have liked nothing more than to give Chip Randolph a run for his money.

'I don't think we've met before, have we?' she said in her attractively husky voice.

'No, I don't think so. I mean, I'm sure I'd remember if we had. Your father mentioned you'd been working abroad.'

She laughed. 'Don't make me sound like an au pair! I manage his land interests. We're thinking of expanding in this direction. Chip's been dutifully giving me the hard sell on one of your properties in the Territory, but it's Queensland that interests me most. I'm planning to fly up there once Daddy's safely on his way.'

'Then you've got to visit the new resort,' said Chip forcefully. 'The main part's still under construction, but there are a few top-class suites ready —' this was news to Ash — 'and the diving's out of this world. I could take you over, show you around.'

Kara smiled coolly. 'Thank you very much. I'll certainly bear it in mind for when I've finished my business trip. What I'd really like is to talk to the Randolph Enterprises' cattle expert.'

'That's Dad. I'll get him for you.' Chip obligingly went in pursuit of his father.

'Actually, I know quite a bit about the cattle operation,' Ash heard himself offer.

She smiled warmly. 'I was hoping you'd say that.' She turned to her father. 'Why don't you go and talk to our hostess, Daddy? She's looking rather lost.'

'I know when to make myself scarce, don't worry.' Waving his glass at them, he made off after Lucinda.

'Don't get me wrong,' said Kara, as she guided them purposefully towards two low chairs, 'I'm grateful for your cousin's help on business matters. The private side's something else. He will not leave me alone! Keeps wanting me to go with him to places called The Pink Pussycat and Moby Dick's. Have you heard of them?'

'I have, but I wouldn't take you there.'

'Really? Where would you take me, just as a matter of interest?'

'Up the Hawksbury in a plane for lunch at a little place I know. Nothing fancy, not the foodies' paradise — somehow, I don't think that's your scene. Or maybe to my father's house on Palm Beach. And if I had time, I'd take you to the family's original property, Yelonga. The old house is still there, slab walls, tin roof, the lot, though naturally we've built a fair bit round it now. It's a two-hour drive away from our nearest neighbours — that's in good conditions, that is. No phone half the time. No distractions at all.'

Kara's smile transformed her into a daredevil tomboy. 'Sound's great! When can we go?'

'Are you normally this direct?'

'When I want something, yes.'

'What do you want, though? Me or my property?'

'Take me there, and we'll see,' she said in a vamp's voice. 'Seriously though, Ash, I'd very much like to visit a working cattle station, and Yelonga's a model of its kind, so I've heard. Is there any chance you could fix to show me around?'

He looked at her regretfully. Normally he'd jump at the chance to spend a weekend on the Randolph Enterprises' showpiece with a pretty girl, but with so much else going on here and in London ... He glanced guiltily at his watch. In a quarter of an hour he should be calling Courtney. There was no way he wanted to do it from Luke's house.

'Look,' he began awkwardly, 'you're going to think me terribly rude, but I have to go now. Business,' he explained, seeing her hurt expression. 'I've enjoyed talking to you and I'd like to show you around, but it's kind of a bad time for Randolph Enterprises at present.'

She looked surprised. 'Chip doesn't seem too concerned.'

'He wouldn't! Kara, give me your phone-number. I'll try and get back to you.'

'I'm at the Sebel Townhouse for next week at least. But it's okay, really. I wouldn't want to impose.'

Damn! The first girl who'd really interested him in a long while, and he was handling it clumsily. 'I'd very much like to see you again. I'll call, I promise.'

She smiled again. 'You'd better! Another week of your

705

cousin is more than any girl should have to bear! Oh no, here he comes.'

Chip threaded carefully through the partygoers towards them, carefully carrying a frothy pink drink garlanded with fruit and fancy straws. Kara looked down at the whisky and soda in her hand, and smiled ruefully at Ash. Chip didn't seem pleased to see them still together. Ash got to his feet. 'Have to go, I'm afraid.'

'Yeah. Wouldn't want to keep you,' Chip smirked.

With a smile for Kara, Ash left them. He was running a little late, but there was no saying his father's operation would be over yet. If he pulled out all the stops on the way back to Paddo . . .

His Aunt Lucinda hurried after him as he walked down the side of the house. She looked nervously over her shoulder. 'When you speak to your family, Ash, my very best wishes to them all, particularly your father. He's in my prayers, tell him.'

There were tears in her eyes, he noticed. 'Yes, of course. But, Aunt Lucinda . . .'

He was about to ask what she and Rhianne knew of Dexter's illness. From her manner, it was obvious she knew how sick he was, and yet neither Luke nor Chip had mentioned it to him, let alone passed on any good wishes for his recovery.

'Lucy! Where the hell's the woman hiding?'

'Coming, Luke. Go now,' she said urgently to Ash. 'He mustn't see us talking together.'

She almost pushed him round the side of the house, out of view of his uncle who came charging down to find her. 'Lucinda, we're running out of ice here. Can't you keep your servants under better control than this, you silly bitch?'

Quite a different face from the affable party-giver of earlier, Ash reflected. But quite probably the one Lucinda saw every day.

★

706

Ash jumped lights and broke speed limits on his way home — only to be told by Courtney that their father was still in the theatre. Ash told him to ring as soon as there was news, and spent the next few hours cooling his heels before the phone rang.

'Ash, it's okay! He's come through. Mums is with him now in the recovery room. Georgie and I are going off for a rest. No one got any sleep last night.'

'They got the bullet out?'

'Yes, that part of the operation is a success, and they're pretty sure he'll have regained the mobility he had before the shooting. We won't know for sure until he comes out of the anaesthetic, of course.'

'Thank God! And, Court, you will keep up the security, won't you? If whoever tried hears this . . .'

'Of course. Anything in particular worrying you?'

'Nothing concrete — only Uncle Luke and the family seem to know everything that's going on in London. I haven't said a word, but Aunt Lucinda and Rhianne seem to know Dad's seriously ill, while Chip and Luke haven't mentioned it directly to me.'

'I don't think you need worry too much. They thought he was coming back with you this time, didn't they? They know how he hates changing plans. When he didn't show, they probably worked out for themselves that it had to be something pretty serious. Luke and Chip are probably pissed off with you for not taking them into your confidence.'

'Yeah — I suppose you could be right. I'll be here for the next ten hours, Court. Call me as soon as there's any news.'

'I promise. Try and get some rest, though. When Dad's back in action, the first thing he'll want to go through is this big new deal.'

'I can't wait. It'll be great to have him breathing down my neck again.'

But the news later that night was not so good. Camilla

707

rang twice to say that though Dexter had come out of the anaesthetic and was talking to her and the nursing staff, there had as yet been absolutely no sign of movement.

She was alarmed when a nurse called her away from the bedside for a conference with Dane Maddigan. 'Before I examine him,' said the surgeon, 'I want you to tell me how he's been behaving.'

'He's quite lucid, he's talked to me a little, moved his head when I gave him a drink. But that's all. It hasn't failed, has it?'

'Lady Camilla, I don't know — which is why you and I are going to have to play a little trick on him. Believe me, it's being cruel to be kind. Don't be surprised at anything I say.'

He followed Camilla into the intensive care cubicle. Dexter had a much better colour, Dane noted, and his breathing was unimpeded. He watched the way the patient moved his head on the pillow to follow his wife's progress around the bed.

'I'm sorry to have to run out on you,' said Dane, 'but I'm afraid I've been called to New York — emergency case. G'bye, Lord Randolph. There's no point in my staying any longer.' He stuck out his hand.

'But you can't leave us now!' cried Camilla in a panic, forgetting what Maddigan had said. She was half out of her seat at Dexter's side, ready to plead her case more forcefully, when she realised what was happening.

Slowly, as if pressed down by an invisible weight, Dexter's hand was being lifted off the coverlet to shake Dane Maddigan's.

'You did it!' she cried in delight, and ran to the door to call Courtney and Georgie, who had arrived for Maddigan's morning round.

With his family clustered around him, all talking and congratulating him at once, it was a while before Dexter could make himself heard. 'That was a mean trick, Maddigan. You're not really walking out on me yet, are you?'

'Not today, anyway, but I will have to leave soon. At least we know you're on the road to recovery.' He smiled apologetically at Camilla. 'I did warn you that sometimes we surgeons have to be a little devious. After a make or break piece of surgery like this, sometimes the patient's too keyed up to put our work to the test.'

'I notice you tactfully don't say "too damn' scared",' growled Dexter.

'It's not a question of being afraid. It's the difference between being able to live a life or merely endure it. I'm sorry to have to chuck you all out again, but do the rest of you think you could leave me alone with Lord Randolph for a minute? I haven't examined him yet.'

Courtney went off to phone Ash. Georgie and Camilla sat in the waiting-room, hugging each other for joy.

'Name any fee you like,' said Dexter as Maddigan was testing the reflexes of his upper body.

'Give it to charity,' said the younger man carelessly. 'I've already told your son — there's a connection between us. You won't remember him, I don't suppose, but my old man once worked for you. Randolph Enterprises was more than fair when Dad died. Reckon I owe you this in his memory.'

'And I owe you my thanks, and anything I can do for you in the future. Anything at all, Maddigan. Just call me.'

'The very best thanks you could give me would be to walk again,' said the surgeon, folding the sheet away from Dexter's feet so that he could prod them.

'But — what are you doing? I don't understand. I'm still paralysed from the waist down, aren't I? They told me when I had the accident that nothing could be done.'

'Nothing could be done — then. New techniques in surgery are discovered all the time, you know. While I was patching up the bullet wound, I did a little bit more repair work . . . Feel that?'

Dexter screwed up his face and concentrated. 'I don't think so . . . I don't know. I've forgotten what feet feel like!'

Maddigan looked at him seriously. 'It's early days yet, and don't get your hopes too high, but when we let the physios loose on you, they'll be tackling your legs as well as the upper body. I didn't want to say anything in front of your family. Sometimes it can be tougher on them even than the patient, hoping for a miracle which doesn't happen. I reckoned you were tough enough to take it, Lord Randolph.'

Dexter could not look at him for a moment. When he spoke, emotion thickened his voice. 'You're quite a man, Dane Maddigan. If you pull this off, I promise you I'll build a whole bloody hospital just for you! Try and stop me!'

'I've done my job. The rest is up to you. Don't force it, but stay hopeful.'

'Thanks, doc, for everything. Oh, before you go — your dad. Wasn't he the little red-headed chap with a pair of specs on him so thick it was like looking into a goldfish bowl? We used to call him Hawkeye.'

Dane Maddigan's grin was one of his most attractive features. 'You've got him! Glad to hear you haven't forgotten the old rip. See you later.'

Dexter settled back on his pillows, remembering. He had a clear mental picture of Bert Maddigan now. Better than that, he could remember dancing with his wife, Olive, at a company dinner dance some time. Little wispy blonde thing ... Funny, neither of them resembled in the slightest their tall bold-faced son.

With the news from England so encouraging, Ash felt free to push full steam ahead with Chimera. It took up the lion's share of his time, so much so that he pushed the Bradbury detective business to one side. In his joy at his father's recovery, he couldn't feel too vindictive towards Lucas and Chip. Let Dexter decide what to do about it all when he was well enough to travel to Australia. And then there was Kara.

He had called her at the hotel and made time to meet her there for a drink. She was just as gorgeous as he remembered, more deeply tanned with just the sort of open outdoor good looks that appealed to him in a woman. She was just as beset by Chip, he gathered.

'The oaf won't take no for an answer! And your uncle's still pushing this Maroonda place, though I've told him time and again it's a Queensland station I want. Your uncle and cousin are like a lot of men. They think if a woman says no, she wants coaxing into saying Yes. Well, they're in for a rude shock, both of them.'

'Good on you!'

She looked askance. 'Shouldn't you be pushing Maroonda, too?'

'Don't see why, when my father'd skin whoever parted with it.'

'You don't see eye to eye with Luke and Chip, do you?'

'You could put it that way.'

'Look, maybe I'm talking out of turn here, but I think you ought to know that they've been saying — not just to me, but all over town. This body that was found on your father's home station ... Luke's let it be known that he has it on good authority the evidence against your father is pretty damning. After the inquest, the Queensland police will have no choice but to charge him with murder, Luke says, and when that happens he intends to step in and run Randolph Enterprises.'

Ash was inwardly seething. No wonder he'd got the cold shoulder at his uncle's party! Financial failure was one thing, but a murder charge was something even the Queenslanders would find it hard to overlook. 'I can't think why Luke's letting the whole thing rattle him so badly.' He tried to laugh it off. 'As soon as my father gets out here, they'll drop the whole business like a hot potatoe.'

'Do you know when that will be?'

'Oh, any time now. But why don't we talk about you? Are you going to be here for long?'

She lowered long silken eyelashes. 'I could be, if I thought it might be worth my while. Daddy owes me a sabbatical, and I like it here. Who knows? You might even decide to show me Yelonga. I know it's not for sale, but one day we could be neighbours.'

'You never give up, do you? All right, we'll make a deal. If you can hang on in Sydney a little longer, I should have some free time at the end of next week.' The Chimera board had asked for a grace period to consider some of the terms of Dexter's financial arrangements and Ash felt he could afford to relax for a few days then.

'Great! I've been reading up about it. Can we go heli-mustering?'

'If one of the pilots is on duty, why not?'

'We don't need one. I can fly a helicopter.'

And ride a motocross bike, he discovered to his amazement. Kara joined in with the stockmen, helping to round up the most stubborn bulls in the outlying paddocks, chivvying them from the seat of a motorbike. It was one of Yelonga's most popular Sunday pastimes, and she took to it like a duck to water. There was no mustering going on that weekend, but he allowed her to fly the station's own old Bell 47, swooping low over the wispy tops of the eucalypts; soaring over high outcrops of red basalt. He was privately glad that the heli-musterers with their superior helicopters were not around. They were a wild mob at the best of times, and with a girl to show off to, the sort of girl who'd think nothing of trying a stunt like swooping down to ground level and opening a gate with one hand while she worked the controls with the other ... He shuddered to think of it.

He was more pleased to discover that she shared his love of horses, confidently mounting one of the quarterhorses which Dexter and he had introduced some years before.

'I rode them in Texas,' she explained.

He shouldn't be surprised, he realised. Kara was a natural athlete as well as an astute businesswoman. In a few days on the station she had pumped him dry on information about the land and the future for the cattle industry.

On their final evening, the manager and his wife had arranged to visit friends on a neighbouring station. Ash and Kara ate some of the cold roast beef — like none she had ever tasted before — and salad left for them, and sat out under the stars, drinking beer and talking like old friends. At midnight, she decided she wanted to swim in the billabong beside the house.

'I don't know,' said Ash doubtfully.

'Oh, come on! Just a dip. Something to remember when I'm back in England, reporting to Daddy on why I haven't bought the perfect station.'

'Why's that?'

'Because you won't sell it to me, of course.'

'Are you going soon?'

She looked at him. 'I don't seem to be getting very far here, do I?'

He took her hand. 'Look, this is difficult for me.'

'Do you mean there's someone else, Ash? Because if there is, just say so and I won't stick around.'

'There's no one, I promise. In fact, you're everything I admire in a woman. I haven't had as much fun in ages.'

'It's not over yet! Coming for that swim?'

'Shouldn't we get our bathers from the house?'

'Ash, it's pitch dark out here! I don't think we'll need them.'

But not so dark that he couldn't appreciate every line of her taut body, which managed to be slender yet voluptuous at the same time. She stood at the water's edge, clothed in nothing but starlight, and made no attempt to hide herself. He shrugged off his own clothes except the boxer shorts he hoped would conceal his instant response to her.

She dipped one toe in the ink-black water, and hesitated.

'You are the loveliest thing,' he said. 'Do you really want to swim?'

She showed the first hint of uncertainty he'd seen since they met. 'Actually, no. Swimming in the dark is the one thing I'm a bit of a coward about.'

'Then why — ?'

'I couldn't think how else I was going to get your clothes off. Now I suppose you'll think me a shameless hussy?'

'A very beautiful shameless hussy! Come here, and I'll prove it to you.'

For the rest of the night he made slow tender love to her, on a bed of leaves, under the stars. The manager's wife, drawing her curtains at five-thirty the next morning, saw them sneaking back into the house and their separate bedrooms.

After breakfast, a Randolph Enterprises plane called to collect them. It would be impossible to talk in front of the pilot, Kara knew. Just before they boarded, she took Ash aside. 'I don't have to go back to England for quite a time. Only, I've grown rather tired of living at the hotel.'

'You could live with me in Paddo,' he said slowly, knowing he was committing himself to rather more than it sounded like. 'But if things get rough with Chimera, you might not see very much of me.'

She threw her arms round his neck and kissed him. 'Thank you, Ash! Just so long as you come home occasionally, I won't nag, I promise. But something else is going on, isn't it? I wish you'd tell me what. Maybe I could help.'

'Sweetheart, I wish I could, but there's too much at stake right now. As soon as I can, I promise.'

She saw she'd have to be content with that, for the moment. To the pilot's disgust, young Mr Randolph made the journey hand in hand with his sheila. Catch ld Dexter being so soft!

Dexter and Camilla were holding hands and kissing when Court called in to see his father. His mother blushed and tried to spring away, but Dexter laughed and pulled her down on the bed beside him.

'It's okay, Camilla. I think he knows we're married.'

Dexter was making such good progress that the hospital had transferred him to a room which was more like hotel accommodation than anything else. No sign of the intensive care apparatus now. Dexter looked fit and raring to go. 'Georgie coming?' he asked his son.

'I don't know. She wasn't at the house this morning. Wonder what she's up to?'

He was answered when his sister appeared, clutching a bottle of champagne in one hand and Guy's arm in the other. 'Look who else has come to see you, Daddy. You met once before at Chester Square, remember?'

Dexter didn't. His daughter had attracted hordes of young men over the years, but he knew this one was very special. He also respected the steps Guy had taken when the scurrilous pictures of Georgie were published. Though Dexter had known little about it at the time, Camilla had later told him how impressed she'd been with Guy. He flew over to be photographed with Georgie, and told the press, who'd been waiting for a bust-up, how much he admired and respected her.

Looking at them together, Dexter could see it was rather more than that. 'Glad to see you brought some champagne,' he said, 'because I've had some goods news today. The hospital's so sick of me they say I can go home for Christmas — with a couple of nurses and that sadist of a physio in attendance.'

'That's terrific, Pa, but when you say "home" ...'

Dexter looked at his son, indicating he needn't say any more. When he was well enough to appreciate the security provisions Court had made for him, he'd been pleased and impressed. With the police confessing themselves baffled still as to who exactly had shot him, Dexter knew they could not afford to take chances.

'I meant Gilmour. Angel's up there now, seeing to things. All being well, your mother and I should be up there next week.'

'Oh, Daddy, that's wonderful. Now we've got three things to celebrate!' said Georgie.

Dexter looked puzzled. 'Well, I'm one.' He looked at Guy, and smiled. 'I think I've guessed what two is. But number three?'

'I've been dropped from the Sarong campaign. Isn't it marvellous?'

Her father looked mystified. 'If you can call dropping two million dollars as well "marvellous", I suppose so.'

'I thought you wanted the job, Georgie,' said her mother. 'It is the ultimate accolade in modelling terms, having a campaign built around you.'

She wrinkled her nose. 'I know, but at the moment it would just get in the way. Anyway, the stuffy old things said Christian's pictures broke the morals clause. I really don't mind at all.'

She smiled lovingly up at Guy, who kissed her on the cheek before announcing solemnly, 'Georgie has just agreed to be my wife. If you have no objections, sir?'

'Take her.' Dexter waved his hand. 'Penniless, reputation torn to shreds — what good is she to me?'

The rest of the family laughed, while Guy looked mystified.

'Now I know you're better!' said Georgie. 'It's okay, Guy. Australian humour. You'll get used to it.'

Court chased up some glasses and they drank the champagne — only a taste for Dexter, to his disgust.

'What about you?' he asked Court. 'You've been a tower of strength, don't think I haven't appreciated that, but isn't there someone waiting to see you? I seem to remember you and that little girl of yours were due to visit her family. What was their name again? Something foreign.'

'Von Stolsenberg, though Chantel's mother's Australian, it turns out.'

'I *knew* I liked that girl. Well, what are you waiting for? Book yourself a flight for after Christmas and get over there. Your mother and I want some time alone together, damn it!'

716

Chantel met Court with a car at John F. Kennedy Airport. They drove to the Fifth Avenue apartment, and spent the rest of the day and all night being reunited.

'When do I get to meet your mother?' asked Court sleepily the next morning. 'She isn't here, is she? Not much of an introduction seeing your future son-in-law stagger blearily off a plane and lock himself in a bedroom with your daughter.'

Chantel giggled. 'It's okay. She's not hiding in a closet waiting to denounce you as a seducer. Mom's cool. She thought we might like some time alone together. We're invited to the New Jersey house for the weekend at least. Does that suit you?'

He pulled a horrified face. 'Does that mean I'm going to have to keep this up for the next three days?'

'Keep what up?' she asked innocently, and giggled again when he showed her.

The next three days were the very best he could remember spending with Chantel. Free from worry, he was able to enjoy himself unreservedly. They visited an exhibition at the Metropolitan Museum, found time to try out a few new clubs and cafés, but most of their time was spent in the apartment, and most of that in the bedroom. They gave the maid a holiday and stayed in bed, watching endless re-runs of old movies on television and dialling out for food when they got hungry. They picnicked on the king-size bed that had become their world.

On their last night in New York Court watched Chantel as she sat cross-legged at the foot of the bed, huddled in his dressing-gown and trying not to let him see the streams of sentimental tears as she watched *Now, Voyager*.

'Chantel — do you like Vietnamese pancake rolls?'

'Mmmm ... Sure.'

'Oh, good. I just dropped one on your side of the bed.'

'Okay ... *What*! Oh, you slob!' Tears forgotten, she growled in mock fury and started to tickle him in revenge.

'Joke, joke! Can't you take a joke?'

'I can see I'm going to have to learn, spending the rest of my life with a joker like you.' Her face looked suddenly serious again. 'Oh, Court, it will be all right, won't it? I do wish we'd come clean with Mom and Dad from the beginning.'

'I know you do, and I'm sorry. Maybe I'm not such a good catch.'

'Don't say that! I love you, Court. I'm never so happy as when I'm with you. The last few days have been like heaven.'

'For me too, darling. Just hang on to that, and we'll wing it tomorrow, you'll see.'

The von Stolsenburgs' Rolls-Royce took Court and Chantel to Coopers's Hollow, their house and 2,000-acre estate in northern New Jersey. The house itself was low and white, with a graceful veranda to the front and two sides, commanding views of lush rolling paddocks where horses grazed peacefully. There were lavish stables to the back of the house. Obviously a horsy household. Court approved.

'I'll show you round properly later,' said Chantel, 'but Mom will kill me if I don't take you in to meet her straight away. It's a shame Dad isn't back from Europe, but we're expecting him in a day or two.'

A dignified English butler showed them through to a charming small sitting-room decorated in the pastel colours and French Provincial furniture which had characterised the Fifth Avenue apartment. There was no sign of the Baroness.

'Typical!' said Chantel. 'Mom, we're home. Where are you?'

The double doors at the far end of the room burst open. 'Darlings! I didn't hear the car.' The warmth of the Baroness von Stolsenburg's greeting was disarming. She hugged them both impartially, then stood back from Court and frankly appraised him. 'Great to meet you at last. Chantel told me you were good-looking. I guess she gets her good taste in men from me!'

Court smiled and kissed her hand. Wasn't that what you were supposed to do with the European aristocracy? Then, when he looked at her, he remembered she was Australian. Funny, but despite her years in America and marriage to a European, she looked it still, with her abundant grey-streaked tawny hair and ocean-blue eyes.

'Now we'll sit down and I'll ring for tea,' she was saying, 'and you can tell me everything about yourself. Chantel's been so tight-lipped. I can't imagine why. I don't even know how you two met. Was it at the Sorbonne?'

'I'm afraid not, Baroness.'

'Linita, please. And do I call you Charles, or Chuck as the Americans prefer?'

'Neither. You see, it isn't my real name.'

Linita looked at her daughter. 'But I don't understand ... You said your boyfriend's name was Charles Hamilton.'

'Chantel, let me explain,' said Court. 'None of this is your daughter's doing,' he told Linita earnestly. 'You asked how we first met. Well, it was through my sister Georgie. She was living in the same hotel as Chantel. They palled up, and one day Georgie brought Chantel along to visit me.'

'I'm afraid I still don't understand.' She frowned. 'You sound as though you were sick or something. Heavens, don't tell me you were in jail!'

There was an awkward silence. Chantel slipped her hand into Court's and he plunged on: 'I was in a private clinic, the Malmaison, being treated for drug abuse. My father takes a very firm line on that sort of thing. He's a self-made man, Australian like yourself. I'm afraid it wasn't the first time I'd been treated — though it will definitely be the last,' he hastened to reassure her. 'My mother and sister knew that if he got to hear I'd started on drugs again, he'd disown me. They had me admitted under a family name — Hamilton — but it's not my own.'

Linita seemed almost to have stopped breathing. 'And that is?' she said.

'My name is Courtney Randolph. My father's Dexter Randolph. Maybe you've heard of him?'

'I think she took it rather well,' Court said, when he and Chantel had been shown upstairs after tea.

Chantel was looking worried. 'She didn't give you a hard time, it's true, but I don't know ... There was definitely something.'

'Well, yes, I must admit I didn't feel it was the time to ask for your hand in marriage,' he admitted. 'We'll wait till your father gets back for that, shall we?'

'Don't feel bad, Court. I'm pleased it's all out in the open, and when she's had time to come to terms with it, Mom will be, too. She's very fair-minded about things usually. If you don't mind, maybe I'll stop by her room before dinner? Have a talk while she finishes dressing. We often do that.'

In her bedroom, Linita's hands were shaking so badly she couldn't manage to dial Wolfie direct in Munich. She rang downstairs and asked Simpson the butler to send up some brandy.

He was surprised. The mistress rarely drank, and never spirits. She must have had a shock. 'Two fingers, madam, or three?'

'The whole goddamned bottle! I need a drink.'

She felt a little calmer after her first generous measure. Chantel's appearance, a few minutes later, started her heart racing again.

'Mom, what is it?' asked Chantel. 'I know it must have been awful hearing that I hadn't told you the truth about Court's name. Believe me, I feel terrible about it, but there was so much at stake.'

'Yes, it was a bit of a blow.'

Linita felt a stab of self-reproach. Chantel was apologising to her when practically since her birth Linita had lied by omission. How many times over the years had Wolfie suggested that now perhaps the time was right to tell Chantel the truth about her parentage? 'It's fairer that way.' Linita had always stubbornly resisted. 'Fairer to whom? Chantel believes you're her father, and she loves you. Dexter Randolph didn't even care enough to check that I'd delivered a healthy baby. Let it go, Wolfie. It's better this way, believe me.'

But when it had seemed that Chantel was getting serious over her fellow student Mark, Wolfie had taken him out fishing one day and told him that Chantel was his adoptive daughter. It seemed to freak Mark out — heaven knew why, since the little pissant was an obvious fortune-hunter and Chantel stood to inherit all Wolfie's wealth, whatever the lack of blood relationship. Mark had dropped her flat, nearly breaking her heart. Later, Linita had heard that he, too, was adopted. Obviously he had some sort of thing about it. The whole experience had left Linita determined never again to risk the delicate family harmony by allowing the note of truth to intrude. Now it had, in the most jarring and horrible way possible. Every time she slept with Courtney Randolph, Linita's innocent child was committing incest.

She smiled painfully at her daughter. It felt as though her face might crack from the effort. 'I won't come down to dinner, darling. I need to speak to your father about all this, and I may be some time. Promise me one thing, though.'

'Sure. If it will make you feel better.'

'Oh, it will! Promise me, Chantel, that while you're under my roof you and that boy won't sleep together.'

'Courtney, Mom,' said Chantel sharply. 'He does have a name.'

'Which he's only just deigned to let me know! Please,

721

baby. I don't mean to be unreasonable, but this is tough for me.'

Chantel thought her mother was over-reacting, but decided to humour her. She'd probably calm down once she'd spoken to Dad, who was always a moderating influence. 'Okay, I promise.'

'Thank you. I'll have the maids move his things while you're at dinner.'

Chantel explained to Court what her mother had requested. He took it on the chin. 'That's okay. I understand. Maybe it would be better if I left altogether.

'No! We're supposed to be telling them we plan to get married. Oh God, I can't believe the way this is going.'

Linita sipped a couple more stiff drinks while she grappled again with the international dialling codes and tried to trace Wolfie from Munich to Frankfurt, back to Munich, and then to Geneva. Obviously the legal battle to prevent another firm from pirating the company's new miracle cancer-retardant was hotting up. Though she left repeated messages, she couldn't get to speak to him.

Finally, in a haze of brandy and exhaustion, she decided she'd sort this one out for herself. After all, it was Dexter Randolph's fault. He'd got them into this hideous mess, treating her like a doormat, hiding her away from the world, and especially his toffee-nosed wife. He should be made to pay for the misery his son and daughter were to endure. Linita intended to see that he did.

At the back of her mind, though, however hard she sought to pin all the blame on Dexter, she knew that it did not rest entirely at his door. She'd never told Wolfie, the kindest, most understanding man in the world, about her second child, David. In her own way, for reasons she'd laboured to convince herself were valid, she'd been just as much a deceiver. The knowledge was too painful to bear unaided.

When her maid came in to hang up the Baroness's clothes and turn back the bed, she found her mistress sprawled across it, dead to the world. The woman wondered if she should fetch Miss Chantel, then remembered the instructions to move her boyfriend's things out of the girl's room. She had problems of her own.

In their separate rooms, lonely and full of trepidation, Court and Chantel wondered what the morning would bring.

Linita greeted them at the breakfast table, pale but composed. 'Morning, darling. Morning, Courtney. I hope you both slept well.' And not together, said the light in her eyes.

'Fine.'

'Very well, thank you.'

'Good, because I'd like to suggest that we should all make a journey. I'm sure you'll understand, Courtney, that if I'm to feel happier about your relationship with Chantel continuing —' God forgive her for being a liar! — 'I'd like the reassurance of meeting your parents and learning what they have to say about things. In the light of your — er, history.'

What was going on? Chantel wondered. She knew her mother for the least conformist of women. Normally, Linita didn't give a stuff for the social niceties.

Court, who did not know this, drew false hope from Linita's request. 'That's an excellent idea,' he said. 'My father's been rather ill lately — ' hell, another evasion when he desperately wanted to come clean — 'but he's been making an excellent recovery. If you wouldn't object to my just checking that he and Mums don't mind receiving guests?'

'Of course not. If it's okay, Simpson has details of flights to London.'

'We'll need to take a shuttle to Inverness after that. The family's at our Scottish home at present. Or maybe Dad will send a plane.'

'That's fine. May I leave the arrangements to you, Courtney?'

'Of course.' He was delighted to have a positive course of action. 'You'll both love Gilmour,' he said enthusiastically. 'And when you've met my parents,' he told Linita, 'I'm sure you won't be worried any more.'

Court glanced at his watch. 'Do you think we ought to wake your mother?'

Linita had chosen a seat away from them, on the upper deck of the 747's first-class accommodation. 'I'm going to sleep the flight away. I won't be much company,' she had told them.

Court was taken in, but Chantel, who knew her for a nervous traveller who rarely closed an eye in flight, was not.

At Heathrow, while they waited for their baggage to be transferred from the jumbo to the Randolph Enterprises Gulfstream which had been sent to fetch them, Linita pleaded a headache and sat some distance away, silent and withdrawn. A car was waiting to take them to Gilmour. At the sight of the watery winter sunshine smearing the lochs' grey surfaces and revealing the harshness of the hills, she shivered inside her sable coat.

Chantel was delighted by her first view of Gilmour's pink granite façade, the Hamilton standard fluttering from a flagpole on the central turret. 'It's so much prettier than I thought it would be! Look, Mom. Deer under those trees over there.'

Linita didn't turn her head. She seemed to be straining forward in her seat, all her attention fixed on the baronial front door. As the car drew up, it swung open. Camilla stepped out, smiling and waving. A very elegant older woman joined her. The two of them then turned back and looked into the house.

Court and Chantel jumped out and ran to greet them —

to stop short in amazement at the sight of the third figure, sheltering just inside the door. It was Dexter. Leaning heavily on a silver-topped cane borrowed from Angelica, his face taut with effort, but actually standing to welcome them home.

'Dad' congratulations! But why didn't you let us know?'

'Wanted to surprise you. Glad to see it worked. What's the matter, Chantel? Don't I deserve a kiss?'

She hugged him, taking care not to pull him off balance, then remembered her mother, still sitting in the car. 'Mom, come and be introduced,' she called.

'Don't stand for too long. Remember what the physio-therapist said,' Camilla admonished him.

He shifted his weight, looking down at his clumsy feet. 'I'm okay, don't fuss. Now I can, nothing'll stop me standing to welcome our guests.'

He looked up. A tall woman in a full-length sable coat and dark wide-brimmed hat had climbed out of the car. She came towards them and stopped six feet away from the welcome party. She made no attempt to exchange greetings, but merely removed her dark glasses.

The smile drained from Dexter's face. 'Oh, Christ, no! It can't be. You mean *you're* Chantel's mother?'

He swayed on his feet. Angelica snapped her fingers, and Webster appeared in the nick of time, pushing Dexter's wheelchair. He sank back into it, staring at their visitor as if his worst nightmare had just materialised.

Chantel had never seen an expression like that on her mother's face. 'Mom, what's going on? Do you two know each other already?'

'Can these explanations wait?' said the Dowager Countess. 'I think my son-in-law should be taken inside. It looks as though he's had a shock.'

Webster wheeled Dexter into the hall sitting-room, the old building's principal reception room. He pushed the chair next to the fire. Dexter seemed unwilling or unable to work the controls himself. Chantel and Court followed in silence.

Camilla stared in bewilderment from her husband to their visitor. 'I'm Camilla Randolph,' she said, holding out her hand with customary good manners. 'Haven't we met before somewhere?'

'Linita von Stolsenburg. We have, though I'm surprised you remember. I brought a collection-tin to the house in Yarrabbee Road once — the house I used to share with Dexter.'

She turned to him. 'It's taken a long time, but it was worth every minute of the wait. It's true what they say. Revenge *does* taste sweet.'

Her taunt seemed to snap him out of a shocked silence. 'Revenge? Are you so blind you can consider only yourself in this? It's two young lives we're talking about here. Whatever our differences, my son loves your daughter.'

She couldn't stop herself. 'Wrong, I'm afraid. Your son loves your daughter.'

There was a shocked intake of breath from Camilla.

'If you'd had the common humanity to check out what happened to me when you left me carrying your child, maybe this could have been avoided,' continued Linita inexorably.

Chantel ran to her mother and stood before her, studying her expression. 'What are you saying, Mom? Dexter's not my father?'

Linita's face softened when she looked at her daughter. 'Baby, I'm sorry. Wolfie's your father in every other sense — believe me you mean everything to him — but this is for real. A long time ago, while I was still living in Australia, Dexter Randolph was my lover. When he found out that you were on the way, he abandoned me. I came to New York with you as a tiny baby. Wolfie married me when you were a year old and formally adopted you.'

'Is this true? Did you know that Chantel was your daughter?' Court's stricken face was almost unrecognisable.

Dexter put up his hands, appealing for forgiveness.

'Believe me, I had no idea. It's true Linita and I were lovers, even after I married your mother, I'm afraid. I'm not proud of this, but when she told me she was expecting a child, I gave her a settlement and left Australia to make my permanent home here.'

'So that was the story,' said Camilla tonelessly. 'I always knew that something forced you to make the break.'

'Now I can see why you were so shocked when I told you my name,' said Court to Linita. 'I make no apologies for my father — what he did to you was inhuman — but please, for your daughter's sake if not mine, tell us truthfully — are you absolutely sure Dexter Randolph is the father of your child?'

Now that she had exacted her revenge, Linita could find it in her to be sorry for Court. He and Chantel were the innocent victims of their father's sins. 'Don't pin your hopes on anything like that,' she said gently. 'No matter what you would like to believe, I was not a gold-digger out to trap any rich man. I loved your father. Too much, as it turned out. After he married your mother, I was stupid enough to go on seeing him. There was no one else but him, until I left Australia and went to New York. Chantel is his daughter and your half-sister. I'm sorry, Courtney. You'll have to stop seeing each other.'

'Seeing each other? We're supposed to be getting married!' Chantel stepped away from him, an instinctive rejection. He looked as if she had struck him. 'This isn't true,' he said, seizing her arms and pulling her towards him. 'She's making it up to get at my father. And even if she isn't, what do we care? We love each other. Isn't that enough?'

Camilla tried to intervene. 'Court, think what you're saying!'

'You keep out of this! It's between me and Chantel, no one else. None of you has the right to stop us — a bunch of liars and hypocrites the lot of you! Come with me now, Chantel,' he said more steadily. 'I won't ask you again.'

She searched his face with pain-filled eyes. 'Darling, I can't go with you. I can't even kiss you goodbye ... Don't look at me like that, Court! You know I loved you.'

'Loved me? You mean you can stop as easily as that?'

'Don't make this any harder,' she pleaded. 'I think we should be apart for now. In a month or two, maybe things will seem clearer.'

His brown eyes looked colder and more distant than she had ever seen them. It was if a light had died inside him. 'Things look clear enough to me.' He turned his back on her and faced his parents, speaking with cold deliberation. 'I want you both to know you've ruined my life. I have nothing left to live for. You —' he pointed to Camilla —' because you knew Dad had someone else and did nothing to stop it.'

'Courtney, please!'

'And you, you hypocritical old goat, because you've sat in judgment over me all my life, letting me know how I failed to match up to the great Dexter Randolph.' It was as if the months of closeness in Dexter's illness had never been. 'Well, don't worry. You won't have to live with this particular disappointment any longer. Don't try to stop me, and don't come after me. I'm finished with the lot of you.'

They stood frozen and watched him go. Outside on the gravelled drive the chauffeur was polishing the car, whistling while he worked. Through the mullioned bay they saw Court approach him, ask a question, and snatch the keys from the astonished man's hand. A moment later, the car that had brought them from the airport roared away.

Angelica was the first to recover herself. 'Poor boy,' she sighed. 'It's been a bad shock for him. And for you, young lady. All this emotion on top of a long flight. Come with me, and we'll see if we can't find you somewhere to rest.'

Linita tried to accompany them. 'Hold on a minute — she's my daughter.'

'What a pity you didn't remember that when you engineered this little scene.' Guiltily, Linita realised the old Countess was right. 'Besides, having come all this way, don't you have things to discuss with my son-in-law? You might as well get them over with. I'm sure you wouldn't want to outstay your welcome.'

When Angelica and Chantel had left, it seemed to be Camilla's turn to take charge. 'Won't you sit down?' Taken aback, Linita did. She'd expected tears and reproaches from the betrayed wife. Instead, she found herself on the receiving end of a cool put-down. 'I don't approve of the way you handled things, but no doubt you felt yourself justified. We'll say no more about it, shall we? Now that you've made your revelation, there are a few things that perhaps I should tell you. My husband has only recently recovered from a serious illness. In a few weeks he hopes to be able to travel to Australia, where the police wish him to help them with a murder enquiry.'

'It's Wally,' Dexter put in. 'You remember him, don't you?'

Reluctantly, unwilling to concede any link between them, she admitted, 'Yes. He was a good sort.'

'The best. You remember how he went missing that time while we were visiting Yelonga? Well, recently they found his body — or what remained of it. There was a bullet-hole in the skull. God knows why, but since Luke told them I fired him, the slope-headed police think there was bad blood between us. The idea of it, between me and Wally!' His laughter sounded strained and false.

'Nasty for you,' Linita commented. 'Why are you telling me all this?'

Dexter looked incredulous. 'Don't you remember what happened when we got back from Townsville?' Her face remained blank. He swallowed his pride. 'Please, Linita. You must try. You could give me an alibi.'

She got to her feet. 'I remember nothing except your betrayal of me, your double betrayal of our daughter. You

729

rejected her at birth, and now you're responsible for wrecking her life.'

She spoke to Camilla with grudging respect. 'You know, the first time I met you I couldn't imagine what he saw in you. If it's any consolation, now I can. I'm sorry for any pain I've caused you and Court. You are the innocent victims in this. But as for you, Dexter Randolph — as far as I'm concerned you're guilty as hell! They can lock you up and throw away the key. What could I possibly have to say in defence of a man like you?'

The phone's insistent ringing woke Ash and Kara early in the morning.

'Hello,' said Ash groggily. 'Who is this?'

'It's me, Court. Just ringing to let you know that the old man's on his feet again.'

'Fantastic! Well worth being woken up at three in the morning for. When did all this happen?'

Court did not reply directly to the question. As Ash's sleep-fuddled brain cleared, he realised that his brother's voice sounded thick and slow. Maybe he'd tied one on to celebrate. God, let it just be that! Court's next words strangled the hope at birth.

'Yeah, thought I'd better warn you. He'll be over in Oz before you know it, trampling all over you. Smashing up your life the way he's smashed mine.'

Ash was beginning to feel uncomfortable about Kara hearing this. Though he knew she'd find it hurtful, he picked up the radiophone and carried it into another room.

'What's the matter, Court? What else has happened.'

'Chantel . . .'

'Is she okay? Court, come on. How can I help if you won't tell me what's wrong?'

He heard a crash, and the line went dead. It sounded as though his brother had dropped the phone rather than hanging up on him, but the effect was the same.

The last Ash had heard from his family had been a phone call from Camilla saying that they were all due to gather at Gilmour, except for Alexander, who was in New York seeing about his divorce, and Georgie who was in Paris. He rang the Scottish number and was put through to Camilla.

'Mums, I've just had a strange telephone call from Court.'

'Oh, thank God. Where is he, darling? Your father's been so worried.'

'I'm afraid he didn't say. We were cut off. Look, I don't know for sure, Mums, but it sounded awfully as if ...'

'My poor boy,' she said, with no trace of reproach. 'What have we done to him?'

'I don't know what's been going on, but he sounded terribly bitter about Dad. Have they had a fight?'

Camilla stayed commendably calm while she told him about the visit from Linita von Stolsenburg and the revelation that Chantel was their half-sister.

'Good God! You're taking this awfully well, Mums, I must say.'

'I nearly lost your father a few weeks ago. I can remember how that felt. Beside it, this is not so very important, except for the pain it's causing Dexter, and poor Court and Chantel. If only your brother would come home! If he could see what it's doing to Dexter.'

'You'd better get some detectives after him fast, Mums. If he falls into the wrong company, like he did last time ...'

Kara loved living in Sydney's Paddington. Walking through the streets of low terraces she was reminded of Hampstead or Chelsea, except that since her arrival the streets seemed to have been bathed in perpetual sunshine and the flowers in the tiny front gardens, spilling out on to the pavements, were the tropical bougainvillaea and poinsettia, hisbiscus and frangipani. Ash's small green-painted Federation house, with its fancy iron lacework outside, polished wood floors and Early Australian furniture inside, was welcoming and fun to live in.

Though he was working very hard on the last stages of the Chimera buyout, he snatched time to show her a few of Sydney's more civilised pleasures: Saturday morning brunch at the Bayswater Brasserie, dinner at Oasis Seros. One Sunday they went to the beach to catch the floatplane, dodging the windsurfers in Rose Bay, and landed at Palm Beach. They spent a long lazy Sunday swimming and sunbathing. Afterwards they called in at the beach house, where Ash introduced her to the pleasures of a real Australian barbie — charcoal-grilled king prawns followed by succulent steaks.

When Ash couldn't be around, she was happy to explore the antique shops, boutiques and Saturday market of the area. She watched the weekly changing of the guard at the barracks — the soldiers in their digger hats drilling rather mutedly in the middle of a rugger pitch — and explored the Italian delis and greengrocers full of mouth-watering tropical fruit and vegetables. She was a fine cook and delighted in experimenting with new dishes, even if Ash couldn't always be home to try them with her.

There was only one thing about their life together that worried her. Although he tried to hide it from her, she could see the burden of worry he shouldered every day. In bed, he was loving and tenderly solicitous. In sleep, he tossed and turned restlessly, his mind still full of the problems of the day. She felt that it was more than just the strain of trying to pull Chimera together, but she did not press him.

One evening he came home early and took a bottle of vintage Australian champagne from the fridge.

'Are we celebrating? What's happened?'

'Chimera — it's all over bar the signing. We'll tie it up tomorrow.'

'Ash, that's wonderful! Congratulations. It'll really put

Randolph Enterprises back on the map, won't it?'

'I certainly hope so — it's my money and Pa's down the drain, if not.' He opened the bottle and poured them both a glass of champagne. 'So where do you want to go and celebrate — Bilson's?'

'Is there any need to go out? I can see you're pretty bushed. What I'd like is a quiet night in catching up on what's really going on round here. I think you could come clean with me now, don't you?'

'You've been very patient, Kara, and yes, I should. The trouble is, you might not feel the same about the Randolphs when I do.'

'Try me.'

She made a simple meal of yabbies, saffron rice and salad, and they finished off the champagne and sat by the french doors at the back of the kitchen-dining-room, screens drawn against marauding mosquitoes but not against the cooling breeze from the Harbour.

'You know I told you my father had been ill?' he began.

'Yes.'

'It's true he was in hospital and had to have some tricky surgery. But I didn't tell you why. Someone had taken a pot-shot at him. Hit him in the chest. The doctors thought he might be paralysed.'

'That's terrible. Who?'

Kara was a businesswoman. She did not ask why he had kept Dexter Randolph's wounding a secret, understanding at once the implications for Chimera and the rest of the Randolph empire if word got out that its chairman was seriously ill.

'The police have no idea who did it. They thought at first Pa had shot himself, and he couldn't help. He's lost his entire memory of the incident. He's on the mend now, though — better than ever, in fact — and cockahoop about Chimera. We need their properties badly. They're already established in the luxury resort market we plan to enter with Bradbury — if the place doesn't beggar us first.'

733

'I've seen you going through the costs. What happened? Did you hit construction problems?'

Ash grimaced. 'Worse than that. It looks as though two directors have been systematically defrauding the company.'

She sighed. 'So that's it. No need to ask which two.'

He told her of the discrepancy he'd noticed on Funswim's paper, and of the report of the private investigator he'd put on to the case. 'Lucas and Chip bought into the company just before it was given the pool construction job. They retained their own firm, allowing book costs to go sky high when real construction costs were probably under a third of what Randolph Enterprises was charged. I have the proof waiting for Pa when he comes over. I want him to decide what to do with them.'

'It won't be just the pool, will it? I had a similar problem with the manager of the ranch. He was milking every source he could. A project like Bradbury's got to have given Luke and Chip scores of opportunities.'

He nodded. 'The figures are pretty dizzying. Hence the grim and abstracted air. You've no idea what a relief it is to talk to somebody here about it. I don't know why I didn't before.'

She looked at him reproachfully. 'Neither do I. It's not something to be ashamed of, having a fraud in the company, and I think you know by now you can rely on my discretion. Funny, I never did like Luke and Chip — too smarmy by half — but their crookedness hardly reflects on the rest of the Randolphs.'

Ash sighed. 'Maybe not, but there's more, I'm afraid. Remember that phone call from Court the other night?'

'Yes, to say that your father was walking again. I couldn't understand at the time why you needed to take it in another room. It was good news, wasn't it?'

'Court didn't think so. You see, he'd just discovered something about our father, something that gave him a terrible shock.'

734

Briefly he outlined the scene when Linita von Stolsenburg visited Gilmour.

'So Court's fallen in love with your half-sister? Awful for them both, but don't you think, given time . . .?'

'I'm afraid time's something Court's running short of. He's been missing since that day. My parents have sent private detectives out after him, but though he's been seen around, his foolishly protective friends are keeping quiet about his address.

'Ash, I know its hurtful when someone cuts himself off in this way, but —'

He stared at her bleakly. 'You don't understand. We've been through all this before with him. My brother's been treated for drug addiction before. The last time he was "cured", the doctors were quite specific: another relapse, and Court could die. We're terribly afraid that in the wrong company, Court's life could be in danger.'

Wolfgang von Stolsenburg flew back from a gruelling series of meetings with his German lawyers and a representative of the Swiss pharmaceutical company who had pirated his company's new miracle cancer-retardant. Their defence was that they had purchased the formula in good faith. It wasn't their fault if the vendor was a disgruntled ex-employee of Wolfie.

Privately he was surprised that the term 'good faith' was even in the vocabulary of a cut-price, cut-throat operation like theirs, but after days of stonewalling he took the words at face value and offered them the deal he knew they couldn't resist: ten million dollars in 'compensation' for the expenses they had incurred in pilot tests and preliminary marketing. He flew back to New Jersey with his cheque-book considerably lighter, looking forward to spending a peaceful few days with his family and Chantel's new boyfriend.

He arrived to find the house strangely quiet. There was

no sign of the young people, and he found his wife sitting in their bedroom. Despite the greyness of the day, there were no lights lit.

'Wolfie,' she said, running to bury her face on his shoulder. 'I'm so glad you're back. I've done something so stupid and cruel. I think I've wrecked our daughter's life.'

He switched on the bedside lamp, seeing the swollen eyes and blotched skin which told of hours of misery. 'It can't be that bad,' he said gently. 'Tell me.'

He had seen Linita cry many times, she was an emotional woman, but the tears she wept now as she told her story frightened him. The accumulated sorrow of years threatened to overwhelm her. Before his eyes she lived again the pain of her betrayal by Dexter, her fear and desolation in the lonely months leading up to the birth of her children.

Although she had contrived the scene with Dexter, its effect had been traumatic. In her blind rush to confront him, she had not realised the seriousness of the attachment between Chantel and Court, or stopped to consider what her revelation would do to them. She blamed herself bitterly for that now, but though she'd tried to tell Chantel how sorry she was, the girl had locked herself away in her room, taking an occasional meal from the housekeeper but otherwise refusing to see anybody.

'What kind of mother am I?' moaned Linita. 'I did a terrible thing, Wolfie. I was blind and selfish, and this is my punishment. I've lost Chantel just like I lost —'

'David?'

For a moment the name hung between them, charging the air. Linita couldn't move, afraid that if she did the whole fragile edifice of her happiness with Wolfie would come crashing down around her. 'Oh God, how long have you known?' She covered her face with her hands, terrified of seeing the accusation that must be in his eyes. 'What must you have thought of me — the kind of woman who could abandon her own son to the care of strangers?'

'Always,' he said gently. 'It makes no difference.' He took her hands and forced her to look at him. He was exactly the same as always, the calm, generous, loving man who had given a new life to her and Chantel. 'Forgive me, Linita. I would not have mentioned it now, but I knew this shock with Chantel and Dexter Randolph would have brought it to mind.'

'But how can you not care? All these years I've lied to you!'

'You did not lie. You simply did not tell me of a situation which neither of us had the power to change. I found out about it because, as I told you on the day I proposed, the basis for success, in business or marriage, is always knowledge. I know why you left David when he was so sick, and I know that when you enquired later he was already established with good and loving parents. You felt you could not reclaim him. It must have been a very painful decision. I love and respect you for it. Linita, don't you know by now? You are everything to me. I could never judge you harshly.'

'Not even for hurting Chantel like this? I can't believe I did that to her, hauling her across the Atlantic so she could hear something as devastating as that. It's all Dexter Randolph's fault! Nothing went right for me after I met him.'

For the first time Wolfie looked reproachful. 'Are you sure about that?'

'Of course I am! The bastard ruined my life.'

She could not quite meet his eyes while she said it.

'Is that all the years with me have been? Second best after Dexter Randolph spoiled things forever?'

Her expressive face was horrified as she realised what her words had sounded like to him. 'No! You're the best and kindest man. I love you dearly.'

'Then why waste even a minute more on this senseless enmity towards Randolph? It was so many years ago, I can't bear to see you dragged down into bitterness and petty revenge. I'm willing to bet he's already suffered greatly.'

'You're right,' she said slowly. 'There was a terrible scene between him and Courtney. He comes off worst in this, and none of it was his fault. He was in a clinic, being treated for drug-dependency when Chantel met him. He admitted it to me quite openly. He was very brave about it, poor boy. When I told him Dexter was Chantel's father, he fell apart. Oh, Wolfie, you don't think he'll do anything stupid, do you? Poor Dexter.'

The words were out before she could stop them. Wolfie smiled.

'That's more like the woman I love! Dexter's a parent, too. Everything you are going through with Chantel, he's experiencing with Courtney. And there's more to come. You have yet to tell him about David, I suppose?'

It had taken Linita years to come clean about the full story of the twins' birth. Wolfie had never told her that his detectives had smoked out the truth before their marriage.

She looked at him imploringly. 'I've kept it secret for so long. Must I tell him?'

'Yes, only this time more gently. I think perhaps it would be best to wait for a while. Perhaps we should trace David's whereabouts first? I have the name of his adoptive parents somewhere, if you'd like to know it.'

'Yes, but not now. Let's have him traced first. I couldn't bear to start thinking about him, imagining what it will be like when we meet — only to find he can't be relocated or that something's happened. And we have to tell Chantel. Wolfie, you do it, please. She won't talk to me.'

'We'll do it together. I know our daughter. She has her mother's warm and loving heart. She won't reject you for long. Come on, Linita. We'll go to her now.'

At his insistence, Chantel let them into her room. She would not look at her mother, but allowed Wolfie to put his arm round her and tell her all about her mother's history and his first meeting with them both.

'I fell in love with your mother on sight, but the fact that she had you was a cause of such joy. I knew that I would never be able to father children. I could not believe that any man would have wanted you both out of his life.'

'Dexter really did that to you, Mom?' said Chantel.

'He did. He felt I'd betrayed him, you see, conceiving when he told me he didn't want me to have his children. Now, I'm beginning to see his point. It's caused some heartache, hasn't it? It was a pretty sneaky thing to do, trying to win him away from Camilla, but believe me, Chantel, I have never regretted having you, not for one minute. If only I'd been strong enough to keep your brother too.'

Chantel's eyes softened. 'You were pretty strong to get through all that. I still can't believe I have a twin somewhere. It's quite a story, isn't it? Stealing your own child while dressed up as a nun! Only you could pull a stunt like that, Mom.'

For the first time since their trip to Scotland, the old affection was back in Chantel's voice.

'Oh, darling, does this mean you've forgiven me?'

Chantel looked grave. 'It means I will do, Mom, but only if you make things up with Dexter. You hurt him pretty bad, and you hurt Court, too. I've tried to call him, but Camilla says he's disappeared. She and Dexter are trying to trace him, but he has to go to Australia soon. Camilla said something about seeing the police.'

Linita looked guilty. 'Poor Wally! I'd forgotten him in all of this. Dexter loved that man. How could those fools of police seriously think he'd have anything to do with murdering his friend?'

'Randolph is under suspicion of murder?' her husband asked.

'Well, not quite. Not yet. But they found the body of an old aboriginal stockman who went missing on Yelonga years ago. They could tell that someone had shot him, so there has to be an inquest. We were up on the station at the time, and the police seem very keen to check what Dexter was doing.'

'Mom, it sounds as though you might be able to tell them,' said Chantel.

'Yes, I could. On the day Wally left Yelonga, Dexter was with me. We flew over to Townsville on business and came back in the afternoon. I wasn't very pleased. I'd wanted a night away because of that sourpuss Lucinda, but Dexter insisted on getting back. While I was lying down — the heat that day was something else,' she added hastily, 'Luke came up and told Dexter that Wally had been sacked ... My God! What did I just say? *Luke* told Dexter that *he* had sacked Wally. Yet when we were in Scotland, Dexter told me that the police had it from Luke that Dexter was responsible. They think there was a falling-out between them. I can see it all now ... Chantel, what's the number for Gilmour? I must speak to Dexter. This could help him.'

'It's okay. I'll call. I want to ask if Court's back yet.'

But when they reached Gilmour, they were told that the family was not in residence. Chantel tried Courtney Park next. A noncommittal voice she recognised as Ford's told her that Lord and Lady Randolph were not at home. Mr Courtney's whereabouts were not known at present. Would she care to speak to Lady Angelica?

Court's grandmother had been kind to her in Scotland, and Chantel knew she kept her finger on the pulse of family affairs.

Angelica sounded pleased to hear from her. 'Chantel, I've been meaning to telephone you myself.'

'Is there news of Court? I've been so worried.'

'Sadly, no. I'll pass it on as soon as there is, I promise. The worst of it is that the press has somehow heard of our enquiries. There've been one or two nasty little pieces in the gossip columns about his time at the Malmaison, and they seem to have heard that he and his father are estranged. Don't worry. Your name hasn't come into any of this. If only we could find him! But it's not that I wanted to speak to you about. I don't suppose there's a chance you could get your mother to speak to me?'

'I think that might be possible! Hold on, please.'

Linita grabbed the receiver. 'Hello, this is Linita von Stolsenburg. Look, I know you don't approve of me, but I need to speak to Dexter pretty urgently. Do you know where he is?'

'I do, Baroness. That is why I wanted to speak to you. Dexter is on his way to Australia. The police have insisted on bringing forward the date of the inquest. Unless further evidence is produced, it seems there is a strong possibility he will be arrested and charged with murder.'

Dexter eased himself out of bed so as not to disturb Camilla. He looked lovingly down at her. She was a reluctant traveller at the best of times but had loyally insisted on facing the long flight to Australia with him. On arrival she had run the media gauntlet at the airport, then gone on to insist that they make this night a memorable one. Although she did not say as much, they both knew it could be his last one free from the taint of a murder charge. His Australian lawyers had tipped him off that the evidence was running against him.

Ash and Kara had come over to the house earlier. Ash wanted to run a few business matters past Dexter, and to introduce his new girlfriend. She talked to Camilla while the men talked shop in the study. Dexter was pretty sure she knew everything that was going on, but she gave no sign. He liked her discretion, and her looks could not be faulted. If Ash had any sense, he'd hang on to her.

They had a few drinks, then Ash looked at his parents' drawn faces and left them to get what sleep they could before the flight to Brisbane in the morning. Instead, they had made love, surprising and delighting each other with the strength and sweetness of their new physical accord. Afterwards, Camilla drifted into sleep.

741

Though his body was resoundingly at peace, Dexter could not follow her. The last few months had seen such a bewildering sequence of reversals. From a crippled embittered man, unable to make love to his wife, he had survived a murderous attack and been restored to health and virility. In the last few weeks, despite the unhappiness over Court, he and Camillas had become closer than ever before. How ironic that tomorrow would see all these hard-won advances hanging in the balance. His lawyer had told him to prepare himself for charging and possible imprisonment before bail could be arranged.

In England, told of Lucas's statement that Dexter had sacked the old stockman, he had at first put it down to nothing more sinister than Luke's perennial inability to carry the can. The fact that he had been the one to dismiss Wally, and therefore the last to see him, would not suit Luke under the heat of a police enquiry, and so he had taken the easy way out and tweaked the facts. It was hardly the first time this sort of thing had happened. At first, Dexter had been confident he would be able to refresh Luke's memory and talk him into telling the truth.

Luke had refused to take a single phone call from him, at the house or at the office. Eventually Dexter's embarrassed Australian lawyer, Rick Danby, had to ask him to stop calling his brother or run the risk of proceedings being started against him for intimidating a witness.

'But that's crap! There's not even a criminal charge yet!'

'That's right, Lord Randolph. Not yet. I'm afraid the buzz is the evidence will go against you.'

'As given by my brother, I suppose?' The suspicion that had lurked half-formed at the back of Dexter's mind took full and hideous shape. 'By God, he actually intends to bury me with this, doesn't he? The bastard intends to stand up in court and blacken me with his lies. I'll see him in hell first!'

Dexter knew beyond a shadow of a doubt that his

recollection of events at Yelonga was accurate. If Luke had played it just a little more cleverly, agreeing that perhaps he could be mistaken, his memory of events a little fuzzy with time, Dexter would have been less sure of his motives. As it was, his contemptuous evasion of Dexter and single-minded determination to blacken his reputation pointed to only one conclusion: Luke was covering his own back. Dexter had always known he was a liar, but in the early hours he'd come to believe that Luke was a murderer, too.

The bedside phone started to ring. He snatched it up so as not to disturb Camilla. 'Yes?'

'It's me, Lucinda. I haven't got long, so listen carefully. Luke knows your arrangements for tomorrow. He thinks you're using a company plane at nine. He's taking Ansett at ten. Please, Dexter, change your plan. Meet me by the Quickbite on Circular Quay. It's always busy, and anyway he won't be having me watched once he thinks you're under way. See you there at half nine.'

'Lucinda, it's the middle of the . . .'

'Dexter, please, for your own sake be there. I know what happened at Courtney Park.' The line went dead.

It was the end of sleep for that night. He went downstairs to the study, where Camilla had broken the news that she was expecting Ash. He smiled at the thought of the son Ash had become. He'd pulled off a miracle in Chimera. Time he was thinking of settling down . . .

The thought of marriage led him to Georgie, in Paris with Guy preparing for a quiet civil ceremony — much to her grandmother's disgust, but the girl had been adamant. 'Grandmama, it's hardly the time for a family celebration!'

For once, her grandmother looked ashamed. '*Le pauvre*,' she agreed. 'They must find him soon.'

Dexter remembered his younger son's horror stricken face as Linita had shattered his hopes of a life with Chantel. His four children . . . two on the right course, two with their young lives in disarray. If only he could stick around to help them through.

He had never before realised what a precious commodity time was. Given time, he felt he could trace Court, ask his forgiveness and get him to come home. With time, maybe Chantel would forgive him for what she was bound to see as his betrayal of her mother. Linita had seemed unswerving in her enmity towards him but perhaps, in time, that too would have changed.

Dexter sat in his study until the first light of dawn painted its fiery opalescence on the black canvas of night. It was the day of the inquest. For him, time had just run out.

Dexter took Camilla's morning tea from the housekeeper and woke his wife himself, telling her there'd been a slight change of plan. 'Got to look in briefly at the office. Ash's just called.'

'Last night he said everything was under control. That's why he wanted to come to Brisbane with us,' she said suspiciously.

Dexter shrugged. 'I couldn't see the point of dragging him up there. It'll be a day or two at the outside. It's not such a big deal.'

'Then why can't this meeting wait till we get back?'

He kissed the tip of her nose. 'You're getting too quick for me, you know that? Okay, Lucinda called late last night. She seemed a bit upset. Wanted me to meet her this morning when Luke was out of the way.' No need to worry her with mention of Lucinda's obvious distress and talk of Courtney Park. 'You go on to the airport about ten. I'll catch up with you as soon as I can.'

Camilla frowned. She had never cared for Lucinda, who had not welcomed her in the early days. 'Can't I come, too?'

'I think she'd talk more freely if I was on my own, sweetie. Lucy and I — well, we go back a long way.'

'Did you love her, Dexter? I mean, before you loved me?'

On another day he might have dismissed talk of the

past. On what could be his final unshadowed morning with Camilla, he felt it was important to tell the truth. 'When I was seventeen I believed I'd never love anyone else. Later, even after she'd married Luke, I still thought that. Everything I did on Maroonda — losing my shirt at first, then making money on the mineral rights and by buying all the properties, including Yelonga — I did it all for her.'

Camilla had guessed as much in the past but hearing it from his own lips was something else. 'Well, if she's so important to you ...'

'Camilla, I was telling you what I felt then. Listen to me, there may not be time for this later, and it's important you know — I have never loved anyone the way I love you. Promise me you'll remember that, whatever happens.'

She smiled tremulously. 'I believe you. And whatever happens, you have my love and trust always.'

'I've always loved you, Dexter, and I always will. Luke dazzled me for a few months. After we married, I let my mother's religion and my own misguided loyalty get in the way, but I soon saw how wrong I'd been. And then I paid. My God, how I paid!'

They were sitting in the café on the Quay, one of Sydney's main commuter centres. Every few minutes ferries and water-taxis brought new arrivals across the dancing water on their morning dash to work. The tables around them were full of smartly dressed secretaries, businessmen in suits, rather cooler counterparts in their work-clothes of shorts, long socks and shirt.

Lucinda looked like a ghost beside the chattering customers who were grabbing a cappuccino and a sandwich on their way to work. Looking at the frail washed-out woman she had become, Dexter was full of pity and regret. She had been such a beauty once.

'Do you remember when you brought that blonde bitch to the station?'

'Linita? As it happens, yes.'

'I cried myself to sleep every night of that visit. I didn't let Luke see, but he knew all right. When he realised what it did to me, seeing you with your girlfriend, and later Camilla, he started to use my jealousy. I couldn't bear to see you happy, so I conspired against you with a man I'd come to despise. It was just little things at first, like falsifying stock records, ordering too many supplies so that we could have refunds on them. The money never saw the accounts, of course. When you put him in charge of the whole Cattle Division, it got worse instead of better.'

He touched her hand. 'There's no need to tell me this, Lucinda.'

'I must! I have to make you see how it happened. I've lived with the shame for so long. One day I added up all the money we'd taken. I was appalled. I told Luke it had to stop. He told me he'd only just begun. One day he'd have the whole of Randolph Enterprises to pay you back for taking Yelonga. Yes, I know you did that fair and square, but it made no difference to Luke. He never forgave you for it. I begged him to stop, which was a mistake. Luke has no pity on someone he sees as weaker than himself. How was I going to stop him? he sneered. Turn myself in to the police? Tell you the truth, feeling about you as I did, despite the jealousy? He dragged me down to his level, in the mire. And he got greedier by the year. I don't know the details of his frauds since you put him in overall control of Australia, as Chip was his lieutenant by then, but I do know he overreached himself on Bradbury Island. When you told Chip that day you were planning to come over and go through the costings, Luke was in a frenzy. If you want to pin anything financial on him, Bradbury's the key.'

'It's okay, Lucinda. Ash and the inquiry agents have got him on that. As soon as this inquest business is over we'll go after him. Don't worry about it any more. I understand —'

'No, you don't! You've never understood Luke — what

746

he's capable of when he thinks someone's done him down. Wally did him down. He couldn't help it. He was the sweetest, mildest man, but he was naturally so much better at everything to do with Yelonga, and Luke couldn't stand that. I've no evidence, I was in bed most of that day with a migraine, but Luke was behind that killing, I'm absolutely sure.'

'So am I,' he said heavily. 'And kicking myself for taking so long to realise it. But what's the use when I've absolutely no witnesses on my side?'

'Not even Linita? She always acted so in love with you? Sorry, I shouldn't be such a bitch. I know I've no claims on you, but you've been the most important thing in my life. That was why I was so appalled when I heard them ...' Her voice trailed off. She looked terrified.

'What did you hear? Tell me all of it, Lucy.'

'Chip and Luke on the phone. I couldn't sleep that night. I'd gone downstairs to make some tea. I heard them talking, and realised it was about Courtney Park — where your rooms were, and Camilla's. What routines did the servants work to, that kind of thing. Then I heard Luke say, "It's either his neck or yours. You're into Clarendon's and the Chelsea Sporting Club for seventy-eight thousand. Do me this little favour, and I'll wipe the slate clean."' Lucinda's manner, which had seemed vague and distracted until now, had altered. She seemed to be making an effort to remember the conversation word for word.

'When was this exactly?'

'A few days after you'd said you were going to look through Bradbury. Two days before you were shot.'

'But how did you know about that? Ash told no one here.'

'He didn't have to. Luke and Chip sat up the next two nights, waiting. On the second night, an Englishman called. I knew something was up. I sat in our bedroom monitoring the calls on the extension. The man said, "Did a bit of rough shooting earlier. Quite a bag. A couple of

747

little bunnies and a great big sitting duck." Luke crowed with delight. He was so excited he broke the code. "You're history, Dexter! You're out of my way." Even then I didn't quite realise. It wasn't until the Englishman said, "I'm afraid it wasn't a clean kill. They've taken him to hospital, but don't worry, the old bugger's well and truly paralysed. He can't possibly come nosing round Bradbury now." Then I realised they were talking about you. I couldn't help myself. I screamed "Murderer!" down the phone. I was hysterical with shock and grief, but I can remember Luke saying, just before he came for me, "It's all right, Mark. We'll keep her in line." Does the name mean anything to you, Dexter? Is it someone in the house?'

'I'm afraid so. It will break his father's heart.'

He looked ten years older, sitting without speaking, searching his own mind for any recollection that would link the estate manager's son, Mark Hayward, with the shooting. Try as he might he could not remember that day, but he felt in his bones that Lucinda was right. It had to be an insider, and it had to be someone with a pretty powerful motive. He'd always known Mark was wild. Paying off pressing gambling debts could well be enough to turn a weak unscrupulous man to murder.

He turned his attention to Lucinda, who sat opposite, silent and remote. He remembered what else she had said. 'What did he do to stop you coming clean before?'

She shuddered. 'Don't ask me that. Please Dexter, I don't want to talk about it.'

He remembered another night, long ago on Yelonga. The awful sounds of Luke taking his revenge on them both. In the morning he had found her numb with horror, looking just the way she did now. He came over to her side of the table and put his arm round her. She leant against him.

'Afterwards, when I threatened to go to the police and tell them about the money and about — the other thing, he made me drink something. I don't know what it was but it left me half crazy. I remember a doctor coming, and Luke telling him I was often like this. The doctor actually advised him to send me away. I could understand everything he said but I couldn't speak. The words came out back to front. When the doctor had gone, Luke told me that unless I did exactly what he said and kept my mouth shut, he'd make sure the whole thing happened again. All of it, and this time he'd let them lock me away. Dexter, I'm sorry. I wasn't strong enough to stand up to him. I told myself I was doing it for my baby. Rhianne's the only one of us who hasn't been touched by this. But the truth of it was, I was too frightened to do anything but pray for your recovery. It was like a miracle when I heard you were better and walking again. But you must be careful. He's tried once . . .'

Dexter nodded over his shoulder. Behind them a thickset man in khaki shorts and a Hawaiian shirt sat sipping a milkshake. When Dexter summoned him with a movement of his hand, he came to join them. A second man slipped into his place.

'Lucy, you are the bravest woman I know,' he told her. 'You have nothing at all to reproach yourself with. Now I want you to go with my friend Mike here, pick up Rhianne and some things for you both from the house. He'll find you somewhere secure and stay with you both till I've put Luke behind bars. Will you go with him?'

She smiled for the first time. 'Gladly. You will get him, won't you, Dexter? I did help by telling you this?'

'You're a heroine, Lucy.'

Dexter knew his own flaws. None better. By clinging to her romantic illusions about him, Lucinda had endured more than any woman should have to. Unfortunately, as Lucas's wife, she would not be able to give evidence against him, but she had given Dexter a very useful lead. Before he left for Brisbane, he would phone the British police and tip them off that Mark Hayward might be able to help with their enquiries.

Life with Courtney Randolph was both better and worse than Maggie Merrilees had foreseen. An old flame from their time in the squat during Court's early London days, she had always carried a torch for him. A once pretty girl whose looks were fast disintegrating from the effects of too much heroin, she had been delighted to bump into him again and had readily agreed to his request to share the Notting Hill flat she was caretaking, in return for bank-rolling both their habits. The plus side of their life together was that Court was prodigal with his money. He paid for everything they did, as well as settling the household bills. The flat was rapidly covered by a slew of discarded clothes, half-eaten takeaways and empty bottles of sweet fizzy drinks. Neither Court nor she had the energy to tidy up, but outside at least they enjoyed a glamorous lifestyle. Court had arrived with only his credit cards and the clothes he stood up in. He bought himself a new wardrobe, replacing clothes with new ones as soon as they become dirty. When Maggie became jealous, he bought her a lot of new things too. They picked up the sort of lifestyle he had led before the overdose — sleeping for most of the day, then joining a group of similar rootless friends for supper at whichever restaurant someone had booked that evening: Kensington Place, the River Café or a Ladbroke Grove Indian restaurant on casual evenings; 90 Park Lane, San Lorenzo or Le Caprice on the others.

Afterwards it was always on to a club — Annabel's, Tramp, Fellini's — or back to someone's house. At some point in the evening it was always suggested that a few lines or a snowball would go down well. Maggie joined in enthusiastically. After all, she wasn't paying for them. This part of life with Court made up for the down side.

Although he'd join in to be sociable, the cocaine rush was no longer enough for him. He wanted to mainline. And yet he was the strangest junkie she had ever met. When he came back to her flat that first evening he didn't seem able to manage for himself — heating a small amount in the bottom of a spoon until it dissolved into a gummy liquid which could be injected. Maggie kept a supply of disposable needles, nobody could say she wasn't punctilious about that, but Court didn't seem able to inject himself. She realised he was still scared of the needle. Funny thing in a junkie.

When she injected him in the arm, she noticed that the skin was smooth and free from puncture-marks. She supposed he could have been injecting himself in the thigh so as not to be too obvious, but from the way he treated the needle she'd had the feeling he was practically a virgin at this procedure.

That had been a few months ago. Now Maggie found it hard to keep him within the limits she considered safe. Court was constantly pushing to take more and more. The social life which she had enjoyed fell away. He didn't feel much like talking or dancing, and the alcohol buzz was trivial and shallow compared to the deep slow security heroin brought — for a few hours at least. But the reassurance seemed more fleeting every time. His dependency made him paranoid. He accused Maggie of cheating him.

Tense and strung out, trying to wean herself off the bigger doses she'd been taking along with him, she scowled at him. With his pale spotty face and red-rimmed eyes, painfully thin so that his clothes hung on him, he was very different from the handsome young man she had met a couple of months ago. He was on the downward slide, it was plain. She did not intend to let him drag her down with him.

'Why don't you stop snivelling and start getting your act together?' she snapped at him. 'I'm sick of you coming on like I'm your nanny, Courtney Randolph. "Start me up . . . be nice to me," she mimicked a little-boy whine. 'You make me sick! Why don't you just piss off out of here and leave me alone?'

It was mostly her own paranoia speaking. Court, shivering and overdue for a fix, was in a hypersensitive state. He heard only the note of rejection. 'It's happening again,' he mumbled. 'What's the matter with me? They all leave me.'

She sank into a chair, feeling too weak and shaky to stay angry at him. She heard him crashing about in the next room, and supposed he was packing his bags. Then she remembered he had no bags to pack. Typical . . .

When she woke up, it was quiet in the flat. The front door stood open as he had left it. Court had gone, taking with him her entire stash, which she had thought she had hidden from him in an old First Aid box on top of the wardrobe. The tin with its red cross was still there. It was empty.

'Fucking junkie thief!' she yelled, hurling it at a mirror, which shattered under the impact. He'd left all his clothes, she saw. He needn't think she'd let him back in to pick them up.

Christ, she needed a fix. Cold turkey could start tomorrow. She got down on her knees and began to scrabble through the expensive designer shirts and suits left where Court had let them fall. She found thirty pounds in cash in the pocket of the suit he'd worn the day before, and an Asprey's credit-card holder complete with all his plastic. Wherever Courtney Randolph was heading, he was going there broke.

Court didn't need money. He had everything he needed right there in the pocket of the overcoat he had pulled on before leaving the flat. It was a bitter night in late February. He hadn't bothered with a sweater or jacket. Just thrown on the coat over his jeans and thin shirt. He was shaking with cold and with the need that seemed to gnaw his bones.

Warmth and light and somewhere to shoot up . . . He staggered into a pub at the seedier end of Ladbroke Grove

She shook her head vigorously. 'You don't get rid of me as easily as that, Dexter.'

As the car drew up, she took off the dark glasses she had hitherto worn in public. Flashlights gave her a headache, but there was no way she was going to slink past the press in semi-concealment today. Proudly she took Dexter's arm and pushed through the press to the relative peace of the room where proceedings were to be held *in camera*.

Rick Danby had indicated that Dexter was to be the first witness after medical and forensics experts had given their opinion.

'Try and give a solid, trustworthy impression. Don't beat about the bush,' he'd advised. 'Stick to the facts as you remember them, and don't forget to look the Coroner in the eye.'

Gloom permeated the proceedings. Prominently labelled 'Exhibit A', the shattered skull of Wallace Wuggalar faced Dexter as he began to answer the Coroner's questions. Camilla had feared Dexter might find it a distraction, but watching the conviction with which he spoke, she realised that it had worked for them. She felt that everyone in the room must realise from the affection with which Dexter spoke that Wally had been his friend, while he himself was the most reliable of witnesses.

She had reckoned without the long reach of Lucas Randolph, which directed the way in which the Coroner put his questions.

'And when did you last see Wuggalar?'

'On the morning of February 12th, 1960. He waved goodbye from the strip as the company plane took me on to Townsville.'

'How can you be so certain of the date after all this time, Lord Randolph?'

'I've made a habit of keeping my business diaries, sir. They reveal that I attended a closing in Townsville on that date.'

'And you returned to Yelonga later that day?'

'Yes. We flew back to the station, but Wally had left by then. My brother Lucas told me it had been necessary to dismiss him after Wally insulted Mrs Lucinda Randolph, his wife.'

'Not unreasonable grounds. And were you alone on this trip to Yelonga?'

'No, sir. I was accompanied by an associate.'

'And their name would be?'

Dexter hesitated. It was noticeable that this was the first time his reply had not been completely fluent. 'Miss Linita Tyrone.'

'May we ask what position Miss Tyrone held? That's enough now!'

There was some sniggering in court at the Coroner's *double entendre.*

'She came to give me secretarial assistance,' said Dexter, though he knew he was stretching the point. The most Linita had ever done in that direction was to type out the occasional note of meetings he'd attended.

'I take it your former secretary can corroborate your version of events?'

'She has not come forward, sir.'

'Then leaving aside Miss Linita Tyrone ...'

The damage had been done, though. Dexter's earlier upright image was already smeared. Having entered the court on his wife's arm, he was already revealed as the sort of man who took female company on a business trip and labelled her 'secretary'. Not a crime, but not strictly honest either. Furthermore, the absence of Linita Tyrone, a witness who should have been able to corroborate his story, was a damaging omission.

The Coroner finished his questioning of Dexter by checking in which direction he had ridden out after Wally. He made the same point as Les Munro, the first policeman on Yelonga.

'I believe Wallace Wuggalar trained you in tracking, Lord Randolph?'

756

'That's true.'

'And yet you were not able to follow the tracks of a man who left the station openly and had no reason for concealment. Did your search take you to Sylvia's Stairs?' This was the rocky terrain in which Wally's remains were eventually found.

'Among other places, yes, sir.'

'Did it surprise you when Mr Wuggalar's remains were found there?'

Dexter thought it was a daft question. He'd been surprised to learn that Wally had been murdered, not so much at where it had been done. 'Well, it's treacherous country,' he said, not wishing to rock the boat.

'So treacherous, it seems, that Wuggalar ended up with a bullet through his skull. Thank you, Lord Randolph. No further questions.'

Lucas Randolph, by contrast, was given a much easier time. He looked confident and relaxed, smartly dressed in one of the Italian suits he favoured. Though his looks had coarsened, he was still an imposing man with an actor's ability to assume any expression he chose.

When he was asked what his relations had been with the deceased, he looked fond and reminscent. 'Excellent. Old Wally was like a second father to me.'

Dexter gripped his wife's hand painfully. Lucas's first lie. It was to be the first of many.

'Why did the deceased leave the station?'

Luke looked regretful. 'On my brother's orders. He thought that Wally had been taking liberties, cheeking my wife and so on. Dexter didn't like that, so he told Wally to roll his swag.'

'Despite his forty years on Yelonga?'

'Yeah, well, I thought it was kind of hard myself, but Dexter was like that where Lucinda was concerned. Very protective of her.'

'A devoted brother-in-law.'

Lucas smiled. 'Very.'

There was a ripple of interest among the spectators.

'I don't believe this,' hissed Dexter. 'Not only is he standing up there lying his head off, he's making a whore out of his own wife.'

'Dexter, please.' Camilla rested a hand on his arm, but did not succeed in calming him before a lynx-eyed reporter noticed his reaction. He nudged his neighbour in the ribs, and further notes were taken.

'Were you surprised to hear the version of events which your brother gave us? That it was in fact *you* who dismissed Wallace Wuggalar?'

Lucas's mobile faced creased into a concerned expression. 'Yes and no.'

'Can you be a bit more precise, please?'

'I was surprised to hear Dexter say I got rid of Wally. I was fond of the old guy — he'd been around since we were kids. But then again, it's a serious matter, isn't it? He was murdered, after all.'

The Coroner rapped on his desk. 'Hold on a minute! I haven't made my ruling yet.'

But the damaging statement had been spoken; the link with Dexter reinforced.

'Thank you, Mr Randolph. That will be all.'

Rick Danby was not in his seat beside Camilla when Lucas was dismissed. The third witness was an aborigine. As he shuffled into court, Dexter did not at first recognise him under the grizzled hair. Then he realised from the run-to-seed bulk of the stooped man that he had once been a giant among his race.

'My God, it's Samson! I haven't seen him since '62. Wonder where they found him?'

Samson had, it was established, been living on tribal lands in the Northern Territory where he had gone after leaving Yelonga. The Coroner asked if he knew what today's proceedings were about.

He pointed to the skull. 'Him feller Wally. You findem feller that killem.'

'First we must prove that a murder was committed.'

With Samson's testimony, it looked more likely. His story supported Luke's in every detail.

'Mr Dexter tell Wally go 'way. Him feller sad. Him people live on-a land long before Randolphs come. Wally roll him swag and go.'

'And Dexter Randolph — what did he do then?'

'Coupla hours, Mr Dexter ride same way.'

Of all the people in court, none but Lucas knew the man as Dexter did. When Samson was lying, he couldn't help looking at his feet. Until the Coroner's final questions he had stood facing out into the body of the room, with Dexter clearly in his line of sight. When they got to the events on Yelonga, he shuffled back and sideways slightly, and sure enough Dexter saw his eyes flicker momentarily downwards. He remembered something else. Samson had had no reason to love Wally since the day the head stockman had struck him for cowardice. Was it far-fetched to believe he bore a grudge against Dexter, too, for showing him up that day?

The Coroner dismissed Samson and consulted the list on his desk. 'We've heard our last witness — '

Rick Danby came hurrying back into the room. 'With your permission, sir, someone else has just requested leave to appear.'

The Coroner glared. 'Well, that's too bad! I need notice in writing within the statutory period.'

'The witness is no longer an Australian citizen, sir. A considerable distance has been travelled at the witness's own expense.'

The Coroner sighed, and gritted his teeth. He could see the snide lefty comments now if he refused them leave to appear! 'It's irregular, but under the circumstances ... Witness's name?'

'Baroness von Stolsenburg, *née* Linita Tyrone.'

The atmosphere was electric as people craned their heads to catch a first glimpse of Dexter's mysterious 'secretary'. Lucas Randolph's expression was thunderous. His son, who had kept a low profile at the side of the room until now, ignoring his uncle, got to his feet to protest. Luke pulled him down, and thinking better of his first reaction, whispered something in Chip's ear. The two of them sat back with smug smiles.

Linita passed Dexter by without a second glance. She had tied back her heavy hair in a white silk scarf, and wore a chic black linen dress and jacket. Fitting, he thought, for a woman who had come to bury his reputation.

'Baroness,' said the Coroner with an appreciative smile, 'Lord Randolph tells us you were once his secretary.'

'That is not true. Do I look like a secretary?'

'Well — ' he looked at the expensive clothes and jewellery — 'I suppose you *could* have been.'

'I was never employed by Lord Randolph in any capacity. I lived with him as his mistress for five years before his marriage to Lady Camilla.'

'And after that?'

She raised an eyebrow. 'I can't see what bearing that has on the matter in hand, but yes, if you must know, I was his mistress afterwards as well.'

The Coroner looked gratified at hitting pay-dirt so soon. The younger journalists were already scrambling over their fellows to hit the newsdesks with the latest development: 'Tycoon's Mistress Spills the Beans'. The older hacks balanced on the edge of their seats, confident there was more to come. They were not disappointed.

'Baroness, do you recall the circumstances surrounding the disappearance of Wallace Wuggalar?'

Before she spoke, Linita's eyes ranged the crowded room. She located Dexter, and directed her answer at him.

'In every detail.'

'What happened that day?'

'Lord Randolph had to attend a meeting in Townsville. I was brought up there, so I took the opportunity to go along

760

for the ride. The meeting broke up early enough for us to get back to Yelonga. I was tired after the flight. I went to wash and lie down. Dexter was sitting outside. I heard footsteps, and then Luke Randolph's voice. I heard him tell Dexter that he had sacked Wally.'

There was a burst of excited comment. Rick Danby clapped Dexter on the back, grinning from ear to ear.

'Thank God! Oh, thank God,' cried Camilla, openly smiling at Linita.

Chip Randolph could not be restrained. 'Baroness, my arse! How much did you pay your scrubber, Uncle?'

'Silence!' called the Coroner, and when he was ignored in the hubbub: 'Pipe down, the lot of you! I haven't finished yet. You say that when you overheard this conversation you were lying down. You'll have to give us some indication as to what distance you were from Lord Randolph and his brother.'

'Very close. Less than ten feet, and the house is very old, slabbed timber. It was the quiet part of the afternoon. I could hear perfectly.'

'She's lying!' Lucas Randolph's mask of geniality had slipped since he gave his evidence. Foam flecked the corners of his mouth as he yelled, 'She can't have heard! Her room was up the veranda, thirty feet away. I made sure we were alone —'

'I think there's been some misapprehension,' said Linita. 'It's true my room was some distance away. I wasn't in it. I was waiting for Dexter in *his* room.'

A chorus of cat-calls and 'Good on yer's' from the press greeted her admission. The reporters shook their heads approvingly. They might have known Rando would have something good up his sleeve. The tide of feeling which had been running against him turned in his direction.

'Have you anything more to add?' the Coroner asked when he could make himself heard.

'Yes. When Luke told Dexter about Wally, he set off after him immediately. As he rode out, I heard Luke talking to himself: "It's no good. Wally's gone. He's gone for good this time."'

She pointed at Luke. 'I don't think I've ever heard anything more chilling than the way that man said those words.'

Lucas had not regained his seat. Face twisted into a feral snarl, he started pushing his way towards her. 'You bloody bitch! Wait till I get my hands on you.'

There was something so coldly murderous about the way he spoke that reporters and court officials moved out of his way. Two policemen guarding the door tried to make for him, but were impeded.

'Mr Randolph, take your seat!'

'And you can shut up! What bloody use were you, allowing this bitch in in the first place?'

'Pa! Watch what you're saying . . .'

Lucas ignored them all, intent on reaching Linita, who stood her ground. He felt a tap on his shoulder and swung round, snarling with rage. Dexter's fist caught him square on the jaw in a roundhouse that sent him sprawling backwards, arms outstretched. Several chairs were shunted into one another and splintered like matchwood. Lucas's head connected with the wall, and he was knocked cold.

Chip took one look at his fallen father and made a bolt for the door. The policemen instinctively hung on to him.

'In the light of these new developments, and until the furniture can be replaced, I declare this inquest adjourned.' The Coroner gathered the remnants of his shattered dignity and left to tear a strip off the police for causing him public embarrassment.

They carried Lucas Randolph away. Dexter hoped it would not be long before the British authorities contacted them with the results of their questioning of Mark Hayward.

Camilla went up to Linita, and kissed her. 'Thank you, my dear. You were magnificent.'

'Mom! Are you okay? What's been happening here?'

The Honourable Courtney Randolph was buried on his birthday. He would have been twenty-eight. Among the flowers was a wreath of white rosebuds bearing the message: 'For Courtney. Love always, Chantel.'

She and Linita stayed away from the service, following Dane Maddigan to New York, where he was retained by a prestigious hospital. He heard Linita's story without censure. As a doctor, he had heard many similar.

'As far as I'm concerned, Olive Maddigan brought me up and so she is my mother,' he told Linita, 'just as Bert Maddigan will always be my father. But there's a place for you and Chantel in my life. I'm not so sure about the man who abandoned you.'

'Don't be hard on Dexter, please. Courtney's death has knocked him sideways.'

'Yes, it would. Court was a good bloke.'

Linita did not push him further. Like his father, Dane felt things deeply. He would be slow to overcome the pain of rejection.

In Olive and Bert Maddigan he had been blessed with kind and loving parents — even if Bert, an inveterate gambler, had frittered away a large part of the money Linita had left with her baby. It was going to take Dane quite a time to come to terms with the idea that he was the by-blow of a world-famous tycoon.

He refused an invitation to Georgie's wedding in the spring, the quiet family affair she and Guy had planned even before news of Court's death.

Ash and Kara came over specially. With Lucas and Chip's forced retirement, Ash was now Chief Executive of the Australian division. Despite his sadness at Court's death, he was busily engaged in recruiting bright new managers, one of whom would be trained up to replace him at the Australian end. Dexter had indicated that he hoped to retire soon. When he did, Ash would return to England and overall control of the company.

Kara was worried. She did not know how much longer

she could stay away from her father's business, and still had not brought Ash to the point of proposing to her. Her heart ached to see the changes in him. At just thirty, he had the looks and mannerisms of a man ten years older. It was a cold grey autumn in Sydney. He needed a spell in the sun, she decided, and made arrangements for them to visit Yelonga again. It had worked once before.

After a week of keeping up with Kara's daredevil antics, Ash was tanned and fit and feeling distinctly outpaced. She was so damned good at everything! Ace pilot, fine horse-woman, more than useful shot ... Was there anything this woman couldn't do? Then he remembered. 'Come on,' he said one night. 'We're going to the billabong.'

'Please, Ash, no. You know I hate swimming at night. All that mud and the slithery things in it. Oh, please don't make me.'

He pulled her round the side of the house. The manager's wife saw them go. 'About time,' she said to herself, and shut the curtains.

'Ash,' Kara pleaded as they reached the water's edge, 'I'll do anything you want, but please don't make me go in there.'

'Anything at all? Even marry me?'

'*Especially* that! I thought you were never going to ask.'

They clung together, kissing and laughing, until Ash began to unbutton her blouse. She shivered as the breeze off the water played over her naked breasts.

'You are a bully! You know how I hate the water!'

'Who said anything about swimming when there are far more interesting things to do ...'

'Promise me one thing,' she said later, staring up into the southern stars which always seemed warmer and less remote than the ones in England.

'Anything you like,' he murmured sleepily.

'I want to come back here every year. I love this place.'

'More than you love me?'

'No, but it's a close-run thing.'

To Angelica's delight, Kara's mother insisted that her only daughter's wedding would be a full-scale affair with the ceremony at St Margaret's, Westminster, and the reception at Claridge's.

Linita, Wolfie and Chantel were invited, and speedily accepted. Dexter started to brood when no acceptance was received from Dane Maddigan.

'But you mustn't, darling,' Camilla told him. 'You don't even know if he's received it, the way he moves around the world.'

Dexter had told the Melvilles to send one to each of Dane's addresses, so he was pretty sure his son knew of the occasion and had chosen not to attend.

Georgianna was Matron of Honour, looking sleek and disgustingly healthy in her fifth month of pregnancy. Alexander was Ashley's best man. In his speech, he made a momentous announcement. 'My nephew and his lovely young bride are very dear to me. I can think of no safer hands than theirs to which to entrust the fortunes of my ancestral home, Courtney Park. As some of you will already know, Ashley is my heir. I hope to hold on to the title for a while yet, but the house is a different matter. I shall shortly be leaving for New York, where I plan to make a permanent home for myself. I see no reason why Ashley and Kara should wait, and hope they will agree to make Courtney Park their English home.'

A wedding photographer caught the moment when Alexander kissed the bride and handed Ash the ornate silver key to the front door of Courtney Park.

'It's a big responsibility,' he told them, 'but don't worry. You've got Maman and your mother and father to see you measure up to it!'

Dexter and Camilla, however, were not to be a permanent presence. After nearly thirty years in England, he was beginning to feel drawn to his native land. He had responsibilities there, too. Lucy and Rhianne depended on him.

When she heard of the part Lucinda had played in catching Mark Hayward, Camilla generously agreed that they must do everything in their power to help her make a new life for herself. They were due to fly to Australia on an extended trip. While they were there, Dexter planned to investigate houses on the Gold Coast with a view to spending half the year between there and Yelonga.

The speeches wound on endlessly. Dexter was relieved to feel a waiter tap him on the shoulder. 'Message for you, my lord.'

'Well, what is it?'

'The messenger's outside. He insists on giving it to you himself, my lord.'

Dexter excused himself to the Marchioness of Cunningham and followed the waiter.

A tall dark-haired man in a drenched raincoat was standing in the corridor outside, his back to Dexter.

'You wanted me?'

'Yes — or rather your money. If you remember a promise you once made me?' He turned round.

'Dane! Jesus, it's good to see you! Ash and Kara will be delighted.'

Dane Maddigan fingered a heavy growth of stubble on his chin, and looked at his soaked shoes and trousers. 'Give them my very best, but I won't come in. Not dressed for it. I've just got in from Sydney.'

'What did you do — swim over?'

'Bloody nearly! We hit a patch of bad weather. While we were being battered around like ping-pong balls, I finally realised what a pig-headed fool I'd been, punishing you and myself. I've been walking around for hours trying to get things sorted out in my head. I'm not going back on what I've said to Linita — the Maddigans will always be Mum and Dad to me — but I'd like us to be friends. We were when you were in hospital, remember? In fact, you offered to build me a hospital.'

Dexter's love and pride in his son were plain. 'The offer

768

still stands, Dane. Whatever you want, whatever it costs, together we'll make the Maddigan into the finest hospital there is.'

'Thanks, but I think you got the name wrong.' Dane's blue eyes and strong-boned faced had never looked more like his father's than when he said: 'We'll name it after Courtney. He'd have liked that.'

THE END

DAZZLE

Judith Gould

Three generations of fire and fame, they were born to
star, born to dazzle!

Senda – she fled the pogrom-haunted woods of her
childhood for the scented palaces of St Petersburg, a
meteoric star of the stage bewitching a generation born to
die in the blood-spattered snow of revolutionary
Russia . . .

Tamara – golden-haired star of the silver screen, her face
was her fortune and Hollywood her kingdom. Who was
she? Where had she come from? Not even she knew. One
man had made her for the dream machine, and he could
save her, or break her . . .

Daliah – the film idol of millions, in her the legend lives
on. Snatched into the crazy fury of a terrorist hell, she is
forced to pay for the sins of her fathers . . .

DAZZLE

Three women as fiery as priceless diamonds
Three lives burning with power and passion

FUTURA PUBLICATIONS
FICTION
0 7088 4293 3

THE LOVE MAKERS

Judith Gould

It was the world's most luxurious hotel empire – a monument to the ruthless determination of four powerful women, counting no cost in the drive of their ambition. They were

THE LOVE MAKERS

Elizabeth – fragile and vulnerable on the surface, diamond-hard beneath, whose struggle to bring up her children in New York caused her to lose sight of her dream . . .

Charlotte – sensuality's slave, who deserted her family for an Italian prince, only to find her ecstacy turned to nightmare in war-torn Italy . . .

Anna – orphaned, anonymous, unaware of her noble heritage, who followed a path of gold from the ashes of World War II . . .

Dorothy – poor little rich girl, target of her father's bitterness, whose multimillion dollar legacy made her powerful, desirable, ultimately invincible . . .

Four stunning women, four passionate lives, four destined for success.

FUTURA PUBLICATIONS
FICTION
0 7088 2917 1

RULING PASSIONS

Susan Crosland

When Daisy Brewster landed in London she was just
another pretty young American out to enjoy a year abroad
before returning home to marry. But before the year was
out, Daisy would take on the scheming world of London
journalism, and be taken on in turn by London's most
eligible bachelor MP.

Though she couldn't know it, she would also take on a
dangerous enemy when she casually flicked off the sexual
gropings of her lecherous boss, pushing a button that
would detonate fifteen years later in vicious innuendo and
blackmail – all aimed at destroying her husband's career
and her own happiness.

Meanwhile Daisy will become a not-so-innocent abroad
as she manoeuvres through the shoals of political intrigue
and sexual misadventure – taking us behind the
scenes at Buckingham Palace receptions, dinners at
No. 10 and top-secret meetings in Whitehall.

'Has all the ingredients . . . sex, ambition, political
intrigue'
Guardian

'A big slick book . . . plotting and intrigue well conveyed'
Sunday Times

'The conflict between politicians and journalists is
beautifully portrayed'
Evening Standard

'Elegant, sophisticated . . . knowing, gossipy'
The Times

'A racy dip into the shenanigans of Fleet Street and
Parliament'
Today

FUTURA PUBLICATIONS
FICTION
0 7088 4471 5

GIRL TALK

Cindy Blake

LADIES WHO LUNCH TOGETHER ...

What do three sparkling, sexy, successful career women talk about in smart restaurants? Men – what else. Who needs them? Sam, Georgia and Eugenie do – that's who. Clinking glasses of champagne, they toast their pact to role reversal, for they plan to outplay men at their own game. Now they will seduce the seducers.

THE HUNTRESS ...

Samantha, gorgeous but unbelievably naive, is tutored by the worldly Georgia and Eugenie in seduction techniques. When they have taught her all they know (and they know an awful lot) she is set loose upon an unsuspecting male victim.

THE PREY ...

Is *homme fatal*, devastatingly handsome gynaecologist John Rankin. As proficient at putting on charm as he is at taking off bras, he is Sam's prime target. But when faced with such a smooth operator, it is inevitable that the huntress will become the hunted. And the hunt becomes more and more intense, until a sizzling climax is reached in St Lucia, where tangled relationships and steamy passions explode in the hot Caribbean sun.

GIRL TALK

One of the wittiest and most perceptive novels for the nineties.

FUTURA PUBLICATIONS
FICTION
0 7088 4356 5

THE THORNBIRDS

Colleen McCullough

The international number one bestseller.

'A heart-rending epic of violence, love, piety, family
roots, passion, pain, triumph, tragedy, roses, thorns . . .
the plot sweeps on in truly marvellous fashion to its tragic
but triumphant conclusion.'
Chicago Tribune

'This book is not a book. It is a marvellous experience.'
David Niven

'A novel that is destined to be one of the biggest-selling,
best-read novels in the annals of fiction.'
Time Magazine

'Miss McCullough's novel is excellent . . . the story is told
superbly . . . Never for one moment does the pace flag.
Never for an instant does her control fail her . . . I read it
with immense pleasure, enjoyed every page, and heartily
recommend it.'
The Times

FUTURA PUBLICATIONS
FICTION
0 7088 1374 7